PALM *of the* MOTHER

PALM *of the* MOTHER

A NOVEL

LINDSEY D. LINDEN

Title: Palm of the Mother

Author: Lindsey D. Linden

Genre: Mythical fiction

©2019 Lindsey D. Linden. All rights reserved.

ISBN: 978-0-9863482-6-6 Trade paperback
ISBN: 978-0-9863482-7-3 Electronic epub format
ISBN: 978-0-9863482-8-0 Electronic mobi format
Format: Trade paperback and e-book
Publishing Date: March 1, 2020

Book 3 of, The Lion of Djibouti, trilogy.

Edited by Nicole R. Klungle

Cover Design and Formatting by Damonza

1

"VERA!"

Rosa stopped to listen for her daughter's voice.

Vera, answer! Dear God, please!

But the sounds of the jungle—squawking birds, the trilling hum of insects, and the raucous chatter of tree-dwelling monkeys—concealed what she was so desperate to hear.

"Vera!" she screamed once more.

Wielding a hatchet like a scythe, she pushed ahead.

Rosa attacked the foliage blocking her way with fervor, each swing of the small axe delivered in wild, slashing strokes. Vines, branches, bushes, ferns—these were her enemies. A wall keeping her from Vera, allies of the brutish soldiers who'd come to remove her family from their farm. So she bludgeoned the vegetation without mercy. But the jungle would not give way without a fight.

Razor-sharp thorns tore at Rosa's flesh and pulled at her hair, while shattered ends of branches ripped her clothing. Blood began to stream down Rosa's taught, sun-browned arms, and it marred her cheeks and forehead with jagged lines of red. But Rosa took no notice of her wounds or the blood oozing from the cuts. Finding Vera before the government soldiers—*the filthy pigs*—was all that mattered. If she didn't find Vera before the soldiers… Driven forward by the unbearable, tormenting thoughts raging inside her head, Rosa bulled her way forward.

Suddenly, something pulled on Rosa's ankle and jerked her down into a clump of ferns. Hoarse, raspy breathing filled her ears. Panic-stricken, she twisted her body sideways and swung the axe back toward her feet, her strokes frenzied and brutal. The Y-shaped vine that held her foot split on the second swing. But the raspy, deep-rooted breathing remained. Placing a hand to her chest, Rosa gulped for air. Her lungs felt raw and on fire. Beneath her breastbone, she could feel her heart furiously pounding.

"Vera!" she croaked.

With her chest constricted into a knot, Rosa struggled to her feet. A wisp of pink—a shred of shiny material lying on the ground near where she had fallen—caught her eye.

"Please, no," she whimpered.

Her hand shook as she bent to retrieve the scrap of cotton, twitching uncontrollably at a distant burst of gunfire. In that disjointed moment— horrific images of what the gunfire meant swirled through her mind—she heard a girl cry out. Snatching the piece of material off the ground, she raced forward.

Rosa swung the axe with renewed urgency, her arms and hands moving in furious symphony; left hand grab, right hand chop. Left grab, right chop. Grab, chop, grab, chop. Blood-tinged sweat streamed down Rosa's face. Her breathing became even more labored and erratic. *Vera!* her thoughts screamed. *Vera, where are you?* Filled with dread, she pressed ahead.

Yellow and pink—ribbons hanging limply from a branch a dozen paces ahead—brought Rosa to an abrupt stop. Overcome with a sense of fore-boding, she reluctantly let her eyes drift down to the jungle floor. There she saw what she didn't want to see: a bundle of white material crumpled atop a patch of green moss—Vera's birthday dress. A muffled cry of "Mama" reached her as a haunted whisper. Rosa looked up.

"Vera," she sobbed.

A grimy, half-naked soldier grinned at Rosa. His sweaty arms pinned Vera's slender, naked body against his.

"Mama!" Vera cried.

Rosa rushed forward screaming, "*Porra de porco! Porra de porco!*" "Fuck-ing pig!"

The soldier laughed. Then, pulling Vera's arms taught behind her back, he bent her torso forward and violently ground his manhood into her groin. Enraged at the sight of her daughter being raped, Rosa raised the axe above her shoulder and leaped forward.

Just as Rosa swung the weapon toward the soldier's neck, something smashed into the side of her face. The force of the blow knocked her backward, to the ground. Stunned, pain shooting across her jaw and temple, Rosa blinked several times. Suddenly, Vera appeared above her, her lithe body held aloft by dirty fingers clamped around her throat. Then the smirking face of the soldier appeared behind Vera. The man's bloodshot eyes bore into Rosa's. She turned her head as Vera cried out in pain.

"*Sikoyo tufi mamá,*" a man she couldn't see taunted with a lustful snicker.

Before Rosa understood what was happening, the soldier holding Vera shifted his grip, placed his hands on either side of Vera's head, and twisted. Horror-stricken, Rosa watched her daughter's lifeless body slide to the ground.

A shadow passed across Rosa's face. The soldier who'd raped and murdered her daughter stared down at her and laughed as he stroked his penis. As tears filled Rosa's eyes, the barrel of a rifle was thrust against the base of her throat. Another man's face suddenly loomed inches above hers.

"You're next," the man whispered.

Saliva drooled from the corner of the man's mouth as he spoke. Rosa felt his free hand probing her inner thighs. She clenched her fists as a sick, hollow feeling spread through her.

With a surge of adrenaline, Rosa lurched upward and swung the small axe with every ounce of strength she could muster. The blade tore into the soldier's upper arm. Howling in pain, the man stumbled backward and pulled the axe from his flesh.

With a feral cry, Rosa sprung from the ground.

A deafening bang and an explosion of pain in her chest stopped her in her tracks. Staggering back, she fought to keep her balance. Her eyes glimpsed a smoking gun. Slowly, she became aware of the sensation of moisture running down her stomach. Then a jolt of utter agony as the wounded man plunged the axe into her shoulder. Rosa fell to her knees.

Two harsh, swift blows to her lower back forced Rosa to the ground. Then hands grabbed her around the waist and yanked her hips up. Her legs were jerked roughly apart. Though wracked with agonizing pain, she managed to turn her head. The soldier holding the blood-smeared hatchet smiled at her as he fondled his penis. Rosa looked away and worked her hands up toward her chest. When her fingers found the bleeding hole in her flesh, she tore at the wound with her fingertips. Blocking out the pain of the rape, she scratched and pulled at the bullet hole until the opening was the size of her fist. Overwhelmed with a sense of utter despair, she pushed her face into the ground and filled her mouth with dirt. Squeezing her eyes shut, she swallowed. Her world turned murky grey as she willed herself to die.

*

Marcos was huddled beneath a burlap sack, his attention fixed on a thin column of dirt seeping through a pin-sized hole above his head. Although the trickle of soil brushed against his lips, he dared not move. His father had told him not to.

"*Escondor*," his father had ordered. "*Até—*" Hide until—

Marcos focused hard on the words *hide until.* Hide until what? He didn't know. His father hadn't said.

Marcos had heard his mother scream his sister's name a few minutes ago, as his father had shoved him into a shallow hole and laid the burlap sack atop him. Then came the sound of a shovel digging into soil. Soon after, he felt dirt piled atop the burlap sack. Then came the rustling of branches—his father covering his hiding place, he assumed. After that, he heard the receding patter of footsteps. There'd been silence for a while. Then Marcos heard his father curse in Portuguese, which meant he was very angry. A burst of gunfire shortly afterward made Marcos pee in his pants. He was embarrassed by what he had done. He knew his father would be angry with him. *Maybe they'll dry before Father returns*, he thought.

Marcos stared at the steady trickle of dirt seeping into his hiding place and thought, *how much longer do I have to wait?* He didn't know. His father hadn't told him.

"*Il est là! Chercher!*"

Marcos shivered. The man yelling wasn't his father. From the smattering of the languages he'd been taught at the school run by the Catholic nuns near Kongolo, he understood the man was yelling in French: "He's here! Search!"

The man's voice sounded close. Marcos began to tremble. He tried not to. But he couldn't help it. His entire body started to shake. The steady trickle of dirt dribbled across his cheek.

"*Ici!*" was shouted above him.

Then something pressed the burlap sack onto Marcos' head. Reflexively, he moved his hands to block it. The burlap was suddenly pulled away. An avalanche of dirt fell into the shallow hole his father had placed him in. Then a hand grabbed hold of his wrist and jerked him upward.

"*Esclave!*"

The soldier who had hold of him laughed and began to examine Marcos like a piece of meat for sale at market.

"I'm not a slave!" Marcos shouted.

Angry, Marcos kicked the soldier in the chest. Two other soldiers standing nearby laughed. The soldier holding Marcos slammed the butt of his rifle into the side of Marcos's face and threw him to the ground. Stunned, Marcos stared up at the man as he shifted the rifle and pointed it at Marcos's head.

The assault of feathered wings came with a rushing *swoosh*. The soldier aiming the gun at Marcos screamed as taloned feet flailed at his eyes. With an ear-splitting shriek, the attacking bird veered upward, hovering for a moment before swooping down toward the soldiers standing nearby. Mesmerized, Marcos watched the broad-winged bird make a diving pass. The soldiers crouched low to the ground, barely escaping the bird's outstretched feet. The eagle-sized bird swooped past them and then, with another shrill cry, flew directly at Marcos.

Scrambling to his feet, Marcos turned and ran deeper into the jungle. A burst of gunfire erupted behind him. He could hear bullets strafing the branches above his head. Grey-white feathers flashed at the edge of his field of vision. Glancing sideways, he saw the eagle-sized owl bank sharply upward and disappear into the tree canopy. Then a second round of gunfire boomed. Marcos felt a fiery, needle-sharp pain in his lower back. He fell forward in a twisted heap. To his surprise, he felt nothing as his body slammed into a spiky-leaved bush. Feeling strangely numb, he stared upward into the trees. Then the barrel of a gun appeared above his head. A moment later, the weapon was fired into his face.

2

SARAH PRESSED HER hands over her ears in an attempt to muffle the awful, pulsating sounds. *Thump thump thump thump thump thump thump*—the blasts of automatic-weapon fire rattled her bones, fraying what little composure she was clinging to. Squeezing her eyes shut, she tried to pretend that the booms were thunderclaps and that the periodic flashes of orange from tracer bullets crisscrossing the darkening sky were some strange sort of heat lightning. But it was no use. Pretending wouldn't change what was taking place. Gun battles, mortar explosions, rocket attacks, roadside bombs. Vehicles and people turned into blackened heaps of shredded flesh and metal. Everywhere she'd been—everywhere Teimbaka had taken her in their search for Claire and Dirk—savage, bloody combat raged.

Everyone, it seemed, was at war. *And for what?* she'd asked herself a dozen times. She didn't know, really. She couldn't quite grasp the concept of total anarchy. She'd heard some fragmented talk about autonomy, of overthrowing the government to reclaim tribal lands. But she'd witnessed little, if any, distinction between those who proclaimed they were fighting for justice and those who were labeled tyrannical oppressors.

She'd encountered her first firefight two days after she and Teimbaka had left Sudan and set out for Djibouti. The battle they'd blindly stumbled into had prompted a near weeklong ordeal of backtracking to evade patrols and scurrying for cover whenever firefights erupted. Over the course of a few days, they realized they were pinned between two brutal factions.

They'd been forced to steal food and water to survive. And they'd witnessed the brutal deaths of scores of soldiers and civilians alike. The carnage had been sickening. Neither babies or the elderly had been spared.

She attributed their survival of that first weeklong ordeal to the grace of God. The days, weeks, and months that followed she attributed to His continued mercy. What she had hoped would be a journey of a few weeks—a month at most—had stretched over nearly six months. And when she and Teimbaka had finally reached the port city of Djibouti, she'd felt a great sense of relief and accomplishment. She had met God's test, she'd thought, and endured the challenges He'd set before her. Having kept His faith, she'd been certain God would reward her for her perseverance. She and Teimbaka would undoubtedly find Dirk and Sister Claire in the first hospital they came to.

But her vision of God's reward hadn't materialized. Dirk and Sister Claire where nowhere to be found in Djibouti. After spending a few months searching that city, she now found herself hiding behind a bullet-riddled wall in a maze of nondescript streets in Mogadishu, Somalia, looking for someone named Bin'ka, waiting for Teimbaka to come back for her and lead her to safety.

Cringing at the ear-splitting melee around her, Sarah pressed her palms tighter to her ears and whimpered. Safety—where was she going to find that here? With a sarcastic grunt, she glanced at the tracer bullets crisscrossing the darkening sky. The notion of safety suddenly seemed as far-fetched as the thought that Dirk and Claire would be waiting for them in Djibouti, swaddled in crisp, white-sheeted hospital beds, with smiles on their faces. God, she'd come to conclude, had forsaken these lands—Ethiopia, Sudan, Somalia—to Satan. And Satan was having a field day spreading his depraved brand of evil. Safety did not exist here.

Scared and despondent, with the sounds of conflict intensifying around her, Sarah began to silently pray.

Blessed Father in heaven, keep us—

The wall to her right suddenly blew inward, the explosion blanketing her in dust and stones. Bullets strafed the sides of the pulverized opening. Shards of rock, plaster, and stone careened in every direction. Figures appeared—dark silhouettes against a dusk-grey backdrop—their murky forms brandishing weapons. Sarah went rigid and held her breath, hoping the combatants—if they spotted her—would think she was dead. A moment later, when she saw the same figures scurry away, she sighed with relief. Then she heard a new burst of gunfire followed by a whooshing explosion that shook the earth beneath her feet.

"*Waxaa aad! Aad!*"

Startled by the close proximity of the shouted words, Sarah pressed her back against the wall and scooted a foot to her right.

"*Jooji! Aad! Jooji!*"

Sarah watched a boy scramble through the break in the wall. He carried a weapon nearly as big as his body.

"*Maxbuus!*" he shouted, leveling the gun at Sarah. "*Aad, maxbuus!*" He jerked the rifle up and down in quick, abbreviated motions.

Sarah raised her hands above her head.

"I don't know what you're saying," she told the boy in a calm voice.

Slowly, she pulled the blue and white scarf Teimbaka had given her away from her face.

"I'm not your enemy."

"*Ingiriisiga?*" The boy edged closer. His hardened features appeared to soften. "English?" he asked. "You *cad*—white?"

The boy smiled. Sarah lowered her arms.

"*Lacag badan,*" the boy said with a definitive nod. Taking a step closer to Sarah, he shook his rifle and laughed.

"I don't know what you're saying," Sarah repeated.

"*Lacag*—money," he told her. Shaking his weapon again, he pointed the barrel at her chest. "*Maxbuus!*" he barked. "You—up!" He poked the rifle into her stomach. "Prisoner!"

Sarah searched the boy's face, looking for the touches of innocence she'd observed in his features when he'd smiled. But she could find no trace of innocence now. To the contrary, his features seemed severe, somber, and unforgiving. And anger—she saw what she took to be anger—flashed in his eyes. Why would he be angry with her? She didn't understand. Her focus drifted to the imposing gun he held.

"Surely you mean me no harm," she said, looking into his eyes as she slowly rose to stand.

Ghostlike, Teimbaka suddenly materialized behind the boy. In one swift, fluid motion, he placed a knife against the boy's neck and wrenched the rifle from his grasp.

"*Ingiriisiga! Ingiriisiga!*" the boy shouted.

Teimbaka exerted pressure on the knife. The boy fell silent as a few drops of blood trickled down his neck. Sarah grabbed hold of Teimbaka's wrist.

"He's just a boy!" she cried.

"He would bring—" Teimbaka glanced over his shoulder at the break in the wall. "He would kill us," he told her, sliding his forearm across the boy's neck. Tightening the crook of his arm around the boy's throat, he added, "Or sell us."

Sarah squeezed Teimbaka's wrist. "You can't just—" She glanced at the bloodstained knife in his hand. "Hasn't there been enough killing?" she asked. She shook her head. "Will murdering him bring us closer to finding Claire and Dirk?"

Sarah glimpsed a sudden movement of the boy's arm: a swift elbow jab into Teimbaka's crotch.

"*Ingiriisiga!*" the boy yelled as Teimbaka lurched backward to avoid the blow.

Slipping out of Teimbaka's chokehold, the boy tumbled sideways and scrambled to his feet. He was through the opening in the wall before Teimbaka or Sarah could react. Shouts of "*Ingiriisiga! Ingiriisiga!*" soon echoed through the alley.

*

Teimbaka sheathed the knife in the folds of his shamma and grabbed Sarah's arm. Pulling her, he hurried across the courtyard toward a narrow wooden door within the far wall. As he thrust out his arm to push the door open, he heard the sharp clap of a closely fired gunshot. A bullet gouged the wall inches from his hand.

"Throw down your weapon!" an angry voice ordered in English.

Teimbaka jerked Sarah in front of him as he swung the AK-47 he'd taken from the boy behind him. Firing off a strafing burst, he pushed Sarah through the narrow doorway and shoved her sideways. Bullets strafed the door as he leaped through the frame. Behind him, the grey, weathered wood splintered into a dozen pieces before the door blew off its hinges.

Sarah yanked on Teimbaka's arm. "What are we doing?"

"Run!" Teimbaka yelled.

They sprinted right, Teimbaka holding tight to Sarah's shirtsleeve as he scanned the way ahead. He estimated they had ten seconds, maybe less, before a shower of bullets would obliterate anything that moved within the alley. Hearing movement behind him, he released his grip on Sarah and twisted left, awkwardly firing off another round. Sarah screamed. Teimbaka swung the AK-47 out in front of him and prepared to fire. But the way ahead was deserted. Immediately he came to a halting stop.

Glancing quickly around, he realized Sarah had left his side. She was a few paces behind him, slouched against a wall, her face buried in her hands. Thirty meters beyond her position, Teimbaka saw five gun-wielding figures deploy into the alley. He fired off a sustained round as he ran back toward Sarah.

"Hurry!" he yelled as he clasped her shoulder.

"I can't!" she screamed, slapping his hand away. "I can't do this anymore!" She burst into tears and slid to the ground.

"Get up!" Teimbaka ordered. Firing off a short burst from his weapon, he grabbed a handful of her hair and yanked her to her feet. "Move! Now!"

After Teimbaka gave her a sharp push, Sarah stumbled ahead. Teimbaka followed close behind, prodding her forward to keep her moving. When he spotted an opening to their left, he steered her into it.

Teimbaka hurried Sarah deeper into a corridor so narrow they could barely stand abreast. When another narrow alleyway appeared on their right, he pulled her roughly sideways. Twenty panicked strides later, a third corridor offered them a path to the left. Without a second thought, he shoved Sarah into it. After running for a few minutes, he brought them to a stop and listened for sounds of pursuit.

Teimbaka was breathing heavily as Sarah's head came to rest upon his shoulder. He could feel her body trembling, sense the fear she was struggling to contain. Understanding the danger they were in, he couldn't help but wonder if the dark angels were lurking nearby, waiting for an opportunity to reap another soul. And if they were, he wondered if he had the strength to protect the haggard, terrified woman leaning against him. With a heavy sigh, he gazed up at the sliver of night sky visible between the buildings. He could see no stars twinkling in the blue-black abyss above him. The slender piece of heaven was empty. Like this city, he mused—empty of light.

Mogadishu. Why did we come? Where is Claire?

He shook his head and took a deep breath.

She isn't here.

He wondered if she ever had been. They'd searched every hospital, every clinic Bin'ka might have taken her to. None had any record of her.

But if she was never here, if Bin'ka never brought her to Mogadishu, then where is she?

A ship's horn blared at the same moment a chorus of animated voices echoed down the alley. Instantly, Teimbaka grabbed Sarah's arm and set off running. A hundred meters later, he pulled her to stop when the alley opened into what appeared to be a dock district.

Clusters of bright lights mounted on tall poles some fifty meters in front of their position compelled Teimbaka to shade his eyes. He noted the nearby cries of seabirds and the smell of diesel fuel. The docks were close, perhaps just beyond the garish lights that ringed what appeared to be an oil storage facility. If they were lucky, they could steal an unattended boat somewhere along the harbor and make their escape. Grasping Sarah by her wrist, he started to move out past the buildings. A moment later, he came to an abrupt stop. He pressed Sarah's body flush against a wall before glancing over his shoulder.

"What?"

"Shhh," he ordered. "Listen."

A flash of white-plumed fire suddenly filled the alley behind them. A split second later, a screeching wall of light streaked up the alley. Sarah covered her ears with her hands and sank to her knees. Teimbaka pulled her to her feet and pushed her forward. As soon as they exited the alley, he yanked her hard to the right and pushed her to the ground. Then he jumped on top of her and covered her head with his arms. Behind them, the shrieking torrent of light grew to a high-pitched wail. The ensuing explosion was earsplitting.

Shockwaves buckled the ground beneath Sarah's body as an avalanche of stone, pebbles and dust fell on Teimbaka's back. A siren began to wail. Searchlights switched on; beams of blinding white light emanated from the oil storage facility. These moved in synchronized patterns, searching along the ground, probing crevices and structures. Teimbaka lifted his head as one of the powerful beams passed over him. Gunshots rang out. People began to shout. He pushed off Sarah's body.

"Are you hurt?" he shouted. Picking up the AK-47, he yelled, "Can you move?"

"I—I think so," came her muffled reply. "I won't really know until—"

Teimbaka didn't wait for her to finish. He slipped his hands under her shoulders and lifted her off the ground.

"Go," he ordered, pulling on her arm.

Sarah slapped his hand and screamed, "Go? Go where?"

She looked past him. The glare of the searchlights revealed the frantic look in her eyes.

"This is insanity!"

Teimbaka slapped her hard across the cheek.

"Do you want to die?" he tersely asked.

*

Sarah wondered why the doctor had slapped her across the face and why he was suddenly wearing black clothing.

Why did he change out of his white coat? she wondered.

Still, she knew he expected an answer. She could tell by the unrelenting look on his face and the slap he'd just administered.

Did she want to die?

What a stupid question. Maybe the stupidest one she'd been asked since she'd been brought to the infirmary. Of course, she didn't want to die. If she'd wanted to die, she would have let the monster who'd captured her kill her too.

Why do you think I cut his fucking throat? Idiot.

She wanted to laugh in his face. But that, she was certain—to laugh at him—would infuriate him and make him suspicious, adding to his skepticism that she wasn't as far along the road to recovery as she would have him believe.

"No," she simply replied.

To Sarah, the next few minutes were mostly a blur. The doctor grabbed her wrist and pulled on her until she began to run. Explosions thundered behind them as they traveled through bands of darkness and light. A voice filled the sky above her head, bellowing over a crackling loudspeaker, yelling words she didn't understand. Then, for whatever reason, the doctor grabbed her around the waist and yanked her to a stop. To her utter confusion, he then fired some spine-numbing weapon she hadn't noticed he was carrying. The spotlight they'd been standing in suddenly went out. An instant later, the doctor made her run again. To her wonder, she felt the dirt beneath her feet magically turn into asphalt. A few minutes later, when she heard the sound of waves breaking against a shoreline, the doctor pulled on her arm, forcing her to a jolting stop.

"Can you swim?"

Sarah studied the doctor's face. For the first time she noticed scores of scars scattered across his cheeks and forehead. How had he accumulated so many, and why was he was asking another a stupid question? Was this a test of some sort?

Can I swim?

"Of course," she scoffed.

She was about to ask him why he wanted to know when she heard shouting behind her. She turned and looked, but she couldn't see anyone. Then the doctor pulled on her arm again. Reluctantly, she resumed running. As she struggled to keep pace with the doctor, she heard the voices behind them grow louder. This upset her, because the voices sounded angry. *What are they so upset about?*

"Do you see that boat?"

Sarah stuttered to a stop as she followed the doctor's pointing finger. The body of water he was pointing toward looked serene. She guessed it was a painting or a mural. She took a moment to admire the moon-kissed wavelets rippling across the surface. Then the doctor grabbed her wrist and yelled, "Do you see that boat?"

Taken aback by his vehemence, Sarah was about to tell him to fuck off, but then she caught herself. *Play it smart.* Turning her attention back to the projection of water, she located the boat she assumed he was referring to: a small ship hoisting a sail.

"You mean that one?" she answered, nodding to the vessel.

"Yes."

A surge of pride ran through her. She could tell he was pleased.

"You must swim to it. Plead for help."

Sarah gave him a quizzical look but shrugged her shoulders as though she was saying *sure.* Before he could reply, a series of explosions occurred. She covered her ears. But the doctor jerked on her arm, and they were running again, heading toward a large stack of giant boxes illuminated by a tall, bright lamp. For some reason, some of the boxes started to explode. Little plumes of smoke rose up from their faces, particles of wood flying into the air. Observing the scene, Sarah suddenly wondered if she was supposed to make a comment. Did he want her to say the explosions reminded her of small volcanic eruptions?

"You have to swim to it. Plead for help."

She listened to the gravity in the doctor's tone as he pointed to the water. She guessed he was referring to the boat again.

Why is he repeating himself? she wondered. *Is this another trick question?*

"I understand," she replied. To reassure him, she squeezed his shoulder. "I'll get there. And I'll ask for help."

"Good," he responded.

She heard relief in his voice. She smiled; she'd passed the test.

A burst of gunfire from the weapon he was carrying startled her. She screamed. The sound of her screeching voice snapped her back to reality.

*

Sarah felt a surge of panic as Teimbaka hurriedly leaned his weapon against the side of a large crate. Bullets whizzed all around them. The sound was maddening. Then Teimbaka suddenly grabbed her by the forearms and yanked her toward him. As her body shifted toward him, he took a huge stride forward. He grunted as he swung her outward and hurled her off the dock.

She closed her eyes.

The ocean sucked her down upon impact. Water rushed over her head and up her nose. It invaded her nasal passages and her throat. She began to choke. Panic stricken, she opened her eyes. She found herself immersed in darkness.

Feeling as though she was suffocating, Sarah began to thrash about, wildly swinging her arms and pumping her legs. Somehow, she managed to thrust her body upward. As she broke the surface of the water, she gasped for air. A wave washed over her face. She spit water from her mouth and coughed. The roar of gunfire drew her attention toward the dock.

"Teimbaka!" she yelled.

She saw him crouched behind a stack of wooden crates, pinned down by heavy gunfire. The crates were being shredded by bullets.

With the grim realization that Teimbaka was about to die, Sarah felt her muscles go weak. She began to sink. Frantic, she furiously began to tread water and looked for something to hold on to. Her eyes latched onto a sail wafting against the backdrop of a star-filled sky. Then she remembered what Teimbaka had told her.

Swim to it! Plead for help!

"Help!" she screamed. With a quick glance toward the dock, she set off swimming.

Arms churning, legs feverishly kicking, Sarah headed for the boat. But the little waves she'd admired a few minutes before fought her every stroke. Salt stung her eyes, blurring her vision. She managed to swim only a handful of meters before she tired. With barely enough energy to tread water, she tried to get her bearings.

"Help me!" she yelled again.

She looked for the sail. She couldn't find it.

Dear God! The boat's gone!

Desperate to locate the sail, Sarah slowly turned in a circle. But the constant onslaught of waves made it difficult for her to see more than a few meters in any direction. A sudden, booming explosion sent a shiver down her spine. The surface of the water around her immediately turned fiery red. Looking back toward the dock, she saw a column of fire billowing upward. She noticed that the crates Teimbaka had taken refuge behind were no longer there. Fiery shards of wood began to rain down from the sky.

"Teimbaka!" she screamed in horror.

As the waves slapping at her face crested crimson-orange, bullets struck the surface of the water in a sequential line a meter in front of her. At the edge of the dock, she could see a group of figures. Some were pointing toward her.

As though caught in the thread of a dream, Sarah numbly watched the featureless gunmen raise their weapons and aim them toward her face. In that instant, she felt her body go numb. Suddenly, her arms and legs wouldn't move. The ocean sucked on her, pulling her downward. Water rushed into her mouth. Coughing and gagging, she willed her limbs to move, desperate to keep her face above the surface. But the water inched higher. A terrible feeling of hopelessness took hold of her. When a resounding clap of thunder sent a shockwave through the sea, she interpreted it as God calling her to her end.

Water splashing in her eyes, Sarah looked up at the sky. She saw angels appear as streaks of blue blazing over her head. The angels were showing her the way to heaven, she thought. But the sound they created reminded her of the sound made by a rocket, the kind she'd seen and heard dozens of times as she and Teimbaka had made their way across Ethiopia. Nevertheless, she found herself mesmerized by the flaming blue-white light and watched in awe as it impacted with the dock. The bone-rattling explosion produced a new cloud of crimson flame.

"Teimbaka!" she screamed. "Teimbaka!"

Suddenly, Sarah was swept up from the sea. As she ascended from the fire-colored water, she believed she had died. The notion was reinforced when she slowly descended into a dark enclosure and found herself surrounded by a multitude of fire-tinged eyes. Then a giant shadow appeared. It loomed over her—a massive dark shape with flaming orbs for eyes.

"You yelled 'Teimbaka,'" the shadow grumbled.

Sarah cringed.

"Were you with him?"

When she didn't respond, the shadow grunted and leaned toward her.

It grasped her arms and lifted her into the air. Sarah studied the reflection of the flames dancing across a black, wide-nosed face.

"The Lion," the shadow-man muttered as he turned and looked toward the burning dock.

"Yes," Sarah stuttered, terrified. "You mean Teimbaka. He—" She grasped the shoulders of the massive figure and pressed her fingers into his flesh. "You must help him!" she implored.

The shadow-man stared at the flaming shoreline for a moment. Sarah watched his brow wrinkle and his nose flare. And then the man snorted. Without a word, he set her down.

The fire-tinged eyes she'd observed moments before moved toward her. She could hear words murmured she didn't understand. As her eyesight started to adjust to her dark surroundings, she realized she was looking upon a score of children.

The sound of the sail snapping full from a strong gust of wind prodded Sarah to look up as the boat surged forward. Glancing aft, she could see the upper torso of the shadow-man. The massive figure was at the tiller, his attention divided between the boat's heading and the fire raging along the dock. Something about his girth and the outline of his imposing frame struck a memory, a snippet of a conversation she'd had with Teimbaka about the man they were searching for in Mogadishu.

"Bin'ka?" she blurted. "Are you Bin'ka?"

She saw the man roll his muscular shoulders and look away. And then someone tapped her on the arm. A child offered her a blanket.

3

"GET THE FUCK away from me!"

Dirk hurled a beer bottle at the manifestation across the room. When the bottle struck the long-nosed animal on the forehead, he chuckled. But the moment of satisfaction passed quickly. The ethereal animal barely flinched as the bottle passed harmlessly through its shimmering body before striking the wall. Dirk sagged back in his chair, despondent. An instant later, he flew into a rage.

"Fuck you!" he shouted. "Go back where you came from!"

The baby ghost-elephant flapped its ears. Dirk pulled at his unkempt hair before interlocking his fingers on top of his head.

"What do you want from me?" he screamed. He glanced around the room, terror-stricken with the thought that there might be more of the ethereal creatures lurking. "Why do you keep bothering me?"

The ghost-beast stared at him in accusatory silence. He felt its hollow eyes boring into his soul.

"I can't help her!" he cried.

The beast's hollow eyes grew wider.

"Go away!"

Dirk grasped the crystal ashtray sitting on the table next to his chair, cocked his arm, and threw the ashtray as hard as he was able. His elbow smacked the floor lamp positioned near the table in the process. The brass fixture crashed into the wall behind him just as the crystal ashtray smacked against the door on the other side of the room. Taken off guard when the ghost-beast began to drift toward him, Dirk curled his legs into the chair and covered his head with his arms.

"I don't want to see her!" he yelled, thrusting his hands out in front of his chest in an attempt to stop the manifestation.

The baby spirit-elephant passed through Dirk's outstretched arms and placed the tip of its trunk against his forehead.

*

Dirk immediately felt the jolting pain of an electric shock as he watched Claire's body go rigid. Emulating what the woman was experiencing, his back arched and his shoulders stiffened just before his arms, legs, and torso began to shake uncontrollably. His mouth went wide as Claire screamed in agony, the 450 volts of electricity knifing into her 16-volt brain an excruciating overload to her senses. When Dirk witnessed her face turn a ghostly white and her body spasmodically jerk against the restraints tied around her wrists and ankles, he began to cry. Seeing the woman tortured in such a way was never what he had intended when he'd taken her out of Africa. Watching her suffer made him angry. It made him want to punch the doctor administering the shock therapy in the face.

"He told me the voltage will be raised to the maximum next week if she doesn't respond to this level."

The prune-faced old woman fingered a rosary as she spoke. When Dirk glanced across his shoulder to acknowledge the woman's presence, she nodded and smiled. Claire's mother—*some mother*—was an unfeeling shell of a human being, a mummified replica of something he assumed once held a capacity to feel. Then his attention snapped back to Claire's image; she was having a seizure. A loud and violent one. She struggled to turn her head to the side as she began to retch violently. Dirk sensed panic in the attending nurse as the white-clad woman hurried to undo Claire's head restraint. It was clear to him that Claire was about to choke to death on the yellow bile gurgling out of her mouth.

"This is such a waste of time," he heard Claire's mother mutter. The old prune sighed heavily before she said, "And for what? Because she took up with a nigger?" She clicked her tongue as she turned toward Dirk. "You're certain they had no children together?"

Children? She's a fucking nun, for Christ's sake! She's your daughter! He stared at her, aghast.

"Because, down the road, if it's proven that she did… Well, that could present a problem." When she reached out and touched the back of his hand, Dirk felt his skin crawl. "Let's follow up on that. Have Adiam check on it."

Dirk turned away from the woman when Claire began to gag. The nurse, he saw, had loosened the head restraint so Claire could turn her head to one side. But the bile coming out of her mouth was heavy. Dirk could tell Claire was struggling to breathe. When she started to whimper, he felt a suffocating numbness in his chest. Dismayed, he hung his head.

"Why doesn't she just sign the papers?" he muttered.

"Oh, she did that weeks ago," Claire's mother replied. "Didn't I tell you?"

Weeks ago?

Without a word, Dirk rose from his chair and left the observation room where he and Claire's mother were seated. He closed the door behind him and stepped across the hall.

"This is to make her forget she ever knew Teimbaka?" he mumbled.

Dirk placed his hands flush to the wall and banged his forehead against the white tile. Desperate for a moment of peace, he immersed his thoughts in the sound of his head hitting the wall, focusing on the dull *knock knock knock* in an attempt to block everything out. For a moment, he experienced a sense of relief. But then the knocking changed. Strangely, it turned sharper, conveying a sense of urgency. Confused, he held his head still. For a moment there was silence. A moment later, the knocking started again.

*

"Are you all right?" a voice outside the door pointedly asked.

Dirk stiffened and looked around. The knocking morphed into an angry pounding.

"Mr. Savage!" a man yelled.

As if waking from a stupor, Dirk looked hurriedly around the room. The small ghost-elephant—the manifestation of his fast-encroaching insanity—was nowhere to be seen. Dirk heard the jingling of keys just before the door to the room swung open. The familiar figure of Mr. Locket—the majordomo of the Waterman estate—stepped into the room. Dirk could tell by the man's expression he wasn't happy.

"The gardener told me he heard banging and crashing and that you were screaming at someone. He called, quite upset. Was certain something was amiss or that someone had broken into your apartment."

Dirk watched the man take stock of the room: watched his eyes drift from the beer bottle overturned in the corner to the ashtray lying by the door to the fallen lamp. Mr. Locket shook his head in a manner that suggested disgust.

"I'll leave you to your vices, then," Mr. Locket said after briefly clearing his throat. "I'll relay to the staff that you were watching a television program with the sound turned up."

Dirk raised a hand as the white-haired majordomo turned to leave.

"Claire," he blurted. "Any— Any word?"

Mr. Locket hesitated at the door. Dirk interpreted his expression as one of disdain when he turned to reply.

"Word, Mr. Savage? I'm afraid I don't follow."

"Is she—"

Dirk rubbed his fingers across his unshaven chin. Mr. Locket raised his eyebrows.

"Are they— The doctor, is he still using— Does she remember, I mean—" Dirk rubbed his hands over his face and sighed. "Is she comfortable?"

"Comfortable?" Dirk realized how strange the word sounded when Mr. Locket repeated it. "Comfortable." He saw the eyebrows of the tall, stately looking gentleman pinch together. "Impossible for me to say, I would think."

"I don't understand. Why is it impossible for you to tell me how she's doing?"

"It's rather simple, Mr. Savage." Dirk felt small and inadequate as Mr. Locket stared straight into his eyes. "Having never undergone electro-therapy while undergoing hallucinogenic psychotherapy, it's utterly impossible for me to say whether Miss Claire is *comfortable* in her situation. And Madam has not been forthcoming about her daughter's progress where it concerns her—" Mr. Locket took a lengthy pause "—memory-related illness."

Dirk found his attention drifting down to the man's black, impeccably shined wing-tip shoes.

"Do you require anything else at the moment?"

Dirk could hear the contempt in Mr. Locket's voice.

"I, uh—"

Dirk nearly jumped out of his chair when he saw the image of an elephant appear in the tip of Mr. Locket's shoes. Unnerved, he blinked a few times and waved his hand across his eyes. He breathed a sigh of relief when the image disappeared.

"I'll leave you to your thoughts, then."

Dirk looked up as Mr. Locket stepped out of the room and closed the door behind him. To his chagrin, the baby spirit-elephant was standing in the corner, staring at him with its haunting, hollow eyes.

*

The stream Mirko was following carved a relatively straight course through the woods. The clear, cold water flowed swiftly, rushing toward the river where he'd set up camp. As he hiked beside the crystal-clear stream, he held fast to the hope that his wife, Gabrielle, was preparing the family's lunch next to the campfire he and his sons—Anthony and Hassan—had meticulously built before they'd left to go fishing.

Smoked turkey on a hard roll with spicy mustard and dill pickle; yes, he could taste the combination as he envisioned it. *And coffee. Strong—black and hot—served in a tin cup.*

The thought of warming his hands on the sides of the cup as the aroma of coffee drifted into the air gave him a jolt of energy; he smiled. And perhaps, if Gabrielle didn't object—and why would she, since they were out in the country—he would light a Turkish cigarette after lunch and enjoy a well-deserved smoke.

Trout fishing. Who knew?

Mirko shook his head and chuckled. What was the show called? *The Outdoors? Wild Adventurer? Wild Kingdom?* He wasn't sure. But his boys loved watching the television program that starred an older white-haired man and his young assistant as they traveled around the globe, filming animals in exotic locations. And after having watched one particular telecast devoted to fly-fishing—and learning that Michigan had some of the best trout streams in America—his sons had relentlessly pestered him to take them on a camping trip. To his surprise, his wife agreed with his sons. "It would be a good thing for the family to do," she told him, "to go camping. It would introduce the boys to nature. Allow them to see there is more to their world than asphalt and cars and the grimy streets of Detroit."

The boys—Anthony and Hassan—had of course wholeheartedly supported their mother's point of view. Finding himself outvoted three to one, how could Mirko say no? So, after a bit of networking, camping equipment had been arranged. And with an offered bribe of four box seats for the upcoming Tigers game on opening day, three fly-fishing rods and reels were procured for a week's use from a local sporting goods store owner.

April—Mirko had envisioned that the weather in mid-April, coinciding with the boy's spring break from school, would be pleasantly warm during the day but still chilly enough at night that a big campfire and crawling into down-filled sleeping bags for a good night's sleep would be warranted.

Spring. Mirko chuckled to himself as his shoes sank into a patch of melting snow. What spring? The temperature was a frosty 38 degrees when he and the boys had hiked up river to the mouth of the stream where they'd been told brown trout might be biting. The temperature was supposed to reach a balmy 55 degrees by noontime, according to the weather report they'd heard on the transistor radio they'd packed. Maybe it was 55 degrees in the sun, but here in the woods next to the stream, the temperature felt closer to thirty.

Trout fishing. He shook his head. *Shit.* A waste of time so far. Not one nibble all morning. And Hassan kept getting his line caught in the branches lining the banks of the stream. And now Mirko's feet were wet and cold from tramping through patches of snow. The boys' feet had to be cold too. Cold, wet, tired—right now, Mirko didn't much care for camping. But the thought of hot coffee and a hearty sandwich gave him some comfort. And yes, whether Gabrielle objected or not, a Turkish cigarette would be in order after he ate.

"How much farther, do you think, Father?"

"You tell me, Mr. Lewis. This was your idea."

"Mr. Lewis?" Anthony—closer to nine now than eight, and bundled up in a puffy green parka—turned and gave his father a confused look. "Why do you call me that?"

"Your mother tells me you two are learning of this man, Lewis, the wanderer, in your American history lessons. Some kind of trailformer, yes?"

"Oh, I get it. Lewis and Clark." Anthony laughed. "And I think you mean trail*blazer!*" he yelled over his shoulder.

"Trailblazer," Mirko repeated under his breath. He shook his head and chuckled.

"I see it!"

Mirko looked ahead at Hassan's announcement. He watched his youngest son—youngest by fifteen seconds—run ahead of Anthony.

"Pizza!" the boy yelled.

"What is he talking about?" Mirko called out to Anthony. "What does he mean?"

"Camp's just ahead!" Anthony yelled back. "Mom must have gone for pizza! There's a box sitting on one of the chairs!"

Mirko looked past his son to their sky-blue tent rising out of the underbrush some thirty-five yards ahead. He didn't see his wife. But, as Anthony said, there was what looked to be a pizza box on the seat of one of the two navy-blue canvas camp chairs they'd carried from the car.

Pizza? Why would she go for pizza? And where would she have bought it? The nearest town is at least a dozen miles away. And Gabrielle doesn't like to drive, especially along roads she isn't familiar with.

"I can smell it! Come on, Dad, before Hassan eats it all!"

Grudgingly, Mirko broke into a jog.

"Pepperoni!"

Hassan held a slice of pepperoni pizza in front of his smiling face before taking a large bite. Then his head exploded like an overripe cantaloupe thrown against a concrete wall. Pieces of skull and brain sprayed every which way. A fountain of blood plumed into the air as the sound of a powerful gunshot reverberated across the river.

"Hassan!" Mirko wailed.

Dropping the three fishing rods he'd been carrying, Mirko sprinted ahead, pushing Anthony to the side.

"Run, Anthony! Run!" he shouted over his shoulder.

"Mama!" Anthony wailed. "Mama!"

Chest heaving, his head a jumbled mess of fragmented thoughts, Mirko came to an abrupt stop. He looked at the tent.

"Gabrielle," he muttered.

He looked at Hassan—or what was left of him. The boy's face was sheared away, the slice of pizza with a bite missing lying on the ground next to what remained of his mouth.

Pizza—he looked at the red garment hanging on the back of the chair above the box. He realized it was the fake Domino's jacket he'd hidden under the floorboards beneath his bed, in the same hiding place where he kept his Desert Eagle handgun. Instantly, he scanned the terrain where he guessed the shot had come from. He almost jumped out of his skin when something touched his hand.

"Where's Mama?" Anthony sniffled, wiping tears from his eyes.

Mirko looked down at his son before shifting his attention to the tent.

"You must go to the car," he told him. Placing a hand to the side of the boy's neck, he ran the tip of his thumb along the rim of Anthony's cheek. "Get help. You understand?"

"But Mama," Anthony whined.

"Go!" Mirko ordered. He pushed his son to move. "Go now!" When Anthony hesitated, Mirko stepped to him and slapped him across the face. "Do as I say!" He gave his son a harsh look before turning away.

Mirko knew what he was going to find before he reached for the flap covering the entrance to the tent. Yanking the heavy piece of canvas away, he saw Gabrielle's bloodstained body slouched in the second of the chairs they'd brought from the car. Her wrists and ankles were tied to the wooden arms and legs. Mirko stared at his wife's ash-colored face for a few moments before his eyes drifted to the knife that had been used to kill her. It was the big butcher's knife they'd brought to clean and gut the trout they were going to catch. The blade was embedded in the center of her throat almost to the hilt.

A second gunshot boomed, and Mirko felt a stabbing jolt of pain at the knee of his left leg. The pain felled him. Laboriously, he twisted his upper torso around when he heard Anthony scream. He vaguely registered the powerful crack of the second gunshot as he stared at the terrified face of his son. The sound, however, was inconsequential to the agonizing pressure penetrating his forehead. And then there was nothing.

*

Chris lined up the scopes' crosshairs on the boy's forehead. His index finger slid across the trigger. He took a deep breath and held it as he waited to see if the boy was going to move. But the boy was in shock, he guessed. He was frozen, staring at his father's body, not moving a muscle. The boy would be an easy shot, one he could make in his sleep. But he hesitated. Then he exhaled. With a sigh, he took his eye away from the telescopic sight. He grunted, then crawled away from the small ridge of hard-packed soil he'd used to steady the rifle. What was left of his conscience told him he was done here. A father, a mother, and a child had been killed. A debt collected: three lives taken in return for the murders of Ed, Elizabeth, and Yutanda Taylor.

*

"Why we gotta meet here? What's wrong with the usual place?" Lucy said as she turned and watched the red cab drive away. "And you bet your sweet ass you gonna pay me back for the money I shelled out to get here."

She gave Goliath a sour look and then nodded over her shoulder to the receding automobile.

"And you best be figurin' on callin' one back here so I can get home." She huffed and grumbled as she stepped through the doorway of what looked to be a warehouse. "And you'll be payin' for that one too."

The daylight that had temporarily brightened the interior of the warehouse disappeared as Goliath eased the door shut behind her.

"Or Mr. Super Freak payin'." She laughed and waved her hand through the air like she was shooing a fly. "Or whatever name he going by this week." She laughed again and raised a finger into the air. "Course, we know who he *really* is."

Turning to Goliath, she put her finger to her lips.

"But, shh," she told him, her eyes going wide. "Don't nobody supposed to know. Might upset the congregation," she whispered, then winked.

Goliath gestured her forward and, when she turned, gave a slight nudge to the small of her back.

"Place smells," Lucy muttered. She took a few tentative steps into a cavernous, dimly lit area. "What is this place? Why I got to come here?" She eyed Goliath as he moved past her.

"Fishery," he mumbled in his gravelly voice. "Went bankrupt a few years back."

"Thought it smelt like an old can of sardines," she said with a chuckle. "Phew—stink like old river water." She laughed and looked up. "Why fish need so much room?" She pointed a finger up to the ceiling and narrowed her eyes. "Can't even see it, it so far up. Where the roof?"

Goliath shook his head but said nothing.

"Now looky here, why—?"

Lucy paused in mid-sentence when she saw Goliath stop next to three large black barrels. She edged a few steps forward when he leaned down behind them.

"What you doin'?"

Goliath straightened, a piece of plywood in his hand. Without responding to Lucy, he placed the rectangular piece of wood over top of the middle barrel. Before she could ask him what the wood was for, he leaned over and retrieved what she thought was some kind of lamp. Giving Lucy a cursory look, Goliath placed the brass object down on the plywood. A small flame flared and then flickered as he struck a lighter and lit the wick of the lamp.

"Gonna read me a story?" she teased.

Lucy pulled the front edges of the orange boa vest she was wearing close together and shivered. She appraised the room; the area seemed darker and more imposing beyond the periphery of the flickering light.

"Hey!" Lucy impatiently snapped, absently scratching her forearms. "Why I gotta come here?"

Goliath smiled and bent down a third time, producing what Lucy thought was some kind of doctor's bag.

"New supplier," he said, plopping the bag down on top of a barrel. "Need your opinion."

"What's wrong with the old supplier?" Lucy asked. "Weren't nothin' wrong with his shit. Why you wanna change?"

"He's dead."

Lucy watched Goliath take a spoon, a syringe, a bottle of water, a section of rubber hosing, a hunk of cotton, and a plastic packet out of the doctor's bag.

"Well, why didn't you just—?"

"Black tar." Goliath held up a plastic packet and jiggled the balloon caps stored inside. "Freak wants to know what you think."

"Oh, he does, does he?" Lucy strutted toward Goliath, her stiletto heels click-clacking on the cement floor. "Since when the Reverend give a shit what I think?"

"Don't call him that," Goliath growled.

Lucy came to an abrupt stop and extended her hands out in front of her chest.

"Calm down, tiger," she said. "Ain't mean no disrespect. I call him Mr. Freak if that make you happy." She opened her arms and looked right and left. "You act like somebody 'round to hear us." She gave a nervous giggle. "Ain't nobody else here but you and me." She leaned forward. "'Less somebody be hiding in the dark somewhere."

Lucy couldn't tell what Goliath was thinking from the look on his face. But she sensed he wasn't happy. A little shiver ran up her spine.

"What kind of fish they make here?" she asked, changing the subject.

She took a long look around, pretending she could see what lay behind the veil of darkness blanketing the cavernous room. A subtle whiff of vinegar drew her attention back to Goliath. She could feel what she called butterfly wings fluttering in her stomach. She took a deep breath. Her heart began to race. Her eyes locked on to the spoon Goliath held over the flame.

"Tie yourself off," he told her with a slight nod to the thin strand of rubber hosing lying on the plywood. "One?" he asked.

Entranced by the amber liquid pooling within the cradle of the spoon, Lucy felt like she was floating as she moved to the trio of barrels. She picked up the section of blue latex and, without a second's hesitation, started to shimmy out of the leggings she wore under a black vinyl skirt.

"One cc?" Goliath gruffly repeated, holding up a needle and syringe.

"What?" Lucy looked at the tip of the needle and felt her heart flutter. "Yeah."

She stepped out of her leggings and kicked them off to the side.

"Got a chair in this place?"

"Sit on the floor with your back against a barrel."

Lucy obediently squatted down on the cement floor and slid a few inches to the nearest barrel. Tentatively, she nudged her back against the metal.

"Feel like a cement wall," she muttered, pushing her weight against the barrel. "What's in these?" she asked Goliath in a loud voice.

"Fish oil," he curtly replied. "You ready?"

"Fuckin' hold on," she grumbled.

Lucy hiked up her skirt and wound the latex around her upper thigh. After pulling it taught, she tied the ends together in a simple knot. Then she gave the back of her leg a few quick slaps with the tips of her fingers and felt along her inner thigh.

"There's a good baby," she said when she located a vein. "Ready!"

She looked up to find Goliath standing over her, holding a needle and syringe. Lucy's eyes widened.

"This where you tell me I got to suck you off 'fore I can have that?" she asked matter-of-factly. "Do a better job if I had a chair."

"Take it," he told her in a gruff voice.

Lucy reached up and snatched the syringe from his fingers. She eyed the cc of liquid pooled in the end of the syringe.

"Black tar, you say?" She smiled, mesmerized by the gleaming tip of the needle. "Where this shit made?"

"China," Goliath told her.

"China." She started to laugh. "Ain't that the shit." Her laughter turned into a cackle.

"What's so fucking funny?"

"Like you see on TV," she told him, modulating her shrill laugh to an awkward giggle.

She lowered the needle and syringe to her leg.

"Chinese New Year."

She pinched the vein behind her inner thigh and inserted the tip of the needle.

"Dragons in the street."

Deftly, she pulled the plunger back ever so slightly. When she saw a miniscule amount of blood draw into the chamber, she pushed the plunger all the way forward.

"Dragons in my veins."

*

Goliath stepped back to the makeshift worktable. When he saw Lucy rest her head against the barrel and look up toward the ceiling, he reached into the black doctor's bag and took out a shallow metal bowl.

"Zoom, zoom, zoom," he heard Lucy mumble as he emptied the contents of five balloon caps into the bowl. "Floatin' on heaven."

Goliath added a touch of water to the bowl. Then, holding the container by its lipped edge, he placed it over the flame.

"Good shit?" he asked as he reached into the black bag.

He shook his head when he heard her mutter, "Zoom, zoom, zoom."

"Hey!" He swished the bowl as his shout faded into the darkness. "Good shit?"

"Fuckin' yeah," Lucy happily replied. "How many of these I get a week?"

Goliath set the bowl down on the plywood platform and picked up the needle and syringe he'd taken from the bag.

"All you want."

He tried not to laugh when she made some kind of sighing squeal.

"Mr. Freak's way of showing his appreciation for you keeping quiet about the child and such."

Goliath inserted the tip of the needle into the liquefied contents of the bowl and slowly drew the plunger back.

"He just asks that you stop referring to him as Reverend when you get annoyed with—" he lifted the syringe and checked the fill lines "—how your day might be going."

"No, no, no, no, no—I'm good, I'm good," she assured him, waving her hand in the air like she was clearing a cobweb. "Yeah, I won't say Reverend no more." She snickered. "I mean, I won't say that *word* no more." She put a finger to her lips. "Shh, shh, shh." She giggled. "I be a good girl and keep quiet." Letting her hand fall to her side, she sighed and closed her eyes.

Goliath leaned down and placed one of his very large hands against the side of Lucy's head.

"Be real still for a second, okay?"

"What ya doin'?"

"Bug. Just going to flick it off you, okay?"

"Yeah, yeah."

Goliath spread his fingers across the side of Lucy's face until his thumb felt the pulse on the underside of her jaw.

"Don't move," he whispered.

Goliath inserted the needle into the vein that ran down the soft area of Lucy's neck just under her jawline.

"Ow," she muttered.

Pressing her head against the barrel, Goliath emptied five cc of pure heroin into her bloodstream.

"Zoom," he heard her whisper.

Extracting the needle from her neck, he stood up straight and checked the time on his wristwatch: 8:30 pm. His shift at the bar started at 10:00 pm. He glanced down at Lucy and saw her shoulders twitch and her head roll to one side. He dropped the needle and syringe back into the doctor's bag and then hurriedly shoveled everything he'd placed atop the plywood into the bag. Using the toe of his boot, he gave Lucy's shoulder a slight nudge. She fell sideways onto the cement floor, her face devoid of expression. Dropping the black bag at his feet, Goliath bent and picked up a crowbar. A foul odor assailed his nostrils as he inserted the toe of the crowbar under the lid of the center barrel.

"Shit," he cursed when he saw the puddle of urine around Lucy's skirt.

He popped open the lid of the barrel.

"Fuck." He lifted the lid. "Should have dumped her in first," he muttered, shaking his head. "Fuck."

4

WHAT WILL I look like when you see me?

Claire stared at the seam in the corner of the room and tried to concentrate.

It was real, wasn't it?

She curled her fingers, rubbing the tips against the inside of her palm. She could feel scar tissue.

That proves it was real, doesn't it? He did ask me. Why won't anyone believe me?

The seam began to waver. Two faces peered out at her from the wide crack that formed. The faces were those of her doctor and nurse. They were shaking their heads and frowning, just like they'd done when she'd first told them about her conversation with the white fire and how she'd come to acquire the scar on her hand. The expressions of ridiculing doubt the doctor and nurse had worn when she'd described the manifestation had unnerved her. How could they not understand? "Don't you believe in God and Jesus and the Holy Spirit?" she'd asked them.

Drug therapy had started the next day.

Claire continued to stare into the expanded seam while she ran the tip of her forefinger along the edge of the butter knife the orderly had mistakenly left when he cleared her dinner tray. The teeth of the blade were unusually sharp for a butter knife. But she thought little more of the knife and its sharpness because she knew something important was about to happen, something that had happened several times in the recent past. So she concentrated a little harder—and waited. The faces of the doctor and nurse dissolved. The scar in the middle of her palm began to tingle. The outline of the seam grew wider. She leaned toward the opening.

Claire flinched and looked over her shoulder, her eyes drawn to the small pane of glass located near the top of a knobless door. She tightened her grip on the knife and pressed the teeth of the blade against her wrist as she looked for signs of movement on the other side of the window—a blurred shape or a shifting shadow that would warn her someone was watching. Seeing nothing, she grudgingly shifted her attention to the corners of the empty room where she was being kept. When she was satisfied no one was observing her from some unseen hiding place, she made the sign of the cross and turned her attention to the seam.

She waited. Beads of perspiration formed on her brow. She could feel tension building within her. She pressed harder on the knife to ease her anxiety. Slowly, the seam widened, growing in increments until it was the width of her body. Claire peered into it. She could see a line of flames burning near a body of water. Above the fire, a group of winged forms began to take shape. Although they were nothing more than dark silhouettes hovering within a band of wavering heat, their outlines reminded her of the gargoyles stationed along the ramparts of Notre Dame Cathedral: human-like in body, with horns and long, spiked tails. She felt a cold shiver run down her spine when the creatures began to swoop low into the flames with their claw-tipped hands. She couldn't help but think they were trying to capture someone or something. It frightened her to think what the creatures would do with their prey once they got hold of it. As Claire contemplated what or who the winged gargoyles might be pursuing, a blue fireball rocketed into the line of flames and exploded, sending streams of fire outward into the surrounding darkness. Claire drew back from the seam when she felt something warm splatter against her neck and cheeks. Reflexively, she wiped her face. When she examined her hands, she saw they were covered in blood. She screamed.

*

"Here we go."

"How much did the doctor give her?"

"Enough to make an elephant hallucinate for a week."

"God. I can't believe she's lasted this long."

"That's why the orderly was instructed to leave the knife."

The younger of the two nurses observing Claire through a ceiling panel peephole frowned and shook her head. She pursed her lips as she reached for the phone sitting atop a coffee table half an arm's length from where the two women were crouched.

"I'll call for medical."

The older woman placed her hand atop the receiver before the younger woman could lift it from its cradle.

"No," she told her in an impassive voice. "Orders are to observe, not interfere."

*

Eden was chewing on a khat leaf when a large centipede crawled atop her foot. She gritted her teeth and tightened her grip on her rifle to fight off the urge to bend and swat the creature away. The centipede—a fat brown specimen with yellow legs, nearly as long as her foot—came to a sudden stop. She held her breath as the insect swept its long antennae across her skin. Unsure if the bug was poisonous, she spit a glob of green-tinged saliva from her mouth. The wad landed on what Eden hoped was the centipede's head. The arthropod scurried away. Eden breathed a sigh of relief. A moment later, she cocked her head to the side and tensed her muscles. Men were approaching, the men she had been waiting for. She could hear their laughter, hear the motor of the truck following behind them. Grinding her jaws together, she yanked back the charging bolt of her AK-47.

Thieves! Murderers! Poachers!

She promised herself she would kill all of them before they had a chance to move off the trail. Their deaths would be a message: ivory and slaves come with a price—a heavy price. Blood for blood, a life for a life. Don't come here. Don't trespass on Bouda's land. Maybe the *ebob caca* would cease to exist if she killed enough of them, she mused. Maybe the elephant killing would stop and women and children wouldn't fear for their lives while they slept. Maybe all killing would stop. She mulled the notion in her head: no more killing. There'd be peace.

Eden spit out the masticated khat leaf and stuffed a fresh one in her mouth.

Peace.

She gnashed down on the new leaf and felt an instant surge of adrenaline.

Peace.

The men's laughter grew louder. She knew who they were, and yet she didn't know. They could be some of George Henry's army, or some of Bacha Alba's mercenaries. Maybe they were soldiers from Mengistu's government, come to rape the land they were sworn to protect. Unconsciously, she shrugged her shoulders; she didn't know and didn't care. Whoever they were, they weren't welcome.

This is Bouda's territory!

She took a deep breath and slotted the AK-47 for auto fire. Then she calmly stepped out from behind the mound of tall grass where she'd been waiting.

Eden took no notice of the terrified faces of the men carrying the ivory tusks. If she had, she would have seen that some were not much older than she. But it didn't matter. Young, old, in-between; strong, weak; intelligent, stupid—whatever they were, Eden saw them as part of the plague that was threatening to destroy the land. And plague had to be eradicated. The land—Bouda's land, her land—needed cleansed.

Eden pulled the trigger.

The eight men who'd been tasked with carrying the ivory tusks were decimated before her ammo clip ran out. As Eden ejected the spent clip, she observed the three men riding in the cab of the truck following the ivory bearers frantically attempting to open the doors. With calculated calmness, Eden slotted a new magazine into the magwell of the AK-47and rocked it backward. When she heard the definitive click locking the new ammunition clip into the weapon, she yanked the charging bolt back and depressed the trigger. The windshield of the truck blew inward under a barrage of bullets. The men inside were reduced to bloody mincemeat in a matter of seconds. With a smile of grim satisfaction, Eden took her finger off the trigger and listened. There was a moment of gratifying silence. And then she heard what sounded like crying children.

*

"Are you just going to sit there like a dumb mute?"

Dirk adjusted his grip on the car's steering wheel and glanced into the rearview mirror.

"God, you're fucking annoying."

He looked over and gave the little ghost-elephant sitting alongside him in the front seat of the Cadillac Fleetwood a condescending smirk.

"But you already know that, don't you? Fucking big-eared, hollowed-eyed freak. See the white inlay on those radio buttons?" He nodded toward the console. "Ivory."

Dirk smiled when the creature turned its head to look at him.

"Probably came from your mother. Poacher probably sawed the tusks off her face while she was still alive." Dirk gave the little ghost-beast a wink and a nod. "Yeah, I thought that might get your attention." He smirked. "Anything you want to say to me now?"

Dirk quickly turned his head away and looked out the driver's-side window when he saw a crystalline tear slide down the ghost-elephant's face.

"Maybe there's a 7-Eleven up the road," he muttered. "Get you a pair of over-sized sunglasses." Dirk looked back at the ethereal entity and smiled. "You know, the ones with the giant lenses." He checked the rearview mirror again before shifting his attention to the road. "Be nice not have to stare into those black holes you call eyes. God, you're a creepy-looking fuck. Was it the same hunter that killed you that killed your mother?"

He saw the ghost-beast turn and look out the windshield.

"Sure. Just sit there and pretend you can't hear a word I'm saying." Dirk blew air between his lips and shook his head. "But you let me know if you need anything. Like if a mud hole pops up along the side of the road and you want to get out and take a roll in it, I'm happy to oblige. God forbid you get upset with me and disappear." Dirk ran a hand through his hair. "Like I could be so lucky."

When the baby ghost-elephant suddenly appeared on the hood of the car, Dirk flinched back into the leather seat and grimaced. As the beast stuck its trunk through the windshield, he slammed his foot on the brake and brought the car to a screeching stop. The ghost-beast—its eyes as wide as the tires of the Cadillac— placed the tip of its trunk on Dirk's forehead. Instantaneously, Dirk was immersed in a vision.

*

"Peter!"

Dirk felt his heart rip apart as he witnessed Genevieve's body arch upward. With the sound of her tortured scream echoing inside his head, he lunged forward in an attempt to break free from the men who'd pinned his arms behind his back. When he couldn't break their grip, he twisted sideways and kicked the man to his left, smashing the toe of his boot into his shin. His effort was rewarded with the butt of a rifle slammed into the pit of his stomach. The pain shooting through his torso doubled him over, but not before he saw the man who was standing above Genevieve thrust a burning torch into her neck.

Suddenly, one of the men holding him jerked his head up by his hair. Hands clamped harshly around his face held it immobile. Forced to stare straight ahead, he could feel the insanity of rage bubble inside of him as two men from the mob who'd chased him and Genevieve into the alley took knives from their robes and cut Genevieve's clothes from her upper torso.

He felt a scream explode from his body but strangely did not hear it unleashed into the sky. In its place: a dull, thudding ring inside his skull. Confused and disoriented, he watched the wall of the alley begin to tilt and sway. The men around him began to laugh, their bodies spun around in circles. Then something was shoved into his face. Flesh was pressed against his cheeks and rubbed across his lips. The taste of blood washed over his tongue. Then a savage blow to his testicles sapped the air from his lungs and strength from his body. He sagged forward and gagged. He longed for unconsciousness, but his head snapped back when something hard smashed against his forehead.

"*Madinatuna!*" someone screamed in his ear. "*Ferenji caca!*"

Groggy, his body wracked with pain, he sensed people lifting him to his feet. A moment later, the back of his head slammed against something immovable. A second blow to his testicles left him shattered. He crumpled to the ground, writhing in pain.

Dirk stared blankly at the sliver of sky above the walls of the alley as warm liquid streamed over his face. A chorus of laughter roared in his ears. The flow of liquid was steady but then slowly subsided, ending with a few dribbling drops. He closed his eyes and welcomed the merciful blackness when he heard someone shout "*Khalass!*" In the ensuing silence, he heard a woman's tortured moans.

Genevieve!

He tried to move.

Genevieve!

He raked his fingers across the hard-packed soil.

Genevieve!

He felt his torso lifted off the ground and propped against something hard.

Genevieve!

He opened his eyes.

Genevieve was kneeling in front of him, blood streaming down her chest. Two men—their faces hidden by the ends of their robes—held her up by her wrists. A third man stood behind her, a handful of her honey-auburn hair clutched in his hand.

"Your lover," a foul-smelling voice sneered.

Dirk watched in horror as the man standing behind Genevieve drew a long, serrated knife from the waist of his robe. As the man standing behind Genevieve began to cut into her throat, a needle was jammed into Dirk's neck. He could barely comprehend Genevieve's agonized scream before a feeling of euphoria exploded throughout his body. All the emotions he was experiencing—pain, rage, fear, horror—turned to bliss and calm. He felt his body floating, as though it were drifting on a gentle wind. The smell of perfume—sweet, heady, sensual—filled his nose. Songbirds sang lovingly in his ears.

It was in a state of ecstasy that Dirk found Genevieve's head nestled in his lap. Lovingly, he ran his fingers through her hair. Her flesh felt like ivory as his fingertips slid across her forehead. Jubilation pulsed through his veins. He tilted his head back and looked up at the sky. He stared at the stars and let his mind go blank.

*

"What happened then?"

Dirk swallowed hard as the vison dissipated. Cautiously, he looked around. The vibration of the car's idling engine rumbled through his body. Outside, the car headlights illuminated a wooded stretch of road. Thirty yards up on the left, he could see a sign. He had to squint to read the words stenciled in block letters, white against a brown background: New Market Clinic. Beneath the name of the clinic, down in the right corner: "2 miles."

"What happened when you woke up?"

Dirk cowered against the car door and bumped the side of his face against the window. Gripped with fear, he unwillingly looked right, where the sound of Genevieve's voice had originated. The small ghost-elephant was staring at him.

"I'm fuckin' losin' it," he said in an exasperated exhale.

In an effort to regain some semblance of composure, he gripped the steering wheel and forced a laugh.

"What happened?"

Dirk brushed his ear when he felt a puff of air against it. His eyes immediately darted to the seat next to him. Genevieve's voice had sounded so close. Surely it was her breath he'd felt against his ear.

"What happened?"

The question posed in Genevieve's voice poked at his memories. He started to shake as the young ghost-elephant pulled its trunk away from his ear.

"You motherfucker!" he yelled. "I don't want to remember what happened!"

He recoiled when the baby ghost-beast extended its trunk toward his ear.

"No!" he screamed. "I don't want to hear her voice! I don't want to hear her voice!"

But it was too late. Genevieve whispered in his ear.

"Tell me what happened."

Dirk felt a shudder in his throat.

"I wish I had died," he croaked.

"But you didn't."

Genevieve's tone was gentle and filled with concern. Dirk closed his eyes. He could smell her perfume.

"Tell me what happened."

"I woke under a blazing sun," he told her. "I was confused. The intense light, the heat. I didn't understand. Two men, they grabbed me by my ears and forced me to look down." Dirk closed his eyes before he continued. "Your severed head was in my lap. Flies—swarming, buzzing, maddening—were everywhere, crawling inside your mouth, probing your eyes. I tried to throw you off me."

Dirk paused and took a deep breath. He rested his forehead against the steering wheel before he went on.

"I couldn't move. I was tied to a post. The men kept my head tilted down, made me watch the flies eat away at you until I vomited."

Dirk lifted his head and looked out the windshield. His eyes scanned the terrain from one side of the road to the other.

"Your mutilated body was three feet away. I— I—" He grimaced. "They pissed in my face. Screamed at me, told me it was their city. Whites, foreigners, *ferenji* needed to go, needed to die." Dirk looked over at the ghost-elephant. "Then they stuck a needle in my neck and—" He shrugged his shoulders. "I wasn't there. But when I regained lucidity, the nightmare was. Only worse, because your face was rancid and decaying. Three more times—" He hesitated. "Three more times they stuck a needle in my neck. And each time I came out of my stupor, your face—it was worse." He laughed, bitterly. "But the fourth, the fourth time was different. I was alone, unbound, your remains scattered next to me across some godforsaken stretch of land. Vultures were everywhere. I scrambled away and watched them pick at your rotting flesh."

Dirk ran a hand through his hair and stared out the windshield. After a few moments, he shifted the car into drive.

"They left me with a needle and syringe full of heroin in my shirt pocket." He took his foot off the brake and eased the car onto the asphalt. "Salt traders took pity on me and took me to a village. From there, it took me three months to make it back to Djibouti. I was a junkie for two years after."

He brought the car to a sudden stop and glared at the ghost-beast.

"You're a fuck!" he blurted. "Not enough you badger me into stealing one of the old bitch's cars—" He gave the ghost-beast an unforgiving scowl. "But you make me relive—" He shook his head.

"Claire needs you now."

Dirk tried to punch the ghost-elephant's trunk away from his ear. But his hand passed through the ethereal beast and struck the side of his head.

"You son of a bitch," he muttered. "Using her voice to do your bidding."

The baby ghost-elephant removed its trunk from Dirk's ear and wrapped it around the top of the steering wheel. It stared at Dirk for a moment before nodding toward the road.

"Do you have a plan to get her out?" Dirk shifted into drive and pressed down on the gas pedal. "Or are you going to be an asshole and go mute again?"

The ghost-elephant didn't reply.

*

Bin'ka understood they were in trouble. As soon as he saw bobbing lights emerge along the fire-line in front of the dock, he knew what they were. And he knew the dhow he'd stolen wouldn't be able to outrun the RHIBs in pursuit. Assuming the attack boats were outfitted with .50 caliber machine guns, he figured he'd be dead within the next thirty minutes. And the woman—who is she? She, along with the kids on board, would be taken prisoner and sold to the highest bidder.

Bin'ka studied the woman for a moment, noting her white skin. Her fate would be far worse than slavery, he guessed. Prostitution was more likely. Perhaps she'd be allowed to finish out her days as a slave if she was lucky enough to survive her years as a whore. But he didn't hold much hope she'd live through that vocation. Most prostitutes died within a few years of being forced into that life, whether it be from disease, an angry customer, drug abuse, or by their own hand. The life expectancy of a prostitute in east Africa—especially a white-skinned one—was, at best, a few years.

Yet, the woman had been with Teimbaka. *Is she a fighter?* he wondered. Surely, she was a survivor. Anyone who kept company with the Lion had to be. But would she fight? He glanced toward the docks; the searchlights were drawing closer.

"Can you use a weapon?" he called to the woman from his place at the helm.

He saw her look back toward him as the first warning shots raked the dark water in front of the boat's bow. In conjunction, the searchlights swung in the same direction, scouring the surface of the water less than fifty meters ahead of their position. The dhow would soon be caught in the light's glare. The old sailboat would be an easy target. As he assessed their predicament, he heard the sudden surge of outboard motors. The boats were separating, he imagined—one headed toward their bow, the other toward their stern.

Bin'ka checked the cut of the dhow's sail and made a slight adjustment to their heading. Then he tied the tiller to an aft cleat to keep the ship on a straight course. Helm secure, he reached for a long canvas duffel lying by his feet.

A second burst of automatic gunfire strafed the water portside. Bin'ka heard the woman scream. He pulled an Uzi and an RPG from the duffel. A searchlight swept across the deck from astern as he looped the handles of the duffel around his forearm. A second light beamed directly into his eyes.

Bin'ka dropped the RPG by his foot and engaged the Uzi. Turning astern, he used the powerful beam of light streaming across his shoulders to pinpoint the exact location of the aft attack boat. He fired a sustained round directly into the light. The light immediately died. He could barely make out the boat's murky outline as it maneuvered toward the dhow's starboard side. He'd swung the Uzi to fire when the dhow's wooden frame shuddered under the force of high-caliber bullets ripping into her planks. The dozen odd children he'd freed from a slaver's pen and placed in the boat's shallow hold began to cry. Someone tugged on his tunic.

It was the woman. Her eyes were wild and unfocused when he turned to address her.

"What are you doing?"

"We'll all be killed!" she screamed.

Then she grabbed the Uzi and tried to wrench it from his grasp. Bin'ka clubbed her across the face with the back of his hand and sent her sprawling to the deck. A barrage of bullets fired from the stern attack boat forced him to dive onto his stomach. He grabbed the RPG and slid the canvas duffle from his arm. Out of the corner of his eye, he saw a boy running toward him.

"Get down!" he yelled.

He watched the boy fly ten feet backward as a bullet hit the center of his chest. Bin'ka shifted his attention to the canvas bag. He quickly rummaged through it until he found what he wanted; a booster charge and a warhead.

"No!" the woman screamed. "You have to give up! You have to surrender!"

Bin'ka scowled at the woman as he screwed the booster charge to the warhead and loaded it into the RPG.

"Slavery is death!" he shouted. "Grab the Uzi and fight if you want to live!"

*

Sarah felt powerless. How could she convince the man to lay down his weapon? One boy was already dead! Shot in the chest. And the man didn't even flinch!

"Please!" she yelled. "You've got to—"

Sarah pressed her face against the deck and covered her ears as a shower of bullets whizzed past her and shredded a portion of gunwale.

"Cover aft!" she heard the man shout.

She lifted her face when she felt footsteps on the deck. Two children ran by her toward the back of the boat. One of them—a girl no more than ten, she guessed—retrieved the machine gun where the big man had dropped it. The boy, she saw, was crouched next to the open duffel. Sarah was about to shout a warning, to tell them to get down, when the girl pointed the weapon toward the back of the boat and fired. Dumbfounded, Sarah pushed up to her knees. Immediately, something plowed into her and pressed her to the deck just as a rush of fire-charged fumes streamed over her head. Disoriented, she looked over her shoulder. The big man was standing over her. He slapped the side of the bulky weapon he held and yelled, "Slide me the bag! Hurry!"

Sarah felt a body scramble across her back. It was a girl pulling the bag toward the man. In the next instant, the girl's throat exploded. Then another bullet ripped into her chest. The impact sent the girl over the gunwale into the water.

"Do you want to die?" the man yelled. Sarah's head banged against the wood planks as he stomped by her. "Fight!"

Sarah ran her tongue across her lips; she tasted blood. Then something warm dripped into her eyes, clouding her vision. Reflexively, she wiped her hand across her face; sticky, gooey moisture clung to her fingers. She was about to throw up when the boat suddenly shuddered under an onslaught of bullets.

"Get down!" she heard a boy scream.

Sarah looked toward the back of the boat. The little boy was armed with a machine gun. He was pointing the weapon directly at her, but his eyes were searching past her, out across the boat's stern. As she crouched to the deck, the sweeping beam of a powerful searchlight exposed him. Sarah looked on in horror as the boy's chest erupted, then closed her eyes when plumes of flesh and blood turned the beam of white light a sickening pink.

"Do something!" the man bellowed.

Sarah's eyes flew open, but she was transfixed by the sight of the little boy's body lying on the deck. When she noticed blood pooling over the wooden planks, she was transported back in time, back into the closet where she'd been defiled. A vision of the hooded man—her captor—lying facedown in a puddle of blood materialized in her thoughts.

A whooshing explosion jolted Sarah out of her stupor. As she struggled to regain some sense of clarity, something metal flashed across her field of vision. She glimpsed a section of rope fluttering behind it. *Grappling hook!*

"Grab the gun!" the man implored.

A little girl ran by. Sarah saw her lunge for the machine gun. To her horror, a knife embedded itself in the girl's back. The child instantly fell to her knees. Then a man—armed with a rifle—jumped onto the deck. A flurry of gunfire ensued.

"The Uzi! Use the Uzi!" she heard the big man shout.

Sarah focused on the machine gun lying on the deck. She was about to scramble for it when she saw the little girl with the knife in her back reach for the weapon. In the next instant, the man who'd boarded the boat pointed his weapon at the girl's head and fired.

"No!" Sarah screamed as she watched the girl's head explode.

Dazed, Sarah dumbly watched the intruder raise his weapon. As he fired, she lunged for the Uzi and hugged it to her chest. When the intruder aimed his gun down at her face, Sarah swung the Uzi upward and pulled the trigger.

*

"Cut the damn bullet out!"

Sarah lost herself to the sky, immersing her senses in the furrows of cotton-candy clouds in the plain of cerulean blue. Certainly, God's hand was on display, for who else could take delicate threads of gold-tinged pink and sew them into fluffy loops emblazoned with day's first light? No one but the Lord, no one but the Lord.

And look below, her imagination invited. *Behold the sunrise of heaven! Absorb the rose-hued light sparkling atop the turquoise water and linger in its beauty.* Sarah breathed deep, absorbing the serenity around her. She felt contentment and peace wash over her, the feelings reinforced with each little wave that rippled against the dhow's wooden hull.

"Stop daydreaming! Get on with it!"

Sarah blinked and clenched her hand.

A seagull materialized an arm's length from where she was seated— a large white-bellied bird with broad, grey-feathered wings—effortlessly floating on a current of wind inches above her head. Captivated by the bird's appearance, Sarah linked her emotions with the motion of the bird. Exhilarated when the seagull was lifted skyward by a gust of wind, forlorn and regretful when it suddenly zoomed out of sight.

"Damn it, woman! What the hell is wrong with you?"

Giggles, children's giggles—she heard giggles.

Children—the children!

Sarah shifted her attention from the sky and sea and looked to the ship's hold.

"*Shange!*" a boy called out in greeting.

The other children—the fourteen who had survived the attack—laughed and waved.

"*Shange!*" one of the girls chimed in.

Within a moment, the ship was filled with squealing voices.

"*Shange bahr!*" a boy shouted above the din. "*Shange bahr!*" the rest chimed in.

Sarah heard the big man laugh.

"What are they saying?" she asked as she turned to face him.

"That's what concerns you?" the man replied, incredulous. "Not this?"

Sarah followed his eyes to the bloody tourniquet wrapped around his upper arm. He grunted and looked skyward.

"Women. Hmph."

Sarah felt her fingers clutch at an object in her hand. She shuddered when she saw she was holding a bloodstained knife.

"I—"

She glanced between at the man's wound and the knife. An image of herself as a teenager trapped in a closet flashed through her head.

"I was—" She gave the man a sheepish glance. "Why are they laughing at me?"

"Laughing at you?" She saw him look past her toward the ship's hold. "Urchins." He frowned and shook his head. "Doesn't make sense. Zulu and Arabic." He huffed. "They probably don't even know what they're saying."

Sarah glanced across her shoulder. She smiled and bowed her head when the children waved to her.

"Jesus Lord, are you ever going to finish digging this bullet out of my arm?"

Sarah immediately sat up straight.

"Why do you speak of Him?"

"Him? I was just— Shit, are you one of those?"

Sarah felt a pang of self-consciousness.

"I— I'm not sure what you mean"

"A religious nut—a Christian."

Sarah abruptly looked out across the water.

"Though, if you are a Christian," he chuckled, "you certainly don't act like one."

She glared at him.

"I am a Sister of the Holy Cross!" she vehemently stated. "I'm a nun!"

"*Shange bahr! Shange bahr!*" several of the children shouted.

And when some of the children roared like lions, she turned and gave them a stern look. Immediately, the ones who'd been making the ferocious sounds fell quiet and looked sheepishly toward their feet. Behind her, the man heartily laughed. Angered she was being mocked, she whirled on him, her expression fierce.

"What are they saying?" she demanded.

He winced as he raised his hands in protest.

"Remember, you're holding a knife." He nodded to the blade in her hand. "No need to—" He shrugged. With a nod toward the children, he touched his wound. "We owe you. No need to be angry. You killed—"

"I didn't mean to," she interjected. She looked down at the knife resting in her palm. "I just—"

"They were scum. Butchers. Slavers. The world won't miss them."

Sarah closed her eyes and tried to concentrate on the sound of the dhow sliding through the water.

"You were slow to act," he went on. "But when you did act, you acted with courage."

She squeezed her eyes tightly shut, hoping the red color swirling on the inside of her lids would disappear.

"*Shange,*" he said in passing. "Maybe the urchins are right."

Her lips trembled and the knife shook when she looked at him and asked in a soft voice, "What does that mean?"

"*Shange*: a Zulu word meaning 'he who walks like a lion.'"

She surprised herself when she giggled.

"And the other?" she asked, somewhat embarrassed.

"*Bahr,*" he said.

She cocked her head to the side when he started to laugh.

"Why do you laugh? Is it a word— Are they— Are you making fun of me?"

He winced as he lifted his wounded arm from the tiller and slightly waved his hand from side to side.

"It's not what you think," he told her. "It's just that the first word is Zulu. The other, Arabic."

"Arabic?"

"*Bahr*: 'ocean, the sea.'"

He shrugged his massive shoulders. Sarah noticed sweat beading on his clean-shaven head. The sun, she realized, had risen over the horizon. She looked up to see that the cotton-candy clouds had dissipated.

"But who knows where they all came from and what languages they speak," he said. He looked toward the ship's hold and added, "Or how long some of them have been kept together." He chuckled. "Lion of the sea." He smiled at her and shook his head. "Children." He grunted good-naturedly.

"Who are they?" she asked him. "Where were you taking them?"

"I don't know who they are," he replied. He absently glanced at his wounded arm. "Don't want to know." He shrugged.

"Then how did you know where— How did you— Why are they here?"

She watched him check the sail and fiddle with the tiller and then adjust the bandage over his wound. Just when she thought he wasn't going to respond, he snorted and mumbled, "Old hag."

"Old hag? I don't understand."

He rubbed the back of his neck and looked across the water toward the shoreline.

"She—" His brow furrowed. "She tells me, she sends a—" Sarah recoiled when he leaned toward her and bellowed in an angry tone, "I just know! That's how they get here!" She saw his hands squeeze the tiller. "They're slave fodder! Currency, profit." She watched his eyes dart to the hold before he looked toward the shoreline again. "Most will probably end up back where I found them. And no one will care. No one will notice."

The weariness she heard in his voice tugged at her heart. She reached out to offer him a comforting touch. He grunted.

"But the people you're delivering them to, surely they care what happens to them."

"People I'm delivering them to?" He sighed and looked out toward the open sea. "There's nobody waiting for them. Nobody wants them." Deep lines appeared on his forehead. "I free them and I let them go. What happens after that—" He looked at her and shrugged.

"But you said a woman—you called her an old hag. She must—"

"She doesn't exist!" he shouted. "Leave her out of this!" He thrust a hand in front of his chest as if he were ordering her to stop. "She's just a—" He lowered his hand and shook his head.

Sarah said nothing as she watched his fingers pinch and release the fabric of his trousers. Then the wind changed direction. Drawn to the sound of a fluttering sail, she shifted her attention upward.

"When will we make port?" she cautiously asked.

She thought his expression odd when he looked at her while he changed the angle of the tiller.

"Won't be docking at any port," he told her. "Stretch of beach north of Merca—that's where we're headed." He glanced up at the stiffening sail. "Be there in an hour if the wind holds. If they're lucky," he nodded toward the hold, "beach will be deserted." He touched the bandage on his arm and then looked at blood on his fingertips. "Give them a chance. A day's head start." He wiped his finger on his pants leg. "Now, can you finish digging this damn piece of lead out of my arm before I bleed to death?"

"What do you mean, a day's head start? What? Who?" She searched the water aft of the boat. "Is someone coming after us? *Them?*"

"They're someone's property," he replied in a dire tone. "Someone always follows."

She watched him adjust the tiller. For a few moments, she thought they were moving toward the open sea. But then the dhow began to angle toward shore.

"Fire might have given us some extra time."

"The fire," Sarah repeated as if she'd just remembered something she'd forgotten. "Teimbaka," she murmured. "Dear God, we were—"

She looked at him as though she was seeing him for the first time.

"Bin'ka?"

She reached out a hand as if to touch him.

"I asked you before, but you didn't answer. Are you Bin'ka?"

She sharply exhaled when she saw him nod.

"Dirk. Sister Claire. Dear God—do you know where they are?" She leaned toward him. "Dirk. Is he— Is he all right?"

"Dirk," he scoffed. He spit on the deck. "Worthless piece of shit."

"Then you know where he is? Where *they* are?"

"Haven't seen them since I put him and the woman on the plane."

Sarah felt her heart sink.

"Plane?"

"Woman was badly hurt. Thought she'd die before we could make it to the airport. Red Cross plane." He chuckled "Adiam." He shook his head. "Got connections all over the world."

"But why not a hospital here?" Sarah heard the anguish in her question. "I mean," she shifted the knife from one hand to the other, "if she was hurt, like you said, why put her on a plane?"

Bin'ka studied her for a few seconds before shrugging his shoulders. "Those were the instructions."

"But where?" Sarah brightened. "They flew her to Addis Ababa, then. Or Nairobi." Hope seeped into her voice. "Yes, that would make sense. If she was as bad off as you—" She fell silent when she saw him shake his head.

"Paris, then America. They're long gone." He looked up at the sail and made a slight adjustment to the tiller. "Like I said, over a year now." He cocked his head to the side and smiled. "You have a thing for Dirk?"

Long gone. Over a year. Sarah felt her body go numb. Her mind began to spin. *Gone. Paris, then America.*

"I wasted a year?" she muttered. "America? Why didn't Reverend Mother tell me?"

"Who?" Bin'ka asked. "And stop mumbling. You going or staying?"

Sarah looked at him, perplexed. "Maybe she didn't know. Maybe she hadn't heard." She searched his face as though the answers she sought were locked away in the lines of his creased brow. She ran her fingertips against her lips. "Before she passed away," she muttered.

Sarah looked past him to the approaching shore. Her eyes grew wide.

"I need to get back home."

"Then you're staying. Though I'm not sure what port would be safe to drop you on your own."

"What?" Sarah eyes drifted over Bin'ka's massive frame before focusing on the bloody bandage on his arm. "You're hurt."

He rolled his eyes. "Oh, god," he groaned.

"God," she repeated. "How can I—?" She looked at the knife in her hand and then looked forlornly at Bin'ka. "I killed three men. How can He forgive me?"

"There," he said with a nod to the hold. "That's how. Now get over here and dig this bullet out of my arm so I can drop them over the side when we get to shallow water." He pinched his eyebrows together as he waited for her to reply. "You'll need to hold the helm while I lower them off the ship."

"I should have taken my vows of Perpetual Commitment by now. I should be back in America." She slowly shook her head from side to side. "I don't understand," she confessed. "My life is with God."

"Hey!" he shouted. "Look around! You see any god here?" His nostrils flared when he snorted. "Now get over here and dig this bullet out of my arm." He took a deep breath and sighed. "*Shange bahr*, my ass." He glared at the children when a few of them giggled. "Maybe your god has other plans for you," he grumbled. He paused before adding, "Or maybe you'll realize there aren't any gods and that you're stuck with what you have."

5

"I HATE MEETING out here."

Rue watched Alexis pull the front of a black sable fur close around her shoulders.

"It's either too hot or too cold." She stomped her feet against the tarmac and shivered. "And the bay always smells like a gas station toilet." He grunted when she buried the tip of her nose into a fur lapel. Her voice was muffled when she asked, "Why can't we ever meet in your office?"

"Trenton? Why the hell would you want to drive all the way down there?"

Rue Thompson ran his hands along the sides of his head, giving his perfectly coifed hair a slight pat at each temple before he continued.

"Too many damn distractions from all the damn bureaucrats and their fool trolls. Better to meet out here away from all that, don't you think?" Rue looked out past the edge of the Toyota Logistics pier toward a massive container ship anchored on the near side of Newark Bay. "Can't get this kind of show in Trenton," he said with a nod to the ship. "Wonder what goodies they'll be offloading tonight?"

He smoothed the sides of his slicked-back hair and chuckled.

"Are you that unorganized that you don't even know what cargo is arriving? Do you even *know* when the next ivory delivery is due?" She frowned. "Maybe I should look for a different supplier. One who has a finger on the pulse of his business, instead of one who has to run off to the state capital every other day to vote on highway bills and day care centers."

"You're one huffy bitch." Rue gave the fur-clad woman a wink. "Course, you already knew that. Now," he brushed a few wrinkles from the front of his knee-length, khaki-colored raincoat. "As far as your next shipment, apparently there's been a delay."

"What?" Alex's eyes narrowed. "That's unacceptable. I have buyers waiting. You told me the shipment would be in—."

"Nothing I can do, Alex. Price of doing business with Africa."

"Just what the hell does that mean?" She looked over her shoulder toward the car that had driven her to their rendezvous. "Do you want me to signal my—?"

"Your punk-ass spic driver?" Rue interjected, following her eyes to the shiny black sedan parked fifty yards from where they were standing. "You think I come out here alone?" His gold and diamond rings caught the light from the giant post lamps lining the perimeter of the expansive pier as he waved his hand toward the hundreds of automobiles parked in the lot. "Look at all those cars," he told her. "I could have men posted in any one of them."

"Or none of them," Alex countered. She glared at him for a moment and then frowned. "But this doesn't get us anywhere. What's the holdup with the ivory?" She pointed a gloved finger at his chest. "And don't bullshit me."

"Somebody's been knocking off the hunters." He raised his eyebrows and shrugged when she didn't look convinced. "That's Akmir's story, anyway. I see no reason why he'd lie."

"Don't be so naive. He's probably getting a better price from somebody else."

"And what? Upset the deal for other merchandise?" Rue sharply exhaled and shook his head. "Can't see him jeopardizing our partnership over a bunch of dead elephant tusks. No." He looked out toward the container ship and stroked his chin. "He told me someone's been waiting for the poachers when they haul the ivory out of the bush. Just mowing them down. They found the last group along a dirt path. Said their bodies were shredded into little pieces. Shell casings all over the ground. Ivory nowhere to be found." He turned back to her and shrugged. "Seems the elephants have a friend."

"Sounds more like someone's reaping profit without doing any work." Alexis tugged at one end of the black silk scarf tied loosely around her head. "Where's the product resurfacing?"

"That's the perplexing part," Rue answered. "Akmir tells me he hasn't heard of any of the confiscated ivory being sold on the markets. It's as if somebody is stockpiling the stuff." Rue turned his head toward the river when the sound of an engine throttling up for power rumbled across the surface of the bay. "Makes no sense," he said as a red-hulled tugboat headed out toward the container ship.

"Maybe they're shipping it or flying it to Asia," she countered. "Maybe Akmir's not as in tune with what's going on as he thinks." Her tone was biting when she added, "Like you not having a clue as to what's offloading tonight."

Rue pulled the collar of his raincoat up around his neck.

"Just settle the fuck down. You can't expect deliveries from halfway across the world to run like clockwork." Rue frowned and shrugged his shoulders. "Just a delay we have to live with."

"I don't like delays," she told him. "And neither do my customers." She turned and walked a few steps away. She kept her back to him when she asked, "What's Akmir doing about this *delay*?"

"Doing?" Rue turned back to the bay. The tugboat was rounding the container ship's bow. "Don't know if he's doing much of anything." The tugboat was edging its nose against the ship's hull. "I'm assuming he'll let the poachers or mercenaries or whoever he's dealing with take care of the problem."

"That's not good enough."

Rue whirled around.

"Jesus Christ, Alexis, what the fuck is your problem? Why can't—?"

"Fifty thousand."

"What?"

"Payable in gold upon delivery of the severed head of whomever's meddling in the ivory supply chain."

"Fifty grand?" said Rue, incredulous. "You'll have every mercenary and every starving villager out beating the countryside for that kind of money."

He looked at her like she was insane. "How will you ever verify they've brought in the right person? You'll be funding a killing spree."

"Like I care about villagers and camel herders." She walked back to stand in front of him. "Let's not fool ourselves, *Mister Assemblyman*. You've had plenty killed to fill your pockets, so don't pretend you care about some innocent peasant in east Africa having his head cut off by mistake." Her face was devoid of expression when she said, "They can all die for all I care. As long as the ivory ships on time."

She glanced over her shoulder and raised her hand in the air. The black sedan's headlights flickered from low to high beam three times.

"Fifty thousand in gold," she told him. "And tell Akmir I'll throw in an extra five if the head's delivered in the next seventy-two hours."

"Look, Alexis." Rue glanced over toward the car as it rolled forward. "I'll make the call, but I can't promise—"

"I want my ivory," she flatly told him. "And if you can't deliver," she turned and started walking toward the black sedan, "then I'll find someone who can."

Rue watched her slide into the back of the sedan. He kept an eye on the car until it drove out through the gates at the far end of the pier. When the car's taillights flickered away, he turned his attention back to the bay.

"Creepy-ass shit," he muttered. The container ship made a slow turn toward the Newark pier. "Fuckin' ghouls worshipping the bones of dead animals." He glanced over his shoulder toward the exit gates. "Hope you do find somebody else to deal with." He crossed his arms over his portly stomach. "Fuckin' creepy-ass shit," he muttered. "Who needs it?"

*

Jim had just shut and locked the front door to the restaurant when his wife screamed from the kitchen.

"Rochelle!" he called out. "What is it? What's wrong?"

He bolted across the narrow half-lit dining room and rounded the service counter. A loud, *tap-tap* froze him in his tracks.

"Rochelle!" he cried.

As he reached to push open the kitchen door, it swung open. A scrawny figure stuck a handgun in his face.

"Shut it," the man hissed.

Jim stumbled across the threshold when the man gruffly pulled him into the kitchen. A moment later, the barrel of the gun pressed into his nose.

"Open the safe, motherfucker," the scrawny man ordered. "You hear me?"

"Keep your fuckin' voice down."

Jim caught a glimpse of another man out of the corner of his eye. Like the man holding the gun to his nose, he was dressed in sunglasses, a black do-rag, and dark clothing.

"Where's my wife? Rochelle!" he called.

The barrel of the gun smashed against his ear. Jim cried out as his knees buckled. But the man kept him from falling by grabbing the front of his apron. Once Jim regained his balance, the man dragged him around a long metal table in the middle of the kitchen.

"That your bitch?" the man with the gun taunted.

He jerked the gun away from Jim's face and pointed it at a heavy-set woman lying on the floor.

"You wanna join her?" he asked, once more pressing the barrel of the weapon against Jim's head.

"You motherfuckin' punk!" Enraged, Jim tried to push the scrawny man away. "You son of a bitch!" He managed to get his right arm up far enough to land a glancing slap across the man's face.

Retaliation was swift. The man smashed the flat of the gun against the side of Jim's head. Then he grabbed him by the back of his neck and pushed him toward the woman's body. The gun boomed. Jim stiffened in horror when he saw Rochelle's body twitch.

"Goddammit," the second man hissed. "What the fuck you doin'? You gonna have the pigs down on us."

The scrawny man placed the gun flush against Jim's face so the barrel pointed toward the woman.

"You want I should shoot the bitch again?" he threatened. "She ain't dead yet, but she gonna be if you don't do what I say."

Jim heard the click as the gun was cocked.

"Rochelle." Jim stared at the blood oozing out of his wife's shoulder. "Don't hurt her no more," he pleaded. "Don't hurt her."

"Then do what I say!" the scrawny man shouted. "Open the fuckin' safe!"

Jim noted the scrawny man's runny nose and beads of sweat around his mouth as he was yanked toward the small office along the back wall of the kitchen. When he and the scrawny man rounded the end of the long, metal table, the man shoved him into the little room.

"Now open the damn safe," he ordered.

"Hurry the fuck up, man," Jim heard the second man say. "This is taking too long."

"Shut up!" the scrawny man screamed. "And you," he shoved Jim in the back. "Hurry up or I'll shoot the old bitch between the eyes."

"I'm hurrying," Jim snapped. "Just gotta move this chair out of the way." He bent to one knee. "No need for any fireworks."

"Whatever," the scrawny man replied.

Jim felt the barrel of the gun press against his neck.

"Just do it and shut up."

Jim glanced over his shoulder as he put his fingers on the combination lock.

"How long you been hittin' the needle, boy?" he asked as he spun the tumbler twice to the left.

"You see anything?" the scrawny man shouted.

"Nothin'," the second man replied.

"Keep your motherfuckin' eyes glued to the street."

Jim felt the barrel of the gun tap the back of his head.

"Hurry the fuck up, old man. You ain't got it open in ten seconds, that fat old bitch of yours getting one between the eyes." Jim heard what sounded like a cross between laughter and a cough. "Better yet, maybe I'm just gonna plug the old cow for the fun of it."

"Wait, wait, wait!" Jim urged. "I'm opening it! I'm opening it!"

A sick feeling flooded Jim's stomach when he heard a gunshot. Filled with dread, he whirled around in time to see the scrawny man stumble and fall against the office wall. Out of the corner of his eye, he glimpsed his wife. She was pointing what he knew was the Glock handgun they kept hidden beneath the stainless steel worktable. Just as he was about to call out to her, a gunshot boomed. He felt his throat explode.

Dazedly, he heard Rochelle scream, "You punk-ass junkie!"

Though his vision was cloudy, he saw the Glock fire. The scrawny man lurched against the wall and then fell to the floor. Half the man's head appeared to be missing. Then the room started to spin. Confused, he searched for his wife. When he located her large frame, he tried to motion to her. But his arm wouldn't move.

As though in the grip of a bad dream, Jim watched the wavering form of his wife swing the Glock toward the dining room door. Then he saw her forehead explode. Rochelle's body crumpled and fell. An icy shiver gripped his body from head to toe. He struggled to take a shallow breath and closed his eyes.

*

"Now what?"

Dirk eased the door closed and looked down the hall.

"I have no idea where she is."

He tugged on the shirt of the powder-blue scrubs he'd stolen from the storage closet and ran a hand across the stiff, flimsy material.

"How do I look?" he asked the ghost-elephant.

He tilted his head to the right and turned from side to side.

"I can't believe I'm doing this."

He ran a finger under the waistband of the slip-on pants.

"*Why* am I doing this?"

Dirk recoiled when the ethereal beast extended its trunk toward his ear.

"No!" He vehemently shook his head. "I don't want to hear her voice. I don't want to—" His chin drooped toward his chest and his voice trailed off to a mutter when he added, "I don't want to go through that again."

"Go through what? Who are you talking to?"

Dirk felt his face flush. Slowly, he turned toward a woman's voice.

"Are you okay?"

A nurse. She looks like a nurse. I think she's a nurse.

"You're a nurse."

The woman's eyebrows pinched together. Dirk felt a stab of anxiety as her eyes wandered up and down his frame.

"Well, that was stupid of me to say, wasn't it?" He smiled at the petite brunette standing in front of him. Running a hand through his hair, he said, "Sorry. First day. A little nervous."

He studied her brown eyes as she scrutinized his face. He'd decided to run for the exit door when she smiled.

"Julie," she said, extending her hand. "Julie Janowitz. And welcome aboard."

Dirk shook her hand.

"Uh, Peter," he replied. "Peter Benson," he told her. "And thank you." He smiled uncertainly. "And sorry you overhead me talking to myself. I was just—" He glanced down at the baby spirit-elephant. "I was telling myself not to screw up." He took a deep breath and swallowed. "I don't really want to go job hunting again anytime soon." He nervously eyed the red neon exit sign at the end of the hallway.

"Job hunting." She nodded her head in agreement. "Yeah, that's the worst."

Dirk's eyes flitted to her breasts. They lingered there for a moment before sliding down to her hips. He wondered what her figure looked like under the stiff, white A-line dress she had on.

"You permanent?" she asked.

"What? Ah, no—temp agency. But I'm hoping."

"Oh, which one?"

"Uh, Philadelphia Medical."

He felt his insides start to squirm when he saw her frown. The exit suddenly seemed very far away.

"Never heard of it," she replied with a shrug. "But that's nothing new. Lower level staff always seems to be coming and going. Don't know where half are sent from. Oh, shit, I'm sorry." She hurriedly placed a hand to her lips. "I didn't mean it to sound—"

"Relax." Dirk reached out and lightly touched her shoulder. "No offense taken. Changing bed pans and sweeping floors isn't the most glamorous of jobs." He laughed.

"Seriously, I'm sorry." Dirk sensed genuine warmth when she grasped his hand and squeezed his fingers. "I'm a jerk for saying something like that. It's just—" He wasn't sure what emotion he was seeing in her expression as she paused. "You know, small clinic out in the country. No public transportation. No benefits to speak of. Crappy cafeteria." She raised her eyebrows and leaned toward him. "Medium-grade loony bin." She looked sheepishly toward the floor and giggled nervously. "I'm awful, aren't I?"

"I take it you've been here a while," he said. Offering a sympathetic smile, he added, "And no, you're not awful. It's always nice to get the low-down from someone who's been around the block."

"What section?" she inquired as she checked her wristwatch.

"Section?" He felt his balls tighten.

"Medical or therapy?" she replied. She looked at her watch again.

"I— Um, I'm not really sure. I just got here."

"Yeah, I saw you drive in." He turned his face to the side and leaned forward when she gestured for him to edge closer. "I was catching a smoke," she said in confidence. She motioned toward the exit with her head. "Last hour of the shift is killer. Nice car, by the way. Cadillac, right?"

"It's a friend of mine's." He smiled. "No employee lounge, I take it."

He experienced a pang of panic when she looked past him. By her expression, he could tell something was wrong.

"Look, I gotta run." With a slight upward motion of her head, she whispered, "Supervisor. Good luck with your shift."

"Administration?" he asked as she started to walk away.

She pointed in the direction she was heading. "Building map up at the intersection."

Dirk saw a taller, older woman dressed in a nurse outfit pause to look at them before she disappeared into what he guessed was an adjoining hallway. "If you get assigned to therapy, maybe I'll see you up there."

"Yeah, okay. Hey, thanks."

When she raised her hand in reply, he looked down at the little ghost-beast.

"She was nice."

Dirk closed his eyes when the baby spirit-elephant shook its head.

"What did you want me to do, come right out and ask her what room Claire Waterman is in?" Dirk paused before expressing his displeasure with a frown. "Fine. *You* lead the way, then." He rolled his eyes when the baby spirit-elephant began to float up the hallway. "After all, I'm just your bitch," he muttered.

*

Dirk alternately studied the building map and the four adjoining hallways. Luckily, as he saw it, the architecture of the clinic was pretty basic: a giant H structure with an extra crossway built between the two exterior wings. Outside of these, on the perimeter of the building, ran a narrow, sickle-shaped parking lot. He'd parked Mrs. Waterman's Cadillac in one of the spaces on the outer fringes of the lot, nearest the entrance to the winding service road that connected the clinic to the highway.

As he shifted his attention from the hallways to the map, Dirk took note of a red dot with YOU ARE HERE stenciled beneath it. Judging from his present position, he gauged he was standing at the crossroads of the medical wing and the administration wing. Therapy—where Julie was working, and where he guessed Claire was being kept—was marked as being at the far end of the nearer of the two exterior wings. But which room was she in? And what good would the information do him if and when he found out?

Dirk looked down. When he saw the baby spirit-elephant staring up at him, he shivered and looked back at the map. To his annoyance, the ghost-beast's trunk appeared in front of the map and touched one of the crossing halls. He gave the ethereal creature a dismissive smile before taking a closer look at that particular section. The words *Restricted Area* immediately jumped out at him.

"Restricted area. How are we—?" Dirk raised his eyebrows and looked down at the young ghost-elephant. "How am *I* supposed to get in there?"

With a heavy sigh, he stepped behind the ethereal beast as it headed toward the restricted area.

*

Dirk stared at the set of imposing metal doors and shook his head. He noted their width and height—wall to wall, floor to ceiling—effectively separating the restricted area from the rest of the clinic. On the wall to his right, about three inches from the closest of the doors and shoulder high, was a rectangular black box with a keyboard face. He glanced down at the shimmering entity standing next to him.

"Know the code?" he glibly asked.

"You there, orderly. What are you doing?"

Dirk took a deep breath.

Just by the expression on the woman's face, Dirk was certain the tall, middle-aged nurse walking toward him was either a person of authority or a bitch. Either way, he knew he was in for a grilling.

"I'm trying to get to the therapy wing," he lied. The wrinkles on her pasty complexion deepened. "But I just realized, I can't go this way, can I?" He smiled and stuck out his hand. "Peter Benson. First day." He gave the woman an innocent shrug. "I'm new."

The woman stopped three feet in front of him with her arms folded across her chest.

"Really." She eyed him suspiciously. "I wasn't aware we'd hired any new employees." Her brows pinched together as she studied his face. "A little old for an orderly, aren't we?" The woman looked at her wristwatch. "And early, too; the morning shift doesn't start for another hour."

Dirk looked past the woman when he saw the ghost-beast begin to walk back the way they'd come.

"Are you ignoring me?"

"No! I mean, no, of course not." It took all his mental strength not to wince under the woman's withering glare. "I'm just having trouble getting my bearings. And, yes, I know I'm early, and I guess I am probably a little older than most orderlies." He shuffled his feet. "I've been working as a freelance writer most of my life." He hurried on when he saw she was about to interject. "Volunteered at a triage facility in Africa for a few months when the money dried up. Thought I'd switch to medicine when I got back to the States. Temp agency called late last night. I drove out early this morning. Not sure if I'm here longer than today or not. I guess that's the office's call. Don't know if the person I'm filling in for has the flu or quit." Dirk raised his eyebrows and shrugged.

"Well, why don't we just take a short walk to administration and find out," the woman replied. "I'm sure we can get you where you rightfully belong in a matter of minutes."

"Uh, sure." Dirk suddenly wondered if the clinic employed security guards. He was contemplating making a run for the exit door when the steel doors swung inward.

"There you are."

Dirk nearly peed his pants at the implication.

"I've been looking for you."

Julie hesitated when she noticed Dirk.

"It's the doctor's special patient," she said to the taller, older nurse. "I thought I'd better find you."

"What is it? What's wrong?"

Julie looked at the older woman and then looked at Dirk. The older nurse shifted her weight and huffed.

"Fill me in on the way," she snapped.

Dirk breathed a sigh of relief when the older woman walked briskly through the doors. An instant later, his heart skipped a beat when she spun back around and barked, "You!" She pointed a finger at Dirk's chest.

"You stay right there. I'll be back for you in what I'm sure will be a matter of a few minutes."

"We could use him," Julie said.

Dirk nearly laughed at the look of annoyance on the older nurse's face.

"An orderly," Julie hurried to explain. She nodded toward Dirk. "She's fallen out of bed. And—"

"And?" the older woman tersely inquired.

"Some of her lines came out. Her wrist bandage unraveled. Bedpan spilled. And—"

"And?" the older woman pressed.

"Her heart monitor showed an unexplained jump in BPM just before—well, I'm guessing—just before she fell out of bed."

"You." The older nurse crooked her finger and motioned for Dirk to follow. "Come with me."

*

"Just lay her down. You don't need to inspect her."

The woman's voice grated on Dirk's psyche. Her words, the tone she used, everything related to how she talked rubbed him the wrong way. And while he would have taken great pleasure in telling the old bitch to go to hell, he refrained. Claire commanded his full attention.

Is this really you? What have they done to you?

Arms trembling, he bit down on his lower lip as he laid Claire's head on a pillow. Mindful of her fragile state, he gently slid his hand out from under her neck.

She's—he gritted his teeth while blinking back tears—*she looks like she's dead. She looks like*—Dirk abruptly stepped away from Claire's bedside and looked dazedly around the room. His breathing became shallow and hurried as he struggled to remember where he was.

"What are you doing?"

Dirk stared dumbly into the older woman's face for a few seconds before abruptly averting his gaze to the floor. His vision blurred as he stared into a puddle of liquid under the bed.

"Looking— Looking for a— A mop," he stuttered.

"Well, we certainly don't store those here."

Dirk winced at the sound of woman's voice. He found it piercing, like someone was pounding spikes into his eardrums.

"In the utility closet."

Dirk looked to his side and wondered who the petite brunette was who was pulling on his shirt sleeve.

"Where you got your scrubs."

Dirk felt relief when he recognized the woman: *Julie!*

"I'll set the security doors to remain open."

"Right. Got it." Dirk smiled uncertainly as he glanced at the older woman. "Do you want me to do anything else before I go?"

"No," the older nurse curtly replied. "And make sure you bring some disinfectant." He watched the woman's face crinkle when she sniffed the air. "The room reeks."

Dirk found himself drawn to Claire's face. He vaguely heard the old bitch saying something more, but he was preoccupied with Claire. As he tried to understand how she'd deteriorated, he found his attention drawn to her hands.

"Jesus, what happened?" he muttered when he noticed a deep cut in her wrist.

"That's none of your concern. Just get the mop and disinfectant."

*

Claire's physical state—sallow complexion; filthy hair; dark circles around her eyes; cracked, colorless lips—haunted him as he traversed the halls to the utility room. By the time he grabbed hold of the doorknob and opened the door, his nerves were frayed.

"Son of a bitch," he gasped. "What the hell are you doing in here?"

The eyes of the baby spirit-elephant seemed more forlorn than he could ever remember. As he gazed into the ethereal entity's dark, forsaken orbs, he wondered how that was possible.

"I'm getting a mop and bucket," he told the ghost-beast, averting his gaze. He was reaching for the mop handle when he felt compelled to say, "I saw her."

Dirk stepped out of the closet when the small spirit-elephant unexpectedly raised its trunk and charged the wall at the far end of the narrow, rectangular room. A white-gold flash of light preceded a tremor that shook the shelves. Dirk stood frozen for a moment, stupefied by the animal's actions. Slowly, he became aware that the ghost-elephant had disappeared. Tentatively, he stepped back into the closet. An odd smell compelled him to stop.

Dirk pinched his nostrils and surveyed the room. As his attention drifted from the shelving units to the floor, he saw an upended bottle of rubbing alcohol. A good amount of the liquid had spilled out and pooled on the linoleum tiles. A can of disinfectant and a can of spray starch had also fallen off the shelves, these lying in the pool of rubbing alcohol with their tops ajar.

"Fuck," he mumbled, annoyed. "Now I have to clean up after the little shit."

Dirk grabbed the handle of a mop but quickly released it when images of fire appeared in his thoughts. The visions clicked through his head like a slide show: the torch used on Genevieve, lines of flames burning in George Henry's camp, the odd combustion when the soldier from the Legion of

God was killed, the pyre Bacha Alba's men had set ablaze to alert George Henry to his location, a truck's gas tank exploding as he and Bin'ka—with Claire in Bin'ka's arms—ran toward the helicopter. He blinked his eyes in an attempt to clear his mind, but the images remained. *Fire*, he thought. *Why?*

The parade of fiery images suddenly grew more intense. Smells, sounds, heat; his senses were overwhelmed. It was if the visons were real, unfolding as he'd experienced them.

"Fire," he murmured, alarmed.

A glimmer of light drew his attention toward the back of the room. The baby spirit-elephant had returned, the ethereal beast standing next to the puddle of rubbing alcohol. Smoke billowed from within the beast's hollow eyes.

"Smoke," he whispered. "Fire. What are you trying to say?"

*

"Finally," the older nurse snapped. "Did you get lost?"

Dirk gave the woman a sheepish glance as he hurriedly pushed a mop and bucket into the room.

"Sorry," he replied, a little out of breath. "I guess the door must have locked after I put on my scrubs." He glanced at Julie as if he was looking for her to confirm his explanation. "Had to find someone who had a key. I came back as quickly as I could."

"Just get on with it," the woman harshly replied. "Mop up the urine and then disinfect the floor."

"Yes, ma'am."

Dirk wheeled the bucket beside Claire's bed. Then the fire alarm sounded.

"What now?" the older nurse complained.

"I'll call the desk," Julie responded. She glanced at the older woman before hurrying out of the room.

"What the hell are *you* doing?"

Dirk nearly bumped his head against the bed as he straightened from the floor.

"I was unlocking the casters on the wheels so we could move the patient out," he quickly explained. "Isn't that procedure when there's a fire?"

"Procedure," the woman huffily repeated. "Just leave the bed be. It's probably nothing more than a drill."

"But I smell smoke," he countered.

"Do you, now?" she haughtily replied.

A shout of "Fire!" echoed down the hallway outside Claire's room. The old nurse frowned.

"Unlatch the wheels and be ready to move her as soon as I come back," she instructed. "And have Julie stay with her when she returns. I'm going to see what this is all about."

Dirk flipped the woman the bird as she strode out of the room. As soon as she was gone, he bent to the job of unlocking the casters. He was wheeling Claire out the door when Julie stepped in front of the bed.

"What are you doing? Where's Nurse McVee?"

"I don't know," he told her. He nudged the bed into Julie's waist. "Move!" he shouted. "Show me where I'm supposed to take her!"

Julie put her hands on the end of the bed. Dirk saw the indecision on her face.

"Parking lot, right? Right, Julie?"

He could feel his jaw clench as she looked to either side of her.

"Julie, there's a fire!" he yelled. "Help me get her to safety!"

*

Julie held the double security doors open as Dirk pushed Claire's hospital bed across the threshold.

"Take her down the hall and then outside to the parking lot," she instructed.

Dirk wheeled Claire down the hall and through the door at the end of the hall. As soon as he stepped outside, he scanned the parking lot for the white Cadillac Fleetwood he'd taken from the Waterman estate. After an anxious few moments to get his bearings, he spotted the big white car just where he'd parked it, near the entrance to the service road.

"Just to the end of the sidewalk!" Julie called out from the exit. "Don't block the lot off in case the fire trucks need to get through."

Dirk's heart was pounding as he reached the end of the sidewalk. A quick glance over his shoulder revealed Julie hurrying toward him. In a moment of panic, he lifted Claire into his arms and started running for the car.

"Peter! What are you doing? Peter! Where the hell are you going?"

Dirk kept on running. He didn't stop until he reached the Cadillac.

"Peter! Jesus Christ, what are you doing?"

Dirk balanced Claire against the car as he fumbled in his pocket for the car keys. He gave Julie a hurried glance as he pulled the key from his pocket and unlocked the door. He could hear footsteps pounding on the asphalt as he slid Claire into the passenger seat and slammed the door shut.

"I'm calling the police!" Julie screamed. She stopped ten yards from the car and stared at him. "Do you hear me?" she yelled.

"Go ahead!" he shouted. "Call them!" He could feel himself getting angry. "I'm sure they'd be interested to find out what you've been doing to her!"

Dirk stared through the windshield at Claire's pallid face as he rounded the hood toward the driver's-side door. Before he yanked it open, he paused and made eye contact with Julie.

"Were you just going to let them kill her?"

"What are you talking about?" Julie took a step toward the car. "Nobody's trying to kill her."

"Really?" Dirk pulled the driver's-side door open. "Look at her!" He pointed inside the car. "You trying to tell me she looks *better* than she did when she was admitted?"

"She's suffering from acute psychosis," Julie feebly offered. "Now, Peter." She took a cautious step forward and extended her hand. "No need to take this any further."

"Bullshit!" Dirk shouted. He slid into the driver's seat and pulled the door shut. As he rolled down the window, he yelled, "You're pumping her full of drugs and zapping her with electricity! That's what she's suffering from! And don't deny it, because I've seen it with my own eyes!"

"How did you—?"

Dirk started the car as he glimpsed Nurse McVee run out of the clinic. He put the Cadillac in reverse and pulled a few feet out of the parking space before easing to a stop. He looked out the window and held Julie's gaze.

"You're killing her," he told her. "And she—" Dirk glanced over at Claire before he said, "She's a nun, Julie. Did you know that?"

"I don't understand." He saw confusion on her face. "How can you know all this?"

Dirk rolled up the window, put the car in drive, and sped out the parking lot.

"Because I'm the asshole who brought her back from Africa," he muttered.

6

NOTHING—NOTHING LEFT, NOTHING the same—nothing.

John stared at the ground as he ran a fingertip along the horn's spiral ridges. Without thinking, he pressed the horn's razor-sharp tip into the crux of his arm.

The laughter the puncture produced was forced and unbalanced. John drifted between states of joy and pain as blood oozed from the wound. Stupefied, he watched a fat, heavy-looking globule drip and splatter on the earth. As the soil absorbed his blood, John felt his heartbeat wane. Stricken with a sense of loss, he pulled the horn from his arm and licked blood from the tip.

"*Kongo,*" he muttered in Amharic.

Fur brushed across his thigh.

"*Kongo Ahndt,*" he said to the animal. "Beautiful One."

A large, female spotted hyena nuzzled her jaw against his chest and began to lick the wound on his arm. Heartened by the animal's show of concern, John hugged the animal's neck.

"*You* are still here," he said with satisfaction. "Not *everything* is gone."

The distant cackle of another hyena off in the distance drew John's and the female hyena's attention. Both looked eastward, where the call had originated. John listened intently while the female hyena raised her snout to the sky and sniffed the air. When the animal uttered a slight squeal and began shifting her weight from one foreleg to the other, John became concerned.

"What does the wind say?"

The hyena took several paces eastward before turning and snarling.

"Men?" John asked.

The animal raised its bristled tail.

"Show me," John said.

*

Tusks of ivory were stacked in a square as tall as a man. John eyed the configuration with suspicion, for the ivory looked too polished to have been newly harvested. Compounding the strangeness of the discovery was the nonexistence of tracks leading to or away from the tusks. *Who would leave a stack of polished tusks unguarded out in the bush?* he wondered. He scanned the waist-high grass rising up behind the ivory, thinking poachers must be nearby. But the grasses revealed little; no bent stalks or darkened areas that might suggest an individual's hiding place. Before he motioned for the female hyena to join him, he meticulously scanned the area. Finding nothing out of place, he signaled Beautiful One to come out of hiding. As the hyena stepped out of the tall grass, John warily approached the tusks.

No sooner had John placed a hand atop a tusk when a series of deep, staccato rumblings erupted behind him. Alarmed, he glanced quickly over his shoulder. Half a kilometer to the east, he saw the dark outline of a helicopter ascend over a ridgeline. As he started to back away from the ivory, the whoosh of blades slicing through air exploded from the west as well.

"*Ehroochee!*" he shouted to the hyena. "Run!"

The first volley of bullets struck the earth just ahead of him. Soil and grass exploded into the air. As John shaded his eyes from debris, he heard a second wave of gunfire. A pain-filled howl sent a jolt through his body. He stopped and turned. Beautiful One was down on her side, blood spilling from a gaping hole in her neck. Enraged, John raised the spiral horn above his head and screamed into the sky. A third burst of gunfire sent bullets deep into his chest and hip, pulverizing flesh and bone. John crumpled to the ground without making a sound.

*

"Silence!"

Eden slapped the stock of her AK-47 and glared at two of the boys she'd discovered in the poacher's vehicle.

"I should have left you in the truck!" she shouted.

She looked on in utter frustration as the boys continued to cry while a little girl dressed in a tattered pink and white kanga incessantly whined and paced in an aimless circle.

"Better that you make your new owners miserable than me! And you!" she barked, focusing her attention to the girl. "You sound like a dying baboon!" Putting a stern expression on her face, she added, "And lions eat baboons!"

To Eden's utter surprise, the little girl plopped down on the ground and proceeded to wail. As she stared dumbfounded at the waif, the two boys dropped to their knees and—as far as Eden could tell—tried to out-wail the little girl. With a shake of her head, Eden pointed the AK-47 up at the sky and pulled the trigger. The violent *boom boom boom* brought an immediate reaction; a moment of utter silence. Eden smiled.

"Better," she said. "Now I can think."

She shouldered the AK-47 and started walking eastward.

"Come," she told the children. Beckoning them with a wave of her hand, she added, "Just over this rise you will see your new home." She nodded when the three children scrambled to their feet and began to follow her. "You have made a good decision in coming with me. The others who were with you—not so much, I think."

She shook her head and fell silent as she thought about the other children she'd discovered in the poacher's truck. Most had been in a state of shock. It wasn't hard for her to imagine what they'd been through at the hands of slavers.

"I don't think most knew where they were going when I freed them," she went on. "Certainly not the three that ran south." Again, she shook her head. "Only bogs and swampland lie that way." She shrugged. "But maybe they knew a path I'm not aware of. And maybe some had an idea of where their villages—"

Eden fell silent as she crested a small ridge. Numbly, she stared at the cloud of vultures circling in the sky a kilometer or so in the distance. Below the grouping of scavengers, a curling band of smoke snaked upward from behind a line of low-lying hills.

"Bouda," she whispered.

When something touched her hand, she slapped at it.

"I'm tired," the little girl whined, rubbing her wrist where Eden had struck her. Wiping a tear from her cheek, she asked, "How much longer?"

Eden glared at the girl.

"Why did I bring you?" she snapped. "I should have—" She shook her head and looked back at the rising smoke. "Keep up," she ordered the girl. "And you two," she barked at the boys. "Hurry."

"But I'm tired," the girl whined.

"Then perish!" Eden curtly replied.

Again she glared at the girl as she un-shouldered her weapon. After engaging the weapon's firing bolt, Eden turned and sprinted toward the smoke.

*

"Bouda!"

Eden gave a wide berth to a pack of feeding hyenas as she reached the area where she and Bouda had agreed to rendezvous. Although she was familiar with the animals—and they with her—she moved cautiously around them, her finger on the trigger of the AK-47.

"Bouda!" she called again.

She eyed the charred chassis of a helicopter with interest, taking note of the machine gun mounted on a swivel arm above the passenger-side cockpit door. She looked for an insignia—the Ethiopian flag or the emblem of the Sudan People's Liberation Army—but could see no paint of any color on the body of the blackened aircraft. Perhaps Bacha Alba had ventured south, she thought, out of the realm of his territory, with designs on poaching ivory and slaves from another warlord. She studied the helicopter more closely; a line of bullet holes ran diagonally from the base of the body to the rotor. *Who fired the weapon that downed the aircraft?* she wondered.

"*Enat!*"

At the cry of "Mother," Eden rolled her shoulders and sighed.

Positioning the AK-47 against her shoulder, she turned a slow circle. She located the pink-clad little girl near an outcropping of stones. The waif, she observed, had wandered dangerously close to the pack of feeding hyenas. A juvenile had risen from the pack. The animal's eyes were riveted on the little girl.

"*Jib! Koomee!*" she yelled.

The hyena looked her way and snarled.

"*Ahhoon!*" she ordered, slapping her weapon. "*Jib!*" With a vehement shake of her head, she motioned for the animal to return to the pack.

"*Enat!*"

"I am not your mother," she crossly told the child as the girl ran toward her. "And where are the boys?"

Eden glanced in the young hyena's direction. To her relief, the animal had moved back to feeding on the kill. Satisfied the hyena posed no danger, she shifted her attention to the girl.

"The boys—where are they?" she asked again.

Eden was confused when the girl pointed a finger at her.

"What do you mean? They're not with me."

"There," the girl replied. "Behind you."

Eden turned and saw the boys trying to lift something off the ground some thirty paces away.

"What are they doing there?" Eden pressed. "And how did they end up behind me?"

"The other hyenas," the girl replied. "They went far around."

"Other hyenas?"

The girl pointed north.

There, off in the distance, partially hidden by clumps of tall savannah grass, Eden spied two groupings of hyenas. Like the group nearest her, these looked to be feeding.

"What are they—?"

Eden took a step toward the near pack of hyenas and tried to see what they were feeding on. When she saw an adult with a boot stuck on its muzzle, she quickly took a step back in retreat.

"A man," she muttered.

Her gaze drifted to the northern group of hyenas. As if suddenly remembering something she'd left behind, she abruptly turned to face the downed helicopter.

"Or men!" she exclaimed.

"*Birr!*"

Startled, Eden glanced over her shoulder. The two boys had arrived. They clapped their hands after dropping a large object on the ground.

"*Birr*—yes?" the boy asked.

"Ivory," the second boy gleefully said. Slapping the fingertips of his right hand into his left palm, he grinned at Eden and said, "Sell for *birr*."

Eden scrutinized the meter-long elephant tusk lying at the boy's feet.

"Where did you get that?" she asked.

The boys' smiles vanished at the harsh tone in Eden's voice. The nearest of the two—dressed in a khaki-colored T-shirt and loose-fitting dungarees—gave Eden a questioning look as he ran a toe across the tusk.

"Why are you angry?" he innocently asked. "It was lying there," he explained, motioning over his shoulder with a sideways nod of his head. "We found it."

"It's ours!" the second boy emphatically stated. "It is worth many *birr*."

Eden met the gaze of who she guessed was the older of the two boys— dressed in a yellow T-shirt with a clean-shaven head and the tooth of an animal looped around his neck—and started to laugh.

"Money—ha! Where will you spend it?" She waved a hand in front of her. "Look where we are. Do you see a merchant's stall? Or a market filled with fruit and bread?"

"We will carry it to market!" the younger of the two defiantly replied. "And then buy what we want!"

"And what of the men I freed you from?" Eden slapped the stock of the AK-47. "They are everywhere. Slavers, thieves, poachers—how far do you think you'll get carrying a tusk you can barely lift?"

"We will—"

"Enough!" She brushed the older boy's shoulder as she strode by him. "The words of children—hmph—like monkeys babbling in the trees." She twisted to face them when she said, "Now show me. Show me where you found the tusk."

"There's no more!" the younger boy yelled as he ran past her. "You see where the tracks end," he told her, pointing to an area ahead of them. "Maybe it fell off the truck." He looked at her with an animated expression on his face and nodded. "Yes, they must not have noticed when it fell."

Eden caught up to the boy. She studied the ground where he pointed. Just as he said, wide tire tracks ran northeast toward the highlands from a spot near a large, square impression outlined in the dirt.

"Not yet hidden by dust," she said of the tire tracks. She straightened and scanned the ridgeline beyond the waist-high grass. "Bouda would have alerted me of a poacher camp," she muttered.

"*Enat!*"

Eden whirled at the little girl's scream.

"*Jib!*" Eden shouted. "*Koomee!*"

Eden leveled the AK-47 and sprinted toward the pink-clad girl.

The same juvenile hyena Eden had warned off a few minutes before stood five meters from the child, body coiled to attack. Reflexively, Eden raised the AK-47 to fire off a warning shot. But her finger froze. A cold shiver ran down her spine as she stared at the object the little girl held in her hands. The hyena snarled and lunged. The AK-47 boomed. The hoots, yelps, and cackles from the hyena clan were instantaneous. The little girl ran toward Eden with open arms. But Eden made no attempt to receive her. She was hypnotized by the spiral horn in the girl's possession.

"That is not yours!" she screamed, her voice filled with anger. "How dare you have it!"

The child dropped the horn as Eden backhanded her. Visibly stunned, the little girl stood frozen for a moment before she started to cry.

"Stop it!" Eden yelled.

She grabbed the girl by the shoulder and shook her.

"Where did you steal it?" Eden quickly shouldered the AK-47 and pushed the girl away from the horn. Grasping the horn, she shouted, "This is Bouda's!" Her body shook as she glared at the child. "Where did you steal it?" She pointed the horn at the girl's face and yelled, "Where?"

The girl plopped down on the ground and wailed. Eden stepped to her and delivered a kick to her side.

"Get up!" she screamed. She kicked her a second time. "Get up!"

The girl rolled to a crouch and shuffled a dozen paces away. When

Eden took a few menacing steps toward her, the girl quickly pointed to an area off to her side.

"There," she hurried to say. "Where the dirt is black."

She cowered as Eden approached.

"I didn't steal it!" The girl placed her arms in front of her face when Eden bent toward her. "It was there." Cringing, she peeked to the side and said, "In the black dirt."

Eden bent to one knee and knelt aside the darkened patch of soil. Tentatively, she touched the stained earth and then quickly pulled her hand away. She rubbed her thumb across her fingertips before lifting her hand to her nose. As she inhaled the aroma of the soil, she closed her eyes. With an audible sigh, her chin drooped to her chest. Taking a deep breath, she traced a finger over the two-inch scar that ran from the base of her palm up her forearm. Sniffling, she roughly wiped her nose with the back of her hand. As a single tear slid down her cheek, she whispered, "Bouda."

Eden ground a foot into the black dirt. Shoulders trembling, she looked over at the carcass of the juvenile hyena she'd killed. After staring at the animal's bullet-ridden body for a few moments, she stuffed the spiral horn into the waist of her brown cotton trousers. In one fluid motion, she pulled the AK-47 from her shoulder and engaged the charging bolt. She eyed the northern groups of feeding hyenas with furrowed brow.

"For Bouda," she whispered.

And then she pulled the trigger.

When the gun stopped firing, Eden yanked the empty ammunition cartridge from the receiver and threw it on the ground. Taking a fresh clip from her pocket, she snapped the new magazine into the weapon and walked briskly to the nearest carcass the hyenas had been feeding on and fired a single round into the heads of the three dead hyenas lying next to it. After briefly inspecting the remains of the kill the animals had been feeding upon, she strode to the area where the northern groups of hyenas had been congregated. As she drew near, she fired a strafing round into the waist-high grass.

Using the barrel of the weapon, Eden sifted through what was left of a carcass and found the partial remains of a shoe. *Not Bouda*, she thought as she straightened and walked to the area where the second group of hyenas had been feeding. *Nor here*, she concluded when she saw a helmet of some sort with what looked to be the remains of someone's head still stuck inside of it lying next to a bloody lump of cloth. *Then where?*

She thought about where Bouda might be as she walked back to the three hyenas she had killed. *Would they have eaten him?* Mulling the thought in her head, she looked over to where the little girl was standing and stared at the patch of dark soil. With a slight nod of her head, she grasped the fat end of the spiral horn and walked toward the downed helicopter. Halfway to it, she veered off and headed toward the area where the boys had found the tusk. As she arrived at the spot where the tire tracks began, she pulled the horn from the waist of her pants. Squatting to the ground, she ran the tip of the horn through the corrugated impressions. She stared at the line in the dirt for several minutes before her gaze drifted to the scar on her wrist.

"My blood is your blood."

Eden felt a shiver run up her spine as she recalled Bouda's voice. She remembered placing her wrist against his as he spoke. For her, the mingling of their blood had been an elixir, transforming her from child to woman. Her body had tingled with energy, as though her skin had absorbed the sun and sunlight was spreading through her veins.

Soon, she recalled thinking at the time, *soon he will take me, and I will bear him a son.*

When the ceremony was finished, when he pulled his wrist away from hers, she grabbed his arm and ran her fingertips along the incision he'd made across his wrist. She recalled how empowered she'd felt when she'd wiped his blood on her lips. The smell, the taste, was intoxicating. She reveled in the realization that she was his; Bouda's woman.

Eden squeezed the horn between her hands as the memory of that moment began to falter. She blinked her eyes several times in an attempt to refocus. But try as she might to hold on to the memory, the image of Bouda blurred. So too did the strength she'd felt in the touch of his flesh, the euphoria she'd experienced when his blood flowed into her body. The loss of clarity unnerved her. Her mood turned dark, her thoughts troubled. Overwhelmed with grief, she took the horn and blindly struck out at the shadows clouding her recollections.

"Is the dirt hurting you?"

Eden whirled on the voice and thrust the horn toward the blurry form standing near her.

"What do you want?" Eden screamed at the figure.

Eden slowly shook her head as the shape took substance. The color pink confused her until the little girl's arms and legs materialized. She stared at the child's face, wondering why it looked so frightened.

"What are you doing here?" she asked the girl.

The child wiped one eye with the back of a hand and then the other. With a sniffle, she looked down at the ground. Her arm trembled as she pointed to the spot in front of Eden.

"What did they do?"

"They?" Eden's face flashed with anger. "Why are you so—?" She fell silent when she saw the deep gouges across the tire tracks.

"You scare me."

Eden pressed the fat end of the horn against her forehead and closed her eyes.

"Go away," she told the girl.

"Where?" the girl meekly replied.

Eden's face twisted into a scowl. She opened her eyes and yelled, "To your village! Anywhere!" She pointed the horn westward. "Just go!"

The girl glanced over her shoulder.

"Will you take me?"

"No!" she yelled. "I have—" Eden lowered the horn. Turning her face toward the highlands, she said in a soft voice, "I have to find him."

"Him?"

"Bouda."

"I'll come with you."

"No!" she snapped. "Now go! Take the boys and—"

"They're gone."

"Gone?" Eden's brow furrowed as she rose to stand.

"When you fired your gun," the girl explained, "they ran away."

Eden stomped her feet and growled.

"When do we eat?" the girl asked. "I'm hungry."

Eden glared at the child. Without a word, she briskly walked toward the highlands.

*

"There is war everywhere."

Kamua gazed into the fire as he slowly stirred a wooden spoon into a small tin cup perched on a rock at the edge of the flames.

"The elephants, the rhinos—they will soon be gone."

He lifted the spoon from the tin and brought it close to his mouth.

"What will they do then, when they are no longer?"

Lips puckered, he blew air onto the brown goo cradled within the spoon. Eyeing the paste, he asked, "Will they sell women? Children? Oil?" He took a cautious taste of the spoon's contents. "Rich *ferenji?*" With a slight shake of his head, he placed the spoon back in the tin. "Is this how they will pay for their wars after they kill all the animals?" He shook his head. In a subdued tone, he said, "We are losing."

A sharp hiss assailed him from an area above and behind him.

"You know I speak the truth."

Sitting cross-legged, he bent to the tin and continued to stir the contents.

"There are too many warlords seeking power. *Tembo* and *vifaru* will perish."

Kamua edged the tin away from the flames. As he waited for the owl to respond, he gazed thoughtfully at the blue-white light flickering on the cup's metal surface.

What will the land be without the ancient beasts? he wondered. *Elephants and rhinoceros have ruled here for thousands of years. The Mother will be heartbroken when they are gone. She will—*

He thought of Teimbaka and the day Selam taught him how to shoot a rifle. How he, Teimbaka, had lamented the use of the weapon. Kamua looked across the campfire and eyed the .50 caliber machine gun mounted on the pickup truck he'd commandeered from what he assumed was one of George Henry's poaching squads.

What would Teimbaka say of this weapon? "*This is not what the Mother wants.*" Kamua grunted as he pictured him expressing his opinion. *Teim-baka*—he sighed.

A gust of air swept across the back of Kamua's neck before rushing over the fire and bending the flames toward the ground. More a shadowed perception than a solid form of flesh, bone, and feathers, the owl flew across the backdrop of a starless night. Though he did not pretend to know where the bird was headed, he followed the owl's path over the fire and beyond, visualizing its powerful wing strokes as it soared toward the mountains.

Pinpoints of color materialized where the wind-bent flames cast their flickering light. These appeared as radiating circles of reddish pink that hovered within the depth of the night's unfathomable gloom. Kamua calmly watched the orbs move toward him, taking note of the phenomena's bobbing gait as they drew near.

"*Tembo roho*," he whispered. "Elephant spirit."

And when several more sets of glowing eyes materialized on either side of the first pair of luminous spheres, Kamua stood and said in greeting, "*Amani.*" "Peace."

As he watched the spirit-elephants materialize, he experienced a sense of both awe and foreboding.

"Why have you come?" he asked.

From a point high in the mountains, the rough-throated *gwok-gwonk-gwokwokwok* of the eagle owl resounded. Kamua glanced up to where he guessed the call had originated: the cave where he'd stored the tusks recouped from the poachers.

"I have done what I can," he said, addressing the spirit-elephants. "The cave is nearly full."

The herd began to waver as he spoke, the outline of their shimmering gold-white bodies destabilizing, as though a stiff wind was peeling streams of luminous particles from their torsos and spreading them into the air.

"I don't know what else I can do," he lamented. As he watched a mass of the glowing specks gather and swirl upward toward the mountains, he added, "I am sorry."

From within the mass of shifting forms, Kamua observed a small shape emerge. Judging by its size and form, he understood it to be a baby spirit-elephant, no taller than a meter in height. As the ethereal shape floated toward him, he was overwhelmed with a feeling of great sadness. For the animal—devoid of feet and hollow eyed—displayed numerous scars across its forehead and torso.

Kamua gasped and staggered a few steps back as the vision of the mutilated animal suddenly disappeared and was replaced with a wall of smoldering red eyes. The anger he sensed emanating from the herd of spirit-elephants unnerved him. Shaking with fear, he sank to his knees and bowed his head.

The cackling hoot of a lone hyena drew Kamua's attention toward the mountains. As the echo of the call faded, he slowly realized that he was alone. The spirit herd had vanished.

"*Amani*," he whispered. "*Amani.*"

Kamua squatted to the ground and sat cross-legged next to the rings of stones he'd placed around the fire. As he stared into the ash on the fringe of the flames, he mulled the different shades of color that lay upon the earth. Grey to black, black to white, white to grey. *What do the colors represent?* he wondered. *Death, rebirth, survival?* He shook his head. He didn't know.

Mindlessly, he extracted the spoon from the tin and took a nibble of the lentil paste.

The cave is nearly full. What else can I do?

The spirit-elephants had started to decompose as he had asked the same question: *What else can I do?* Their bodies had dissolved, swirling upward toward the cave. Ethereal forms transformed into a cloud of heavenly particles, a new entity. Taken with the notion of transformation, he observed embers of the fire as they drifted up into the night sky. *What do tiny bits of flame and wood become when they reach the point they can no longer be seen?* he mused. *What do they become then?* The question prodded him to ponder the flesh of the living; when death calls and time and elements erase the skin from your bones, what is it a person becomes when their spirit is no longer constrained within a body? *Is this what the spirit-elephants are trying to say to me?* he wondered. *Are they showing me they need to evolve—transform—before they can be free of this world? And their tusks—what do I need to do with them before the spirit beasts find peace?*

Kamua pondered these thoughts as he placed the spoon back into the tin and looked toward the mountains. *The cave—what more do the spirit-elephants want me to do*? Drawn by the flickering light of the fire, he gazed once more into the embers. As he studied the residue of wood and flame, a small gust of wind stirred, blowing dust and ash into the air.

Dust to dust, ashes to ashes.

As he watched the dust and ash settle back to earth, the baying of several hyenas echoed along the ridgetop at his back. Envisioning the cave of tusks, Kamua sensed what he must do, what the spirit-elephants wanted of him. But he did not have the means with which to accomplish the task.

*

"Pay me."

"For what?"

The man demanding payment—tall and bearded, with a sky-blue turban wrapped around his head—dropped a bloodstained bundle on Akmir's desk. With a grunt and a nod, he said, "The head of the one you seek."

Akmir barely glanced at the item before returning his attention to the papers spread out in front of him.

"And?" Akmir inquired.

The turbaned man shifted his weight from one foot to the other and cocked his head to the side.

"What do you mean, 'and'?" he inquired. "Bounty." He smacked the top of the desk with his hand and once more nodded to the bloody bundle. "You pay. Twenty thousand!" In a raised voice, he added, "*In gold!*" Slapping the stock of the AK-47 slung across his chest, he exclaimed, "You pay!"

The man's jaws began to tremble when Akmir laughed.

"You mock Mosi?" he shouted.

Mosi slid the AK-47 off his shoulder and pointed the muzzle at Akmir's head.

Instantly, an arm wrapped around his neck. The sharp edge of a machete pressed against his throat. Simultaneously, the nose of a handgun nudged his temple. Calmly, Akmir raised a hand as if to say *Stop*. At once, the two uniformed men who'd come to his defense lowered their weapons and stepped away.

"You go by Mosi?" Akmir asked. "That's Swahili, yes?"

Akmir's brow furrowed when the man didn't reply.

"Don't mock you, is that what you said? Don't make a fool of you?" Akmir glared at the man as he adjusted the sleeves of his white cotton thawb. "Yet, you would do this to me?" He took a pencil from the cup on the corner of his desk and poked the bundle. "A head." With a nod to Mosi, he added, "Undoubtedly—but whose? A goatherd's? A farmer's? A fisherman's?"

"It is the elephant protector," Mosi curtly responded. "That's whose head I have brought you."

"Ah, the elephant protector." Akmir nodded as if in agreement. "Then the rest is outside, yes?"

"The rest?" Mosi's face took on a perplexed expression. "You mean the body?"

"The ivory," Akmir clarified. "Surely you have it—or know of its whereabouts—if you have indeed—" he pointed to the cloth-wrapped bundle with the pencil "—brought me the head of the elephant protector."

Akmir rose from his chair and rounded the small makeshift desk positioned in the center of the large khaki-colored tent.

"The one responsible for killing a dozen hunters and confiscating the tusks in their possession," he explained. He gave Mosi a wry smile. "So, you must have it—the ivory—yes?"

Mosi hesitantly looked at each of the five faces in the room.

"Because if you don't have it—or know exactly where it is stored—" Akmir reached into the sleeve of his thawb and withdrew a thin-bladed knife. Holding the stiletto an inch below Mosi's right eye, he exclaimed, "then you are just another murdering *muhtāl* dishonoring yourself and your family with a lie!"

"I didn't—!"

"Do you know how many heads have been brought to me?" Akmir shouted. Touching the tip of the blade against Mosi's nose, he continued, "And how many *thieves* have tried to con me for the gold by telling me the same lie as you?"

Akmir's eyes narrowed to smoldering slits. With a flick of his hand, he cut a line along the side of Mosi's cheek with the knife. When blood began to ooze from the shallow wound, he grunted.

"And you—you dare tell me not to mock *you*?"

Akmir placed the stiletto underneath Mosi's chin. Mosi stiffened but held his ground. Akmir studied the man's eyes before he turned and walked to the far side of his desk.

"I lost three men," Mosi angrily retorted as he wiped blood from his cheek. "And a helicopter," he went on, his teeth clenched. "To bring this to you." His body trembled with anger when he said, "I do not lie!"

"Of course, you do," Akmir replied matter-of-factly. "We all do." With a dismissive wave of a hand, he added, "Now take whoever's head this is out back and throw it in the pit with the other hundred that were brought to me this week."

Nearly in unison, the four men guarding Akmir leveled their weapons when Mosi jerked the AK-47 in a threatening manner. Akmir shook his head and frowned.

"You are all the same," he said, addressing Mosi. "Not a businessman in the lot of you. Kill, butcher, steal." Akmir shook his head and sighed. "Is there anything you and those like you won't do for money?" He poked the bloodstained bundle with a pencil. "Someone you knew? Or just some poor villager you happened upon?"

"It is the elephant protector!"

"Of course it is," Akmir replied. He smiled. "Just as all the other heads brought to me were." He gave a final poke to the cloth-wrapped bundle. "Now get out."

"I lost three men and a helicopter!" Mosi vehemently complained. "The bounty calls—"

"Enough!" Akmir slapped the head off his desk. "No ivory, no gold! Now get out before I have *your* head removed!"

Akmir pulled on the sleeves of his robe and sat down in the chair behind the desk. His tone and manner were even-keeled when he said, "There are a score like you already back out on the hunt. I might suggest you join them instead of wasting my time." Akmir directed his attention to the papers spread out before him. With a wave of a hand, he added, "You are dismissed."

*

Mosi strode out of Akmir's tent and was immediately joined by a gangly man dressed in a red T-shirt and camouflage pants. A good six inches shorter than Mosi, the man rose up on the tip of his toes so he could grab Mosi by the shoulder and place his mouth next to his ear.

"The gold?" he whispered.

Mosi glared at him and thrust his bloody bundle into the man's stomach. With a curt shove to the man's chest, he ordered, "Throw it away."

The man stared at the bloody bundle for a moment before shrugging his shoulders.

"It was worth a try," he said to the cloth-wrapped bundle. "Worth a try."

7

"PUFFER'S DEAD."

Tanya stopped rubbing her eyes and took a step back as a tall man with a black do-rag on his head pushed the door open and stepped into the entranceway.

"What you talkin' about?"

As the man swept past her, she pushed the metal door closed and secured the deadbolt. With a worried glance over her shoulder, she pressed her ear to the door and listened. After a moment, she hurried after Gerard.

"What do you mean?" she pressed. "What the hell you talkin' about? What you two do?"

"Shut up, bitch! Let me think." Gerard put his hands to his face and kneaded his fingers into his forehead. "Shit," he said, "shit, shit, shit."

The woman took a hesitant step across the brown and cream linoleum floor and gently placed a hand on the man's upper arm.

"Gerard." She quickly withdrew her hand when Gerard flinched and gave her a confused look. "You jonesin'?" She stepped in front of him so she could look into his eyes. "Sweet Jesus, boy. You crashin' hard, ain't ya?"

Gerard wiped his nose and squinted. Pulling on the front of his shiny red Chicago Bulls jacket, he shuffled his feet and bobbed his head.

"Weren't nothin' s'pose to happen," he blurted.

As though he suddenly lost his balance, Gerard stumbled past the woman and flopped his six-foot-four frame down on the chocolate-brown couch.

"I don't even know how," he muttered. "You said they were—"

Gerard's left eye begin to twitch.

"Easy street, ya know? Like grabbin' a soda from a—"

Gerard ran a hand across the stubble on his chin. His eyes glazed over when he tilted his head back and stared up at the ceiling.

"What do you mean, I said?"

She pulled the sash of the purple terrycloth robe tight around her waist and sat down next to Gerard.

"Who was supposed to be easy street?" She placed a hand on his arm. "Who killed Puffer?" She gave Gerard's arm a light push. "Gerard? Was it gang shit? I thought you were done with that." She leaned across Gerard's chest and looked into his face. "Was it Bloods?" She squeezed his arm to get his attention. "Where were you when it happened?"

When Gerard offered no response, Tanya sat back and sighed. With a frown, she studied Gerard's face. She took note of the little beads of perspiration running along the bottom edge of his do-rag and observed the clenched muscles at the back of his jaw.

"When was the last time you hit it?" She rolled her eyes when he didn't answer. With a shake of her head, she muttered, "Probably dreamed this shit up while you were high. You and Puffer always talkin' shit when you on. Puffer probably fell off sleepin'. And you so fucked up you think he dead."

She giggled and looked across the room. She focused on the face of the USMC eagle-globe-anchor clock on the upper tier of the low shelving unit that ran the length of the opposite wall. When she noticed the time—6:35 am—she pursed her lips and shook her head.

"Daddy be home in an hour or so." She ran a finger along the inside of Gerard's thigh. "You got any juice in the stick?" she teased. "Maybe Puffer come back to life if you shoot one out."

Gerard jolted off the couch when the woman grabbed his crotch.

"Goddammit, bitch!" He looked down at her, incredulous. "Bro done took two bullets to the chest and you fuckin' wanna play with my dick? What the hell wrong with you, Tanya?" Gerard leaned toward her and bunched his right hand into a fist. "Puffer was my boy! We tight! And that fat old cow you call Mamma just shot his ass! Now he dead!"

Gerard suddenly clutched his stomach as if he'd been punched. He staggered back and doubled over. Tanya got up from her seat and pushed Gerad back to the couch.

"You tellin' me you fuckin' tried to rob Jim's?" Tanya slapped Gerard hard across the face. "You stupid, brainless ass! They see your face?"

She raised her arm to strike him again but stopped short of hitting him when Gerard heaved a blubbering sigh and started to cry.

"Sweet fucking Jesus," she muttered. She ran a hand back over her head and clasped a handful of the silver beads dangling from the ends of her cornrow braids. "If they recognized you—"

Gerard sniffled and wiped his nose with the back of his hand.

"Don't matter," he mumbled.

"Don't matter?" Tanya mocked. "You fuckin' crazy? Course it matters. They seen you with me before! All they gotta do is put two and—"

"They dead."

Tanya's jaw dropped and her face went blank. Then, in a burst of anger, she directed a flurry of slaps to the side of Gerard's head.

"What the hell you do?" she screamed. "You killed 'em?"

Gerard cowered away and covered his head with his hands.

"Jesus Christ, Gerard!" She slapped his hands. "They part of the hood! They family! How could you fuckin'—?"

"It's your fault," he whined. He rubbed his head where she'd struck him. "You were the one said how they crazy for having so much cash laying around at the end of the day. You the one said they ripe for the pickin' if somebody walk in with a gun and rob 'em."

He curled into a fetal position when Tanya took a menacing step toward him.

"You to blame," he whimpered. "Never said the old fucks had a fuckin' Glock."

Tanya's expression went from anger to disgust. With a heavy sigh, she loosened the sash of her robe and pulled on the bottom of her white T-shirt. She checked the time on the clock before she turned to Gerard and asked, "Anybody see you? Cops on your ass?"

Gerard shook his head.

"Better not bring no fuzz here," she warned. She glanced at the clock and rubbed her forehead. "Jesus, Gerard! What the hell did you do? Why the hell you gotta go kill two fine folks like Jim and Mamma? What the hell wrong with you and Puffer?"

"Not like we wanted to," Gerard retorted, his tone defensive. "Puffer in some deep shit with the Brotherhood. He say they gonna come down on him hard if he don't throw some cash their way." Tanya shook her head when she saw tears sliding down his cheeks. "We thought it would be easy." He shrugged and wiped his eyes. "Pay the money and have some green for some shit, you know?"

Tanya folded her arms and frowned.

"Easy," she said. "Shit, three people dead and now you gonna have the cops on your ass."

"They don't know nothin'," he shot back. "Don't even know they all layin' there. Ain't nobody come."

"What you mean, ain't nobody come? You hang around and watch?"

Gerard sheepishly nodded his head.

"Been by a few times since—"

Tanya watched him slide his fingers across his lips as his eyebrows pinched together. He stared off into space for a few seconds before he mumbled, "They all dead." She watched his face twist into an expression of disbelief. "Puffer. The old man. The fat woman."

Tanya took a step back when Gerard raised his arm and shaped his hand into an imaginary gun. She felt a jolt of fear shoot through her when he pointed a finger at her forehead and dropped his thumb as though it was the hammer on a revolver.

"Pow," he said in a faraway voice. "Damn forehead exploded like—" He chuckled and tilted his head back onto the cushion. "Like I don't know, man." He balled his hands into fists and then thrust his fingers out. "Just, pow, you know?"

He laughed and then abruptly stopped. Tanya watched his bottom lip quiver and his eyes tear up. His mouth opened like he was about to say something, but no words came out. When he started to scratch his neck, she took a step toward him.

"So, nobody saw you and the cops don't know yet. Is that what you're telling me?" She glanced back at the Marine Corps clock. "You can't stay here, Gerard. You hear me? You gotta go."

Gerard wiped his nose before cupping one side of his face with his hand. Tanya shook her head as his thumb and fingers slid up and down his cheek as though he was wiping crumbs from his skin.

"I need a taste."

Tanya sighed and shook her head.

"You holdin'?"

"Gerard."

"You know, just enough to get me through. You know."

"Gerard," she repeated in a frustrated tone. "You know I don't keep no drugs here. My dad find any shit in this place, he'd whip my ass but good. And then he'd drag me to the candyman and beat *his* head in."

"Shit, girl, I gotta have some." He clutched his stomach and bent forward. "Front me," he croaked. "Enough for a taste."

"Sorry, Gerard, I'm tapped out. You know my dad has Jim hold my work money and tips 'fore he go and collect it at the end of the week."

"You shittin' me."

"No." She stood up and put her hands on her hips. "I've told you a dozen times. You just not listenin', is all. Ever since he had to bail me out with that bookie, he keeps all my dough under lock and key and divvies it out on Sundays like the miserly old tyrant he is."

Tanya huffed and gave Gerard an angry look when he started to laugh.

"That's right," he snickered. "You 'bout got yourself turnin' tricks for life bettin' on hoops." He sat up and put his hands to his chest when his laughter turned into a hacking cough. "That's what you get for bein' a Knicks fan," he wheezed.

"Go ahead and choke to death, fool. You be gassin' soon anyway, cops find out you killed somebody." Tanya pulled on the ends of her sash. "Now I ain't got no job *and* no money 'cause you and Puffer go shoot up the place I work and kill the owners." She tightened the sash around her waist and grunted. "How I gonna make a livin' now?" She glared at him. "And you asking me to front you—shit." She made a fist and leaned toward him. "You done fucked up!" she snarled.

"T."

Tanya whirled around.

"Marcus," she said in a soft voice.

Marcus—dressed in Superman pajamas with a stuffed figure of Kermit the Frog pinned under one arm—looked uncertainly between Gerard and Tanya.

"I forgot you were here."

"Who the fuck is that?" Gerard asked.

"Oh, my God." Tanya put her hand to her mouth and turned to look at Gerard. "Jim and Rochelle—their grandkid. I was babysitting him like I do some nights." She turned and took a step toward Marcus. "Hey, little man," she said in a cheerful voice. "Guess Gram and Pops had a late night and decided to pick you up sometime later this morning." She glanced over her shoulder at Gerard and raised her eyebrows. "Probably too late to come get you by the time they closed up," she told the boy.

"How old is he?"

Tanya gave a start when she realized Gerard had moved from the couch and was standing next to her.

"Two and a half. Three maybe," she replied.

"Talk yet?"

"Nah." She shook her head and laid an arm on the boy's shoulder. "Just startin' to figure shit out." She bent down and lifted Marcus into her arms. "He real quiet." She smiled at the boy and ran a finger down his cheek. "Probably why I forget he even here."

"Then he don't know what we been sayin', right?"

"Nah, just a bunch of noise to him." She playfully placed a fingertip to the boy's nose and then did the same to Kermit. "Ain't that right, little Marcus?"

"Shit, woman, stop actin' like you his mama." Gerard rubbed a hand across the back of his neck and groaned. "Forget about him. I need—"

"Forget about him?" Tanya interjected. "Who gonna take care of the boy now?" She leaned toward Gerard and whispered, "Now you kill his folks?"

"Why I give a shit who take care of the boy? Send him back to his real mama."

"She dead."

"How you know?"

"Cause they told me, that's how." Tanya lifted Marcus into her arms and started to pace the room. "Daddy some fugitive or somethin'," she muttered. "They don't know where he is and he ain't worth shit, as far as Jim say." She gave Gerard an ornery look before adding, "Like most men I know."

Tanya sighed as she watched Gerard grab his stomach and stagger back to the couch. She took a quick look at the clock.

"Gerard, you need to go."

"Go where?"

Tanya's shoulders drooped when she saw the distraught look on his face.

"You gotta help me, T. I need a fix—bad." His voice was near pleading when he extended a hand toward Tanya and said, "Your dad gotta have some cash stashed somewhere 'round here, girl. Think. Please."

"Ain't no cash nowhere in this place, Gerard. He take it all with him when he go to work. Only time we got cash lying around is when he bring mine home from Jim and Rochelle's and give me my allowance."

"Then let me have whatever you got left, girl. Even—"

"Uh-uh," she told him with a definitive shake of her head. "Long gone. Ain't nothin' left." She frowned and raised her eyebrows. "Supposed to get paid tomorrow. But that ain't gonna happen now, is it?" She looked away from Gerard and continued to pace the room. "Money probably just sittin' in a drawer," she mumbled as she patted Marcus on the back. "Not doin' nobody no good." She gave Gerard a pointed look when she said, "Least of all, me." When she saw Gerard inspecting his hands as if he didn't understand what they were, she muttered, "Sweet Jesus."

"What's that?"

"I said, 'sweet Jesus.'"

"No, 'bout money sittin' 'round not doin' nobody no good. Sittin' where?" he pressed. He moved to the edge of the couch. "Where money just sittin'?"

Gerard abruptly stood and moved toward her. She watched his expression change from one of pleading to one of anger as he clamped a hand around her wrist.

"Where the money at?" he demanded.

Tanya froze at the anger in Gerard's voice.

"Where the money?" he shouted.

Tanya flinched when he twisted her wrist.

"What money?" she snapped, jerking free of his grasp. "You fuckin'—"
She quickly turned away from Gerard when Marcus started to cry. "Now
look what you done," she said in a calming voice. "There, there, little man.
No need to—"

Marcus wailed when Gerard pulled him from Tanya's arms and put
his head in a chokehold.

"Jesus god, Gerard, what you doin'? What you doin'?" She reached out
for the boy and yelled, "Don't you hurt him, you hear me? Don't you—"

"Where he keep it?" Gerard yelled. "Tell me or I'll pop his head right
off his neck!"

Gerard slapped the boy's head.

"Tell me!" he screamed.

"I don't know where!" Tanya cried.

She started to shake when Gerard slapped the boy again.

"I don't know, Gerard!" she sobbed. "Somewhere in their crib, I guess.
How you expect me to know?"

"Where their crib at?" Marcus started to choke as Gerard exerted pressure on his neck. "Where it at?"

"Twelfth Street!" she blurted. "Near the cemetery!"

She fell to her knees when she saw bubbles come out of Marcus'
nostrils.

"451 12th Street. 6A." She looked up at Gerard with tears streaming
down her cheeks. "Please, Gerard, don't," she begged.

Gerard dropped the boy to the floor and placed a foot against his head.

"You got a key?" he asked. His eyes narrowed. "Give it to me or I'll
flatten him."

Tanya bunched her hand into a fist. Her arm coiled to strike, she
launched herself at Gerard.

"You fuckin' bastard! You touch—"

Gerard's fist smashed into her right breast. She stumbled backward, pain shooting through her chest. Marcus screamed. Horror stricken, Tanya looked down to see Gerard's foot grinding the boy's face against the floor.

"Stop it!" she wailed.

"Key!" he yelled. "Give me the fuckin' key to their crib!"

"I don't—"

"Don't lie to me, girl!" Tanya felt as though she was going to faint when Gerard raised his foot above Marcus' head.

"Okay, okay, okay," she sobbed. She staggered over to him and grabbed hold of his arm. "I'll get it, I'll get it. Just don't stomp on the boy."

"Then get it," he ordered, shoving her away. "And don't make me wait, or—"

Tanya ran down the hallway to her room. By the time she returned with the key, Gerard was down on one knee suffering a bout of dry heaves. Marcus, she saw, was lying on the floor. She couldn't tell if he was dead or alive. When Gerard noticed she was back, he staggered to his feet and stumbled toward her.

"That it?" he asked, trying to focus on the object she was holding between her thumb and forefinger.

He reached for her hand but Tanya swung her arm to her side and walked to the front door.

"You think I'm playin'?" he snarled.

Before she realized he'd followed, Gerard grabbed her hair and threw her against the wall.

"Give it to me!" he demanded.

Tears streaming down her face, Tanya jabbed the key into his side.

"Take it," she hissed.

Gerard slapped her across the face before wrenching the key from her hand. Without a word, he went to the door and pulled it toward him. When it didn't open, he pulled on the knob several more times to no avail.

"Why don't it fuckin' open?" he blubbered.

Tanya brushed him aside and angrily slid the deadbolt to the side.

"Gotta unlock the bolt, fool," she replied. "Now get the hell out. And don't ever—" She gasped as Gerard bulled past her and ran out the door. "And don't ever," her bottom lip trembled as she closed the door and slid the deadbolt in place, "come back."

*

Mr. Locket turned in to a gravel parking lot off Route 23 east of Leola, Pennsylvania, and eased the car to a stop. He glanced down at the piece of paper in his lap and then looked out the windshield at the grime-covered billboard connected to the roof of a square two-story building. The words *Zack's Motel* were written in a putrid color of orange on the face of the dingy white sign.

Mr. Locket cleared his throat as he checked the time on his gold wristwatch. Lifting his foot off the brake pedal, he maneuvered the car into a slow arcing turn and parked it next to the only other car in the lot, a white Fleetwood Cadillac. After turning the car off, he studied the piece of paper in his lap one more time before folding it in half and slipping it into the inside pocket of his black suit coat.

When his phone had rung at 6:25 that morning, he'd assumed it was Mrs. Callahan calling to let him know that Madam was up early and would undoubtedly be asking his whereabouts shortly. He'd been very much surprised when he'd heard Dirk's voice on the other end of the phone instead of Cook's. He was more surprised—shocked really— when the man asked for his help. *Help, indeed,* Mr. Locket had thought. *Presumptuous laggard, to be asking me for help when all he has done for the past year is live off the generosity of Madam and make a nuisance of himself with the staff.* But when Dirk mentioned Claire's name—Miss Claire, as Mr. Locket thought of her—he had immediately agreed to the man's request.

As Mr. Locket knocked on the metal door with 5G painted on the front, he could feel his pulse quicken. *How did such a worthless dolt like Mr. Savage come to be in the company of such a wonderfully educated and kind woman as Miss Claire?* he wondered. *Sister Claire,* he reminded himself. Odd that she would be released from the clinic and not be brought straight home. And why in the world had she agreed to accompany Mr. Savage to such a seedy, out-of-the-way motel? Mr. Locket stiffened as the door opened only as far as a chain security lock would allow.

"You came."

"I am a man of my word," Mr. Locket briskly replied. He eyed the portion of Dirk's face he could see with an air of disdain. "Have you asked me here to hold a conversation through a locked door?"

The door eased shut. Mr. Locket heard the chain moving before the door swung open. He hesitated before entering the dimly lit room. Upon crossing the threshold, he stopped to allow his eyes to adjust to the lack of light.

Mr. Savage, standing to his immediate right, was dressed—oddly, Mr. Locket thought—in sky-blue medical scrubs. He was somewhat dismayed when he didn't see Miss Claire standing next to him. He had been expecting her to greet him upon his arrival.

"On the phone, you relayed that Miss Claire would be appreciative of my service," Mr. Locket said, repressing the urge to place his hand over his nose when he got a whiff of the musty smell in the room.

Dirk reached past him and closed the door.

"Brace yourself," he said.

And then, to Mr. Locket's confusion, Dirk extended his arm toward the room's single bed.

"I don't understand."

With what little morning light shown through the east facing window, the pale illumination was enough to reveal the haggard features of a woman lying motionless on the left side of a double bed.

"God have mercy," Mr. Locket muttered as he took a tentative step toward the bed. "What have you done to her?" He gave Dirk a threatening glare.

"Miss Claire." Mr. Locket knelt to one knee at the side of the bed. "Miss Claire," he said again. He reached out a hand as if he was going to touch her cheek when Dirk spoke.

"They were going to kill her."

Mr. Locket furrowed his brow.

"She needs more help than I can give. Do you know of a doctor in the area?" Dirk hurried to add, "One you trust?"

"What nonsense are you spouting?" Mr. Locket protested as he rose to stand. "Good God, Mr. Savage, what have you done? Why have you brought Miss Claire to such a despicable location when she obviously is in need of a hospital bed? You will certainly pay a heavy price if Miss Claire suffers for your irresponsible actions."

"They were *killing* her," Dirk repeated. "Look at her!" Dirk pointed to the bed. "Take a look at her right wrist."

Dirk abruptly turned and walked to the far corner of the room. Mr. Locket raised an eyebrow when he heard the man mumble something unintelligible.

"I would think you are in a very serious situation if you have, for some reason, taken Miss Claire from the clinic against her will."

"Me?" Dirk replied, incredulous. "Why are you making this about *me*? I thought you gave a shit about her."

Mr. Locket stiffened when Dirk stepped to the bed and abruptly yanked the covers halfway down Claire's body.

"Take a look at her, Locket."

Mr. Locket positioned his body nearer to the edge of the bed. When Dirk's movements seemed to indicate he was about to touch Claire, Mr. Locket pointed a finger at his chest.

"Don't touch her," he warned.

Mr. Locket grunted a curse word when Dirk bent to one knee and grabbed Claire's hand.

"I told you not to—"

Mr. Locket fell silent as Dirk displayed the inside of Claire's wrist. The wound he revealed resembled an open sewer: a foul-colored line of festering browns and blues streaked with a slimy film of yellow-green. The laceration—even to someone like himself, who knew nothing of wounds—looked highly infected. The flesh was swollen and inflamed, with red rivulets flaring into a forearm the color of a pale moon.

"I'll show him."

Mr. Locket eyed Dirk with a mixture of curiosity and concern. *Why is he looking over his shoulder when he talks?* As he tried to assess Dirk's state of mind, he observed the man gently release Claire's arm and move his hand to her head. Mr. Locket cleared his throat and pinched his eyebrows together when Dirk brushed a few strands of limp, oily hair away from a spot on her scalp.

"Here," Dirk said as he ran a finger over a discolored circle imprinted in Claire's skin. "She has four of them evenly spaced around her head. More on her arms and body." Mr. Locket noted Dirk's distraught expression when he added, "They even placed them on her—" Dirk shook his head and lowered his eyes. "On her—" He couldn't finish.

"You've inspected her without clothing?" Mr. Locket disdainfully asked. "That's disgusting. Perverse."

"Will you stop making this about me?" Dirk shouted. "Pull your head out of your ass! Look at her! She needs help!"

Dirk abruptly stood and moved to the foot of the bed.

"I thought from the conversations we've had over the past year that you cared for this woman," he said, pointing to Claire. "Am I wrong?"

"I am devoted to Miss Claire, as I have always been," Mr. Locket calmly replied. "As I have been devoted to the entire Waterman family for most of my adult life." Mr. Locket paused to pull the bedding up so Claire's upper body was covered. "But I am not a doctor, Mr. Savage." He gently tucked the covers behind Claire's shoulders. "I really have no understanding of what you want me to do. Or what you expected of me when you asked me to come here."

Dirk ran both hands through his hair and then pressed his palms against his temples.

"What I want you to do?" he repeated. He shook his head and looked at Mr. Locket with disbelief.

"Jesus, man—look at her!" He thrust out an arm and pointed to Claire. "I want you to help me save her from the people who are killing her!" Mr. Locket flinched when Dirk swung his arm and pointed a finger at him. "I want *you* to help me *save* her!"

"Calm down, Mr. Savage." Mr. Locket frowned and stroked his chin. "The issue here is the best course of action to take."

"Best course of action?"

Mr. Locket had edged back toward the head of the bed when Dirk suddenly turned and pointed to the far corner of the room.

"You showed him helping her!" he screamed. "He's not helping!"

"Mr. Savage."

Dirk turned and glared at Mr. Locket with clenched fists.

"I believe everything will turn out satisfactorily if you will just calm down." Noting the perspiration on Dirk's forehead, he asked, "When was the last time you slept?"

Dirk looked up to the ceiling and shook his head

"When was the last time—?" he muttered. "Are you fucking—?"

Mr. Locket watched Dirk's face go ashen as the door to the room burst open and two burly men dressed in hospital whites rushed in. Pointing a finger at Dirk, Mr. Locket said, "That's him."

Before Dirk could move or open his mouth to protest, the men grabbed his arms and yanked them behind his back.

"I believe he will need to be restrained," Mr. Locket said.

Mr. Locket took a defensive posture when Dirk wrenched an arm free and pushed one of the men holding him. But a powerful blow to Dirk's kidney from the second man brought an immediate halt to the struggle. And when a subsequent, equally powerful punch was delivered to his stomach, Dirk doubled over and slumped forward.

Mr. Locket stood passively to the side as the two men bound Dirk's hands behind his back. A moment later, Mrs. Waterman walked into the room. She was followed by a short, olive-skinned man dressed in a charcoal pin-striped suit. He carried a doctor's bag.

The woman scrutinized Dirk for a moment before shaking her head.

"Ah, Mr. Benson, the orderly," she said.

"What have you done?"

Mr. Locket felt a moment of confusion when he heard the anguish in Dirk's voice.

"He's taking care of the Waterman family," Mrs. Waterman replied. "As he has done for many a year." She acknowledged Mr. Locket with a slight nod. "And quite admirably, I might add." Shifting her attention to Dirk, she said, "But I'm afraid there is nothing admirable in your actions, Mr. Savage, as events have revealed." She looked over at the man with the doctor's bag and motioned for him to move past her. "You are very much a disappointment."

Mr. Locket eyed the olive-skinned man, who he guessed was a doctor, as he filled a syringe with a clear liquid and held it up to the light streaming in the doorway.

"But life is filled with disappointments, isn't it, Mr. Savage?" the elderly woman commented.

"If I may interrupt, Madam," Mr. Locket politely interjected, "Miss Claire seems in need of immediate medical attention."

"Mrs. Waterman doesn't give a shit about Miss Claire," Dirk bitterly interjected. "Who do you think is doing this to her?" He shook his head, "You just signed her death warrant, you stupid bastard. She'll be dead within a—"

Mr. Locket surmised that the needle inserted into Dirk's neck hurt a great deal, for the man gasped and kicked out with his legs. Given the expression on his face—which Mr. Locket perceived as a mixture of agony and disbelief—he felt certain Dirk would no longer be slandering anyone. Indeed, as he watched Dirk's eyes close and body go limp, he nodded with satisfaction.

"Shall I accompany Madam to the hospital?" he politely inquired.

"That will not be necessary," the elderly woman replied.

"We have an ambulance waiting outside, Mrs. Waterman."

Mr. Locket raised an eyebrow when a woman dressed in a nurse's uniform strode into the room. As the woman bent and placed a hand to Claire's forehead, he edged slightly away from the bed to give her room.

"She's only been gone for a few hours," the nurse stated. "Once we get her in the ambulance, she should be fine."

"The laceration on her wrist looks quite infected," Mr. Locket interjected. "And she's not been conscious since I arrived."

"Everything will be taken care of," the nurse responded without bothering to look at Mr. Locket.

"Charles."

Mrs. Waterman gave Mr. Locket a slight shake of the head.

"It's been quite a long morning for all concerned. You've been of great help." She placed a frail-looking hand to her chest and patted her heart. "As you always are. But allow the professionals to do their jobs."

"Yes, Madam," he said apologetically. "Of course." He watched impassively as the two orderlies dragged Dirk from the room. "The authorities, they've been—?"

"Waiting for him at the clinic," she responded.

"Very good, Madam."

"I didn't foresee him becoming such a nuisance," she muttered.

Mr. Locket observed a slight wrinkling around her eyes as the lady of the estate focused her attention on the activity outside the door.

"I don't know why I allowed him to stay on," she continued. "Part reward for bringing her back from that dreadful place, I suppose." He caught the slight shrug of her shoulders when she added, "And, perhaps, a small amount of guilt."

Mr. Locket waited for her to say more. When she seemed lost in thought, he softly prodded her.

"Guilt, Madam? I'm not sure I understand."

"For allowing her life to unravel to the delusions she now suffers, Mr. Locket. Her constant harping on orphans and famine and death, as though they are the only issues that exist in the world." She gave him a disconcerting look. "And her obvious infatuation with that— that—" She shuddered. "Filthy nigger."

Mr. Locket looked down at the toes of his shoes and cleared his throat.

"So, keeping him around, I suppose, was—"

Mr. Locket looked up to see her wringing her hands. Her expression, to him, seemed ambivalent when she said, "My way of trying to help her back to some semblance of her former self, I imagine. By using Mr. Savage as a bridge between what she needs to leave behind and what she needs to focus on going forward." Mr. Locket felt a pang of anxiety when he saw her face twitch. As well, her eyes seemed vacant to him when she asked, "You see that, don't you?"

The sound of tires crunching over gravel preceded the reappearance of the two burly men rolling a gurney into the room. As they maneuvered past Mrs. Waterman toward the bed, she turned her back to them.

"I will attend to matters at the clinic and then return home," she announced in a detached manner. "See to it that the Cadillac is ferried back to the property, if you would, Mr. Locket."

Without so much as a parting gesture, Mrs. Waterman walked out of the room. A moment later, Mr. Locket experienced a sense of remorse as Claire was wheeled out the door.

To the background noise of doors closing, engines turning over, and tires rolling on gravel, Mr. Locket gave the room a cursory inspection. Finding nothing he could attribute to Miss Claire, he was making his way toward the door when what sounded like the whimper of a small child compelled him to stop. A quick glance back into the room revealed what appeared to be the translucent outline of a small elephant shimmering in the light flowing through the window. But as he blinked his eyes to bring the object into better focus, the image disintegrated into particles of dust. Suddenly feeling very fatigued, Mr. Locket decided the aberration of light and dust was a product of stress and the reference by Madam to the dark and wild continent where Miss Claire had contracted whatever disease it was she was suffering. Without giving the anomaly another thought, he walked out of room 5G and pulled the door closed behind him.

*

"Money."

Gerard didn't know exactly what was inside the Quaker Oats container, but he knew it wasn't dried oats. He shook the cardboard cylinder one more time just to be sure he wasn't deluding himself before placing it on the counter. Sweating profusely, his body twitching, he popped open the lid and tilted the canister on its side.

"Fuckin' A."

He smiled widely as he shoved a shaky hand inside the drum and pulled out an envelope containing a wad of bills bound with a rubber band. He'd just begun to count the money when he glimpsed a black and white police cruiser pull up to the curb on the opposite side of the street. Reflexively, he drew back from the kitchen window.

Using the key Tanya had supplied, Gerard had entered Jim and Rochelle's duplex—situated at the end of a line of similar row houses at the corner of 12th Street and Woodland Avenue in west Newark—through the front door. He didn't know if he'd been seen going into the premises, and he didn't much care if he had. Desperate for his next fix, he'd ransacked the bedrooms on the second floor before making his way down to the lower level to pull open every drawer and cabinet in a frantic attempt to find the stash of money Tanya had alluded the dead restaurant owners kept in the house. The kitchen was the last room he searched. As it was located right off the front entrance and faced the street, he had a perfect vantage point from which to observe the comings and goings of the neighborhood.

When Gerard saw a cop slide out of the police cruiser with his eyes riveted to the front door of the duplex, Gerard slipped the rubber band around the wad of bills and set it and the envelope down on the counter. A slight clunk drew his attention away from the approaching officer to the envelope. Curious, he ran a finger over a small protrusion near the bottom of the envelope. Judging by the feel and form of the object, he deduced it was a key. He had half a mind to open the envelope and see exactly what type of key it held, but out of the corner of his eye he saw the approaching officer draw his gun. Grabbing the money and envelope, Gerard ran to the back of the duplex. In a matter of seconds, he was out the back door and sprinting down a narrow alley. His plan was to cut through the nearby cemetery up to 18th Street and then over a few blocks to Lincoln Park. There, he intended to connect with a dealer he knew kept early morning hours. With a smile on his face, he tightened his grip on the envelope.

8

DARKNESS NEED NOT be a barrier. Darkness need not be a fear. When the path to salvation is blocked, what choices will you make?

*

"Seven percent is piss."

"Indeed. A trifling, a pittance, an insult. But that, in reality, is what Mr. Thompson is paying you for your services."

Goliath's eyes wandered over the sculpted animal figures scattered on the desk between him and Alexis Taylar.

"And your loyalty, I might add." She smiled. "You understand what I'm saying, don't you?"

Goliath's attention drifted to a bank of television monitors on the wall behind the desk.

"But you don't understand, do you?"

When Alexis approached the desk and picked up a figurine of a tiger, he observed how slender and delicate her wrist was, how easy it would be to reach out and snap it in half.

"Do you know what this is?" she asked.

She grasped the base of the tiger figurine between her fingertips and held it out toward him.

"Tiger," he grunted. "Bengal."

"You know your animals."

With her free hand, she motioned to the walls of the room.

"As you can see, I am a collector of sorts. Skins." In sequence, she pointed to a leopard hide displayed on the wall behind him, the lion pelt he was standing on, and a zebra hide stretched between two long spears mounted on the wall at her back. "Artifacts, artwork, knick-knacks. But what I really love," she said, holding the figurine of the tiger up as if she were displaying it to a crowd, "is ivory."

"Ivory," she repeated with a degree of pride. "Exquisite, aren't they?" she asked with a nod to the desktop. "All these beautiful pieces: ivory."

Goliath reached down and grabbed a figurine of an elephant. He nearly laughed when he slipped the piece into a side pocket of his army surplus jacket and her smile changed to a frown.

"That particular piece is worth—" She looked at his jacket pocket like it held some sort of treasure.

"Keep it. It's yours." She smiled as she placed the tiger figurine back on her desk. "I want you to get a sense of how you would be treated— how I treat everyone who works for me—if you were to decide to—" she reached a hand up past her cheek and rubbed the slender white piece of jewelry dangling from her earlobe "—realign your priorities."

Goliath studied her attire—admiring the sparkly material of her clinging blue dress, the matching makeup applied above her eyes, and the bright gloss of her crimson lipstick—while trying to decide what she wanted from him.

"I have everything I need," he told her. "Reverend been taking care of me for years."

"Really? Taking care of you? Seven percent of the profits from a seedy bar on the waterfront is taking care of you? Didn't you just say that 7 percent was piss?"

"It's extra," he argued.

"Seven percent is 7 percent. Whether it's tip or part of your salary, it's shit."

"So, you say."

"And extracurriculars? What about those?"

Goliath rolled his shoulders and grunted.

"Extras," she clarified. "What about extras?"

Goliath averted his eyes and pretended to study the ivory figures on the desk.

"I'm not asking you to divulge how much powder you skim off the poundage that goes in and out the backdoor of the bar." She gave him a quick wink. "Don't look so surprised. I've been observing your operation for some time. Clever, using empty beer kegs to move product." She gave him what he considered a smug smile.

Goliath tensed when the woman made an abrupt movement toward the wall at her back.

"Come with me."

Like in a scene from an old spy movie, a section of the wall opened under the woman's touch. The woman beckoned for him to follow as she stepped into a passageway.

"Our main focus is the distribution of ivory."

Goliath warily entered the dimly lit corridor. Out of habit, he placed his hand at his belt buckle and fingered the release button located under the prong. If the need arose, he could spring the wire-thin stiletto resting within. He'd used the four-inch blade at least a half dozen times to take out an adversary's eye.

"But we deal in a variety of other merchandise."

She turned and motioned to a group of doors evenly spaced along the right-hand wall.

"Come take a look. Perhaps you'll see something you like."

*

Alexis studied Goliath with a mixture of amusement and curiosity as he approached the first door. He was enormous and in prime physical condition. If she didn't have need of his services, he would make a fine addition to her stable. Perhaps, she mused, when he was of no more use to her, she would make the notion a reality.

"Pretty, isn't she?"

Alexis studied the inflections of his eyes and mouth as Goliath peered through a small window just above the center of the door.

"From the Netherlands." When she noticed no change to his expression, she added, "A virgin. Fifteen, I'm told."

She suppressed her disappointment when he gave her what she construed as a disapproving look and moved to the second door.

"Asian," she said, when he stepped to the second door and looked through the window. "From Thailand. A virgin, like the first."

She saw him grimace and move away. The next girl, she knew, was a new arrival from Africa, smuggled over on a freighter out of Libya. Perhaps she, being closer to the color of his skin, would appeal to his desires. She deflated when he gave the third door what could best be described as a cursory glance before grunting and moving on.

Door four—she experienced a twinge of sexual excitement when she saw his reaction to the contents of room four. The man inside was in his prime. Twenty-three to twenty-five years old, she'd been told. A refugee from Syria. Ruggedly handsome and muscular. A specimen that would fetch a pretty penny, she knew, whether from some homosexual looking for a slave, a wealthy dominatrix seeking a pleasure toy, an underground fight promoter in need of fresh meat, or some sick fuck making a snuff film. Whomever the buyer turned out to be, the Syrian was a prize she intended to charge a high price for. And while she'd be remiss for not collecting on what she felt the man was worth on the black market, the fact that Goliath was showing interest in the specimen meant she was closer to achieving the first step toward her goal. A step she found personally exciting. Watching two muscular men fuck each other was one of her most pleasurable pastimes, especially when foreplay consisted of one beating the other bloody and senseless before celebrating his dominance by violently thrusting his engorged cock into the defeated man's ass and—

"Why is he locked up?"

Startled, Alexis quickly moved her fingers away from her groin and tried to sound businesslike.

"Wrong place at the wrong time," she said.

She couldn't help feel depressed when Goliath seemed to lose interest in the man and moved to door five. Knowing that older women were kept in the next three rooms—five, six and seven—she didn't have any illusions that he would find any of the merchandise desirable. And when he passed by those rooms, showing as much interest in their contents as a door-to-door salesman passing by a row of boarded up houses, she began to feel exceedingly anxious. *Maybe the man can't be bribed*, she thought. But then came door number eight.

It was as much the slight movement of his hand toward his crotch as it was his licking his lower lip that cemented her conclusion that Goliath was a pedophile.

Had he been born with the perversion? Or was his sexual attraction to young boys a product of his upbringing? Had he been raped and sodomized by a father or uncle? Or was he reacting to some form of rejection by the female sex? Perhaps his dick was too small, or he couldn't get an erection, or he had a premature ejaculation problem. She didn't care. She was happy to have found the lever she would need to help her get rid of the middleman—Reverend Rue Thompson—in the ivory trade.

"He's around ten, we think. Clean and scared. We took him off the streets day before yesterday."

She gave him an even, non-opinionated smile when he looked at her.

"He's been bathed and fed. He's quite innocent looking, isn't he?" She saw his hand clench and unclench as he continued to stare through the window. "Kind of has a California look to him." She saw his eyes close. "Door's open. None of them are locked. Each subject is bound to the wall by a four-foot length of soft-coated plastic twine tied around an ankle. We can't afford any blemishes." She nodded when his hand moved toward the doorknob. "Go ahead," she prodded. "We can talk after you've finished."

*

Alexis hurried down the hall as soon as Goliath entered room eight and closed the door. She hadn't told him the doors were left unlocked because each room was kept under constant video surveillance. Besides, having to unlock a door for a client seemed to dampen the moment, as if the time it took to have a key brought to her tempered the insatiable lust bubbling just beneath the client's façade, leading to a moment of second-guessing and—in some cases—squelching the prospective deal altogether. An unlocked door, however, offered the client instant gratification. But those observations were of little consequence to her at the moment, for watching a grown man have sex with a child was also an act she found personally arousing.

As she neared the end of the slave corridor, Alexis began to fantasize about what she was going to see on the monitor for room eight. She hoped Goliath was prone to roughing up his subjects before consummating his lust. She smiled broadly.

*

Rue Thompson stared into the gold-plated face of Jesus Christ, the Savior, before bringing the chiseled depiction of the Son of God to his lips. As he softly kissed the face of Christ, he murmured, "Thanks for another fine day, my man." With a nod, he rested the gaudy, three-inch crucifix atop the upper curve of his portly stomach and then stuffed it—and the lower few inches of the gold chain it hung upon—inside his shirt.

"Now," he said, rubbing his hands together and then reaching for the McDonald's bag sitting on his desk, "let's eat."

Rue stacked the different-colored Styrofoam boxes he took out of the bag into a tower with Big Mac at the base, Filet-o-Fish in the middle, and Quarter Pounder with Cheese on top. He built the structure solely as a base to lean the super-size container of french fries against so the fries wouldn't spill out and leave grease marks on the papers lying on his desk.

This evening's reading material, a report containing the latest statistics on poverty levels in the district he represented, was of particular interest. While fairly bland reading, Rue looked past the numbers and neighborhoods represented in the report and saw a dilemma: converging pockets of poverty-level households indicated that the market for illicit drugs was centralizing. Therefore, the drug distribution area he and some of the other cartels shared was shrinking. A power struggle, he reasoned, was imminent. So, as he munched on a fry and flipped open the lid on the Quarter Pounder with Cheese, he began to weigh the pros and cons of mounting a coup.

The first bite of the burger brought the crunchy tang of pickle doused with mustard and a hint of ketchup. As Rue sat back and savored the culinary assortment of flavors on his tongue, he put the notion of a potential gang war on hold. Abruptly, as though he'd forgotten something, he straightened and scrutinized the remainder of the Quarter Pounder.

"Goddammit," he muttered when he lifted the bun and inspected what was underneath. "I asked for extra pickles." With a grimace, he replaced the bun and took another bite. "Son of a bitch," he mumbled while he chewed. "Probably left 'em off the others, too."

As he thought about how he was going to ream out the worthless teenager who'd taken his order, a small red light on the bank of monitors to the right of his desk began to blink. Taking another bite of his burger, he leaned closer and disdainfully studied the figure attempting to break into the back of the warehouse. The moment brought him a sense of déjà vu.

"El gato negro," he muttered as he reached for a fry.

And then he stuffed the fry in his mouth and licked the tips of his fingers.

Has it been a year since that son of a bitch came to my office? As he reached for another fry, he flipped through the events of the past twelve months.

Yutanda, C, Akmir—playing the part of Super Freak. What a complicated mess that affair had turned out to be. Too many corpses, too much attention from the police when Griper snuffed that woman cop. And his run-in with C—*el gato negro*, as the man liked to go by—that was a mistake. Trying to frame a hired killer for kidnapping a child—what was he thinking? Compounding that mistake, he'd hired a stupid, junkie whore to tell the cops she witnessed the man stealing the kid before blowing up the apartment building councilwoman Yutanda Arbagna lived in. At least he didn't have to worry about *her*—the junkie whore—anymore. Thanks to Goliath.

But C and the kid had disappeared—an aspect of the situation Rue found disconcerting. Not knowing the man's location or what his thought process was in regard to extracting revenge, Rue had plenty of reason to fear for his life. So, as he nibbled on his dinner and watched the baseball-cap-wearing figure begin to climb the staircase to his office, Rue wondered if the man he'd framed for kidnapping, arson, and murder had hired this punk to do his bidding. With that thought in mind, Rue reached under his desk and extracted the Glock handgun strapped beneath the center drawer. As the door to his office swung open, he released the safety and snapped the slide back to load a bullet into the firing chamber.

"People usually knock." Rue pointed the gun at the man's face. "Unless they asking to get shot."

"Ain't carrying, bro," the lanky youth replied.

Rue noted the slouch in the man's shoulders and his foot-dragging lazy demeanor as he plopped himself down in one of the two chairs in front of his desk.

"What up, bro?" the young man brashly asked.

Rue reached for a fry but changed his mind when he observed the amount of acne on the man's face.

"Dig the Micky D scene, I see," the man quipped, nodding at the tower of Styrofoam containers. "Mind if I nibble?"

Rue pointed the Glock at the man's head.

"Mind if I blow a hole in your face?"

"Be cool, be cool." The youth raised his hands in surrender. "No reason to get all uptight. Just bein' social, ya dig?"

"God, you're an ugly motherfucker," Rue remarked. "I ought to do the world a favor and put you out of your misery. But I'm assuming there's a point to this unannounced visit." He waved the barrel of the gun in tight circles before he asked, "You have a name, or should I just call you *boy*?"

"My crew call me Jame Ain't."

Jame Ain't flashed a crooked-toothed smile and scratched his chin before flashing some kind of signal with his fingers.

"What the hell is that supposed to mean?" Rue inquired.

ASL, bro." Jame Ain't made the same signals with his fingers again, only slower. "Mean, from the ghetto," he explained. "You from Mars or somethin', Rev?"

"Can we just cut the street-nigger jargon and get to the point?" Rue motioned to his food with the gun. "As you can see, you've interrupted my meal."

Jame Ain't studied the gun for a moment before answering.

"They said you gettin' old." He tugged the brim of his black Nike baseball cap. "Said you wouldn't want to hear no shit." Jame sat up straight. "Fine with me. Get right down to business, then." Folding his arms in front of his chest, he said, "I want your powder come under my wing."

"Don't know what you're talking about," Rue quickly replied. "I'm a servant of the people, Assemblyman for the 29th district."

Rue felt an itch in his trigger finger when Jame Ain't started to laugh.

"Rev, you bust me up." Jame Ain't turned the brim of his cap so it protruded over his ear. "Servant of the people, my ass. Other way around, ain't it?"

Rue pointed the gun at the youth's nose and then motioned with it toward the door.

"Unless you have some actual district business to discuss, I suggest you find your way back to wherever it is you came from. As you can see," he said, nodding to his desk, "I've got work to do and don't have time for whatever nonsense you're up to."

"Nonsense?" Jame Ain't leaned forward. "You wanna talk nonsense, bro?" Pointing a finger at Rue's chest, he said, "You full of shit, ya know?" He motioned to the room around them. "Sittin' up here in your ivory tower like you be something you ain't. You done lost touch with what's real."

Rue laughed and pulled the crucifix from under his shirt.

"Ivory tower," he scoffed. "Since when did a small office in a warehouse along a run-down old pier constitute an ivory tower?"

"Got heat, ain't it? Bet you even got AC when it's hot."

Jame Ain't stood and moved to stand behind the chair. Without warning, he grabbed it and violently swung it to the side.

"Got motha-fuckin' food!" he shouted. "And a car and cash and rings, ain't ya? Even got a motha-fuckin' tiny gold Jesus hangin' 'round your fat-ass neck!"

Rue stood up and slammed an open palm on the desk.

"Get the hell out of here, you pimple-faced punk! Take your scrawny ass and—"

"When the last time you visit one of the buildings you represent, Rev?" Jame Ain't shouted. "You bring fries into one of them," he said, nodding to the food on Rue's desk, "rats be bringing the ketchup 'fore you even put the first one in your mouth." Calmly taking a seat in the remaining chair, he continued. "Cold as fuck in the winter, hot as shit in summer. Hallways smellin' like an outhouse. Junkies hangin' out in the hallways. People gettin' robbed, 'fraid to go out their doors."

"I'm calling the police."

"Go ahead, cuz, pick up the damn phone and call piggy. No sweat off my back. Ain't nothin' to keep me from tellin' them 'bout Gripe and his crew takin' a hit for you."

"I don't know what you—"

"Damn, bro, you really is a fossil, ain't ya? You trippin', you think wearin' a chick wig and moon-shades keeps people from knowin' you. But I tell you what, cuz," Jame Ain't said, leaning forward in his chair, "ain't no reason your world gotta be shattered. All you gotta do is what I'm proposin'. Time all the powder be runnin' out one door, dig? So, what you say, old timer? You in? Or I gotta do something crazy, make you fall in line?"

Within the confines of Rue's office, the Glock was deafening. Jame Ain't covered his ears, then slid them over his face when the splinters from the impact erupted under his feet. When the reverberations from the discharge faded and silence blanketed the room, Rue pointed the smoking barrel at Jame's crotch and said, "Next one goes right in your prick."

He gave Jame Ain't a wide smile when the visibly stunned, pimply-faced youth lowered his arms.

"Nothin' would make me happier than to see you squirming on the floor, squealing like a pig while you bleed to death from where your dick used to be." Rue extended the gun toward Jame Ain't. "You dig where I'm coming from, *bro*?"

Jame Ain't tilted his head a little to the side and frowned.

"My, my, my, Rev—you as uncooperative as they said you'd be." Eyes glued to Rue's gun, he slowly rose out of the chair. "You sure you ain't wanna throw in with me?" He edged toward the door. "'Cause I ain't playin'. I'm givin' all the players a chance to throw in with me 'fore I—" Jame Ain't grabbed the doorknob and pulled the door open. "Well, you know," he said with a wink.

Rue was tempted to follow the punk out into the hall and put a bullet in the back of his head. But he didn't. Wouldn't be smart, he knew. Better to do some digging around and see who Jame Ain't was and what part of town he was doing business in before he took any drastic action. Maybe the boy could be of some use in the future—a diversion for the cops, or a patsy to take a fall with a rival. With a Cheshire cat smile on his face, Rue sat down and placed the Glock on his desk.

"Paybacks are a bitch," he muttered with a two-handed pat to his stomach.

Looking over at the video monitors, he nodded with satisfaction when he saw Jame Ain't exit out the door he'd entered.

"Fuckin' punk," he groused. "Won't be so arrogant when Goliath puts his hands around your neck or the Bloods cut you up for fish bait."

Satisfied his run-in with Jame Ain't was finished, Rue shifted his attention from the monitors to the food on his desk. He grimaced when he reached for a french fry. "Cold," he grumbled. "Damn fish sandwich probably hard as a rock. Fuckin' punk-ass motherfucker." The bubble light atop the bank of monitors started blinking red. "What now?"

Rue scrutinized the screens one by one.

"Son of a bitch."

Jame Ain't stared into one of the several security cameras mounted around the perimeter of warehouse. With what Rue construed as a shit-ass smile on his face, the pimply motherfucker raised his hand in front of the camera and flipped the bird. Rue picked up the phone and punched 911 as Jame bent down and momentarily disappeared from view. A few seconds later he reappeared holding a bulky rectangular container. Rue saw him smile into the camera just before he poured what Rue figured was gasoline from the container. Rue was debating whether to stay on the line or hang up and run downstairs and shoot the punk in the head when Jame Ain't lit a match. He felt his balls tighten when Jame Ain't tossed the match out of view. The burst of flames was nearly instantaneous. Rue stared at the TV monitor in disbelief. The video feed went black just about the same time the warehouse fire alarm began to wail. A woman's voice came over the telephone receiver.

"You've reached emergency services. How may I help you?"

*

Tanya bent and brushed away several damp leaves from her mother's bevel marker. Straightening, she attempted to pull the front of her tight-fitting black denim jacket together, but there wasn't any give to the fabric. She settled for rounding her shoulders inward and stuffing her hands under her armpits. With a shiver, she looked down at the name engraved on the face of the pink marble slab and tried to picture the woman buried beneath it.

"Wish to hell I could remember you, Mama," she whispered. Her eyebrows—mostly makeup—arched, then bunched, then arched again. "But I don't."

Tanya shivered a second time as she looked out across clumps of dead grass, toppled headstones, and overgrown patches of weeds. Out of habit, she scanned the row of leafless trees that lined the east perimeter of Woodland Cemetery alongside Rose Street. The graveyard was both a depressing reminder of the city she lived in and her life: neglected, forgotten, unkempt, frayed, and in desperate need of attention. She shivered anew and shrugged.

Maybe it had been the chill of the early November air that had prompted her to visit her mother's grave. Or perhaps the somber pallor cast upon the morning from a cold drizzle that streaked the windows with tears had stirred memories of a woman she couldn't quite remember. Countless times, as she'd walked along the trash-strewn streets on her way to the cemetery, she'd tried to conjure the face of her mother. But the image proved elusive. The inability to connect with her mother's memory put her in a dour mood. She felt as pale, lifeless, and grey as her surroundings.

"Daddy say you was a big believer in God."

Tanya took note of the dirt collected along the contours of her mother's chiseled name and the brackish-colored markings the wet leaves had left on the marble. The stains, the dirt, and the dreary landscape made her feel as if she was standing in the middle of a dying world, one where sympathy and empathy didn't exist.

"Lotta good it done you," she said. "Look where you ended up."

Tanya pressed her arms closer to her sides and shivered a little harder. She willed her mind blank as she watched wisps of condensation form and dissipate in front of her mouth. Absently, she rubbed her right breast. Two days had passed since Gerard had hit her, yet her flesh was still tender and sore.

"Why you gotta die before I even know you?"

She could feel herself getting angry. It wasn't often she thought about her mother without that particular feeling stirring inside her.

"Daddy don't know shit about girls. Hmph. Fuckin' wish I were a boy. Then at least him and me have somethin' to say to each other."

Tanya turned away from her mother's grave and focused her attention on the bell tower that graced the dilapidated building at the entrance of the cemetery. She imagined the structure must have looked like a stately medieval castle when it was first built, what with its tall spire and the grand archway that spanned the width of the entry road and the way the stone-framed windows came to pointed ends.

"Done look like an old, used-up whore now," she muttered.

And it suddenly struck her that maybe that's where she was headed, that maybe that's what she'd turn into if she didn't get her act together: an old, used-up whore. And she wondered, as well, if things didn't change, if all the other girls she knew weren't going to end up like the once-beautiful building that had turned into a part-time crackhouse and a place to exchange a blow job for a dime bag and the few hours of numbness the weed brought. Maybe that's what all poor nigger girls were destined to be, she thought. Old, used-up has-beens, their better days behind them, clinging to life as some sort of worn-out shell of themselves as they waited for someone or something to come along and put them out of their misery.

"Is that what you were before you died?" she inquired of her mother. She glanced over her shoulder at the bell tower before addressing the bevel marker again. "Somethin' that used to be, 'stead of somethin' that is?"

A sudden gust of wind sent a push of chilly air through the spindly crests of the winter-browned grass that grew knee high in places between the headstones. Beyond the row of stark grey trees that ran along Rose Street, a siren blared and then abruptly ceased. Tanya spotted the jagged reflection of the vehicle's swirling red light traveling from treetop to treetop on its way toward 18th Street. She followed its progress until the trees gave way to glass and concrete and the muted beacon disappeared.

"That your answer?" Tanya put her hands on her hips and gave her mother's marker a look of disapproval. "Came here to talk, not get attitude."

A single leaf fluttered down through the sky and came to rest on her mother's first name. Tanya stuck out her foot and pushed the leaf away with the toe of her ankle boot.

"Don't need ya disappearin' right now." She stuffed her hands into the pockets of her black denim pants. "Daddy always seem mad when he talk about you dyin'. Why is that? You two have some big argument or somethin'?" She shuffled her feet before she whispered, "He hit you? Is that how it happened?" She bunched her right hand into a fist and cupped it in her left palm. "Seem like that what all men like to do." Rubbing her breast, she muttered, "Fuckin' Gerard." The silver beads in her hair made a dull clicking sound when she shook her head. "Fuckin' pussy. Kick his ass next time I see him."

Tanya took a deep breath as she gazed at her mother's name. It didn't mean much, she realized, knowing a person's name but having no memory to put to with it.

"Wish I knew what you looked like. Daddy don't keep no pictures of you 'round the apartment."

"A fine lookin' lady she was."

Tanya nearly stumbled over her mother's marker in her haste to move away from the male voice coming from directly behind her.

"No need to be afraid, young lady," the man quickly said as she turned to face him. "No need at all."

"Jesus, goddamn, Mister. What the hell you doin'?" Tanya didn't know whether to run away or hit the man. "'Bout scared the livin' shit outta me."

The man doffed his chocolate-brown beret and bowed his head a little.

"I sincerely apologize, young lady. Didn't mean to scare you. No, ma'am," he told her in a meek voice. "Meant no harm at all."

Tanya took stock of the man as he placed his beret back on his head.

Old, she could see. But how old? She couldn't tell. His deep-brown face was creased with wrinkles. But there was some kind of youthful presence to it—which made no sense to her. His wiry grey hair, thinning at the crown, coupled with his wrinkled face; a wrinkled corduroy jacket over a hunched, stocky frame; and wrinkled hands—Tanya thought they looked like two old leather gloves with dirt caked under the nails—gave her the impression that the old dude was a homeless wino who'd decided to make the cemetery his turf.

"I ain't got no money," she blurted, "if that's what you want."

The man cast his eyes toward the ground. With a shake of his head, he replied, "Didn't come here for no money. No ma'am, not a beggar. Saw you standin' talkin' to yourself." He gave her a sheepish glance. "Thought maybe you needed a little company."

A wheelbarrow was parked a few steps behind him. Tanya noted the tools it held: shovel, pick, hoe, steel rake.

"You work here?"

"From time to time," he replied with a nod to the wheelbarrow. "When somethin' needs tendin'."

"Then you be behind," she bitingly remarked. Shifting her attention to the unkempt grounds near her mother's marker, she added, "Like, really, really behind."

"Always somethin' needs doin'," he good-naturedly replied. "Yes, ma'am. Always somethin'."

Tanya studied his face for a moment before she replied. She observed a clean-shaven chin, eyes bright and lively.

"Well, I'm sure you have a lot of work to do, Mister."

"Brown," he said with a slight nod of his head. "Mr. Brown, I go by."

"Mr. Brown, then." With an awkward little chuckle, she said, "I suppose I should be on my way too." She glanced down at her mother's marker before she started to walk away.

"Leave this for her if you want."

"What?"

Tanya let out a little gasp when she saw the man holding a white rosebud in his hand.

"Might make you feel better." Tanya saw his brow furrow as he looked at her mother's marker. "I know she'd appreciate it."

"Where'd you get that?" she asked. "I didn't see you holding that before." She looked at the rose again—there was a pink blush at the tips of the petals—and tried to remember if she had seen him holding it when she'd studied his hands. "And how you know she like flowers?" She took a step toward him with a questioning expression on her face. "And how you know she— What did you say about her? She a fine-lookin' lady? You knew her?"

Mr. Brown held her gaze for a few seconds before he answered.

"Know her like I know you," he said in a soft tone of voice.

And then he looked past her over toward Rose Street and seemed to lose himself in thought. Tanya waited for him to say more, but he seemed content taking the scenery in.

"Do I know you?" she inquired. She glanced over her shoulder to see what he was looking at. "'Cause if I do," she said, annoyed, "I don't remember."

She crossed her arms as she waited for him to reply.

"You hearin' me?" When he showed no outward sign that he'd heard what she'd said, she impatiently tapped her foot against the ground. Angry that he seemed to be ignoring her, she barked, "Hey! Old man! You trippin'?"

"Child be like their mother," he calmly replied.

Tanya rolled her eyes and shook her head.

"Spend those months together, on their own." Mr. Brown glanced at her before shifting his attention to the cemetery entrance. "Just the two of them. Form a bond that lasts until—" Tanya thought he looked a little lost as he paused and tilted his head to the side. "Till one parts and the other is left to remember."

"I don't—" She shook her head, confused. "What you on about?"

"That's why you're here, isn't it? Why you came today? The remembering?"

She rubbed the spot on her chest where Gerard had hit her.

"She looked just like you, don't you think?"

When Mr. Brown reached out and gently took hold of her wrist, Tanya's initial instinct was to pull away. But she didn't. And when he turned her arm over so the palm of her hand faced the sky, she felt her body relax. A warm sensation spread over her skin as Mr. Brown placed the rosebud in her hand and closed her fingers over it.

"Don't need no picture to see what she looked like," he said. "Heart don't change between when you're born and when you pass on." She felt herself start to tremble when he turned and walked to the rear of the wheelbarrow. "Mighty beautiful, she was, by the looks of you." He nodded to the bevel marker near Tanya's feet. "No question 'bout it."

"Wait," she said a little stronger than she'd intended.

Mr. Brown smiled as he lifted the back of the wheelbarrow off the ground.

"Umm." Tanya's eyes flitted between Mr. Brown and the flower in her palm. "Umm, you never— I mean—" She lifted the blossom level to her chest. "You never said where you got this."

"Pretty," he remarked. "Simple and pure." She took a step toward him as he said, "That's why I picked it for her."

"Picked it for her?" Tanya looked out over the winter-drab landscape. "Where you pick somethin' like this," she said, nodding to her open palm, "in a place like this?"

"Tree over yonder," he replied with a smile. With a slight nod toward Woodland Avenue, he said, "Blooms almost year-round, it does." He chuckled before adding, "If you know how to look."

"How to look?" she repeated, perplexed. "I don't see nothin' growin' out there but—"

"Girl, what you goin' on about?"

Tanya turned with a start and slapped away the hand on her shoulder. "Why you—?"

"Shit, Gerard? What the fuck?"

"Be cool." Gerard raised his hands in surrender. "Didn't mean to startle you. Just wanted—"

"Fuck you!" Tanya shouted. Taking a menacing step toward him, she yelled, "Get the fuck away from me!"

Tanya lunged forward and threw a punch at Gerard's head, but he grabbed her fist before it could hit his face. But he wasn't quick enough to sidestep the kick to his crotch. The blow caught him on his inner thigh.

"Goddamn it, girl! What you on?" He pushed her fist to her side and rubbed the spot where her foot had landed. "Damn, T, that shit hurt. Why you wanna try and kick old Hercules?" He rubbed his crotch and grinned. "He never done nothin' but treat you good," he added with a wink.

"Why I wanna?" Tanya heaved a frustrated sigh and rubbed an open hand across the right side of her chest. "You hit me!" she yelled. "And about killed that little boy!" Coiling her arm like she intended to throw another punch, she feinted a step toward him and shouted, "So fuck you!"

Trembling, her eyes blurred with tears, she slowly lowered her arm. Wiping her eyes, she took a deep breath and exhaled.

"Sorry you gotta hear all that, Mr. Brown," she apologized. "Didn't mean to lose my cool. Just that Gerard, here—"

She stopped in mid-sentence when Gerard started to chuckle.

"What you find so funny?" she yelled. Furious, she punched him square in the chest.

"Hold up, hold up, hold up," he laughingly told her. "And gimme some of whatever you on."

"What you sayin'?" she demanded.

"Must be some good shit you on, girl. 'Bout had me rolling on the ground."

"What you talkin' about? Why you lookin' at me like I'm some kind of crazy woman?"

"I been watchin' you since you got here, girl. You been talkin' to someone who ain't here."

Tanya felt an icy shiver shoot down her spine.

"But looky here," he said, his laughter abating. "I got somethin' serious I think you and me need to talk about."

Ignoring Gerard, Tanya slowly turned her head and looked over her shoulder; Mr. Brown wasn't there.

"Found a key in the old folks' crib."

She vaguely heard what Gerard said, but paid him no mind.

"Where the old man go?" she muttered.

"Looky here, girl," Gerard went on. "You need to listen. Those old folks, they like a bank. Had a wad of cash stashed in a cupboard in their kitchen."

Utterly confused, Tanya did a slow turn as she searched for the wheelbarrow and Mr. Brown.

"Girl, what you on?" Gerard grabbed Tanya by her wrist and pulled her toward him. "What you lookin' for?"

Tanya jerked her arm free and pushed Gerard back. With a bewildered look on her face, she held her arm out, turned her fist up, and unfurled her fingers.

"What—?"

Tanya stared at the mound of dark soil sitting in the middle of her palm. For a moment, she was certain the soil held the shape of a rose, but when she blinked her eyes, the outline of the flower blurred into an ill-defined mound of dirt.

"Yo, I'm talkin' to you." Gerard slapped her hand downward, spilling most of the soil to the ground. "Where the kid?"

"Goddamnit, Gerard!" Tanya cupped what little soil remained in her palm and clutched it to her chest. "Why you gotta be such an asshole?"

Gerard's slap to her face was lightning quick and harsh. Stunned, Tanya teetered a step backward and rubbed her cheek.

"I ain't playin', girl!"

Gerard grabbed Tanya by her wrists and threw her to the ground. Teary-eyed, she looked up to see a rose petal drifting slowly downward through the air.

"Get up!" Gerard yelled. And then he yanked her to her feet by her hair. "I asked you a question!"

Trembling, Tanya kept her eyes on the rose petal as she struggled to find her balance.

"The kid!" Gerard pressed. "Where the little fuck?"

Just as the petal came to rest on her mother's bevel marker, Gerard grabbed Tanya by the shoulders and shook her.

"The kid!" he screamed. "Ain't gonna ask you again!"

Tanya drove her knee up into Gerard's crotch with all the violent power she could muster. As the lanky man released his hold on her and doubled over, Tanya punched him twice in rapid succession on the side of his head.

"Fuck you!" she shouted. "Get the hell away from me!"

Gasping, Gerard staggered back a few steps and held his arm out toward Tanya.

"I sorry, I sorry," he hurriedly said.

Tanya took a menacing step toward him.

"No more, no more," he implored with a frantic wave of a hand. "I had it comin'—I had it comin'. I did." Gerard suddenly sagged to one knee and spit a gob of saliva on the ground. "Been just about the worst person you know, haven't I?" he rasped. "Serves me right you want nothin' to do with me no more. I just a— Just an asshole."

She shook her head and frowned when he looked at her with what she recognized as his *poor, poor me* expression.

"Stop actin', Gerard." With a grunt, she gave him swift kick to the side of his butt. "And yeah, you *the* worst person I know." She crossed her arms and huffed. "Specially now Puffer dead. You right up alongside him being the stupidest asshole I know. Serve you right somebody put you in a box and bury you in the weeds."

"You right, you right," he quickly agreed. Gerard slowly rose with his eyes locked on the ground and his chin drooping toward his chest. "Been a fuck-up, I been. One damn mistake after another. Don't know why you even give me time o' day."

"Oh, shut the hell up and stop your blubberin'. Only thing worse than you actin' like you some mafia nigger is when you pull this shit and pretend like you some innocent boy done lost his way home."

"Yeah, yeah—you right, you right. That's why I here, though." She met his sheepish glance with a stony expression. "Make it up to you some- how." He shrugged his shoulders and shuffled his feet. "Make it all good."

"What you on about, boy?" she scoffed. "And stand up straight and try not to squirm around like you standin' on a hot plate with no shoes."

Gerard grudgingly pulled on the lip of his baseball cap and stood up straight.

"The boy," he said. "He got some kind of guardian angel or somethin'."

"Stop talkin' shit."

"No, no, hear me out. Found a note with the key." He patted the side pocket of his jacket.

"What key?"

"Key I told you about. And a note." Gerard slipped his hand into his jacket pocket and leaned toward her. "Somebody write down 'Five thousand a month' and then give a PO box number. Figure the key go to the box. Boy got somebody lookin' out for him, he does," he said with a definitive nod of his head. "All we gotta do is—"

"Slow down, Gerard," she ordered. "What you mean, *we*? I don't want no part of whatever shit you dreamed up in that fucked-up head o' yours."

"T-baby, don't you get it?" Gerard put an arm around her shoulder and hugged her to the side of his chest. "This our way out. Five Gs a month. Think about it." He squeezed her close. "Enough to see us outta the projects, outta this fuckin' nowhere dump of a city."

Tanya forcibly pushed him away.

"You dreamin', you think we ever gettin' outta here," she said. "You already in the shit, boy. Or you forgettin' you killed two people? Now you wanna what? Kidnap a kid and collect some mysterious cash coming to some mysterious box in a post office we don't even know where?" She folded her arms across her chest and scowled. "You trippin', is what you are. Might as well climb in the hole Puffer in, the way you goin' on."

"Don't gotta be like that," he countered. "Don't no one gotta know what's up. Figure the kid knows where the post office at. Figure fat mamma or grandpa take him there when they go collect the money." He shrugged his shoulders and pulled on the lip of his cap. "Don' t gotta take the boy or nothin'. Just have a little conversation with him, ya know?" He took a step toward her. "So, where he at now? They put him in some home or somethin'?"

"What?" She grunted and turned away. "You mean social services? Hmph, bunch o' lazy-ass motherfuckers." She eyed Gerard with disdain. "Marcus still at my place. My dad watchin' him right now. Cops come 'round about four or five hours after you left and told us about Jim and Rochelle gettin' shot in some robbery where the stupid-ass thieves didn't even take no money."

Tanya paused to make a jerking movement toward Gerard like she intended to hit him.

"Said somebody be around for the boy." She grunted and silently mouthed a curse word. "That was two days ago. Haven't seen or heard from nobody since."

"You shittin' me?" Gerard excitedly asked. "That's motherfuckin' golden. Like a motherfuckin' angel is watchin' over us."

Tanya bent and picked up the rose petal that had drifted out of the sky and landed atop the first letter of her mother's name.

"Boy done climbed into a shell when we told him about his grandparents," she remarked as she straightened.

"Come on, girl," Gerard grabbed her arm and pulled her toward him. "Time to celebrate." Tanya tried to push him away, but Gerard held his ground. "Scored some prime shit. We gonna be flyin'!"

"I don't wanna get—"

"That's right," he teased. "You already high." He laughed. "Talkin to people what ain't here. Spooks done take over your body and make you see shit. Maybe I get you high enough, I put you on a stage and sell tickets." Cupping his hands around his mouth, he announced, "Step up, everybody! Come see the bitch who talk to invisible folk." He held his stomach as he laughed. "Come see—!"

Tanya snapped her arm out of Gerard's grasp and turned her back to him. As she tried to block out his ridiculing laughter, her attention drifted to the perimeter of the cemetery along Rose Street. The trees, she saw, were shrouded in a swirling silver mist. Here and there, she spied limbs poking out. Branches—bare and gnarled—gave the appearance of skeletal fingers rising from a grave. The illusion made Tanya shiver and shift her attention elsewhere. Briefly, she searched the drab landscape for Mr. Brown and his wheelbarrow. But she couldn't spot either.

"Come on, T." Gerard took hold of Tanya's hand and pulled on her so hard she was forced to move. "Fuckin' startin' to rain again," he muttered, glancing up at the sky. He pulled her toward the cemetery entrance. "Get inside and smoke this fatty burnin' a hole in my pocket."

As Tanya reluctantly allowed herself to be pulled behind Gerard, she couldn't shake the feeling that somebody was watching her. For a moment, she was tempted to glance over her shoulder. But she settled for staring at her hand and wondering how a rose petal had fallen from the sky.

9

YOU SIT IN despair. Yet you do not cry. Nor will your faith to vanquish your inner foe. Hear the pounding of the drum. Feel its power in your heart. Embrace the silence between each beat, for there is where your strength resides. Teach yourself to live.

*

"Shit, are you praying again?"

Sarah hugged the necklace close to her chest and closed her fingers around the silver cross attached to the chain.

"I find it comforting," she replied. "And could you please stop cursing? You remind me of—"

"Him?" Bin'ka smirked as he rolled his sleeping blanket into a cylinder. "I thought your life was devoted to your god." He gave Sarah a wink. "Or is that only when Dirk isn't occupying your thoughts?"

Sarah rose from her knees.

"Will we make the border of Kenya today?" she asked.

Bin'ka frowned as he watched her fiddle with the necklace. The symbol of her faith was not welcome where they were headed.

"Won't get close to much of anything if that damn thing draws attention."

Sarah turned to him with an expression on her face that made him feel he'd spoken blasphemy.

"I don't understand why we didn't just sneak back into Mogadishu after you threw the children off the boat," she complained. "It's been two days, and we don't seem any closer to this Lamu place than when we started out." She took a deep breath and sharply exhaled. "Why couldn't we have at least *sailed* to Kenya, instead of wasting all this time trudging along this—" she swung an open hand out in front of her "—desolate stretch of—"

He chuckled as she surveyed her surroundings with a lost look on her face.

"Ugh. Where are we?"

"North of Buur Gaabo and south of Kismayo," he replied good-naturedly.

"Bur-goo what? Where?" Sarah closed her eyes and cupped the cross in both hands. "That tells me nothing."

Bin'ka placed his rolled-up blanket beneath the straps of a large field pack.

"Now yours."

He could sense her anger when she opened her eyes and looked at him. Unmoved, he pointed to the blanket spread out near her feet.

"Please."

Her brow furrowed and her lips turned downward as she bent to one knee and began to roll up the blanket. He nearly laughed out loud when he heard her mutter, "Good mind just to walk back to Mogadishu and find my own way home."

"You wouldn't make it past the first *muharrir* you came across," he told her as he motioned for her to throw the blanket. "Did you learn nothing in the year you walked with the Lion?"

"The lion?" she questioned, perplexed. "You mean Teimbaka?"

He motioned again for her to toss him the blanket.

"He must have gone to great lengths to keep you from falling into the hands of the warlords whose territory you crossed. And Mogadishu," he said, shaking his head and rolling his massive shoulders. "How did you survive? You said you were there for *months*, searching for Dirk and the nun." He glanced down and gently touched the bandage wrapped around his upper arm. "Barre death squads," he said, "squabbling clans, hired thugs, zealots, assassins." He gave her a questioning look. "You must have been invisible to have gone unnoticed. Where did he hide you?"

"Hide me?"

Sarah's eyes drifted to the side. Bin'ka assumed she was remembering.

"We mostly moved at night," she began. "At least, I did. Through alleys and side streets where there wasn't much light. Teimbaka, he—" she looked to him as if she expected him to say something "—he would find a room, or a corner of a courtyard in a— How did he know which people would welcome us?"

Bin'ka said nothing.

"I would sleep and be given food while he—"

He studied her face as she looked down at the ground. Her expression reminded him of times when he, too, had searched among pebbles for answers that didn't exist.

"I don't remember ever seeing him sleep." She ran the toe of her sandal through the loose, sandy soil and looked toward the ocean as she twisted the silver cross between her fingers. "He was always on the move, always searching, always asking if anyone had seen—"

"Sister Lady," he finished.

"Funny name," she remarked.

"Funny?"

"Well, I don't mean—" She ran a hand through her dirty, unkempt hair. "What was she like?" She tossed him her blanket. "Sister Claire?"

Bin'ka snatched the blanket out of the air with one of his massive hands. He squeezed the coarse fabric between his fingers before he answered.

"She was—"

Picturing Claire's face made him uncomfortable. Although many years had passed since Susenyo had ordered him to pin her to the floor while he injected heroin into a vein on her upper thigh, the look of torment he'd seen in her eyes when the drug had entered her bloodstream was like nothing he had ever experienced before. It was as though he'd been witness to the death of innocence, as if he were taking part in the rape of a newborn child. The moment had changed him, had made him conscious of the fact that he didn't like to hurt those who could not protect themselves.

The first sighting of the Lion had occurred later that same day. He remembered the roar of the beast, how angry it sounded. Rumor was that the Lion was injured and was searching for those who had inflicted the wound. Months would pass before he would come face to face with the beast. When he did, when Teimbaka had come to free the nun, the event was as much terrifying as it was mystifying.

But the woman—Sister Claire—had suffered greatly. The time spent under the rule of Susenyo had cost the woman her soul. As poorly educated as he was, Bin'ka had recognized the total destruction of her will. Her addiction to the drug had dismantled the fabric of who she was and all she believed in. How she had recovered from her ordeal, he could not fathom. That she had survived to become a figure of lore, an angel to children beset by famine and war, he could not comprehend. *The Lion and the nun.* He shook his head. Now they were gone.

"She was—?" Sarah prodded.

Bin'ka gave her a sour look.

"She was a nun," he said with a shrug. "Just like you."

"That doesn't tell me anything. Women from all walks of life are nuns. I meant, what kind—?"

"Ask Adiam or Akmir." He dropped to one knee and slapped her rolled up blanket atop his. "Or your precious Dirk." He grunted. "If you ever see him."

"Adiam lied to us."

"I'm sure he did," Bin'ka retorted. "Just as we all do."

"And who's Akmir?" she asked. "I don't recall—"

"Someone you don't want to come across," he replied. "Adiam's partner, before—" He paused as he used his uninjured arm to push off the ground. "He's somewhere on the outskirts of Mogadishu trying to unify the clans and street scum into some sort of government. He wants a kingdom." He grunted. "With him as lord and *master.*"

He bent to grab the field pack, but then abruptly straightened. "'What was she like?'" he mimicked Sarah in a whiney voice. "'Why didn't we go back to Mogadishu?' What do you care what she was like? If I can't get you to Lamu, it won't matter what she was like. And I didn't *throw* those kids off the boat! And *she* would have gone with them! *She* wouldn't have left them on their own to—"

A subtle but distinct click made Bin'ka pause and reach for the assault rifle lying on the ground next to the field pack. Before he could grab it, he glimpsed movement behind Sarah. Then something hard pressed against the back of his head.

"You will not touch the gun, *abeeb*, is that understood?"

Bin'ka stiffened at the man's use of the Arabic word for "slave." Nodding slightly, he said, "You won't find much of value here. Only the woman." Bin'ka motioned to Sarah with a quick jerk of his head. "Fetch a good price in Lamu." He chanced a hesitant glance behind him. "I know a few traders who'll pay gold for a white virgin."

"Virgin?"

"So she says," Bin'ka replied.

Slowly, in acknowledgement to the rifle barrel pressed to his head, he rose to his feet.

"But what woman doesn't say she is pure when a man presses his cock to her thigh?" He chuckled. "Do you not know this to be true?"

Bin'ka smiled at the Arabic-speaking, keffiyeh-clad man as he straightened to full height. With an expression of alarm, the man jerked the rifle upward and pointed it at Bin'ka's neck.

"Step back!" he ordered.

Bin'ka nodded in obedience and took a step back. He glanced over toward Sarah and saw two other men—South Somali tribesmen, he guessed, part of the Dir clan, or perhaps Bimaal—holding the woman by her shoulders. Each held a long knife in his free hand.

"You are *abeeb*!" the Arab shouted. "How is it you are in possession of this woman?"

"Payment from my master," Bin'ka was quick to reply. "For service given in good faith."

"What does an *abeeb* know of faith?" the Arab said, shaking his rifle. "What *service* does a slave perform for a master to be given a white woman as token?"

"A Barre death squad had taken his two eldest sons prisoners. They were to be executed. I was fortunate enough to have the blessings of Allah, blessed be he—" Bin'ka placed his hands together in a sign of prayer and bowed his head "—when my master ordered me to save them."

"*In sha Allah*," the Arab man said in a reverent tone.

Bin'ka heard the two Somalis murmur the same phrase. Then the Arab—gaunt-faced, with a dark, full beard—took a step closer to Bin'ka.

"You saved his sons?" he inquired. "Your master, he was—?"

"Sudanese." Bin'ka paused before adding, "Northern Sudanese."

"You are—?"

"In service to the one who owns me," Bin'ka replied in a submissive voice.

"Then the woman—" Bin'ka saw the rifle dip a few inches as the man looked over at Sarah. "She is yours to do with as you wish?"

Bin'ka kept his expression impassive as he looked over at Sarah and nodded.

The two Somali men, he noticed, were admiring her body.

"Do you want to fuck her?" Bin'ka casually asked. "If you would show deference to the blessings of Allah and not mark her with bruises or scratches, the traders won't know she has been plucked of her innocence." He paused to laugh. "Nor will they care after they sell her."

"You would allow us to penetrate her?" the Arab asked, somewhat astonished. He looked at Sarah with wide eyes and then looked at Bin'ka. "A white woman?"

"She has angered me this morning," Bin'ka said with a dismissive glance toward her. "If it pleases you, stick your cocks into her while I eat breakfast and finish my morning prayers to the Holy One. Perhaps she will be less argumentative on the rest of our journey if she is taught submission."

"Yes, this is true!" the Arab was quick to agree. "Women must be taught that men are their masters as we are formed in the likeness of the King of Kings." Bin'ka could see the lust in the man's eyes when he gazed at Sarah. "White women in particular, they must—"

"She is an infidel," Bin'ka interrupted. The Arab's mouth opened wide as if to express disbelief. "She wears the symbol of the false god around her neck." Bin'ka gave a casual nod toward the woman. "She is a pig."

"My God is not false!" Sarah blurted. "He is all powerful and loving and fills this world with—"

Bin'ka crossed the space between himself and Sarah in three swift strides. Mindful not to strike the Somali men holding her, he swung his open hand and slapped the back of Sarah's head. As she stumbled forward, he yelled, "Silence, infidel!"

With a harsh tap to Sarah's forehead, he returned to stand next to the Arab.

"Here," he told the man. Bin'ka bent and loosened the straps on the field pack holding the blankets. "Use these." He held the blankets out for the Arab to take. "They will help prevent markings on her back." He gave Sarah a contemptuous look and laughed. "And on her knees," he added.

Bin'ka faced away from the Arab and bent once more to the field pack. After rummaging through the contents, he extracted a folded piece of tanned animal hide tied with a length of coarse yarn. As he untied the binding and carefully unfolded the hide, he said, "Take her near the water. The ground there is less rocky."

He stood, turned, and took a bite of the antelope jerky he'd unwrapped.

"That way, she can bathe herself when you are finished with her." He smiled at the Arab before nodding toward Sarah. "I suspect she'll put up a struggle." He held the piece of jerky up in his hand as though it was a finger. "But, please, in deference to the Holy One, if you could see your way clear not to mark her." Bin'ka nodded in a manner that conveyed respect. "May I suggest holding her by her wrists and ankles with her own clothing while you take turns."

The Arab looked at Bin'ka as though he was witnessing a revelation. Securing the blankets between his arm and chest, the man shifted the rifle to one hand and gripped it by the base of its long barrel.

"Strip her!" he ordered the two Somali men. "And bring her close to the water," he instructed.

Bin'ka took another bite of jerky and watched the Arab head down the sloping shoreline toward the sea.

*

Although the sun was hot against her skin, Sarah felt ice spread through her body. Bin'ka's betrayal left her stunned and humiliated. The big, black monster—Bin'ka—was nothing but a liar and a deceiver, just like all the other men in her life had been—including Dirk. She glared at him, hoping he could feel her anger. But the big ape—the buffalo-faced sinner—wouldn't meet her eyes. He was content, it seemed, to chew on his food and stare out over the ocean.

Dear God, she silently pleaded. But before she could continue her silent prayer to the Lord, the two men holding her arms pulled her blouse away from her body and stuck their knives into the fabric. In one quick, violent motion, they sliced into the fabric and then, in unison, ripped the shirt from her body. She screamed when she heard Bin'ka yell, "Gag her!" One of the men—bug-eyed and panting—balled up a piece of her shirt and jammed it into her mouth. Struggling to breathe, the first jolt of panic twisting her muscles into knots, she glimpsed the glitter of a knife before her bra straps were cut from her shoulders. When she felt her skirt cut from her waist, she closed her eyes and whimpered. An instant later, her underwear was cut and yanked away.

"Aye-ya!" she heard a male voice exclaim. "*In sha Allah!*"

Sarah screamed again when she was lifted off the ground and her legs were jerked apart. Overwhelmed with feelings of shock and uncontrollable rage, she looked up through teary eyes to see the Arab man stroking his hard penis and leering down at her. When he saw her looking up at him, he knelt between her legs and pushed his fingers against her vulva. Sarah shuddered at the look of lustful evil in the man's eyes.

The Arab died in the blink of an eye, skull cracked by the wooden stock of a rifle. An instant later, an ear-splitting boom brought a spray of blood and goo that splattered her face and upper body. She turned onto her side, wrenched the gag out of her mouth, and vomited. Vaguely, as she struggled to breathe, she caught sight of a man running away. Then suddenly he stopped and flopped forward. Blinking away tears, she observed a knife sticking out of his back.

Whether seconds or minutes passed before she saw Bin'ka drag the wounded man into the water and push his head beneath the surface, she couldn't tell. In a state of utter shock, she watched the man's arms and legs thrash wildly before abruptly going limp. When Bin'ka rose from the sea and moved toward her with a blood-stained knife in his hand, she closed her eyes, certain she was about to die.

*

"Get up!"

Grabbing Sarah by her hair, Bin'ka pulled her toward the ocean. When she slapped his hand away, he bent and slipped his uninjured arm around her waist. To the sound of her moans and grunts, he lifted her from the sand, waded into the surf, and unceremoniously tossed her into the water. For a moment, after she sank below the surface and disappeared from his view, he contemplated diving in after her. But an instant later, she popped back up, gasping for air.

"Wash the blood from your hair and body," he told her.

He recognized the look of rage on her face before she hugged her shoulders and sagged forward. When she began to sob, he extended a hand toward her. But the cry of a gull squelched his act of compassion.

"Be quick," he told her as he looked to the sky. Several gulls were hovering above the dead bodies on the shore. "Before the sharks get a whiff of you."

Her response was silence and a blank expression. Her face was as pale as a fading moon, her eyes devoid of emotion as she blankly stared at him. He felt compelled to use a gentler tone of voice when he said, "Use the blankets to cover yourself when you are finished. Hurry."

As Sarah washed the blood and tissue from her skin and hair, Bin'ka dragged the corpses of the Arab and the Somali man he'd shot closer to the surf. After a quick search of their clothes for weapons and anything of value, he stripped them bare and laid them face up in the sun. Tossing their clothes into the surf, he returned to where he'd left the field pack and retrieved a length of rope. Sarah was trudging out of the ocean when he placed the rope and a one of the Somali's knives on the edge of an unrolled blanket. As she drew closer, he turned his back to give her some privacy.

"Use the knife to cut an opening for your head," he said in a loud voice when he sensed she was close. "The rope is to tie the other blanket around your waist. I'll find you something more suitable when there is opportunity."

He could hear her breathing—distressed, a mixture of shivering exhales and stuttering inhales—and wondered if it was the shock of what she'd just been through or the temperature of the sea causing her discomfort. When she remained silent for what he considered an overly long time, he imagined she was turning the knife over in her hand and contemplating slitting his throat. He chuckled at the thought.

"You would have let them rape me."

He heard condemnation in her words, but sensed hurt in her tone.

"They would have regardless," he replied. "But I didn't feel like dying at the hands of one who thought me a slave." He glanced over his shoulder to look into her eyes before he said, "And I didn't think you would survive a life as a whore."

"But you let them strip me."

He shook his head and faced away when she started to cry.

"And touch me where—"

When he heard her sob, he sighed and ran a hand over his forehead.

"I needed them to drop their weapons." He started to turn his head to look at her, but decided against it. "Besides, you weren't hurt. It ended satisfactorily."

"How can you—? You killed them!" He could hear the angst in her voice when she added, "And let them touch me, see me naked!"

"See you naked?" He laughed. "Why do you speak of that as though it is a crime? You are a woman."

"I am a nun!" she shouted. "I'm not to be—!"

She immediately fell silent when Bin'ka turned and eyed her as if she were an item for sale at a marketplace.

"You are a woman," he repeated, surveying her from head to toe. "What you do with your life doesn't change what you are." He chuckled when she hugged the blanket close to her body and smoothed the material so it covered her torso. "You have full breasts, and hair between your legs, and hips shaped to bear children. No different from any other woman I have seen or lain with. Except that your skin is white. And pink where—"

"Stop it!" She covered her face with her free hand and sniffled. "How can you talk this way when—?"

"Here. Look."

"What are you doing?"

She cowered when Bin'ka removed his tunic and started to pull his pants down.

"Letting you see *me* naked," he told her. He let his trousers fall to his ankles and spread his arms. "Behold a man of Africa," he said with pride. "Am I any different from the white men you have seen?"

"From the white men I've—?"

He didn't know what to make of her when she placed her hand over her mouth and looked as though she had been punched in the stomach. And when she dropped to her knees and shook her head in a violent manner, he looked over toward the flock of feeding seagulls as if they, in some manner, might help him understand her actions.

"What's wrong?" he asked. "Why are you so—?" He frowned and scratched the side of his head. "Nuns," he muttered in exasperation. "Confusing." He bent and pulled up his trousers. "Or confused," he said, with a pointed glance at Sarah. "But no matter. We need to move."

The squawking cries of seabirds drew his attention to the sky. More gulls had arrived. And higher up, circling, surveying what the birds were feeding on: vultures. Crabs would soon emerge from their holes, eager to claim their portion of meat. The area would soon be thick with scavengers, all squabbling for a place at a feast that would attract the attention of anyone who might pass near.

"Get dressed," he ordered.

He braced for a biting response, but Sarah said nothing and made no move to clothe herself. With her eyes cast downward, head listless, her shoulders drooped forward, she looked to be suddenly taken ill or struggling with an injury he couldn't see.

"We passed the most dangerous part of our journey when we crossed the Juba River," he gently assured her. "If we stick near the coast, two, three days of travel will bring us to the border of Kenya."

Her voice was barely a whisper when she replied, "Three days."

"Once we cross into Kenya and are clear of the border guards, we'll secure a boat and be in Luma before nightfall. Once there, I'll get a call through to Adiam and he'll send transport for us the following day."

"Adiam?" He was surprised by the degree of anger he heard in her voice when she suddenly blurted, "I wouldn't be here if it weren't for him! If he hadn't lied about Dirk and Claire, I'd be home!" She swiped at the beach with a cupped palm and sent a plume of sand into the air. "I want nothing to do with him."

"You have money, then?" he teasingly remarked. "Or something with which to barter your way onto a plane or a boat? And your visa and passport—" He pursed his lips and placed a finger to his temple. "Ah yes, I remember seeing them, but I can't recollect where. Do you recall where you left them? Somewhere on your body, perhaps?"

Sarah bunched a handful of the blanket closer to her chest and stared off to her side.

"If you want to get back to Djibouti, he's our only means."

"Djibouti?" She looked up at him, confused. "Why can't we—?"

"Money and papers." He shrugged. "Unless you have them hidden in a place I—"

"But Mogadishu is closer," she complained. "They have an airport there, don't they? Why can't he send a plane there?"

"That place is hell." He glanced over at the mass of seabirds and vultures before bending and picking up his tunic. "Adiam won't chance sending one of his planes or helicopters there." He wiggled into his clothes before adding, "Your way home goes through Djibouti." He took a deep breath and patted his chest. "Now get dressed. We need to move."

Bin'ka moved to pick up the field pack when she faintly asked, "Why?"

He turned and pointed to the raucous mass of birds feeding on the corpses.

"So we are not still here when someone comes along to investigate *that*," he told her, somewhat exasperated. "Or do you—?"

A change in Sarah's expression made him stop in mid-sentence. The distraught woman he'd been addressing suddenly morphed into a little girl: vulnerable, eyes questioning and uncertain, lips slightly parted, trembling as if her heart was breaking.

"Why?" she tearfully whispered.

And then she let the blanket fall from her grasp. Bin'ka watched her clutch the silver cross as if it were all she had left in the world. She seemed not to care that her breasts were bared, and he, in a moment of awkward embarrassment, shifted his gaze downward.

As Bin'ka gazed into the sand, his thoughts drifted to the day the Lion had come to the alley of the three doors. Sarah—in her vulnerable state— became Sister Lady, broken and lost. And he, Bin'ka, became Teimbaka, determined and strong. Yet, in pretending, he remembered the moment when the Lion and the nun attained their freedom—the instant Susenyo had taken a bullet to the head. There had been confusion in the Lion's eyes, as if Teimbaka realized—though they were free of the evil that had drained the soul from Claire—the uncertainty that lay before them. The same uncertainty that he and Sarah now faced.

Bin'ka scrunched his face into a scowl and stared harder into the sand. *Why am I remembering the day of the Lion now?* he wondered. He shook his head and looked at Sarah anew. *What is she? A woman, a nun, a little girl?* Jaded, yet innocent. Resilient yet broken. Was she so different from any woman he'd ever known? With a grunt, he pulled the tunic from his body and tossed it at her.

"Now that you no longer smell like a camel, you can wear that until we find you other clothes," he told her. "I'll make do with one of the blankets."

Startled by the garment hitting her face, Sarah swatted it to the sand.

"Smell like a camel?" she snapped.

Bin'ka laughed and slapped his rounded stomach.

"Saltwater cleanses the flesh where prayer cannot," he laughingly told her.

"How dare you!"

"Enough!" he bellowed. "Put on the shirt and get ready to travel."

Without waiting for a response, he bent and retrieved the field pack. Then, as Sarah slid the tunic over her head, he leaned forward and grabbed the blanket at her feet. Using the Somali's knife, he sliced a hole in the middle of the fabric and then placed it over his head.

"Three days," he said.

Sarah nodded.

With a grunt of approval, Bin'ka slung the pack over his shoulder. As he slid the Somali's knife into the backpack and retrieved his automatic weapon, he gave Sarah an admiring glance. When and if they were able to reach Djibouti, he would inquire if any of the brothels employed a white whore. Seeing the nun in the nude had aroused him. A woman with white skin would need to be sampled.

*

Jeer. Awraris. Obhejane. Vifaru. The animal had many names. The one she was observing looked as big as a mountain, with a front horn the size of a small tree.

The little girl in the pink and white kanga sat in silence as the rhino tugged leaves from the branches of a bush and folded them into its mouth. The slow, sideways grinding motion of the beast's jaw reminded her of a particular elder from her village, an old man who had so few teeth he needed to pulverize whatever he ate before he swallowed. Thinking about the elder brought a smile to her face. She'd been fond of the old man. He was a storyteller, one who gathered the children in the evening to pass down old tales of their land and their people. She remembered his voice: smooth and warm, easy to listen to. But her smile faltered and then disappeared altogether when she recalled the morning things fell from the sky and blew apart her village. Had the elder survived the attack? She didn't know. She didn't know if anyone, other than she, had been so fortunate.

A loud, snorting grunt drew the girl's attention to the feeding rhino. As she gazed at the massive animal, a tickbird landed on its head. When the small, red-beaked bird began to peck behind one of the beast's hair-tipped tubular ears, she giggled. Immediately, she wished she hadn't, for the animal rotated its ears directly toward her, dipped its massive horn to the ground, and raked the soil with one of its front hooves. And then it charged.

As the earth beneath her rump began to shake, she looked from side to side in search of an escape route. But the clamor muddled her thoughts. She felt as though a thunderstorm had exploded in her head. Every trembling bush and patch of jarred earth became part of a frightening, inescapable nightmare. Instinct screamed at her to run. But as she leaped to her feet and turned to flee, someone shouted, "Juba! Stay!"

The girl in the purple dress—Enat, the one she called Mother, the one she had been following for the past week, the one who carried the horn of an antelope like it was made of precious stone—was motioning to her from behind a tree.

Who is Juba? she wondered.

"Don't move!" the girl yelled.

The girl in the pink and white kanga froze. The charging behemoth was seconds away from trampling her. She opened her mouth to scream—but the beast came to a sudden, dirt-spraying halt. Through the swirling dust, she watched the animal flare its nostrils and rotate its ears toward the girl with the antelope horn. An instant later, the massive beast turned and cantered into the bush.

"Juba!"

Enat extended a hand.

"Come!" she called.

The girl gave her a curious look.

"Juba! Hurry!"

"Who is Juba?" she answered, perplexed.

She saw Enat shake her head and frown.

"You are Juba," the girl told her. "That is what I have decided to call you."

"But that is not my name. My mother calls me—" She paused and gazed at the ground. "She calls me—" She quickly wiped her eyes and sniffled.

"You will be Juba now," the girl told her in a stern voice. "Do you hear? Juba."

"But I—"

Juba crouched low to the ground when the sky suddenly shuddered with a roaring whoosh of wind and the rumbling bellow of a motorized machine. Around her, trees and shrubs flattened. A dark shadow streaked menacingly across the ground. Thunder filled the air. She could feel the world around her shake. Then, just as suddenly as the outbreak occurred, it ended. Stunned and confused, Juba slowly rose.

"What was that?" she asked.

The unexpected boom of a powerful, close-fired gunshot sent a jolt through Juba's body. Before she knew what to make of the thunderous clap, Enat slung a big weapon from her shoulder and bolted off through the tall grass. Juba watched her go, uncertain. She stood immobile for a few minutes, wondering what to do. Enat had disappeared into the bush. Why had she run toward the gunshot? It made no sense. Gunshots were never good. Puzzled, Juba slowly surveyed the terrain around her. Although nothing made sense at the moment, she decided she did not want to be alone. With a shrug, she jogged after Enat.

*

As Juba followed Enat further into the bush, the first ridge of the highlands they'd been traveling toward came into view. Sight of higher ground compelled her to pause, for Enat had spoken of the area—a land of beautiful tree-studded ridges and grassy plateaus—when she had allowed Juba to walk with her one evening. She also told her that she and a man named Bouda had made a home there. Bouda, she'd said on this occasion, would be waiting for her among the first grouping of hills. She was certain of this, she'd said. And Juba hoped it was true. For Enat had seemed upset when she'd told Juba this. In Juba's opinion, the girl had seemed troubled since she'd shot the hyenas.

At the crest of a small hill, Juba paused to rest. As she searched the area for Enat, she was surprised at the change in the terrain; sparse patches of grass, weed clumps, and thorn bushes had given way to slender trees within a sea of head-high, tawny grass. The difference was striking and, for Juba, disconcerting. Everywhere she looked, it was though she was staring into the surface of a shiny pool of water: each section of grass a mirror image of the next, every tree a duplicate of the one beside it, each sphere of terrain identical, an optical illusion that skewed her sense of depth and perception.

Perhaps this section of land has been conjured by a shaman, she mused, *as an elaborate spell to lure unsuspecting travelers into its midst.* From stories she'd heard, the notion might well be true. For shamans, it was told, were in constant need of hearts, livers, and gizzards to cast their charms, and therefore they would need an enchanted place to capture specimens. So, as she looked out over what she considered a landscape of mirrors, she decided the stand of wood and grass she was about to enter might very well be a place of dark magic. The notion made her extremely uneasy.

The booming echo of another gunshot sent Juba into a crouch. Around her, the landscape came alive with the cries of startled birds and calls of alarm from animals hidden within its cover. Just as she was thinking of turning back—back to where the remnants of her village lay—she heard a snapping crack, like the sound of a log splitting, and observed a wide swath of movement in the grass some fifty paces in front of her. Fearing it was a shaman come to collect her, she got down on her knees and prepared to beg for her life. When the wall of grass parted ten paces from where she stood, panic exploded in the pit of her stomach. An instant later, she was overwhelmed with sorrow as the massive rhino she'd encountered minutes before stumbled toward her, front and back horns sheered away, its snout awash in blood.

Juba immediately understood the rhino was in utter agony. Blood oozed freely from the gaping wounds, splattering the ground with every step the animal labored to take. And as the rhino drew nearer, the gaze of the beast held her still, the anguish conveyed in its eyes rendering her incapable of movement.

Gunshots—a loud sustained burst followed by a sharper spurt—sent Juba sprawling to the ground. As she flattened her body against the soil, the agonized scream of a girl pierced the air. Juba stared at the dirt, trembling, not knowing what she should do.

A sudden, violent explosion drew Juba's attention upward. Above the trees and grasses, somewhere among the peaks and plateaus of the highlands, she could see a massive cloud of dust rising into the sky. Had a volcano erupted? Or had someone set off an explosion? Adding to her uncertainty, the air-machine that had flattened trees and shrubs with its wind suddenly thundered across the sky. Juba reflexively ducked her head when its shadow flickered across her position. Then just as before, the flying machine—with the wind, the noise, the shadow it produced—was gone.

Juba took a deep breath and held it. When all remained quiet, she pushed up from the ground and stood. Again, she took a deep breath and listened. As she softly exhaled, she scrutinized the shaman landscape.

Where was Enat? What did the gunshots mean? What caused the explosion in the highlands? Wary of what lay ahead of her, she turned and surveyed the way she had come. *Maybe I should go back*, she thought. *Maybe I'm not meant to follow the girl into the mountains.*

As Juba mulled her options, sunlight glinting off puddles of blood beckoned her eyes downward. Somewhere amongst the scrub, the rhino lay dying, she knew. And though she felt compelled to go to the animal and offer it what comfort she could, she did not relish being a witness to the beast's slow, torturous death. Turning toward the highlands, she warily took stock of the shaman's mirror landscape.

"Enat!" she abruptly called out.

She listened, but heard no reply.

And then she remembered: a girl had screamed.

10

RAIN IS EVERYWHERE, yet it does not fall. The wind, catching each drop before it reaches the ground, whisks it to the kingdom above. There, in the realm of sun, sky, cloud, and star, a crown of light is bestowed upon each droplet so forever there will be a glimmer of hope when darkness extends its reach. You have felt this hope many times. It has glittered upon your skin while you've slept. Why now do you hang your head and pretend it does not exist?

*

"I heard a boy once say, "When the last elephant is gone, we will be no more."

Kamua watched the shadow of the owl shift from tree to stone without the dark impression of its form imprint a silhouette upon soil or air. Emerald eyes blinked open within solid rock—their centers flared with yellow flame—before vanishing in a puff of shiny dust. Wind gusted in bursts of motion devoid of sound, while the crystalline shape of a massive spirit-elephant stood impassively on a stationary cushion of translucent mist. Equating the real to the imagined and the imagined to the real, Kamua struggled to discern whether he had actually heard a woman speak or was suffering a delusion.

"You say we are losing the battle."

The despair in the woman's tone shook Kamua to the marrow of his bones. As though a squall of black thunderheads had formed overhead and unleashed a torrent of hail and wind upon him, he hugged his shoulders to his chest and gripped his arms in an attempt to weather the icy chill shooting through his veins. Stricken by crushing sorrow, he tilted his face to the sky and wailed with the grief of a thousand tortured souls.

"But there is more we must do."

More we must do. The phrase gnawed at his psyche. *More we must do!*

"What more must I do?" he cried.

His words came back to him in waves, echoing off the peaks around him. The hollow reverberations seemed to mock his voice as it faded into insignificance. An arm's length above his head, a glint of vibrant color appeared, a speck of metallic green that flitted in the air as though dangled by the strings of a puppeteer. Weary of visions and hallucinations, Kamua covered his face with his hands and hung his head. But the hum of an insect whirring close to his ear prompted him to swat the air above him.

"Get away!" he hissed.

Two, six, twelve, twenty; he watched in resigned disbelief as the dot of green zoomed to a spot several paces in front of the vehicle where he was seated and multiplied to a number he could not fathom. Like a body of shimmering water flowing over the edge of a cliff, the green wave cascaded to the ground and pooled across the soil. There, in a soundless explosion of heatless flame, the metallic green mass ignited and burned until it became a pile of ash.

Flakes of residue—grey, black, and white—fluttered through the air as though stroked by a fickle breeze, then settled. In a swirling levitation, the grimy mass gathered and congealed, forming a mounded shape prone upon the soil. A blaring cry from the gargantuan spirit-elephant shook the air and ground. In the aftermath, the charred mass lying prone upon the soil blossomed and took the form of a person.

Adolescent, adult, child, elder—the entity standing before Kamua seemed all of those and more. Each feminine age blurred within the features of the others to form a creature of innocence, wisdom, strength, and compassion he struggled to comprehend. The entity was at once beautiful and terrifying, provocative and demure, with flowing hair the color of moonlight and fire, skin the tone of sand, earth, mud, and tar. These colors twined around her torso like the coils of a snake. In her eyes, Kamua glimpsed the hues of every form of water he had ever known:

sun-splashed raindrops, blue oceans, emerald streams, slate-grey rivers, and moon-bathed pools shrouded within a dark veil of midnight rain. Kamua observed all manner of creature and flora within the woman's pupils: beasts of land and sky, fish of sea and stream, insect of forest and swamp—all moving within a forest of flowers, trees, grass, and vegetation born of water that drifts with the currents of the seas. Wind, rain, sky, and sun were the essence of the feminine entity—a collage of life, light, and sound.

Overwhelmed by the splendor radiating from the creature before him, Kamua slid out of the driver's seat and knelt to the ground. As he lowered his head in homage to the godlike creature, she extended a hand, her palm raised toward the sky. Images of spirit-elephants materialized at the tips of her fingers, their forms encased within a luminous sphere fashioned of sea mist and the light of a rising sun. Crystalline in appearance, the ethereal beasts were gathered near the base of a snow-capped mountain surrounded by a sea of golden grass.

Suddenly, black clouds appeared, the ominous forms tethered to the wings of man-like creatures descending from the heavens. Dark angels, these beings resembled, their figures hollow-eyed and grim, mouths twisted with malevolence, taloned fingers disfigured from the work of sin. The dark angels assailed the spirit-elephants one by one, shattering their bodies under an onslaught of silver-rain-steel projectiles. With each death of a crystalline beast, the landscape grew pale. When the last of the spirit-elephants was destroyed, the sky rumbled and the ground buckled and cracked. And then the mountain erupted, spewing flame and ash into the air. Lava rose from the earth, setting fire to the grass.

Black and grey, grey and black; Kamua could see little difference between the earth and sky. But as ash and smoke cleared and a semblance of land appeared, he trembled with fear. For there was nothing left to see. No plain of grass or snow-capped mountain or crystalline beast or any remnant of the beauty that used to be. Without color or life, the landscape was now barren and stark, gloomy and desolate. As Kamua grappled with the vision, a child spoke in a voice he'd heard before; a boy whispered what the woman had said.

"When the last elephant is gone, we will be no more."

Kamua covered his face with his hands as a funnel of wind surged down upon him. Soil rose up. The ground trembled and stirred. The air whooshed and whirred, the sound growing to a crescendo in his ears. Fearful of the hallucination he was experiencing, he pressed his palms against his ears, squeezed his eyes shut, and bent forward until his head touched the ground. Engulfed in a vortex of dust, wind, and whirring thunder, Kamua placed his mouth to the earth and screamed. As though his display of emotion had shattered the illusion in which he'd been immersed, calm ensued. The vision had run its course.

In a moment of reflection, Kamua wondered if hallucinating the demise of the spirit-elephants correlated to his sealing the tusks into the cave. Perhaps the vision had been delivered to him by the owl as a way of bringing closure to a task he had unwittingly undertaken since the day Tengene and Selam were killed. The tusks of a thousand murdered elephants were now sealed within a highland cave. Perhaps, he hoped, their spirits could rest in peace.

A man shouted, "*Sharmuta kalb!*" and delivered a sharp blow to Kamua's kidney.

Stunned by the pain shooting through his lower back, Kamua rolled over onto his side and thrust his arm upward. A harsh kick to his ribs caused him to curl his body into a tight ball.

"You killed my men!" the same man screamed.

Disoriented and distressed, Kamua tried to focus on his assailant. He noted the man's sky-blue turban just before he glimpsed the butt of a rifle streaking toward his head.

"Where is the ivory?" the man shouted.

The blow to Kamua's head rendered him unconsciousness.

*

Mosi examined the skewer of sizzling meat before handing the kebab to the man sitting across from him on the other side of a small fire.

"Go on, Amin. Eat," he encouraged when Amin frowned.

Lifting a second kebob from the low-burning flames, he placed it beneath his nose.

"Ah," he sighed. "Smells just like a whore's pussy." He burst out laughing. Amin did not.

"What, Amin, you aren't one to sample the *kas* after you have worked it?" Mosi tore a piece of the meat from the skewer and, winking, plopped it into his mouth. "Better if you douse it with wine," he joked. He flashed Amin a lecherous smile and licked his fingertips. "It takes away the smell." He bit into another chunk of meat before adding, "But not the taste so much."

As he watched Amin examine his kebob with a dubious expression, Mosi's attention drifted toward the man tied to the grille of a pickup truck parked several meters away. Amin observed his focus and glanced over his shoulder.

"I hope he can talk," he remarked. "You should not have hit him so hard."

Mosi glared at the prisoner for a moment before replying.

"He is a dead man," he said.

"But Mosi, if he is to tell us—"

"He will give us the ivory," Mosi interjected, "and then we will remove his head."

Amin lifted his kabob to his mouth as if to take a bite. With an audible sigh, he lowered the skewer to his side and shook his head.

"I can't," he said, eyeing the stick. "Eating rhino meat is like chewing on a baboon's ass."

Focused on the prisoner, Mosi didn't immediately reply.

"Fucking Akmir," Mosi mumbled.

Amin stared at him while stroking his scraggly beard.

"I will dump the ivory on his desk and then cut the head from the man's neck while he watches," Mosi said and then grunted. "Then he will pay us the gold."

Mosi heard Amin say something in response, but he didn't bother to listen. In his eyes, Amin was stupid—a man of little intelligence and less imagination. *He would still be plowing a field behind the ass of a buffalo and planting yams in shit-laden soil if it weren't for me*, he mused. *Or lying in a ravine along the border of Sudan with a Turkana spear stuck in his throat.*

"Did you not hear me?" Amin inquired. "I said, 'If he doesn't awaken, how will he lead us to the ivory?'"

Mosi blinked several times before shifting his attention from the prisoner to Amin.

"What will you do with your share of the gold?" he asked, his mouth full of food. "Return to your fields to grow more roots?" He gave a short laugh before saying, "Or buy a fleet of boats and become a fishmonger?"

Amin studied his kebab with a wrinkled nose before taking a tentative nibble of the meat.

"God, this tastes worse than a whore's pussy," Amin said. "Couldn't you find anything else to eat?"

"Why go to the trouble?" Mosi countered. "The stupid beast left a trail a child could follow. Besides," he said, pointing his skewer at Amin, "I needed to retrieve my knife." He tapped the leather sheath strapped to his thigh. "The animal was less than a hundred meters from where we left the girl." His forehead wrinkled as he looked into the fire. "Odd there wasn't a scavenger at either body. But maybe she wasn't to their liking." He shrugged, chuckled, and gave Amin a wink. "Maybe they are like you, and don't care for skewered meat."

Again, Mosi laughed but then abruptly stopped and looked over each of his shoulders.

"What is it?" Amin whispered, reaching for the rifle lying an arm's length from where he sat.

"Her weapon was gone when I returned," Mosi explained. "As were the ammunition belts strapped across her chest." He faced Amin with a troubled expression. "I didn't think of it till now. Someone took them."

"Maybe it was another hunter," Amin suggested. "Or a ranger."

"Ranger." Mosi scoffed. "Dog-loving whores. They would rather wipe the ass of an elephant than see a man provide for his family."

"Even so, if—"

"If one pays us a visit, it will be the last he sees of the world. I'll put his head in the sack with the girl's." He slapped the sheath tied to his leg and looked squarely at Amin. "If it is a ranger, let him come. His reward will be death."

Amin held Mosi's gaze for a moment before shifting his attention to an area of heavy brush.

"What?" Mosi inquired. "What are you looking at?"

"I—" Amin stroked his beard and gazed into the fire. "What if it was a scout from the OLF that took the girl's weapon? I want no part of them again."

"Agreed," Mosi replied with a nod. "I don't know which is worse: the Oromo or Mengistu's henchmen."

"This country is—"

"Better to have no country," Mosi interrupted. "Or any allegiance. Be it the Oromo or the Tigray or the Afar or the scum from south Somalia—none are worth the time or effort."

"Akmir."

"Fuck Akmir," Mosi said. "He's no Somali. He's just another piece of Arab shit come to extract money and blood from a people that aren't his."

"He has power and many men," Amin pointed out.

"Paid thieves and rabble," Mosi countered. "No match for those of us who fought with Garang to rid Sudan of Islamic rule."

Mosi watched Amin's eyes search the fire. By the somber expression on the man's face, he imagined what Amin must be thinking.

Mosi and Amin had witnessed hundreds of thousands die in a year's time. Blood and gore had run ankle deep within a fifty-kilometer area just west of the Ethiopian border. Corpses had been piled in mounds along desolate footpaths that led to nowhere. Villages were burned and pillaged. Women were raped and murdered or sold as slaves. Boys were forced to kill their fathers by blade or suffer the same fate while they watched their fathers gutted, their organs fed to packs of wild dogs.

The year they had fought alongside one another—a year of butchery beyond their imagination—had taken its toll. Fighting for a cause, they soon came to realize, was not a life either of them wanted. This was especially true for Mosi, who quickly grasped there was no money to be made in the killing of women and children. Luckily, when he'd decided poaching and ivory running were a far better way to provide for one's family, Amin had possessed the brains to follow him.

"I don't want to go back to Sudan," Amin said in a quiet voice.

Mosi slid the final chunk of meat from his skewer and plopped it in his mouth. He chewed several times before he met Amin's gaze.

"Once the Arab has paid us, we can go wherever we want and do whatever we please."

"But if it was a patrol that stripped the girl of her weapon, we could be forced to choose a side and—"

"We won't."

"How can you be so sure?"

Mosi met Amin's question with silence and a stare. After a moment, he threw his stick into the fire and stood.

"I need to take a piss," he said. Looking over toward the prisoner, he added, "And I know just where to do it."

Mosi pulled the zipper of his bush pants down and stepped around the fire. As he approached the unconscious prisoner, he heard Amin prime his weapon.

"Preparing for a visitor?" he joked.

"You said it yourself; there is someone out there."

"Then make yourself useful. Check the far perimeter while I douse the *abeed* with my flow."

*

Mosi stopped two meters from the unconscious prisoner. The flow of his urine began with a terse command.

"Wake up, dog."

A nearby burst of automatic gunfire caught him by surprise, and he tripped over his own feet as he turned. Steadying himself against the pickup truck, he heard Amin emerge from the brush.

"How many?" he called out as he slung his assault rifle from his shoulder.

Amin shrugged and offered a sheepish grin when Mosi turned to face him.

"How many?" Mosi pressed.

With his eyes cast to the ground, Amin stepped into the firelight and said, "A bird."

"What?"

"It was an owl or something," Amin said.

"You fired at— At a bird?"

"It had strange eyes," Amin replied.

"Bitch, dog!" Mosi muttered. "Now whoever is out there will know exactly where we are! *Khara!* How could you be so stupid?"

"It was like no other—"

"And now I have pissed all over myself! *Khara!*"

Just as Amin started to laugh, the deep-throated call of an owl came from somewhere in the bush. Both men fell silent, for the rough-throated *gwonk-gwok-gwok-gwok-gwonk* echoed with an air of foreboding.

"You see," Amin said in a hushed tone. "Does that sound like—?"

Before Amin had a chance to finish, Mosi fired a sustained round of bullets into the dark wall of undergrowth. The booming roar of gunfire rolled off the ridgelines at their backs like thunder. When the rumbling faded, Mosi slapped the stock of his gun and then nonchalantly zipped up his pants.

"Now who is the bitch, dog?" Amin chided. "Are you not—?"

"You can't kill them."

Mosi and Amin turned and looked toward the pickup truck.

The prisoner's voice was weak. He mumbled, "They're already dead."

Mosi moved toward the prisoner.

"The dog awakens," Mosi muttered as he strode past the fire. "He'll wish he'd stayed asleep."

*

The man in the blue turban—maybe I'm still dreaming.

"You killed my men!"

The kick to the bottom of Kamua's foot was so hard, the pain shot up into his thigh.

"And stole my ivory!"

Kamua winced when the man slapped his face.

"Where is it?" the man screamed.

And then the back of Kamua's head slammed against something hard. He squirmed as a hand clamped around his throat and started to squeeze.

"Don't kill him!" he heard someone yell.

The man in the blue turban turned his head.

"Mosi! You said it yourself."

A man clothed in a red T-shirt appeared over Mosi's shoulder.

"The ivory first, remember?" the man in the red T-shirt said.

Kamua gulped for air as Mosi released his throat and waved a knife in front of his nose.

"I will just cut off his ears, then," Mosi said.

Kamua jerked his head back when the blade pressed against his cheek.

"He doesn't need them to tell us where the tusks are hidden."

Sensing malice in Mosi's voice, Kamua lurched left when the blade flashed upward toward the right side of his face.

"*Neik!*" Mosi grunted. "I will cut your balls off if you move again!"

Mosi grasped Kamua's face with his hand and squeezed. Little by little, he forced Kamua to turn his head until their eyes met.

"Do you hear me?" he screamed. "Look at me!"

Kamua closed his eyes and chuckled.

"You mock me?"

Kamua opened his eyes and saw fury on Mosi's face, but his attention drifted past the man's shoulder.

"What are you looking at?" Mosi shouted.

"There's so many of them," Kamua muttered, confused. "They didn't go."

"What's he saying?" Kamua heard the man in the red shirt ask. "Who didn't go?"

Kamua looked to the second man. When he met his gaze, he said, "The elephants."

"Elephants?" the man questioned. Kamua saw him glance over his shoulder. "What elephants?"

"Why do you speak to this dog, Amin?" Mosi snarled. "He is nothing but a murdering thief!"

Kamua began to feel lightheaded when the eyes of countless spirit-elephants began to swirl in the shadows beyond the fire. Resting the back of his head against the truck, he watched the spinning orbs accelerate, their shapes elongating and flattening until the motion blurred into lines of whirling red. Layer upon layer, the lines linked and then fused. The joined shapes formed a ruby wall.

"Do you hear me?" Mosi squeezed Kamua's face and spit on his cheek.

"You are a murdering thief!" The blade of Mosi's knife flashed before Kamau's eyes. "I will cut off your balls and stuff them down your throat before I take your head!"

"The ivory!" Amin shouted. "Remember the ivory!"

"He will give us the ivory!" Mosi spat. Glaring into Kamua's face, he pressed the tip of the knife into the skin just below his right eye. "Or he will suffer."

A strange, haunting cry came out of the bush as Mosi's blade drew blood from Kamua's flesh.

"What was that?" Amin whispered.

"Nothing," Mosi snapped. "Let me—"

A second cry—forlorn, like that of a gravely wounded animal—compelled Mosi to pause. With the third tormented cry, Mosi stood and sheathed his blade.

"This is the work of a—"

Mosi silenced Amin with a sharp, downward motion of his arm. As he slipped the assault rifle from his shoulder, the bush exploded with unnerving calls of countless unseen creatures.

To Kamua, the proliferation of tormented voices coincided with a throbbing pulse within the fabric of the ruby wall. When the first rippled current shot across the barrier of pink-red light, he thought it an illusion, a result of having sustained a blow to his head. But as the forlorn cries multiplied, so too did the concurrent movement within the wall, as though each cry of an individual animal was synced to a visual beat. Both awestruck and terrified by what he perceived to be a myriad of undulations that mirrored the pulse of a thousand beating hearts, he whispered, "We are doomed."

Shouting "*Ek ras!*" Mosi stepped toward the clamor of cries and fired his weapon until the ammo clip was empty.

"This is witchcraft," Amin muttered in fear. "A *sihr* has come to avenge the girl's death. I told you not to take her head. I knew it was wrong."

"Quiet, fool. You speak like an ignorant woman who's walked too long behind the ass of an ox. *Sihr*," Mosi scoffed. "Shamans, witches, boudas, *shabahh*s. Have you not lived long enough to have outgrown such childhood fears?"

Mosi ejected the spent ammunition clip and snapped a new one into the weapon. Striding confidently toward the dark area of bush, he said, "Let's see what my bullets struck."

*

A ruffling of feathered wings prodded Kamua to look upward. Just then, something sharp jabbed the underside of his wrist. Reflexively, he tried to jerk his hand away, but as they were tethered to the truck's grille, he could barely move. A second painful prick to the same area made him flinch and softly cry out. In the same instant, a scowling Mosi—knife in hand—returned from the bush. Again, a ruffling of feathers prodded Kamua to look up. The owl, he saw, was airborne.

The flight of the broad-winged bird of prey was a blur, a shadow moving within the glow of the campfire. Mosi saw it too and crouched low to the ground. But his action was too late. The owl plucked the turban from his head and flew into the bush. Cursing in Arabic, Mosi sprinted after the owl. Kamua couldn't help but chuckle.

"Shhh," a voice whispered. "Be still."

Kamua jerked his head to one side in an attempt to see who was behind him.

"Don't move!" a child—a girl, Kamua guessed—softly commanded.

The sensation of small fingers pressing against his forearm preceded a series of vibrations running through the rope tied around his wrists. Understanding someone was cutting him free, he shifted his attention to the dark area of underbrush where Mosi and Amin had disappeared.

"Hurry," he whispered.

A burst of gunfire sent a jolt through Kamua's body. He tried to pull his hands apart, but they were still bound.

"Hurry," he urged again.

With a rattling of branches, Mosi stomped out of the brush with Amin right behind him.

"Fuck the bird," he said as he shouldered his rifle.

Kamau felt the rope go slack.

"It's witchcraft," Amin added. "The work of a *sihr*."

"Enough about the stupid bird," Mosi replied. Twisting the handle of the knife sheathed at his side, his attention fixed on Kamua, he said, "Time to make this dog talk."

Kamau felt something hard thrust into his hands as Mosi drew his blade and strode toward him. Fighting a wave of panic, he clamped his fingertips around the metal object and slid it toward him. Round, long, cold. The protrusion of a sight. Realizing he'd been given a rifle, he swung it to his chest and braced the butt against his shoulder.

"He has a rifle!" Mosi warned.

Kamua aimed the AK-47 at Mosi and pulled the trigger. To his chagrin, nothing happened.

"Damn!" he spat. The weapon's safety was still engaged.

Bullets strafed the soil near his legs. Rolling left, he scrambled around the back of the truck. Using one of the rear tires for cover, he positioned the AK-47 parallel to the ground and fired off a burst. He felt his heart skip a beat when something tugged on his arm.

"We must go!"

Kamua stared open-mouthed at the little girl with ammunition belts coiled around her body.

"There is more we must do," she told him.

To the sound of bullets striking the metal body of the truck, Kamua took hold of the girl's outstretched hand. Together, they ran into the cover of darkness.

11

FAITH DOES NOT flow from rock or seep from words spoken in haste. Down—down where darkness and doubt reign—a fragment of light burns. Eternal in nature, the flame weathers what elements it is forced to bear and does not falter in the breath of an angel's despair. Crusade or crusader, it does not care which you are. Free it from the depth of misgiving and cup the fire within your palm. Hold it close to your chest so it may melt the sorrow in your heart. Rekindle the beat of the drum and let the timbre of its voice bring hope. Woe is not your course. That path serves those who lie in wait for broken souls. Awaken, and feel the song of the Mother upon your flesh. Woe is not the way.

*

"She was such a beautiful child."

Mr. Locket stiffened when he realized he'd spoken out loud. Quickly, he placed the gold-framed picture of Claire as a little girl back on the mantle and pulled a white handkerchief from the breast pocket of his charcoal suit coat. With a flurry of hand movements, he pretended to dust the picture frame, all the while keeping his gaze focused on the little girl in the photograph.

He guessed Claire had been five when the photograph was taken. *Five years and nine months,* he corrected himself. At least, that's what he believed. Mrs. Waterman, however, disputed that calculation.

He'd broached the subject of Claire's age with Caroline Waterman only once in the forty-some years he'd worked for the family. She'd flown into a rage. Shortly thereafter, she'd taken the girl to Europe. "To introduce the child to a more refined culture," Mr. Waterman had relayed to the staff.

Mr. Locket never brought up the subject again.

Several weeks had turned into a year, hadn't it? And when Madam and Miss Claire had finally arrived home, the now six-year-old girl was whisked off to the first of many boarding schools she would attend throughout her young life, leaving Mr. Locket little chance to get to know her or keep abreast of her accomplishments except through conversations he would overhear between her parents, or upon the rare occasion when the young lady would return to the manor house on an odd holiday when a family vacation had not been planned. It was on one of those occasions that Mr. Locket had first caught an inkling of Miss Claire's infatuation with the Almighty.

The day in question was Easter of the second year after Claire had returned from Europe. He remembered the day exactly because he'd been serving her and her father tea in the sitting room. The late rays of a March sun streamed through the large picture window facing the western portion of the sprawling estate grounds. Miss Claire was seated in one of the two high-backed leather chairs placed at angles in front of the large picture window so one could gaze out at the two-acre, gorgeously landscaped pond fifty yards from the house proper. Nestled at the bottom of a gently sloping dell adorned with a stand of white birch trees on the far shore, the pond was a favorite vista for Claire and Mr. Waterman.

Mr. Locket had paused as he'd entered the room, for the sunlight flowing through the window framed Miss Claire in such a way that she appeared to be shrouded in a heavenly veil of radiant gold. He couldn't recall having ever looked upon a scene of such quiet beauty: Miss Claire, her chestnut-brown hair swept back across her shoulders by a pink and white ribbon, her face the quintessential picture of innocence and youthful curiosity. He would mull the image of her on that day for several years afterward and come to understand that it was on that late afternoon in March, when the sun bestowed on the girl all its glory, that he was seeing the young woman for what she was and what she was always intended to be: a person of divine quality that was not meant to be kept from the world.

"He spoke to me, Father."

Mr. Locket kept his attention focused on the placement of saucer and cup as Claire spoke. Although he wanted to look at the girl's face when she made the comment, he understood it wasn't his place to acknowledge her. So he poured tea—Miss Claire's favorite, a blend of chamomile, honey, and fresh mint—into her cup while he waited for Mr. Waterman to reply. He thought it odd and a trifle dismissive when the master of the house did not give his daughter a response.

"We were in Arles," Claire went on in an innocent, excited tone. "Mother had brought me to see the works of Van Gogh. By chance, we happened upon an old chapel that had been converted into a museum." The warmth of the teapot had seeped through the material of Mr. Locket's white gloves as he straightened and took a step back from tea service. "Have you been there, Father, in Arles?" Claire had asked.

Again, Mr. Locket was somewhat perplexed when Mr. Waterman gave no reply.

"I was reading a very old parchment written in hand by one of the apostles—I can't remember which at the moment—when He addressed me."

"Indeed," Mr. Waterman said after sipping his tea. "He?" Mr. Waterman glanced up and winked at Mr. Locket. "And what did the old boy have to say for himself? Happy with how the world has turned out, I hope," he joked.

Mr. Locket couldn't help but look over at Miss Claire for her reaction. He remembered the girl shaking her head in a most serious manner before saying, "Not at all, Father. On the contrary, he told me there is much more we must do."

"I dare say," Mr. Waterman lightly replied. "And did he give you any hint of how that might be accomplished?"

"It was beautiful, Father, His voice," she continued. Mr. Waterman had given his daughter a look of genuine concern when she'd sought out his gaze. "It was like a song, only more so. Rather like an orchestra. Made up of different melodic winds flowing through the crest of a wave."

The clink of china cup to saucer preceded Mr. Waterman asking, "And what did this voice say to you, Claire? What words did wind and water conjure?"

"It was a trifle confusing at the time, Father." Mr. Locket felt the urge to take a knee and wrap the little girl in his arms when she looked at her father with an expression of utter sincerity. "I was only five, after all. But now that I am older, I think I understand what He meant."

"By *He*, you mean God?"

"Yes, of course, Father. The Lord."

Mr. Locket wondered what Mr. Waterman was thinking when he gazed out the window and ran a hand over the top of his head.

"'Take care of my children,' He said." As Claire paused to follow her father's gaze to what lay outside the window, Mr. Locket blinked against a sudden reflection coming off the surface of the pond. "'Take care of my children,'" he heard the girl softly repeat.

Neither father nor daughter spoke for a time following Claire's revelation, for after coating the surface of the pond in a blanket of gold, the fading rays of the sun emblazoned the wings of a dozen geese in a halo of fire as they entered the vista of the window and circled to land. The breathtaking image placed thoughts of tea and talk of God aside, or so Mr. Locket thought. But as the large birds touched down and ripples broke the water's glittering crust, Claire continued speaking in a soft tone.

"Those who hope in the Lord will find strength. They will soar on wings like eagles. They will run and not grow weary. They will walk and not be faint."

"Claire." Mr. Locket felt a pang of awkwardness when Mr. Waterman reached across his chair and gently clasped his daughter's hand. "Where did you learn to speak like that? Your words, what—?"

"Are we spouting scripture again?"

The icy tone of the woman's voice was like a black cloud passing in front of the sun; the room fell abruptly silent, the air held within its walls tinged reticent and unsettled.

"Really, Claire."

Mr. Locket flinched when he turned and saw the look of reproach on Mrs. Waterman's face.

"Must you bore your father with whatever dribble they are teaching you in that accursed school?"

"I was telling Father about Arles, Mother. You remember, when I—"

"Yes, Claire, I remember."

Mr. Locket was somewhat taken aback by the terseness in Mrs. Waterman's tone.

"The recordings of the monks you talked yourself into believing was the voice of God."

Mr. Locket remembered clenching his fists when the elder woman stepped by him with a dismissive laugh.

"Really, young lady, I thought you had outgrown that silly notion."

Although Mr. Locket—and indeed, Mr. Waterman, he was sure—was embarrassed for how Claire must have felt at the way her mother spoke to her, he was quite astonished and, dare say, proud at the way in which the seven-year-old responded to her mother's condescension.

"I can understand how those recordings could be construed as what you think I heard, Mother, but I have examined each word spoken to me while I was reading that parchment."

Mr. Locket found himself leaning toward Miss Claire as the girl met her mother's stern glare before shifting her attention to her father, who seemed, in Mr. Locket's opinion, to be hanging on his daughter's every word.

"Take care of my children, for there is more we must do." The sunlight caught the amber flecks in Claire's eyes as she looked down toward the pond. "The birds, the sky, the oceans, people of all walks of life—all are his children." She had turned and looked into her father's eyes before she'd said, "That is what He meant, Father: *all* are his children."

Father and daughter shared a moment, then, an unspoken feeling of understanding that was not to be analyzed or commented upon. It was quite like observing two people watching each other exhale outdoors on a frost-layered morning, when breath is to be marveled at as the sun briefly frames the crystals of warmth it holds before their brief existence dissipates into the elements. A moment of fragile beauty. One which, unfortunately, was short-lived.

"Mr. Locket will see you to your room, Claire."

He watched Claire's gaze fall to the floor at the cold tone of her mother's voice. It had pained him that her father did not intercede on her behalf.

"Mr. Locket."

He had to summon all of his restraint before he could answer the woman in a polite tone.

"Mr. Locket."

How he had degraded himself by allowing her to…

"Mr. Locket!"

Mr. Locket removed his fingers from the gold-framed picture of five-year-old Claire Waterman, replaced the white kerchief in the breast pocket of his suit coat, and turned toward the person addressing him. It took him a moment to process that the woman standing in the foyer of the sitting room was the cook, Mrs. Cavanaugh, and not a younger version of Mrs. Waterman.

"Yes, Mrs. Cavanaugh?" he inquired.

"Mrs. Waterman called. She said everything is as it should be, and she will be home by the dinner hour."

"Did she say how Miss Claire was?"

Mr. Locket received no reply, for Mrs. Cavanaugh, message delivered, was already heading back down the long hallway toward her beloved kitchen. Left to his own thoughts, he turned his attention back to the photograph of Claire. Her childhood seemed so long ago. Another time altogether. *All the years that have passed,* he lamented. And as he took a step closer to the picture of Claire and brought her face into better focus, he suddenly wondered where time had gone.

*

"What will become of you now?"

Dirk blinked his eyes at the sound of a woman's voice but continued to stare at the white ceiling tiles above him.

Forty-seven, he counted. Pinholes or pattern holes, or whatever they were. Forty-seven holes. Part of the panel's design, he decided. But why in the world would someone think forty-seven holes placed within an off-white square of sound-absorbing material was attractive? And why that number: forty-seven? How did someone come up with that? Were the holes supposed to represent stars? He closed his eyes and tried to shake his head. Whoever created the design, he concluded, must have been on drugs.

Wait, a little voice in the back of his head whispered. *Why can't I move my head?*

He blinked his eyes open wide.

"Try to stay with us this time, Mr. Savage. Or have you reverted back to your given name, Mr. Benjamin?"

Dirk tried to speak but found his mouth and throat were so dry he could barely produce a sound. He tried to move his head again—to lean it forward so he could see where he was—but as before, he found it immobile. Ever so gradually, he became aware of pressure pushing down across his forehead.

"Thirsty?"

Dirk focused his eyes on the shape looming above him. He squinted in an attempt to get the wrinkly features he was seeing to smooth.

"Don't look so troubled. You won't be denied basic needs."

Mrs. Waterman. Dirk started to remember what had happened. His eyes followed the figure of the old woman until she moved out of his field of vision. Then someone else was standing next to him. Someone wearing white. He blinked a few times as he tried to remember if he knew who the person was. He felt something touch his lips—something plastic, cylindrical—just before a gruff voice said, "Drink."

Dirk cupped his tongue around the tip of a straw and sucked. Water— god, did it feel good. Although it was room temperature and had a metallic taste to it, damn if it wasn't clearing out the layers of cobwebs clogging his pipes. He ran his tongue over his lips when the straw was suddenly extracted from his mouth. The white-clad figure moved away, and Caroline Waterman came back.

"Ready to discuss your—" he saw a smile form on her face "—imminent future?"

"Kidnapping is a felony," he responded.

"Oh, please, Dirk," she countered. "*Kidnapping* is such a distasteful term. Besides, how can it be kidnapping when no one knows you're missing?" He felt her hands on his chest. "Or knows to look for you?" He felt a finger brush the tip of his chin. "It's the old tree-in- the-forest scenario, isn't it?"

"I don't—"

"Oh, come, come, Dirk. Get that beautiful brain of yours working." He tried to jerk his head away when her face invaded the space a few inches above his. "Does it make a sound when no one is around to hear it fall?" she said in a sing-song cadence. Her breath smelled minty. "Same for you—or anyone, for that matter." His eyes followed what portion of her he could see as she moved out of his line of sight. "Are you really here if no one knows you are? I mean, how does one miss something if one doesn't know it's gone missing?" Her laughter sent a quiver down his spine.

"Someone knows I'm here," he told her. "Staff, the goons that drugged me, Mr. Locket. That shoots your tree theory all to hell."

"Oh, they don't count, Dirk. Come on, think about it. None of them care who you are or why you're here. You're just another patient, another loony tune. So don't flatter yourself."

"Is that what Claire is?" he shot back. "Is that why she's being tortured? Because you think she's a whacked-out crackpot?"

Dirk heard the woman sigh deeply before she spoke.

"Claire, Claire, Claire. Why is it always about Claire?" she asked in a surprisingly dispassionate tone. "A girl who treated her station as if it was flaw rather than privilege." Dirk heard her sigh again. "Drove poor Walter to an early grave."

Dirk tried to move his hands but found they were strapped to the gurney.

"Walter?" he inquired.

"Don't play stupid, Dirk. You've heard me talk about Walter several times over the past year." Caroline's face suddenly appeared above his. "Claire's father. My late husband." He saw her eyes glance down toward his feet when he tried to move his legs. "And stop wiggling," she told him as her face disappeared. "They assured me you're strapped in tighter than a…"

He waited for her to finish, but when she didn't offer an analogy, he prodded, "Tighter than what?"

He flinched when the white-clad figure who had offered him the straw appeared next to him and rubbed something wet on the crook of his arm.

"What are you doing?" he asked the orderly.

"What were you going to do with my daughter if you managed to escape with her?" Dirk sensed a change in Caroline's tone; playful banter had been replaced with acidity. "Did you think she would just claim her trust fund and then pay you some outlandish sum as a reward for saving her?"

Dirk saw the white-clad figure—a muscular man—hold a needle and syringe toward the light. The amber liquid inside the syringe jiggled when the man flicked his index finger against the plastic tube.

"Or were you planning on whisking her back to that continent of niggers and wild animals and reuniting her with her lover?"

"Her lover? Teimbaka was never—"

"Don't say his name!" Caroline delivered a stinging slap to his face. "Don't make him real!" she hissed. Her face was quivering with rage when she peered down into his eyes. "Filthy, soulless—" Her angst-filled voice drifted into a series of grunts as she moved out of his line of sight.

"He's suffered so much," Dirk said without thinking.

He pictured him then, remembering Teimbaka as best he could from the only occasion he'd ever seen the man: bloodied, frail, filthy, scarred—so many scars. He'd wondered at the time what the man must have endured.

"He could be dead for all I know," he muttered. "Probably is."

"Then why did you take her?" Caroline shouted. "Why did you call Mr. Locket and stick your nose where it doesn't belong?" He felt the needle pierce his skin as Caroline's footsteps drew near. "You've made it all worse!" she yelled. Her face seemed a little off kilter when it reappeared next to his shoulder. "She was babbling about him on the way back to the clinic." Dirk didn't understand why her lips were suddenly pulsing as if they were alive. "All that therapy shot to hell because you stuck your nose where it didn't belong!"

"Belong." Dirk's mind latched onto the word and examined it. "Djibouti, Ethiopia— Belong—" He saw Claire in the helicopter seated next to Bin'ka, then experienced a pang of guilt when she weakly grabbed hold of his arm and asked him what he'd done. Accused him.

"She does belong there," he managed to say before a numbing rush of what felt like electricity jolted through his head.

"A little late for second -guessing your actions."

Dirk cringed when he saw Caroline's face take on the features of a hyena. White, wrinkled flesh became polished mahogany with piercing, blood-red eyes framed by a mane of bristle-like fur.

"Enjoy your reward," the hyena face said. "We'll talk in a day or two."

To his relief, the hyena face disappeared. Then, what light there was in the room dimmed to a comforting level. He thought he heard footsteps, but he wasn't sure. The next thing he knew, something soft clamped over his ears. Left to his thoughts, he let his eyes drift upward where, once again, his attention was drawn to the holes decorating each square ceiling panel.

As if by magic, light began to flicker from the holes in the ceiling—bluish where it exited, then taking on various hues as the beams washed over and around him. Where the particles of light merged with one another, shapes began to materialize, these taking on human form. As the human shapes evolved into men, the men became a mob of taunting faces, all assailing him with curses and insults. The faces, the voices—he was back in that alley in Mogadishu. The alley where the torch-wielding mob had cornered him and Genevieve. *Genevieve!* The curses and insults built to a fever pitch just as a woman screamed his name. Genevieve—she was with him, next to him. He recognized her even though her features were distorted by waves of energy flickering across her face. Her presence sent a tingle through his flesh and an awful ache through his heart.

One man thrust a torch at Dirk, and the flame passed so close to his face he could feel the skin on his face singe. Then three balls of flame struck Genevieve, lighting her on fire. The smell of burning flesh as she cried out in agony brought tears to his eyes. Out of nowhere, a flash of metal—he saw it clearly, the blade of a sickle-shaped sword—severed Genevieve's head from her neck. Her blood-garbled scream brought a merciful and sudden end to the vision.

Dirk held his breath and clenched his fists as bolts of electricity shot through his body. Just as he felt his head would explode, the current stopped. Pain addled, he stared up at the ceiling panels and tried to control his stuttering breaths by counting the holes within each bordered frame. He achieved a state of normalcy as the lights in the room dimmed to a comforting darkness. Then, as if by magic, soft blue light began to flicker from the holes in the ceiling tiles. As blue morphed into an array of lighted colors, the voices of an angry mob began to build in his ears.

*

Claire felt a sense of déjà vu as she watched the light from a candle flicker across a wrinkled sheet of paper. Words penciled on the paper faded in and out of focus as the flame wavered. The vision reminded her of the particular night she'd written a letter to her parents by candlelight. She'd heard the distant beat of a solitary drum. The sound of the instrument had sent a chill through her body.

Drum-man. The name floated in and out of her thoughts. Drum-man. Who was he, and what did he mean to her?

Claire murmured the name *Drum-man* as a figure began to come into focus. In the next instant, she watched her image flee the enclosure where the candle sat upon a makeshift table. She could sense an urgency in her image's actions as an overwhelming sense of foreboding washed over her. Drum-man. He needed to be warned. But why? She attempted to call out to him, but she could not conjure her voice.

"Is there something you wish to say?"

Something's wrong.

Claire's eyes fluttered as the vision began to dissipate.

"You've caused everyone a great deal of distress."

Claire willed her consciousness to remain within her dream.

"I'm hoping your time away from therapy wasn't as costly as your mother thinks."

Claire opened her eyes and saw a figure peering down at her.

"What do you believe, Claire?"

What do I believe?

Claire studied the man standing over her. His olive skin, oily hair, and white coat reminded her of someone, but she couldn't quite make the connection. But when a woman dressed in a nurse's uniform appeared next to his shoulder, she thought she knew where she was.

"I don't want to leave Africa," she told the doctor and nurse. "I don't want to go back to America. Please don't let the plane take off."

She gazed up at the faces staring down at her. *Why aren't they showing any expression?*

"What do you believe, Claire?" the olive-skinned man asked her again. Claire saw him glance over at the nurse before he added, "Just tell us as best you can."

What do I believe? Reflexively, Claire reached for the silver cross she had worn about her neck for most of her life. She struggled for a moment when she found she couldn't move her arm. But then she remembered where she was: strapped into a gurney in the cargo hold of a Red Cross plane preparing to take off from Mogadishu.

"Claire?" The man was speaking again. "What do you—?"

"Believe?" Claire muttered.

She rubbed her forefinger against her thumb; the outline of the metal cross she believed to be there felt reassuring.

"I believe in one God, the Father Almighty, maker of heaven and earth and all that is seen and unseen. I believe in the Lord, Jesus Christ, his only begotten Son. And of the—"

"No, Claire." Somewhat startled, Claire looked at the olive-skinned man with a mixture of surprise and confusion. "Not what you believe *in*; what you believe. Who's standing next to you when you see yourself in that special place you most long to be?"

"Drum-man," she heard herself say.

She stared past the man's shoulder up to the ceiling tiles. The holes punched into the panels reminded her of stars. She found the vibrant blue light pulsing from the pin-sized holes to be hypnotizing.

The sensation of something hard being forced into her mouth made her gag. The object pressed down on her tongue as a bolt of lightning shot through her body. Her every muscle tensed in an agonizing spasm. Momentarily suffocating, she tried to lurch upward. But she couldn't move. Terror stricken, she bit down on the object in her mouth and screamed. A second, jarring jolt of electricity exploded in her head. Twitching uncontrollably, Claire gasped and choked as she fought to draw in the smallest breath.

"You must not to say his name." The man's voice sounded far away, as if he was speaking from another room. "You must not remember him."

Claire barely noticed a prick to her arm before something soft clamped around her ears. She thought, for a moment, she was drifting off to sleep when the light around her dimmed to a comforting darkness. The reprieve was short-lived, however. A child wailed inside her head.

The sound of an explosion soon followed the child's scream. These coincided with a searing pain that swept across her forehead and down into her skull. Flashes of light appeared above her, bathing her in bars of colored light. Figures materialized—children—their torsos flickering in and out of focus. Once they formed, however, their bodies scattered apart in a macabre dispersal of limbs and heads. Screams—agonized and tortured—assailed her. As a surge of excruciating pain sucked all the breath from her lungs, the voice of Peter Gunstard suddenly echoed through her skull.

"Drum-man allowed the children to die," he said. "Teimbaka allowed the children to die. Teimbaka allowed the children to die. Teimbaka allowed the children to die."

*

Mr. Locket ate his dinner in silence as he blankly stared at the scheduling calendar hanging from the employee bulletin board. Written neatly within the left-hand margin were the names of the estate staff. Kitchen, household, chauffeurs, groundskeepers, groomers, barn personnel. Phone numbers were listed next to names. Each individual's scheduled times for arrival and departure were noted in the calendar's dated squares in abbreviated notations so the information would fit within each day's allotted space. Normally, the calendar—and the neatly written schedule inscribed within its borders—held more than a passing interest to Mr. Locket. Being the author and caretaker of the document, he took great pride in executing his monthly responsibility. Possible conflicts to the schedule were noted and the schedule changed accordingly. His penmanship—exquisitely precise with a nuanced artistic quality—conveyed a deep sense of duty and an unfailing attention to detail. But tonight, as he dazedly consumed the food Mrs. Cavanaugh had provided, the calendar held no meaning. Other matters weighed on his thoughts.

"Not at all like it used to be, is it Daniel?"

Distracted, Mr. Locket almost let Mrs. Cavanaugh's remark pass as she placed his dinner in front of him. "Dinner used to be a time of such—"

Mr. Locket cut her off by giving her a stern look of reproach. But inwardly, he agreed with her observation. So he supplemented his unforgiving expression with a slight nod and an arching of eyebrows. The gesture seemed enough to put Mrs. Cavanaugh at ease, and she smiled at him—knowingly, as he took it—gave him a pat on the shoulder, and said her goodnights. He watched the woman depart with a mixture of relief and sadness. Left to himself, he shifted his attention to the dinner plate she'd left for him.

Beef-burger, chips, and *petit-pois*. Or, as Miss Claire would refer to them, hamburger, fries, and baby peas. Mr. Locket couldn't help but chuckle as he recalled conversing with the five-year-old about the silly names British people gave American food.

"Indeed, Mr. Locket, if the sandwich in question was a *beef* burger, then Wimpy would not have referred to them as hamburgers, would he? And what about those roadside diners with the golden arches? They advertise selling *hamburgers*, do they not, Mr. Locket?" She'd been sitting on a masonry wall—stonewall, as the Americans called it—at the edge of the formal garden, twirling one of her brown curls around her finger. "On this side of the Atlantic, Mr. Locket, we give our food real names. So, it's hamburger, french fries, and peas. Not beef burger, chips, and whatever French term you choose to affix to small peas."

Mr. Locket took a bite of his beef burger and sighed. Mrs. Cavanaugh had been indisputably correct in her observation. Dinnertime at the Waterman estate was not what it once was. Ever since Mr. Waterman had passed away, there had been no setting of the dining room table for a formal meal, no china or crystal placed upon linen tablecloths. The sumptuous concoctions from Mrs. Cavanaugh—and what was for a time a handful of kitchen helpers—were no longer slowly savored in a refined setting over congenial, unhurried conversation. And the music—oh, how Mr. Locket missed the music that Mr. Waterman would play on the phonograph system while enjoying an aperitif before the evening meal. Gershwin, Shaw, Mancini, and—in the later years, before Miss Claire left for France—folk, jazz, and soul. All of those genres had wafted through the rooms of the estate on any given evening, often culminating with the joyous beat of some flamboyant British Invasion band—as they were called back then—before Mrs.

Waterman raised a protest about headaches and prohibited Mr. Waterman from playing what was commonly referred to as rock 'n' roll.

Ah, yes, dinnertime at the estate: a glorious time of day—an event actually—that the entire staff looked forward to. But that seemed like eons ago. Many other aspects of the once-vibrant Waterman estate had long ago disappeared in an ending of an era. But there was no disputing the cause for the demise of daily pleasantries: Claire's disappearance and presumed death had been catastrophic.

The family had never received any concrete news regarding Claire once she'd landed in Ethiopia. The Sisters of the Holy Cross were unnervingly silent on her whereabouts—and the whereabouts of the other young novice they'd sent to help bolster the staff of some third-world hospital in a remote region of the famine-ravaged country. And with no government agency having any in-depth information on the comings and goings of the two women—two nuns—the Watermans were left to imagine the state of their daughter's welfare.

Mr. Waterman had been visibly distressed by the lack of information regarding his daughter. Indeed, with each passing day the man seemed to fall deeper into despair. Mrs. Waterman, on the other hand, had exhibited a completely different attitude toward Claire's wellbeing. Where her husband seemed to grow more despondent as weeks passed without word of his child, the lady of the house had taken a more cavalier attitude toward Claire's situation, almost making a mockery of her daughter's devotion to God.

"It's in God's hands," she would say. Or "God works in ways we cannot understand." Or "God will lead her back to us."

As was to be expected, the parents' conflicting attitudes soon came to a head. He remembered the breaking point well, for it happened on the eve before Radnor Hunt was to convene on the property, several months after Miss Claire had seemingly dropped off the face of the earth. A formal brunch had been planned at the house following the hunt over the grounds and the adjacent properties. The Hunt was a social affair of such magnitude and stature that only a few, select members of the Hunt were offered the privilege of hosting the event. But Mr. Waterman, citing despondency over his daughter, canceled both the Hunt and brunch a few days prior to the date they were to be held. And did so without the knowledge or counsel of his wife. To say Mrs. Waterman had been livid at his decision would be an understatement. And it was at that point that a deep and irreparable chasm formed between husband and wife.

When Mr. Waterman subsequently succumbed to an aneurism brought on by his constant and ever heightening state of worry over the welfare of his daughter—so was the doctor's opinion—Mrs. Waterman received his death in what the staff deemed a state of aloof casualness. But the negative opinion held by the staff—as well as friends and business associates—toward Mrs. Waterman soon came to a halt when the lady of the house suffered a stroke, the severity of which depended upon whom one spoke to. But the absence of Mr. Waterman from social and business circles closed a door on what was once a prestigious and glamorous lifestyle.

Although Mrs. Waterman was too prideful to publicly show the hurt she felt from being snubbed by her husband's former friends and associates, she began to shun all social functions from that time on, no matter how small and insignificant the gathering. This new behavior—coupled with her growing reclusiveness—indicated clearly that her time as part of Main Line society had come to an end. In a matter of months, almost all of the people Mr. Locket had once welcomed to the estate as frequent guests had ceased coming to the house altogether. A few months later, Mrs. Waterman issued her first orders for the estate to begin downsizing. Mr. Locket had been shocked that so many loyal employees were let go with barely a nod of gratitude for their years of service. Now—three years after Mr. Waterman's death—just Mr. Locket; Mrs. Cavanaugh; and Mr. Lopez, the gardener, remained from those who had served the Waterman family for decades.

Supported by a few part-time employees who kept the grounds looking halfway respectable, the estate had turned into a reflection of the woman who owned it: isolated and stark.

And then a phone call from someone named Adiam had come out of the blue. Miss Claire had been flown back from Africa under mysterious circumstances, accompanied by some second-rate newspaperman Mr. Locket had taken an immediate dislike to.

Dirk. What did he mean, I just signed her death warrant?

Mr. Locket bit into a chip and pondered the implications.

I have nothing to do with Miss Claire's care. She is Madam's daughter. And why in God's name would she want to do her own child harm?

Out of habit, he reached for a shaker of malt vinegar but found his hand clamping air.

"We do not put vinegar on our fries, Mr. Locket."

Mr. Locket chuckled as he remembered the afternoon Claire had made the comment. Her face scrunched up as if she had just placed something sour in her mouth. "You might try dipping them in ketchup, instead." And then she had gone so far as to grab a bottle of Heinz from the refrigerator and hold it out to him as if she was displaying it for a commercial.

And an old Irish sod like me doesn't use that foul American concoction on chips, he remembered thinking at the time. Taking another bite of his fry, as Miss Claire would call it, he stared into his mound of peas and lost himself in thought.

*Miss Claire did look awful. What are they doing to her in that place? And that deep cut on her wrist—it was infected, wasn't it? And why was that nurse so dismissive when I pointed out the injury? And those marks on her body—*he shook his head—*Mr. Waterman would be aghast.*

Mr. Locket took a bite of his burger. He was mulling over Dirk's accusation when the household intercom box to the right of the calendar crackled.

"Mr. Locket, if you can hear me."

Mr. Locket naturally assumed Mr. Lopez was using the intercom to inform him that he was leaving for the day. He was perplexed, however, when the master gardener's voice relayed the following: "A car just passed through the security gates. I didn't buzz it through. Since you didn't alert me to any expected visitors, I thought I would let you know in case the system has malfunctioned."

Mr. Locket stared at the speaker as it crackled and went silent. He immediately rose from his stool and headed across the expansive kitchen toward the long hallway that connected the rooms on the first floor on the right side of the house to the entrance foyer. He was just passing under the kitchen arch when he heard the front door open. He quickened his pace toward the entrance hall.

"Come in," he heard Mrs. Waterman say.

Mr. Locket was nearly at the end of the hallway when he glimpsed a very large person stepping into the foyer.

"Through those doors into the study," Mrs. Waterman said.

"I apologize to Madam for not hearing the door," Mr. Locket called out as he approached the foyer.

Mrs. Waterman raised a hand as if ordering him to stop.

"That's quite all right, Mr. Locket."

He came to an abrupt halt when she shot him what he considered a hostile look.

"I won't require your services. You may retire to your quarters."

Somewhat dumbfounded by Mrs. Waterman's stern tone of voice, he gave the woman of the house a questioning glance before shifting his attention to the very large man who was in the process of pulling open the study door. He noted the individual's massive physique before his eyes were drawn to the tattoo of a dragon's head peeking out above the man's T-shirt on the back of his neck.

"If there is anything Madam might need," he offered.

Mrs. Waterman showed no hint she'd heard Mr. Locket's overture as she followed the giant of a man into the study and closed the door behind her.

1 2

THERE WILL COME a time when you will question whether you were ever here. You will place your tongue to the earth in an effort to taste soil, but you will not find the essence where you think it should be. Salt from your sweat will irritate your wounds and sting your eyes. You will find no peace in your thoughts or solace in your anger. Time will be neither friend nor foe but remain true unto itself—a measure to be gauged from different perspectives. Your self-pity will either worsen or find salvation in the words you take to heart, not those you offer.

Where does the lion walk when a thorn is lodged in his side? What form of shade best offers refuge while he tends his wound? Where does his spirit rest when it is tattered and weary? When will starlight, once more, shine upon the lion's face?

*

"Cause Jame Ain't said so. And when Jame Ain't say you ain't gonna do somethin', motherfucker, then you ain't gonna do it, ya hear?"

Jame Ain't pursed his big lips and ran long, bony fingers across one side of his acne-pocked face. He waved the handgun he was holding in front of the woman sitting across from him, but he kept his eyes focused on the man standing behind her.

"That how I got my name." He winked at the man before lowering the gun so the barrel pointed to the woman's crotch. "You ain't got permission

from Jame to do somethin', then you ain't got permission, dig?" He chuckled and then set his expression to deadly serious.

"So, when I says to you, 'Pablo, brother, you ain't got permission to
sell this bitch and the product you been peddlin' on the street no more,'
then you ain't gonna do it, right?"

Pablo—slight of build with light brown skin, dressed in a shiny red
shirt and white pants, eyed Jame Ain't with contempt. The woman—a girl,
really, judging from the youthful look of her heavily made-up face—was
also brown skinned with long, dark hair. She wore a white halter top and
a pair of red micro-shorts that fit so tight the outline of her vulva was evi-
dent. Jame Ain't thought the two looked like a pair of contestants right
off the set of *Dance Fever*. Under different circumstances, he might have
laughed and asked the two to show him some of their dance moves. But
as this was a business meeting, he wouldn't allow himself to show any hint
of weakness.

"Since when you own the street, motherfucker?" Pablo asked, his
words heavily accented. "I been working that corner for a year or more."
He nodded to the three men slumped against the wall behind him before
adding, "I told your boys that when they got in my face last week. That
corner belong to the Ñetas, negro, or maybe you need some of the *guerreros* to come down here and remind you."

"Oh, you think we negotiatin'?" Jame Ain't sat up straight in his
wooden chair. "And did you just call me a motherfucker?" He looked
past Pablo to the three men leaning against the wall. "Did he just call
me motherfucker?"

Before any of the three had a chance to answer, Jame Ain't fired his gun
into the woman's crotch. The girl fell off her chair and began to scream. As
blood from her wound began to pool around her waist, Jame Ain't stood
up and fired a bullet into her head.

"Hate fuckin' women who scream. Don't you, Pablo?" Using the barrel
of the gun, Jame Ain't motioned for the three men to approach. "Drag
this señorita over to the window and throw her ass down into the street,"
he instructed.

The three men looked at each other before taking a few tentative steps
toward the girl's body.

"But, Jame, man," the smallest of the three men said, "it's still daylight. Everybody gonna see."

"Damn right everybody gonna see, Jacko." Jame Ain't took a step closer to Pablo. "Ain't that right, Pablo? Everybody gonna see? Gonna see Jame Ain't mean business. Gonna see Jame Ain't ain't playin'. Gonna see Jame Ain't one bad motherfuckin' hombre. Ain't that right, Pablo?"

Pablo looked at Jame Ain't and then looked at the dead girl lying on the floor.

"Why you do that, man?" he asked in disbelief. "She weren't nothin'." He shook his head. "Just a trixie and a part-time mule. She didn't know nothin'."

Again, Jame Ain't motioned with the gun for the three men to pick the woman up off the floor.

"Should've thought of that before you bad-mouthed me, Rican." Jame Ain't turned his back on Pablo and sat down in his chair. "Next time Jame Ain't say somethin' to you, you gonna listen, right?"

"You in deep shit, bro," Pablo told him. "The *guerreros* gonna come down on you somethin' hard."

"That right, Pablo?" Jame Ain't said. And then he shot Pablo in the shoulder.

"Throw 'em both out the window!" he yelled to the three men huddled around the dead girl. "And hey, Pablo!" he yelled. "If you survive the fall, you can tell your amigos that everything runs through Jame Ain't now, ya hear? The turf consolidatin'."

Jame Ain't pointed the gun at Jacko.

"Get this shit out my office." Winking at Jacko, he added, "Ladies first."

Jame Ain't watched impassively as the three men dragged the woman's body over to one of the windows that lined the third floor of the old brick warehouse where he'd taken up temporary residence. He was staring at the blood on the floor when he heard the window slide open.

"You sure, boss?" he heard Jacko ask.

With a curt movement of the gun, he gave Jacko the signal to go ahead. A few grunts and the sound of shuffling feet prompted him to look over toward the wall. Pablo, he saw, was putting up resistance to being thrown off the third floor.

"Hey, Pablo!" he yelled.

Pablo, Jacko, and the other two men stopped scuffling and looked over at Jame Ain't.

"You either fly or die, motherfucker." Jame Ain't pointed the handgun at Pablo's head. "Your choice."

"*Pedazo de mierda! Chupame el pito!*" Pablo yelled.

Jame Ain't cupped his gun hand in his left. Eying Pablo's head down the barrel of the gun, he counted, "One. Two—"

Before he could count to three, Pablo pushed away from Jacko and jumped out the window. Jame Ain't kept his face expressionless until he heard a muffled thump—which he assumed was Pablo hitting the ground—followed by a whimpering squeal.

"Guess the motherfucker survived," he said with a laugh. "Message delivered to the Ñetas." Sticking the gun in the waist of his black jeans, he stood. "Time to move on, brothers. Need to convey our intentions to the FPs and the Bloods now. Let's move."

As Jame Ain't headed across the expansive room toward the metal door at the north end of the cavernous enclosure, Jacko hurried to his side.

"Gonna be a turf war, boss," he said in a tentative voice. "We gonna need more numbers or we gonna be—"

"Got it covered, my brother," Jame Ain't assured him without breaking stride. "Got it covered."

*

Tanya woke in a cold sweat to the sensation of a million ants crawling over her body. Muddle-brained and frightened, she rubbed her bare arms as she stared blankly at her surroundings. A beam of neon-blue light flashed through the slats of the venetian blinds and then flickered off. Open mouthed, she waited for the light to return. When it did, she blinked her eyes and inspected the room.

The pair of red Converse sneakers lying on the floor by the side of the mattress she recognized as hers. Same was true for the pair of Gloria Vanderbilt jeans and the bright red Nike T-shirt folded next to the sneakers. When she noticed a lacy bra crumpled on the rug, she reflexively lifted her right hand to her chest. A quick glance toward her midriff brought a sigh of relief; she was still wearing underwear.

Suddenly besieged by another bout of what felt like a multitude of ants crawling over her skin, she abruptly stood and frantically wiped the invisible, imagined pests off every part of her body. As she shook her hands out, a different beam of neon-blue light caught her attention. She followed the shaft to the corner of the room and was unnerved when it revealed a rather odd-looking shape.

"What the fuck?" she muttered.

Tanya rubbed her eyes, thinking she was going crazy. To her utter disbelief, when she refocused and looked closer, the floppy-eared, long-nosed, pink-eyed animal she was hallucinating was still there.

"Jesus. Goddamn," she whispered as she took a frightened step back.

With the step back came a new vantage point. That's when she noticed a bulging lump beneath the blanket atop the mattress.

"Gerard," she hissed. "Gerard, wake up." Tentatively, she shifted her attention to the corner of the room. "Somethin' fucked-up with the shit we did." She stared at the pink-eyed animal, not quite certain what she was seeing. "Fuckin' giant long-nosed mouse or a rat or somethin' sittin' in the corner of the room." She took a step toward the door when the creature with the large floppy ears started to move.

"Gerard." She gave the mattress a kick with the side of her foot. "Gerard. Gerard, wake the fuck up."

Tanya did her best to quiet her misgiving by telling herself that she was probably still high and in the midst of a coke/hash/pot hallucination. So, when the creature stepped into a beam of neon-blue light and begin to glide toward the window, she breathed a sigh of relief.

Thank god I didn't wake Gerard, she thought as she watched the beast float out of the room through a crack in the blinds. *Fuckin' would have slapped me silly for wakin' him.*

Although somewhat relieved by the departure of the hallucination, she couldn't help but feel a bit curious as to where the dream-beast had gone. Before she realized she had moved, she found herself standing at the edge of the window and easing back the blinds.

The glare from the nearby liquor store's sign bathed everything below her in a shade of electric blue. The cracks in the asphalt two stories below, the storefronts, the cars parked along the street, even the air between the buildings seemed imbued with the color. The glaring blue light also shone on another object.

To her utter amazement, her hallucination was floating in a stream of neon blue about ten yards above the ground. Just as she was about to wake Gerard to come see the strange manifestation, the neon sign flickered and then went out altogether. Without the neon light, Tanya lost sight of the illusionary creature. She pushed aside the venetian blinds and pressed her face against the glass. As she waited for the neon sign to come back on, she searched every part of the street for the ethereal entity, but to no avail. She breathed a frustrated sigh and eyed the neon sign with annoyance.

"Why you stop workin'?" she complained.

Suddenly feeling the chill of standing next to a window in the nude, she was about to turn and crawl into bed next to Gerard when a car pulled into view. Curious, she kept her vigil and watched the car come to a stop a few spaces from the boarding house entrance. Three people exited the car. All were hunched low to the ground and looking around.

"Skinny," she mumbled, when one of figures straightened.

Not hard to pick that stupid fuck out of a group, she thought, *what with his big square head attached to a skinny-ass body with a bump between his shoulders like he has a football taped to his back. What the hell he doin' here?*

While she ran through some of the reasons Skinny might show up at Gerard's in the middle of the night—drug drop, place to crash, a meeting she didn't know about and Gerard obviously forgot—she saw him look up and point a finger at Gerard's building. Reflexively, she stepped away from the window, holding the blind so it wouldn't jiggle.

"Gerard!" she called out in harsh whisper. With a glance toward the bed, she raised her voice and said, "Gerard! Why Skinny here?"

Slowly spreading the blind slats with her fingers, Tanya put her eye to the crack and peeked outside. Skinny and the two people he was with were nowhere to be seen. With an uneasy feeling growing in the pit of her stomach, Tanya stepped away from the window and sat down on the edge of the mattress. She shook Gerard's ankle while she picked up her bra.

"Gerard, wake the fuck up!"

She shook Gerard's leg again and put on her bra.

"Gerard!" She grabbed her T-shirt and pulled it over her head. With a smack to Gerard's ass, she yelled, "Wake up!"

"Jesus fuck, woman!" he snarled. "What the hell's the matter'?"

"Get up!" She grabbed her jeans and bolted from the mattress. "Fuckin' Skinny here—and he got people with him."

She almost lost her balance sticking a leg into her jeans, but managed to stay upright. She slid her other foot through her pants leg, then plopped down on the mattress and shimmied the designer denims up past her hips.

"What you doin'?" she asked when Gerard rolled out the opposite side of the bed and stuck his hand under the mattress.

She hurriedly slipped on her tennis shoes and was lacing one up when Gerard abruptly stood. He was holding a gun.

"What you do now?"

"Stop accusin' me of shit and shut the fuck up, would ya?"

Tanya felt her body stiffen when Gerard eased the Glock's slide-bar back. As he motioned with his free hand for her to move to the wall on the other side of the doorway, she heard footsteps on the set of stairs connecting the first and second floors.

"What they—?"

"Shh," he hissed. And then he reached up and yanked the chain he was wearing from his neck. "Hide this in your bra or panties," he told her.

Tanya shot Gerard a questioning look but caught the flash of gold he tossed at her—the little brass PO box key Gerard had taken from Jim and Rochelle's apartment.

Then it hit her. Fuckin' Gerard must have run his big mouth off about the money they'd collected from the post office little Marcus had taken them to just before social services had finally claimed him.

"You, stupid motherfucker," she whispered.

Gerard angrily motioned for her to shut up. Tanya took a defiant step toward him but heard mumbling outside the door. She stuffed the necklace down into her underwear just as the door burst open and pinned her against the wall.

The first gunshot sent an icy chill through her body. The second goaded her to action. Putting her shoulder to the door, Tanya threw the weight of her body into it. When she felt it slam into something, she yanked the door back and then violently pushed it outward. When a third gunshot boomed within the confines of the small room, Tanya didn't hesitate. She yanked the door back, rounded the edge, bunched her body into a crouch, and bulled her way through the person blocking the doorway. She'd reached the stairway landing when a fourth gunshot rang out. Caught off guard, her arm suddenly throbbing with pain, she lost her balance and tumbled down the stairs.

*

Streets, buildings, the cemetery, car headlights—fear turned everything Tanya was seeing, hearing, and sensing into a disjointed haze of sound, color, texture, and emotion. How she had made it across town without being caught by Skinny and his Bloods pals, she didn't know. Maybe her luck was turning. Maybe she could get into her dad's apartment and clean up the gunshot wound on her arm before he got home. If she was really lucky, her dad would be so tired from his shift at the base he'd go straight to bed and wouldn't check in on her like he did most mornings. Then her thoughts strayed to Gerard. The sound of gunshots in his room was still fresh. Skinny hadn't shown up at Gerard's place to play. He wanted something.

Damn Gerard and his big mouth.

She could feel the key necklace in her underwear. Skinny had come for *it*.

Beleaguered and exhausted, she raced past the little kid sitting on the top step of her dad's stoop and threw herself at the front door. She pushed and pulled at the knob several times before it dawned on her that the door was locked.

"Shit, mother fuck," she muttered. She pounded on the door and yelled, "Let me in! Let me in!"

Then she remembered; her hand flew down to her front pocket. With sweat breaking out on her forehead, she crammed her fingertips into the pocket and felt her copy of the house key.

"What's the rush, T?"

She nearly fainted.

"Skinny." She turned to face him, her eyes frantically searching for a way to escape. "Don't hurt me," she pleaded.

Skinny said nothing.

"Where's Gerard?" she asked as a wave of panic spread through her.

Skinny shifted his eyes to the ground and smirked. "He where you gonna be, you don't give up the key."

"Key?"

Skinny reached into the right pocket of his Oakland Raiders jacket and pulled out a snub-nosed handgun.

"I thought you was smarter than that dumb nigger you bangin'." Skinny scratched the tip of his nose with the barrel of the gun. "*Was* bangin'," he added. He aimed the gun at Tanya's chest. "Thought maybe you wanna stay out of shit ain't none of your concern. But no matter," he remarked as he shifted his aim to her leg. "Boys pullin' up now." He motioned with a quick tilt of his head to a car slowing to a stop in the middle of the street. "We finish this somewhere—"

Tanya shouted "No!" as the boy she'd passed on the stoop grabbed the sleeve of Skinny's jacket. In a state of shock, she dazedly watched Skinny bash the flat side of the handgun down across the boy's head. The boy instantly crumpled to his knees and rolled down the steps.

"Hey!"

Tanya's head turned toward the sound of a familiar voice.

"What the hell is going on?"

"Jesus Christ. Dad."

No sooner had she said "Dad" than Skinny jumped down next to the boy and aimed the gun at her father. She barely had time to realize her dad was pulling his own weapon—he always kept it in a holster snapped to the back of his pants—when she heard the loud clap of Skinny's weapon. She put her hands to her ears and screamed when Skinny fired off three more rounds in quick succession. When she saw her dad fall face forward onto the cement, Tanya dropped to her knees and wailed. With her mind slipping into a state of surreal confusion, she saw Skinny grab the boy by the back of the neck and put the gun to the child's head.

"You want he should die too?" he yelled at Tanya.

Skinny swung the gun and aimed it at her face. The sound of a gunshot sent a violent jolt down her spine. Then she heard Skinny scream.

*

With a contented sigh, Reverend Rue Thompson patted his portly stomach and gave a cursory north-to-south review of the Toyota Logistics pier before shifting his attention to the waters of Newark Bay. Drawn to the reflection of the Bayonne skyline glittering on the choppy surface of the Upper North Reach, he couldn't help but equate the wavering lights to the flickering flames of a fire. Rue's thoughts turned to the inferno that had engulfed his warehouse and to the pimply-faced son of a bitch who'd set the blaze. Even thinking about the man and what the asshole had cost him made Rue snort with displeasure.

Punk-ass-motherfucker, he thought. *Uppity, pretentious, self-serving piece of…*

"Settle down," he murmured out loud. Rue ran his hands back across his temples, smoothing his hair down. "Payback time is coming."

Jame Ain't. He pictured the man's ugly face. *Lame Ain't would be a better name for the little thug.* Rue grunted. *To those who wait come the spoils*—he chuckled—*or something along those lines.*

Looking south and upward, Rue spotted a pair of red and blue lights heading toward his location. Guessing it was the helicopter he was expecting, he glanced over his shoulder and gave a thumbs-up signal to the Town Car that had delivered him to the pier. For a fleeting moment, he wondered what the man silhouetted behind the wheel—a twenty-year-old intern from Rutgers named Jamal, whom Rue had taken on to help with the menial tasks of running the day-to-day operations of an assemblyman's office—must be thinking. He doubted the young man had ever expected to act as chauffeur, but Rue thought it would do the college student some good to see what long hours a servant of the people put in to make government run. After all, there was a crime epidemic sweeping through the streets of Newark—as Rue had been quoted as saying many times in the press—and he was about to show the young man just what kind of perseverance it took to do something about it. At least, that's the story Rue had told the kid.

Rue felt a peculiar mixture of anticipation and detachment as he watched the silver and blue police helicopter touch down on the tarmac. Although familiar with the passenger the aircraft was delivering—an ATF agent Rue had helped rise up through the ranks of Newark law enforcement by supplying the man with timely bits of information about his drug competitors—Rue was a bit apprehensive about seeing him again. Rue was looking forward to the day when he would no longer have to be an active participant in what he now viewed as a sordid side of society.

Fulfilling his duties as an assemblyman in the statehouse in Trenton for the past year and few months had given him a new sense of purpose. No longer did he wish to be a drug kingpin and live in a world of violence. There was a bigger game to play, he'd come to understand. One that garnered respect, prestige, and a good deal of money—if one knew how to work the system. And Rue knew how to work the system. Having decided he wanted to move up the ladder of his new profession, Rue had set his sights on a seat in the U.S. House of Representatives. As his felony conviction for bribery had long been forgotten by his constituents, all that was left for him to do to win a seat in Congress was detach himself from the Brotherhood and all the illicit business dealings the group had their fingers in.

But he was getting ahead of himself. First things first. There was unfinished business to take care of. And one unfinished piece of business was dealing with the pimply-faced punk who'd made the mistake of fucking with him. Jame Ain't needed to be taught an unforgiving lesson. It was payback time.

The ATF field supervisor Rue was about to meet with was named Mallard Crenshaw. When Rue had first met the man, he was a common beat cop working the dock district. That was over five years ago, by Rue's recollection, before all the shit had gone down with Menelik Arbagna and the stupid public defender who got himself shot on stage at the debate Yutanda Taylor had organized in front of city hall.

Rue had recognized a weakness in Mallard Crenshaw as soon as he'd met the man. Afflicted with what Rue called black chip syndrome, Mallard, like too many brothers and sisters, carried a sense of persecution on his shoulders. He bore a heavy feeling of racial woe, like slave chains, that preyed upon every facet of his daily life. So it had been rather easy for Rue to sway Mallard with talk of the Lord and the Good Book while enlightening him, so to speak, on the ways the Brotherhood was sticking it to the white oppressors by funneling drugs into whitey's safe, elitist, milk-pure world.

And Mallard Crenshaw had eaten Rue's self-promoting, pompous racial sermons up like a Sunday dinner of fried chicken with a heaping mound of mashed potatoes and gravy. The man couldn't seem to get enough of the racial inequality stuff. And Rue made sure the beat cop had plenty to chew on, believing he was empowering the black race by helping the Brotherhood keep hold of their turf at the port and on the streets of Newark while keeping the other gangs in check.

The tipoffs officer Crenshaw had provided about surprise drug raids and spot customs inspections had been well worth the percentage of profits they had cost the Brotherhood. Prostitutes, cash, drugs—and a monthly take from the bar down on the waterfront—had saved the organization hundreds of millions of dollars. Ironically, Crenshaw had reaped rewards from the police department Rue hadn't envisioned.

Because of the gang arrests Crenshaw spearheaded, he'd attained the rank of sergeant by his second year on the waterfront beat. And then, in year three, he applied to and was accepted into the ATF, where by year five—this year—the man had been promoted to field supervisor of the entire Newark ATF district. And while it was true the busts Mallard had initiated and planned were not big enough to put any of the organizations on the docks out of business, the headlines and television coverage of some of the more flamboyant operations had certainly gone a long way toward furthering his career. Not bad for a brother who'd barely made it through Delaware State University with a degree in journalism, Rue had often told the man.

Yes, Rue acknowledged with a nod of his head, *Mallard Crenshaw had done himself good. And who was to thank for the man's success? Why, the Reverend Rue Thompson, of course.*

"Reverend!"

Mallard Crenshaw—six-foot-two, two hundred and twenty pounds, dressed in black slacks and a black flak jacket—extended his hand and shook Rue's firmly. "Always good to see you."

"Mallard," Rue replied, giving the man's fingers a squeeze as he broke their handshake. "Good of you to meet with me."

Mallard looked over Rue's shoulder toward the bridge that carried Interstate 78 over Newark Bay into Bayonne. The man's age-lined eyes shifted left—to where the Town Car was parked—before settling back on Rue.

"Why the remote nighttime meet, Reverend? Haven't heard from you in quite a while. Thought you'd retired."

"Just a college kid trading time for experience," Rue replied with a nod to the Town Car. "And this conversation isn't one for a phone. If all goes the way it should, you might never hear from me again." Rue gave the man a little smile. "Least not in an unofficial capacity, if you follow."

Mallard's eyes became predatory, their initial warmth disappearing in an instant. Rue felt a little shiver run down his spine.

"What do you have?" Mallard asked in a serious tone of voice. "Something big?" His eyes scanned left to right in a calculated manner, as if he was meticulously searching a quadrant of terrain.

"Big enough." Rue replied. "Turf war interest you?"

Rue saw the man's eyebrows furrow and the corners of his lips turn down.

"Turf war—*puh*—get one of those once a week. Ain't no biggie."

"Ain't," Rue repeated with disgust. "You know the punk?"

"What are you talking about?" Mallard reached into the front pocket of his flak jacket and pulled out a soft pack of Marlboro Reds. "You're not making very much sense." He took a cigarette from the pack and put it to his lips. "Ain't cheap flying one of those around, you know." He nodded back over his shoulder toward the helicopter.

After placing the pack of smokes back in his jacket, Mallard rummaged through his pants pocket for a lighter, put flame to tobacco, and drew deeply. The breeze blowing off the water blew some of the cinders from the cigarette's tip in the direction of Rue's Town Car.

"So, tell me why a beef between a couple of gangs should interest the ATF."

Rue took a step back as Mallard exhaled a stream of smoke. Out of habit, he reached for the big gold cross that normally would have been lying atop his rotund stomach. But he'd shed the large gold chain and the cross it bore a few weeks back. All of his gaudy rings and bracelets were gone too. The decision to rid himself of all his jewelry was calculated; a prospective member of the U.S. House of Representatives didn't wear such baubles.

"Not a *couple*, Mallard." Rue rubbed one hand over the other. "All of them. That big enough to interest the ATF?"

"All of them?" Mallard asked disbelievingly. "I don't understand. Why would all of them be in each other's face at the same time?"

"'Cause some pimply-faced punk is making a play for the whole territory. He's trying to force consolidation. Apparently, he doesn't give a shit about the consequences."

Mallard took another deep draw on his cigarette and looked out across the bay.

"That could cause some shit to fly," he commented as he exhaled another stream of smoke. "Could mean a lot of dead bodies."

"Doesn't have to go down that way. Prevent the whole thing from happening if you take out the little thug."

Mallard took a short drag on his cigarette before flicking the unsmoked portion to the ground.

"Got a name?"

"Yeah—if you want to call it that. Goes by the handle Jame Ain't." Rue grunted. "Runs his operation from the east side of Ironbound, near as I can gather."

"When's all this taking place?"

"Soon," Rue told him. Stepping over to the man, Rue put his arm around Mallard Crenshaw's shoulder and said, "Let me tell you what I know."

*

Rue watched the running lights of the helicopter dwindle within the dome of yellow glare that perpetually hugged the nighttime sky above Jersey City and Manhattan some distance beyond. His attention shifted from the

Jersey City skyline to the bridge looming above him. Like the steel archway of the structure, Rue's plan to take down Jame Ain't while averting a full-fledged gang war was based on a strong foundation. The four cornerstones of his plan were greed, revenge, misplaced honor, and above all else, macho bravado. If all went as planned, not only would Jame Ain't never see the light of day again, but the headline-grabbing drug bust would go a long way toward furthering Mallard Crenshaw's career—all the while shining a glowing light on the part Assemblyman Rue Thompson had played in eradicating crime from the streets of his district.

The first gunshot scared the living shit out of Rue; it came without a telltale boom, arriving as a burst of sparks on the asphalt three feet from where he stood. As he looked to the Town Car and frantically motioned for Jamal to drive the vehicle toward him, two more shots blew chunks of asphalt up into his face. Compelled to flee, he made a break toward the bay, screaming over his shoulder for the car.

"Bring the car! Bring the car!"

But the car didn't move.

Five more bullets hit the asphalt in sequence behind him, each one hitting a little closer than the previous, all of them driving him forward. If the two huge Toyota parking lots that composed the eastern half of the pier had been filled with cars—as they were 70 percent of the year—Rue could have changed direction and headed for the cover of a thousand parked vehicles. But the north lot was nearly empty, so Rue headed toward the perimeter fence in the hope that he could find an unlocked gate and hide in the narrow stretch of wooded marshland that served as a buffer between the bay and the pier.

Rue took it as a sign of good fortune when he spotted a wide gash in the link fence as a new flurry of bullets pinged off the asphalt around him. He'd pushed through and reached the first few feet of grassy buffer when two more bullets hit the ground by his feet. He dove into the dense foliage and lay perfectly still. But it was as though his assailant had a video camera mounted in the bushes somewhere. No sooner had Rue put his head to the ground than a bullet nearly took his nose off. Rue rolled away from the impact point and slithered back toward the water. Panting, his face lathered with perspiration, he stopped. Once again, he lay perfectly still.

Splat splat splat—the next three bullets hit in a semi-circle near his head, sending him scurrying backward. Then all at once he was tumbling down a steep embankment until he hit the water with a loud splash. The water's icy current enveloped his body.

Rue had never learned how to swim, and the thought of drowning threatened to paralyze him. Heart racing, he flailed his arms and kicked his legs while desperately gasping for air.

"Help!" he shouted.

When his head dipped beneath the surface and water rushed down his throat, he flapped his arms and thrust his legs up and down until, to his great relief, his mouth broke the surface. Disoriented, choking and gasping, he stared wide-eyed into a powerful beam of light. Just as he felt himself slipping back under the water, something splashed next to him. He glimpsed a length of rope sliding past. Immediately, he thrust out a hand and grasped it.

Rue clamped his fingers around the coarse rope and clung to it with all of his strength. With a massive thrust of his legs, he launched his body forward and wrapped the rope around his forearm. Feeling somewhat secure, he shifted his attention upward and called out.

"I've got it! I've got it! Pull me up!"

The rope tightened around his forearm, and his body began moving toward the bank. Afraid of being pulled under, Rue probed the bottom with his feet. Able to keep himself from falling by pulling on the rope while he pushed off the rocky bottom, Rue made it to shore. Exhausted, he flopped face first onto the dirt embankment, wanting nothing more than to lie still for a few minutes and catch his breath. But the person or persons at the other end of the rope kept pulling. The upward jerks upon the rope were so strong he felt the fibers cutting into his flesh.

"Hold up!" he cried.

But the rope kept exerting pressure. From the light of the powerful flashlight, he could see blood oozing from several areas on his arm and hand.

"Goddamn it! You're hurting me!" he shouted.

"Hurry!" a gruff male voice shouted down to him.

Spurred on by the thought that the shooter might still be in the area with a scope trained on him, Rue scrambled up the bank as quickly as he could, huffing and puffing. Behind the glare of the powerful flashlight, he could make out the outline of a very large person.

"Goliath?"

A massive hand grabbed Rue under his arm and lifted him up to level ground.

"Goliath!" Rue gushed. "How?" Rue loosened the rope wrapped around his arm, and then bent and placed his hands on his knees. Out of breath, he asked, "How did you—? Did you see—?" Rue straightened and looked into Goliath's eyes. "What the hell's going on?"

Reflexively, Rue tried to move away and duck his head when he saw Goliath's fist moving toward his face. He'd managed to take a single step back when Goliath's hand clamped around the back of his head and jerked it forward. Rue glimpsed a metallic flash before a searing pain blinded him in one eye and then the other. He managed a garbled, "Why?" before a flurry of brutal blows slashed his windpipe to shreds. An instant later, Reverend Rue Thompson tumbled back toward Newark bay. He was dead before he hit the water.

13

"SOMETIMES I CAN see no further than now. And now brings me no closer to what I can see."

Within the walls of a narrow alley, far from the bustling docks of Djibouti and the tranquil waters of the Gulf of Aden, the muted cry of a seabird sounded out of place.

"I watch for him. Every day I wake and feel this will be the day he arrives. Yet he does not come."

A rat—pink eyed and brazen—slipped from one pile of refuse to another, barely pausing as it passed.

"And at night, at night while you whimper in your sleep, I ask that he forgive me for the hurt that I have caused. Because, you see, it must be my fault—something I have done that has brought us to this place. Here," John Too said, sweeping his arm out to encompass an alley littered with trash and reeking with urine, "everywhere I look, there is despair. We have lost our way. Do you hear, Etiyopiya? Lost our way." Looking up to the sky, he said, "The sun dims where it should be bright. The rain goes where none is needed. Crops fail where there is famine. And the moon, even she has become lifeless and cold when she once bathed the land with heavenly beauty. The day, Etiyopiya? What has happened to the day?"

John Too turned his head and studied the ragged figure huddled next to him. To see beyond the man's bandages, to look once more into the eyes of the Lion—even this small hope seemed out of reach. He could not help but think: the day had changed.

*

Sarah couldn't get the picture of Bin'ka's body out of her mind. She'd tried prayer—countless recitations of Hail Mary and Our Father—and had even tried picturing the giant man dressed as a nun, a mother superior who would beat her palms with a ruler if she entertained impure thoughts. But nothing so far had erased the image of him standing naked on the sand with his arms stretched out like the wings of an eagle ready for flight.

She was angry with herself—and disappointed. She was a failure as a nun, her ineptness ordained the day she was kidnapped and forced to suffer the filthy sex acts her captor had inflicted upon her. Then had come Dirk and the wet bodily yearnings she immediately felt when she was in the man's presence. And now Bin'ka. His big black penis swayed inside her head like a cobra dancing to a snake-charmer's flute. Sex, sex, sex. Why was God torturing her so? Had she not completed enough penance both before and during her time spent in Perpetual Commitment? Had she not begged for His forgiveness over and over and over for taking her captor's life? What more must she do? What more did the Lord want of her? What hadn't she done to show Him she had changed?

Distraught that she could not dismiss the image of nude Bin'ka from her thoughts, Sarah gouged her fingernails into her thigh until blood appeared.

"What are you doing?"

Immediately, Sarah curled her legs up toward her waist and pulled the tunic down over her knees. Barely able to meet Bin'ka's probing stare, she gave him a slight shrug.

"What witchcraft do you practice where you puncture yourself?"

"Witchcraft? You misunderstand, I was trying—" She could feel her face going flush. "There was something I was— It wasn't—" She gave him a sheepish glance and then looked to the floor. "I was trying—" She could sense his eyes upon her. She placed her hand to her stomach and bunched some of the tunic in her hand.

"Trying?" he prodded.

She looked up and met his gaze. She reluctantly answered, "To rid myself of sin."

She searched his eyes and waited for his reaction. When he burst out laughing, she felt as though she'd been punched in the stomach.

"Well, then. I better get you to a hospital," he joked, "before you drain all the blood from your body."

"Ugh!" she said, pouting. "How can you laugh?" She held her bloody fingertips up toward his face. "I'm trying!" she cried. "I'm trying!"

"Trying to do what?" he bantered.

"To please the Lord!" she shouted. "To prove I am worthy!"

The awesome power of his strength was surreal, putting her in state of utter shock as he swept her off the floor and pinned her to a wall.

"That is nonsense," he snarled. "Who cares what God thinks?" His face was so close to hers she could feel his breath on her cheeks. "Do not say such a thing again." She whimpered as he squeezed her arms.

"Worthy," he scoffed. "Worthy of what? To get to a place that doesn't exist?" He lightly pressed her against the wall before he released his hold on her. "Don't make me…"

"What?" she angrily countered. "Don't make you talk about what you believe in, about what religion *you* follow?"

How like some great beast he is, she thought as he grunted and rolled his massive shoulders. *A big, dumb ox that only understands eating and sleeping and fornicating.* She wasn't aware she'd moved until she found herself standing right behind him as he stood staring out the window of the room he'd arranged for them to stay in until the next morning, when Adiam's plane would arrive to take them to Djibouti. *What is he hoping to find on the ocean?* she wondered. *Or is he hoping I'll just shut up?*

"Surely you believe in God," she tentatively offered. "Or Allah, if you were raised Muslim." She moved her hand as if to touch him on the shoulder but then let it fall to her side. "Some deity of lore perhaps, a god or goddess of the jungle. I—" she gently placed her fingers on the side of his arm. "Your tribe. Did they practice some sort of ancient ritual?"

She nearly tripped and fell backward when he whirled on her and bellowed, "Ancient ritual? Are you so—?" His nostrils flared, and he snorted like a bull readying to charge.

"My tribe?" he repeated, incredulous. When he bunched his hands into fists, she cowered away. "I don't know what my *tribe* practiced. I wasn't interested in what the *holy men* did after working the coffee fields from the time I woke until the time I fell asleep. Their practice of burning grubs in a fire and reading what the smoke trail told them didn't mean much to those of us who were used as pack mules."

"I didn't mean to make you angry," she told him. "I simply meant to say that you must believe in—"

"Some made-up entity that has nothing in common with the people he demands worship from?" he retorted. "Is that what you meant?"

"God does not demand—"

"Don't be stupid!" he yelled. "Of course he demands! They all demand! Just look at what you were doing when I walked into the room."

"That's different," she argued. "That had nothing to do with Him."

"The hell it didn't. You said you were trying to rid yourself of sin, didn't you? Who put it in your mind that you'd committed some sort of sin?" She gasped when he grabbed her by the arms and shook her. "Who decided what your sin was? It wasn't your god," he mocked, shaking his head. "He had nothing to do with it. What a load of—"

Sarah slapped the back of Bin'ka's hands until he released his grip. Trembling, she pushed him away. She could feel tears forming in her eyes as she struggled to say, "Of course God decides what sin is."

"You fool yourself," he immediately shot back. "Gods don't write things. They don't put ink to paper and spell out warnings and taboos."

"They speak through—"

He thrust his arm toward her with his palm level with her face.

"Don't say it," he told her. "Don't talk to me of holy men. They're all the same. All cut from the same cloth as the grub-burning, smoke-reading, dribble-mouthed lout that sat in his hut all day and napped while his *flock* was out working until they couldn't see straight."

"Jesus is not a grub-burning lout!" she shouted.

Infuriated, she rushed him and struck him in the chest with her fist. Bin'ka grabbed her wrist and jerked her against him. When she tried to pull away, he grabbed her by the collar of her tunic and tilted his head down so their faces were inches apart.

"How do you know what Jesus was or what he wasn't?" he snarled. "Tell me, woman. How do you know?"

"Because He—" She looked away from him when her eyes blurred with tears. "Is the son of God," she blurted.

"A fairy tale," he scoffed. "A story written by some pretend holy man to make people believe what he wanted them to."

"How dare you blaspheme Christ!"

She was tempted to slap the back of his head when he turned away from her and walked to the window. He took a deep breath and exhaled.

"It is the same for all religions," he said in a calm voice. "You said as much yourself when you asked if my *tribe* believed in some jungle god and followed some ancient ritual that you, as an outsider, would find ridiculous."

She took a step toward him when he placed his hands on the window ledge and rested his weight against it. She felt as though she was listening to him recite something he'd been taught when he said, "Christians, Jews, Muslims, whoever, whatever—their religions are all based on stories written by men. Call them scribes or seers or prophets or holy men—whatever name you wish to crown them with. They are still men." He shrugged. "They lie and cheat and steal and kill just like any man does. Yet, what they do best, what they practice until it becomes art, is twisting words to influence people who want to believe in some entity of supreme knowledge, power, and wisdom. A simple con game played upon simple-minded people who believe their lives are guided by a higher power. And so they follow whatever fairy tale these word-twisters—these creators of psalms and commandments and holy books—invent to dictate how best they should live their lives." He grunted.

"So don't ever question whether you are worthy, or whether you have committed some *sin*," he sneered. "You have seen enough of this world," he said, turning to face her, "to know what you are and what part you play in it. Famine, drought, disease, war, rape, slavery, murder—this is the world gods and religions have given us."

Sarah felt a dull throbbing in her chest as he said, "The only sin in this world is if you do nothing to counter its despair."

Sarah bunched the sides of her tunic into her hands and tugged.

"He is—" she released the tunic and placed her left hand over the silver cross dangling from her necklace. "God is not a fable," she timidly offered. "Nor has He brought upon this world that—"

Three loud knocks at the door to their room caught Sarah and Bin'ka by surprise. Puzzled by the look of alarm on Bin'ka's face, Sarah reached out and grabbed his arm as he moved past her.

"Adiam?" she whispered.

With a terse shake of his head, he grunted, "No," and pushed her away. Before he took another step, the door burst open.

Sarah threw herself against Bin'ka and grabbed his hand as three armed, uniformed men moved quickly into the room. She could feel Bin'ka's body go tense as the men fanned out in a semi-circle in front of them.

"Is this woman married to you?" the man in the center sharply asked.

"What business is it of yours?" Bin'ka shot back.

"Directorate of Security Intelligence," the man stated. "Papers, now." he ordered with a slight upward jerk of his rifle. "Or." The man smiled.

"Or what?" Sarah innocently inquired.

"Or money," Bin'ka told her.

"But we have neither," Sarah replied, confused.

The man's smile disappeared.

"Then you are under arrest." The two men on either side of Bin'ka raised their rifles and aimed them at his chest. "You will both come with me."

*

Sarah could still feel the sting of the lash on her back as she curled her legs into her body and shivered on the floor of her cell.

"You affront Allah by committing *zina* with a man who is not your husband."

The scene was still a blur to her: a small room devoid of furnishings save for a thick wooden pole standing erect in the center of a dirt floor, a heavy steel ring protruding from the post an arm's length above her head. She had pulled on the ropes binding her wrists to the steel ring as a bearded man with a beaked nose and eyes as dark as coal studied her with what she could only interpret as contempt.

"You are infidel," he'd said.

"I am a nun," she'd blurted out. "A woman of God!"

"Heretic!" the man screamed.

And then the first lash of the whip had stung her bare back. After that, she could only recall pain. Faces, words, voices, events; they held no meaning. She'd blacked out, she presumed, and had awakened in a dark, smelly place cold, frightened, and in pain. Where was Bin'ka? What had they done to him?

I am in the bowels of the devil, she thought upon hearing an echoing scream that seemed to come from somewhere near. And as she huddled on the floor and shivered and endured stinging aftershocks of pain across her back, she became aware of other sounds: cries of agony, pleas for mercy, voices begging for food and water. As her mind raced with the implications of everything she was feeling and hearing, she nearly dismissed the sound of a door creaking on its hinges until a band of light passed across her face.

"Who's there?" she asked.

When she tried to move her head to look up, she found she'd been tethered to the floor by something encircling her neck. She groaned.

"Wait!" she cried when she heard the door creak again and the light passed back across her face.

She shivered anew and stared wide-eyed into the darkness. When something swished close to her ear, she gasped.

"As-salāmu 'alaykum," a female voice said.

The flare of a match revealed a portion of Sarah's stark surroundings: a coarse stone wall, an earthen floor, a narrow door. A brief whiff of sulfur preceded a second burst of flame, and a candle was placed on the floor a few feet in front of her face. Sarah strained against the neck restraint in an effort to look up, but she could see no more of the person than the tips of their sandaled feet protruding from the bottom of a white robe.

"Be at peace," the woman told her. The voice, Sarah noted, sounded more like that of a mature woman than that of a girl. "I come to tend your wounds."

Sarah closed her eyes and sighed.

"Why?" she whimpered. "Why was I beaten?"

"For lying with a man who is not your husband."

Sarah involuntarily jerked her head forward when she felt the touch of fingers on her neck. She relaxed when the restraint around her throat loosened.

"Can you sit up?"

A hand nudged her shoulder off the floor while another grabbed her arm and gently eased her upward.

"But I didn't," Sarah said. She felt a surge of anger churning in her stomach as she added, "Whoever accuses me of such a thing is lying."

A stinging slap to her back sent a wave of pain through her. She bent forward and gasped, then yelped when the woman grabbed her by her hair and yanked.

"I would watch what you say," the woman harshly whispered into her ear. She gave Sarah's hair another harsh tug before adding in a whisper so soft Sarah barely understood what she was saying, "They hear everything."

"I did not sleep with him," Sarah replied.

A slap to the side of her face, and the woman proclaimed in a loud voice, "The Imam decreed your sin. Be thankful he shows you mercy."

"Shows me mercy?" The flame of the candle flickered violently as Sarah exhaled and shook her head. "But I did nothing wrong!"

Again the woman slapped her open palm against Sarah's back.

"Silence!" she snarled. And then she jerked Sarah closer to her by her neck. "The Imam has extended you the mercy of Allah. One would think you would show your gratitude by quiet reflection upon your sin."

"Gratitude?"

"Reflect, *ferenji*."

Sarah fell silent as the woman applied some oily liquid to her skin. Her head drooped forward when the smell of lavender filled her nose and the sensation of warmth replaced the burning pain crisscrossing her back.

"Reflect, *ferenji*, reflect," she repeated in a soothing voice. "Allah, blessed be he, once again shows his infinite compassion by allowing you your freedom."

"Freedom?" Sarah tilted her head back and took a deep breath. "Bin'ka and I will be released?"

"I know nothing of a Bin'ka," the woman replied. "I only know you are to be made presentable by morning."

"Adiam?" Sarah said in a hopeful tone.

"I do not—"

"He runs Djibouti," Sarah interjected.

"Djibouti?" the woman questioned. "That is far from here. I do not know of this warlord."

"Oh, he's a businessman," Sarah quickly corrected.

"Businessman, warlord—they are the same, are they not? Power, money, control—both desire false treasures to be acquired by whatever means, yes?"

"I never—"

"The folly of men," the woman wryly commented. "Committing sins against the teachings of Allah in their lust for possessions that hold no meaning in the true life."

"True life?"

"Jannah," the woman quickly replied. "You cannot reach Jannah if you have committed bad deeds in your worldly life."

"Oh, you mean Heaven," Sarah said.

"Jannah," the woman corrected. "I was told you worshiped the false prophet."

"Jesus is not a false prophet," Sarah countered.

Sarah cringed when she felt the woman's fingernails rake her flesh.

"No, I mustn't," the woman said. Sarah felt a fresh application of oil at the spot where the woman had scratched her. The woman said, "I am not to judge. Besides, I am sure you will be made to see your error once you reach Somali."

"Somalia?"

The woman chuckled before saying, "*Somali*, not Somalia. Ethiopia— you are to be delivered to Somali Ethiopia."

"Ethiopia? That can't be. Bin'ka and I—"

"Phew! When was the last time you bathed?" the woman interrupted. "You smell like a donkey's— Never mind. Come." Sarah stiffened when she felt something looped around her neck. "I will tell them you need to be washed."

Sarah started to speak but found her words choked off when the woman tightened the noose against her windpipe.

*

The Karamajong warriors had arrived without warning. Brutally efficient, they showed no mercy in taking what they'd come for. Though many were armed with rifles, they'd used their long spears to herd the children working the coffee fields toward a waiting truck. Bin'ka remembered that one of the older boys who'd been given the task of guarding the water supply had stood his ground and hurled a rock at one of the Karamajong. And though the stone barely glanced the warrior's shoulder, the man had killed the youth with a quick jab of his spear. The killing was cruel and needless, but the show of force and the spilling of the boy's blood had put a quick end to whatever thoughts some of them might have entertained about escape or resistance. From that moment on, they'd behaved like a herd of docile pack animals and had been loaded and on their way to the slave market within minutes.

"I was told that you and the other children from your village were sold for one cow."

Bin'ka watched Susenyo plop a sweetmeat into his mouth and take a sip from the silver chalice that never seemed far from his hand. Bin'ka didn't respond to his master because Susenyo hadn't asked him to.

"How is it that a tribe of warriors prizes a cow above human life? An interesting quirk of human nature, don't you think?" Susenyo barely glanced at him before continuing. "And what lesson should we derive from such an equation, where the seller sees more value in one cow than the buyer sees in a dozen slaves?" Before Susenyo gave him the answer, he took a sip from the chalice.

"Shortsightedness and, perhaps, a lack of confidence, I would venture. For with the money the Karamajong could have made from selling the slaves outright—without involving a middleman—they could have purchased several cows and come out far ahead in the deal."

Susenyo motioned for Bin'ka to approach him with the tray of freshly cubed papaya he been tasked to hold. As he'd been instructed, he kept his eyes cast down toward the floor while Susenyo sampled the fruit.

"A middleman is a cost one does not need," he said while licking his fingertips. "Remember that for the future, Bin'ka, on the slight chance that one day you will be in a position to utilize my experience."

Following the instructions he'd been given on how to serve his new master, Bin'ka gave a slight bow and began to back away. Susenyo cleared his throat and added, "But your kind has proven—on a whole, mind you; there are exceptions, of course—to be dimwitted and slow to grasp the concept of supply and demand or even the basic principles of value and worth. There is a saying I've heard."

Susenyo had chuckled for several seconds before continuing, "They say the darker the skin, the smaller the brain. And by all that is holy in life, the Karamajong are some of the blackest people I have ever done business with." Again, Susenyo chuckled for what seemed to Bin'ka to be an overly long time. "Though the people of your village are a close match. One might say you're even blacker than the Karamajong."

Bin'ka recalled how empty he'd felt when Susenyo had remarked, "Born to be slaves, obviously. Must make you feel rather—" Bin'ka looked up when he heard Susenyo slurp from the chalice. "A mundane life, slavery. Better that you are indoctrinated to it at an early age, yes?"

The look Susenyo had given him at that moment had stayed with Bin'ka for many years afterward. It wasn't until the fateful day when Adiam had put a bullet in Susenyo's forehead rather than the Lion's that Susenyo's trademark attitude of superiority began to fade from his memory. Everything had changed the day Susenyo had died.

Or so Bin'ka had thought. But as the months after the man's death elapsed into a year and then into a good chunk of a second, he'd come to realize that nothing had changed. He still took orders from people who acted superior to him. The only difference was that it was no longer Susenyo giving the orders. It was Akmir and, to a lesser degree, Adiam and Talia. And he was certain the rest of the Consortium—before Akmir had them murdered—saw him as nothing more than a big, brainless mass of muscle kept around to do their dirty work. In other words, as a slave.

"Traded for a cow," Bin'ka grumbled as he rested the back of his head against the cellblock wall. "Not even a whole one, at that. Better if I'd been the one who threw the rock," he muttered, thinking back to the boy who'd been killed by the Karamajong spear. "Now look at you." He surveyed the stark cell the security forces had placed him in—earthen floor; dank-smelling stone walls; narrow, iron-barred door—and shook his head. "What would Susenyo say to you now?"

He smirked as he pictured his former master plopping a handful of nuts into his mouth and washing them down with a big gulp of wine. "He'd say, 'You're a worthless *abeed* that will never amount to anything. A big lumbering ox with a brain the size of an ant.'" Bin'ka grunted and looked around the small rectangular cell. "Who could argue?" He shook his head.

If he'd had a mirror to look into, he would have searched his eyes for some glimmer of intelligence or spark of self-esteem. But as he had no such means of reflection, he was left to muse about his past and wonder what he'd become.

Are you free?

Hearing the recurring whisper in his head, he suddenly wished he'd never gone to the old dock in Djibouti on the evening Muhammad had tried to kill him with the RPG. *The damn cat, the damn old lady, the damn sea*, he thought. *Why do they torment me so?* Why did they choose him—*him*—to place his life in peril to save a few dozen kids from slavery? And where were they now, these mystical figures, now that he was imprisoned in a cell in a country where he didn't know anyone? Was this it? Was the old woman leaving him to rot because he'd decided to help the stupid nun?

Sarah. He found himself shaking his head as she slipped into his thoughts. What the hell was she doing here? Why on earth would she agree to come to such a—? Djibouti, Ethiopia, Somalia—he couldn't imagine three countries in the world more desperate or desolate. War, famine, drought, poverty, disease, slavery... *And she's worried about being worthy of her god. What foolishness she clings to.*

"Why *did* she come?" he muttered.

He rolled his massive shoulders and yawned.

Why did she come?

He thought about what she had told him: "I was sent by Reverend Mother to find Sister Claire, to bring her back to America." *But why?* Then he remembered Talia telling him about the payment the other nun's family was making before he'd put her on the plane with Dirk. And Sarah had been traveling with Dirk. Did that mean Sarah had taken part in the plan to extort money from the nun's—Sister Lady's—family? Or was she really just the pathetic do-gooder she seemed to be? Bin'ka shook his head; he didn't know.

"Don't be fooled into believing that everything doesn't revolve around money or power, Bin'ka. Even though people may seem sincere in their motives—and quite possibly believe their own sincerity on a given day— the love of riches lies in the belly of us all, corrupting the intentions of even the purest of heart. Again," Susenyo said, holding up a finger to emphasize the point he was about to make, "there may even come a time when you do not wish to believe the worst about someone—or yourself, for that matter—but don't be blind to the true nature of man. People always want what they can't have, and the price for attaining what is out of someone's reach is invariably their soul."

Susenyo had been teetering on the brink of passing out in a drunken stupor before he'd jerked awake and given Bin'ka this piece of unsolicited advice. He'd motioned for Bin'ka to fill his chalice with more wine before adding, "Not that it will ever come to pass, but what would you give for your freedom, Bin'ka? And mind you, when I say *freedom*, you must understand what a constrained and ambiguous notion that concept is. For no one is ever really, truly free, are they, my boy?"

Bin'ka had stood and waited for Susenyo to answer his own question as his master took another long drink from the silver chalice. It wasn't until he saw Susenyo's triple chin press into the top of his chest and Susenyo began to snore that Bin'ka understood there would be no further talk on the subject of freedom or the immoral nature of man.

He'd forgotten all about Susenyo's oration on the nature of humanity until he'd heard the voice of the sea ask him if he was free as he stood on the pier in Djibouti. And when the sea had taken on the guise of an old woman and pointed across the harbor to the slave boy who resembled Bin'ka as a child, Susenyo's question had come rushing back to him: "What would you give for your freedom?" He felt as though Susenyo was taunting him from the grave when the old woman kept pestering him with the same question: *Are you free?* And how had he answered? He shook his head as he remembered; he'd described freedom to the woman in terms of money, cars, and food. *What a fool I am.*

"The Karamajong had it right all along," he mumbled.

With his head cast down toward the floor of his cell, he glimpsed a slight movement outside the bars.

"Someone there?" he inquired.

He scrutinized the area outside his cell, waiting for an answer. When none was forthcoming, he dismissed with a grunt the notion that he'd seen something. Suddenly realizing how tired he was, he rubbed his eyes and sighed. He nearly slammed the back of his head against the wall when he looked back at the base of his cell door and saw a pair of candle-flame yellow eyes peering through the bars.

"Zanzibar!" he softly exclaimed.

In the few seconds it took for Bin'ka to get up from the floor, the tattered grey cat with distinctive orange-yellow eyes disappeared. Bin'ka rushed to the door and pressed his face against the bars.

"Zanzibar!" he whispered. "Where are you?"

He looked up and down the dark hallway outside his cell, but there was no sign of the cat. Despondent—entertaining the notion that he'd fooled himself into believing the cat had really been there—he leaned his forehead against the bars and stared blankly ahead. *Damn cat, damn old hag*, he thought, *even now you torture me.*

A shadow moved within a shadow in the section of wall across from his cell. As he stared at the rough-hewn stone, a glow of light brightened and wavered across the wall's surface. Realizing the flickering glow was caused by some sort of approaching lantern or torch, he turned his head sideways. Pushing his face as close to the bars as possible, he peered in the direction from which the light originated.

A dozen or so meters down from his cell, he could just make out the juncture of two adjoining hallways. There, a person appeared within the sphere of light illuminating the intersection. Shortly after, a second person holding a candle followed. Something else, Bin'ka noticed: a length of rope running from the first person's neck into the hand of the second. The two had nearly crossed the juncture by the time Bin'ka noticed how the first person was dressed.

"Sarah!" he called out. "Sarah, is that you?"

For the briefest moment, Bin'ka thought he heard Sarah yell something in return. But when he focused and listened, he could hear nothing. A moment later, the glow from the candle dimmed, and soon after, the wall outside his cell reverted to darkness.

*

But I'm not a virgin!

Sarah had wanted to shout the proclamation and then laugh in his face. But she was afraid to, afraid to tell the man with dark eyes and a beaked nose that she'd been repeatedly raped when she was thirteen, her virginity taken without consent. She'd often wondered what it would have been like if she'd had a choice in losing her virginity. Sex, intercourse, foreplay—would she have found them enjoyable? It made her angry that she would never know. She'd wondered about a lot of things after she'd been raped, but mostly, she'd just blamed herself for…

She'd never asked anyone what it was like the first time they had sex with a boy. She'd been terrified to. Besides, people didn't want to talk with her because she was marked: dirty, a slut, a stupid piece of teenage filth. Worse, she was a killer. A murderer, some people had called her, a deranged psychopath who'd taken some perverse joy in slitting her captor's throat. *Like I had a choice in the matter!*

But she did have a choice—at least that's what one of her doctors had told her. She could have just stabbed the man in the arm or something and then run for help. She could have, she supposed. But the old fossil of a doctor who'd told her so wasn't a thirteen-year-old girl who'd been raped and sodomized and forced to suck a man's filthy penis while a knife had been pressed against her throat. Easy for some white-haired, wrinkly-skinned old man to say from a behind a desk—*you could have.* A little different when you'd endured countless acts of sexual abuse for fourteen days and nights and were beaten before and after each instance. *You could have.*

I could have done a lot of things, she'd often thought, *but I did what I did. I killed my captor.*

She hadn't known it was her nextdoor neighbor—a man her father played golf with every other Saturday when the weather was warm. Even when she'd run up the steps and out the nearest door and saw her house standing twenty feet away, she still didn't connect the proximity of her home and where she'd been held prisoner. It wouldn't be until later, when she was made to go to the morgue and identify the bloody corpse she'd left in the doorway of her closet prison, that she realized her abductor had been her neighbor, Mr. Bassett.

"Is this him?" some serious male voice had asked her. "Is this the man who—?"

She remembered looking up at the uniformed man with tears in her eyes as her body began to tremble. *"Is this the man who—?" The man who what? Raped me until I bled and then beat me for staining the floor? Is that who you mean?*

Shrieking like an angry ghost, she'd run out of the police station in a state of utter panic. *Is this him? How would I know? He wore a fucking mask over his head!*

At first—in the first few days after she'd been abducted—she'd wanted to know who had kidnapped her and why. Oh, she got the sex part. She understood that the person who'd taken her was some freak with a sex fixation. But she'd wanted to know, why her? What was she to him? Why pick her? But after she'd been beaten a few times for talking, she'd lost all interest in knowing who it was. Trying to find out who was behind the black cloth mask meant pain and punishment. It was all about survival after she'd endured the first few beatings—survival and finding a way to escape.

He'd kept her hands tied behind her back except when he made her clean the closet floor. He had a thing about cleanliness. Even though she'd been forced to relieve herself through a hole in the back of the closet where he kept her—giving the enclosed room the permanent stench of a sewer—if her excrement or urine spotted the wood planks, he'd beat her and then make her clean it up. All the while pressing a large knife into the back of her neck.

Had she thought about refusing his absurd cleaning orders and letting him kill her? Sure. But every time she felt as though she might have the nerve to dare him to take her life, the pain he inflicted changed her mind. She'd have done most anything to make the pain from his beatings stop. Cleaning up after her "mistakes," as he called them, became part of her ordeal.

"Untainted flesh demands a high price."

She was stunned when the little man with the beaked nose and dark lifeless eyes—Imam, the woman addressed him as—had made the comment. More so because she was naked and in the midst of being hosed down by the woman when he suddenly appeared in the room to ogle her. *Untainted flesh! Dear God, if you only knew!*

Her captor had kept her hands and feet tied when he spoon-fed her. For two weeks, she lived on baby food—strained peas and applesauce and some kind of foul-tasting paste that made her want to vomit. But God forbid she vomit the crap back up. Because after he beat her for making a mess, he'd make her eat what she'd puked. She thought about attacking him when he untied her hands a number of times, but her captor was a big man, and strong. The beatings, the minimal food, and the near para-lyzing fear left her without the strength or the fortitude to overpower him. No, it wasn't going to be her physical prowess that won her freedom, she'd realized. It was going to have to be something subtly cunning—an act that her captor would find pleasing—that would ultimately give her the opportunity to be free of him. She thought about what she could do for several days before she settled on the disgusting plan that eventually led to her freedom. She didn't like the plan—she didn't like it at all—but in the end it had served her well.

Yet she had never forgiven herself for what she had done. And what was worse, she didn't think God had ever forgiven her, either.

"I want to hold it."

The slap to her face for talking was instantaneous, as she knew it would be. Weathering the stinging repercussion for talking, she dared to say, "I want to fondle you while I'm sucking it."

He'd kicked her in the stomach so hard she couldn't breathe and then stepped out of the closet and slammed the door. In that moment, Sarah thought her idea was shit, that she'd read the man's desires all wrong. In short, she felt like she'd taken a beating for nothing. And then the door to the closet reopened. And he'd stepped back into the tiny room. Slowly, as she regained her ability to breathe, her captor unbuttoned his madras shorts and pulled them down to his knees. His penis was erect. She knew she had him. It was only a matter of time.

It took several sessions over the course of a few days of her servicing him before he ultimately reached behind her and untied her hands. And she wanted to die—literally die—every time she had to endure his penis thrust into her mouth. But she didn't die. Even when he grabbed her by her hair and made her swallow every last drop of jism that dribbled out of his shriveling prick, she didn't die. But her fear of him changed. Her fear of being kidnapped and abused by some masked freak changed to anger, and then that anger evolved into rage. By the time he reached behind her and untied her hands, she was ready. When the opportunity presented itself, she didn't hesitate.

"You will know the power of Allah when you give yourself to him."

Sarah tried to move away from the imam when he stepped toward her to rip the silver cross from her neck, but the woman hosing her down tightened the noose and kicked the back of her knee. Sarah was barely able to keep her balance, much less ward off the imam's hands. Now her cross was gone, her link to God broken. Maybe she was never supposed to have a link to God. Maybe she never had a chance of building one after what she'd done. *Give yourself to him*; yes, she'd given herself to him. And her captor had paid the price for it.

When she'd placed her fingertips on Mr. Bassett's testicles, she could feel his entire body stiffen. And when he began to moan, she began checking his grip on the knife at her throat. As the thrusts of his penis intensified and his moaning grew in volume, she noticed his grip on the knife handle began to loosen and his arm began to tremble. Ejaculation arrived with an audible gasp and a slight drooping of posture. It was in that moment of ecstatic weakness that his grip on the knife relaxed to the point where the handle was precariously balanced on the inner joints of his fingertips. With a final tantalizing run of her tongue along the underside of his penis, Sarah snatched the knife out his hand.

Slashing the blade upward, Sarah cut her captor's scrotum just below the shaft of his penis. And when he bent down toward her with his hands poised to grab her head, she lunged upward and rammed the point of the blade into his throat. With a gurgling shriek, he stumbled backward.

Feeling nothing but the burning fever of revenge running through her, Sarah pounced on him and plunged the blade into his neck over and over and over.

Then suddenly it was done. Her energy was spent. She was numb. Covered in her captor's blood, she threw the knife to the floor and ran past his corpse. When she saw a stairway, she ran up it without thinking. Less than a minute later she was opening the back door of her house. She remembered her mother fainting when she saw her and her father looking at her like she was some sort of devil creature come to steal his soul.

Sarah wearily rubbed her cheeks and turned away from the corner of the cell she'd been staring into. Reflexively, she reached for her necklace. When her fingertips touched skin, she leaned forward and began to sob.

Why have you forsaken me? she wanted to scream. But she didn't. She knew very well why God and Jesus and the Holy Spirit had forsaken her—she'd known since she was thirteen. When the Virgin Mary had appeared to her in a vision some months later, she'd embraced the significance of the divine appearance and understood what her course in life was to be—what it had to be. She would become a nun of the Order of the Holy Cross and devote her days to chastity, charity, prayer, and sacrifice. She would atone for her sins through the grace of the Virgin Mother.

But now the strange little man with the beak nose and dark, beady eyes—the imam—had taken her cross and was telling her she was to become the property of some man she did not know and did not want to know. It was as if she was to relive the ordeal of the closet and her kidnapper all over again. She could not let this happen. No, she would not let it happen.

*

Bin'ka concentrated on the hum of propellers as the city of Luma receded from view. Tired of thinking, wondering, and dreaming, he willingly gave in to the haven of sameness created by the constant drone of the engine. There would be time for second-guessing and what-ifs in the days ahead. Right now, losing himself in something abstract was keeping him sane.

"She's just a woman, Bin'ka—a nun at that. There was nothing Adiam or I could do." Bin'ka sighed and closed his eyes. "The price was outlandish." Bin'ka grunted and shook his head. "Besides, she was already gone by the time I arrived. They must have moved her before dawn."

"I saw the cat."

"What? What cat? What are you talking about?"

Bin'ka rested his forehead against the thick-paned window of the airplane and stared down at the passing terrain. For a brief moment, the sun caught the glass in such a way that he could see the reflection of his face. His expression mirrored the surprise he felt at mentioning the tattered grey feline to Talia.

"Zanzibar," he said in a daze. "She was there."

"You're not making any sense," Talia calmly replied. "You and Adiam must be afflicted with the same disease."

Bin'ka grunted and tried to melt his thoughts into the hum of the engines. But images—brief flashes of faces: Sarah and Zanzibar—kept popping up in his head. He couldn't seem to shake them, couldn't seem to separate one from the other. It was like they'd been bundled together, a package—which made no sense to him because he didn't think the two had ever seen each other.

"A good deal has changed since you left Djibouti."

"I imagine it has," he muttered.

"We've nearly doubled our payloads to the U.S. and Europe and expanded our supply lines into Iraq and Iran. We source triple what we used to."

What was it the old hag had said on the dock when the ship's horn sounded? "She's lost. Looking for her way home." He was sure she'd been referring to Claire.

"Don't be too impressed," Talia sarcastically commented. "Just because we've grown the business to a worldwide operation and your net worth is now a hundred times what it used to be. No need to thank us or even be appreciative of our efforts."

Bin'ka glanced to the woman sitting across from him: dark hair pulled back in a bun; fine, chiseled features; almond-shaped eyes; skin the color of honey-sand; the sensuous curves of her slender body beautifully sheathed in a sky-blue suit of what he knew to be Egyptian cotton.

"Talia," he said. And then he stared at her as if he didn't know who she was.

"You all right, Bin'ka? Did they do something to you in that place?"

"I saw her," he told her. "She was there."

Talia cleared her throat and then leaned across the aisle.

"You just sit back and relax," she said with a slight touch of her hand upon his arm. "Try to get some sleep. You look tired." He thought her expression guarded more than concerned when she added, "You'll feel better once we reach Djibouti."

Djibouti. He shivered just thinking of the place. The dock, the sea, the cat, the old hag. He knew they'd all be there, waiting to torment him.

14

HE PLACED HIS ear to the ground and held his breath. Could it be? Could there be a river running beneath the alley? Curious, he scratched the surface of the earthen street and loosened a pinch of soil. After rubbing the granules between his fingertips, he brought the dirt to his nose and sniffed. With a grimace, he wiped his fingers on his robe and repositioned his back against the wall behind him. He wondered if he was losing his mind when he felt a rushing current of air flowing from the stone into the rear of his skull.

"So, you feel them. Not many do."

"Untello," he immediately murmured.

Odd, that that particular memory would pop into his head. He hadn't reflected upon those words—or Untello, for that matter—for many years. Not since the two had conversed at the mouth of the cave where they'd been storing the harvested tusks.

Pile after pile of ivory stretched from where daylight broke the threshold to the very depths of the dank, foul-smelling cavern. Death was there. He remembered feeling its presence, remembered trying to run from it. But Untello had grabbed him and made him stay, made him face his fear. The episode had unnerved him, but it had also opened his eyes and his heart. It had been his first encounter with the baby spirit-elephant, his first true interaction with the Mother.

"Something is wrong," he whispered.

Hoping he was mistaken, he placed his palms flat against the ground and felt for tremors. But the earth was oddly quiet. There was nothing for him to feel, no telltale sign that a spirit-elephant was near.

"John Too?"

His hand trembled as he tentatively placed his fingers to the bandage covering his eyes. Tentatively, he lifted the bottom edge of the cloth above his brow.

"Are you here?"

He blinked several times and waited. Nothing.

"John Too," he repeated.

Unsteady, he rose to his feet and, using the wall as a guide, began to move. After a few cautious steps, he stopped and tilted his face to the sky. Wind and sun; he invited them to touch his skin, caress his cheeks, forehead, and lips, to give him some direction. But as it had been with the earth, the air was still, offering him no hint of breeze or ray of sunshine to follow. Undeterred, he moved on, slowly making his way to... he didn't know where.

He hadn't gone more than a few paces when he tripped over something and fell. He hit the ground hard, landing on his shoulder and hip. From a point close by, he heard someone chuckling.

"John Too?" he said. "Is that you?"

The chuckling stopped.

"Stupid leper," a male voice gruffly replied. "Go back to your place on the wall and die."

"The boy. The boy who was with me. Do you—?"

Teimbaka flinched when something struck him on the cheek. He put his hand to his face and felt where the object hit him.

"Cover your ugly face," the same male voice ordered.

And then Teimbaka heard what he guessed was a brief rustling of cloth before something smashed against the side of his head. The blow was sharp, the pain stinging. Immediately, he tried to slide away, to go back in the direction from which he had come, but something blocked his way, something oblong and cylindrical and, from what he could ascertain, nearly half the length of his body. As he attempted to move the object away, his fingers touched the smooth contour of what felt like animal hide stitched taught around a circular surface. Inching his hand over the skin, he tapped the base of his palm against the object. He knew well the sound his action caused. The reverberation of the drum pulsed through his body as if it was bound in his blood.

*A harsh "Shut up!" was quickly followed by the sound of something strik-
ing the wall near his head. Granules of what felt like pieces of stone or hardened
mud hit him in the face and neck. Reflexively he ducked and moved farther
away. Cradling the drum in his lap, Teimbaka slid across the ground using the
wall as his guide. When he felt safe enough to stop, he rested his head against
the stone and sighed. He was both surprised and confused when he felt a current of air flowing from the wall into the back of his skull.*

*

Kamua nearly laughed at the girl's appearance: a pink and white kanga, an
antelope horn tied to her waist by a piece of twine, two oversized ammunition belts hanging loosely across her chest—drooping so low the bottom
edges scraped the ground. She was holding a rifle out by her side as if she
were using it to measure her height. But he didn't laugh. The girl had just
saved his life. And now he was trying to understand how that had come
to pass.

"Why are we wasting time talking?" the girl asked. "We should be
running. They will come for us."

"I have nothing they want," Kamua replied. He held his arms out from
his sides as if to show her he wasn't hiding anything. "I have nothing." By
the expression on her face, Kamua could see she wasn't convinced. "What
are you called?"

He tried to hide his smile when she puffed out her cheeks and scraped
the dirt with the toe of her sandal.

"I think I am someone else, but *she* called me Juba."

"She? You mean your mother?"

"No, *her*," she told him. And then she pointed down the ridge to a
spot in the woodlands below.

"Why isn't she with you?"

He could see it on her face—a mixture of sadness and fear. He recognized the expression. He had seen it many times before. The girl—Juba,
she said her name was—had seen something awful. He was sorry he'd
made her remember.

"She's dead. They killed her."

"They? You mean the men that—"

"The same who were going to kill you. The man in the blue turban. Now," she paused and narrowed her eyes, "can we go?"

Kamua looked up toward the peak of the mountain before he said, "I have nowhere *to* go."

He could see her jaw tremble as she shook her head. Her shoulders slumped forward. She pulled the rifle close to her body and leaned on it.

"Where is it you belong?" he asked. "Is your village close?"

She shrugged.

"Don't you know where you live?"

He thought she looked puzzled when she met his gaze. Pointing past Kamua's shoulder toward the western horizon, she told him, "Somewhere that way. Past the villages of the ghost people."

"Ghost people? I don't—"

"But it's gone now. The bad men burned everything." She jerked her head as if she suddenly felt a sharp twinge in her neck. "I was— There was screaming. And guns. I—" She abruptly turned her face and grasped one of the ammunition belts. "I was in a truck." He could see a teardrop sliding down her cheek. "My village—" She shrugged.

Juba shifted her attention upward at the cackling howl of a lone hyena.

"*Jib*," she muttered.

Kamua noticed she moved her hand from the ammunition belt to the antelope horn as she spoke. He studied the horn for a moment, wondering where he had seen it—or one like it—before.

"Where did you get that?"

She shuffled back a step and yelled, "I didn't steal it!"

Kamua raised his hands to show he meant no harm.

"I didn't say—"

"It was in the black dirt! She took it from me!"

When Juba plopped down on the ground and started to cry, Kamua rolled his eyes.

"She said it was Bouda's," she whined. "Now she's dead." Grabbing the horn with both hands, she held it out to him. "Take it. I don't want it. I don't want it."

The hoot of the lone hyena sounded once more. Several other hyenas soon joined in. Seemingly spooked by the sudden outburst, Juba threw the horn to the ground and hastily stood.

"It's a shaman's charm," she said in a fearful tone. "It's possessed."

The cackling cries of the hyenas grew louder. Kamua approached the antelope horn and bent to take hold of it.

"What are you doing?" Juba asked. "Leave it. Leave it for the beasts."

Kamua lifted the horn off the ground and brought it close to his face. "I know this horn."

As he inspected the horn, the vision of a black serpent appeared in his head. The image called to memory a dream he'd had, one where a man wearing rotted hyena pelts was fending off an enormous black snake.

"Tell me where you found this," he said to Juba. "You spoke of Bouda, a hyena-man."

A distant burst from a high-caliber automatic weapon prompted Juba to crouch to the ground. Kamua, however, moved a few steps closer to the edge of the trail they'd been traversing and looked down. In the aftermath of the gunshots, he heard the distinct sputter of a motor turning over.

"It's them." Juba said. "The bad men. They're coming." The distress in her voice was unmistakable when she stated, "They will kill us."

"Your weapon, does it work?"

Juba nodded. "I saw her use it. It's loud."

Kamua looked up toward the peak of the mountain.

"Come," he said. "The truck can only make it up the trail so far." He glanced back down toward the base of the ridge. "After that, they will have to travel by foot." He placed one of his hands on the barrel of the AK-47. "The path narrows the last hundred meters or more, with little cover for a man to shelter behind." Nodding to the weapon, he gently took it from her grasp. "When we reach the top, you can tell me how you came by the horn."

*

"What happened here?" Juba studied the pile of boulders and stones for a moment before looking at Kamua. "Was that from the explosion I heard?"

Kamua aligned the sight of the AK-47 to the section of the path he'd described to Juba.

"Why did you blow up rocks?" she asked. "Were they mean to you?"

Kamua chuckled for a moment but then fell silent. With a heavy sigh, he rested his head against the rifle barrel.

"I buried—" He closed his eyes and found waiting for him the memory of the day Teimbaka had fired a gun for the first time. "I buried part of the Mother," he explained as he studied the images parading through his thoughts. "But I can't seem to stop—" Kamua shook his head and opened his eyes. He looked at Juba with a furrowed brow. "I can't stop them from being killed," he told her. "So, I'm left to gather their souls to try to give them peace."

Juba stared at Kamua like he had just told the biggest lie she had ever heard.

"You don't make any sense," she told him. "What mother are you talking about?" She shook her head. "And what souls? Souls don't live in the mountains." Her expression seemed troubled when she tentatively reached a hand out toward his shoulder. "Are you— Are you *ibidi*? Should I have let those men—?" She quickly looked away.

Kamua latched onto the word *ibidi*—"crazy." He remembered Tengene grabbing him by the arm and asking him what he knew of Mother Africa, of the old ways, the day Teimbaka had fired the Lee-Enfield carbine. "The Mother cries for help," Teimbaka had said. "What would you have me do?" And then he, Tengene, and Selam had driven the poor bastard near the border of Sudan, where George Henry and his rebel militia were sure to find him. The man had been willing to give his life to try to save a herd of elephants. At the time, Kamua had thought Teimbaka crazy, a fool.

"I was blind," he muttered.

He saw Juba run a finger along the grooves of the antelope horn.

"He's there," he said to her. When she looked up to meet his gaze, he nodded to the pile of boulders and stones. "Buried along with a thousand elephant tusks." He eyed the antelope horn and said, "He'd probably like to have that. Looks like he used it as a weapon."

He watched Juba slide her hand down the length of the horn and lightly place the tip of her finger atop the razor-sharp point.

"You say you found it in black dirt?"

He noticed her brow furrow before she answered.

"Enat was mad. She slapped and kicked me." Juba rubbed her cheek where Kamua guessed she'd been struck. "Said it was his, Bouda's. But everyone was dead. How could it be anybody's when they were all dead?"

"Everyone was dead. You mean— Was there a wrecked helicopter? Is that where you found the horn, the place where Enat slapped you?"

"She wasn't Enat," she replied. "That's what I called her. Her name was Eden, I think. But she only said it once. So I don't know. It could have been—"

"But was there a helicopter, a wrecked one? Are we talking about the same place?"

"There were big metal blades sticking out of the ground near a burned machine."

"The helicopter I brought down."

"And there were dead soldiers lying in black dirt."

"Must have been dried blood."

"And hyenas." He could tell by the expression on her face that the memory scared her. "They were eating the dead men."

"Hyenas? And they let you near them?"

"She could talk to them. Order them, I think."

"She?"

"Enat. Eden." Juba shrugged. "She would yell at them and they would listen."

Kamua looked at the antelope horn as if seeing it for the first time.

"Maybe you're right. Maybe it is—"

"One had no head."

"A hyena?" Kamua questioned. "Why would one of the hyenas have no head?"

"One of the *men*," Juba corrected. "One of the men had no head."

Kamua instantly thought of the man with the blue turban, Mosi. He vividly recalled the man threatening to take his head off.

"Where do you think it went?" she asked. "What does someone do with a head?" Juba clasped the body of the horn and then released it. "Maybe someone needed it to mark their land."

"Mark their land?"

Juba shrugged. "You know, put it on the end of a spear and stick it in the ground."

"Oh, I don't think—"

"I didn't see it, though. I guess they took it."

"Who?"

"The people who killed the men."

He hesitated before telling her, "I killed those men."

Juba laughed.

"Why is that funny?"

"You? How could you have done that on your own?" she scoffed. "*Ibidi*, I think, or a story maker."

"I'm not making… What's wrong? Why are you crying?"

Juba sat down on the ground and covered her face in her hands. When he saw her begin to rock back and forth, he knelt to one knee and put a hand on her shoulder.

"What did I say?" he gently prodded. "Why have I made you cry?"

Juba wiped her eyes and took a deep breath.

"They have it," she told him in a trembling voice. "They put it in a sack."

"They have what? The man's head?"

"No!" she shouted. "Hers! They have *her* head!"

"Calm down."

"I heard them talking!"

"Keep your voice—"

"Before the rabbit appeared." She sniffled and wiped her eyes. "Before she sang to me and told me what to do."

"Rabbit?" Kamua grasped her shoulder and gave it a shake. "You mean the one with eyes like the sun?"

Juba nodded.

"Where?" Kamua asked with a sense of urgency. "Where was the rabbit?"

"Near to where the men had you tied up. She told me what to do." She looked at him with an expression that he interpreted as quizzical. "How do you think I found you?"

Kamua rubbed his chin and smiled. Then, in the next instant, he ruffled the top of Juba's head and laughed. Juba stared at him wide-eyed like he was, indeed, *ibidi.*

"Why are you so happy about a rabbit?"

"Because she hasn't deserted me."

"Deserted you? Is she your pet?"

"My pet?" He chuckled as he stood, then shook his head. "No, she's nobody's pet. She's—"

"Why do you call her *she*? How do you know it's a girl?"

"How do I know she's a girl?" He turned and looked out over the darkened terrain below the mountain. "Let me tell you how I know."

At first, he didn't know where to begin, but as he fumbled for the right words to tell Juba what he knew of the rabbit, he realized the story began with him. And so he told her that he was a good deal like her—an orphan, a survivor of a village burned to the ground by some warlord he knew nothing about. The death of his mother and sister by fire—his father had been shot while defending the village—enraged him. He'd headed north in hope of catching up to the killers. Which is how he had come to cross paths with Tengene and Selam and ultimately, under the guidance and tutelage of the two older rangers, become a park ranger for the country of Ethiopia.

"Why would they take you?" she interrupted. "How old were you?"

"I was a man," he immediately responded while puffing out his chest. But then he shrugged and with a slight smile told her, "I was a boy who wanted to be a man."

And he went on to explain that because there was a shortage of rangers at the time, he was given the job without anyone questioning his age or country of origin. Being a ranger, he went on to say, meant putting his life on the line for little pay under harsh conditions. It was an unspoken fact about the job, that each day in the bush might very well be the last. Between poachers and hunters and the men who paid the poachers, deaths among rangers were common, nearly an every-other-day occurrence. Older, more experienced rangers like Tengene and Selam took great care to never choose a course of action that courted death, whereas the younger rangers, or those with little experience, reacted more on adrenaline than intelligence and were therefore prone to making mistakes—which in all too many instances meant loss of life.

"'Can't help the animals if you're dead,' Tengene would always say," Kamua told her. And with a slight chuckle, he walked to the end of the bluff and looked into the darkness below. "And there was already too much of that."

"Too much?" Juba questioned.

"Death." Too many elephants, rhinos, zebras, lions—even giraffes, he told her. Scores killed daily. It wasn't uncommon for him, Tengene, and Selam to look up and see a sky darkened by vultures, spinning and circling like storm clouds gone mad. And when they would follow the trail of those who had done the killing, they would often find themselves outnumbered twenty to one or pitting their single-shot carbines against automatic weapons and mortars and grenades and helicopters. Rangers often didn't stand a chance, he said. It was like fighting a war with spears and rocks against an enemy made of fire and steel.

"What?" he asked, when he looked over and saw her frowning.

"You're saying a lot of words but not saying anything about what we were talking about."

"What we—?"

"The rabbit, remember?"

"Right. Her."

They had driven toward a particularly large mass of swirling vultures one afternoon, he told her, and they'd found a man tied to the trunk of a tree. The man was in terrible shape. He'd been whipped to the point of death. Selam had insisted they cut him down and see to his wounds.

"What does that have—?"

"Shush."

An enormous lion and a mountain-sized elephant guarded the man, he went on, and they couldn't for the life of them ever recall wild animals acting in such a manner. Every hour, he told her, the lion would roar and the elephant would trumpet, and they would not leave the man even after he'd fallen asleep next to the fire they'd built. Kamua, being the youngest of the three rangers, was elected to keep first watch.

"First watch?"

To guard against a prowling lion or hyena and to keep watch for the men who'd used a whip on the poor bastard they had found, he told her.

"They must have been bad men," Juba muttered.

"I was wondering who the man was—why someone would do such a thing—when she appeared."

"She?"

How odd it was, he'd thought at the time, to see a savannah hare wander toward a campfire at night. Odder still that the animal focused its attention on the wounded man, edging closer to him as it kept a wary eye on Kamua. So bold was the rabbit, he explained, that the animal set her paws on the man's back and smelled his wounds.

"But how do you know she was a—?"

"I found myself staring into her eyes," he said. And then he went on to tell her that he thought he was hypnotized or, as Selam and Tengene had later theorized, had a spell cast upon him. For as he stared into the animal's eyes, he saw them as a sea of rolling sand dunes with flecks of sun sparkling in the center of each. And just before he lost consciousness—or fell asleep, as Tengene had chided—he saw the image of a woman standing next to him. She'd cradled his head to the ground as he closed his eyes. He vividly remembered the smell of her perfume as she gently laid his head to rest upon the grass.

"A shaman," Juba whispered.

Stranger still, he went on to tell her, was that when he awakened, the man who had been whipped to near death was healed, his open wounds now scars.

"He was making coffee," Kamua said with a shake of his head. "I didn't know…" His brow furrowed as his gaze fell to the ground. "It was her, the hare. She had made him whole."

Juba fiddled with the twine wrapped around her waist.

"He must be special. The man," she explained when Kamua looked at her. "Who is he?"

"His name was Teimbaka," he replied. "He was—"

"Was? Is he dead too?"

"I don't know. We left him. There were bombs and gunfire. I don't know what happened to him."

"He must have been *somebody* for a shaman to heal him."

"So many scars," Kamua recalled. "Like he'd been punished for believing in old Africa. He's a link to the past, Selam said, a bridge to the world of the Mother and spirit-elephants." He nodded to the horn in Juba's hand. "And hyena-men."

"Spirit-elephants? What are they?"

Kamua studied her face for a moment before he said, "They're the animals' souls."

He smiled when Juba placed a finger to her chin and shook her head.

"I didn't believe it either when Teimbaka first talked about them. But then..."

"But then—what?" she pressed when he let his sentence trail off.

The memory was still vivid: the taunting jeers of the soldier who'd fired the RPG into the Range Rover, Selam and Tengene's burnt and mangled bodies, the blinding white light and the blaring wails of the ghost-elephants as they stampeded over the hill.

"Then they came." He shrugged and turned his head a little to the side. "They allowed me to see them." A flash of anger shot through him when he heard the girl giggle. "They're there!" he defiantly told her. And he pointed to the rubble piled against the mountain behind them. "A thousand tusks buried in a cave along with your hyena-man!"

*

Juba eyed the fuming ranger as he walked to the end of the bluff and looked over the side. *Ibidi*, she thought. That, or the bad men had done something to him to make him act crazy. Either way, spirit-elephants sounded like a tale an elder would spin around the village fire to settle the children before they were called to sleep.

Souls. Spirits. She shook her head before glancing at the pile of boulders. She wondered what had lived in the cave before the ranger blocked the entrance. Looking left to right, she realized the cave faced west, the direction of sunset. Sunset, a time of magic, of storytelling and lore. Eyeing the cave, she suddenly wondered if she was standing in a holy place.

The bluff was a huge slab of level stone some twenty meters wide and ten meters deep bordered by waist-high boulders and the weathered remnants of thick-trunked trees. Exactly like the holy places the elders of the village described when they wove their tales of ancient beasts and mighty warriors. She remembered sitting wide-eyed and open-mouthed as the elder's voice slowly melded into the movement of the flames, enticing her and the other children sitting around the fire into a dreamlike state where everything that could be imagined became real.

Stricken with a pang of melancholy, Juba walked to the front of the bluff and sat down on one of the barrier stones. Resting her hand against the gnarled skeleton of a weatherworn tree, she gazed out over the foothills below.

A hint of yellow in the sky, wisps of silver mist ensnared within tree tops, a pall of muted light creeping over her shoulders—these were signs alerting her that a new day was near. Turning, she saw the top of the mountain was obscured behind a bank of puffy, fast-moving clouds. Carried by a wind she could not feel, the vaporous mass gave her reason to imagine that an ancient beast from one of the elder's stories had taken refuge within them, and that as soon as the sun rose, the clouds would disperse and she would see what creature of lore stood upon the mountain's peak.

Amused by the whimsical thoughts running through her head, Juba looked over to the ranger with the hope that he might ask her why she was smiling. But when she saw him brooding—staring over the bluff with a frown on his face—she shrugged and followed his gaze to the vista below.

Juba took a deep breath and tightened her grip on the skeletal tree. For as far as she could see, from the base of the mountain to the horizon, a blanket of mist lay across the land. Here and there, small puffs of fog rose into the air, these swirling and twisting upward toward the pre-dawn sky. At her back, spreading south to north and moving west, the first rays of sunshine slipped over the horizon. With the infusion of light, the mist began to glitter, the canopy filled with shining droplets colored silver, ivory, and gold. Lines began to materialize atop the luminous surface, these forming subtle outlines of mounded shapes that moved counter to the spreading light. Squinting against the sudden glare, Juba tried to blink away the myriad pinkish dots popping into view. But her attempts to clear her vision only seemed to strengthen the phenomenon.

Silver, gold, ivory, pink, and red—individual colors drifting atop the mist began to shift and realign, intermingling within the outlined shapes. Crystalline, these entities glittered with shards of silver and gold. As Juba stared open-mouthed at the manifestations, ivory tusks grew out of feather-like streams of vapor. Set behind these, pairs of pink-red eyes stared upward toward the mountain.

"*Tembo*," she whispered, awestruck. "So beautiful."

"Beautiful?"

She started when she found the ranger standing next to her.

"You see them?" he asked.

Confused by his harsh tone of voice, Juba nonetheless nodded.

"They are so beautiful," she remarked. "I have never seen such—"

"They're dead," Kamua interjected. "Nothing beautiful about them. Nothing beautiful at all."

"But look at them," she countered. "They look like they are made of precious stones."

"They're dead!" he yelled. "Don't you understand? Look at them! How many do you see?"

Confused by his anger, Juba cautiously asked, "How many?"

Slowly, she looked left to right and then back to the left.

"I can't count that high," she admitted. "They're too many."

"Generations," he spat. "That's how many there are. And who do you think killed them?"

Juba became somber as she looked down at the infinite herd of spirit-elephants. "Bad men?" she hesitantly offered.

Nodding, Kamua grumbled, "Bad men." Bending to look into her eyes, he added, "And no one's been able to stop them."

Juba's brow furrowed as her gaze shifted back to the spirit-elephants.

"Spirit-elephants," she murmured, "Maybe that's why she healed him." She looked up at the ranger. "Maybe he is the one," she said. "Maybe that's why."

"What are you talking about?"

"The man the shaman healed. Maybe he can—"

The ranger abruptly motioned for silence. She studied his face, confused, as he tilted his head to the side with an expression of worry and slid the rifle from his shoulder. A strange, whistling hum sounded in the sky just as he yelled, "Mortar!" Before she could move, he tackled her to the ground and lay on top of her.

The frightening explosion shook the rock beneath Juba's stomach and sent a shower of debris into the air. She yelped when stinging pellets hit her flesh.

"Are you hurt?" the ranger yelled.

Before she had time to answer, he pulled her to her feet and pushed her toward the cave. He yanked her behind a big boulder as a second mortar shell exploded. Pushing her into a crouch, he yelled, "Keep your head down!"

Juba shuddered from the tremor running through the stone. A shower of debris fell on her head and shoulders as streaking projectiles ricocheted off the rocks around them.

"Stay here!" Kamua ordered.

Terrified, she watched the ranger scurry several meters to his left, keeping low to the ground. When he neared the lip of the bluff, he dove toward the barrier stones. Taking cover behind one of the large slabs of rock, he slid the rifle up to his shoulder.

Juba heard a third mortar shell descending from the sky as the ranger began firing the rifle. The ensuing explosion, to Juba, seemed closer, louder, and more violent than the previous two. The shower of debris that followed came over her in a wave. Coughing, wiping dust from her eyes, she suddenly realized the ranger's weapon had stopped firing. She held her breath, fearing he'd been killed. Then the boom boom boom of the rifle started up again. Relieved to hear the gunfire, she edged her way around the boulder to see if the ranger needed help. That's when she felt a tug at the bottom of her kanga.

Juba screamed and tried to scoot away, but the hyena lunged and clamped its jaws around the horn fastened to her waist. Panic-stricken, she slapped the hyena's muzzle and tried to kick it away. But the animal kept its jaws tight around the horn.

"Ranger!" she screamed.

A fourth explosion drowned out her voice. Desperate, she coiled her legs and then thrust them into the hyena's chest. But as before, the beast would not let go.

"Ranger! Help me!" she pleaded.

Afraid to look into the hyena's eyes—afraid she would see the last seconds of her life within the beast's wild, ravenous gaze—she turned her head away. Anticipating awful pain when the animal bit into her flesh, she tensed her muscles and wailed. A few moments passed before she realized nothing had happened. A tug to the horn prompted her to address the hyena.

"What are doing?" she shouted.

The animal seemed to study her before it lowered its head and uttered a low growl.

"*Jib*," she said in a calmer voice.

The hyena released the horn and sat back on its haunches. With its ears straight up and turned toward her, the beast tilted its head.

"*Dehna.* Good," she told it.

Chancing a quick glance over her shoulder, she called for the ranger. She received no answer. The hyena growled anew and took a few steps toward the lip of the bluff.

"What are you—?"

Juba stopped in mid-sentence when several more hyenas appeared.

"Ranger!" she screamed. "Where are you?"

To Juba's bewilderment, the pack of hyenas began to hoot and cackle. Removing the antelope horn from the twine tied around her waist, she extended it toward the first hyena. She and the animal flinched at a fresh burst of automatic gunfire. The familiar boom boom boom of the ranger's rifle answered. Then, abruptly, silence. Juba loudly whispered, "Ranger? Ranger? Are you alright?" When she received no reply, she scooted close to the edge of the boulder. Again, the hyena clamped its jaws around the horn. Reflexively, she slapped the animal on the snout.

"No!" she barked.

The beast snarled but released the horn and inched back.

"You want this?" she asked. She held it out toward the beast. "Then take it."

She didn't understand when the hyena turned away.

"I don't know what you want from me," she whined. "But if you want the horn, you can have it."

The hyena showed no indication that it understood. Frustrated by the animal's behavior, she shifted her attention to the ranger.

"Ranger?" she tentatively called.

Again, no response. Taking a deep breath, she scooted out from the cover of the boulder.

She assumed the ranger was dead as soon as she saw his body prone on the ground, with blood smeared across his forehead and shoulder. Immediately, she moved to help him. But a tug on the horn prompted her to stop and look down. The hyena—ears flat against the side of its head—stared intently into Juba's eyes. Again, confused by the animal's behavior, she petted the beast on the snout and then walked quickly to where the ranger lay. Cautiously, before she bent to check on his condition, she peeked over the edge of the bluff. Fifty meters or so below her, she glimpsed a man wearing a blue turban. Curious, she leaned farther out to get a better look. A round of bullets blasted into the rock below her feet, sending her falling backward on her rump.

She was immediately set upon by the hyena. With a sharp growl, the animal took the antelope horn into its jaws and pulled.

"I don't—" The hyena released the horn and turned toward the cave. Following the animal's gaze, she said, "I don't— How did you—? What is it you want?"

Her attention fixed upon the entrance to the cave, she noticed one of the hyenas separate from the pack and scamper behind a large configuration of boulders near the far side of the bluff. Curious, she took a few steps to follow but then abruptly stopped. The ranger.

Juba sprinted back to where Kamua lay and bent to one knee.

"Get up!" she yelled. Pulling on his pants leg, she again shouted, "Get up!"

Without warning, the hyena knocked her away. Enraged, she swung her arm out to smack it.

"Go away!" she screamed. "The shaman told me to save him! Go away!"

The animal snarled but to her surprise turned its head and uttered an odd call. Four hyenas came running. Fearing an attack, she stood and swung the horn as though wielding a sword.

"Stay back!" she screamed. "*Koomee!*" she shouted.

But the animals didn't stop.

Juba crouched and back-pedaled. Jabbing the horn in the air over the ranger, she attempted to keep the beasts away. But they separated into pairs and swiftly moved around her. Not knowing what else she could do, she ran toward the nearest hyena with the horn poised to strike. She gasped when the lead hyena blindsided her and knocked her to the ground. When the animal clamped its jaws around the hem of her kanga and dragged her toward the cave, she was overcome with panic.

"*Jib!*" she screamed. "*Koomee!*"

To her utter shock, the animal immediately released her. A flurry of movement drew her attention to the ranger. Scrambling to her feet, she cried, "No!"

But when the four hyenas dragged the ranger past her, she saw their jaws were clamped around his clothing.

"*Dehna, jib*—good!" she yelled.

As the all-too-familiar whistling-hum in the sky alerted Juba to another incoming mortar round, she ran to the lip of the bluff and grabbed the rifle and ammunition belts. In the next instant, she was hurtling through air with a terrible explosion echoing in her head.

*

Grey to black, black to white, white to grey; sky was earth, earth sky, each beginning and ending on the shore of a lifeless sea. Fire burned in the distance—orange flames against a background of black—flickering off and on as though a door was opening and closing. In the air, the stench of rotted flesh. When he inhaled, a bitter taste clogged his throat. Surely, he thought, he was on the doorstep of Jahannam.

"Where am I?" Kamua croaked.

Barely conscious, Kamua felt his lips gently part and liquid trickle into his mouth. Thirsty, his throat parched, he raised his hand to his mouth, desperate for more.

"Slow," a child's voice said as his hand was slapped down. "Drink."

And so he did. A few drops became a sip, a sip a gulp. Then suddenly it was gone—the water stopped.

"Teach me," the child said.

"What?"

Kamua grasped his head between his hands in an attempt to make the ache in his skull go away.

"Open your eyes," the child ordered. It was a girl's voice. It sounded familiar. "Teach me," she repeated.

Squinting against the glare of a campfire, Kamua groggily opened his eyes.

"Teach me." The blurred outline of a girl in a pink and white kanga thrust what looked to be an AK-47 assault rifle toward him.

"I don't—"

"I want to know how to kill."

15

"THE WORDS OF hope are dead. Do not shake your head as if you believe it is not so. Look, listen, feel; you sense it—the light is gone. Shiver and cower into your wall if you will. It does not alter what you cannot change. Altar. Now there's an interesting word—a place where offerings are burnt to an invisible entity. Perhaps the word was invented as a slip of the tongue or a jab at the folly of belief. What do you think? No, no—no need to answer if even entertaining the thought makes you tremble. But you must acknowledge the irony of burning a living animal as a way of paying homage. Barbaric, wouldn't you say? Altar—yes, a very interesting word. But, where were we? Oh yes, hope—or rather the lack of it.

"You thought I was gone, didn't you, when Gunstard was killed by that demented child? But she knew I wasn't dead. She clutched her pathetic cross and prayed that I was—but she knew better. That's why she was always afraid, always doubting, always—ha ha—praying. And you—fixated on spirits of beasts that have no place in this world or any other. Archaic remnants of a time fast moving toward annihilation. Did you ever stop to think you were wasting your life? Don't look so aghast. No one wants them. Your kind kills them for their tusks to make trinkets that yellow and fade until they are completely forgotten. Oh, not you personally, but rather those akin to you: men, killers, toothless braggarts who would sell their world for a penny and a whore. And when the beasts are dead—hollow-eyed and decayed, their spirits trapped between what she calls heaven and hell—there's nowhere for them to go. They cannot stay here with you, in the world where they were murdered. And they

are not welcome in antithesis. Where, you ask? A place you cannot fathom because it doesn't exist. Hope is dead. That's all you need know.

"She's dead too, by the way. You knew as much, didn't you? Oh, don't cry. Tears won't bring her back. And she wouldn't want it anyway—to come back. It was excruciating the way she perished: slow, deliberate, torturous, and agonizing—yes, agonizing. She suffered—unspeakably—for months until she finally succumbed. In the end, she cursed you, damned you to fire, wished your soul to hell. But that would be too easy, to take your soul without you understanding what you have done. There, there, now, no need to weep. I am not swayed by your pathetic display of weakness.

"You are useless, a failure. Everything you have touched withers and dies— or wished it had. Did you know the other one is a slave? Yes, her, the one you tossed into the sea. A few years slaving as a whore is what you condemned her to. And then she will end it. She will take her own life. But not before she has cursed you, not until she wishes your soul to me. Pity they both trusted you, believed in you. Look what you've done to them.

"Shall we talk about the boy you destroyed? You know the one. Gnarled feet, broken heart, unstable mind. You killed him too. Oh, not so much with your hands, but you killed him. Better for him if you'd shown mercy and plunged the horn into his throat when you fought over her on the edge of oblivion. But you, you in your magnanimous wisdom, you let him go on living so he could suffer a life of addiction and sorrow. His broken heart killed him in the end. And now his soul is trapped in a dark place that not even I can reach, buried in a tomb along with the amputated remains of a species that no one wants.

"Why are you looking around? He's not here. He's deserted you. Call to him if you will. He won't answer. He doesn't want to. He no longer believes in you. You are dead to him, as he is dead unto himself. Again, I say: the words of hope are dead."

Something clammy slid across Teimbaka's sandaled feet and slithered up his ankles. So cold and repugnant was the sensation, his flesh recoiled from the biting edge of every scale that wound its way up his torso. Tighter and tighter the coils became, pressing breath from his stomach up and out through his throat. And when the whispered hiss of a viper flickered in his ear, he slapped at his head as if it were on fire and screamed as though he was a witness to Claire's slow and torturous death.

"No!" he wailed in anguish. "No!"

A shout of "Damn you to fire, leper!" was delivered with a vicious blow to the side of his head. Trembling and in pain, unnerved by being struck, Teimbaka turned his face to the wall and began to sob.

"Etiyopiya! Etiyopiya!" John Too shouted. Teimbaka felt a hand grab his shoulder. "What's wrong?"

"She's dead," he whimpered.

"Who? Who's dead?"

Teimbaka lightly touched his lips where Claire had kissed him; he could no longer feel her presence.

"Claire," he softly cried. "Claire is dead."

"How do you know?" John Too challenged. "Who told you this?"

"A man—a man's voice." Teimbaka tilted his head a little to one side as though straining to hear a sound. "He's here. He was right next to me. He struck me."

John Too paused before he said, "We are alone, Etiyopiya."

Teimbaka hugged his arms to his chest as an intense shiver ran down his spine.

"There is no one here but you and I. We are alone."

*

Goliath noticed the headlights soon after he left the Waterman estate. It wasn't hard to spot them. Any set of headlights appearing in his rearview mirror on a near-deserted stretch of highway would have drawn his interest. But this particular set had followed him as he'd wound his way through the back roads of Pennsylvania, Delaware, and New Jersey. They were impossible to miss—and ignore.

Who is the amateur behind the wheel? he wondered. And what the hell did the person want? One thing was certain: whoever the fucker was, they were in for a big surprise when they reached Trenton. Considering it was going to be a little past midnight when he crossed Calhoun Street Bridge to the Jersey side of the river—and the confusing cloverleaf of exits that fed off of it—he figured there'd be ample opportunity to lose whoever was tailing him. And if he couldn't lose them—well, the Delaware River would be in close proximity in the event he could arrange an ambush. The river had never refused to accept a dead body into its cold currents before, so he didn't see why it would start now. But Jesus fucking Christ, had the trip to the old lady's place been a setup? Was Alexis trying to screw him over? Or was some other player stepping onto the scene now that Rue was dead?

He knew word on the street traveled fast. Rue's unexpected departure from the landscape had left a big hole in the power structure that existed between the competing drug-trafficking factions. And though he was sure there were more than a few posers who were ready to take Rue's place, he didn't know if any of them had the balls to make the move so soon or had enough muscle behind them to make it happen. Sure, he'd heard the static on the street about some new punk with a pimply face who was trying to consolidate everybody's action, but that wasn't going to happen. Fat chance any of the big players were going to give up their piece of the market just because some greedy son of a bitch thought it made sense. There was too much bad blood—and far too little trust—between the gangs and the syndicates for them to come to a consensus on pricing and distribution. Goliath chuckled at the thought: Bloods trusting Five Percenters, spics trusting blacks, and so on and so forth. The world would have to be about to end for that to ever come to pass. No, there was going to be some heavy shit hitting the fan now that Rue was dead. And unfortunately—or maybe fortunately, if he played his cards right—he was right in the middle of it. Alexis had made sure of that.

Alexis—he'd wanted to strangle the bitch when she'd shown him the video she'd taken of him sodomizing the boy and then beating him to death. He'd wept at first. Like he always did when he'd realized what he'd done, when his lust was finally sated and he found himself naked in a room with the battered corpse of some boy he'd done unspeakable things to. And then he became enraged when he heard someone laughing and looked over and saw it was her. Judging him, thinking he was some perverted mon-ster who was to be looked upon and treated like a fucking circus freak. But before he could put his hands around her throat, she'd told him to sit down. With a businesslike expression on her face, she showed him foot-age of three other boys in three other cells. Three boys she'd just taken off the streets. Three boys who'd be waiting for him when he returned from the errands she was giving him carry out. One boy in particular—no more than seven or eight, with blonde hair and full lips—had given him an instant erection. His rage had been replaced by his insatiable need to fulfill his sexual desires.

He'd already delivered a note and package to the old fossil who lived on the big estate out in the countryside of Pennsylvania, and he'd delivered a pound of heroin and enough psychedelics to throw one hell of a party for a few weeks to the clinic out in the boondocks in Delaware. And now he was nearing Trenton—where he hoped to complete his third task of the evening—breaking into Rue's office at the statehouse and leaving an envelope on top of his desk. But the tail he'd picked up after leaving the old lady's place was troubling. Who the fuck had been following him for the past few hours, and what the hell did they want? That was the troubling part: he didn't know.

*

Daniel Locket's given name was Daniel Shane O'Loughlin, and he was the youngest of three boys born to Shane and Mary O'Loughlin of County Cork, Ireland. Although Daniel was brought into the world in the town of Kinsale, he didn't recall much, if any, of his time there, or much of his early youth, for his family moved to Belfast when he was five. What memories of Kinsale he might have wanted to hold on to were soon buried under the layers of anger and humiliation accrued from being a Catholic child raised in the Protestant world of Northern Ireland.

His father, a welder, had been lured to Belfast to work for the Harland and Wolff shipbuilding company in the mid 1940s with the promise of a steady job, good pay, and the prospect of bringing his sons into the fold of one of the top shipbuilding companies in the world. Unfortunately, the move to Belfast—a stronghold of Unionists, Protestants, and British loyalists—put Daniel, his two brothers, and his mother in an oppressive atmosphere. His father, a quiet, hardworking man, was normally too tired and too focused on his job to understand what his family was going through.

"Try to get along," and "show your good Catholic side," were his normal responses to any complaints Daniel or his brothers brought up about the environment they were living in. And his mother, God rest her soul—well, Daniel had been too young and hot-headed to understand what the woman was going through: making a home for her family with the stigma of being Catholic. Needless to say, Belfast wasn't Kinsale—and the Irish Republic wasn't Northern Ireland.

By 1961, after a troubled decade of fistfights, expulsions from school, and acts of rebellion against the Crown, Daniel Shane O'Loughlin was on the lam from British authorities for taking part in the beating of a Unionist judge who'd sentenced one of his brothers to ten years hard labor for speaking out at a public gathering in Derry. Not knowing where to turn for help or where he could escape the long reach of British law, he went to his father, seeking guidance. His father, now close to retirement age, had seemed at best indifferent to his youngest son's predicament. At one point in their conversation, he even went so far as to blame Daniel for the death of Daniel's mother two years earlier.

"You killed her with your conniving, rebellious ways," he said to him in a monotone. "I'd see you rot in Hades where you belong, but I promised her before she died I would do my best to see you straighten yourself out." And he'd given Daniel a hard, sobering look. "You're a dark cloud, boy," he'd added. "But I intend to do right by your mum."

And so he took Daniel to the docks a few days later and, with the help of some old, toothless night watchman, smuggled Daniel aboard a huge ocean liner. His father had worked on the ship—the SS *Canberra*—for the past two years. Daniel was put to work as a boiler stoker when the vessel was transferred from Belfast to Southampton, Great Britain, whence it would soon set sail for Australia. The working papers his father had silently stuffed into his hand when he'd turned him over to one of the ship's stewards said his name was Daniel Locket.

Daniel Locket first met his future employer, Charles Waterman, on the *Canberra*'s maiden voyage. Waterman, a young American of some wealth with a penchant for horses and gambling, had bribed his way into a below-decks boxing match that several members of the engine crew had organized. He'd arrived at the makeshift ring in time to see what he later described to Daniel as a wiry, tow-headed youth in his twenties matched against a burly Greek who looked to have a forty-pound advantage and ten years' experience on his younger, thinner adversary. Daniel recalled Charlie laughingly telling him that as soon as he saw the two combatants set to go a few rounds, he placed twenty pounds on the Greek to win by a knockout.

"Easiest money I ever made," he boasted to Daniel. "What did you last, all of three minutes?"

Daniel remembered nodding at the question—though he didn't recall much of the fight—and then downing the shot of Irish whiskey the American had bought him from a purser who was skimming the ship's liquor. But although Daniel didn't remember much of his first fight with the big Greek, he did remember squaring off against the man three more times before making port in Australia. And he clearly recalled—proudly so— that Charlie Waterman had lost all three of those bets.

One week after the *Canberra* made port in Melbourne, Daniel landed a job at Flemington Stables on a whim. He responded to a flyer taped to a hardware store window seeking a track rider, assuming the notice was an advertisement for a position driving tractors on a farm. Slightly taken aback at the prospect of straddling a horse and galloping around a race course, he decided to give it a go and found, much to his surprise, that he was a natural born rider. It was there he crossed paths with Charlie Waterman again. Only this time the circumstances weren't as enjoyable for Charlie as they had been when he'd first met Daniel.

A serious bookie keeps all hours, as Daniel had learned over the course of his life. Whether said bookmaker personally shows up to collect what is owed or delegates the job to someone else—perhaps two or three people— there really isn't a time of day or night when a debt can't be held due. On one early morning, when Daniel was off to the loo for a morning sab- batical after exercising a three-year-old colt, he ran across the American. Charles Waterman was in one of the outer barns away from the track and in the process of having the stuffing beaten out of him by three rather large gentlemen armed with a cricket bat. From the heated words exchanged between the four men, Daniel knew the altercation was over a betting debt. Recognizing Charlie from the *Canberra* and having experienced first- hand an unfair fight, he threw himself into the fray and came to the aid of the American. Within a matter of minutes, one of the bookie's goons was on the ground with a broken leg, a second was on one knee nursing a broken jaw, and the third was running for the nearest phone while yelling how the two of them—Charlie and Daniel—would pay for crossing some bloke who went by the name of Magnum Jake. As Daniel would soon learn, Magnum Jake was the biggest bookie in Melbourne, and had, by all accounts, a score of hardened criminals on his payroll, as well as a local constable and a several policemen at varying precincts around the city. Needless to say, it was the last morning Daniel worked at Flemington Stables, because within twenty-four hours, he and Charlie Waterman—at Charlie's insistence—had traveled to Sydney, where they boarded a plane bound for Cairo.

By the time Charlie and Daniel landed in Cairo, Daniel had decided to find employment on a freighter or an ocean liner as a boiler stoker and make his way to Singapore or Hong Kong. There, he'd been told, a race industry was blossoming, and he was certain that he could find steady work as an exercise rider; one day in the future, perhaps a trainer would be willing take him under his wing and show him the ropes of becoming a first-class horseman. Daniel had realized in the short time he had spent at Flemington Stables that he enjoyed being around horses and the people who were involved in every aspect of the racing vocation.

Charles Waterman derailed those plans. Love, or the thought of being in love, often alters how a person thinks and acts; level-headedness and logic fly out the window, rational behavior is happily discarded on impulse, and prudence is pushed aside for confusion. Charles Waterman had dabbled in his fair share of relationships with the female sex, but all manner of reason left him the day he met a young socialite passing through Cairo on her way to Paris.

Daniel wasn't in the hotel lounge on the afternoon Charlie fell in love with Caroline

Dunhill Abernathy. He supposed if he had been, the intricate charade that Charlie concocted in the wake of that meeting might never have come to fruition or even entered the man's head. But as it was, Charles Waterman felt very deeply in his heart—or rather in his loins, Daniel thought—that fate had brought he and Caroline to the same hotel desk at the same time on the same day in that exotic locale; the two were destined for each other. Because Charles felt the need to present himself as a man of equal standing to Miss Abernathy, a distant heir to the Dunhill fortune who was traveling with an entourage of chaperone and handmaiden, Charles needed a valet. He talked Daniel into posing as his for the few days Caroline was in Cairo before continuing on to Paris.

Little did Daniel (or Charlie, for that matter) know that the few days in Cairo would evolve into a fortnight in Paris. Charlie suddenly needed to be addressed as Charles.

The charade of Daniel posing as Charles's valet continued when Charles followed Caroline back to America, promising Daniel that he would help him find employment at a stable in Kentucky immediately upon entry to the country. Having no better offer at the time or means by which to enter America without a sponsor, Daniel reluctantly agreed.

And so began the next thirty-odd years of his profession: taking care of Mr. and Mrs. Waterman; overseeing the estate the newlyweds were gifted by one of Caroline's relatives on their wedding day, six months after they arrived back in the U.S.; and shouldering the responsibility for a stable of horses the Watermans acquired along with the estate for the very important purpose of joining the foxhunting set.

By Daniel's reasoning at the time, while becoming the majordomo of the Waterman estate was not his life's dream, it wasn't a bad short-term position, either. He had his own private quarters and three meals a day prepared and served to him by the estate cook. He oversaw beautiful grounds and a household staff of ten. And of course there were the horses. He figured a year or two on the job would allow him to save enough money and make contacts with trainers so he could strike out on his own as a horseman. And Charles, ever cognizant of the fact that Daniel was doing him a favor, went out of his way to make things right by Daniel, always treating him as a friend and never placing Daniel in a situation where he might feel he was being treated as a lesser human being.

Caroline was a quite a different matter. Born with a silver spoon in her mouth, Caroline Dunhill Abernathy treated people according to their station in life. Persons she deemed of equal standing—both socially and intellectually—were favored with impeccable manners, respected, graced with her sharp intellect, and showered with a self-effacing charm that put the most dour personalities at ease.

Those Caroline deemed lesser—servants, cooks, stablehands, clerks, and especially anyone black or Hispanic—saw a different side of Caroline.

*

"Mr. Locket, the lady of the house would like wine served with her meal this evening."

Mr. Locket pulled the car over to the curb and flicked off the headlights. As a fine mist had developed the closer he'd driven toward the Delaware River, he turned on the windshield wipers and drifted back into the memory of the evening when he'd gotten a firsthand look at the what lay in the heart of the lady of the house.

He'd stepped away from the horse he'd been brushing out and given Mrs. Cavanaugh a perplexed look.

"I told her I would be happy to fetch it myself, but she insisted that you were better suited to select something appropriate."

Daniel raised an eyebrow at that.

"She's dining on roast pheasant this evening."

He was formulating a protest to being pulled away from his horses when Mrs. Cavanaugh gave him a slight curtsy and then hurried out of the stables. He shook his head and reluctantly followed her up to the main house. It wasn't until he'd stepped into the kitchen to access the wine cellar that Mrs. Cavanaugh informed him that Mrs. Waterman had decided to take dinner in her bedroom.

"She seems a bit out of sorts this evening, Mr. Locket. I wouldn't keep her waiting."

Not knowing anything about wine except what he had picked up from being around Charles, Daniel grabbed a bottle of white Bordeaux, snatched a wine glass from the pantry shelf, and headed for the Watermans' bedroom.

"Tray, Mr. Locket, tray," Mrs. Cavanaugh had reminded him.

Mr. Locket noted the time on his watch when the large man he'd been following the past few hours exited his car and entered the alley on the side of a building with a set of large wooden doors. Not wanting to be seen by the large individual, Mr. Locket turned off the wipers to allow the mist to cover the windshield. Intensely curious about the link the large individual shared with Mrs. Waterman, the clinic in Delaware, and what he assumed was a government building in Trenton, he kept his eyes glued to the big wooden doors.

"It's Mr. Locket, madam," he'd announced upon knocking on the Watermans' bedroom door. "I have your wine."

He'd blushed when he saw her; she was wearing just a nightgown.

"Ah, Daniel, do come in," she said. "Why don't you tell me something about yourself as you open the wine."

He'd thought her neither pretty nor unattractive as he watched her walk across the room to take a seat in a red, cushioned chair. But she was young, with a young woman's body: slender, slightly muscular, with an ample bosom and curvy hips. He hesitated to enter because, well, something felt wrong about him being in her bedroom.

"Well, don't just stand there, Mr. O'Loughlin. Do come in and pour my wine before my dinner gets cold." Upon hearing his real name, he gripped the stem of the wine glass so hard he felt certain it was going to break.

"Yes, I know all about your sordid past," she said in a dismissive tone of voice. "Now pour my wine before I lose my patience."

When Mrs. Waterman had called him O'Loughlin and intimated she knew of his checkered past, he'd felt squirmy, like an annoying little shiver was running up his spine. He was experiencing quite the same feeling tonight—uneasy, a little off-balance—sitting in a car on the side of a road, wondering if the person he was watching was performing some type of unsavory act. Reflexively, he wiped the back of his neck with his palm. A sudden glare of headlights across the misted windshield reminded him of lamplight reflecting off the wine glass he'd set on the table in front of Mrs. Waterman.

"That was—" he'd stammered from the doorway of the Watermans' bedroom.

"The judge you brutally beat with those other men is paralyzed, you know."

He stiffened as the headlights from an oncoming car glared right into his face.

"There's an active warrant out for your arrest back in Ireland."

He was temporarily blinded when the car flashed its highbeams into his eyes.

"What do they do with common Irish trash in a British prison?" she'd asked.

He'd broken into a cold sweat and run out of the Watermans' bedroom to his small office in the stables.

The window by his face shattered a millisecond before he heard a gunshot. He slouched down in his seat, put the car in drive, and pushed the gas pedal. His heart felt like it had stopped beating for a moment as he raced away with mist blowing in through the damaged window.

After several blocks, Mr. Locket flicked the car headlights back on and checked the rearview mirror to see if he was being pursued. Balling one hand into a fist, he pushed down on his crotch to relieve the stress he was experiencing. Just about the same time, he saw a dimly lit sign alerting him that a Route 1 exit ramp to Pennsylvania was coming up on his right. Without thinking, he took the exit and headed back across the river.

*

It was a game Alexis liked to play: how long could she teeter on the brink of orgasm before she allowed herself to go over the edge? She indulged in the exercise because she knew that once the initial ecstasy of climax had passed, there would be a slight lull in her lustful urges—a lull that invariably led to a moment of self-examination. Normally, that moment of self-examination made her feel unclean. And she didn't particularly like feeling unclean or anything close to it. She grabbed a handful of the girl's hair and lifted her head.

"Wait," she whispered when the girl tried to push her face back into her groin. Alexis took a deep breath and arched her hips upward. "Slow," she whispered.

And then she lowered the girl's head back between her legs and moaned when she felt the girl's tongue flick across her clitoris. Closing her eyes, she began a slow gyration of her hips. Her breathing had just become erratic when there was a knock on the door. She ignored it, putting both hands on the back of the girl's head and pressing harder. The knock came again.

"Boss," a male voice called out from the other side of the door. "Sorry to bother you."

With a sigh, Alexis pulled the girl's head from between her legs. "What?" she barked.

"Overseas call. You said to find you no matter what."

"I know, I know. Shit—okay."

"Did I do something wrong?"

The girl was what, twelve or thirteen? A little on the thin side, but pretty—and she was clean. Her hair had been recently washed, and she smelled like—well, she smelled young and fresh. She was sure the girl was still a virgin.

"What's your name?" Alexis asked as she arranged a lock of the girl's straight brown hair behind her right ear.

"They call me Junebug," the girl replied in a southern drawl. "'Cause of my blue eyes," she explained, playfully batting her lashes. "What's yours?"

Alexis stiffened when June placed her hands on the soft flesh of her inner thighs and lightly ran her fingers upward. She grabbed June's wrists and shook her head.

"Later," she told her. She gently pulled the girl to her feet as she rose out of her chair. "We'll do something special," she told her. And then she stared into June's eyes as she closed the front of her sarong and tied the sash around her waist. "Would you like that?" she asked. Bending forward, Alexis pulled open the top drawer of the black and gold lacquered work desk. "I hear you like candy." She held up a small, square plastic bag partially filled with white crystals. "This should take care of your hunger until I have time for you again."

Eyes widening, June slowly reached out to take the bag from Alexis.

"Did you enjoy what you did to me?" Alexis asked as June took the bag from her fingers.

June nodded without hesitation.

"You tasted sweet," June said. "I liked it."

Alexis bent and kissed her on the forehead. A third knock came at the door.

"Guy says he's hanging up," the same voice told her. "Said there are other buyers if you don't want the ivory."

*

"How soon?"

Alexis placed the finger she'd run between June's legs under her nose and closed her eyes. While she listened to Akmir's reply, her imagination wandered to various erotic scenarios involving Junebug and sex toys.

"What did you say? No, no, that won't do. I have impatient buyers who have already waited too long." She tapped a foot against the floor and slapped the side of her thigh. "Well fly it out or pay off another ship's captain to ferry it across!" She sighed and shook her head. "That's not my problem. Nor can I do anything about that from my end." Her lips went tight as she frowned. "What do you mean, maybe you're dealing with the wrong person?" She gripped the phone so hard the inside of her palm turned white. "I just arranged fifty thousand in gold to be transferred to you. I'll gladly spend another fifty to have your head sent back to me with your balls stuffed down your throat if you think for one minute that—"

She wrapped the phone cord around her wrist and then unwrapped it. Her eyes narrowed and widened as her forehead crinkled and then smoothed.

"Well, if that old fool could charter a Red Cross plane, why can't you do the same? You're always telling me how better connected you are then he is. Prove it." She held the phone away from her ear and rolled her eyes. "Blah blah blah blah blah. And fuck Allah and any other god you want to hang an excuse on! We rule our own domains, Akmir! People like you and me *are* god and the devil wrapped in one. So, don't give me some pathetic crap about what Allah will allow and what he won't. *You* call the shots, don't you? So, you get me the first shipment of this huge cache of ivory you say your men have found within a week, or I'll be looking for a new partner to do business with! You hear me? I'll expect—"

She groaned and turned toward the bank of TV monitors arranged on the wall behind her. Her eyes reflexively scanned each and every image the monitors displayed, unconsciously taking note of the condition of each young inhabitant of the cells.

"Yes, I know you're trying to negotiate your way into becoming a nation within a country," she said in a placating tone of voice. "And that's all fine and well. But in the meantime, Akmir, we have business to take care of. You understand? Sometimes visions of grandeur have to wait."

As she listened to Akmir talk, Alexis pulled out the small address book she kept in the desk drawer and quickly flipped toward the back of the book.

"Look, Akmir, I'm sure the situation over in Somalia is as dire as you say, but I can't stress the point enough that business is business. With that as the sole basis of our relationship, you have a week to get me the first shipment of tusks before you give me no choice but to make other arrangements." She held the receiver away from her ear before shouting into it, "You know very well what I mean! Call me when the merchandise is on the way!"

With that, she put her finger down on the hook button and ended the call. She waited five seconds before lifting her finger off the button. When she heard the low buzz of the dial tone, she punched in an exceedingly long number.

"Salaam," she said when the call went through. "Talia? It's Alexis, Alexis Taylar."

*

Honeysuckle. He was sure of it, though he hadn't smelled the blossoms of the wild vine in a long time. Still, he thought, there was nothing quite like the aroma and the inevitable memories that floated into one's thoughts as the sweet, pungent fragrance invaded one's senses.

"How dare you leave without permission."

Mr. Locket looked out through the bullet-splintered window next to his head and into the dark field that lay on the north side of Church Road as Caroline's voice came to life within his head. He'd been stunned that she'd followed him from the manor house to the barn. And equally taken off guard by her angry demeanor.

"I am not some piece of tawdry Irish trash you can turn your back on," she'd spit. *"You leave when I say you leave and do what I say you do."*

Her voice was cold and bitter, but her face was hot and flush.

"Mrs. Waterman," he'd calmly countered, "let's get you back to your bedroom and call it a day."

"Oh, you'd like that, wouldn't you?" He was startled when she grabbed his forearms and looked into his eyes. *"Get me in bed."* Her breath smelled

of wine and— He turned his face and tried to push her away. "Shag me but good; isn't that the term?" she'd baited, refusing to let him go. "Fuck me till I can't stand straight?" When she slapped him across the face, he was shocked. "Oh, I bet you'd like that," she went on. "I've seen the way you look at me when Charles isn't watching."

"You're out of your fucking mind," he angrily blurted. "Get away from me."

But she pulled at him instead, eyes wide, her expression irrational. He didn't know if she meant to, but she caught the side of his eye with one of her nails when she reached up to give him another slap. He'd punched her in the mouth before he was aware he'd reacted to the pain of his injury.

"Good," she said when she put a fingertip to her lips and saw blood. "Now they'll believe me when I say you assaulted me, tried to rape me."

Mr. Locket stared out through the splintered glass and thought how dark the night seemed when one was away from the glaring lights of a city—or any light for that matter. Almost as dark as the inside of the invisible box he felt Caroline had lowered him into when she raked her nails across his neck and wiped the blood she'd drawn onto his shirt.

"If I tell them."

His brain couldn't work fast enough as he tried to think of a way to get past her and out of the office without physically hurting her.

"What do you think they would do to you, Mr. O'Loughlin—an immigrant criminal fugitive—if I were to tell Charles and the local authorities that you attacked me and tried to rape me while he was away on business?"

"Why?" was all he could think to say.

"Criminal, servant, stall-mucker," she continued. "And you dare to turn your back on me before I give you permission?"

She acted like some mad animal, the way she grabbed a riding crop from the tack pegs and began striking him across his upper arm with wild-eyed furor.

"Irish scum!" she screamed. "And you want to have me? You?" she taunted. "Impotent, I bet!"

And then she took the riding crop and struck him square across the face. He'd reacted on impulse and sheer anger, ripping the front of her nightgown away from her breasts while knocking the riding crop out of her hand.

"That's right, fuck me!" she yelled.

She tried to slap him again, but he pinned her arms to her sides, lifted her off the ground and threw her over his shoulder. Before he even made it outside the barn, he'd torn the rest of her nightgown away. Once outside, in a darkened paddock away from the windows of the stable, he threw her to the ground, stripped off his pants, and threw himself on top of her. The sex they engaged in was primal and fierce. They were like two dogs in heat, the way they pawed at each other and ground their bodies together to the point of physical pain. And when it was done—when he had no more energy left and she could barely move—he carried her back to her bedroom and dumped her into bed.

The fragrance of honeysuckle had been heavy in the air as he'd walked back to the barn in the hour before dawn. He remembered the fragrance so clearly because he associated it with the guilt that started to weigh on him with each step he'd taken and that had never left him. He'd left himself so open and exposed to the future whims of others.

Morning found him sober and somber. He knew what he'd done was wrong—disgustingly so. That he would confess to Charles and accept punishment was a foregone conclusion. But he hadn't anticipated that Caroline, upon Charles's return to the property, would convince her husband to take her on an immediate and impromptu vacation that lasted for six weeks. And when Daniel finally came face to face with Charles, the urgency to confess and cleanse his soul had dimmed with time. Whether by chance or planning on Caroline's part, he did not see her for six months after the Watermans returned from holiday. By then, the announcement had been made that she and Mr. Waterman were expecting their first child. Claire was born two months later. From that point on, Daniel's life was governed by guilt and a sense of responsibility for a child that was—or was not—his.

"Claire," he whispered with the hope of visualizing her as the five-year-old little girl in the gold picture frame.

But the shattered glass next to his face wouldn't allow him to see Claire in her youth. The jagged lines running across the window reminded him of the deep cut he'd seen on her wrist and the wicked bruises that discolored her ankles and marred the flesh on either side of her forehead. Who was the giant black man who had visited Mrs. Waterman, and what did he take into the clinic where Claire was being cared for? What business did the man have at the State House in Trenton in the middle of the night? And who had taken a shot at him? Had someone meant to kill him, or was he just in the wrong place at the wrong time?

Mr. Locket rubbed his eyes and checked the rearview mirror for what seemed to him to be the hundredth time. Satisfied that he was alone, he turned the ignition key and started the car.

What was going on? Everything—Miss Claire, Dirk Savage, Mrs. Waterman, the clinic, the giant black man—suddenly confused him. How did they all fit? Where did the pieces meet? And most of all, what part was he to play in the scheme that was developing?

As Mr. Locket flicked on the car headlights, he thought back to a moment when a young Miss Claire had offered an observation beyond her years. It had been the afternoon when Mrs. Waterman had curtly dismissed her daughter from the sitting room where Mr. Locket had served tea to Claire and her father as the two looked over the pond and shared conversation. He'd accompanied Claire to her room, as the lady of the house had instructed. And though he—Mr. Locket—had felt terrible about the way the child had been treated by her mother, Claire had exhibited no signs of harboring hurt feelings. The child had indeed seemed unperturbed by the incident, for she had, upon entering her room, gone straight to her chest of drawers where her toys and such were stored and pulled out a jigsaw puzzle of the earth which, in Mr. Locket's opinion, was far too mature for her to attempt. Yet the child unabashedly dumped the entire contents of the box on the floor and immediately sat down next to what looked to be a thousand intricately cut pieces.

"My, Miss Claire," he remembered commenting, "that looks quite challenging."

"I dare say it shall be, Mr. Locket," she replied.

"How will you—?"

"By understanding where it all begins, Mr. Locket," she confidently said. "That's the trick, isn't it? To find the piece that all else follows?"

16

"FOR THE FIRST time in my life, I am afraid of the Father."

Teimbaka twisted a frayed piece of fabric dangling from his sleeve and listened to the sounds beyond John Too's voice. The river current—or so he thought the continuous rushing whoosh that flowed from the wall at his back— was there, but there was something more, something that reminded of him of distant thunder. No, not thunder. More the sound of heavy artillery laying down a patterned bombardment some distance away. Out of habit, he looked up to where he imagined he would find the mountain range that straddled the border of Eritrea to see if the glimmer of war flashed amongst the peaks. He remembered hearing the same sounds before. He'd been holding Claire within his arms as she tried to sleep while artillery raged in the distance. If he imagined hard enough, he could still feel her body trembling against his. The memory was bittersweet.

"It feels odd to be afraid. He sent the boy, after all."

Teimbaka rubbed the bandages covering his eyes and tugged at the hood of his robe. As he sniffled and cleared phlegm from his throat, he was certain he heard the cooing of a dove.

"But I have not seen the boy since—"

Teimbaka felt along the ground on either side of him as though he had lost something.

"My dula, John Too. Where is it?" he asked.

"Your dula?" John Too inquired, confused. "The boy— The boy has your staff."

"How is that possible?"

"He said you lost it. He says he is keeping it for you until—"

Teimbaka tilted his head to better hear the rest of what John Too said.

"Until? Until when?" he pressed.

"Until you are ready to carry it."

Teimbaka grunted and turned away. Folding his hands across his lap, he closed his eyes and tried to picture just where it was he'd left Tafari's walking stick. A wide ribbon of green color appeared in his thoughts, spreading from his forehead to the back of his skull. Oddly, the metallic hue began turning red—as if an incision had been made down the middle of the mass and blood had seeped from the wound—before bursting into flames and disintegrating.

"Where did you go?" Teimbaka abruptly asked. "The morning you left— why didn't you tell me you were leaving?"

The sound of the river current seemed to strengthen in the silence before John Too replied. A sensation of wind blowing sand against his face prodded Teimbaka to tilt his head toward the ground and gather his hood close about his cheeks.

"I went to the Danakil, where the boy said he would be. Deep in the salt flats I found him, traveling with a small band of traders who barely noticed his presence. He was barefoot, his feet blistered and bloody. He used your staff to hold himself upright.

"Where are your sandals?" I asked him.

"I discarded them," he told me, "so the sin I have walked upon might be burned from my flesh."

I asked if I should do the same.

It was a curious sound, Teimbaka thought, the unfurling of a sail. Or was it the muffled, prolonged click of a cotton fan opening and closing? Farther away, some distance from the flutter of noise that had piqued his interest, the soft coo of a dove came and left him within the time it took to turn his head.

"'Your burden is not the cross," he told me. "Though the scars upon your back will be as deep."

The cross—Teimbaka could see it clearly. He almost wished he couldn't. For the image of it dangling from Claire's hand, aglitter in moonlight— though joyous in a way he could never put into words—had become a memory steeped in torment. The cross had been a beacon of faith in a time of doubt. He remembered she'd been praying, asking the Father to keep the children safe, to keep the Mother from harm. He'd known for some time that he'd fallen in love with her, but it was in that specific moment, as she rose from her knees and held the small silver cross close to her heart, that his bond to her became eternal, his devotion complete. And when they'd kissed, his soul had joined with hers in a melding of passion, courage, and faith that had set his spiritual being aflame.

"This is why I am afraid, for I can no longer see the boy or hear his voice. And I cannot help but wonder what the Father will yet place before me."

Teimbaka cupped his face in his hands as a vision of the cross slipping from Claire's hand and falling to the ground manifested within his thoughts. As he watched the silver medallion sink into the earth and disappear, he felt his spirit retreat, wither, with a pain in his chest so severe he felt as though his ribs had cracked. The cross and Claire were gone, vanished from his life before he had a chance to understand how much they'd meant to him. He was nothing now—just a blind beggar squatting in an alley littered with refuse and sewage.

"How cruel and wicked the Serpent is," he whispered.

"What did you say, Etiyopiya? My mind was somewhere else."

*

"Is that the only animal the kid knows how to draw?"

Tanya rubbed a hand over the bullet wound on her arm as she watched Marcus draw what looked to be another pencil outline of a miniature elephant. It was the boy's latest addition to the dozen or more he'd already sketched. She thought it peculiar, a child of—what was he now, three?—drawing a zoo animal. Most kids his age were lucky if they could draw an elongated V for a flying bird or a crude outline of a dog or cat with a long tail and pointed ears. Least that's all the ones she'd babysat could draw. And why did Marcus keep looking over in the corner of the room like he was actually looking at an elephant as he drew on the paper? Skinny had hit the boy hard on the side of his head. Maybe he thought he was in daycare or something, where they had pictures of animals on the wall.

"You still whacked out?"

Tanya gave Chris what she hoped he interpreted as a belligerent look and grunted.

"What's it to you what he knows how to draw?" she replied. "What's the kid to you, anyway? Not like you know him or nothin'."

The man she knew as a sometime customer of Jim and Rochelle's restaurant looked at the boy with what seemed to be a little too much concern on his face. Maybe he did know the boy. Maybe he was more to the boy than he let on. *And why he show up at my place same time as Marcus?* Maybe he followed Marcus from wherever the city took him to stay after they finally came and collected him. Tanya studied the man's face for a moment, then gave Marcus's features a good hard look. She didn't see any resemblance between the two, but shit, maybe he *was* the boy's father.

"Just wondering," Chris replied. "Since he doesn't seem to know how to talk, either." Tanya followed his movements as he cautiously approached the only window in the room. "Maybe Jim and Rochelle took him to the zoo a few times," he commented as he peered out the window from a good three feet away from it.

Tanya looked at all the elephant drawings Marcus had made and thought about the hallucination she'd experienced just before Skinny had shown up at Gerard's apartment building. She shivered and squeezed her eyes shut.

"Course, that had to be before you and your dead boyfriend blew them away."

"I had nothin' to do with that!" she snapped. "I just—" Tanya froze when Chris reached behind his back and pulled a gun from the waistband of his pants.

"I ought to just shoot you right now for the lying piece of shit you are," he said. She stiffened when he took a menacing step toward her. "Blow a hole in your forehead like you did to Rochelle."

When Chris put the barrel of the gun to her head, she reached for Marcus and started to tremble.

"It was a mistake," she whimpered as she pulled Marcus across the floor and brought him to sit next to her. "No one was supposed to—"

"What was a mistake?" he replied. "You being born, or everything that came after?"

"Fuck you," she hissed. "Like you all that." She grunted and gave him a defiant look. "Fuckin' street pimp, for all I know." Cupping one breast in her hand, she said, "I seen the way you look at me. Don't take no mind reader to know what you want." She ran her hand along his thigh and winked. "Maybe I let you between my legs if you let me go."

Chris slapped her hand from his leg and pressed the barrel of the gun harder against her head.

"The only thing I want to put between your legs is a bar of soap," he snarled. "Fucking bitch."

In one quick motion, he clipped her across her cheek with the butt of the weapon. "You one fuckin' stupid—" He took a few steps away from her and shook his head. "You even give a shit that your old man's dead? Or your boyfriend? Or Jim and Rochelle? You give a shit about anything?"

Tanya put her hand to her cheek and felt the area where Chris had struck her. Her fingertips came away with blood on them. In a blur of motion, she shoved Marcus away and lunged at Chris. Chris easily sidestepped her and punched her in the head as she flew by. Tanya landed on the floor with a loud thud and didn't move. Chris stood over her for a minute before he stuck the toe of his boot under her shoulder and rolled her over so her face was pointed up at the ceiling.

"Dumb bitch," he muttered.

As if he'd just remembered Marcus was in the room, Chris sighed and looked over at the boy.

"She's lucky you're here," he said. He stuffed the gun into the back waistband of his pants before adding, "And lucky that you like her."

*

Marcus saw the man talking at him, but he didn't understand what he was saying. Nor did he care. He glanced over at his babysitter and saw she was sleeping on the floor. Maybe they—she and the man—would stop pushing and pulling him and taking him to places he didn't really want be. He was tired and his head hurt. It made him feel icky. He just wanted to draw and maybe make friends with the animal in the corner of the room—if the grownups could just be quiet for a few minutes.

The animal made him feel good. He liked the way it was kind of sparkly and kind of invisible at the same time. Its long nose was funny looking but seemed a perfect match to its big, flappy ears. And the animal's eyes—small and round, the color of some flowers he'd seen in a store—well, he felt like they could see right down into his stomach. Which was a little scary and a little special at the same time. Maybe the animal would let him pet it—if the grownups were done making noise.

Marcus noticed the man turn away from him and move toward the window. The animal saw it too, was watching the man. So Marcus picked up his latest drawing and held it up to the animal. When the animal looked his way, it raised its long nose in the air. Marcus giggled at that, because it made the animal look like it was raising a hand to ask a question. But when he saw the man turn and look at him with a frown, Marcus lowered the sketch and shifted his gaze to the floor. Putting pencil to a different sheet of paper, he started another drawing of the animal he hoped might become his friend.

*

When Chris saw the boy start another drawing of an elephant, he shook his head in disappointment. *Kid's retarded*, he thought. He'd probably been that way since the day that hitman had blown up the gas line in his apartment building and sent everybody to their deaths. It had probably done something to the kid's brain when he hit the ground.

It was obvious to Chris that the kid had been cursed with bad luck. All you had to do was look at the people who'd been killed during his short life: his mother, grandparents, fake grandparents (Jim and Rochelle), Tanya's boyfriend, and Tanya's father. He figured there'd undoubtedly be more people killed in the future because of the kid. The kid attracted death like a magnet.

Shit, he thought. If he'd known how many people were going to lose their lives because of Marcus, he never would have bought the kid from the junkie whore who'd found him after the explosion. Or maybe the kid *was* really cursed. His old man was African, right? So maybe some witch doctor cast some kind of voodoo spell on the kid's father and the incantation got passed down to the son when the father was killed. *Shit, the father was murdered too, wasn't he?* Maybe there was more to the curse thing then he imagined. He gave Marcus a wary look and frowned; damn if he wanted to die because of some cursed, retarded kid.

Chris shifted his attention from Marcus to Tanya when she moaned. What the hell was he going to do with her? If it was up to him, he'd put a bullet through her skull and rid the world of another stupid, junked-out teenage bitch. But as it was, because the kid felt attached to her—and because there wasn't anybody left he knew of that might take the boy in and raise him—he felt like he didn't have any choice but to let her live and get her out of whatever mess she'd gotten herself tangled up in. Of course, he was still going to have to convince her to take Marcus. But first things first.

How deep in the shit was she? And what would it take for her to make a commitment to the kid? He searched her exposed skin for gang markings and tattoos. So far, all he knew about Tanya was that her boyfriend and the other punk who'd killed Jim and Rochelle were dead. He'd heard one of them had taken a bullet during the robbery, but Tanya's boyfriend—Gerard—and her father had both been killed because of gang-related business. At least that's how he saw it. And if that was the case, he figured he'd have to make sure the three of them—Tanya, Marcus, and himself—kept invisible until he could get her and the boy relocated where the Bloods or the Brotherhood or the Fiver Percenters—or whatever chapter of losers Tanya was involved with—didn't have a chapter. Even then he couldn't be certain that some banger trying to earn his place wouldn't be given the job of finding Tanya and snuffing her out to settle whatever beef she had with the big skinny dude he'd shot in the hand.

Links of a gold necklace showing out of the top of Tanya's shirt reminded Chris of Super Freak. Word on the street was that the reverend had been butchered on the Toyota Logistics pier to make a statement. There'd be some heavy jockeying for power, what with the elimination of a big wheel like Rue. Somebody must have their eyes on his piece of the drug action—and everything else coming through the docks. But which faction—or who—he didn't have a clue.

The chain. Chris took a closer look at the gold chain showing from under Tanya's shirt. Curious, he bent down and slid the chain out of her shirt. When he saw a key attached, he lifted it to eye level.

The key was small and looked like it fit one of those inexpensive padlocks you buy in a hardware or grocery store. Closer inspection revealed a group of letters chiseled on the key: USPS. United States Post Office. *Shit*, he thought. Could it be? For several months, he'd been sending Jim five grand a month to a PO box in Elizabeth City, New Jersey. Was this the key to that box? If it was, it meant Tanya knew about the cash Jim was collecting every thirty days, and more than likely she knew why the money had been sent.

He turned the key from side to side as he pondered what else Tanya might know. And worse, whom she might have told. Is this what the big skinny dude wanted from her? Was a gang aware that she had a key to a PO box where five thousand in cash showed up the first of every month? Is that the reason her boyfriend was killed—because they wanted the key? And if he was, if the gang killed Gerard because they wanted the key and money that came with it, did that mean they knew the boy was the reason the money was sent? Was Marcus now the target of a gang?

He nudged Tanya's shoulder with his foot.

"Wake up." He nudged her a shoulder a little harder when she didn't respond. "Hey, wake the hell up."

When he saw her mouth move like she was chewing on a blade of grass, he straddled her face and let a wad of saliva drop out of his mouth. *Splat*. She wiped the moisture from her cheek and opened her eyes. He dangled the necklace and the key a foot above her head.

"Where'd you get this? And why'd you have it stuffed down your bra?" He pressed a foot down on her shoulder when she tried to roll over onto her side. "Don't bother trying to move until you tell me what I want to know."

"Fuck you," she snapped. She jabbed two fingers into his calf and snarled, "You gonna beat me front of the boy? That what you gonna do? Show Marcus what a big man you are by slappin' me around?" She reached up and grabbed hold of his wrist. "Go ahead, then," she said, pulling on his arm. "He seen me knocked around before. Ain't gonna freak him none."

Chris had half a mind to oblige her, but because of the boy's presence, he merely kicked her extended arm to break her grip. With a grunt, he stepped away and allowed her to stand.

"Why you bring me here?" she snapped. "And why you let Skinny live after what he done?" She folded her arms in front of her chest and frowned. "You scared of shootin' somebody dead?"

"What gang are you a part of?"

"I ain't."

"Fuck you ain't."

"I ain't," she said. "I ain't in a gang. And ain't never been in one."

"Who's Skinny? What group of losers does he belong to?"

Tanya turned to face the unadorned wall behind her. "Skinny just be—"

"Your dumb-ass boyfriend part of the same gang? Is that why's he's dead? 'Cause he went shootin' his mouth off about this?" Chris dangled the key in front of her face. "Is that how you came by that gunshot wound on your arm? Is that why Skinny was about to blow your head off before your father showed up?" Chris raised the key a little higher. "How many people know about this? What do you know about it?"

"What *you* know about it?" she retorted. She turned and took a step toward him. "Just what you know about all this shit? Why were you at my place? What's the boy to you? You his father or somethin'?"

Chris smirked and then looked down at Marcus.

"Promised somebody I'd keep an eye on him when I could. Just happened I was in town when I heard about—" He gave Tanya a withering look as he moved toward the window. "You know what I heard." He reached behind his back and tapped the gun he carried. "Ought to waste you right here for what you did."

"I didn't—"

"Shut up!"

"I wasn't there!" she yelled. "So go ahead and shoot if you think that's gonna change anything!" He heard her mutter something as she glanced down at the floor. "Never would have happened if soul-daddy didn't keep so much dollar around. Every junkie on the street knew he only dealt in cash. Like a fuckin' candy store, he was."

"What do you mean, you weren't there? Then how—?" He held the key up. "How'd you get this?"

She folded her arms across her chest and then unfolded them. She rubbed absently at her chest when she answered.

"Fuckin' Gerard came poundin' on my door. He was flyin' but on the down. Goin' off about Puffer being dead and how shit got outta hand." She nodded to Marcus. "Marcus was there 'cause I was watchin' him for the night. Soul-daddy—Jim—supposed to come get him after closin'." She paused before adding, "Never showed."

"Because your man offed him," he coldly reminded her.

"I told you I wasn't there!"

"Whatever," he replied. "Get on with it." When she flipped him off, he calmly responded, "The key."

He saw her eyes flit toward the door before she cleared her throat and continued talking.

"Like I said, Gerard was comin' down hard. Started to lose it. Started talkin' shit about needin' cash for a score. Started gettin' rough. Got pissed when I told him my old man don't let me keep none of the cash soul-daddy pay me for watchin' the kid."

"What do you mean, rough?"

"Shit," she scoffed. "Don't play no dumb nigger with me. You from somewhere I ain't?" She rolled her eyes and sighed. "Rough," she said, "like pow-bang-slap."

Chris grunted.

"But then he freaked."

"What do you mean, freaked?" he pressed.

"Started beatin' on Marcus. Started chokin' him. Thought he was—" She looked into his eyes but then quickly looked away. "I ran and got the key to their crib—soul-daddy's—before he killed the boy. Grabbed it out of my hand and poof, he was gone before—" She sighed and turned to face the wall behind her. "Next I see him, we trippin' on some prime and everything good." She shrugged. "Then Skinny and his crew show up and— He tossed me that necklace just before they busted down the door and started shootin'." She shrugged again before turning to face him. "Don't know what the boy done to make Skinny so mad, but yeah, he knew about the key, and I suppose he knew about the money." Her eyes shifted to Marcus. "Kid like a bank," she muttered. "Too bad he never knew he had an account."

"Yeah, too bad," Chris sarcastically agreed.

"So now what?" He saw Tanya's brow furrow as she scanned the room. "What is this place? Ain't no motel." She took a few steps toward the door.

"Go ahead," he goaded. "I'm sure Skinny and the other—what, Bloods? I'm sure they can't wait to see you walking the streets." He smiled when she glared at him. "Of course, they'll blame you for Skinny getting shot. And they'll want the key." He winked as he stuffed the key and necklace in the pocket of his jeans. "And they'll probably want Marcus, too—once they figure out he was the boy on the stoop."

He balled his right hand into a fist when she took a few aggressive steps toward him and yelled, "I'll just tell 'em it was—" She stopped abruptly. "Tell 'em—"

"Tell them?" he mocked. "What you going to *tell* a bunch of brainless punks? What do you think they're going to do to you next time they see you? Especially when you consider the fact that they already killed your boyfriend, murdered your father, and were about to pull the trigger to blow you away when I showed up." He gave her a dismissive shake of his head before adding, "You better wake up, sister. Your time in this town is over."

Her eyes narrowed as she bit down on her bottom lip. He figured she was about to break down.

"I'll just give you up."

He looked at her like he didn't hear her right.

"What's that?"

"Yeah, that's right. I'll tell Skinny and the boys you took the key, took Marcus, and laughed about it, sayin' what fools they are for thinkin' they could get one over on you. I'll say you called 'em a bunch of dumb-ass niggers got their cocks in their ass." She puffed out her chest and gave him a definitive nod. "Yeah, that's what I'll do." She pointed at him and smirked. "They'll be on yo' ass lickety-split. And I'll be dancin' free and clear."

He wanted to shoot her, wanted to pull the Glock from his pants and blow a hole in her face. Instead, he nodded toward the door.

"Go ahead," he told her. "Go strut your ugly ass out on the street and see what happens."

He didn't flinch when she took a few steps toward the door, nor did he show any expression when she abruptly stopped and glanced at Marcus.

"No need to concern yourself with the boy," he said. "He'll be fine with me."

Her brow furrowed, her tone accusatory, she asked, "What the hell you gonna do with him?"

"Doesn't concern you." He motioned with his hand for her to continue on to the door. "You run along now, give my regards to Skinny and his boys."

"Maybe he don't wanna go with you. Maybe he better off with me."

He shook his head. "You'll be dead before the day is out, so that don't wash."

"But I—"

"Go on," he told her. "Go reap the rewards for what you've done."

Tanya rubbed her chest as she glanced at the door.

"What you gonna do? You know, after I go?"

"What do you care?"

"What you gonna do?" she repeated. "It's just a damn question." She folded her arms across her stomach and huffed. "Just a damn question," she said again. "Ain't no big thing."

"Well then, seems—"

"He need to eat."

"Say what?"

"Marcus." She pointed to the boy and frowned. "He need to eat. When you gonna feed him?"

"When I get around to it," he replied.

"Safe to say you ain't got nothin' here." She raised her eyebrows. "Not like you got a kitchen or nothin'. So I'll stay with him while you get him somethin'."

"I don't think you're seeing things straight. You—"

He shook his head when Tanya sat down next to Marcus and put her arm around the boy's shoulders.

"What do you think you're doing?"

Eyebrows raised, she shook her head and said, "Told you I'd stay with him till you bring him somethin' to eat. So I am." She gave Marcus a hug. "What you want, little man? Hotcakes?"

"Don't play me, girl. If you think for one minute—"

"Well I can't go," she interjected. Rolling her eyes, she explained, "You say yourself I'll be dead if I do." With a quick look around the room, she shrugged. "Besides, I don't know where the hell I am. But you do." She nodded toward the door. "So go already. And bring extra syrup. Little man, here," she hugged Marcus again, "likes extra with his hotcakes."

"You're out of your fucking mind if you think—"

"Probably a golden arches right around the corner." She glanced up at him before shifting her attention to the paper Marcus was drawing on. "Got more McDonald's in this city than grocery stores," she mumbled. "Wouldn't mind a Diet Coke and a sausage biscuit while you're there. Don't remember last time I ate."

Heavily sighing, Chris closed his eyes and shook his head. Jaw clenched, he reached for his gun. Before he could get his hand on it, he heard her mumble.

"What's that?" he asked.

"I said, 'You got a toilet?'" She winked. "'Cause I gots to go."

*

"Listen up. This is how it's going down."

Jame hated most everything about his reflection: the pimples; the wide, flat nose; the protruding, overly round nostrils; and the wiry jaw attached to cheekbones that reminded him of prehistoric man. Yeah, he was an ugly son of a bitch, no doubt about it. In fact, he'd been told he was an ugly blankety-blank so many times in his life he pretty much expected to hear the phrase uttered by anyone he came in contact with. If it wasn't for his eyes—mellow brown, he'd heard them described as, sharp and keen like a hawk's, with just the right touch of iciness, like if you looked into them deep enough and long enough you'd see the goddamn spirit of a cobra—there wasn't a redeeming factor about him. But shit, man, his eyes, his eyes were his equalizers, able to hold someone's full attention without allowing it to wander to any other destination on his face.

"I'll shoot you in the motherfucking balls while you hypnotized by my stare."

He gave his reflection a wink and a big toothy smile.

"That's right. The name's Jame Ain't, motherfucker, and you just done got yourself killed 'cause you got lost in my dreamy-ass eyes."

He laughed, but then wiped his hand down his face from his forehead to his chin. By the time the knuckle of his thumb passed his lower lip, his laughter and smile were gone, replaced by a stony expression.

"Y'all been running your own game for years and years. Gone through turf wars and piles of dead bodies to show for it. You know it and I know it. Profits are good, no denyin'. But some years are better than others, right?"

Jame turned away from the mirror and looked at the weapons he'd laid out on top of the toilet tank: a .44 Magnum pistol, a switchblade, a razor ring, and the small stun grenade he'd picked up at an army surplus store. Having cleaned the gun, sharpened the knife, and inspected the razor casing for any weakness, he was satisfied the weapons were 100 percent ready for action. He wasn't nearly as certain about the reliability of the stun grenade, but he figured it would have the proper effect on people whether it worked or not. Because who in their right mind was going to stand around and wait to see if a grenade was going to go off? Nobody, he figured. So it was a good piece of armament to carry along.

"But let me point out a few things." He pointed at his reflection as he turned back and looked into the mirror. "Your distribution is piecemeal, your pricing inconsistent, quality control nonexistent, and security left to whatever gang-bangers and street thugs you got on your payroll. Most of you losing product between point A and point B because your mules and middlemen skimmin'. Or you losing entire shipments because you got poorly designed methods for getting shit from port out into the city."

Jame puffed out his cheeks and leaned toward the mirror. Brow furrowed, he put a big frown on his face and cleared his throat. When he spoke, his voice was deep and threatening.

"What you sayin'? Why I should listen to a punk-ass ugly motherfucker like you?"

Jame leaned back from the mirror and stroked the few long whiskers growing out of his chin. He gave his reflection a long, thoughtful look before he replied.

"'Cause this ugly motherfucker gonna show you the way to stream-line your operation and put more green in your pocket, that's why. Gonna tell you how distribution can be handled so y'all not competing to hire the same people to run the same routes. Gonna introduce you to price control, too, so crack cost the same in Blood turf as it do in Chinatown. And quality: quality gonna be consistent; same shit hit the streets in Philly as in Brooklyn. And security," he paused and shifted his gaze from one area of the mirror to another like he was looking at a group of people standing around him in a semicircle, "security gonna be handled by an organized army of professionals instead of by a bunch of hotheads running around shootin' people 'cause they high on the shit they supposed to be protectin'."

"Sound like you talkin' con-sol-o-dation."

Jame looked at the cold, street-hardened face staring back at him from the mirror and was tempted to reach for his .44. He knew there was going to be pushback from somebody for what he was saying, and he was ready for it.

"Ain't gonna happen," the same street-tough persona went on in a threatening tone. "Things cool the way they are—the way they always been. Don't need no outsider—a motha-fuckin' ugly one at that—trying to squeeze in on the action. You playin' us for fools?" Jame heard anger in the dude's voice. He put his hand on the .44. "That what you think we are? Fools? Maybe I show you how to streamline your way to the grave."

Jame moved with the quickness of the cobra he was certain lived inside him. He grabbed his pistol and pointed it at the man's face before it could change expression.

"Just be cool, brother," Jame told the imaginary adversary. "Ain't gotta go down like this. Ain't nobody have to eat it." He stared into the mirror and gave himself a look he hoped would convey a mixture of understanding, strength, and seriousness. "You hear what happened to Super Freak, right?" He slowly looked from left to right and nodded to the imaginary people standing around him. "He didn't want no consolidation either." Jame gave what he hoped would be seen as an innocent-but-telling shrug. "And look what happened to him. Pity he was blind."

"What do you mean, he was blind?" It was the frowning guy talking again, the one with the deep, menacing voice.

"Didn't see the possibilities consolidation offers. Couldn't see the danger of not consolidatin', either. Must be awful not to be able to see the future." Jame paused to give an odd sounding laugh. "Course, don't need eyes if you dead—if you know what I mean. Now somebody else got his piece of turf, collecting his cut, tasting his treats. And where he at?" He looked around at the imaginary people again with a questioning expression on his face. "At the bottom of the river is where. Carp pickin' the meat from his bones."

"You saying that was you, *negro*?"

Jame caught the heavy Spanish accent in the new speaker's voice, but there was something else, some other sound that he picked up on too. No doubt in his mind, he just heard a Glock locking in a round.

"Cause Freak was an *amigo* to me and my *compadres*. It ain't no good he was killed the way he was."

Jame turned and didn't flinch when he met the gaze of the non-existent Ñeta gang member.

"Funny, he didn't say nothin' about spic compadres when he was rolling down the bank into the river. Think he was kinda glad to have it all over with. You know, leading the double life like he did and all. Stress must have been somethin' awful. Don't you think, Pablo, or whatever the fuck your name is?"

Jame stared into the mirror. With a stony expression, he raised his left hand and snapped his fingers. As he imagined a dozen guns being cocked, he allowed his mouth to form a thin wisp of a smile.

"You go ahead and live in the past with a dead fat man, if that's your thing, spic-boy. But you gonna find out real quick what it means to cross Jame Ain't if you do." Once more, Jame Ain't paused so he could gaze into the face of each imagined ringleader, boss, crew chief, and *jefe* standing around him. "Now, if there ain't no other objections or comments, what say you all to puttin' our operations under one roof so we can generate some real power and double our cash flow?"

The knock upon the bathroom door was so unexpected Jame Ain't whirled round on the balls of his feet and fired a shot from the .44 point-blank into the wood.

"Fuck! It's me!" he heard a familiar voice yell. "Don't shoot! Don't shoot! It's Jacko!"

Jame Ain't yanked the door open and thrust his weapon in front of him.

"Thought I said I didn't want no interruptions!" he shouted. "What the fuck you want?"

Jacko—slight of build with a light brown complexion and orange-dyed, short-cropped hair—peeked around the frame.

"Meet's set," he said.

"When?" Jame Ain't asked.

"Half-hour," Jacko replied.

"Players in place?"

"They on their way."

Jame shoved Jacko to the side as he existed the bathroom. "Where we headin'?"

"Bar down by the pier."

"Got a name?"

Jame Ain't abruptly stopped, turned, and headed back toward the bathroom.

"Well?" he inquired.

Jame retrieved some items from the top of the toilet tank and stuffed them in the pockets of his pants and jacket.

"Ain't—ain't got no name, far as I, far's I know," Jacko replied. "Been, been there a while, though. Big, big h-h-h-uge motherfucker run it."

"That so," Jame replied as he pushed past Jacko.

"Yeah, yeah, that's what I heard. Big son of a bitch. Goes by the name Goliath."

"Goliath, huh?" Jame glanced over his shoulder and winked. "Well Goliath about to meet David, then," he remarked. He displayed the .44 like he was holding up a trophy. "'Cause it's showtime!"

*

Chris couldn't help but feel like he'd been pussy-whipped. He felt as though he'd reverted to Noah Kunda and was reliving the days when he'd bring dinner to Yutanda's apartment under the pretense of dating her. He was sure to anyone who might be watching that he looked like some lame-ass delivery boy, what with the way he was walking down a litter-strewn street with a bag of food under each arm and a damn diet soda clutched in his hand. *"Bring extra syrup,"* he silently recited to himself. *"Little Marcus like to dip his pancakes in it."* *Well fuck little Marcus,* he thought. *Kid's a goddamned retard! And he's cursed, too!* Chris shook one of the McDonald's bags like he was trying to get the wrinkles out of the paper. *But you're too damn high all the time to notice, aren't you?*

Chris shook his head and let out a frustrated sigh.

"What in the world have you gotten yourself into?" he mumbled. *Why am I even bothering with this kid anymore?*

Why? Good question. Why *was* he continuing the charade? He looked at the bags of food and shook his head. He didn't know why, and that gnawed at him. What was worse, he couldn't for the life of him figure out a reason he'd listened to the teenage junkie slut who more than likely would be dead by now if it wasn't for him sticking his nose in her business. He didn't really expect her to be waiting for him when he got back to the place he'd rented out near the bridge, did he? Not likely. Not likely at all. Then why leave her there alone with the kid in the first place to run to the McDonald's on West 63d for an order of pancakes and a couple of sausage biscuits?

There it was again: that *why* word. He rolled it around in his head for a few seconds—*why*—before reaching a conclusion. *Hell if I know.*

When he'd scooped Marcus—Menelik was the kid's name, he reminded himself—up from the sidewalk and dragged Tanya to the car he'd hot-wired to follow her father home from McGuire Air Force Base, Chris had reacted so fast to the events that had transpired—Tanya's father shot, the boy clubbed and having a gun put to his head, Tanya on the edge of get-ting blown away—that he hadn't had time to process his surroundings. He didn't know if other gang members—lookouts and spotters, capable of calling for backup and having him followed across the river—had been posted on Tanya's street. But it suddenly dawned on him that maybe he hadn't seen any suspicious cars slowly cruising down Mina Street because they already knew where he was and were just waiting for the right oppor-tunity to move on the kid, Tanya, and the key. With that thought in mind, he started walking with a little more purpose.

When Chris saw a big, black four-door sedan come barreling off of

Mina Street onto Sycamore Avenue and head right toward him, he pulled his gun and scurried behind an abandoned car parked a few feet in front of him. As the big sedan drew closer, he tried to see who the occupants were, but the windows were tinted smoke-grey. Just before the big four-door drew parallel to him, he saw a rear window edge down a few inches and caught a glimpse of a gun barrel. Bracing for gunshots, he pressed his body against the abandoned car and tucked his head. As the rumble of the car's engine grew louder, he chambered a round in his Glock.

"Fuck you, man."

Chris looked up over his shoulder just in time to see the flash of a metal bar.

17

*THERE IS AN aspect to my blindness I did not foresee. While the affliction
has placed me within a dark and sightless place, I was not expecting the monsters it has unleashed: terrible beasts whose sole purpose is to torment me in the
innermost corners of my soul. What weapons do I possess to repel fear and beat
back the relentless waves of doubt that seek to penetrate the very essence of my
being? What words exist that will sway the tide of cowardice flowing through
my veins? I have witnessed the silver cross sink into the Serpent's sand. How
then, am I not to believe that Claire has perished?*

*

"Do you remember what I said to you the first time we spoke?"

The voice elicited a mosaic of colors backlit by diffused sunlight. Claire
grappled with the image, wanting to cherish its sublime beauty but torn
away by the waves of intense pain shooting through her skull.

"I— I," she was able to stammer before her throat constricted to a
point where she couldn't breathe.

As she choked, a tattered piece of paper manifested within the center
of the colored light. She focused on it and found herself—her much
younger self—transported, standing in front of a glass display case featur-
ing an ancient parchment. In the vision, she observed herself gazing at
an ancient parchment through a display case made of glass. Curious what
was written on the tattered page, Claire tried her best to concentrate on
the script. The words were written in Latin, and her younger self had not

yet learned Latin. Yet she had been able to understand the words, for she distinctly remembered the scene she was witnessing. On the afternoon she and her mother had visited the chapel in Arles, the words on the parchment had flown into her head as if carried on the wings of angels.

"Remember?"

Claire blinked her eyes several times as shafts of brilliant sunshine broke through the mosaic of colors. Awestruck by the spectacle, she followed the golden rays from origin to destination. What she saw within the light brought tears to her eyes. She remembered the evening well.

She had left the twelve boys—John Too, Thomas, and the other orphans—to say her evening prayers. The moon had just risen above the horizon, bathing the highlands in a heavenly light. A shadow appeared beside her as she knelt. But she wasn't afraid, for she knew well the silhouette.

"What do you pray for?" Teimbaka asked.

She was filled with hope that evening, her faith in God strong and unwavering. She felt emboldened when she said, "For the suffering to end. For the famine, drought, and killings to stop."

He smiled and lightly placed a finger against the side of her chin. He kissed her then. It was unexpected but magical. She felt the power of the world beating in her heart as their lips touched for the first time. She remembered wishing she could linger in the sweet tenderness forever. And when the kiss had run its course, when their unspoken vows of devotion had seamlessly linked their souls, they'd looked out across the highlands and witnessed the manifestation of hundreds of spirit-elephants in crystalline form. The moment was spellbinding. Never before had Claire felt such majesty and beauty. Oh, how she had longed to see the spirit-elephants again since that evening. And now here they were, spread out across a field of bright green grass, embellished by shafts of sunlight begot from a stained-glass sky.

And then, to her utter horror, the ethereal beasts caught fire. Flames burst from under their feet, withering their crystalline bodies into pools of murky grey ooze. The field of green grass was shrouded in a haze of black ash as cinders swirled across her sightline.

"The children, Claire." It was the voice speaking to her again—His voice—His words portrayed as a vision of a burning tree set against a back-drop of utter darkness. "I asked you to take care of them."

As if gasoline had been misted into the air, the swirling cinders ignited into brilliant bits of orange flame before they fell into ash. Claire, left staring at an emptiness that seemed to have no beginning or end, felt her heartbeat become erratic. Her heart beat faster and faster in an uneven rhythm. Laboring to breathe, her heart fluttering at a maddening pace, she was gripped by an overwhelming sense of panic. She gasped for oxygen in large, spasmodic gulps. Her body twisted and arched. And then, in the immediate aftermath of what felt like an axe cleaving open her chest, Claire's afflictions ceased. Disoriented, she watched the shafts of sunlight disappear, the colors fade, the spirit-elephants vanish. Surrounded by dark-ness, Claire's thoughts drifted into a black, soundless void.

*

"Finally."

"Is she—?"

"From all indications." Nurse McVee touched the bridge of her glasses as she leaned forward. "She certainly deserves to find some peace after the way she's suffered."

"Not that her treatment helped in that regard."

"Is that your professional opinion, Nurse Janowitz?" Nurse McVee snapped. "Or are you just spouting off?"

"Sorry, I was just—"

"When you become a certified clinical psychologist, you let me know."

The room where Nurse McVee and Nurse Janowitz were seated wasn't much larger than a storage closet. Furnished with a desk and two black Samsonite folding chairs that faced a wall of television monitors, the area often made those who'd been tasked with patient surveillance feel uncom-fortably close. At the moment, Julie Janowitz felt claustrophobic.

"I was only—"

"Trying to undermine the doctor?"

"No, of course not. It's just—"

"We're paid—*you're* paid—quite handsomely to work here." As hard as it was for Julie to believe, the lines on nurse McVee's face seemed harsher than usual. "That can all change."

"I'm sorry, I'm sorry, I'm sorry," Julie rushed to say, reflexively reaching out a placating hand. "Please, you know how much I need the money. I didn't mean— I shouldn't have. I suppose it's the stress."

"Stress," her superior scoffed.

Julie looked at the monitor depicting Patient W's room before glancing over at nurse McVee. Odd, she thought, that the woman seemed to be looking at a different patient's room monitor. Following her gaze, she realized Nurse McVee was observing the man who'd kidnapped Patient W.

"I wonder how much longer *he's* going to be with us." Julie put her hand over her mouth as soon as she saw Nurse McVee's brow furrow and her jaw begin to tremble. "It's just that he frightens me so. Thank God you're on staff to take care of patients like him."

Julie felt a sigh of relief when she saw Nurse McVee's expression soften.

"Yes, well—" Nurse McVee dipped her head and cleared her throat. Briefly fiddling with the nurse pin she wore above her heart, she said, "I imagine he'll be remanded back to the state police in a day or two. I believe the doctor is just about finished with his assessment." Nurse McVee patted Julie on the arm. "Not to worry. He'll be out of here soon."

Nurse McVee nodded toward the monitors. "Now, go find Dr. Haraji and inform him of Patient W's condition. And," she said, briefly grasping Julie's wrist, "best get a couple of orderlies to her room." Nurse McVee nodded to the monitors again. "We'll have to move her to cold storage until arrangements can be made with the family."

*

Dirk had lost all sense of time. Not only did have no clue what time it was, he had no idea what day it was or how many days he'd been at the clinic undergoing what he'd been told was an assessment of his mental state as ordered by the county judge who'd reviewed his case. Problematic for him was that he had no recollection of having been brought before a judge. Nor could he remember ever speaking to anyone—defense attorney or policeman—about his reasons for taking Claire out of the clinic and driving her to a motel in the Pennsylvania countryside.

It had taken him several days to process that, in fact, he had not spoken to any authorities or appeared before a judge. By the time he realized he was being held against his will, he also realized the clinic had purposely re-addicted him to heroin. And that had put a whole different spin on his dilemma.

Reliving Genevieve's death had been traumatic for Dirk. It was traumatic every time—and he'd relived it what seemed like hundreds of times. But once he became aware he was showing signs of heroin use—a runny nose, watery eyes, nausea, profuse sweating, chills, disorientation, paranoia, alternating between feeling ravenous and nauseated—he was able to come to grips with the repeated visions of her murder and reach the conclusion that he was purposely and systematically being driven toward insanity.

He supposed he would have already lost his mind if he weren't a former heroin addict who had lived through a torturous withdrawal. But he'd traveled that road before. The thrice daily routine he was now enduring—being strapped to a gurney, wheeled into a room where he was given an injection, and then induced into hallucinating Genevieve's murder— wasn't as damaging to his sanity as it could have been. Nor had it shattered his psyche the way he supposed was intended.

He didn't let on that the so-called treatment hadn't succeeded in making him crazy. Somewhere in his jumbled brain, he knew his only hope of getting out of the clinic—and freeing Claire, if she was still in the facility—was to convince whoever was overseeing his treatment that they'd driven him over the edge. He knew, if he played his part well enough, he would be viewed as being so mentally useless that he wasn't a threat to anyone. In which case he figured the plan would be to drive him to some remote location in the middle of the night and leave him to perish. And who'd be the wiser? They probably figured he'd be listed as a homeless junkie who'd met his end in a cold ditch by the side of a road—if he was found.

Mid-morning, late afternoon, and a little before evening shift-change were the scheduled times of his sessions. He didn't see much of the staff. He had an occasional run-in with Nurse McVee, but otherwise most of his contact was with an assortment of male orderlies who seemed to rotate every few days. And they didn't have much to say. Actually, most didn't say anything at all except "You done?" or "Time to go." He'd seen Julie once or twice from afar, but never close enough to try to speak to her. And for her part—at least as far as Dirk saw it—she didn't seem too interested in going out of her way to say hello to him. Just as well, since she hadn't believed him when he told her they were trying to kill Claire. *They.* Hell, she was part of *they*, wasn't she? How deep a part, he didn't know, but she didn't ask questions. That much was clear.

Dirk knew it was morning by the meal he'd recently been served: pasty oatmeal, a piece of dry white toast, scrambled eggs—powdered and cold, as usual—and a quarter of an apple sliced in thirds. He would have killed for a cup of coffee. He'd asked for coffee a few times—three times that he could remember—but on each occasion he'd been rebuffed with cool silence. So today he nearly stood up and hugged the orderly who'd delivered his breakfast tray with the sentence, "Someone will be in to collect your tray when you're done."

Dirk had wanted to ask the man a thousand questions, but he thought better of it. *It's a trap!* his thoughts screamed. *They're testing you!* So he didn't react, didn't change expression. He just continued to stare up at the ceiling and count the little dots inside each panel of soundproof tile. Forty-seven dots; who came up with that number? He'd been asking himself that same question since the day he arrived.

*

Julie ground one cigarette into the grass as she pulled another from the pack. She put flame to tobacco and sucked in as much smoke as her lungs would allow. After a brief pause, she exhaled with a heavy sigh.

"Damn," she hissed before taking another quick drag off the cigarette.

As she blew smoke from her nose, she replayed in her head the encounter she'd just had with Dr. Haraji.

No more than five minutes after she'd informed Dr. Haraji of Patient W's death, she was summoned back to his office via the facility's PA system. The doctor seemed agitated when she entered the room—odd, since he'd been relieved when she told him the news of Patient W just a few minutes before.

"Am I in trouble?" she'd asked.

"No, no, no," he assured her. "Not in trouble, so to speak. But I am disappointed—somewhat alarmed, actually—that you would inform me that a patient has died without first verifying the diagnosis via thorough physical examination."

Her mouth dropped open.

"I was just reporting— I mean— Nurse McVee— We were watching— She seemed— I mean—" She told herself to try to sound rational, to keep eye contact with him. "You mean she's not dead?"

"No, she is not," he told her. "And I am quite troubled by the fact that you and Nurse McVee reached such a dire conclusion about the patient in such a cavalier manner. It gives me reason to wonder whether the two of you need to be retrained."

When Dr. Haraji leaned forward in his chair and pushed his glasses closer to his owlish eyes, she reminded herself that owls, however they might be portrayed as noble and wise, were silent predators who regurgitated the bones of their prey.

"I can understand the confusion I've caused by our misdiagnosis. I don't know what to say, Dr. Haraji, except that I was only following orders and that it won't happen again. "

But before she could further explain, he'd raised his hand in a signal for silence. Minutes passed while he wrote in a notebook. She felt like an insignificant fool, just standing there, waiting for him to continue. Finally, after clearing her throat twice in futile attempts to get him to acknowledge her, she found the courage to speak.

"Shall I continue with my duties, Doctor?"

He looked up from what he'd been writing and gave her a little smile.

"Duties?" he'd said. "I would phrase it more as an experiment."

She'd fled the room. What the hell was he going to do to Patient W? What was he *already* doing to Patient W? She took a final drag off her cigarette and threw the butt down in the grass by her feet. She glanced out at the cars parked in the wraparound lot and located her white Ford Taurus. With a shake of her head, she ground the smoldering butt into the grass and hissed, "Damn."

*

Dirk was confused. He'd finished eating everything but those vile eggs more than an hour ago. But no one had come to collect his tray. Maybe he'd done something wrong. Maybe he was supposed to eat everything on his tray today if he wanted someone to come back to his room. Or maybe he was supposed to have engaged the orderly in some sort of conversation when the man spoke to him. "Hey, how long have you worked here?" or "How you feeling today?" But maybe his treatment or assessment was changing. Maybe this was a new tactic to— He grunted.

To what? Drive me nuts?

He eyed the mound of cold scrambled eggs he'd left on the plate and then looked up at the ceiling tiles. Forty-seven dots in each soundproof square. How many of them were fitted with a tiny camera? And why did they give him powdered eggs every morning when he never ate them? He was toying with the idea of using the eggs to cover the dots in the ceiling panels when the door to his room opened. When he recognized Julie standing in the doorway, he had an urge to run to her and embrace her. But before he could act on his impulse, two very large orderlies appeared behind her with a gurney in tow.

"Good morning, Mr. Benson."

Dirk shifted his attention away from Julie to the cold lump of eggs he'd left on his breakfast tray.

"I'm not sure you remember me."

Out of the corner of his eye, he noticed Julie wringing her hands.

"We met— Uh, we met the day of the fire. Remember the fire, Mr. Benson? You helped save one of the patients."

Dirk glanced over at the two orderlies when he heard the metal restraints clang against the gurney's steel frame.

"My name is Julie. Nurse Julie. Remember?"

Dirk didn't reply.

"I'm afraid I have some news."

He stiffened when he saw Julie motion to the orderly closest to him. The man opened a pouch attached to the belt wrapped around his waist.

"Bad news, I'm afraid."

Dirk glanced at Julie before fixing his gaze to the mound of cold eggs.

"The woman—the patient you helped during the fire. I'm afraid she passed away."

Dirk focused on the dots within the tile located directly above his head. Starting in the bottom right corner, he counted them.

"One, two, three—" At three, he felt the grasp of strong hands on his upper arms. "Four, five, six, seven—" At seven, the orderly dabbed something moist on a spot on his neck. "Eight, nine, ten—" His mouth was forming the word *eleven* when the sensation of a needle pricking his skin made him wince.

"I'm sorry," he vaguely heard a woman's voice say.

And then all the dots in the ceiling started to move around in a chaotic zigzag fashion. Having lost count, Dirk closed his eyes. In a dreamlike state, he felt his body levitate. He sensed his torso floating sideways for a moment before his back came to rest on something firm.

*

She felt cold. Unusually so. But there was something more that struck her as odd, something more than the freezing chill that seemed to have filled her veins with ice: she felt no pain. Not in her head, not at her wrists or ankles, and not even in her heart, which had been broken for an eternity.

How had she gotten to this state? *Through God's will*, her thoughts replied. God. Of course. She had offered her life to Him. And He had accepted it. He had been her path forward ever since.

"Why are you here?"

She opened her eyes, expecting to find darkness, anticipating having to contend with an overwhelming void. His voice, the voice addressing her, would be represented by flame—an eternal omnipotent arc of fire. She was surprised to be greeted by sunlight and a tug on the wrist.

"Are you lost?"

Claire scrutinized the face of the boy staring up at her. Did she know him? Or was she supposed to know him? The more she studied his features, the more she realized he looked like hundreds of boys she had crossed paths with. Gaunt, protruding cheekbones; slightly bulging eyes; dry, cracked lips—every aspect mirrored those of countless other boys she had cared for over the years in various refugee camps or observed walking on the side of the road in one of the endless lines of the forgotten. The forgotten—the displaced, the sick, the wounded. Poor souls clinging to some minuscule hope they would be able to find a semblance of a normal life even in a place they were not welcome.

The boy was no one she knew, yet he represented all those she had interacted with. As she stared into his eyes, she sensed that he could tell the story of every child who stood in the line of the forgotten: those who carried the burden of famine, drought, and war in their souls and hid the scars of those indignities behind a mask of melancholy.

"Am I lost?" she repeated. She reached for the silver cross that had hung about her neck for most of her adult life but found it wasn't there. "Perhaps I am."

"You should not be here," the boy replied.

"Why?" She looked quickly to the left and right. "Where should I be?" The terrain ahead of her—stretches of pale sand nestled between ridges of granite—reminded her of a place where she had once been happy. But she could not recall where.

"Working your way back."

Confused that the boy was now standing some distance away, Claire took a few uncertain steps toward him.

"My way back?" she asked. "Back where?"

The boy shouted his reply. "He isn't here!"

Claire felt a pang of anxiety spread through her when she saw the youth turn and walk away.

"Wait!" she called.

But the boy did not heed her call. Claire hurried after him and caught up near the crest of a wind-furrowed dune. She was reaching for his shoulder when he turned to look at her. She immediately dropped her arm. Startled, she blurted, "John!"

The boy gave Claire a quizzical look.

"I am Tafari," he said. "John is somewhere else."

"Tafari?"

Claire searched her memory and found herself sitting across the fire from Teimbaka. He had been one of three brothers, he'd told her. Tafari was the oldest. Hope swelled inside of her.

"Then you know—"

Claire fell silent when she saw that Tafari was again standing some distance away. As though bidding her goodbye, he raised his right arm. How she had missed seeing the long walking stick he held above his head, she didn't know. The long shaft of wood returned her thoughts to the night she had sat at the fire and listened to Teimbaka talk about his family. He had abruptly stood and swung his staff into the darkness just beyond the reach of the fire's light. She'd thought he was playing a mean trick on her, so she'd turned her back to him in a huff.

"Creatures of the night," he'd explained in a grave tone. "Those who venture out in darkness to steal the spirits of the living."

She hadn't believed him at first, and she scoffed at him for confronting what he could not see. But the ensuing years had changed her beliefs. She knew better now. The minions of the Serpent took on all shapes and forms, including those not visible to the human eye. How foolish she had been in her younger years. How Teimbaka must have thought her a spoiled, ignorant child. That night, after Teimbaka had spoken, she'd heard a terrible howling, like that of a wild animal suffering a mortal wound. In the same moment, a cold wind had stirred the fire. Embers swirled off the flames and gathered to form a cloud. Then, as if guided by the breath of God, the fiery cloud enveloped them, shielding them from the forces of the dark.

"Teimbaka," she whispered at the memory. "Where are you?"

"He's not here."

Tafari was standing next to her now, the staff held outward by his side, presented so the ends touched both earth and sky.

"You know where he is?" she asked.

The soft clang of a bell drew Tafari's attention toward the horizon. Following his gaze, Claire saw a small herd of goats grazing near the base of a granite outcropping.

"There," he told her, pointing to the goats. And then, as if he'd suddenly remembered something, he shook his head and opened the hand he'd used to direct her attention. "And here," he told her, nodding to his open palm.

"I'm confused."

"Where *she* is," he explained. "Where she holds those who protect her."

"She?"

Tafari smiled. "The Mother," he told her. "Here," he repeated, again nodding to his open palm.

"But where?" she asked. "Where is *she*?"

Claire thought him confused when his brow furrowed and his attention shifted toward the ground.

"You must know," she gently pressed. "Teimbaka spoke—"

"Yes," he said with a definitive nod. "Yes, with him."

"*With* him? How can he be—?"

"Now go."

Claire reached out and grabbed hold of the staff.

"Go where?" she asked in earnest as she wrapped her fingers around the wood.

Contact with the staff sent a jolt through her body. Heart palpitating, her pulse racing, she was suddenly overcome with a feeling of suffocation. As she lurched upward, gasping for air, she heard a woman scream.

"Sweet Jesus!" she heard a woman exclaim. "She's alive!"

*

Julie looked down at her notebook and sighed.

"Seems pointless," she muttered.

"What's that?"

Somewhat embarrassed she'd spoken out loud, she gave the orderly a slight shrug and shook her head.

"Nothing," she said. "Just thinking out loud."

The orderly responded with a little grunt while he continued to push Dirk's gurney down the hall.

"Dude looks like he's sleeping," he muttered.

Julie looked up from her notebook and glanced down at Mr. Benson. *More comatose,* she wanted to correct the orderly's observation. But she didn't. After her exchange with Dr. Haraji, she decided it was best to keep her opinions to herself.

"Why didn't we inject the guy in his room like we always do?" the orderly asked in a conversational tone. "Doc weaning him off?"

"Actually, Dr. Haraji—" Julie caught herself before she said any more. "He's—" she shot a nervous glance to her notebook. "We're injecting him when we get to the observation area today." She gave the orderly a guarded look. "Those are the instructions. I really don't know any more than that."

Although she did know more, she certainly wasn't going to divulge the information to the orderly. Even though she'd seen the man around the clinic for a few weeks, she didn't know who he was. She thought his name was Bill, but she wasn't 100 percent certain. And though he'd seemed quite capable the few times she'd asked him to help her with a patient, she had no clue if she could trust the man to keep his mouth shut about what she might have to say about a particular patient.

"So, I get to stick him, right?"

"Stick him?"

She heard the orderly chuckle before he said, "Yeah, you know: put the needle in his neck."

Julie gave the man a stern look before tapping the open page of her notebook.

"Do you mind?" she responded. Nodding to the open notebook, she added, "The instructions are pretty specific."

"Yeah, yeah," the orderly hurried to say, "I was just—"

Julie raised her hand to signal the man to silence as they neared the end of the hall. She stopped just to the right of a large set of stainless-steel doors. Above the door was a white tile square etched with a black number one.

"Middle of the room, please," Julie instructed as she pushed the doors open. "I'll prepare the syringe."

*

Julie eased the plunger back until the pale brown liquid reached the 3cc level. Satisfied with the measurement, she removed the needle from the ampule and held the syringe perpendicular. Then, with a deft movement of her thumb, she applied a minuscule amount of pressure to the plunger until a drop oozed out of the needle.

"Patient secure?" she inquired as she turned away from the medical cart she'd been working off of. She saw the orderly shift his attention from the patient to the needle and syringe.

"Ready to go," he replied.

Julie studied the orderly's face as she walked toward him.

"Doctor's instructions are for you to inject this slowly—I repeat, slowly—while I—" Julie stopped and put her free hand to her face. Covering her nose and mouth, she turned her head to the side and groaned. "What's that smell?"

Before the orderly could answer, she saw what could only be urine dripping from the gurney onto the floor. "Oh, no! He didn't, did he?"

"God, that stinks," the orderly complained.

Julie took a step backward. "Oh my God!" she exclaimed. "He's got diarrhea!"

"Shit," the orderly grumbled.

"Didn't you take him to the bathroom before I arrived?" she cried. "You know he's supposed to be taken to the facilities before he's brought to the treatment room!"

"The guy was out of it!" the orderly explained. "What was I supposed to do?" Julie watched his face turn pale as he looked down and saw drops of greenish-brown slime next to his feet. "He wouldn't wake up!"

"Okay, okay, okay!" she snapped. "Nothing we—oh, dear God!" She covered her face with her hands and backed farther away. "You'll have to clean him up before we can continue. Ugh," she moaned. "Please hurry."

"You want me to roll him back to his room?"

"No!" she barked. "No—his next treatment needs to be administered on time!" She gave the orderly a stern look. "Dr. Haraji won't be happy with either of us if he hasn't been prepped for the second part of his treatment."

"I hear you," the man said with a nod.

"Go down the hall and get a mop and a bucket." She glanced at Mr. Benson and shook her head. "And bring a new gown and some sterile wipes." She grimaced. "We'll have to clean him."

"I'm on it."

Julie watched the orderly leave the treatment room.

"You're on it," she mumbled in a mocking tone. "Last time I work with you." She shifted her attention back to the patient lying on the gurney. "Jesus," she sighed. "Damn."

When the orderly came back into the treatment room with the mop and bucket, Julie checked her wristwatch.

There's still time, she assured herself. *Haraji normally waits a half hour after the injection before he arrives to administer the second part of the treatment. Only ten minutes have passed. And with the added dosage he's prescribed for this session, the patient should be well under if we can get the shot into him in the next ten minutes.*

"I'm gonna need help cleaning him up," she heard the orderly say. "You're gonna need to steady him on his side while I," the orderly chuckled, "wipe his ass."

"He still out of it?" she asked as she turned and walked toward the gurney.

"You tell me," the orderly replied.

Julie stopped an arm's length from the gurney and studied Mr. Benson's face. Tentatively, she extended her hand toward him.

"Mr. Benson?" she inquired. She lightly touched his cheek. "Mr. Benson, can you hear me?" She gave his chin a little shake. "Mr. Benson?" she said a little louder. "Can. You. Hear. Me?"

She drew back, startled, when Mr. Benson muttered something unintelligible and jerked his head a little to one side.

"Dude's out of it," the orderly said. Julie gave him a disapproving glance just before he added, "Now you know why I didn't take him to—"

"Fine," she interrupted. "Whatever. Let's just get this done." She gave the orderly a forgiving smile. "Undo the straps and roll him onto his side, and I'll steady him while you wipe his— While you clean him up."

"Got ya."

As the orderly undid the straps binding Mr. Benson's arms and legs, Julie thought back to the morning when she'd first met the man. He seemed so pleasant then, she recalled, so normal. Quite the actor, she supposed. She would have never guessed he was a loony tune by the way he presented himself. Harder still to believe he was so off kilter that he would start a fire in the building and kidnap a patient. It had never crossed her mind that he was mentally unstable. Even now, as she admired the rugged handsomeness of his face, it was hard for her to see him as one of the clinic's crazier patients.

"You ready?" the orderly asked.

She looked the orderly in the eye and nodded. "On three, okay?" He nodded back. "One, two…" Julie cupped one hand under Mr. Benson's upper arm and placed her other on the side of his hip. "Three."

The orderly pushed Mr. Benson up onto his left side while Julie steadied his lower torso.

"You got him?" the orderly asked.

"Yeah, I think so."

The orderly released his grip on the patient's leg and shoulder and shuffled a few steps back. Keeping his arms extended and his hands open, he gave Julie a quick smile.

"Yeah, I think he's balanced," he replied. Julie noticed a puzzled expression on his face as he glanced over each of his shoulders. "Keep him steady. I'll be right back."

"Be right back? Where are you going?"

"I forgot the wipes and the gown," he said.

Before she could respond, he darted out of the room.

"Hurry!" she called out. She glanced down at Mr. Benson and shook her head. "Stupid idiot," she muttered.

No sooner had the words left her mouth than she felt Mr. Benson's body begin to jerk. Immediately, she widened her stance and tried to secure his lower body.

"Steady," she said as she used the weight of her body as an anchor.

Inexplicably, Mr. Benson's lower leg slid completely off the padded table, which in turn, pulled one side of his hip off the edge. Julie tried to gather him back, but Mr. Benson slipped off the gurney and fell to the floor. Exasperated, Julie put her hands on her hips and sighed.

"Great, just fucking great," she said.

Frustrated, she was about to bury her face in her hands when she caught a whiff of her fingers. They were covered in diarrhea. She went to wipe them on her uniform but realized her scrubs was stained with the same smelly, greenish-brown slime. Thoroughly annoyed, she snapped,

"Christ, Bill. Where are you?" as she moved hurriedly toward the stainless steel doors.

Using her right elbow, she nudged one of the doors open a crack and peeked into the hall.

"Where are you, Bill?" she hissed. "Or whatever the hell your name is."

Easing the door shut, she took a deep breath—and winced from a sharp pain in the back of her neck. When she reached back, someone grabbed her wrist and twisted her arm. Her scream was cut off when her assailant threw her into the wall.

18

"I WISH TO be buried beside my brother."

Teimbaka tugged the edges of his robe close around his face and bowed his head. As he waited for John Too's reply, he envisioned his brother's resting place and recalled how the wind had blown down off the mountain, how the air had gnawed at his flesh as the light of a pale moon turned the realm of the highlands a ghostly shade of white. Shivering, he'd stared at the crude wooden cross Claire had set at the head of Menelik's grave and breathed in the aroma of newly turned earth. Just beyond the cross, he could see a shadow hovering in mid-air. As if alerting him to the presence of this darkness, the ring of dried beetles Claire had draped over the arms of the cross began to emit a soft, emerald light.

"Ras Dashen is far from here," he heard John Too say. "The journey would be long and arduous. Your smell would worsen along the way. Better that you are dumped off the docks so the current can take your rotting carcass far out to sea."

Teimbaka quickly covered his ears with his hands when John Too began to laugh. Stung by the boy's response, he curled his legs beneath him and wrapped his arms around his body. Turning his face toward the wall behind him, he began to gently rock back and forth.

Gradually the laughing subsided and then—mercifully—ended. In the silence that followed, Teimbaka was certain he heard the screech of the cave wraith that had tried to keep him from finding the book of words. Unnerved by the recurrence of the unholy cry, he thrust his hands out in front of him as a shield.

"The souls of the lost have been forsaken."

"What?" asked Teimbaka.

"Like the sand within a mountainous dune, they are imprisoned, each indistinguishable from the next. Yet, each particle desires to be swept into the heavens and cherished for what it is."

"I don't understand what you mean."

"She who gave them life has turned her back on them. They are nothing to her."

Teimbaka experienced a moment of numbness as he grappled with what John Too was saying.

"You are one of them."

"One of—?"

"Those she does not see."

"That is not so!" he retorted. "The Mother has—"

"Left you to rot in an alley of piss and shit. That you believed you were ever more to her is laughable."

Morbid, piercing, and full of anguish, the death cry of an elephant reached Teimbaka's soul and sent him spiraling toward despair. Overcome with a sudden spell of dizziness, he slumped sideways on the ground. He curled his body into a fetal position and focused on the sounds he recognized: his breathing, the hum of blood rushing through his veins, the beating of his heart, and the whoosh of the current flowing from the wall at his back. But the voice of John Too was like the stinging bite of a green-headed fly—unwelcome, relentless, and sharp.

"Better that you wander into the desert and wither under the sun or wade into the sea and let the tide swallow you," John Too said. "You are worthless. The beetles are dead. You are worthless."

Although the soil beneath Teimbaka smelled of human waste and the remains of some maggot-laden carcass, he welcomed the stench into his senses as recompense for his failures. Claire was dead; the elephants decimated; the land ravaged by famine, drought, and war. John Too was right. He was worthless. There was no longer a reason for him to be alive.

Deep within the soil, concealed beneath layers of what once existed, he could hear what he believed to be the Mother's sorrow: the haunting cackle of a hyena, the death wail of an elephant, the shriek of a cave wraith, the whimpering pleas of starving children, and the chilling whisper of dark angels as they whisked the souls of the damned to the Serpent. He wept as he listened to Her cry, for he could not help but think that he was partly to blame for Her misery. Gripped with shame, he acknowledged he had betrayed Her trust. She had tasked him to keep Her children safe. Yet, because of his failings, they were lost, doomed to wander a mist-shrouded world that existed in neither light nor darkness.

"You are worthless," John Too repeated. "Worthless."

*

Bin'ka did not turn at the sound of the muezzin's call, nor was he tempted to look over his shoulder at the setting sun to witness the painted minarets transformed into spires of flaming gold. Even when a flock of gulls dove toward the sea and directed their grating cries at a fishing boat sailing into harbor, Bin'ka kept his eyes riveted on the water below him, his attention focused on the black blob wavering upon its surface. And though he wasn't overly interested in seeing the features of his reflection with any clarity, he stared into his watery face nevertheless, for he entertained the notion that if he concentrated on the image long enough, he might draw a crumb of wisdom from it.

When he'd decided to walk down to the old dock after meeting with Adiam and Talia, Bin'ka had no idea why—or what he might accomplish. As he made his way through the streets and alleys of Djibouti, he realized that poverty within the city proper had worsened in the time he'd been away. Or maybe he'd been fooling himself all the years he had lived here. Maybe the conditions had always been as squalid and bleak as he saw them to be now.

He'd been taken aback by the number of children who'd assailed him on the way to the harbor, hands extended, voices pleading as they clamored for money. Their eyes sought his in hopes they might stir his guilt, or they focused on his clothes and the polished shine of his shoes, the children no doubt imagining what he'd done to acquire such finery and wondering if they too might someday own such expensive items. But what troubled him more than the despair he saw around him were the signs that slavers were actively working the streets. Of course, there were no physical signs of their presence, but the evidence of their activity was easy enough to spot.

Bin'ka recognized the fear in the faces of the children as they solicited passers-by for money, and he understood their habit of constantly looking over their shoulders when they stood off on their own. How many of them had lost a friend, a brother, or a sister? How many of them would disappear in the coming days, never to be heard from or seen again? It wasn't lost on him that he'd accomplished very little in rescuing the children he'd freed from the slavers' holding cells and ferried to the beach south of Mogadishu. Most had likely already been lured back into the slavers' clutches. From what he'd seen and heard, the slave trade was as strong as ever, and he doubted, no matter what he or anyone might do, that would ever change.

"What do you see when you look at your reflection?"

The voice of the old hag no longer affected him as it once did. He was used to her now, used to her ways, used to her popping up unexpectedly, prodding him with questions about things that made no sense or taking endless digs at his morality. As of late, he'd begun to wonder why she bothered with him, for after all she had coaxed him into doing, nothing had changed. The realization that he was of little consequence in the grand scheme of things had made him feel hopeless. So he did not welcome her sudden appearance on the dock. Nor did he have any great interest in engaging her in conversation.

"What do I see? Nothing," he grunted.

"Yes," she said. "It can be harsh."

Out of the corner of his eye, he saw the sleeve of her grey robe flutter near the handrail he was leaning against.

"Deflating as well."

Bin'ka shifted his weight from one foot to the other and turned his head away from her. He was not surprised, however, when he found her standing on the other side of him—a grey-cloaked figure pointing a slender finger at his reflection.

"Whittle away, little by little."

He heard what he guessed was a sigh—her sigh—but it reminded him of something more. Without warning, a picture came to mind of an alley with three doors at its end. He vividly remembered the doors and the small cul-de-sac where they stood, and he experienced, for the briefest of moments, the wind blowing through the entrance of the center door and swirling into a room filled with treasures. It was the night of the Lion, the night Adiam had put a bullet into Susenyo's head, the night Teimbaka had freed Claire from her chamber and carried her into the desert.

Bin'ka closed his eyes and rubbed his face with one of his massive hands. The memory melded into the murmuring sea and disappeared.

"Calming, isn't it?"

Bin'ka ignored her question and concentrated on the waves lapping against the rocks beneath the pier.

"Little by little," she said. After a pause, she muttered, "Eventually."

Bin'ka opened his eyes and looked down at the water; his reflection was no longer there. With a grunt, he shook his head.

"It's still there."

Perturbed, he snapped, "What is?"

"Everything you believe in."

"Leave me be," he retorted. "You make no sense."

"Little by little."

"Little by little *what*? What does that mean?"

"Live and grow, age and die; just what you were thinking."

"I wasn't thinking that."

"I could see it in your eyes," she told him.

Bin'ka twisted his hands around the railing and flexed his shoulders. "What drivel do you speak now?" He turned to address her but found she was no longer standing where she had been a moment before. "How would you know what I was seeing?" he asked as he turned to face her.

"Because you told me."

"Told you?"

"'Nothing,' you said."

Bin'ka took a deep breath and bellowed toward the sky. When he regained his composure, he quietly said, "Go away."

"Little by little."

Bin'ka dipped his head toward the rail and blew air from his nose.

"What do you want of me?" he asked.

"What you want of yourself."

Bin'ka snarled, "I want—"

He eyed the hooded figure standing next to him and then looked down into the darkening waters of a twilight-hued sea. His reflection was there again, floating on the surface, an imposing figure dressed in a white thawb. When his image puffed out its chest and rolled its shoulders, he smirked.

"For all the strength you possess—"

He wiped his eyes with the back of his hand and sighed. He opened his mouth to speak but found he had nothing more to say. After glancing into the eyes staring up at him from the water's surface, he dipped his head and gazed at his shoes.

"It can be harsh."

"What can be harsh?"

"To not see yourself—even though you are there."

As twilight crept toward darkness, the giant lamps positioned along the perimeter of the loading dock across the bay began to flicker to life. A little to the north, where the waters of the Gulf of Aden and the Red Sea mingled, Bin'ka could see the running lights of cargo ships glittering against the murky seascape. With a sense of melancholy, he embraced the vista, admiring how the light and darkness subtly altered the colors of ocean and sky. From his vantage point atop an ancient dock that had withstood nature, time, and war, he suddenly felt invisible, as though he was an insignificant piece of a puzzle no one had ever assembled.

"There's still time," the old hag quietly offered.

Bin'ka closed his eyes and tried to savor the touch of a warm breeze upon his face.

"Little by little," she murmured.

Bin'ka squeezed the guardrail between his hands. "Little by little *what*?" he demanded.

Sand brushed stone and wind gusted through foam-splattered waves. Where ocean and land collided in a never-ending tussle, the voice of the old hag spoke to him in whispers, each word applied as if it was a delicate stroke of a painter in the throes of creation.

"Waves tumbled and broke but then gathered and renewed. Sun

touched water, and water rejoiced. A spark became light, and light became creator of unfathomable beauty. My breath became the wind. My touch became the earth. And from the essence of my being came the fabric that would color them all. One became two, then two became many, until my hands cradled a multitude born of me."

The sea began to swirl with the sound of the old hag's voice, and as Bin'ka listened to her talk, he saw the running lights of the freighters begin to bob upon the water, their shapes transformed into small orbs of radiant color that swelled and dipped with the flow of her words. White-tipped mountains magically appeared behind these colored spheres to tower above an ocean of the purest blue. Fields of green fanned out from the ocean's shore, each a different shade and texture, their boundaries defined by swaths of sun-tinged gold. Cliff-faced shores—some sun-dappled, some sprinkled with stars—rose out of the sea, their crests veiled in a silvery mist. Bin'ka looked upon the vision and sighed. For he saw it as the world he had always imagined. One he'd hoped to escape to after he'd been sold as a slave.

"Creatures great and small lived side by side and shared what had been given. Water, wind, sun, and stars; these were the threads that bound each to the next."

When the old hag didn't speak for a time, Bin'ka looked over. She flicked a sparkling stone into the sea. The water rippled where the moon-colored rock disappeared beneath the surface, and with the rolling motion, the woman's voice changed. Gone was the innocence of hope in her words. Her tone gained a hard edge. A rumble of thunder far out across the water sent a shiver down his spine.

"A feather plucked, a horn butchered, a hide stripped, a tail severed. Slaughtered for trinkets and hats."

A flash of lightning lit up a vast portion of the sky far out toward the horizon, and within the moment of ghostly illumination, Bin'ka saw the white-peaked mountains of his imaginary world crumble and fall.

"One became two and two became many. What had been created began to seep from my hand."

A sudden boom shook the dock beneath Bin'ka's feet. Unnerved, Bin'ka grabbed hold of the old hag's drooping sleeve. A thousand points of stinging pain shot through his palm as if he had wrapped his hand around a beehive.

"I tried to keep them," she hissed in earnest.

Bin'ka released his hold on her robe and rubbed his palm across his chest.

"I tried to find a way."

The sound of a ship's horn not far from the mouth of the harbor drew Bin'ka's attention away from his smarting flesh. Looking beyond the giant cranes, out past where he'd seen the freighter lights morph into novae of color, Bin'ka searched for the cliffs that had risen out of the ocean. But from one end of the horizon to the next, a murky grey-brown haze obscured the line between ocean and sky.

"Many have been lost."

The sound of a churning sea drew his attention to the water directly below him.

"Little by little."

Bin'ka tightened his grip on the railing as he watched the turbulent water break against the rocks.

"They seep away."

He scraped the toe of his shoe across the pier and blew a stream of air through his nose.

"I know you feel what I say," she told him. A brief flicker of silver light shot across the water just before she added, "Now that she's gone."

"She?"

A gust of swirling wind blew through the railings and swept across the pier. Its sound, hollow and forlorn, pushed past him. In its wake, Bin'ka was overcome with a sense of emptiness. Feeling isolated and alone, he looked back over his shoulder in hopes of finding some comfort in the lights of the city. But the same grey-brown haze he'd seen clinging to the eastern horizon shrouded the buildings along the shoreline.

"What sorcery have you cast?" he asked the old woman.

Where the old hag had been standing, a trace of sea mist lingered. And as Bin'ka searched for the grey-robed woman, the wispy fog slowly dissipated. With a shake of his head and a sigh of frustration, he turned his attention once more to the sea. To his relief, every aspect of the ocean, port, and sky looked normal; stars twinkled down from above, the giant cranes across the bay were engaged in moving cargo, the running lights of the freighters out on the water shone steady and true, and the grey-brown haze that had obscured the horizon was gone. Pleased that his encounter with the old hag seemed to be over, he was just beginning to think about what she had said to him when he heard gunfire in the nearby streets. Immediately, he thought of Adiam's café and what had taken place there the last time he was in Djibouti. Without a second thought, he pushed off the rail and started to walk briskly inland. He had taken but a few hurried strides when a scrawny figure stepped out of the shadows.

"*Francs, monsieur?*"

Bin'ka rose to his full height as he gazed down at the waif of a girl standing in front of him. He looked at her outstretched hand and open palm and snorted.

"Go away," he told her in English.

He tried to sidestep her, but she moved with the deftness of a cat and blocked his path.

"*S'il vous plaît, monsieur.*" The girl thrust her open palm toward him. "*J'ai faim.*"

She couldn't be more than seven years old, but as Bin'ka took stock of her pencil-thin frame crowned with matted jet-black hair, he was struck by how aged her eyes appeared, the sullenness of her gaze, and the dark lines of weariness that shaded her skin just below her lower lids.

"You shouldn't be—"

A distant burst of automatic gunfire stopped him mid-sentence. Searching the streets nearest the dock, he tried to move by the girl. But once more she nimbly slipped in front of him and pushed her hand against his thigh.

"*S'il vous plaît , monsieur, s'il vous plaît ,*" she begged. "*Un franc. Un franc.*"

Another burst of gunfire set Bin'ka on edge. Without realizing what he was doing, he pushed the girl to the side and moved to get past her.

"*Ici!*" she yelled as she grabbed hold of his wrist. Bin'ka tried to pull away when he felt her nails dig into his skin. "*Prends le!*"

Jerking his arm free, he balled his hand into a fist and raised his arm to strike. But something he felt in the middle of his palm stopped him from cuffing the girl on the side of her head. Confused, he lowered his arm and opened his hand.

"*Pour toi*," she said in a quiet tone. Nodding to the necklace in his hand, she wheedled, "*Franc, oui?*"

Bin'ka stared at the small silver cross she had placed in his hand and said nothing. He had seen only two such necklaces before in his life: one around the neck of the nun the children called Sister Lady and the other around the neck of the woman he'd fished from the harbor in Mogadishu—Sarah.

"Where'd you get this?"

The girl glanced at the cross and then smiled up at him.

"Who'd you steal it from?" he asked.

The girl took a step back and shook her head. With what Bin'ka interpreted as a sad expression, she pointed to the cross and then to the sky.

"*Du père*," she said. "*Du père.*"

"Father?" Bin'ka mumbled, confused.

Another burst of gunfire—sounding farther away—drew his attention back toward the city. When he saw nothing of immediate concern, he distractedly asked, "What father do you speak of?"

He didn't receive an answer, for the girl was no longer standing in front of him.

East of him, a flash of heat lightning turned a vast portion of the horizon an eerie shade of yellow-green. Drawn to the phenomenon, he traced the outline of the cross against his palm as he watched the sky flicker back to darkness. With a last look around for the girl, he turned to head for the city. A whisper made him stop and turn back to the sea. There on the rail, precariously perched on a coupling joint, was a matted grey cat with yellow-flame eyes. Spellbound, he muttered, "Zanzibar."

He took a tentative step toward the animal but stopped when it abruptly stood. Slowly, he raised his arm and let the cross dangle from his hand.

"What are—?"

A sudden explosion startled Bin'ka. He looked over his shoulder to see a fireball shooting up into the sky.

"What in Allah's name?"

As Bin'ka watched a column of fire rise high into the sky, he wondered if he was witnessing the beginning of the conflict that had been building between the Afar and the government over the past few years. Talk of the Afar claiming the lands of their fathers and creating their own country had veered toward calls for action as of late. Gunfire in the streets, an explosion within the city—surely these were harbingers of what was about to unfold.

"An unsettling night," he muttered as he turned back to Zanzibar.

But like the girl who had given him the necklace, the cat was nowhere to be seen. With a shake of his head, he flipped the cross into his hand and started back toward the city.

*

Lavender, she thought. Lavender and something more. Some other heady fragrance invaded her senses when she took a deep breath.

God, what do you have in store for me now?

Surveying the room she'd been escorted to, Sarah knew God need not answer. An oval bed beneath a canopy of colorful fabric. Perfumed air. The tray of fruits and the two silver goblets that stood beside it. The sheer white robe she'd been ordered to wear after her bra and underwear had been ripped off her body.

She was sure—because of the lavish comforts on display—that she was expected to accept her situation with humility and a degree of gratitude. But regardless how her owner wished to view what was about to take place, Sarah saw it for what it was: she was going to be raped. By whom, she didn't know. She hadn't met the man who'd purchased her from the hawk-nosed imam in Kenya. In fact, she hadn't held a conversation with anyone since she was taken from the bathing cell and forced into a plane.

Sarah remembered being shackled by her ankles to a seat inside what she assumed was a cargo plane, judging by the cavernous expanse of the aircraft's interior and the various crates stacked within. She was given a flask of water and a small round of flatbread stuffed with some sort of stewed meat by the man who'd shackled her into her seat. He departed without saying a word, and since she was hungry and thirsty, she ate and drank everything he'd left her.

She remembered nothing of the flight and could recall nothing of how she arrived in the room she now found herself in. Dry-mouthed, groggy, and nauseated, she'd required a few minutes to remember who she was. But as snippets of her memory began to slide into place, she realized she'd been drugged. There was no other explanation for her blackout. And when she realized she had no idea where she was, she started to panic.

The old woman who appeared out of the shadows at the sound of her first whimper offered no words of comfort or explanation—just a chilled, perfumed towel. No matter what Sarah said to the woman or how much she pleaded for an answer, the woman said nothing. Even when she'd crumpled to the floor, sobbing, and beseeched the woman in the name of both Allah and the Lord for a shred of mercy, the silent woman's line-weathered face remained impassive, her dark brown eyes devoid of emotion. Only after Sarah had calmed and stood did the silent woman show any sort of concern for her, and that, Sarah concluded, was because she had been instructed to prepare Sarah for what was to come.

Brushing her hair, sponge-bathing her where her body showed the slightest bit of grime from her journey, offering her a robe after two gun-toting men had removed her undergarments, dabbing perfume on her breasts and inner thighs; all of these acts were carried out with one purpose in mind: to ready her for her new owner.

A slave, Sarah thought.

"Slavery is death." Wasn't that what Bin'ka had yelled to her when they were escaping from Mogadishu? It had all seemed so abstract to her. Slavery had always been just a word. It was certainly abhorrent to keep someone against their will and treat them as a piece of property. But she had never given it more thought than that, never tried to imagine what it must feel like, what it must make people think of themselves when they found their lives no longer held meaning. But now, imprisoned and subject to the whims of a person she knew nothing about, she felt utterly despondent. She should be outraged, she knew, or terrified, or a mixture of both. But what would it serve to embrace those feelings? What purpose would it serve to fall victim to her emotions? Deep down, she wondered if she had the courage to fight back, as she'd promised herself she would.

The avenues of escape were next to nonexistent. Blinking back tears, she could hear Bin'ka's voice as if he were standing in the room next to her.

"Slavery is death," he'd said.

But he'd also yelled something more that day, something that Sarah desperately latched on to: "Fight!" he'd implored as the slaver's boat drew near. "Fight!"

Sarah clenched her fists as she scrutinized the room anew: one window and one door. The door was locked; she had heard the old woman latch it. But the window? It was shuttered, but she didn't know if the shutters were locked. Nor did she know what she might find on the other side of the window. Bolstered by Bin'ka's appeal to fight, she started toward the window.

The door to the room opened.

The silent woman entered the room holding a white rose in her wrinkled hands. Barefoot, she walked the dozen or so paces across the stone-tile floor, bowed her head, and held the rose out to Sarah.

"And why would I want this?" Sarah asked her.

The woman did not respond or look up to meet Sarah's eyes.

"Look at me," Sarah ordered. "Look at me and tell me why I am to have it."

The woman did not move or make a sound.

"Look at me!" Sarah shouted.

Trembling, the woman slowly raised her head just enough to meet Sarah's unflinching gaze.

"You're—" Sarah touched the woman on her shoulder. "You're frightened. Why?" The woman immediately tilted her head back toward the floor. "Tell me," Sarah said as she took hold of the woman's shoulder. "Tell me why you are afraid."

At the sound of footsteps in the hallway, the old woman thrust the rose into Sarah's hand and, head bowed, retreated several paces. A moment later, two armed soldiers entered the room and stood at attention on either side of the door. They clicked their heels at the arrival of an imposing figure dressed in what Sarah thought looked like a color guard uniform bedecked with copious amounts of medals.

"Ah! My virgin!" the man boomed. "Welcome to your new home!"

Sarah took in the girth of the man and flinched at his lecherous expression. Her skin crawled when he rubbed his hands together as though he was ravenous and about to enjoy a lavish feast.

"I demand that you free me!" Sarah blurted out. "I am a nun!"

The man's eyes grew small as he scrutinized her. But a moment later, with a clap of his hands, he let loose a loud belly laugh.

"All the better!" he exclaimed. "We can discuss the merits of your beliefs after you have satisfied me."

With a confident swagger to his step, the man moved to the table where the goblets and food had been laid out.

"Bring wine," he ordered no one in particular as he sampled a grape.

Sarah saw the old woman leave the room.

"Nuns drink wine, do they not?" he mischievously asked. "We'll have just enough to warm your skin." He took a bite of papaya and smiled. "Of course, if you'd rather not wait, I have many pressing matters to which I can turn my attention."

He looked strong. Too strong to overpower. But he was educated, or seemed to be. He spoke English. Maybe there was a chance she could reason with him.

"Whom do I have the pleasure of addressing?" she asked in the calmest voice she could muster. "My name is Sister Sarah. And you?"

She was confused when the man chuckled.

"Will you scream my name when I penetrate you?" he joked. "Is this why you ask?"

Stunned by his response, Sarah shook her head and looked toward the window.

"They are not barred," he said. "There is a partial view of the harbor if you stand to the side looking south."

She gave him a quizzical glance.

"You will be tempted, of course. They all are. But you will find you are close to twenty meters up—sixty feet in American thinking. And with no ledges or outcroppings to drop to, the height is— Well, it is imposing. Most have not survived the jump." He turned toward the door as the silent woman came back into the room with an ornate jug in her hands. "Ah, the wine is here."

Sarah turned away as the man beckoned her to join him.

"Come, sample a few sips of what I have chosen. I think you will find it pleasing."

Sarah folded her arms across her chest and took a step closer to the window. "Pleasing?" she retorted.

"I remember one broke her neck in the fall." He laughed. "Another broke both legs. I allowed them to live for their effort. But when the pain became unbearable, they begged for me to kill them."

Sarah swallowed hard when she heard the clinking of the goblets.

"I must admit, however, that I have thrown a couple out the window myself."

Sarah felt a hollow pang in her stomach.

"When they no longer pleased me. So, the choice is yours."

Sarah turned to face him when she heard his footsteps approaching on the stone floor.

"What name shall I use when I beseech God for your forgiveness?" she challenged. When I ask Him for the reclamation of your soul?"

The man smiled, and just before he was an arm's length from her, he shifted the goblets so he could hold them both in one of his large hands. With a slight bow of his head, he slapped her hard across the face with an open palm. The jarring blow dropped Sarah to the floor.

"You will from this moment on address me as Your Eminence or General Adhib or Master, whatever may be my whim."

Her eyes filled with tears, her face stinging, Sarah looked into the face of what was surely a manifestation of the devil. Wishing she were dead, that God would send a lightning bolt through the window and blow a hole in her chest, she started to tremble.

"Get up," the man snarled.

She yelped when he grabbed her by the hair and jerked her to her feet. He yanked her flush to his body and forcibly pressed his lips against hers. Repulsed when she felt his tongue thrust into her mouth, she pushed against his chest and struck him on the side of his head with her open hand. Breaking free of his grasp, she shuffled back a few paces and screamed, "No!"

He laughed and extended one of the goblets for her to take.

"Drink," he told her, with a nod to the goblet. With a lecherous smile and a wink of his eye, he added, "I grow hard."

Sarah suddenly felt light-headed. Her vision blurred, her balance faltered, and a chill swept through her body. Still trembling, she began to mumble the Lord's Prayer.

"Slavery can be pleasant," General Adhib said as he pressed a goblet into her hand. Closing her fingers around the stem, he added, "Or unpleasant, if you displease me."

Sarah felt numb as she stared into the goblet. The dark ruby color of the liquid reminded her of blood. The myriad images it conjured made her shudder. She recoiled when the man brushed his hand against her cheek.

"Drink," the general said again.

Sarah didn't move.

"Now," he ordered.

She was still.

"Very well," he hissed.

When he grabbed her breast, she snapped.

Taking a step back, she splashed wine onto the general's chest and hurled the goblet at his head. The silver chalice struck him square above his protruding eyebrows. Blood appeared where the lip of the cup cut into his skin.

The general's reaction was immediate and fierce. Roaring like an enraged lion, he lunged at Sarah and cuffed her on the side of the head. Once she'd fallen to the floor, he kicked her stomach. Writhing in pain, she gasped for air.

"White bitch!" the general shouted. "You cut me!" And then he grabbed her by the hair and jerked her head off the stone. "I should kill you!" he raged.

"Do it!" she croaked. "Kill me!" Clasping her hands in front of her chest, she blubbered, "I am God's servant. I am God's servant."

"You are my slave!" he bellowed. "You are mine! And you will learn to obey!"

"I will never!" she spat. "You will never own me!"

She cried out in pain as he tightened his grip on her hair and shook her head. Sarah dared to meet his eyes and found them smoldering with rage.

Sensing the devil in the man, she braced herself for the violent beating she was certain would come. When the general snorted and coiled his arm to strike, she closed her eyes and she steadied herself for a vicious blow. But nothing happened. Confused, she opened her eyes. She didn't know what or how to feel when she saw the general leave the room.

*

"I'm telling you, Bin'ka, there were no gunshots this night. Or an explosion, as you described, that shook the streets of the city."

"But I *heard* them," Bin'ka forcefully replied. "And *saw* the sky light up with a tower of fire."

Adiam lifted the snifter from the table and swirled the amber liquid it held. He scrutinized Bin'ka's face before responding.

"Perhaps there were fireworks I did not hear," he said with slight shrug of his shoulders. "I *was* indisposed for a time while I relieved myself." He raised the snifter in a toast and, with a good-natured smile breaking out on his face, added, "I would recommend not using my private—"

"Stop." Bin'ka ordered. He shook his head and motioned for Adiam to cease. "Just—" He mumbled something Adiam couldn't make out.

"Why does this distress you so?" Adiam took a sip of bourbon. "One would think you would be happy to know there have been no firefights in the street this night."

Placing the snifter back on the small, marble-topped table, Adiam reached for a cigarette. Before his fingers found the pack of Camels nestled in his shirt pocket, he started to cough.

"You sound like a clogged drainpipe," Bin'ka said. "Talia told me you'd stopped smoking."

Adiam pulled a handkerchief from his pants pocket and placed it over his mouth. He hacked wetly into the cloth.

"Talia says many things," Adiam wheezed. "Too many, sometimes." He took a sip of bourbon and sighed. "But she is a woman, after all. Do they all not talk too much?"

Bin'ka looked toward the harbor but said nothing. Adiam pulled the pack of cigarettes from his pocket, lit one, and set it on the table next to his drink.

"What troubles you, my friend?"

Adiam opened his eyes and smiled as he blew a stream of cigarette smoke from his nose.

"You stare at the sea as if expecting someone to emerge from its depths. Who is it you are looking for?"

Bin'ka rubbed his face with his hand and sighed.

"There was—"

He placed the necklace with the silver cross on the table.

"You've become Christian," Adiam remarked.

Bin'ka snorted. "Don't be foolish," he replied.

Adiam raised his eyebrows and turned his palms to the sky. "Then?" he asked.

"A girl. Some waif." Bin'ka nodded toward the harbor. "Stuck it in my hand." His brow furrowed. "Then disappeared." He placed a finger along the bottom edge of the cross and moved the symbol from side to side. "I've only seen two such as this."

"A trinket sold in every market where Christians sell their goods. Don't let your thoughts run—"

"I saw her," Bin'ka interjected. He covered the cross with his hand and shook his head. "She was—" He fell silent.

"She?"

Adiam took a deep drag off his cigarette and tilted his head to the sky. He blew smoke from his mouth and chuckled.

"We are both getting too old, Bin'ka," he teased. "I fear we see and hear things that aren't there."

"Zanzibar."

Adiam's expression made it clear he didn't understand.

"The cat," Bin'ka explained. "The old grey cat that has lived in this city since I can remember." Bin'ka picked the cross up from the table and held it between two fingers. "She appeared right after the girl disappeared." Bin'ka stared at the cross for a moment. "I've only known two like this," he said again, nodding to what he held. "The first—"

"A trinket from a girl and one of many cats that skulk around the merchant shacks for scraps of fish. Why are you—?"

"The *Lion*. The cat of the Lion. It was Zanzibar. Do you not remember the roar that filled the alleys the night the Lion came for the nun, the night you killed Susenyo?"

Adiam's attention drifted to the ring on his right forefinger. His gaze lingered on the ruby-and diamond-encrusted lion head for a few moments before he replied.

"It does not sparkle as it once did," he remarked. "The time of the Lion is no more." Adiam's voice grew sad. "As so much has perished in our time, my friend, the world to which we were born is no longer. The winds of the deserts never cease to alter what they touch."

Drawn to the stare of the ruby-eyed lion, Bin'ka immediately thought of the fire on the dock of Mogadishu and the woman he had pulled from the sea. *Shange bahr*, the children had called her: Lion of the Sea. Where was she now?

"I heard he was killed by one of the clans fighting for control of Mogadishu," Adiam told him as he gazed into his snifter. After taking a sip of bourbon, he added, "Akmir's grand folly."

"Folly?"

"Trying to unite the warring clans of a divided city." Adiam placed the snifter on the table and leaned forward. "It's one thing time does not seem to change." He paused to tap the silver cross lying on the table. "The ignorance of men. The winds cannot seem to keep them from embracing stupidity. It is though violence and prejudice have been sewn into the very fabric of our souls."

Bin'ka's gaze shifted from the ring to the cross to the harbor and then farther past the giant loading cranes out to sea. *Shange bahr*, his thoughts whispered. *Shange bahr.* Why couldn't he stop thinking of the name? Of *her*?

"But you are not interested in what ails mankind, are you? You search for someone who—" Adiam raised an eyebrow and tilted his head to one side. "Who is it you seek?" Adiam asked. "Who is it that calls to you?"

Bin'ka placed a hand over the cross.

"You never told me why you didn't return to Djibouti after taking Dirk and the nun to Somalia." Adiam tapped the tabletop with his finger. "What was there that made you stay?"

The breeze off the water stiffened. A cat growled from somewhere in the shadows across the street. Bin'ka closed his eyes and pressed his hands over his ears when he heard the old hag's voice whisper, "Are you free?" He nearly toppled backward out of his chair when someone grabbed his wrist.

"Are you ill?" Adiam inquired.

Bin'ka opened his eyes and looked sheepishly at Adiam. Sighing, he placed his hands on the table and grunted. His fingers traced the outline of the cross before he spoke.

"The slavers," he began. He paused as Adiam pulled his chair closer to the table. "Children—so many children—taken, imprisoned, sold." His brow furrowed and then smoothed. "She—" He picked the cross up by its base and held it so it stood upright. "'Are you free?' she asked. 'Are you free?'"

Bin'ka shook his head when a glint of white light reflected into his eyes. He wondered if Adiam noticed that no matter how he angled the cross, light reflected off the metal.

"I'd heard Sister Lady cast a strong spell," Adiam remarked. "I wasn't aware that she was conscious before she was flown out of the country."

"Not her," Bin'ka replied. "She's not the one I hear."

"Ah, hearing voices." Adiam nodded. He took another deep drag off his cigarette. "And seeing things, as well." He blew smoke from his nostrils and then flicked the cigarette butt into the street. "You remind me of him," he said, tapping the lion-head ring. "He could hear the Mother's voice. Perhaps you are as lucky." Adiam nodded to the silver cross. "Or unlucky, depending on what you hear Her say."

Bin'ka blinked his eyes against the gleaming light shining in his eyes. He set the cross back on the table. His brow furrowed.

"If she speaks of slavers and freedom, I fear you will not be with us long."

Bin'ka looked at Adiam as though the aging Arab had just hurled an obscenity at him. He clenched and unclenched his fists as he glowered at the older man.

"Perhaps she is asking you to make amends for your dealings in the trade," Adiam said.

"I had no part in imprisoning woman and children!" Bin'ka vehemently hissed. "You and Akmir—"

"Yes, Akmir," Adiam casually countered as he pulled another cigarette from the pack. "Your partner—*our* partner. Did we not both stand and watch as he gathered and sold those who live in the streets?"

"Akmir," Bin'ka snarled. "The *khinzir.*"

"Pig or no pig, he is a businessman with no conscience." Adiam lit a second cigarette and inhaled. "He almost killed us, yes?" He chuckled. "And simply set up shop in a different locale when his plan did not play out as he'd hoped."

"I would like to squeeze his throat until his eyes pop out."

"I hear he is surrounded by a small army of mercenaries."

"Maybe one of the lunatic warlords jostling for control of Mogadishu will take his head," Bin'ka mused.

Adiam cupped the base of the snifter and eased it off the table. He swirled the bourbon before raising the glass to his lips.

"From what I have been told, he sells to all of them to garner their support. Weapons, drugs, women, children—even ivory, or so I am led to believe." Adiam took a sip of bourbon and then set the snifter down. "The woman you were with—the second nun. I hear he brokered her sale."

"You mean Sarah?"

Shange bahr!

"Was that her name?" Adiam asked. "Poor girl. I hear Adhib bought her."

Bin'ka slapped his hands on the table.

"That butcher?" Bin'ka snarled. *Shange bahr, shange bahr, shange bahr!* "She will not survive—"

Bin'ka swept the cross into his hand and clenched it in his fist. As Adiam took another drag off his cigarette and began to cough, Bin'ka stood and walked briskly toward the harbor.

*

Sarah dipped her finger into the drops of wine splattered on the floor and pressed the liquid onto her chest. She repeated the action nearly a dozen times until the white cotton robe she was wearing bore the symbol of a cross above her heart. Kneeling below the window, murmuring the Lord's

Prayer, she briefly noted her handiwork before clasping her hands and bowing her head.

Prayer brought her the vision of the hilltop where John had taken her after she'd been shot. The sky that morning had been a heavenly shade of blue, the flora along the river as green as any emerald she had ever seen. The swaying grasses of the plain shown sunlit gold as they swayed beneath a gentle breeze, while animals of all species grazed peacefully along the banks of a sparkling river. Sarah closed her eyes and embraced the image. Comforted by the serene beauty, she repeated aloud what she'd recited in silence.

"Thy kingdom come, thy will be done on earth as it is in heaven."

A voice of a child—muffled but distressed—broke her train of thought. Alarmed, she held her breath and listened, but she heard no repetition of the sound. Dismissing the incident as a product of her state of mind, she looked up at the window. Eyes fixed on the wooden shutters, she muttered a quick *amen* and made the sign of the cross.

"Blessed Mother," she murmured. She took a deep breath and blinked back the tears welling in her eyes. "Since I have not heard from you in some time, I realize you are in agreement with the Lord." She gazed at the shutters as her bottom lip began to tremble. "Penance is not enough to erase my sins." Tears began to trickle down her cheeks. "I know that now. I know there is no redemption for my soul. I—" She bowed her head and, making a fist, softly struck it against her heart as she choked back a sob. "I ask that you understand. I cannot bear to suffer. I ask that you— That you—" She hastily wiped her eyes and cleared her throat. "Help me," she pleaded. "Help me."

Bowing her head once more, she slowly made the sign of the cross and rose, unsteadily, to her feet. With a heavy sigh, she took a step forward and pulled open the shutters, whispering, "May God forgive me."

Sarah closed her eyes as she edged closer to the window ledge. She did not want to see sky or buildings or sea, for she wished to focus on the vision she'd created in her mind. Why she had conjured the memory of the hilltop where the hyena-man had taken her, she did not know, but she was grateful for the beauty it offered. Since her ordeal in the closet, life had been dark and filled with torment. She'd suffered enough, she'd decided. And God and the Holy Mother—by their silence—had made it clear that she was not forgiven for the sins she had committed. The grace of heaven could not be obtained in this life, but perhaps the hill of the hyena-man could be attained in death. With a deep breath, she grabbed the sides of the window frame.

"*La!*" a woman shrieked.

Startled, she turned to see the silent woman running toward her. Her expression was one of extreme distress.

"*La!*" the woman gasped as she grabbed hold of Sarah's shoulder. There were tears in the woman's eyes as she looked into Sarah's and pleaded, "*La!*"

Stunned that the woman she thought was mute could speak, it took Sarah a moment to react. But in a flash of anger, she slapped the woman's hand away and said, "So you talk."

Tears streamed down the woman's face as she blurted, "*Ana asifa.*"

Struck by the raw emotion in the woman's voice, Sarah's anger immediately waned. Lightly cupping her hand along the woman's slender jaw, she said, "I wish I knew what you meant."

"She says you must learn."

General Adhib had returned. The old woman bowed her head and backed several steps away.

"I don't think that's what she said," Sarah replied.

The general responded with a lecherous smile. And then he snapped his fingers. Three children appeared in the doorway. Confused by their appearance, Sarah asked, "Why are they here?"

"To teach you." The general moved a few paces closer, his attention drawn to her chest. He ogled her breasts as he said, "To imprint upon you the value of obedience."

"I don't—" Sarah glanced at the children. Taking a closer look, she noticed their hands were tied behind their backs. When she saw their ankles were also hobbled by what looked to be wire, she let out an alarmed gasp.

"Why are they bound?" she demanded. "What are you going to do?"

Sarah recoiled when the general attempted to touch her cheek with his finger. Undeterred, the man took a step closer and clamped a hand behind her neck. The sensation of his sweaty palm on her nape made her cringe.

"The lessons they will teach you depend on how quickly you learn," he told her. Shifting his hand from her neck to her cheek, he said, "Let me demonstrate." She felt his thumb slide along her jaw. "Kiss me."

Sarah slapped the general's hand off her cheek and retreated a pace. She shook her head. "I— I won't. I won't kiss you."

The general clapped his hands together and smiled.

"So, you say," he replied.

A flurry of movement at the doorway drew Sarah's attention. A soldier—slight of build and armed with a long stick—ushered the children into the room and then took a position a few feet in front of them. Sarah didn't understand why the children were whimpering until she saw traces of blood where the wire wrapped around their ankles.

"What have you done to them?" she blurted. "Dear God!" She started to move past him, but the general grabbed her roughly by the arm and held her still. "Let me go!" she demanded.

"Obey!" the general retorted.

Sarah's attention snapped back to the children when she heard one of them cry out in pain. The middle child yelped when the soldier cracked the stick against the side of his face. Before Sarah could react, the soldier raised the stick, moved slightly to his left, and smacked the next child square on the ear.

"Stop!" Sarah screamed. "Stop it!"

As she watched in disbelief, the soldier then struck each child square in the face with the long, thick stick. Wailing from the pain of the blows, the children moved away. Their cries grew louder. The movement, Sarah realized, exacerbated the cuts from the wire binding their ankles; she saw blood oozing where wire sliced into skin.

"Will you kiss me now?" the general casually asked.

Sarah looked at him as though he were a manifestation of Satan. She could feel the blood rushing from her face as she stared, disbelievingly, at the man.

"You're— You're—" She ran a hand over her head and whimpered. "I can't believe—" She looked at the children and shook her head.

"Very well."

When Sarah saw the soldier raise the stick above his shoulder, she immediately looked toward the general. The man had his arm poised as if to signal the start of a race.

"No!" she screamed.

But it was too late; the general dropped his arm. The sound of wood smacking against flesh and bone was immediate. One of the boys screamed, "*Shange bahr!*" The middle child was staring at her, his pleading face smeared with tears and blood.

"So, you know one of these slaves!" the general roared. "All the better!"

Sarah could feel her heart breaking as she gazed at the boy. *Shange bahr*, he'd cried. Bin'ka had been right. Some if not all the children they had put ashore on the beach the next morning had been recaptured and sold into slavery. "Slavery is death," he'd unequivocally stated. She could feel tears welling in her eyes as she began to understand his full meaning.

"Bring the boy forward!" the general commanded.

Sarah shook her head and edged toward the window. She could take no more suffering. God might damn her to hell for what she was about to do, but what difference was there between hell and the life she'd been living? Perhaps she would get used to the pain of eternal damnation. Holding on to that notion, she turned and leapt toward the window.

"Kill the boy!" she heard the general shout. "Cut his throat from ear to ear!"

Stricken by the malice of his tone, Sarah came to a sudden halt. Horrified, she whirled to face him.

"Three lives for one," he barked. "The price of disobedience." He nodded to the boy the soldier had brought forward. "That is the lesson you will learn."

Sarah saw him motion to the soldier with his hand. The solder pulled a long knife from a sheath attached to his waist. He held the blade aloft for a moment as if showing it to her, then put it to the boy's throat. The boy looked at her and began to cry.

"*Shange bahr*," he whimpered.

"You might find obedience pleasurable," the general snickered. "Or—"

Sarah's mind whirled with snippets of her life: the hooded man, the closet where he kept her bound in her own waste, the blood that poured from his throat when she stabbed him, Dirk coming to her rescue in the streets of Djibouti, the kiss he gave her as he lay her on his hotel bed, the eyes of the Afar warrior before he died, the hideousness of the hyena-man when she woke after being shot, the wild cackling of the hyena pack as they raced down the hilltop, the crucifix that hung in the chapel on the grounds of the Solitude of the Savior, the eyes of Christ as he hung dying for the sins of man, the purity of the Holy Mother the night she appeared to Sarah and offered her refuge, the carnage she witnessed as she and Teimbaka crossed Ethiopia on their way to find Dirk and Claire, the fires she walked through at the beckoning of the man dressed in a black robe. All these images swirled round and round in her head as she glanced between the boy, the window, and the man extorting her for obedience.

"Take the boy's head," the general ordered.

"No!" Sarah screamed.

"Then disrobe and get on the bed!" the general yelled.

Sarah began to tremble.

"And remember, if you do not please me, you will find the boy's head in your lap."

Sarah met the general's eyes. A shiver ran down her spine.

"Rest assured, I will—"

Sarah gathered her robe and pulled it over her head. Her stomach churned as she walked slowly toward the bed. She could feel herself go cold as she lay down.

"Very good," she heard the general say. "Remember, you must please me if you wish the boy to live."

Sarah swallowed hard, closed her eyes, and spread her legs.

"That will not please me."

Confused, Sarah opened her eyes and looked at the man. She winced when she saw him staring at her as he stepped out of his pants.

"Turn around and get on your hands and knees," he told her. She looked away when she saw him stroke his hardening penis. "Do it now," he ordered. "And remember: obey."

Fighting back a wave of nausea, Sarah slid to the end of the mattress and rolled over on to her stomach.

"Up," she heard him command.

Tears welled in her eyes as she pushed off the mattress and positioned her body as she'd been instructed. Numbness enveloped her heart when she heard him laugh.

"I will fuck you like the infidel you are," he said. She bit down on her lower lip when she felt him grab her hips and brush against her vulva. "Then you will lick your stench from me with your tongue." She hung her head. "After that—"

Warm, wine tainted breath blew against her ear. A hand stroked her breasts and rubbed them from side to side.

"I will take you while you gaze into my eyes." Sarah fought to keep her sanity when the general began to grunt. "Or together we will watch the children die one by one."

19

HE SAW THEM from afar.

Men. Surely, they were men, he thought. But he was mistaken. While the figures heading toward him looked like men in all manner of shape and form, what sort of man moved without walking and cast no shadow beneath the sun? What type of man left no footprint in the sand and stirred not a grain of dust along a dry dirt road? Nay, these were not men—at least not men of this earth. More like ghosts, they were, the way they seemed to drift on air, the way light passed through their torsos like a breeze through tall grass. Ghosts, then. Where did they come from? Where were they headed?

So many their number, so different their dress. Some wore a soldier's uniform, some the robes of the church. Still others wore the tattered rags of the poor and calluses on their feet. Young, old—all marched westward toward the desert, the procession as silent and gloomy as any Teimbaka had ever witnessed.

"You see yourself amongst them."

"Who are they?" Teimbaka asked. "And where are they going?"

"Who are they?" John Too mocked. "Open your eyes."

"But I am—" Teimbaka placed his fingers to the cloth bandage on his face. "I'm blind."

"Are you?" John Too scoffed. "Then how is it you can see the forgotten?"

"The forgotten?" Teimbaka questioned, uneasy.

"Look again," John Too instructed after a lengthy pause. "Tell me what you see."

Confused, Teimbaka again patted the cloth covering his eyes.

"Where are you, Teimbaka? Tell me what you sense."

"I am in an alley. You told me yourself when—"

"Listen. Feel."

"I don't understand."

"The wind, Teimbaka, the wind."

"I— I don't—"

"Listen."

Wind suddenly gusted around his shoulders. Within the swirling current, he heard a muffled, intermittent cry—one that stirred memories from his past.

He'd been lying awake, staring into the fire. Hours had passed since Untello had shown him the cave where the tusks were stored.

The feel of death was everywhere in that cave, the morbid presence so strong it seemed to reach into his soul. He tried to run as soon as he felt its presence, as soon as his blood turned cold, but Untello kept him from moving and told him he must face what part he'd played in harvesting the tusks. He heard it then—the whimper of a baby spirit-elephant—coming from deep within the cave, hidden behind a mound of ivory. Overcome with fear, he pulled free from Untello's grasp and raced out of the cave. When he once more stood beneath the blazing sun, he thought he'd escaped, thought he would never again hear the heartbreaking cry of the tormented beast. But he was wrong.

He hadn't known what to make of the tiny pink lights that appeared beyond the campfire later that night. Bugs, he thought, or a species of flower that glowed in the dark. There were so many—everywhere he looked. He suddenly found himself surrounded by pink-red orbs that appeared to float several meters off the ground. Then, slowly, as if emerging out of a pool of water, elephants began to materialize out of the night air. They were massive crystalline animals with eyes that reminded Teimbaka of the sun after a dust storm. Overwhelmed by the appearance of the ghost beasts, he'd panicked and frantically searched for a route to escape. But the spirit-elephants closed ranks and encircled him. A moment later, they assailed him with their death wails: blaring, tormented sounds that paralyzed him. And as he waited for the ghosts to extract their revenge upon him for the part he'd played in killing their kind, a sound that tore at the very fabric of his soul began to supplant the elephant's deafening calls.

Sad, forlorn, distressed, heartbroken. The tormented whimpers of the ethereal beasts were too much for him to bear. He remembered closing his eyes and crying. And as he wept, he could sense the elephant's spirits pass through him, as though each was imprinting its grief upon him.

Untello found him, unharmed but forever changed, at dawn. And though Teimbaka had grown quite fond of the men who had taken him under their watch after his parents died, he left them later that day. Sickened that they had turned him into an elephant poacher, he killed Bawa in a fit of rage and then fled. The man's death haunted him, but Bawa's life was only the first he would sacrifice to keep the remaining elephants from harm.

"Look now," John Too bade. "What do you see?"

Snowflakes flitted across a mound of newly turned earth. A few of the pristine white flakes had collected on the necklace of metallic green beetles that adorned the wooden cross Claire had placed at the head of his brother's grave. He would have liked to have taken a few moments to admire the beauty of the scene, but the cold wind blowing in his face made him turn away. As he shivered and rubbed his arms, he glimpsed a procession of figures in the distance. Men. Surely they were men.

"Look closer," John Too's voice instructed.

Tattered figures of men blurred to slate-colored shapes that quivered into outlines of thick legs, long trunks, and floppy ears.

"Elephants," Teimbaka mumbled.

"Watch."

Now crystalline in appearance, the ethereal beasts moved atop a road of milk-white mist in numbers too great to count. West, toward the desert, the spirit-elephants traveled, and as Teimbaka turned to study the path they followed, a shadow—a dark mass that covered both earth and sky—appeared on the horizon. Black and ominous, thunderheads materialized over the procession of crystalline beasts. Soon after, jagged bolts of lightning shot down from the clouds and struck the elephants en masse. Wherever an elephant fell, there was an explosion of light. As his heart filled with despair, Teimbaka watched the ethereal beasts shatter and crumble, one by one, into the mist.

"Save them," John Too urged. "Save them before they are gone."

"But I am—"

"Were you not chosen to protect them?"

"Yes, but I—"

"Look how they perish in your care. Look who steals their souls."

Taloned and gruesome, dark angels descended from the sky to hover just above the mist. These minions of the Serpent reached down into the fog with long, sinewy arms and lifted the elephants' tusks from where the spirit-beasts had fallen. Once they had secured the ivory in their ghoulish hands, the dark angels ferried it into the clouds.

"You've failed them."

Teimbaka hid his face within the folds of his robe.

"You can see, but you choose to look away."

Teimbaka vehemently shook his head but remained silent.

"Who will help them if not you?"

"I am blind!" he angrily replied.

"The sick, the hungry, the innocent, the ravaged—you see them, but you turn away."

Teimbaka turned to face John Too. What felt like stinging pellets of ice blew cold against his face.

"The forgotten search for one who will help them find their souls. What will you say when the Mother asks where you have gone, Teimbaka?"

*

"Should we ask for more?"

Mosi studied a clipboard before he replied.

"Ask?" He gave Amin a dismissive smirk. "I'm not in the mood to ask."

"But I have never seen so many tusks. How many does each truck hold?"

Mosi slowly ran his finger down the sheet of paper.

"The full-beds carry twenty, half-beds ten. The older pick-ups can only take the weight of five to seven, depending on the condition of their suspension."

Amin shaded his eyes and looked down the mountain toward the caravan of vehicles assembled.

"I count seventeen trucks—ten full-bed."

Mosi watched as Amin extended each of his fingers one by one on both hands and mumbled. His brow furrowed.

"So, a hundred and fifty or so?"

"Plus a hundred more." Mosi glanced at the mouth of the cave behind them. "With probably triple that still inside."

"A fortune," Amin said.

"A fortune," Mosi agreed.

Amin looked down toward his feet and fingered the hilt of the knife sheathed at his waist.

"A fortune for Akmir," he commented. "You would think our cut would be worth more than twenty thousand pieces of gold."

Mosi studied Amin's face for a moment before replying.

"One would think, yes."

"Then perhaps," Amin rubbed his chin, "perhaps you will ask him?"

"Ask? Ask who?"

"Akmir," Amin replied. "Perhaps you will ask Akmir."

"Ask him what?"

Amin clutched the hilt of his knife. "For more gold. Money. More."

Mosi shook his head. "I told you, I am not in the mood to ask."

"But we are being cheated!" Amin stressed in a restrained voice.

Mosi observed him eyeing the men nearest them—some of the score they'd hired to load and drive the ivory to Akmir's base on the outskirts of Mogadishu.

"We are the ones who found it. We are the ones who were shot at." Amin took a few steps toward the lip of the bluff where they were standing before abruptly turning and retracing the steps he had taken. "If it wasn't for us sending a few mortar rounds into the rocks, no one would have ever known the cave existed."

"Yes, no one would ever know," Mosi agreed. "But now they do."

"We deserve more!"

"Keep your voice down," Mosi tersely replied. He grabbed the collar of Amin's T-shirt and pulled him closer. "Do you want everyone to hear?" he whispered.

"What does it matter?" Amin knocked Mosi's arm away. "We are fools! Fools for giving it away!"

Mosi ground his jaws together and glared at Amin.

"Yes, I am looking at a fool. One who—" Mosi stopped talking when he saw one of the hired men approach. "What is it?" he asked the man.

"We've loaded as much as we can," the man replied. "The trucks cannot handle any more weight."

"Then start for Mogadishu," Mosi told him. "You know the way to Akmir's camp, yes?"

"Yes, but don't you want to—?"

"We'll be right behind you." Mosi reached into his waist sash and extracted a key. Holding it level to the man's eyes, he said, "We'll take the last full-bed truck." He nodded his head toward the cave. "We'll catch up after we pull some underbrush in front of the opening. Now go. I don't want the sun to set before we show Akmir what we bring."

He saw the man look toward the cave.

"Something else?" Mosi inquired.

The man shook his head.

"Then get going."

Amin was silent while he and Mosi covered the mouth of the cave. And he remained quiet on the walk down the mountain to the waiting truck. Even when Mosi slid into the driver's side of the cab and started the engine, Amin sat in the passenger seat with his lips closed tight and a stony expression on his face. They sat in silence for a few minutes, each man staring straight ahead out the windshield. When the last of the dust trail from the convoy of trucks disappeared from view, Mosi spoke.

"How far ahead do you think they are?"

Amin turned his head away and shrugged his shoulders.

"Five, ten minutes?"

"I don't—" Amin shifted his weight. "What does it matter?"

Mosi put the truck in gear and pressed his foot against the gas pedal. The truck backed up several meters before he turned the steering wheel hard to the left.

"What are doing? Mogadishu is that way," Amin told him, pointing toward the convoy of trucks.

"We are not going that way." Mosi smiled at Amin as he braked, shifted gears, then turned the steering wheel hard to the right. "We have a different destination."

"What are you saying?"

Mosi gave the truck some gas and turned the steering wheel so the truck was pointed away from the convoy.

"I said I wasn't in the mood to ask, remember?" He chuckled. "But I am always in the mood to make a better deal." He reached over and slapped Amin on the thigh. "We are going to be rich, my friend! Rich!"

*

Kamua's leg throbbed. And when he placed his hand where the shrapnel had torn into his thigh, he could feel heat rising off the swollen tissue. He understood he was in trouble. He needed a doctor. But his wound would have to wait. They were on the move, following a laden truck. The ivory needed to be recovered.

Neither he nor Juba had understood why sixteen of the vehicles loaded with ivory had gone in one direction while a single truck had taken a completely different route. And while they'd both wanted to recover the full cache of ivory the men had stolen from the cave, they were realistic enough to acknowledge their limitations. Two stood no chance of stopping a convoy of sixteen trucks and a score of armed men, but stopping one truck and two men seemed highly achievable. Especially when the two men in the truck's cab were the two who had tried to kill them.

The girl—Juba—had made it plain she wanted to kill the man wearing the blue turban. She said she owed it to the girl she'd been traveling with. "She could talk to the hyenas," Juba told him. "And she had this," Juba added, holding up an antelope horn.

Eden, the girl had been called. Kamua believed Eden had been some sort of bouda—a hyena-man.

It was clear Juba thought that the antelope horn held some special power.

"You take the gun," she'd said when they'd decided to follow the lone truck. "I have the horn." She'd run a finger from the tip of the horn to the base, tracing the spiral grooves. "And because of it," she'd gone on, "I have them."

Kamua had followed her nod to the pack of hyenas lingering near their encampment. He didn't pretend to understand the odd relationship between the girl and the animals, nor was he convinced the hyenas were safe to be around. They were brutal, vicious beasts; he'd observed their ruthless behavior a number of times when patrolling the bush. Their presence was unnerving. And he wasn't convinced some old horn taken from some poor antelope held any power over them.

But the girl trusted them, so maybe he should too. She said they saved his life, pulled him to safety before another mortar round fell. He was grateful—at least he told himself he was. But he didn't trust the beasts. That would be unnatural. But regardless of how he felt about hyenas and their instinctive traits, he had no choice but to accept their presence. For it was as Juba told him: the hyenas were drawn to the horn and therefore to her. He didn't need any more proof than what he was witnessing.

Now Juba was fifty meters ahead of him, standing in the midst of a score of hyenas, animatedly waving for him to join her. They'd decided that once the single truck made the turn north, they would follow it. The decision allowed them to track the vehicle while the dust left in its wake hid them from view. Juba had somehow communicated to the hyenas that she wanted some of the pack to run alongside the truck to keep it within eyesight.

"We must stop them!" she called out as he labored to reach her position. "They're loading the tusks into a plane!"

Kamua scanned the terrain behind Juba.

"A plane?" he questioned, out of breath. "How—? Where?"

Juba pointed directly behind her. "There. Two-hundred paces or more. Hurry."

"Wait," he told her when she began to move away.

"There is no time!" she yelled, breaking into a run.

"How many men are with the plane?" he shouted. "What weapons are they carrying?"

But Juba didn't answer. Kamua shook his head and limped after her.

*

Juba motioned for Kamua to get lower.

"You move like a tortoise," she told him as he gingerly crouched beside her. She glanced at the large bloodstain on the leg of his pants. "Maybe there is medicine on the plane."

Kamua winced.

"Medicine," he repeated. "And how would we get to it?"

She pointed toward the boxy-looking, twin-engine plane parked some distance from their position.

"There are only four men," she said. "You could shoot some of them and make the others run away."

"What about their guns? Don't you think they'll shoot back?"

Juba was silent for a moment.

"They could help," she replied, nodding to the hyenas on either side of her.

Kamua glanced left and right. He could barely discern the score of hyenas hidden in the steppe.

"I think this was a mistake." He rubbed his leg and grimaced. "I think we should go back. We won't be able to—"

"Go back?" Juba balanced the antelope horn in the palm of her hand. "Some things can't go back," she told him, eyeing the horn. "There isn't a way." She shifted her attention to the four men, pointing with the horn toward one. "Blue-head is there. He killed Eden and cut off her head. He was going to do the same to you." She glanced at the horn before adding, "All the dead elephants we saw when we were on the mountain? Their souls? You said bad men killed them. You said no one has been able to stop them." She plunged the tip of the horn into the ground. "Don't you want to try?"

"But—"

"They're only four."

"With guns."

"We," she nodded to either side of her again, "are many. And they do not know we are here."

"They'll know as soon as we—"

"We have to try."

Kamua shifted his weight so he could kneel on his uninjured leg.

"And what if we die? What then?" He nodded to the horn. "Who will look out for the living, the ones who need our help? Men like Blue-head are everywhere." He tapped the AK-47 strapped over his shoulder. "They kill without conscience. Elephants, rhinos, lions—the animals don't stand a chance."

"All the more reason to strike." She extracted the horn from the dirt before forcefully plunging it back in. "Bad men. Bad men must die."

Kamua tousled Juba's hair and chuckled.

"Agreed. Bad men should die," he told her in a wistful tone of voice. "Too often, though— Hey! Come back!"

Kamua lurched out of the underbrush and swung the AK-47 from his shoulder. He engaged the primer just as Blue-head spotted Juba running toward him with the antelope horn raised above her head. A score of hyenas ran with her, fanned out on either side.

"Shoot!" he heard Blue-head yell.

Kamua fired his weapon in a tight arc from right to left. The man dressed in the red T-shirt took a round to his shoulder and fell to his knees. Kamua fired another burst in his direction and the man fell face forward into the dirt.

A staccato round of gunfire sent a line of bullets into the soil just to one side of Juba. Tracing them to their source, Kamua saw Blue-head standing behind the truck, slapping an ammo clip into his assault rifle. He glimpsed another man to the left of Blue-head roll under the plane and scramble out the other side. He didn't see the remaining man. A new burst of gunfire from Blue-head sent two hyenas to the ground, squealing in pain. Juba screamed. And then the air around him seemed to explode.

A terrible pain ripped into his stomach. Suddenly, he couldn't breathe. As he fell, his eyes focused on the wisps of smoke lingering above the barrel of a large caliber machine gun protruding from the back door of the plane.

*

Juba screamed and covered her ears. The thunder gun was deafening. Hyenas to either side of her squealed and jerked sideways amidst sprays of blood. Then something hit Juba's side and knocked her to the ground. Spun at an angle, she glimpsed the ranger lurch backward as several bullets tore into his body. In a state of shock, she watched Kamua fall.

Blood everywhere, the death squeals of hyenas filling her head,

Juba covered her ears. But the thunder gun kept firing. Suddenly, nothing seemed real. Nothing made sense. So much death. What had been the point?

Slowly, she became aware that she was moving, carried by one of the hyenas. She threw the horn to the ground and began to sob.

*

Talia clicked off the radio receiver and scanned the sky to the west. Out of habit, she checked the positions of her personal guard: seven well-armed men who'd accompanied her from the city, as well as three others she knew to be positioned within a triangle of 100 meters from where she stood. Akmir's attempted coup the previous year had taught her a valuable lesson: one couldn't be too careful. And since Akmir was by no means the only threat in the region, she believed in taking extra care where it pertained to her survival.

What she'd just heard from the pilot she'd sent to rendezvous with the ivory seller only served to reinforce her belief. But it baffled her how a girl and a park ranger could have known where the ivory buy was going to take place. She'd contacted the man the day before, and the exchange had been arranged less than eight hours ago. It made her wonder if she had a mole in her operation—though it wouldn't surprise her if she did. She wouldn't put it past Adiam to insert one of his own men into her inner circle to keep an eye on her.

As to why the girl and the ranger had ambushed her men, no doubt they wanted the ivory for themselves. But where and to whom were they going to sell it? As far as she knew, only she and Akmir were dealing in ivory in the region. Was there another buyer she wasn't aware of? Or was this some bizarre attempt by Adiam to stop her from dealing in the product?

Certainly she'd misheard what the pilot had said about hyenas. There was no possible way wild animals had taken part in the assault. Perhaps they'd simply come running when they'd heard shots and smelled blood. The whole matter was a curiosity. But she'd come to accept the unexpected as part of her business. She'd have been dead long ago if she hadn't.

Business, she mused, *who would have thought? A trash scrounger, a street girl from Khartoum. Look how far I've come.* She allowed herself a little smile as she scanned the sky for the bush plane. It would be landing soon. He couldn't be more than a few miles away, judging by the clarity of the transmission, and once he was on the ground and she'd inspected the merchandise, she'd have to make decisions quickly.

Transporting the tusks to the United States would be the first order of business. Judging by the quantity she'd been told was on offer, the transport would need to be capacious.

The *Jameel* was still docked in Wilmington, Delaware, and not due to return for another week to ten days. Space on one of the other Conglomerate transport vessels would have to be arranged. *Which ship is due to leave port first?* she wondered. *Talisman* or *Inshallah*? She would call Adiam to find out. She'd have to come up with some excuse for asking, but since Adiam was getting sicker by the day and somewhat confused about the day-to-day specifics of the Conglomerate's business, she didn't think there would be much of a problem.

Besides, Adiam was too involved in trying to become legitimate to probe too deeply into her request. The last thing he wanted to hear was that she was smuggling ivory again. She found it a little peculiar that he had no qualms dealing in drugs, weapons, stolen art, or jewels but was adamantly against trafficking ivory or people.

How many times had she heard him say, "Everything has a price, so everything is for sale"? Why he had abandoned that doctrine, she didn't know. But for Adiam, ivory and slaves were taboo commodities. Which was fine with her, because it left an entire market for her to monopolize.

"There," she heard one of her guards say.

She heard the drone of engines before she spotted the plane.

The DeHavilland DHC-3 twin-engine aircraft coming into view had been one of Talia's first personal acquisitions, and the bush plane had repaid her investment a hundred times over. Able to take off and land in nearly all types of terrain while carrying a payload upwards of four thousand pounds, the plane enabled Talia to deal in and transfer merchandise of all types across national boundaries without having to worry about police, customs, the military, or the Conglomerate sticking their nose into her affairs. The purchase of the plane had enabled her to amass a small fortune outside her holdings as a Conglomerate partner. And with that small fortune, she'd hired an array of employees: pilots, thieves, poachers, slavers, guards, and crew for a small contingent of sailing vessels.

She'd expanded her dealings in human trafficking, prostitution, and ivory smuggling from the horn of Africa down through Kenya and up into Sudan. To carve out her own fiefdom within the region—aside from what property she held as a partner in the Conglomerate—she would need a small army to seize and hold regions undergoing internal upheaval. But buying an army wasn't the same as commanding it. She needed to find someone she could trust to oversee a paramilitary operation. As of yet, Talia had not found that individual.

Talia's grander plans for the future included the takeover of the Conglomerate and overseeing the worldwide operations—both legitimate and illegitimate—Adiam had meticulously built over the past decade. Taking control of the Conglomerate immediately would require Adiam's removal, so she'd set those plans aside for the present. She was patient. The man was sick, his demise near. Her moment would come sooner rather than later. And when it did, she would be ready. But for the time being, she needed to focus on growing her resources and expanding her blossoming business empire. Africa had taught her that power and control could be obtained by force, but they could not be maintained without money. Money was the key.

"Everything has a price. Everything is for sale."

She thought about how true Adiam's favorite saying was as she watched the plane land.

*

"Excellent."

Talia ran a hand across one of the twenty large tusks stacked neatly in front of her and smiled.

"How many can you carry in a load?"

The pilot—a grizzled man with a wrinkled face and sunburnt nose—replied, "Fifteen optimal; twenty, max weight."

"No more?" Talia inquired.

"Not unless I strip what's in the bay."

"Then do it."

"Won't," the man stated.

Talia's smile faded. "You'll do what I tell you."

Touching the brim of his cap, he said, "No, madam. Sorry. Won't fly without my big gun. Especially not after what just happened."

"Your big gun?"

"Browning M2. Fires—"

Talia motioned for him to stop. "Never mind. I understand." Looking west, she asked, "How many trips can you get in before dark?"

"Depends on the other end. There were only two men unloading the merchandise, and now one's dead. Don't know how fast the remaining one can work or if there's others helping him."

Talia frowned.

"For my part, I can go and return three, four times before we lose the light—if he's waiting with the goods each time I land."

"Did he say how many he has to sell?"

The pilot shook his head. "Wasn't much in a talkative mood when we arrived. Less so after those animals charged." The pilot removed his cap and ran his wrist over his balding head. "Damnedest thing I've ever seen. Some little waif in a pink dress surrounded by a pack of hyenas and a—"

"Let's get these tusks loaded on the truck," Talia interjected. "You and you," she said to the two guards nearest the plane. "You'll fly back with—" She looked at the pilot.

"Yaroslav, madam."

"Back with Yaroslav and help with the loading and unloading. Understood?"

If the men were perplexed or unhappy with her instructions, they nonetheless nodded their compliance without hesitation. Turning her attention back to the pilot, Talia said, "I'll contact the seller and let him know you're on the way back. I'll update you by radio if there's to be any holdup in the transfer." She tapped one of the tusks. "Understood?"

"We haven't discussed—"

"Same as what I paid you for this trip. Half again more for every load you can bring me after the next three."

Yaroslav stroked his chin for a moment.

"You didn't warn me there might be problems. My price would have been substantially higher if I'd known there was going to be a firefight."

Talia studied Yaroslav's face for a moment before she laughed.

"Mr. Yaroslav," she said. "You're in this country because of your expertise in weaponry and war. I would think a few gunshots fairly routine." She paused long enough to frown. "After all, this is Africa, Mr. Yaroslav. When isn't there trouble?"

*

Juba ran a stick through the dirt and stared at the line it made. Nothing within the center of it, nothing at either end. Same as what was in her mind—nothing. Nothing left, nothing to look forward to, nothing to cling to. Nothing that might kindle a spark of hope. Nothing. Her village destroyed, her parents killed, Eden butchered by Blue-head. And now the ranger and most of the hyenas were gone. Dead. Nothing. Nothing left. Everything had become nothing. Nothing was all she had left. She took the stick and scratched another line in the dirt next to the original one. The second line didn't change anything; everything had become nothing.

A shadow passed across the lines. Juba thought little of it until the shadow reappeared and remained stationary. Glancing upward, she saw a broad-winged bird hovering above her. With a sigh, she shook her head.

"Come to pick my bones," she mumbled. Turning her attention back to the lines in the dirt, she tapped each with the stick. "Waiting for me to become nothing."

When the shadow moved away, Juba didn't bother to look up to see where the bird had gone. She didn't care. It didn't matter. Nothing mattered. Off in the distance, she heard the yelp of a hyena. The pained call of the animal sent a shiver down her spine. Overcome with sadness, she placed her hands over her ears and closed her eyes. She didn't want to be reminded. She didn't want to hear. She didn't want to relive what she had witnessed. In the nothingness of the moment was where she wanted to be, where she wanted to remain.

"What is it you draw?"

Startled, Juba opened her eyes. A hunched figure in a hooded grey robe—a woman, judging from the strands of long, white hair sticking out of the hood—was crouched several paces across from her. Like Juba, the woman was scratching the soil with a stick.

"When did *you* get here?" Juba asked.

The woman briefly pointed her stick toward the sky.

"Just resting," she replied. "A few moments to reflect before the sun slips away."

Juba glanced over her shoulder and located the sun; she calculated less than an hour of daylight remaining.

"Well?"

Something about the woman's voice struck Juba as familiar. She was certainly old. Might she know the woman? Had the old lady visited her village when Juba was younger?

"Well?" the woman repeated.

"Well?" Juba asked, confused.

"Your drawing? What is it?"

Juba glanced down at the lines in the dirt. She could feel the aura of nothingness oozing from the gouged soil. When her vision blurred, she blinked and quickly wiped her eyes.

"Nothing," she said. With a shrug, she repeated, "Nothing."

"Ah. Nothing!" the woman replied. "Difficult, yes, to draw nothing."

Juba stared and waited for her to say more. But it was clear the old woman was focused on what she was scratching in the soil.

"What are *you* doing?" Juba softly inquired. When the woman didn't respond, Juba spoke a little louder. "What are you drawing with your stick?"

The woman lifted the stick up to eye level as if inspecting it.

"In the dirt," Juba explained. "What are you making?"

"Oh," the woman replied as if she had just realized what Juba meant. "That." The sleeve of the woman's robe covered her hand as she placed the stick back into the dirt and continued to draw. "Everything," she said. "A story."

"A story?" Juba craned her neck in an attempt to see the woman's etchings. "How do you draw a story?"

"By connecting nothing to everything."

Juba wrinkled her forehead and squinted. She tapped her stick against the soil several times and sighed.

"That makes no sense. How can nothing be everything?"

Juba sensed the woman was disappointed with her question by the way she shook her head.

"Like the wind," she told her, pointing the stick skyward. "Don't you see?"

Juba gazed up at the sky and frowned. Somewhat annoyed, she asked, "See what?"

The woman resumed drawing. Juba huffed and folded her arms across her chest.

The woman said, "Look again. Tell me if you see it."

Juba pursed her lips and rolled her eyes but did as the old woman instructed.

"I see the sky," she replied. Placing her hands on the ground behind her, Juba arched her back and tilted her head back as far as she could. "Nothing else," she told the woman. "Just the sky."

"Close your eyes."

Juba sighed.

"No need to huff. Not if you want to see."

Juba reluctantly closed her eyes.

"Now tell me."

With a sharp exhale, Juba sat up straight, eyes still closed, and folded her arms across her chest.

"Tell you? Tell you what?"

Annoyed when the woman didn't reply, Juba wobbled her head from side to side and flapped her elbows up and down. She waited for the old woman to reprimand her, but the woman said nothing.

A wisp of air nuzzled the back of Juba's neck before swirling around her ear to her cheek. Soft and silent, the current glided upward to caress her brow before sliding off her forehead to linger on her chin. Enamored with the breeze's soothing touch, Juba sought to hold the current in her hand. Unfolding her arms, she reached up to grasp it, but her fingers curled around nothing. Disappointed, Juba opened her eyes and stared at her empty palm. As she gazed at her hand, a shadow crossed over her fingers. Looking up, she saw the broad-winged bird had returned—floating on a current of wind.

"Is that what you mean?" Juba asked as she stared at the bird. "The wind? Something that is nothing that touches everything?"

She noticed the first star of the evening had appeared. In the same moment, the breeze gusted before settling to a constant, calming push. Juba closed her eyes and took a deep breath.

"Did I guess right?" she asked.

Distant, distant, distant, Juba caught the faint but unmistakable call of an elephant. The sound drifted in and out of her hearing as the wind ebbed and flowed to the rhythm of her breathing. Around her, grasses swayed, leaves rustled, and branches creaked. With a nod, Juba sighed and opened her eyes. The evening star was a bit brighter, as were the colors of the impending sunset.

"Nothing becomes everything," she whispered in awe.

And she cupped her fingers around the vision of the setting sun and pretended to squeeze it into her palm.

The sudden boom of a gunshot echoing across the plain prompted a chorus of startled cries from bush birds. As a bevy of wings rose out of the steppe, Juba heard an elephant wail. Troubled by the gunfire, Juba sought comfort in the earth, focusing on the nothing contained within the lines she'd drawn. Though she tried to keep her thoughts blank, she couldn't keep the images of tusks, the dead ranger, Blue-head, and bullet-ridden hyenas out of her mind.

"I didn't want them to die!" she blurted. "Why did they have to? Why?"

With tears blurring her vision, she looked to the old woman. But the old woman was no longer squatting across from her. The stick she had been using was there, however, standing upright, one end stuck firmly in the ground. Wiping her eyes, Juba stood and stepped over the lines in the soil to see what the woman had drawn.

Outlines of an elephant, a giraffe, a wildebeest, an antelope, and a lion stood side by side on an earthen canvas. Above the animals, the woman had drawn a broad-winged bird. Near these figures was the depiction of a river that ended at a waterfall near the base of a mountain. Along the far bank of the river stood an expanse of trees that ran from the edge of the river to the mountain's far slope. What appeared to be a series of sand dunes came next, but as Juba studied the curved lines running spiral, she noticed they originated from a closed point, then incrementally expanded. Tilting her head from side to side, she adjusted her stance to alter her viewpoint. Studying the curling lines from a new vantage, she realized she was looking at the depiction of a horn. The same type of horn she had taken from Eden. The same type of horn she had thrown to the dirt in despair. The revelation was sobering, for the woman had drawn the horn as a boundary, placing it between the idyllic scene of nature she'd created and a blackened stretch of barren earth.

Bewildered by how the old woman had managed to depict a burnt wasteland, Juba pressed a finger into what looked to be scorched earth. Finding the ground painfully cold to the touch, she quickly pulled her finger away. It was at that moment she heard the drone of a plane. Reflexively, she looked toward where the ranger had been killed. At the distant call of a hyena, Juba closed her eyes and wished everything would go away.

A sudden gust of wind swirled at Juba's feet, prodding her to open her eyes. Glancing down to the ground, she was alarmed to see a dust cloud spinning near the old woman's earthen canvas. Grain by grain, the animals, the landscape, and the horn disappeared under a layer of dark soil. Dismayed, Juba looked to the sky. Daylight was nearly gone, the brilliant colors along the western horizon fading to subtle hues of yellow, white, and blue. With a parting nod to the woman's vanished creation, Juba headed back to where she had left the horn. Where everything, she believed, had turned to nothing.

20

"WHEN WILL YOU go?"

"When the moon is shaded by the sun."

John Too contemplated how the sun—a burning, blinding orb of fire— could possibly shade the moon, an object that shone at night. While he tried to make sense of such a notion, he followed the flitting dance of several moths around the fire he was tending. Perhaps the boy had misspoken. Or he himself had misunderstood what was said.

"I don't understand."

John Too wished the boy would move closer to the fire, but he remained standing at the edge of the roof, his back turned, staring up at the sky. Waiting, as he had for the past few months, for a sign from the Father.

"An affliction of age."

John Too sighed. The boy talked in riddles of late. The boy. John Too slowly exhaled. The boy was no longer a boy. He was a man now. The change was troubling. If the boy, growing older, had changed his appearance and viewpoint, might aging have affected John Too as well? He could no longer see the past or the future. He could no longer see clearly what had always been so clear. Troubling.

"Age?"

John Too placed a branch on the fire and stoked the embers with the metal rod that hung from a spike along the side of the stone hearth. From the rooftop of the house where the boy had been offered lodging for the night, they could see both the harbor and the desert. He watched as the trail of smoke rising from the fire split into two columns; one plume drifted toward water, one plume toward sand.

"Age: the perception of the journey from child to man." John Too could barely make out the boy shaking his head as he spoke. "Rain is no longer rain, stars no longer stars," he said with a gesture to the sky. "Awareness is a gift I sometimes wish to have never unwrapped."

John Too silently mouthed the words rain no longer rain *while he watched the trails of smoke slip into their respective areas of darkness.*

"When is rain not rain?" he asked.

The boy did not answer right away. John Too wished the boy had a name. Although he had asked the boy several times what name he could use for him, the boy had always shaken his head and told him he wished to remain without one. His old one, he explained, the one people remembered him by, was of another time and served no purpose in the Father's plan. Eventually, he said, the Father would tell him what he was to be called. But that time had not yet arrived.

"Rain," the boy began, "puddles to splash, drops to catch, a song amongst leaves. Rain—how we remember it, how it is intended to be."

The boy gathered the ends of his robe and sat down on the low wall that ran along the perimeter of the roof. John Too saw him look down. The small change in posture made him think of Teimbaka, who was sleeping in the alley below them.

"But now it has become a possession: gathered, bottled, and stored. Used as a means of commerce and bribery. Worse, it is a weapon of war." The boy stared at the sky directly above him. "Innocence lost. Why must it be so?"

John Too stirred the base of the fire and watched the embers cling to the tip of the metal pole.

"And the stars?"

The boy stood and walked to east side of the roof. Gazing toward the harbor, he said, "A ship's beacon, a child's wish, the soul of the sky—objects now argued over and claimed, used as a base for war or seen as a destination to lay waste for riches and then discard when it is dead." The boy turned. John Too could sense his eyes upon him. "What was never intended has now come to pass: man goes where he was not invited. Father waits to judge while the

Mother wrings her hands and wonders why she has been betrayed, her faith balanced in a child's hand."

Voices from the alley drew John Too's immediate attention. Wielding the metal pole like a weapon, he quickly moved to the south side of the roof and looked over the edge. The dark shape he knew to be Teimbaka was moving fitfully against the far wall.

"He hears the Serpent's voice," the boy said.

"We must go to him."

"He will find no comfort in our presence."

"How can that be? Surely he would be eased by knowing we were there."

The boy shook his head.

"He would hear only you," he said. "And the Serpent has stolen your voice."

*

He wondered where Grandma and Grandpa were. He hadn't seen them in a long time. He wondered if they'd forgotten him—or worse, didn't want to see him anymore. Maybe he'd done something wrong. *Had* he done something wrong? He tried to remember what he'd been doing the last time he saw them, the last time he was at their apartment. But he couldn't remember things like he used to. Ever since the man with the big head had hit him, things were kind of fuzzy. Like everything was there, but kind of not at the same time. But Grandma and Grandpa. Where were they?

Maybe they'd moved or something. Maybe *that's* why he hadn't seen Gran-Jim or Gran-Chelle for so long. At first the thought kind of made him feel better, but then the same thought made him feel a whole lot worse. If they'd moved, they'd left without him. Which meant they didn't want him with them. Which meant they didn't like him. And that made him feel yucky.

He *must* have done something—but what? He couldn't remember. Everything was kind of fuzzy. Worse, he didn't know where he was. And he didn't know any of the grownups he was with, except his babysitter, Lady T. Maybe she would tell him—if he could ever get her attention. But she'd been acting kind of weird ever since they'd run out of the room with no furniture and found the man with the big head. Now she was sad, staring down at her feet or off into nothing. What was she sad about? Maybe he could ask her that, too—if he could get her to look over at him.

Marcus tapped on the floor. Nothing—she didn't flinch. He did it again, but this time with a little more urgency.

"What the hell you doin', boy?"

Marcus looked over at the big fat guy sitting in a chair across the room. The fat guy patted the gun stuffed in the waist of his pants.

"You make any more noise and I bust you up the side of your head." The man's little round eyes widened as he nodded. "You dig what I'm saying?" He tapped the gun again. "Now shut the hell up."

Marcus stared at the man but didn't respond. He shifted his attention back over to Lady T. He tried to smile when he saw she was looking at him, but he couldn't seem to make his lips move. It didn't much matter, though, because Lady T turned her head and went back to staring at nothing. He frowned. What was wrong with her?

*

Shit. You in the shit now, girl. Tanya focused on the door to the right of Big Larry while her mind raced with unsettling thoughts. She kept her expression blank—at least she hoped it appeared so. If she showed the least bit of fear, it'd make things worse for her and Marcus. The boys—Skinny, Fat Larry, and the rest of the low-life scums—would see it as a weakness to be exploited, something to be used against her to make her do things she didn't want to do. And she knew what they wanted to do. Skinny for sure wanted to bang her. Fat Larry too if he could still find his dick under the mounds of fat hanging over his crotch. She nearly laughed at the image of him trying to get his penis out from under his rolls of fat, but she didn't—because it wasn't funny. Fat Larry had a reputation for treating women bad. She was certain he'd find a way to make sure his dick was satisfied before he— She didn't want to think about it. So, she thought about something else. *I wish little Marcus was older. Wish he knew how to shoot a gun.* She glanced over at Fat Larry and immediately wished she hadn't.

"You lookin' for a place to stretch out?" Fat Larry laughed. "Good spot over there." Tanya pretended she wasn't looking at him, but she saw him nod to a stack of crates. "Use that nigger you were with as a mattress." He laughed again. "Little lumpy, but better than that fine ass of yours banging against the floorboards." She cringed when he licked his lips and his beady little eyes nearly disappeared beneath his fleshy cheeks.

What did he just say? The nigger I was with? She took a closer look at the crates. *What the hell is he talkin' about?* Then she saw the pair of boots positioned heels flat on the floor with somebody's ankles still inside them. She hadn't noticed them before. She hadn't noticed much of anything since Skinny stuck a gun in her face when she and Marcus ran down the steps from the unfurnished apartment. She'd been too scared and too preoccupied with her situation to notice where Fat Larry had driven her and Marcus. Where the hell was she? *Think, girl! Open your eyes and ears!*

Tanya took a quick survey of the room. From the cases of beer stacked near the back and the large tins stored on metal shelves behind Fat Larry, she figured she and Marcus had been brought to a restaurant or a bar. The place reminded her of the storage room at Jim's Soul Food Restaurant, but bigger. Like maybe five times the size, with a lot more stuff packed in.

Thinking about Jim had a sobering effect. She suddenly wished she was far away, someplace quiet and remote where there weren't any gangs or guys like Gerard to fuck up her life. For some odd reason, Mr. Brown came to her thoughts. But what the hell could an old man do for her in the circumstance she was in now?

Old men—men in general—not enough good ones. And way too many bad ones. And a whole lot of substandard ones in between. Lucky if you could find one who wasn't using. Incredibly lucky if you could find one who hadn't been tainted by some bitch who was lookin' for a ride to glam city and all the drugs, money, cars, houses, and power that came with the package. You'd have to find one Marcus's age before that happened, and even then—she shot a glance at the boy—it might be too late.

*Men—assholes—*her attention drifted to the pair of boots sticking out from the crates. *Just like you,* she thought. *Why you botherin' with us, anyway? Bullshit story about promisin' somebody to keep an eye out for the boy—fuckin' bullshit. Well, you in a shit-storm now. Done shoot Skinny in the hand. Probably be dead before long.* She kept her eye on the boots for a second longer to see if they moved. *Maybe you already dead.* She quietly sniffed the air; she didn't smell any awful aroma. *You lucky.* She looked from the boots to Fat Larry to Marcus and then to the floor between her feet. *Ain't nobody lucky. Least not anybody in this room.*

*

The little shiny, half-invisible animal with the long nose and flappy ears appeared to Marcus at the same time he heard a bunch of voices yelling from behind a door. Holy cow, they sure sounded mad. But then the little animal started to move. And that was something, because it looked to Marcus like it was floating on air. Cool! Really cool.

The animal stopped moving when the big fat man got out of his chair and went to the door. The man looked scared as he pulled the door open a crack and peeked out. But then Marcus glimpsed the animal moving again. Past a stack of green and white boxes. Past a group of silver barrels stacked one atop another. Past a wall of red, white, and blue boxes with blue letters printed on the side. When the animal got to a stack of brown crates, it looked over at Marcus before making a turn.

Boots—Marcus saw boots—and then he remembered seeing the fat man throw the empty-room man behind the crates. He rubbed his head because it hurt remembering.

How did the animal know the man was there? And why did it care about the man? And why was it using its long nose like a finger and pointing to the man and then motioning for Marcus to come over? Everything seemed fuzzy again because his head hurt.

Marcus felt a jolt shoot through his body when he heard a loud slap from behind the door. He saw Lady T react the same—jerky—like when he stuck a finger into the square thing on the wall where Gran-Chelle put the end of the toaster cord. He remembered he'd cried cause his finger hurt bad after. Gran-Chelle had hugged him and talked to him in a real soft voice. But then she got mad and yelled at him to never do it again. Gran-Chelle—where was she? The see-through animal motioned for Marcus to join it again. Marcus checked to see what the fat man was doing before he started to crawl on his hands and knees toward the shiny animal behind the stack of crates.

*

Tanya motioned with a sharp wave of her hand for Marcus to stay where he was. She knew Fat Larry would go off on the boy if he saw what Marcus was doing. What *was* he doing? Looked like he was crawling over to the man she knew as Chris—a customer of Jim's who always left a big tip. But why? What did he think he was going to do once he reached Chris? Did he think he could help the man?

Out of the corner of her eye, she glimpsed Fat Larry pull the gun out of the waist of his pants as he cracked the door a little wider. The voices coming from the next room became clear. She listened intently for a moment. *Somebody spoutin' some shit*, she thought, but she didn't recognize the voice of the man who was talking.

"Unify and fly," she heard the man say, "or stay separate and be raped. Raped by your own compatriots. That's right. That's what I said. Fucked by your competition, undone by your own egos. So, I'm gonna explain how it's all goin' down from here on in."

Her attention shifted back to Fat Larry as he closed the door. She averted her eyes when he looked her way. She got a bad feeling in her stomach when she sensed him moving toward her.

"Sound like somebody takin' over," she abruptly said. She nodded to the door. "Ain't you gonna listen to what's goin' down?"

Fat Larry frowned as he stuffed the gun under his waistband at his back.

"Don't need to listen." He winked. "No need to pay them no mind, neither. We got time before—" He grabbed the zipper of his pants.

"Before what?" she asked, pretending she'd not seen the gesture. She pointedly peered over his shoulder toward the door behind him. "Somethin' big goin' down?"

Fat Larry rubbed his crotch.

"Yeah, somethin' big goin' down." He chuckled.

Tanya looked away.

"Hey—where the kid? Where that little fuck go?"

Tanya immediately stood up.

"We was playin' hide and seek," she rushed to stay. She raised her hands in front of her placatingly. "So he hidin'."

Fat Larry reached around his back for his gun.

"Ain't no need for a gun," she told him. "He ain't botherin' no one."

Tanya took a few steps closer to Fat Larry. "He like to hide, is all." She put a hand on his arm when he started to move past her. "Just let him be." She looked into his beady little eyes and smiled. "He can sit quiet-like for a half hour or more before he gets fidgety and asks what goin' on."

Tanya tried to guess what Fat Larry was thinking, but it was hard to tell. To her, he looked both angry and confused. She knew her impromptu story about Marcus playing hide and seek sounded weak, but at least it'd kept him from pulling his gun. What the hell did little Marcus think he was doin'? *Little fuck gonna get himself killed.*

"Half hour, huh?" Fat Larry said. "Sounds about right."

"What?" Tanya asked, confused. She stopped thinking about Marcus and focused on Fat Larry's face. "What you on about?"

Fat Larry grunted.

"Gerard always braggin' bout how you give good head. Time to show me." She wanted to puke when he ran his tongue across the top row of his teeth. "Go on and sit back down," he told her. "Unless you more comfortable on your knees."

Tanya looked at him like she hadn't heard him right. But when she saw him pull at his zipper, she decided to set him straight.

"You dreamin'. You gots to be crazy if you think I'm gonna touch that little piece of salami between your legs." She shook her head and folded her arms in front of her chest. "You go on and jerk yourself off while I—"

Fat Larry pulled the gun from the back of his pants and fired off a shot so quickly it took Tanya's breath away. Stunned, she turned to see the air muddled with dust from the crate that Fat Larry had shot. A chunk of wood lay on the floor nearby.

"Marcus!" she yelled. Fat Larry elbowed Tanya just below her neck as she tried to run past him. She staggered back, clutching her chest.

The door flew open. Skinny stepped into the doorway with a gun in his hand. He looked at the wheezing Tanya and then turned his attention to Fat Larry.

"You good?" he asked.

"Yeah, we good," Fat Larry replied. With a little wave of his gun, he glanced at Tanya. "Just makin' things clear."

Skinny nodded before he took a step back into the other room and closed the door behind him.

"Like I said," she heard Fat Larry say. Fat Larry waved the gun in her face. "Time to prove Gerard right." She was just about to spit in his face when he added, "Or I can find the boy and stick this .44 down *his* throat."

*

The sound of the gunshot and the impact of the bullet into wood nearly made Marcus pee his pants. If it weren't for the glittering animal wrapping its long nose around his shoulder, Marcus would have scrambled out from behind the crates and raised his hands in surrender. But his fear subsided when the animal touched him. With the animal's help, Marcus edged a little closer to the man who'd taken him to the empty room.

The first thing he noticed about the man was the big lump on the side of his face. The discolored bulge that ran from his ear to his eye made him look like a monster, as did the jagged line of dried blood that ran along the top of the lump. After a more thorough examination of the man's swollen eye, Marcus shivered and shook his head; he didn't know how the man would ever see out of that eye again. Then he heard Lady T shout his name. When he went to stand up to show her where he was, he felt a tug on his arm. The animal had its nose wrapped around his wrist.

"But she—" The animal hushed him by placing the tip of its nose against his lips.

Marcus questioned the animal with his eyes. The animal shook its head before looking down at the man and resting its long nose on the man's hands. They were bound with plastic strips. The animal tapped on the plastic strip and then looked at Marcus. Marcus nodded.

Marcus didn't have any trouble finding the spot where the plastic strips were joined. Problem was, no matter how Marcus pulled or pushed, he couldn't get the plastic strands to budge. After several attempts to loosen the man's bindings, he sat back on his haunches and sighed. He looked up at the ceiling and said, "I can't do it."

Marcus stared at all the pipes that ran in every direction across the ceiling and wondered what they were all for. He never knew pipes came in so many sizes. Some were no bigger than a fifty-cent piece, while some were so big he was certain he could crawl through them. Curious, he followed the path of one of the bigger pipes across the ceiling, but he lost track when he heard Lady T giggle. A second later, he heard the unmistakable sound of a hand slapping flesh.

"You think it's funny?" he heard the fat man shout.

Marcus clenched his fists when he heard a second smack.

"Wait!" he heard Lady T say.

"Take it!" the fat man barked.

Marcus waited to hear what Lady T would say, but she didn't say anything. Then the fat man spoke.

"There you go. Remember, this is for the boy. So make it good."

Marcus heard what sounded like a little girl's whimper. It reminded him of sounds he used to hear in the dark when he was told to go sleep. Memories of being so hungry his stomach ached were never very far away, nor were the imaginings of shapeless monsters who'd wait for him to close his eyes so they could sneak up on him and suck the blood from his body. He wanted to cry out when he felt scared—wanted to call out for his mama—but no one had ever told him she was his mama. So he'd shiver under a blanket and sniffle until either he fell asleep or the morning sun shooed the shadows from the room and chased the monsters away.

But the whimpering he was hearing at the moment was different. It was sad. Really sad. And that made him angry. Fists clenched, Marcus started to stand. But then the man with the balloon face groaned.

"He's waking up," Marcus whispered. "What should I do?"

Confused when he realized the animal was no longer standing next to him, Marcus looked around. A quick search of the nearby boxes, crates, barrels, and shelves didn't reveal its whereabouts, but a twinkle of light at the back of the room snared Marcus's attention. He saw it first at the gap between the floor and the door at the back of the room. From there it moved into the shadows behind a stack of brown boxes. A moment later, Marcus watched it zip across an open space before it came to rest atop a large silver can. Spinning like one of those plastic windmills he'd seen in people's yards, the light hovered above the can for a moment, then burst outward into countless particles of glitter. Mouth agape, Marcus watched the glitter shift and sway as if caught in a twisting wind. Then, like a snake curling around a pole, the configuration shot upward several feet before cresting into the shape of a tattered mushroom. Just before it began to descend, the particles gathered into a cloud. Like a sheet of rain falling through a moonbeam, the slivers of light fell back toward the floor. Just before impact, they came to a halting stop. Dangling on a protrusion jutting from a cardboard box, the particles of light condensed into a sphere, then shrank to the size of a raindrop. With colors of ivory and gold twinkling from its surface, the dollop of light was spellbinding. Putting thoughts of the ballon-faced man, the shiny animal, Lady T, and the fat man aside, Marcus quietly slid across the floor, intent upon touching the sparkling orb.

The nearer he drew to the sphere of light, the more it reminded him of a clear marble rolling in sunlight. He'd played with one once. He couldn't remember where or when, but he recalled that the clear marble had a white wavy center. The sparkles the marble produced when it rolled through the sun reminded him of fireworks. And fireworks were neat; he liked them.

And now here was something that looked just like the marble he'd played with. Mesmerized by the moondrop, Marcus reached for object and positioned his fingers around the sphere. But a deafening boom from the outer room made him gasp and jerk his hand away.

*

Chris couldn't find any correlation between the pain throbbing in his head and the cases of Budweiser stacked next to him. He stared at the red, white, and blue boxes with the familiar name scripted on the side, wondering what their presence meant. He blinked a few times in an effort to clear the watery film blurring his sight, but he stopped when the effort produced a sharp needle-jab of pain deep in the nerves behind his left eye. With a grunt, he turned his head away from the Budweiser boxes and sighed.

Calm. He took a deep breath and willed himself to calm. Calm would bring clarity, he hoped. Calm would buffer the pain pulsing through his head. Slowly, he took a look around. His last memory was of crouching behind a car and using it as a shield. Somebody in a speeding car was shooting at him. Then there was… He couldn't remember.

Boxes. So many boxes. He tried to make sense of all the stacks of boxes around him. How did he get here? And where was *here*?

Jumbled. His thoughts were jumbled. Then he caught a glimpse of something that made him question his state of mind.

The shimmering image of a small, semi-transparent elephant had to be a hallucination. What else could it be? Certainly, it wasn't real. But why hallucinate a near-invisible elephant, of all things? Then he saw the retarded boy kneeling next to the illusion. *No wonder*, he thought. *Fucking kid drew so many pictures of elephants, of course I would imagine one had come to life*. He stared at the kid a little harder. What was he doing? What was he was reaching for?

A loud gunshot would have jolted him to his feet—but he couldn't even move his arms. Lifting his hands, he saw his wrists were bound with a heavy plastic tie. The image of Marcus reaching for something exploded into his thoughts.

"Kid," he hissed.

"Get down on the ground!" he heard a man yell.

Chris saw Marcus jerk his head in the direction of the man who'd yelled. He tried to get the child's attention by moving his arms up and down.

"Move and I'll put a bullet in your head!" the man shouted.

Chris noticed the boy's eyes flitting from side to side as if he was trying to look at two things at the same time. Chris waved his arms again: nothing. The boy was focused on whatever he was looking at. Then Chris heard a chorus of muffled voices—angry male voices—coming from somewhere nearby. The disruption broke the boy's focus. Chris animatedly moved his arms up and down one more time. Marcus saw him. When the boy made eye contact, Chris nodded to the object Marcus had been reaching for.

"Bring me the cutter," Chris silently mouthed.

Chris could tell the boy didn't understand what he'd said by the confused look on his face. A second gunshot produced a moment of utter silence. Chris shook his head and pointed as best he could to the box-cutting tool stuck in the edge of a brown cardboard box. He felt a tinge of panic when the man who'd yelled before called out.

"Where the hell you at, kid! Get your ass out where I can see you or I'll put a bullet in the girl's head!"

Chris saw Marcus place his hands on the ground as if he was about to push his body up off the floor.

"No!" he urgently whispered. He pointed as definitively as he could to the box cutter when Marcus looked toward him.

"I ain't playin'!" the man barked. "Get your ass out here!"

"The cutter," Chris whispered as loud as he dared. He nodded to the oblong metal tool right above Marcus's head.

"Now!"

"Throw it to me," Chris hissed.

"I hear you, you little fuck!"

Chris saw Marcus's eyes go wide. Then he heard the familiar sound of a bullet sliding into a Glock's chamber.

"The cutter!" Chris silently mouthed.

"There you are, you little fuck! Get over here!"

Chris closed his eyes when he saw Marcus raise his hands in surrender. He stifled a groan when something smashed against the bottom of his right foot.

"Still out cold," the man who'd been yelling grumbled. "Move, kid!"

"Don't hurt him!"

Tanya. Chris recognized her voice.

"Now!"

Chris heard the scuffle of feet and then silence. He could feel his adrenaline wane as the hope of getting the box cutter faded. Then he felt something settle on his stomach.

*

Tanya cleared her throat and spit. She thought about sticking her finger down her throat so she would vomit, but she saw how little Marcus was looking at her. So, she cleared her throat and spit again. She shot Fat Larry an angry look when he started to laugh.

"The taste that lasts a lifetime," he taunted. She wanted to die when he winked at her. "Better get used to it." He laughed again.

She hugged Marcus as the boy wrapped his arms around her leg.

"Don't be afraid, little man," she told him. "Lady T here for you."

"Lady T," Fat Larry mocked. "You mean Lady C, don't ya?"

"Fuck you!" she yelled.

She tried to keep Marcus close to her when Fat Larry took a stride toward her, but the boy broke free of her grasp and headed straight for the fat man. Fat Larry swung his gun hand and caught Marcus flat on the side of his chin. The boy flew backward and screamed as he landed with a thud on the concrete floor. Overcome with rage, Tanya pounced on Fat Larry. But he stopped her cold with a vicious punch to her face. Stunned by the blow, she staggered back, blood spurting from her nose.

"Stupid bitch," he said. "You with a man now."

Tanya covered her nose with her hand. She angrily wiped tears from her eyes as Fat Larry moved to a stack of boxes, reached down into an open box, and lifted out a bottle of Crown Royal. She looked away when he unscrewed the top and smiled at her. Disgusted with herself, she bent down to tend to Marcus. Her voice breaking, she said, "Come on, little man. You okay. You fine now."

Tanya nearly jumped out of her skin at the sound of breaking glass. She looked over her shoulder just as Fat Larry fell to the floor with blood gushing from his throat.

*

Overwhelmed by the pain throbbing through his head, it took everything Chris had to steady his legs and maintain his grip on the bloody box cutter. He nearly fell to his knees at a deafening burst of automatic gunfire from the doorway behind him, followed by a jarring explosion that shook the floor. A shout of "He's a cop" barely registered. He heard the door slamming open against the wall directly behind him and an angry shout of "Fuck."

"Get down!" Tanya screamed.

A bullet whizzed by Chris's ear. He saw Tanya pointing a smoking gun. He turned to find Skinny slumped against the doorframe, a weapon by his feet, blood oozing from his chest. Beyond Skinny, from what he could see through the open door, the outer room looked like a war zone. A couple of bodies were lying on the floor beneath a haze of smoke. The smell of gunpowder hung heavy in the air. He saw two men running, then one fell like he'd been shot. Bullets tore into the doorframe just above Skinny's head. Chris reached for Skinny's weapon at the same time he saw a guy running toward him with a gun.

"Hold it right there!" the guy yelled.

Chris grabbed Skinny's gun and fired off a round. The bullet struck the man in his shoulder. Chris caught a glimpse of something shiny dangling from a chain around the man's neck.

"Police!" the man shouted.

The cop flashed the shiny object dangling from the chain: his badge.

"Throw your weapon down!"

Chris pointed his gun directly at the cop's head and waited a second before he fired. The cop dived to his right, and Chris stepped to the door and slammed it shut.

"Let's go!" he shouted.

As he ran toward the back of the room, he grabbed Tanya by the arm and pulled her along. Barely breaking stride, he bent low and jerked Marcus to his feet.

"Keep up!" he yelled to the boy.

When they reached the back door, Chris shoved Tanya and Marcus behind him. He put his ear to the door for a moment before unlocking the two deadbolts above and below the doorknob. Grabbing the knob, he glanced back at Tanya.

"Be ready to move," he told her.

The door next to Skinny started to open. He swung the gun back across his shoulder and fired off a round, splintering wood. He yanked the back door open and, with one hand on Tanya's wrist and the other holding the gun ready near his chin, he stepped outside.

"Freeze!"

"Don't shoot! Don't shoot!" Chris yelled.

"Drop your weapon! Now!"

"Undercover! Undercover! Coming out with hostages!"

Chris pulled Tanya out into the alley.

"Both of you on the ground!"

"I got a kid! Don't shoot!"

Chris made eye contact with the cop shouting for him to get down as Tanya edged Marcus out in front of her. The uniformed policeman was crouched behind a patrol car, his weapon pointed at Chris. Chris read the hesitation in the man's face as the cop eyed the boy.

"Call it in," Chris urged. "Officer down, multiple casualties. Gonna need multiple med units."

"Put your weapon down!" the cop demanded.

"Stay cool. Stay cool." Chris slowly lowered his gun hand toward the ground. "Here ya go, here ya go. But shit, man! Call it in!"

As soon as Chris saw the cop edge up from his crouched position, he swung his gun hand up and fired off three quick rounds. The cop's shoulder jerked back as one round tore into his upper arm, then he tumbled backward when a second round blew a hole in his chest just below his collarbone.

"Let's go!" Chris shouted.

Pulling on Tanya, he yanked the cruiser's driver's-side door open and pushed Tanya and Marcus into the front bench seat.

"Get over!" he yelled.

Chris slid behind the wheel. He put his foot on the gas pedal as he slammed the door. The cruiser jerked forward. He gave the car more gas when he saw flashing lights ahead at the end of the alley.

"We're gonna die!" Tanya screamed.

"Shut up!" he snapped.

Chris turned the rooftop flashers on, then flicked on the siren and slammed his foot on the gas. The cruiser sped down the alley, heading straight for the center of the cop car parked in the middle of the road.

"They're gonna kill us!" Tanya screamed.

Chris saw two cops crouched behind the hood of the car with their guns pointed straight at him. As he turned the steering wheel to the right with his left hand, he thrust his right arm over Marcus and Tanya and pushed them toward the floor. He ducked down just as a bullet blew the glass out of the window next to his head. The cruiser slammed into the tail of the car blocking their exit and spun it outward. Chris turned hard right and floored it. The police cruiser jolted forward. Lights flashing, siren wailing, the car sped down the street. As he flew through the next intersection, he glimpsed the framework of a familiar structure off in the distance. Realizing he was somewhere near the seaport, he took the next left. He switched off the lights and the siren and sped toward the water. It would be a snap to dump the cruiser at the Toyota pier and switch cars. Once he pulled back out onto Corbin Street, he knew he could mirror Interstate 95 South. North Elizabeth was a matter of minutes away—if he could get to it.

*

"If it weren't for you—"

Marcus reached over to pet the floppy-eared animal but pulled his hand back when the man with the balloon face and Lady T started yelling at each other. He shook his head and sighed. The creature stared at him with its pink-red eyes. He wondered if it understood what was going on.

"I'm hungry," he said. "Are you?"

The animal gave no indication that it had either heard or understood him. So Marcus sat back in the passenger seat of the big truck the balloon-faced man had put him in and sighed again.

What was he doing here? Why had Lady T and the balloon-faced man brought him to a truck museum? And when were they going to eat? He glanced over at his animal friend, thinking it might point him to some food, but the glimmering sheen that swept across the creature's outline as a ray of sun crept into the cab distracted him. Captivated by the animal's sparkling skin, he unconsciously rubbed his stomach.

Lady T and the balloon-faced man were standing a few feet away from the truck the man had placed him in. For a moment, he was tempted to roll down the window and tell Lady T that he was hungry, but she and the balloon-faced man were still arguing. Why were they mad at each other? Their constant arguing made his head hurt and his thinking fuzzy. He covered his ears. Couldn't they just shut up? Or maybe just talk softer. Was that so hard to do? Tired of listening to their angry voices, tired of being hungry, tired of guns going off and of sitting in speeding cars, Marcus rested his head against the door panel and closed his eyes. But it didn't help. He could still hear everything Lady T and the balloon-faced man were saying.

"Why you gotta take the boy? Why can't you leave him with me?"

"With you? Are you stupid?"

"What you mean? I ain't the one shot those cops."

"You shot Skinny. And for all the cops care, you were helping me when I shot two of theirs."

"I'll just tell 'em—"

"Damn, you're dumb. What color your skin? You think the boys in blue gonna listen to you? Shit, how much blow you put up your nose?"

"I ain't put no—"

"Stop fixin' on you. Boy needs to get out of here. Needs to start over."

"He'll do just fine if he stays with me."

"He'll be in a state-run orphanage ten minutes after the cops throw you in jail for accessory to murder."

"Murder! That's bullshit."

"You're black. That's the way it'll go down."

Marcus kept his eyes half closed as he peeked out the window. Lady T and the balloon-faced man were looking away from each other. Lady T looked sad. The man didn't look like he was feeling anything. Marcus turned his head and quickly wiped his eyes with the back of his hand. *Why is everybody mad? Why do big people have to yell? Why won't they play with me? When is dinner?* He searched the unblinking gaze of his friend. Where were Gran-Jim and Gran-Chelle? He rubbed his temples. Why did his head still hurt?

"It'll be dark soon," he heard the man say. "I'm heading out. Stay or go."

"Where? How you—"

"Out of the country."

"How you gonna pull that off?"

"I got my ways. You'll just have to trust me."

"Trust you? Shit. You must be trippin'."

"Whatever. Like I said, stay or go."

Marcus yawned and rubbed his eyes. The big people were suddenly quiet—finally. Still—he wondered what that meant. Was it time to eat? Time to go? And go where? He looked over at his near-invisible friend as he thought about everything and nothing at the same time. The little animal had taken on the appearance of glass with gold sparkles running through it. But like all the other thoughts running in and out of his head, his friend's appearance occupied his thinking for a split second before dissipating into a consciousness rooted in a make-believe world where everything meant nothing—and nothing offered a world of possibilities.

"You hungry, little man?"

Marcus met Lady T's gaze as she stepped up into the truck.

"Stay low when I pull out onto the road."

"Boy needs food," Tanya said as Chris slipped into the driver's seat.

Marcus glanced over at the man and suddenly wondered who he was.

"Have to wait till we get to Wilmington," Chris replied.

"Wilmington?"

Marcus looked up at Lady T and wondered what Wilmington was.

"Know a place. Be there under two hours."

Lady T seemed mad when she looked over at the balloon-faced man. But then she turned her head toward the window and sighed.

"Best be invisible till we get off 95."

Marcus saw the man shrug his shoulders and put his hands on the big steering wheel. When the truck started to move, Marcus looked out the front window and smiled. He wondered how hard it was for his animal friend to stand on the front of the truck while it moved.

21

I STAND IN the moment before dawn when night and day claim equal share of the sky. I see a star kissed by daylight and ponder all the dreams I have not yet imagined while clinging to memories I do not wish to forget. The wind stills in a moment of calm—an interlude filled with grace and hope, a forgiving caress that lingers on my brow. Melancholy—I cherish the moment and nurture it to a bittersweet end. The wind suddenly gusts; a troubled start. It blows dry off the desert then turns, carrying hints of salt and sea. Interlaced within the current I hear voices of kingdoms swallowed by time.

The boy is leaving, and I don't know what to say. I am frightened in this moment, frightened by the sound of my own voice. For if the Serpent can steal my words and speak as me, what can I say that won't be interpreted as cruel? What can I whisper that won't cause pain? I am lost—lost, tired, and scared.

"Your thoughts are troubled."

John Too stoked the embers of a fire long cold. Where there had once been flame and warmth was the chill of grey ash and a feeling of loss. He could not find the courage to look at the boy.

"Would you say nothing to me?"

John Too pulled his robe close about his neck and rubbed the edge of his thumb across his chin.

"I am—" He dipped his head and stared at his feet. "What dare I say when the Serpent has my voice?" he mumbled.

John Too bit down on his lower lip while nervously shifting his weight from one foot to the other.

"I did not mean—" John Too turned to the boy. "How could you allow it?" he blurted. But the boy was no longer standing beside him.

A forceful current of wind stirred the remnants of the fire. Dead embers reignited. Flames leapt skyward from lifeless ash. Startled, he backed away. Then, in a blinding flash of ivory light, the blaze inexplicably died. Mouth agape, John Too watched a curling wisp of smoke gather above the hearth before rising slowly toward the heavens. As though tugged aloft by unseen hands, the swirling column of grey haze dispersed in a myriad of directions, drifting north, south, east, west, and all points between. But the wind had ceased the moment the flames had died.

*

Moonlight gave the liquid contained within the syringe a milky sheen and turned the needle a sparkly silver-white. Trees stood like watchtowers outside a ring of foot-soldier bushes as starlight twinkled through openings in the leaves. Dirk huddled next to a boulder worn smooth by weather and time. His concentration wavering, he tried to keep his arm steady as he guided the needle toward a slender vein barely visible in the muted light. The sudden hoot of an owl nearly caused him to miss the mark as the needle broke the surface of his skin. He hesitated for the briefest of moments before depressing the plunger.

The feelings of pleasure and dread arrived together, slithering through his body as though on the back of a flaming snake. The sensation of a fiery entity moving inside him made him fitful. He shifted his body to one side and then the other. He stared up at the trees, wondering where he was. When the air around him started to whine, he didn't understand. Then he recognized the sound: sirens—perhaps several—blaring somewhere in the distance. He surveyed the line of bushes encircling the small clearing where he'd stopped to rest. Would they shield his hiding place? Would they prevent him from being caught? His attention wandered to the nearest tree. Would it alert him if someone approached?

Where moon nor star could not pierce the canopy of leaves, Dirk was wary of the dark. Imagining shadows moving within shadows, he sensed ill lurking where there was no light. The nomads of Ethiopia had told him tales of night-stalking spirits that feasted on human souls, hideous creatures with voices like shrieking cave-wraiths and eyes crafted of smoldering embers. Suddenly overcome with chills, Dirk curled his body into a ball and closed his eyes. With a wistful chuckle, he willed himself invisible and then entertained the notion that he could fly. As he dreamed about drifting amongst the stars, a voice came to him—a voice he did not relish hearing. Genevieve was calling his name—over and over and over.

It was an easy thought to entertain, the wish that he could die. He was a coward, after all. Genevieve knew it as well as he. It was why she tormented him, he'd come to believe, why she'd driven him to the brink of insanity. She knew as well as he that he'd been nothing since the moment he'd led her to her death. In his mind, he was worse than slime, lower than the most despicable sinner. He was a coward. Even in his imagined state of invisibility, he could not hide from the fact. Slipping into a state of utter self-repudiation, he began to cry. But his tears did not mute the sound of Genevieve's voice.

"Curse you!" he wailed.

Without warning, his body shook and his stomach burned. Undone by what he had dared to utter to the woman he loved, he wrapped his arms around his torso to keep his body from shaking apart. Distraught, he placed his hands around his throat and squeezed. Oh, why hadn't he done this before? Why hadn't he taken his own life? It would be so easy. And he deserved to die. He was a coward, after all. Genevieve knew.

But why was she crying? He listened to her sobbing and shook his head. Why did she care after what he had done? Why was she so upset with him trying to take his own life? She should be egging him on so she could watch him die and then taunt his soul as his body slowly rotted away. He didn't understand. Why was she grasping his hands and pulling them from his throat?

"Let me die," he blubbered, slapping the air in front of him.

Overwhelmed by the depth of his perceived flaws, Dirk felt his stomach churn and then the contents hurtle up his throat. He turned his head and violently retched upon the ground. Desperate to rid the bile taste from his mouth, he spit several times, but his mouth and throat were so dry he ended up hacking air. Coughing, choking, and wheezing, he slumped to the ground and let his head drop to the soil. Half out of his mind, he stared blankly into darkness.

Tiny torches raced across his sphere of vision. The bad men had arrived. The evil men—the men who tortured and murdered Genevieve—had come back for him. But what did they want from him? She was dead. She was dead. *She was dead.* He could envision nothing but her decapitated, dismembered body lying in a pool of blood. Her lifeless head appeared in the crook of his arm. He stared into her face, felt his spirit being sucked into her lifeless eyes. The world into which she pulled him was dark and icy cold. He began to shiver. When an owl hooted, Dirk took it to be a greeting from Genevieve's ghost. He licked his lips in preface to reply.

Bits of soil clung to his lips and the tip of his tongue. Finding the taste of dirt foul, he began to laugh. *I'm already underground,* he thought. *Genevieve has pulled me into a grave without me being aware. A fitting end. A deserved end. I'm a coward, after all.* What better way to escape this wretched life than to crawl into the earth and die? He closed his eyes and waited for death to arrive. He began to imagine what it would feel like to be dead. He hoped it would be a relief. He was tired. Tired of pain, tired of remembering, tired of trying to forget, tired of living life as a coward.

The sensation of fingertips brushing lovingly across his brow soothed his tortured thoughts. The feeling was sublime. Submitting to the moment of pleasure, he sighed with relief. Then the feeling abruptly stopped. He furrowed his brow when what felt like soft pin pricks traced a path down his forehead and tickled the tip of his nose. When the same pattering feeling crossed his upper lip, he blew a stream of breath upward out of his mouth. A subtle puff of air crossing his chin prompted him to jerk his head back and open his eyes.

The bad men, the cruel men, the ones who had murdered Genevieve had arrived; those were his first thoughts. But then he noticed the torches they carried: small and burning moon-dappled white, with a hint of green around the edges. Perplexed by the odd appearance of the tiny fires, he propped himself up off the ground and tried to focus. Certain he was hallucinating, he blinked several times.

At once frightened by the formidable-looking pincers jutting out of gaping jaws, Dirk scuttled back a few inches to put some space between him and the three bright-green bugs in front of him. Lit by moonlight, the insect's shells glittered deception. Torchlight was rendered to spark-like glitter; evil men were transformed into metallic-shelled beetles. Mystified by the presence of the bugs, Dirk sought enlightenment amongst the bushes and trees. To his disappointment, the foliage was silent. But then the owl hooted for a third time. He sought the bird's whereabouts.

Genevieve's ghostly image sat on the lowest limb of the nearest watcher-tree. She smiled when their eyes met, and Dirk immediately felt compelled to call out to her. But before he could utter her name, she looked away, directing her gaze toward the ground. Captivated by her beauty, awe-struck by her heavenly aura, he watched in adulation as she swept her arm out in front of her and closed her hand around a beam of moonlight. As though she were dropping pebbles into a pool, she plucked a moondrop out of her palm and tossed it to the ground. Dirk shook his head in wonder as the three glittering bugs immediately scurried toward the bit of gleaming light. As the bugs converged on the glittering spot and absorbed its energy into their bodies, he rose to his feet.

Above him, Genevieve giggled and tossed a second moondrop from her hand. The three beetles once again scurried over to the object and drank the light. Genevieve dispensed a third moondrop, but this one did not fall straight. Either carried by a breeze he could not feel or thrown sideways by Genevieve, the glowing drop of milky light landed somewhere ahead of where he stood and disappeared behind a line of sentry bushes. Instantly, the beetles crawled away toward the line of bushes. Above him, he glimpsed Genevieve move. Like an angel gliding on the breath of God, she drifted off the limb and floated toward one of the corridors of darkness.

"Genevieve!" he called, alarmed.

But she did not answer or give him any indication that she had heard his voice. Unnerved, he called her name once more.

"Genevieve!"

As Dirk stood and listened to the echo of his voice subside, he saw Genevieve toss another moondrop into the corridor of darkness. A feeling of dread surged through him when he saw her drift farther into the depths of shadowland. Panicked at the thought that she might be harmed by monsters lurking in the dark, he stumbled after her. The line of sentry-bushes parted to let him pass.

*

Mr. Locket was in such a tizzy he could barely concentrate on the road.

Miss Claire dead? Preposterous. What a horrible mix-up. She couldn't—She can't be dead. Not before she knows. Damn you, Locket! Why did you never speak up? What has the old bitch done to her? Oh, dear God! Let me have the chance to tell her I'm her father!

The car's steering wheel felt like some cruel pillory: his hands were stretched apart, frozen to circular beams; his head locked in a stationary position; his eyes confined between the invisible walls of what appeared to be a never-ending tunnel. He felt trapped, frozen in an eternal moment of nightmarish thoughts. Arriving at the clinic before he reached an unforgiving state of despair seemed impossible. Was Miss Claire dead or alive? In an attempt to keep his wits about him, he examined each tidbit of conversation, dissected each crumb of information, so he might discern a thread of logic or truth.

Was it just yesterday? Had that much time elapsed since Mrs. Cavanaugh's unnerving, conflicting announcements? Or was it earlier today, late in the afternoon? Mr. Locket retraced his actions to slot the events as they'd unfolded.

"Are you certain you're feeling well, madam?" Mr. Locket had asked as he poured Mrs. Waterman's tea. "You seem out of sorts." The woman turned her head away from him when he sought to make eye contact. "Something to do with Miss Claire?"

"Why would you say that?" she snapped. "She's perfectly fine, from what I've been told." She slowly turned toward him. The expression on her face was stern. "Just serve the tea, Mr. Locket. You needn't concern yourself with family business."

Mr. Locket glanced at the mantle. The gold-framed photograph of Miss Claire looked out of focus. He knew it wasn't.

"One of the several phone calls you received yesterday?" he casually remarked. He withheld a smirk as he heard the phone begin to ring down the hall. "I thought perhaps—"

"*Keeping count of my calls, are you? Nothing more pressing in your duties?*" *He placed the cup of tea on the end table to the right of the high-backed wing chair where she was seated. "Perhaps we should relegate you to part-time status."*

Mrs. Cavanaugh's scream—more a wail, now that Mr. Locket had time to reflect upon it—startled both he and Mrs. Waterman. The woman of the house looked as though she had seen a ghost when Cook rushed into the study.

"*Mrs. Waterman! Mr. Locket! Oh, dear God!*" *The woman was wringing her hands so hard Mr. Locket thought she might pull her fingers from their sockets. "The phone— The clinic— I— I told them you weren't taking any calls."*

The oddest look came over Mrs. Cavanaugh's face then. She was probably terrified by what she was about to say. Mrs. Waterman must have interpreted the expression the same way, for she smiled disdainfully at the woman and said, "Has the world come to an end, Mrs. Cavanaugh? The look on your face is quite morose."

Then Mrs. Waterman took a sip of her tea.

"*It's Miss Claire,*" *the woman said in a rush. "They called to say she's passed."*

Mr. Locket experienced a jabbing pain in his chest.

"*She's dead.*"

Although Mr. Locket had seen people make the sign of the cross thousands of times in his life, when Mrs. Cavanaugh performed the blessing, the action made no sense to him.

"*God rest her soul,*" *she said.*

And though Mr. Locket thought she wanted to say more, Mrs. Cavanaugh began to sputter and then broke down and cried. Covering her face with her hands, she went running back down the hall toward the kitchen.

Mr. Locket felt numb. He stood motionless for a few minutes, his gaze locked on the photo on the mantle. How he came to physically hold the gold-framed photograph in his hand, he had no recollection. Yet, he'd found himself staring into the little girl's eyes as if she were standing inches from him. He wondered how he could have missed it—the resemblance.

"*My little girl,*" *he sorrowfully mumbled. "It can't be. Don't let it be."*

He wasn't certain how long he'd been staring at Claire's photograph when he heard Mrs. Waterman sigh. The sound pulled him out of his stupor. He looked down, expecting to see her weeping. Instead, she was calmly sipping her tea as if nothing had happened. When she muttered, "Well, that's that," he didn't know quite what she meant. Reflecting back on the moment, he couldn't help but wonder what would have happened if he'd just let the comment pass. But he hadn't.

"That's what?" he'd asked.

She waved her hand as if shooing away a fly. "The whole sordid affair," she said, sounding exasperated.

Mr. Locket was as perplexed by this comment as he was by her previous. As he tried to unravel the meaning of her cryptic responses, she continued speaking, her tone of voice becoming more animated.

"Traipsing around the world. Acting as though she were Mother Teresa or some such nonsense. Lowering her station by associating with those kinds of people. Sullying the family name by cohabitating with a— with a—" She paused to shake her head. "A filthy nigger. Dear god—what was she thinking?"

It was all Mr. Locket could do to keep his emotions in check when she glanced up and made eye contact.

"Well." Her shoulders lifted then drooped as she sighed. "It's over now." She took a sip of tea and shook her head. "How the pure are drawn to sin." She chuckled. "I dare say, I'm sure she thinks the gates of heaven will be flung open for her. Won't she be surprised when she's greeted with fire and brimstone instead."

Mr. Locket cleared his throat.

"I don't follow," he responded.

"One doesn't get into heaven by fornicating with niggers, Mr. Locket." She made a clicking noise with her tongue. "No, I dare say, the Lord frowns upon that." Mr. Locket could feel anger rising from his bowels when she began to laugh. "He'll see the little you-know-what for what she was. Oh yes, you mark my words."

"Little you-know-what?" Mr. Locket glanced at the photograph of Claire and then glared at Mrs. Waterman. "What does that mean? How can you say something like that?" He became so angry the photograph began to shake in his hand. "She's your daughter, for God's sake!"

A pang of crushing sadness drew him back to the photograph. There were so many words he wished he'd said to her. So many years had gone to waste.

How does a man tell a little girl he is her father when the little girl knows another man by that name? But the resemblance, the look in her eyes—he wasn't dreaming. He knew he wasn't. She was his—and now she'd never know. In a daze, he wiped tears from his eyes.

"My little girl," he whispered.

He thought Mrs. Waterman was choking at first, but then he realized she was spitting tea out of her mouth as she laughed. She was mocking him, he realized. Laughing at him. He felt like punching her in the face.

"You certainly flatter yourself, don't you, Daniel? Your little girl?" She shook her head and grunted. "Where on earth?" But when he looked her in the eye, she turned away. "Preposterous," she grumbled.

"You know it's true!" he blurted. "She's mine! I can see it in her eyes."

Her mocking cackle made him feel as though he'd swallowed a worm. And that worm had broken into a thousand pieces, and each piece had grown spikey arms and was wriggling through every cell of his body.

"See it in her eyes?" The spikey worms shot into the pit of his stomach. "I don't know how that could be."

"Because I—" Mr. Locket gritted his teeth as he placed Claire's photograph on the mantle. "Are you going to deny?" He took a step closer to her. "You're not going to try to pretend that we didn't— didn't— fornicate, are you?" he challenged. "And that nine months later—nearly to the day—you bore a child?" Mr. Locket stared at Mrs. Waterman for a moment before pointing to Claire's photograph. "Are you going to deny that she's mine?"

He could see her lips moving, silently repeating the words she's mine. *Then, as if she'd been struck by a mild case of indigestion, she lightly patted her chest.*

"No," she casually admitted. "No, I can't deny that she could be yours." She arched her eyebrows as she took a sip of tea. "But neither can I confirm it."

"But I—" Mr. Locket rubbed his chin. "The sex we had— It was so raw, urgent. Surely—"

"—your semen shot right up and impregnated me? Is that what you mean?" She chuckled. "Of course it is. You're an Irish male, for God's sake. Of course you'd think your sperm holds some supernatural quality."

He felt numb, just plain numb, as he listened to her giggle.

"Well, I hate to shatter the image you've created of yourself, Daniel. But

you're not the only one I exchanged my passion with, so to speak, during the period in question." She smiled at him.

Mr. Locket's jaw dropped. What was she implying? He hadn't been the only one?

"I don't believe—"

"Believe what you want, Daniel. You obviously already do." She glanced up toward the mantle. "I suppose you would see yourself in her. But then so might the gardener or that big strapping boy you employed in the stable for a few months all those years ago. I believe he was from Virginia. I don't remember his name."

"You're lying," he snapped. "I would have known if—"

"Oh, please, Daniel," she scoffed, dismissing his words with a flick of her hand. "You don't give me enough credit. You weren't on the property 100 percent of the time. And Charles—dear lord, poor Charles—he couldn't find enough excuses to be away." She cupped her hand to her mouth. "Homosexual, you see." She nodded. "Poor man didn't realize it until we were on our honeymoon."

"I don't believe that for a minute."

"Oh, there you go again, Daniel—what you believe…" She shook her head. "He hid it quite well, I dare say. But trust me, he'd rather have a man's penis in his hand than my breast." She paused for a moment. "But he was proud, Very proud. He didn't want anyone to know." She raised her eyebrows. "Especially his good friend, Daniel Locket. Oh, yes, he went to great lengths to keep it from you. He would have been crushed if you'd known. Would have lost face. Is that the saying?"

"But then—"

She shifted her body ever so slightly to pick up the cup of tea.

"Oh, I assured him Claire was his. You see, if I got him drunk enough and got physical with him, he'd get physical right back and—" She glanced out the window, her brow furrowed. "Well, let's just say he would treat me as if I was one of his male counterparts."

Mr. Locket grasped for something to say. But he was at a loss. Everything she was telling him was too much to comprehend.

"But regardless of who the father is—or was," she went on, "Charles loved the girl. And I must say, so did I, up to a point." She let out a sharp giggle.

"Thank God she wasn't born with any Latin influences. Otherwise I would have had to give her up for adoption, wouldn't I?" She nodded as if deep in thought. "But she came out rather nicely, didn't she?"

"She was beautiful," he quickly replied.

"And then she found God. Ugh. And that was the beginning of the end." She clicked her tongue. "The path to heaven runs aside of hell," she said with a sigh. "I suppose it was inevitable."

Mr. Locket was suddenly struck by the memory of Claire and her father sitting in the study, staring out the window as a flock of geese settled on the pond. He remembered quite vividly the sunlight shrouding the girl in a dome of golden light and how pure her voice sounded when she spoke.

"She was touched by heaven," he said without thinking.

"And has no doubt ended up in hell."

"Dear God." He closed his eyes and shook his head. "What's wrong with you?"

"What's wrong with me?" She gave him a quizzical look. "Odd of you to say."

For the life of him, he didn't know what she meant. He stared back at her in silence.

"Now that I think about it, she very well might be yours. After all, you did have a hand in beating a man to death, didn't you, Daniel? Perhaps that's what your overrated Irish sperm carried to my egg—a penchant for sex and violence with glorification of God thrown in." She nodded. "Indeed, that would explain the child's abhorrent behavior."

"Abhorrent? She took care of orphans and the sick! Sacrificed everything to help people she didn't know! Didn't you listen to anything Mr. Savage told us? Weren't you touched by the stories he told of her? Good God—Miss Claire was a saint, by all accounts! A saint!"

She motioned for him to lower his voice.

"There, there, Daniel," she calmly replied, "I would expect you to say nothing different, since you believe the girl to be yours. But I am her mother, after all. And mothers see and feel things others don't about their children. I see what she is."

It was all he could do to stop himself from bashing her across the side of her head.

"I suppose I should have expected it," she went on.

Mr. Locket rubbed his forehead and closed his eyes as he waited for her to say more. But to his surprise, she fell silent.

"And what was it you should have expected?" he reluctantly inquired.

She raised a finger toward the ceiling and shook it.

"I didn't foresee her infatuation with God. No, that was a surprise. But turning out to be a common whore…" She paused to look up at him, realization dawning on her face. "The apple doesn't fall far from the tree, does it, Daniel?" Then her expression soured. "But I draw the line at sleeping with niggers. No, no, no. That falls below the threshold of decency. No, it's better this way." She lifted her cup toward him and motioned with a slight nod for him to pour. "Dead. Yes, better that she's gone. I suppose arrangements will have to made." She looked up. "Would that interest you, Daniel?"

Mr. Locket looked from the photograph of Claire to the ceiling and then out the large picture window that framed the pond. His childhood in Ireland, Charles, the estate, Claire, the night of sex he'd shared with Mrs. Waterman, the years he'd dutifully taken care of everyone and everything for the Waterman family—why did none of those memories seem to hold any meaning? He'd wasted his life.

"Daniel?"

A repeated clinking noise wormed its way into his thoughts. Confused, he blinked and looked around the room.

"Daniel," Mrs. Waterman repeated. She tapped her spoon against the saucer. "Tea, if you would," she said when he made eye contact with her. "I suppose we could ask the clinic to take care of it."

Mr. Locket shook his head.

"Take care of it?"

"Her disposal. Perhaps they have a crematory on the premises."

It was at that moment Mr. Locket realized that his opinion of Mrs. Waterman, up until this point, had been shaped by his observations of her. But now, now as he took a moment to reflect upon her as she might regard herself, he got the inkling that the woman must consider her life one of hardship: a lonely, mundane subsistence in an arcane society in which image meant everything. He wasn't sure if he should feel sorry for her or slap her across the face.

"Scatter her ashes out in the woods," she commented, sounding distracted. "Yes, that would be best."

"You can't be serious," he replied. "Certainly, you would want—"

Mrs. Cavanaugh's second shrill scream startled them afresh. Mrs. Waterman dropped the cup and saucer. Mr. Locket grabbed hold of the mantle and looked toward the hall.

"She's alive! She's alive!" he heard Mrs. Cavanaugh shout. "It was a mistake! A mistake! It was all a terrible mistake!"

Mr. Locket slammed on the brakes as a figure stumbled into the car's headlights.

"Dear God," he gasped.

He fumbled for the switch above the armrest and pressed it.

"Mr. Savage! Mr. Savage!" he shouted as the window slid open.

Mr. Locket saw Dirk shield his eyes from the glare of the headlights and run across the road. He shook his head in disbelief as he watched the man disappear into the bushes.

*

The crack in the corner of the room was dark. And, as far as Claire could tell, empty. She'd been staring at it for hours. Or was it days? She couldn't fathom. Yet she had seen no flames or glimpses of Teimbaka. What did it mean? Why wouldn't the seam widen and show her a link to her past, to what she felt most attached to, to what gave her joy? Was the past dead? And if it was, when did it die? When did the link between her present and her past disintegrate? And, more troubling, why? Why was the seam dark? Why could she no longer see into it?

Her fingers sought the silver cross hanging about her neck as she bowed her head. The skin of her chest felt cold. Something was wrong. Something was terribly wrong. The cross wasn't there, wasn't hanging on the simple chain the Order had issued her when she'd undertaken her vows of novitiate. The revelation left her numb. Was she no longer a nun? Had she forsaken her vows? She clasped her hands and began to tremble. Her mouth went dry when a confusing, distressing thought entered her mind: had God cast her out of grace? What had she done? Is that why the seam was dark? Because it didn't want to show her what sin she'd committed?

Again she clutched at her chest, desperate to feel the cross in the palm of her hand. But as before, her fingers clamped around nothing. The empty sensation was unbearable. She tilted her head toward the ceiling and wailed.

*

Dirk came to an abrupt stop as a tortured cry reverberated in the darkness. Immediately he squatted and looked about. Indistinguishable shapes loomed everywhere. *They're trees and bushes*, he told himself, but he wasn't sure. And the more he studied the murky objects, the less convinced he was. Monsters, ghouls, goblins, zombies—the vague shapes suddenly took on ominous characteristics: gangly appendages, sinister and deformed. Panicked, he searched for the woman he'd been following. Where was Genevieve? Where were the moondrops? He examined the ground around him. Where had the green bugs gone?

"Mr. Savage!"

Dirk dropped to his hands and knees. A tree! A tree was calling his name! He scrambled back a few feet when the tree began moving toward him. He looked on in fear as a cluster of gnarled twigs reached down and took hold of his shoulder. Falling to the ground, he curled his body into a tight ball and whimpered, "Genevieve."

He cringed when he felt the twigs press into his flesh.

"Genevieve!" he cried.

What he perceived as a tree-branch cuffed him on the side of his head.

"Dear God, man," he heard the tree grumble. "Get hold of yourself."

*

Mr. Locket kept one eye focused on the pathetic figure slumped in the passenger seat as he slid into the driver's side of the car and pulled the door closed. Now he understood what the term *death warmed over* meant, for Dirk Savage looked as if he'd been imprisoned in a coffin for the past several days. His complexion was pallid and he had dark circles around his eyes and an obvious aversion to light. He also seemed to be hallucinating. What had happened to the man?

He scrutinized Dirk—soiled hospital scrubs, bare feet—and deduced he'd managed to escape from the clinic. A grievous error on the facility's part. Perhaps that explained the unforgivable phone communications regarding Miss Claire's death and her sudden, miraculous revival. Perhaps the clinic was a poorly run institution that did not warrant Mrs. Waterman's confidence. If that was the case—and the circumstances certainly bolstered his line of thinking—Miss Claire's transfer—or, better yet, her discharge from the substandard facility—would need to be arranged immediately. Certainly Mrs. Waterman would not stand for incompetence where it concerned her daughter's care. Regardless of the old woman's ramblings and shocking revelations, she wouldn't stand to have her daughter's health endangered. Of that he was certain. Still, he couldn't dismiss a lingering concern: if Dirk Savage had come from the clinic looking like death warmed over, what must Miss Claire look like?

Dirk muttered a name from the passenger side of the car.

"Who's Genevieve?" Mr. Locket cautiously inquired.

Dirk looked wide-eyed at Mr. Locket.

"Where? Where is she?" Dirk urgently asked. Mr. Locket shook his head as Dirk's eyes searched the surroundings. "Is she okay? Is she hurt?"

"You misunderstand, I'm—"

Mr. Locket leaned away as Dirk grabbed hold of his arm.

"Is she hurt?" Dirk demanded.

"Leave off!" Mr. Locket snapped. He winced at the pressure Dirk exerted on his bicep. "You're delusional! I don't know who you are speaking of!"

"Genevieve!" Dirk yelled. "She's here!" Dirk's eyes frantically shifted from side to side. "She's— She's—" Dirk's hand slowly slid off of Mr. Locket's arm. "She was here," he said. "I saw her." Dirk peered out the windshield. "She was—" he pointed toward the front of the car. "She was out—" Dirk paused and glanced over at him "—there."

Mr. Locket cleared his throat.

"Mr. Savage. You're obviously not well. You need— Please, let me get you some help." Dirk suddenly looked like he might cry. "Thank God I found you before— Um, I mean, thank God our paths crossed before you came to some harm." He reached over to take hold of Dirk's hand. When he saw the man's head droop forward, he changed his mind. "I was heading to the clinic to check on Miss Claire," he cautiously said. "We can be there in a few minutes." He paused. "They can help you."

"Help me?" Dirk muttered.

"Yes."

"With Genevieve?"

The man sounded so hopeful, Mr. Locket paused before replying.

"I suppose they could," he told him.

Dirk appeared confused by his answer.

"They?" Dirk turned his head to look out the window "They?" he repeated. "Who are they?"

"The staff, the doctors." Mr. Locket caught a glimpse of Dirk's face reflected in the window; the man looked terrified. "You know, the people at the clinic. They can help you." Mr. Locket deftly hit the car's electronic lock switch when he observed Dirk's hand canvassing the door panel. "You know," he explained, "like how they are helping Miss Claire."

"No!" Dirk exclaimed. "She'd dead! They killed her!"

Dirk lunged toward him.

"I can't go back! I can't go!" Dirk blurted. "They— They—" Dirk's expression suddenly went blank, his eyes glazed. "That's where they kill Genevieve."

Dirk suddenly threw his upper body against him and thrust something narrow and pointed toward his eye.

"They kill her!" he screamed. "They kill her!"

Mr. Locket brought his hand up and jabbed Dirk in the throat. Shifting his weight into Dirk's body, he attempted to push him away. But he couldn't budge him. He screamed when Dirk lanced something sharp into the soft tissue just beneath his right eye.

"They sent you!" Dirk yelled. "They sent you to hurt her!"

"No! What are you talking about?" Mr. Locket thrust Dirk angrily away and put a hand to his face. "I was going to see Claire!" He pulled his hand away and examined his fingers. "Claire!" he angrily repeated. "Do you remember her? Jesus, God, man," he fumed, "you stabbed me!" In a fit of rage, he delivered a rabbit punch to Dirk's jaw. "You fucking lunatic! You could have blinded me!"

Mr. Locket prepared to unleash another punch. Then he noticed a tear sliding down Dirk's face. With a frustrated sigh, he shook his head and sagged back into his seat.

"You're crying. Pathetic bastard."

"Crying?"

Dirk slowly placed a finger to his cheek. The discovery of the teardrop seemed to spark some memory in the man, for Dirk suddenly looked blankly out the windshield as though in a trance. "She's gone."

The depth of emotion in Dirk's voice caught Mr. Locket off guard. He shifted uncomfortably in his seat as Dirk slowly raised his other hand level to his eyes. A needle sparkled in the ambient light.

"They're gone," Dirk muttered.

"They?" Mr. Locket probed. He studied Dirk's face, puzzled by the man's pained expression.

"Genevieve," Dirk absently replied. "Claire. Both— Both gone." Dirk's lips began to quiver, his eyes clouding with tears. "Dead," he said. "Both dead."

"No, no, you're mistaken! They made a mistake. You see—"

"I've seen her!" he cried. Dirk's expression became defiant. He pointed the syringe at Mr. Locket and yelled, "They make me watch! They make me see it! They make me—" Dirk looked at his lap. "Her head," he sniffled. "They— They—"

"Miss Claire's alive," Mr. Locket forcefully assured him. Tentatively, he placed a hand on Dirk's wrist and lightly pushed downward. His eyes on the syringe, he said, "It was a mistake. The staff erred."

Dirk slowly shook his head.

"I remember—" Dirk paused and looked out the windshield. "She told me— She told me she died."

Mr. Locket's brow furrowed.

"She?"

"The nurse." Dirk rubbed his forehead as if trying to soothe a headache. "Julie." His eyes blinked several times. "Julie," he repeated as though in some discomfort. "Julie's her name."

"Well, Julie was misinformed, then, along with everybody else." Mr. Locket nodded definitively a few times. "Miss Claire is alive. Mrs. Waterman received—"

"We have to go there," Dirk said in earnest. "We have to make sure."

Mr. Locket shook his head and sighed.

"That's what I've been trying to tell you: I'm heading there now. I'm going to the clinic to make certain Miss Claire—"

"No!" Dirk interrupted. "Not there. Never there." He adamantly shook his head. "Never go there."

"Preposterous! Of course I'm going there. Miss Claire—"

Dirk placed the needle in front of Mr. Locket's eye. Although Dirk's hand was unsteady, he seemed newly focused and determined.

"Drive," Dirk curtly ordered. "She has to be the one."

"The one what?"

"Drive!" Dirk shouted, jabbing the tip of the needle against Mr. Locket's cheek.

Mr. Locket snapped his head back.

"Shit," he said, rubbing the spot where the needle had punctured his skin. "Jesus Christ." He glared at the syringe for a moment before directing his anger at Dirk. "And where is it I'm to drive you?" he inquired. "Some slum in Philadelphia where you can get that filled?"

Dirk turned the syringe from side to side, an odd expression on his face.

"Get it filled? What are you saying?"

"Jesus, God, man! Don't you understand what's happening? Don't you realize why we're out here?"

"Out here?" Dirk repeated vaguely. Mr. Locket was tempted to grab the syringe, but Dirk muttered, "*She*," his expression turning abruptly hostile.

"She has to do it," Dirk spat, jerking the needle in front of Mr. Locket's face. "She's the only one who can get her out. Now, drive!"

"Where?" Mr. Locket asked, exasperated. "You're not making any sense!"

"To the house."

"The house?"

Dirk gathered the front of his scrubs close about his neck. He stomped his feet against the floorboard and began to shiver.

"To see the old prune," he said through a clenched jaw.

"The old—?"

"Mrs. Waterman, you fuck."

Dirk's expression was full of spite when he looked over at him. "Don't you understand what's happening?" Dirk said.

He glared at Mr. Locket.

"Now, drive," he ordered. "Drive."

22

FORSAKEN. *TEIMBAKA MULLED the word over in his thoughts. He remembered Claire using it to express her dismay toward the plight of the orphans. Who would look after them once she was gone? she'd ask. Who would see to their needs: their health, their education, their spiritual wellbeing? What fate would befall them? She would gaze deep into his eyes as she waited for him to answer. He, in turn, would take her hand and squeeze it affectionately.*

"The Mother will see to their needs," he would gently reassure her.

And she would rest her head on his shoulder and wrap her fingers around his arm. That she trusted him, believed in him, had made him feel whole, given him a sense of worth. He was Teimbaka—the Lion of Djibouti. Yet he felt incomplete without her. Her absence had crystalized that realization for him. She had nurtured his spirit, given him courage, pointed to the need for sacrifice, and steadied him with words of faith. He could not have withstood the wounds inflicted upon him by Gunstard and the Serpent without her strength. She meant everything to him—and now she was gone.

Oh, how he had failed her in the final days they were together! How he had let her down! How disappointed in him she must have been when he didn't return from Ras Dashen to save her from imprisonment.

But no more disappointed than he was in himself. For how could anyone view him as more of a failure then he? To have followed a troop of monkeys to the edge of the highlands instead of returning to Claire when John Too begged him to...

Teimbaka put his hand to his arm and closed his eyes. If he pretended hard enough, he could feel Claire's touch upon his flesh, the softness of her breath upon his neck. He could sense her spirit intertwining with his. The notion that she was sitting next to him was sublime. Yet it was also cruel, for he knew it to be a falsehood, an illusion. The reality that she was no longer part of his life left him empty and cold. Gathering his robe tight around his neck, he huddled against the alley wall. Forsaken. *The word seeped into his bones.*

"But what of Claire, Etiyopiya? Where is she?"

Teimbaka squirmed at the asking. He did not want to imagine Claire's state—where she was, what she was doing. She was gone. And though his sense of loss at her departure was devastating, worse was the crushing anguish that overcame him when he realized she would not be returning. He was alone. She did not want to be with him. These were the thoughts that ran over and over through his head. It was enough to make him wish he had died in the explosion in Mogadishu.

Why had John Too pulled him from the water?

"Better that you walk out into the ocean until the currents pull you down to the bottom."

Isn't that what the boy had said? Why save me, then? Why go to the trouble to nurse my wounds and see to my needs if, in the end, you want me to die? To see me suffer—is that the reason you've stayed with me, kept me from wasting away? To celebrate my undoing, to witness the unraveling of my spirit, to rejoice in the rotting of my flesh? Are these the reasons you keep me—a blind, feebleminded cripple tormented by his past—in this sewer of an alley?

Forsaken. *Teimbaka placed his fingertips against the alley wall and shuddered. He could barely feel the current emanating from the stone. Soon, the link he shared with the Mother would break. The thought that She would soon abandon him suddenly made him feel more alone than ever, even more than when he was a boy wandering in the river of sand after the lion had killed his brother.* Forsaken. *Wearily, he struggled to stand. Using the wall to steady himself, he took one shaky step and then another. The sea beckoned. He would answer its call.*

*

Jame Ain't pressed his hand to his side and winced.

"Damn," he hissed, "where the fuck you at?"

With a grimace, he raised his hand to his face. "Mother-fuck," he said, staring at his blood-stained fingers. "Somebody gonna pay. Somebody gonna pay with their motherfuckin' balls."

Jame looked back up at the wide steel girders and cubes of dark, empty space above him. Industrial light fixtures—steel-colored rectangles wrapped in mesh— glowed with neon brightness. Though the air hummed with electricity, the cavernous room, to Jame, felt freezing cold. Tucking his hands under his armpits, he gently rocked back and forth.

"Where the fuck you at, Jacko?" he grumbled. "Where the fuck you at?"

With a heavy sigh, he leaned back and looked around.

The room where Jacko had left him, from what he could see, was mostly empty. Other than a group of large wooden barrels stacked against the opposite wall with what looked to be a collection of nets hanging behind them, there wasn't much to indicate where Jacko had brought him after the ambush. The only other clue was the room's peculiar smell.

"Smell like a can o' sardines," Jame muttered. "Must be an old fishery or somethin'." He wondered how Jacko had known about it.

A creaking floorboard drew his attention to the door twenty yards to his left. As the knob turned, he drew the Glock from the waist of his blue jeans and slid the weapon's arming bar back, loading a bullet into the chamber. Hand shaking, he took aim at the entranceway. The hinges creaked as the door swung inward. Jame held his breath and curled his finger against the trigger. When Jacko stepped across the threshold, he let out a heavy sigh.

"Damn, boy. Where the fuck were you?" Jame asked. He squinted to see if anyone was behind Jacko. "Where the fuckin' doctor I sent you for? Don't tell me you came back here without one."

Jacko thrust his hands out in front of him in a placating gesture.

"Be cool, brother, be cool," he urged. "It's all good, it's all good."

"Man, what the fuck you sayin'? You ain't the one *shot*." He waved the gun at Jacko's face. "What you mean, it's all good? Shit, can't you see I'm bleedin'? You fuckin' blind or somethin'?"

"Sorry, boss, I just—"

"Where the fuckin' doctor?" Jame snapped. "You better not tell me—"

"He's comin', he's comin'," Jacko hurriedly interjected. "He—" Jacko paused and glanced over his shoulder toward the door. "He's— He's—"

"He's what?" Jame sneered.

"Parkin' his car." Jacko wrung his hands as he took a few tentative steps toward Jame. "Yeah, that's right. He's parkin' his car."

Jame eyed Jacko with suspicion.

"Why you actin' like it's a surprise?" Jame pointed the gun at Jacko's groin. "Why you look so nervous?"

"Why do I look nervous?" Jacko's left eye twitched. "'Cause we almost got killed!" He opened his hands toward the ceiling in a pleading gesture. "Lotta motherfuckers bit it back there, man. Why else you think I stressin'?"

Jame slowly lowered the gun. He gave Jacko an unapologetic sneer.

"Well, the motherfucker better be here—"

Jame abruptly swung the Glock toward the door, prompting Jacko to duck out of the line of fire.

"That's him now," Jacko interjected just before the door swung open.

Jame kept the gun aimed at the entrance as a large black man stepped into the room.

"You a motherfuckin' doctor?" Jame suspiciously asked.

"Yeah." The man's answer sounded more like a grunt.

"You don't look like no doctor I ever seen."

"He ex-army," Jacko hastily explained. "Field medic. All I could get on such—" Jacko glanced over his shoulder toward the door. "You know, after— I mean— The way things went down."

"The way things went down," Jame smirked. "Like somethin' happen to *you.*" Jame waved the gun at the big man. "You know your shit?" he asked.

The big man nodded and took a step toward Jame.

"'Cause if you don't," Jame warned, "I'll shoot your motherfuckin' balls off your dick. Dig?"

The big man paused for a moment as he stared at the gun in Jame's hand. With a grunt, he nodded and then took the few remaining steps to the corner of the room where Jame was seated.

"You have pain?" the big man asked as he took a knee.

"What kind of fuckin' question is that?" Jame replied. "What you think, motherfucker? Yeah, I have pain." Jame shook his head and then looked at Jacko. "Where you find this dude?"

Jame glanced at the big man as he rummaged through the doctor's bag he'd brought with him.

"Am I in pain?" he mocked. "Shit."

The doctor extracted a syringe from his bag and raised it to Jame's eye level.

"What's that?" Jame asked.

"Morphine," the doctor replied, glancing down at the wound in Jame's side before he added, "for the pain."

Jame nodded.

"Now what you hear about that motherfuckin' narc pig who showed up at the meetin'?" Jame asked Jacko. "Anybody know who he is? How he found out about what was goin' down?"

"Haven't had no time to ask, boss," Jacko said. "Place a motherfuckin' war zone after you popped that grenade. Fuckin' place—"

"Was a motherfuckin' setup, is what it was."

The doctor rubbed a cotton ball on his arm just above his elbow. Jame winced when the doctor stuck the needle in his arm.

"How the fuck did that pig know where we were meetin' when it was arranged all hurried-like?" He gave Jacko a harsh look. "You told me it was just decided, didn't you? So how the hell did the nigger arrange a raid on such short notice?"

Jacko rubbed his brow but didn't respond.

"Who was it decided the where and when?" he pressed Jacko. "You had a say, didn't you, since we the ones who called for the meet?" Jame aimed the Glock at Jacko's head. "You fuckin' narced us out, didn't you?" Jame accused him. "Had to be you."

Jame felt himself slump a little to his left. He put two hands on the gun when it started to shake.

"Why I feel—?"

He blinked several times, then abruptly jerked his head up when it started to droop forward.

"Dizzy," he mumbled.

His right arm sank toward the floor. His eyelids fluttered. His speech was slurred when he muttered, "You set me up."

His head tilted to one side as the Glock fell out of his hand.

*

"He dead?"

"Will be," the big man replied.

Jacko took a step toward the big man to look over his shoulder; the man was pulling items out of the doctor's bag.

"What's that stuff?" he asked.

The big man didn't answer. Jacko watched him lift a second syringe from the bag, then a short, flat piece of finished wood.

"You gonna hit him with that?" Jacko asked with a nervous chuckle.

The big man remained silent, rummaging through the doctor's bag as though he hadn't heard a word Jacko had said. Jacko nervously shifted from one foot to the other as the silence between them dragged on. The dragon's head tattoo on the back of the man's neck drew his attention.

"You get that tattoo in the army?"

The man's massive shoulders rose and fell.

"Get lost," the man growled.

"Just askin'."

"Go report to the woman."

"What woman?"

Jacko took a quick step back when the big man turned and glared at him.

"The one who paid you to turn on your boss," he replied. "Now get lost."

"Sure, sure, sure," Jacko said with a nod.

Jacko started to turn toward the door, then changed his mind.

"You need help taking him—I mean his body—somewhere?"

The man glanced toward the stack of barrels across the room.

"No," the man responded.

Jacko saw a flickering light reflecting from the wall next to Jame's head.

He rose up on the tip of his toes and peered over the big man's frame. The man held a lit lighter in one hand and a spoon in the other.

"You gonna OD him?"

"You still here?"

Jacko edged back a few steps when the big man shifted his weight as though preparing to stand.

"Got plenty here for two," the man threatened. "Plenty of barrels, too."

Jacko took a few nervous steps toward the door before breaking into a run.

*

"I'm afraid it might be time."

Mallard Crenshaw listened to the female voice on the other end of the phone and tried to place where he'd heard it before. He grabbed the remote off the coffee table to turn the sound down on the television.

"Who is this?" he asked.

There was a slight pause. Then the woman replied, "You know very well who this might be."

Mallard sat back on the couch and placed a hand to his shoulder. He gently massaged the bandages covering his bullet wound.

"I'm in no mood for any shit, lady. So I suggest—"

"She warned me you might be cross."

"What?"

"But she didn't say anything about cursing."

"Cursing?"

"I'd heard stories about policemen using foul language, but I never thought it was true."

"You don't like cursing?" Mallard angrily retorted. "Well hold your ears, lady. 'Cause I'm about to go off."

"Go off? I don't follow."

"You don't? Well, let me—"

"Could you please stop talking? The situation could already be unraveling, and you're wasting time."

"Wasting time?" Marshall pulled the phone away from his ear to stare into the mouthpiece. "Do you know who I am?" He vaguely heard the woman saying something in reply, but he didn't listen. "This is Field Supervisor Mallard Crenshaw of the ATF! You know what ATF stands for, lady?"

He gave the phone a curious look when he heard a clicking noise come from the receiver.

"Are you feeling all right, officer?" the woman calmly inquired. "She didn't say you were a hothead."

"She?"

"Yes. You know." There was a slight pause before she said, "*She*. A."

"A?"

"Yes. You know." Mallard pinched his eyebrows together when he heard the woman tsk him again. "A. The ivory woman. You know, the one who has the import-export business in northern New Jersey?" Mallard heard the woman giggle. She added, "No names—isn't that the rule?"

Mallard shook his head.

"Are you talking about Alexis? Is that who gave you my home number?"

"Oh my," the woman responded, sounding confused. "So much for secrecy, I suppose. I don't think she'll be happy to hear you used her name."

Mallard rubbed his forehead several times and sighed.

"Look, whoever you are, I've just been—"

"So, will you take care of it?" the woman pressed. "A said you would."

"A."

Mallard stared at the TV, blankly absorbing the images flickering across the screen as he tried to make sense out of what the woman on the other end of the phone wanted from him.

"Said I would *what*, exactly?"

"Take care of my butler," the woman frankly replied. "Mr. Locket. He's heading there. He left an hour or so ago. He should be arriving there soon."

"I'm not sure I—"

"Unless you can have a squad car detain him beforehand, of course. Yes, that would be best, I suppose. Stop him before he causes any disturbance. Or—you know—uncovers our secrets."

Mallard sat up straight.

"Secrets?"

"Why, yes—you know—the D and M and such." The woman paused before adding, "You don't want me to say anything out loud, do you?"

Mallard gingerly touched his wounded shoulder before cradling his forehead in his hand. Bits of the woman's rambling conversation began to fall together.

"Let me get this straight," he began. "Alexis Taylar gave you my home number and told you to call so I could take care of your butler, who's heading for a clinic where you're afraid he might cause some disturbance or uncover—"

"Exactly," the woman interjected. "Finally. Now you see."

"I'm afraid I don't see. I think it best if you start from the beginning. Why don't we begin with you telling me who you are?"

There was a long pause. Mallard heard what he imagined was the woman clicking her tongue against the roof of her mouth. She sighed and said, "W. I suppose you can call me Mrs. W."

*

Junebug moistened her index finger, wiped it across the section of the glass tabletop where several granules of cocaine remained from the line she'd just snorted, and smeared the residue across her upper gums. Licking her lips and giving a hard sniff, she sat back on her heels and closed her eyes. As the numbing, tingling sensation the drug produced washed over her, she smiled.

"Let's do more," she suggested.

Alexis snickered. "What's in it for me?"

Junebug seductively slid her tongue across her lower lip. "We could sprinkle some there," she replied, eyeing the woman's groin. "Then we each get something."

Alexis smiled. "Smart girl, Junebug. Hold that thought."

Junebug. What a stupid name. She ran her tongue across her pleasantly numb teeth. *Better than Harper, though. Shit, anything's better than who I was.* Junebug sniffled twice and then rubbed the tip of her nose. *More, I want more.* She gave Alexis a pouty look when she picked up the phone and started pushing numbers on the keyboard.

Get off the phone! Junebug focused on the little slit of a pocket angled at the hip of Alexis's snug-fitting, red silk knee-length dress. She'd seen Alexis slip the foil packet into the inconspicuous opening. Junebug shifted her attention to Alexis's face; the woman looked serious. She decided it might be best to listen in on the conversation before trying anything.

"I hope I didn't wake you," Alexis said. "I know it's before dawn there, but—"

Alexis wrapped the phone cord around her finger as the person on the receiving end of the call spoke.

"This is excellent news. When can I—?"

Junebug smiled when Alexis looked down at her and winked.

"So soon? How is that possible?"

Junebug ran a hand across her breasts as Alexis rounded the big wooden desk to sit on the edge of the cushioned armchair.

"Philadelphia? Why there? Why not somewhere closer to—"

Alexis crossed one leg over the other and rubbed a hand across her knee. Junebug edged closer.

"I'm concerned with arousing suspicion. One overseas flight originating from Ethiopia might not be cause for concern, but more than that would surely rouse someone's curiosity."

More coke. Junebug wanted more. Setting aside her concerns, she reached out and placed her hand on the back of Alexis's calf. *Get off the phone!*

"Of course, I welcome the merchandise arriving as expeditiously as possible, but not if that puts it and *us* in jeopardy. Need I remind you that we own Customs in Newark? And although—"

Junebug softly ran a finger up and down the back of Alexis's leg. She could feel a flush of warmth spreading through her flesh.

"We do? I wasn't aware of that. Good to know he's doing more to earn his money than just looking the other way. But I still don't like the idea of multiple air shipments. What's the outlook by the normal mode? Were you able to enlist another vessel?"

Junebug slid her hand up the back of Alexis's thigh. Alexis uncrossed her legs and spread them a few inches apart.

"Excellent. So can we agree that you'll ship the bulk of it in this manner?"

To Junebug's pleasure, Alexis reached down and caressed her cheek.

"Excellent. I'll send some of my associates to retrieve what you're flying in and wait to hear from you about the freighter's departure date."

Junebug could feel heat emanating from Alexis's crotch. The woman reached into the little pocket on the side of her dress and extracted the foil pack containing the cocaine.

"My buyers will be ecstatic to hear there's going to be a reliable source moving forward. And I believe," she chuckled, "that will justify a hefty price increase."

Alexis's thighs quivered when Junebug placed her finger atop the lace panties she was wearing. *Get off the phone!*

"I have to get off the phone now," Alexis said as she placed the foil pack of cocaine on the desk. "I'll look to hear from you soon."

Alexis lightly brushed a finger over Junebug's lower lip.

"And Talia." She paused when Junebug began to suck on her finger. "I apologize for calling so early."

Alexis hung up the phone and shook her head.

"Naughty girl," she teased as she slowly extracted her finger from Junebug's mouth. "I think you need to be punished."

"Punished?" Junebug slid her finger off Alexis's crotch and said, "That doesn't sound very nice."

Feigning sadness, she leaned forward and rested her cheek against Alexis's knee. She began to trace little circles on the woman's inner thigh with the tip of her finger.

"How can I get you to change your mind?" she asked. "What did I do that you didn't like?"

Alexis grabbed Junebug's arm and pulled the girl's hand out from beneath her dress.

"I can't have distractions when I'm trying to conduct business," she told her.

Junebug was confused by Alexis's tone of voice until she saw a little smile forming at the corners of her mouth.

"I have to concentrate, be focused. I can't have you—"

Junebug abruptly stood.

"What's wrong?

Junebug crisscrossed her arms in front of her, grabbed the bottom of her maroon T-shirt, and pulled it over her head.

"What are you—?"

Junebug sensually ran her hand across her breasts. Arching her back, she closed her eyes and lightly pinched her nipples.

"Is this some kind of strip show?"

Junebug slid her hands from her breasts down her bare sides to her waist. With a slight forward thrust of her hips, she undid the button of her cut-off denim shorts.

"You little tramp."

Junebug gazed into Alexis's eyes as she pulled down the zipper. She slid her tongue across her lower lip before letting the shorts fall to the floor.

"Still want to punish me?" she asked as she brushed her fingers over her pubic hair. "Or is there—?"

Junebug gasped as the door to Alexis's office suddenly swung open. Reflexively, she covered her crotch with one hand while hiding her breasts with an arm. She quickly averted her eyes when she noticed the odd-looking man with orange hair and mulatto skin ogling her.

"What the fuck is this?" Alexis snapped.

Alexis was pointing a gun at the man. Junebug started to edge out of the room but stopped when another man ran in and blocked the way out.

"Sorry, boss," the second man blurted to Alexis. "I told the gringo—"

"It's done," the mulatto man interjected, his attention focused on Alexis. "We did it."

Alexis slowly lowered the gun.

"Did what?" she inquired.

"Snuffed him," the man with the orange hair replied. "J-j-j-j-j-Jame's gone. Your-your-your man took him out."

Alexis smirked and placed the gun in a desk drawer.

"You witnessed it?" Alexis asked.

The orange-haired man's eyes shifted between Junebug and Alexis. Unnerved by the way he was looking at her, Junebug bent and picked up her clothes.

"Y-y-yes, ma'am," he said. "Watched him stick a needle in his arm."

"And the body?"

"I-I-I—"

Junebug edged back when the orange-haired man took a step toward her.

"Answer me," Alexis snapped.

The way the orange-haired man reacted reminded Junebug of the boys in her sixth-grade class when they got in trouble with the teacher: his eyes went to the floor, his head drooped, and he shuffled on his feet, pulling at his fingers.

"Put it—put it in a barrel, I think."

"You think? You're not sure?" Alexis pressed.

"I-I-I didn't stick around," the man hurried to say. "But-but we on the river, you know, so-so—"

Junebug turned her back on the orange-haired man when he abruptly shifted his attention from Alexis to her. She stepped into her cutoffs as he continued his explanation.

"Like that hooker I hear about a few weeks back. Word on the street she was stuffed in a barrel with cement and dropped to the bottom of the river."

"How do you know about that?"

Junebug pulled on her maroon T-shirt. When she turned back around, Alexis was sitting at her desk, staring at the orange-haired man while shifting the pack of cocaine between her fingers.

"Street got eyes," the orange-haired man said with a shrug. "Figure Jame headin' for the same place. Don't need to be watchin' to know how it gonna go down."

Junebug edged toward the door. She gasped when the orange-haired man reached over and grabbed her by the arm.

"What are you doing, asshole?" She looked nervously toward Alexis. "Let go of me!"

When Junebug heard Alexis say, "Let her go," she felt a huge sense of relief.

"You said, whatever I want," the orange-haired man contended as he squeezed Junebug's arm. "You said you'd give me what I want if I give you Jame."

Junebug cowered back when the orange-haired man pulled her toward him. She looked confusedly at Alexis.

"Tell him to let me go," she implored. "He's hurting me."

Junebug's stomach balled into a knot as Alexis's attention shifted between her and the orange-haired man. A pang of dread shot through her when Alexis raised her eyebrows and sighed.

"I suppose I did," she reluctantly agreed. "But perhaps I could interest you in a different girl. I have a few—"

"I want this one. I like 'em young."

"No!" Junebug cried as she tried to break free of the man's grasp. "Please, Alexis. No."

For the first time since she'd run away from home, Harper Janakowski wished she'd never left. Although her mom was a pill-popping drunk who treated her like shit and her father was a junkie who hadn't bothered with her since she was five, she suddenly longed to be back in the trailer park ten miles outside the Pittsburg city limits, scrounging for a joint while she bemoaned how much her life sucked.

"Take her, then."

The orange-haired man yanked her close and put a hand on her breast. Teary-eyed, she looked to Alexis, but the woman had her back turned toward her. She heard the woman say, "A deal's a deal."

"No!" Junebug sobbed.

She scratched the man's arm and tried to push away, but he slapped her across the face and clamped a hand around the back of her neck. Her knees buckled when Alexis said, "Take them to room seven, Jose."

The orange-haired man pulled her toward the doorway. But when she heard Alexis tell the man to wait, she straightened her shoulders and lifted her head.

"Take this," said Alexis, tossing the foil pack to the orange-haired man. "She'll do anything for the stuff." Alexis winked.

Junebug felt the blood drain from her face.

"And Jacko," Alexis added. "You best be right about your boss."

*

Alexis frowned as she watched Jacko push Junebug out of the room. *Pity,* she thought. *The girl had a way about her.*

"Business is business," she mumbled.

Still, the thought of the girl being forced to have sex with such a low-life bothered her. But not enough for her to follow the two down the hall and tell the scumbag he'd have to settle for another girl. She sighed. *Oh well,* she thought. *There's plenty more where she came from.* She smiled. *There always is. Besides...*

She turned toward the wall at her back and scanned the bank of video monitors. Movement in room number seven: Jacko was forcing Junebug to her knees. He was in the process of pulling the zipper down on his pants when she heard the soft beep of her private phone line. With a dismissive shake of her head, she turned and picked up the receiver.

"Yes?"

Her brow furrowed as she listened to the angry male voice coming through the receiver. With a slight glance to the monitors behind her, she sat down on the cushioned chair. Reflexively, she reached for the nearest of the ivory figurines scattered haphazardly about her desktop. Junebug left her thoughts. She absently rubbed her thumb along a giraffe's ivory neck.

"Don't threaten me," she said. "That's not going to do either one of us any good. I gave her your number because—"

Alexis held the receiver away from her ear and frowned.

"She's half senile," she interjected. "Or didn't you pick up on that when you spoke to her?"

Her head tilted slightly to the right as she tapped the giraffe's hooves on the desk.

"Look, Crenshaw, isn't it obvious what needs to be done?"

Mallard Crenshaw shouted his reply. With a roll of her eyes, she exchanged the giraffe figurine for a lion.

"We don't need her anymore," she said. "We've been bypassing her for months. I've just been humoring her, keeping her involved to make her believe she's still vital to the operation. Better that than have her become disillusioned, don't you think? Knowing how the old bird likes to run her mouth, it would be just like her to allow an unfortunate slip of the tongue outside our circle of influence."

She listened to Crenshaw's response and sighed.

"Look, I'm already dealing with the repercussions of your little raid." Her expression hardened. She squeezed the lion into her palm. "I've already taken care of *him*!" she snapped. "And I'm in the process of smoothing over the *shit* your little show of force stirred up amongst the other parties. So, don't tell me you can't deal with the old bird and her butler!"

Alexis exhaled sharply and put the lion on the desk.

"Look." She sent the ivory lion sliding across the glass desktop with a flick of her finger. "That's up to you," she said. "Send one of your men if you don't want to—"

She rolled her eyes and shook her head.

"She's expecting *you*, not me. So go. I doubt she'll give you any trouble."

With a smirk, she twisted the phone cord around her finger.

"But watch your back with the butler," she said. "Goliath told me he looks to be in his sixties. Maybe he—"

She covered her mouth with her hand and turned her face away from the phone as she suppressed a giggle.

"Well, then, pay him off if you don't want—" She paused for a moment to let Crenshaw vent. "Of course I'm joking. We can't afford any loose ends on any front of the operation. And that's exactly why *you're* the perfect choice for this little hiccup."

She closed her eyes and held the phone away from her ear. She waited for Crenshaw to stop talking before she continued.

"Because you know how to stage these things. Draw on your past experiences. Make it look like a robbery."

She tapped her finger on the desk, opened the top drawer, and eyed the gun lying within. She shook her head at Crenshaw's response.

"Don't be stupid. We all have a great deal to lose. Stop acting like you're the only one being threatened by this. Do your job."

She rested a hand on the gun.

"The one you're being paid for! The one you agreed to with the fat reverend all those years ago!" She sighed. "Or do you need a reminder of how deep you are in this?"

She abruptly stood and grabbed the edge of the desk.

"Don't force me to make a decision detrimental to both of us." Her eyes narrowed. "You know exactly what I mean."

Her gaze lingered on the big cats—a lion, a leopard, and a tiger—within her ivory collection.

"I believe I've made myself clear, Crenshaw. I expect you to handle the situation. If I don't hear from you personally, I assume I'll be made aware of the outcome in the newspapers." She gazed into the eyes of the ivory leopard for a moment before adding, "Good hunting."

With a sigh, Alexis hung up the phone. On a whim, she moved the figurines of the lion, the tiger, and the leopard to one side of the desk, placing them in a line opposite the remaining figures in the collection. She noted the antelope, the zebra, the giraffe, the wildebeest, and the water buffalo seemed unaware of the peril aligned against them. How typical of the herd to be so naïve.

Alexis was taken by surprise when the door to her office opened without so much as the courtesy of a knock. But when she saw Goliath enter the room, she merely nodded her acknowledgement before turning her attention to the monitor for room number seven. Jacko, she saw, had Junebug completely naked, pressed flush against a wall with her neck in a choke hold. The expression on the girl's face was a mixture of terror and revulsion. Alexis entertained a momentary feeling of sympathy for the girl, for she assumed she would have experienced the same emotions if she were the girl's age and found herself being violently raped by a low-life scum like Jacko.

"It's done," Goliath grunted.

Alexis nodded to the monitor and said, "So I was told."

Goliath took a step toward her, angling his body to get a better view of the monitor. He watched silently for a few moments before he spoke.

"Trash."

Alexis nodded. "Agreed."

"Piece of shit."

Alexis shook her head in disgust as Jacko slapped Junebug before slamming her into the wall.

"Then you wouldn't mind?" she said.

"Mind?"

Alexis looked up and met Goliath's questioning gaze.

"Getting rid of it," she replied.

Goliath looked at the monitor and grunted.

"What about the girl?" he inquired.

Alexis took a deep breath and sighed.

"I have no further use for her."

She gave the monitor a final glance before she turned and sat down at her desk.

"Dispose of them both."

*

"I suppose I should have sent you to public school." Caroline Waterman tapped a wrinkled finger along the side of the gold picture frame. "You might have turned out completely different if I had." Out of habit, she clicked her tongue against the roof of her mouth. "You might have gravitated toward cheerleading or home economics. Yes, some *acceptable* vocation. Perhaps even taken up with a boy." She chuckled. "That would have been a great surprise." She raised her eyebrows at the girl in the photograph. "Would have gone a long way to silence the rumors of your— Of your being a lesbian."

Caroline studied her daughter's face before lowering the photograph to her side. She cast her eyes about the room, vaguely feeling as though she had misplaced something, but unsure what it might be, before crossing the room to the large picture window. Invariably, at this time of the evening, her gaze was drawn to the glimmering strand of lights strung across the small pier that jutted out into the pond. She found their soft reflection upon the surface of the water to be quite soothing

"I couldn't have allowed you stay." She turned the face of the photograph toward her. "You understand, don't you? Your father would have doted on you, ignored his responsibilities, his business dealings and such. Threatened our social—"

She suddenly yearned for a cup of tea.

"Mr. Locket!"

She scrutinized the photograph as she waited for Mr. Locket to answer. Who *did* she resemble? She closed her eyes in an attempt to conjure the image of Claire's adult face. But she couldn't quite bring the woman's features into focus. She found her inability to visualize her daughter as a woman in her thirties to be unsettling.

"Mr. Locket!" she shouted with a bit more urgency in her voice.

Why isn't he answering? Where the hell is he? Maybe Cook is still here.

"Mrs. Cavanaugh!"

She took a step toward the hallway and then stopped and looked down at the photograph.

"Don't mock me," she cautioned the girl in the picture. "You think you're better than me? Think you're holy?" She gave her daughter's image a spiteful look. "Drove Charles away," she grumbled, "then flew off to some barbaric country to shack up with a nigger. So much grief, so much pain. And now you come back? Now? After what you did? What you became?"

Caroline threw the framed photograph across the room. The dull thud it produced when it landed irritated her.

"So like you," she griped. "Disappointing. Immoral. Shameful."

Her eyes began to tear as she stared at the discarded object. With a huff, she wiped them away. Pulling the collar of her robe close about her chest, she made a hesitant turn toward the picture window before abruptly halting.

"Mr. Locket?" she tentatively called. "Mrs. Cavanaugh?"

She clicked her tongue and blinked her eyes several times. No sounds of approaching footsteps. Neither the butler nor the cook appeared. *Where are they?*

Whispers came to her then, the hollow-sounding voices arising from each corner of the room, tugging on her torso as if with their every word they'd attached strings to her limbs. She turned in circle after circle until, quite disoriented, she came to a trembling stop.

She shivered. All was silent.

"Who's there?" she asked. "Who is it?"

She kept perfectly still and held her breath as she listened for a reply. When she heard none, she swept the room with her eyes for anything that looked out of place. The empty spot on the mantle where a photograph of Claire had always stood drew her attention. Alarmed that the photo was not in its designated place, she was about to call out for Mr. Locket when she saw the gold frame lying on the floor.

"What in the world?" she muttered.

She approached the overturned photograph with apprehension, bewildered as to how the picture had ended up on the floor. Wary, she glanced over each of her shoulders twice before bending to pick up the frame.

"You," she said when she recognized the face in the photograph. "Must you always be so troublesome?"

Grudgingly, she placed the photograph on the mantle and gazed into her daughter's eyes.

"You really were a darling girl. For a time, anyway." She furrowed her brow and then pointedly asked, "Why *did* you find God? Was it something I said or did?" She shook her head and clicked her tongue. "It ruined everything."

She grew pensive, her thoughts weighted with the memory of Claire's announcement that she was devoting her life to the Lord.

A complete waste of time, she'd thought then, *and a waste of a good education. But good riddance. Go hide in some convent and spend your day saying the rosary.*

"Even now," she told the girl in the photograph, "your habit of disrupting my life continues. Well, I won't have it. I won't allow you—"

Her voice trailed off.

"No," she flatly decreed. "You're to stay there until you are either—"

She abruptly turned her head to make a quick check of the hallway. Finding it empty, she grunted.

"One left after dinner," she reminded herself, "and the other went to check on—"

With a heavy sigh, she turned back to address the photograph.

"You, always you." She clicked her tongue several times before she continued. "Well, not anymore," she said with a shake of her head. "No, not anymore."

23

"ETIYOPIYA."

John Too searched the alley in both directions before focusing his attention on the old kebero perched against the wall. The crude figures of hyenas and elephants on the walls of the drum had been clumsily carved by Teimbaka; the drum was his. Yet Teimbaka was not sitting next to it, as he should have been. Alarmed, John Too called out.

"Etiyopiya! Etiyopiya!"

If Teimbaka replied, John Too did not hear it over the grumblings of the other inhabitants of the alley—a score of homeless souls trying to sleep off the hardships of the previous day. Where had Teimbaka gone? John Too slung the drum over his shoulder and started walking down the west-running branch of the alley, then suddenly changed his mind. Abruptly turning east, he headed toward the harbor. He would come across Teimbaka before long.

"I couldn't stand the stench of urine and feces any longer," he imagined Teimbaka might say when he found him. "I would have waited for you to return before moving, but I didn't know when you were coming back. Where were you all night?"

The boy, *John Too thought,* I was with the boy. One day I will bring the two of you together and you will see for yourself—

"Are you lost?"

John Too shifted the weight of the drum on his shoulder. Two men were blocking his way.

"Who's with you?" one of the men asked.

John Too noticed a jagged scar running the length of the man's chin. His tunic smelled of petrol.

"I'm looking for someone," John Too replied. "Let me pass."

The man with the scar on his face reached out and gripped John Too by his arm.

"Why so rude?" he inquired.

John Too pushed the man's hand from his arm.

"I'm not being rude," he hurriedly replied. "I'm searching for a friend. Did you happen to pass a blind man as you came this way?"

"A blind man?" the second man—dark-skinned, heavyset, with weather-lined features and a mouthful of yellow teeth—asked. Addressing his companion, he said, "Was the man blind?"

"Who do you mean?" the scar-faced man replied.

"The penniless beggar who insulted you. The one you—"

"Oh, he was blind? Well, that would explain why he didn't duck when I—" the man smiled at John Too "—fended off his weak assault."

"Assault?" John Too questioned. "Etiyopiya would not—"

The punch to John Too's stomach knocked his breath from him. One of the men shoved him harshly backward, and he fell awkwardly to the ground. Dazed, he rolled over onto his stomach and tried to stand. But a sandaled foot jammed firmly against the side of his face pinned him to the ground.

"How clumsy of you to have fallen," he heard one of the men taunt. "We best take you to a place where you won't do yourself any more harm."

"Etiyopiya!" John Too gasped. "Etiyopiya!"

One of the men flashed the blade of a knife in front of John Too's eyes before nicking his lower lip.

"Blind men. Penniless cripples," he heard one of the two men mutter. "Not worth a single franc. But you, *my young friend—"*

John Too groaned as his arms were roughly bound behind his back and a ball of cloth stuffed into his mouth.

"You'll fetch a decent sum. Yes, a decent sum."

*

The allure of the sea was a paradox to Bin'ka, whose origins lay in a remote area of a landlocked country. Perhaps his infatuation stemmed from the years he'd run errands for Susenyo. The Djibouti harbor, after all, had been a constant part of his life. Fishermen, dockworkers, merchants, smugglers, and a faction of officers of the Ethiopian Navy had been mainstays of Susenyo's black-market empire. From diesel-powered warships transporting slaves down the coast to single-masted dhows silently running contraband under the cover of darkness, all those who did business upon the sea—and the sea itself—had been a part of Bin'ka's world since he'd been sold into slavery.

Still, Bin'ka found the sea's appeal confusing. What was it about the turquoise water that stirred his imagination and put thoughts of noble deeds in his head? And what was it about the sound of the waves that transported him to distant shores in search of his rightful place in the world? Truth be told, he didn't know. But the sounds, the smells, and the power of the waves instilled Bin'ka with a sense of worth. Holding on to that sea-spawned self-belief, Bin'ka tied a line from the dhow he'd booked passage on into port to one of the many bulkheads interspersed along the southernmost stretch of the Mogadishu pier.

"Wait for me," he told the solitary figure approaching from the stern.

"Wait for you?" the man asked.

Bin'ka eyed the weathered Somalian with irritation.

"That's what I paid you for," he grumbled.

"So, you did, my large friend." The man smirked fleetingly before bowing his head in deference. "But we agreed," the man continued, as he lifted his head to meet Bin'ka's gaze, "only till first light."

"Your point?" Bin'ka snapped.

The man placed his hands in front of his chest as though praying and said, "Forgive me, but I do not think you will be returning."

Bin'ka's first instinct was to grab the skinny fisherman by the throat and throw him into the harbor. But something in the man's tone, the way he offered his observation—casual, as though he were giving directions to a stranger—made him instead inquire into the man's reasoning.

"And why is that?" he asked, folding his arms across his chest.

The man bent and checked the knot Bin'ka had tied around the cleat before he spoke.

"Though you said little when you paid me to bring you here, it doesn't take a seer to understand what you've come to do."

Bin'ka followed the man's eyes as the fisherman surveyed the lights of the city.

"You insisted we dock after nightfall on the outer fringe of the port. You instructed me to wait for your return with the boat ready to sail."

The man's weather-lined face was nearly black, his eyes darker than his skin. The man took stock of Bin'ka's appearance.

"You are massive—but alone. From the weapons you carry, you are either a deserter from the army or a mercenary."

The man looked once more toward the city before he continued.

"Warlords rule here," he said with a nod. "Everything you see belongs to them."

The man gazed into Bin'ka eyes as his finger pointed first to the short sword sheathed at Bin'ka's side and then to the handle of the gun peeking from inside Bin'ka's robe.

"You've come to take something from one of them." The man paused before cautiously adding, "I fear you will not succeed."

Take something from one of them. Bin'ka mulled the words. *Shange bahr. She may already be dead.*

"I paid you for a service, not your—" Bin'ka grunted "—wisdom."

"As you say," the man replied with a slight bow of his head. "I was only—"

"Be here when I return," Bin'ka warned. "That is all you need do."

"Yes, certainly," the man replied.

Bin'ka followed the man's gaze as the fisherman turned his attention to the sky.

"The moon is troubled by clouds," he observed. "I feel there will be a change in the wind before long." Shifting his attention to Bin'ka, he asked, "What course should I plot upon your return? It would be helpful to know in case you—"

The fisherman's voice trailed off as he looked to the open sea.

What course? Bin'ka clutched the hilt of his sword. He hadn't thought of where he would take Sarah if she were still alive. Back to Djibouti?

Down the coast to Kenya? Or somewhere along a deserted stretch of the Somalia coast, where they— *Where they? They?*

He suddenly wondered if he wasn't mad, if it wasn't lunacy to try to save a woman he barely knew from a city ruled by violence.

"Time passes," he heard the fisherman mutter. "Night will fast be gone."

Bin'ka grasped the bulkhead and, using it as leverage, pulled himself up to the dock.

"Be here when I return," he gruffly told the fisherman. "If you leave—"

He slapped the hilt of his sword. The man smiled and bowed his head.

*

Bin'ka watched the dhow sail out of the harbor from the darkened alcove of a bullet-pocked building some two hundred meters up from the harbor's edge. A torrent of curse words flowed through his thoughts as he visualized cutting the fisherman's throat. But revenge would have to wait. Sarah, according to Talia's informants, was nearly a half kilometer away. And he would need to cross some lesser warlord's territory to reach her. And the fisherman—loath as he was to admit it—had been right: time was passing. Night would too soon give way to day.

*

Sarah remembered what the psychiatrist assigned to her case had told her about the human psyche: "There is an element of defense within the human mind where a person who has suffered violent trauma is able to create an alternate existence for themselves, allowing the individual to cope with an emotionally devastating situation that might otherwise prove fatal to said individual's mental health."

But she wondered—as she had so often of late—if that statement was true or just something the doctor had concocted to make her feel better. Or perhaps it was a standard spiel recited to a patient in the custody of the court to make the judge believe the doctor was an expert of his or her profession. No matter how hard Sarah tried to find the sanctuary the doctor had spoken of—a quiet, peaceful place where the songs of angels could be heard—she could not even come close to obtaining entry into the promised mystical, cerebral domain.

Having been repeatedly raped and sodomized by General Adhib, she no longer clung to any hope of finding a paradise within her mind. Nor did she believe she would ever be free of suffering. God's plan for her was clear now—abundantly clear. She was to die by her own hand and, in doing so, condemn her soul to eternal damnation. Only then would the suffering she had both caused and endured come to an end.

She had envisioned her body broken on the street below her room many times over the course of the past few days. And if it hadn't been for the old woman, she would have already thrown herself to the cobblestones and ended her pathetic existence. But each time Sarah contemplated suicide, the woman seemed to materialize behind her, jabbering at her in a tongue she could not understand while pulling on her wrist to keep her from jumping out the window.

"Go away!" she'd scream at the woman. "Leave me alone!"

But the woman wouldn't leave her alone.

At first, Sarah assumed the general had placed the woman in charge of Sarah's wellbeing. But the more Sarah interacted with the woman, the more she came to understand that it wasn't Sarah's safety that concerned the old woman. The woman's only interest was ensuring someone else's safety; the woman grew frantic each time the general summoned children into the room as leverage.

Sarah had soon learned that simply fornicating with the general was not sufficient. Whenever she balked at some of the perversions he demanded, the general would clap his hands and a few children would be paraded into the room, their hands and ankles bound in barbed wire.

"Which shall I kill to teach you obedience?" he would ask.

She would look at the children and see terror in their eyes. And the old woman would tremble, her eyes filling with tears as she pounded a fist on her chest. Sarah had come to believe the general was holding one of the old woman's family members—a grandchild or nephew, she imagined—on the threat of death or torture if the old woman didn't carry out the general's wishes.

The general had come before sunrise on her third day as his sex slave, bursting into her room and ordering her to spread her legs. He smelled of wine and sweat. He appeared agitated and, in her opinion, borderline insane. She obeyed but was too slow to comply with a more perverse demand.

Four boys were immediately ushered into the room. An instant later, the soldier who'd escorted them slammed the butt of his rifle into the face of the nearest boy, bashing the weapon into the child's head until the floor was covered in the goo of his brain. Sarah screamed and crumpled to the floor. The general kicked her in the stomach and shouted for her to obey. Before she could rise, a second boy was struck, blood gushing from his nose and mouth as he fell to his knees. The old woman rushed to Sarah's side and helped her to her feet. Sarah immediately pleaded for the general to stop, promising she would do as he wished. The general laughed, but mercifully ordered the soldier to stand down. He then raped Sarah on the floor next to the boy's shattered skull.

It was in that moment that Sarah had understood her future. Suicide was to be her means to salvation. God had made her fate clear: burning in the fires of Hell was her only escape from her life of sin.

Focusing on the slatted shutters covering the window, Sarah's thoughts flitted disconnectedly between God, the old woman, the general, her sins, and the unattainable refuge the psychiatrist had spoken of. *Twelve.* There were twelve slats to each shutter. *Twelve.* The number meant something, but she couldn't pinpoint its significance. Twelve people, twelve objects, twelve years, twelve months.? The connotation escaped her. Unconsciously, she put her hand to her neck, where she had always worn her silver cross. At the very moment her hand grasped nothing, a soft light filtered through the slats of the shutter. What little solace she had found in thoughts of suicide disappeared. The purity of the moon's light was a mockery. Unable to contain her anguish, she tilted her head toward the ceiling and screamed. A hard cuff to her shoulder shocked her.

"*Askat! Askat!*"

Alarmed by the intensity of the old woman's anger, Sarah grabbed her wrists and pushed her away.

"Leave me alone!" she screamed. "Let me—!"

Sarah flinched as the door to her room burst open and two armed soldiers rushed in. A moment later, General Adhib followed, a scowl on his face.

"Can you not keep her quiet?" the general snarled at the old woman. "And you."

Sarah flinched as the general raised a hand as if to strike her. With a grunt, he lowered his arm and shook his head.

"Filth," he muttered. Again, the general shook his head as he took stock of Sarah's appearance. "Why has she not been bathed and given a change of clothes?" he grumbled.

Out of the corner of her eye, Sarah saw the old woman offer a trembling bow.

"She smells like a whore."

Sarah recoiled with a start when the general reached out and grabbed a handful of her robe.

"You dare keep yourself clothed in robes stained with my scent?" he bellowed. "You do this to mock me?" he spat. "Is that your intent, to present yourself as a common whore? To ridicule me with your filth? And you," he growled, turning his attention to the old woman. "You allow her to do this when you know I hold—?"

Sarah gasped as the general abruptly lunged at the old woman and slapped her hard across the face. With a whimpering moan, the woman fell to the floor, where she babbled and pawed at the general's boots. With a sharp kick to the woman's side, the general pushed her away.

"You disgust me," he sneered. Turning to Sarah, he spat, "And you are worse."

Sarah cowered when the general raised his hand and took a step toward her. Anticipating a blow to her face, she covered her head with her forearms.

"Virgin," she heard the general scoff. Sarah cautiously lowered her arms. Apprehensively, she looked into the general's eyes.

"You are a great disappointment to me," he said.

"More so to myself," she muttered.

The general frowned. "I paid money for a virgin—a white virgin! And what did I buy?" He squeezed her breast harshly, then pushed her away. "A dour-faced cow with the scent of pig."

With a shake of his head, he turned to leave but then abruptly spun back around. With an accusatory finger pointed at her face, he shouted, "I have been cheated! Cheated! You are not worth a tenth of what I paid! You are like fucking a— like fucking a— a crippled goat that hasn't eaten in a week!"

Sarah's mind went blank as she listened to the man rant. She felt numb in both body and mind. *Cheated.* She briefly acknowledged the word. *Cheated…*

"I should send you back to Akmir and demand my money back! But even he, a man who would sell his own sister for a franc, would say there is no profit to made from the likes of a pig-smelling whore! He would tell me—"

Sarah averted her eyes as the general scrutinized her with an expression of disdain.

"He would say, 'Only a drunken beggar would lie with one such as this. Why not take her to the soldiers' barracks to make your money back?'"

Sarah could hear the general talking but blocked out his words. *Twelve* slid in and out of her thoughts like a needle, sewing fragmented images into a tapestry depicting a paradise. Angels—luminous beings with wings of silver-tinted clouds—hovered above a landscape lush with flowers and fruit trees. Ribbons of sunlight cascaded atop lakes and rivers of the deepest blue. Animals intermingled in the tawny valleys between tree-covered mountains capped in snow. Gentle breezes carried the voices of songbirds through an azure sky. *Twelve.* She focused on the slatted shutters and the beam of moonlight beyond. *Salvation. Redemption.* She felt the allure of the words in the pale, pure light. Sarah made the sign of the cross over her chest and leaped toward the window.

She was tackled from behind and pulled to the floor. Frantic to attain the paradise contained within the moonlight, she kicked and punched her assailant. She could hear the old woman whimper with every blow, but she would not let her go.

"Get up!" the general roared. Grabbing a handful of her hair, he jerked Sarah to her feet.

"You didn't like what I said?" he taunted. "You would rather split your skull on the street below than spend a night pleasuring my men?"

Sarah stared stonily at the general, then slapped him hard across the face. Rage flashed in the man's eyes. Just then, a booming explosion shook the shuttered window at Sarah's back.

"General!"

General Adhib sneered at Sarah before turning to address the soldier who'd run into the room.

"What is it?" he growled.

"The barracks are under attack!"

"What? Who?"

"We don't—"

"How many?"

"I'm not—"

"Idiot!"

Sarah saw the soldier's face flash with fear as the general strode toward him.

"Give me your walkie-talkie!" the general ordered.

Sarah tried to edge toward the window, but the old woman had hold of her ankles.

"Where is Major Jama?" the general shouted as he ripped the walkie-talkie from the soldier's grasp. "Come with me!" he ordered.

Sarah bent and punched one of the old woman's wrists.

"Whore!"

Sarah immediately straightened. The general, she saw, was looking at her with an expression of contempt.

"You two," he said, nodding to the soldiers who'd preceded him into the room. "Have your fill of the woman before I send the rest of your comrades."

Sarah felt her stomach turn when the general smiled at her.

"She is a whore," he said to the men. "Treat her as such."

*

Twelve. Sarah focused on the shuttered window as the men ripped the robe from her body and pushed her toward the bed. *Twelve.* She heard the two men laughing and grunting like pigs as they pawed her breasts and slid their fingers between her thighs and buttocks. *Twelve.* She watched a band of moonlight stream into the room as a man pressed his genitals against her lips and another forced her legs apart. *Twelve.* A man with a beard lay on top of her. *Twelve.* She blinked away tears. Moonlight faded to shadow. Her last shred of self-esteem evaporated when the man on top of her thrust inside her. *Twelve.* She wished she had died in the closet all those years ago. She wished her kidnapper had slit her throat. *Twelve.* The color red filled her eyes. A hard slap to her face brought the taste of blood. *Twelve.* The notion of suicide—suicide as salvation—superseded all her other thoughts and emotions. The struggle for survival ceased. She lay perfectly still. *Twelve.* She closed her eyes and prayed for the blood of the Lamb to wash over her. *Twelve.* The tapestry of paradise turned crimson with a choking cry. *Twelve.* She breathed deeply and willed Hell to take her. *Twelve.* She felt her body rise.

She opened her eyes. Satan had come.

"Hurry," he told her. "We must flee."

Wild-eyed, she looked for the flames of Hell. But there was no fire or brimstone. There were no lines of sinners wailing in pain. Instead, she saw puddles of blood and two men with their heads nearly severed from their necks. Satan set her gently on the floor and pushed a garment into her hands.

"Put this on," he said. "You'll have to clean up later."

Sarah looked down at herself and gasped. Her breasts, her stomach, and her thighs were covered in blood. She put her hands to her face and screamed. Satan clamped a hand over her mouth.

"Quiet!" he hissed.

Sarah stared into Satan's black face. His eyes, oddly, were full of compassion.

"Get dressed. Hurry."

Dazed, Sarah watched Satan move toward the window. In a terrifying display of power, the ruler of Hell ripped the shutters from their moorings and threw them out the window. When he turned and beckoned her to join him, she immediately complied, slipping into the robe he had given her as she made her way toward him.

When he asked, "Can you climb down on your own?" she didn't understand.

"The rope," he said, motioning with his head to the window ledge. "Do you need help?"

"*La!*"

Sarah recoiled when she felt a hand grab her ankle. She looked down to find the old woman struggling to her knees and staring into her face.

"*La!*" the woman shouted as she grabbed Sarah's arm. Rising unsteadily to her feet, she yelled, "*La!*"

Satan brushed Sarah to the side and bashed the old woman across the chest. With a heartbreaking moan, the woman crumpled to the floor. Sarah saw Satan glance toward the door before he turned his attention to her.

"Go!" he urged. "Go!"

"*Sa'eidni!*" the old woman croaked.

Sarah felt the strength in Satan's arms as he ushered her to the window and put a rope in her hand. His touch was gentle when he lifted her and set her on the window ledge.

"*Sa'eidni! Sa'eidni!*"

Startled by the ferocity of the old woman's shouts, Sarah nearly lost her balance. But Satan grabbed her shoulder and kept her from falling. As she turned to thank him, he took a gun from the waist of his robe and fired it. Out of the corner of her eye, she saw the old woman come to a halting stop. A dark stain appeared on the woman's maroon robe just before she fell to the floor. Satan cast his eyes downward when he turned back to address her.

"Go now!" he commanded.

And then he slid an arm beneath Sarah's rump and cradled her out the window. Gently, he lowered her to a section of the wall a few meters below the ledge.

"Take the rope with both hands."

She'd never imagined Satan could sound so kind. The caring tone of his voice brought a fleeting smile to her face.

"Go down one step at a time," he instructed. "But move as fast as you can." He glanced over his shoulder before adding, "I'll be right behind you."

*

Sarah squatted next to one of the shutters Satan had thrown from the window and cautiously placed a finger atop the crack running down the center. *Twelve.* The twelve slats were broken, each split down the middle. She glanced above her to see Satan descending the wall. *He did this*, she thought. She lightly ran her finger along the break in the wood, wondering why he had. She sensed it was important she know. *Twelve, twelve, twelve—twelve what?* Automatic weapon fire off in the distance broke her concentration. Voices—excited, angry—burst into the night sky from the window above. Satan, she saw, had almost completely rappelled down the side of the building. He was jerking his arm sideways and looking at her as though he wanted to harm her. Was he angry?

"Run!" he yelled. "Run toward the harbor!"

The urgency in his tone alarmed her. She looked in every direction but didn't see a harbor. *Water!* her thoughts screamed. *Where's water?* Satan jumped from the wall and landed next to her. Gunshots rang out and bullets traced a line in the ground to her right. Satan grabbed her by the arm and pulled her close to him at another burst of gunfire. More bullets pummeled the ground both left and right of where they stood. Sarah heard Satan grunt and felt his body flinch. Then they were running.

Sarah tried as best she could to keep up with Satan, but she found she could barely move her legs fast enough. More than once, Satan had to slow down and jerk her forward. They traveled down a dark street that ran between rows of squat, flat-roofed buildings. Behind them, she could hear men shouting and sporadic gunfire. She wondered how far they needed to travel. She was tired, and as of yet there was no sign of a harbor. Satan's breathing was labored, and the way he moved seemed unsteady. She could sense they were slowing. She hoped they would be able to rest before—

Satan came to an abrupt stop as torches appeared in the street ahead of them. The muscles in his arm tensed, and he pushed her toward a building. When he glanced over his shoulder, she did the same. A dozen or more torches were bobbing in the street behind them. Even in the wavering firelight, she could see that the men holding the torches were armed.

"Your cross," Satan blurted.

Sarah was dumfounded. "What?"

Sarah heard a boom, and then a piece of the building they were next to shattered right above their heads. Satan covered her with his arms and pushed her forward. She heard a man shout, *"La!"* before more gunfire erupted. She almost fell when Satan nudged her sharply from behind.

"Hurry. Move," he ordered.

Bullets raked the side of the building ahead of her. She hesitated.

"There!" she heard him exclaim. "In the alley!"

Her shoulder scraped the wall as he swept by. His massive hand swallowed hers when he took hold of it and pulled her into a corridor between two buildings. She heard bullets explode just above and behind them. A few particles stung her neck. She yanked on Satan's hand.

"Stop!" she wailed. "No more. No more."

He grabbed her chin with powerful fingers and looked into her eyes.

"We have to keep moving! They're right behind us!"

"What does it matter?" she sobbed. "I'm ready. I'm ready." She squeezed his forearm. "I want damnation."

Without warning, Satan jerked Sarah ahead of him and pushed her forward. She turned and slapped his hand from her shoulder.

"Send me to Hell!" she screamed. "I deserve it! I deserve to go!"

Satan pushed her hard against the wall and pinned her to it.

"What's wrong with you?" he roared. "Have you lost your mind?"

Sarah stared deep into Satan's eyes as she searched for the answers to his questions. Surely he knew what was wrong with her. Surely he was aware of her sins. With a shake of her head, she blurted, "You know what I've done! You know the sins I've committed!"

"What?" he bellowed.

Gunfire heralded another round of bullets ripping into the walls around them. Satan grabbed Sarah by the shoulders and pushed her ahead. Reluctantly, she jogged toward the end of the alley, with him following right behind. When torches appeared at the far end of the alley, Satan pulled her to a stop.

"Trapped," he muttered.

Sarah ducked and covered her ears when Satan raised a gun next to her shoulder and fired two shots toward the end of the alley.

"Over there!" he shouted.

Satan herded her across the alley toward a dark recess. He pushed her low to the ground and then rammed a darkened area with his shoulder. Sarah heard wood splinter. Several men with torches ran toward them.

Satan yanked her to him. Blinking her eyes, she fell against him.

"Your cross," he said in labored voice.

Sarah glanced over her shoulder. The approaching torches cast an eerie glow on the alley wall. "My what?"

"Your cross," he repeated. He pulled her farther into the darkness. "Listen."

She flinched when he squeezed her shoulders.

"Your cross."

Her body trembling, she shook her head and said, "I don't know what you mean."

"Your cross. The one you wore around your neck."

Sarah's lips parted as though she had something to say. She placed a hand to her throat.

"I wrapped it around a latch," he struggled to say. "On a door. Close to the harbor."

The nearby sound of angry voices made it difficult for Sarah to concentrate on what Satan was telling her. Vaguely, she retained the words *cross, latch,* and *harbor.* But something was wrong. By the light of the torches, Sarah could just make out the features of Satan's ebony face. Blood oozed from the side of his mouth. She could see red-tinged bubbles at the corners of his lips as he spoke.

"You need to find it. They're waiting for you." He took a ragged breath and wiped his mouth with the back of his hand. "Up the street from the old fort."

Cross, latch, harbor, fort. Cautiously, Sarah placed a finger to the line of blood trickling down his chin.

"You're hurt?"

Satan cupped her face between his hands and looked deep into her eyes.

"You must run!" he told her. "Run as though the devil is chasing you!"

He pulled a sword from the waist of his robe and turned toward the doorway. Men had gathered at the entrance. The alley wall at their backs looked to be on fire.

"Run!" Satan yelled as a man burst into the room.

Sarah cowered and screamed as Satan's sword sliced through the air and cut into the man's neck. Retreating from the spray of blood, she stumbled backward.

"Say my name!" she heard Satan yell.

Sarah bumped into something solid just as a gun fired. As she struggled to regain her balance, a man screamed. An instant later, she saw a figure fall to the floor.

"Run, Sarah! Run!"

Metal clashed and men cursed, but Sarah barely noticed. Muttering the name *Sarah*, she looked at her hands as though they were a stranger's before turning her attention to the powerful man wielding a sword.

"Bin'ka?" she whispered. She took a tentative step toward him. "Bin'ka?" she shouted. "Bin'ka!"

Their eyes briefly met as Bin'ka glanced over his shoulder. Then, in the flash of a close-fired gunshot, he was down on one knee, blood gushing from his shoulder.

"Bin'ka!" she screamed.

With a ferocious upward swing of his sword, Bin'ka struggled to his feet. He'd barely fended off the thrust of a spear when an attacker hacked a long steel blade into his upper arm. Bin'ka recoiled for a moment and then with a guttural scream bulled his way forward. Sarah stood mesmerized, in awe of the speed of Bin'ka's blade as he swung it mercilessly at his assailants. Back he drove them, back toward the doorway and the alley beyond, where the fire of the torches had turned the dark of night into hell-like day.

Sarah reached out toward Bin'ka as tantalizing images of escape passed through her head. Bin'ka would soon dispatch the rabble sent by General Adhib, and she and he would gain their freedom. By boat or plane, they would leave the cursed city of Mogadishu and head home. *Home.* The word was a paradox of paradise and Hell: the Virgin Mother welcoming her into a life of prayer and servitude contrasted against a past steeped in blood and sin. *Home.*

Where, she wondered, did that exist? And as she reached for Bin'ka, to draw him near, to touch his wounds and heal them if she could, she wondered if home included him, if it *could* include him. The notion fanned a flickering ember of hope in her heart.

The ear-splitting staccato of an automatic weapon jolted her out of her thoughts. Horror-stricken, she watched Bin'ka stagger backward, his bloodstained sword falling from his hand. Wild-eyed, his face spattered in blood, he turned and rasped, "Run!" Then he lurched back toward the door and fell into two men trying to squeeze through the entrance.

To the sounds of gunfire and angry men and her own wail of grief, Sarah turned and fled, feeling and sensing her way through the building where Bin'ka had brought her, until she found herself on the threshold of a double door. With a surge of adrenaline, she pushed it open.

*

The street Sarah faced was a murky collection of shapes and shadows. Frantic, she looked left and right. Her eyes were drawn to a faint light running along the underbelly of the night sky off her right shoulder. Dawn was approaching. The harbor lay eastward. Without hesitation, she ran toward the light.

The image of Bin'ka's bloody, pain-riddled face lingered in her mind as she scoured the buildings for a glint of silver. The cross—*her* cross—how had he come by it? How did—? Her thoughts came to a halt when a half dozen torches appeared some fifty meters ahead. Her stomach churned at the sound of male voices shouting her name. "Sarah! Sarah! Sarah!" Their whoops, hollers, and laughter set her mind spinning. She fled to the opposite side of the street and turned into the first alley she came upon.

As she ran down a narrow passageway strewn with litter, she recalled how Teimbaka had led her through the streets and alleys of Mogadishu in search of Claire and Dirk. They had endured months of war to reach the city in hopes of finding two people who, unbeknownst to them, were thousands of miles away. Why had God engaged her in such folly? Was the ordeal to reach Mogadishu part of His punishment for her? Had He inserted thoughts of Dirk into her head so she might experience the aching hollowness of unfulfilled desire? How could God be so cruel? And worse, why was it necessary for God to take the life of Teimbaka in the process of punishing her? Did He intend she carry the burden of Teimbaka's death to her grave? And Bin'ka—was he too to be part of her eternal misery? Was his bloody death to be emblazoned upon her soul as the fires of Hell melted her flesh?

Bin'ka. She'd barely known the giant of a man. Yet he'd come for her. Saved her. Twice he'd gathered her into his arms and swept her away from harm. And now he, like Teimbaka, was dead, suffering a violent end so that she might live on.

Live on. What a farce that two men of noble fiber need perish so a sinner who had committed unspeakable acts might survive. It was a sham of faith that could not be justified as the will of God. No, Sarah thought, the mercilessness God had shown in the brutal deaths of the two men was abhorrent, if not unforgivable.

Unforgivable. She had been taught that there was no act that could not be forgiven. Murder, rape, kidnapping, even torture—she had experienced it all. But from the moment the Virgin Mother had entered her life, she been asked to forgive the trespasses against her.

Forgive. A life of prayer, sacrifice, and devotion to God's word. What had it brought her? Unspeakable misery.

The stench of urine brought Sarah to an abrupt halt. Disoriented, she blinked to focus. A figure dressed in a ragged T-shirt was pissing on the alley wall. The man—dark-skinned and young—stared at her with a lecherous grin on his face. He tucked his penis inside his shorts. A moment later, he pointed a knife at her chest.

"*Ferengi,*" he muttered. "*Abaidh bashara.*"

The man was suddenly next to her, pressing the knife against her throat as he pawed at her breasts with his free hand. Repulsed, Sarah staggered back and fell against the wall. The man leaned in and pressed his mouth against hers. Sickened by the feel of his tongue on her lips, she pushed him. The man stumbled backward but quickly regained his balance. He circled the knife in the air in front of her, then sprang toward her.

Sarah kicked. The man came to a stuttering stop, his free hand clutching his crotch.

The knife dangled loosely in the man's hand. Just like the knife she'd taken from her neighbor the day she'd escaped from the closet he'd kept her in. Rage coursed through every fiber of her body. She wrenched the knife from her assailant's hand, slashed at the man's crotch, and then, with all the strength she could muster, plunged the blade into his throat.

Sarah felt the warm spatter of blood on her face as a gunshot echoed down the alley. She heard a bullet whistle past her ear. She looked back down the alley. Torch flames filled the entranceway. Men were yelling her name. A second shot rang out, the bullet grazing her shoulder. A third bullet hit the alley wall behind her. She started running.

Sarah ran the length of the alley to where it ended at a cross street. Out of breath, she looked east. The glimmer of light she'd seen in the sky minutes before had grown into layered tones of yellow and red. Dawn was near. The city would soon awaken. Daylight would expose her. Bin'ka's words flooded into her thoughts: *cross, latch, harbor, fort.* Remembering the urgency in his voice, she raced toward sunrise in search of a glint of silver.

She glimpsed the uppermost turret of an old fort just as a group of armed men streamed out a side street ahead of her. Her way suddenly blocked, she searched left and right for an alley to escape into. But there was none. A glance over her shoulder revealed a dozen armed assailants racing toward her. Trapped, she brought the knife close to her chest and closed her eyes. The damnation she'd petitioned Satan for was nearly upon her.

A burst of automatic gunfire followed by a chorus of jeering laughter startled her into casting about once again for an escape route. A broken door hanging precariously in the entranceway of a building on the far side of the street caught her eye. The flimsy wooden barrier—constructed of branches bleached white-grey by sun and salt air—was primitive, and the building itself—a squat narrow structure with no windows—looked more like an oversized closet than a place where she might find refuge. Still, with little choice, Sarah nervously shifted the knife between her hands and then sprinted toward it.

A burst of gunfire brought an explosion of bullets at her feet. Reaching the building in a panic, she flung the door open and rushed inside. Instantly she knew she had made a mistake. The box of a room—bare save for mounds of sand in the corners and a lone door in the center of the back wall—was no larger than the bed of a pickup truck.

Sarah shook her head, not knowing whether to laugh or cry. Surely God was mocking her. She stared at the door at the back of the room, knowing what God wanted from her. Making the sign of the cross, she walked the few steps and pulled the door open. As she knew it would, the door revealed a closet. With a slight bow of her head, she stepped inside and pulled the door shut behind her. Squatting to the floor, Sarah brought her knees up against her chest and placed the knife on the floor under her thigh. As she waited for her pursuers to arrive, she rested her head against the back wall and closed her eyes. When the floor suddenly gave way, she screamed.

24

TEIMBAKA DISMISSED THE sound of gunfire with a tired sigh. Fleetingly, he wondered if Mogadishu would ever find peace, if the people of the accursed city would ever know a day without bloodshed. With a slight shake of his head, he turned toward the rising sun. Finding some small solace in the warmth on his face, he willed his mind blank. Drained both mentally and physically, he found thought burdensome. But the continuing sporadic bursts of gunfire would not allow his mind to rest. The Mother, he concluded, had washed her hands of Mogadishu long ago. As had the Father. The city belonged to the Serpent now. And it was teetering on the precipice of hell.

Long ago, the ancient port might have been something grand. Exactly when the city had been anything other than a cesspool of warlords and slavers, he didn't know. Still, as he stood in the shallows of the harbor with the morning breeze blowing off the ocean and the rising sun upon his face, he sensed the energy the city must have once possessed and felt sorrow at the state in which it now found itself. This dull throb of regret channeled his thoughts toward Claire. Suddenly, the morning felt cold. His feeling of regret multiplied tenfold.

Little by little, the constant lapping of waves at his knees prodded him from melancholy and reminded him why he had traveled from the alley: there was no longer a reason for him to be alive. Claire was gone, the spirit-elephants were doomed, he himself had been abandoned by the Mother, John Too had deserted him. The beetles were dead. He had watched them burn. What more proof did he need that his life had become worthless? Hope was dead, extinguished when Claire was taken.

He took a moment to reflect upon the role he had played in everything that had transpired. It was then that the soft murmur of the waves became nagging whispers. He was nothing, the voices said. Claire was dead, they said. Hope was dead. The beetles were dead. And though the waves spoke with a soft and soothing voice, their message was maddening. Distressed and despondent, he pressed his hands against his ears to block the voices out. But like the water seeping into his pores, the whispers flowed into his soul.

Teimbaka dropped to his knees as an image of Claire's silver cross sinking into sand manifested in his thoughts. He could feel his spirit wane as he watched the symbol of Claire's faith slowly disappear. Raising his arms out to his sides, he fell forward. The sea accepted him with barely a splash. He sank to the ocean floor.

Gradually the whispers of the waves diminished to a rhythmic, unintelligible murmur. Teimbaka felt a blanket of calm envelop him. The solitude of the moment was bliss. Embracing the sensation of becoming nothing, he contemplated the ending of his life. Convinced he would find peace in death, he opened his mouth and let the water rush in.

Having followed him through the streets of Mogadishu, the Serpent slithered into the sea and wrapped around Teimbaka's chest. As it tightened its coils, Teimbaka experienced the sickening sensation of suffocation. His body, roused from its false sense of tranquility, began to contort. As he choked on the water pouring down his throat, he felt a cold aura of darkness surround him. Faced with the last moment of life, he summoned his most precious memory: Claire, rising from prayer, her face awash in moonlight, beckoning with an outstretched hand. Teimbaka reached to grasp it, wishing nothing more than to die in her embrace. There was a pull on his arm. He broke the surface of the water, sputtering for air.

"Be gone!" boomed the voice of a child.

Feeling light-headed as his chest was constricted, Teimbaka began to lose consciousness.

"Do as I command!" the boy bellowed.

Unconsciousness came to Teimbaka with the heartbreaking sensation of Claire's hand slipping from his.

*

Juba stared at the two lines she'd scratched in the dirt. Unlike the lines she'd drawn with a stick a day ago, these had been drawn with her antelope horn, and they did not convey the same sense of emptiness. The nearer of the two—short and deep—denoted her immediate objective. The farther—longer and shallow—signified a much more protracted challenge. With a tap of the horn atop the shorter line, she studied the faces of the animals around her. The eyes of the hyenas glowed metallic shades of red, green, and yellow, depending on where the animal stood or sat in the light of the small fire she'd built. Juba found the effect otherworldly.

"This," she explained, glancing down at the short line, "is Blue-head." She paused long enough to make eye contact with each hyena before continuing. "And this," she said with a tap to the longer line, "is the ivory he takes."

With two swift swipes of her hand, she erased the shorter line and then did the same to the longer.

"They must be no more," she told them. "You understand? It must end."

*

Talia stood at the window of Adiam's third-floor office with a lit cigarette in hand. Drawing deeply on it, she looked south across the port until she located the bow of a certain freighter. Then she smiled and slowly exhaled.

Inshallah was due to sail within the hour. The cache of ivory stored within the false bottoms of a score of shipping containers stacked on board would reap millions. *Inshallah*—"God willing." An apt name. What more did the almighty have in store for her? Time would tell.

In a few week's time, *Inshallah* would dock at the Port Elizabeth/ Newark harbor. Alexis Taylar would receive the first of many planned ivory shipments. A week later—assuming *Jameel* departed Wilmington on schedule—a second shipment of tusks would be loaded aboard that freighter and sent back across the Atlantic. The profits from the two shipments would be considerable—enough to acquire the armaments she needed. Her dream of chiseling out a kingdom for herself would be closer to fruition. But obstacles remained.

Akmir—though hundreds of miles away and seemingly occupied with taking control of Mogadishu—was an immediate threat. She'd heard how angry he'd gotten at the double-cross over the cache of tusks. And though she placed the blame for the soured business arrangement squarely upon the Sudanese-Arab—the Mosi fellow with the blue turban—apparently Akmir didn't see it that way. From what Talia had heard, he'd sworn to kill her, his rage multiplied tenfold by what he deemed an unforgivable affront to his manhood. Outmaneuvered by a woman. Talia drew deeply on her cigarette and chuckled.

Adiam and the Consortium—each nearly synonymous with the other—would also need to be dealt with. The group presented an entirely different problem than Akmir. Where Akmir took a personal approach to business transgressions, Adiam and the Consortium structured their retribution more along economic lines. At least, as of late, that had been their chosen course for dealing with transgressions against their domain. But that hadn't always been the case, as she was well aware—at least not while Bin'ka had been in his prime.

The old days. Bin'ka. Talia tapped the ash from the tip of her cigarette and watched it float down to the street. Bin'ka—neither she nor Adiam had heard from him since he'd flown back to Somalia after what Adiam described as a strange conversation at his café. What had been urgent enough to send him back to where he'd been imprisoned? And what was he hoping to accomplish in Mogadishu, a city on the brink of all-out civil war?

If Akmir could not succeed in uniting the warlords, a bloodbath loomed. And that would benefit no one. Commerce in the port town would be interrupted. Profits would suffer. There would be a period of uncertainty until a ruling faction was established. Would Akmir prevail? She didn't know. And while a part of her completely disdained the man, she wondered if, in some manner, she could assist his rise to power. He would make for a strong partner in the ivory and slave trade. Something Adiam and the Consortium were not. As she took another drag off her cigarette, she decided she would send out feelers to her contacts in Moga-dishu. *Inshallah*—God willing—she could affect a shift in power.

Thinking of shifts in power, Talia directed her attention away from the freighter and toward the northern rim of the Djibouti harbor. A surge in the Eritrean war for independence was at hand. The sudden withdrawal of Soviet troops, which had been supporting the Ethiopian forces, had offered an opening for the Eritrean rebels to step up their offensive. Would the conflict spill over into Djibouti? Would harbor commerce be affected? And if so, for how long? All the more reason to see the conflict in Mogadishu end, for the two main ports serving the Horn of Africa—Djibouti and Mogadishu—were vital to the region. Landlocked countries such as Ethiopia and Sudan could not function without access to the sea. At least one port would need to stay open.

Talia took a final drag on her cigarette and flicked the stub into the air. She watched it tumble to the pavement, where it landed in an explosion of sparks and prompted thoughts of Sudan and Ethiopia; both were embroiled in civil war, as was the entire Horn of Africa. It was an opportune time for any shrewd, courageous businessman—or businesswoman. The upsurge in turmoil and violence corresponded to an uptick in all manner of commerce. Not only did the conflict offer the perfect opportunity to profit from arming each warring faction, it created the optimum framework for the acquisition and sale of unprotected men, women, and children. Nothing disguised a large-scale roundup of human beings better than war. The slave trade—her slave trade—should be running full bore. But it wasn't. Because Adiam frowned on the practice—which meant the remaining members of the Consortium also wanted nothing to do with it. Which left Talia scrambling for secretive ways in which to transport human cargo.

Lighting another cigarette, she weighed the pros and cons of putting the profit from the elephant tusks toward the purchase of armaments or a freighter. With a freighter of her own, she could carry whatever cargo she saw fit and sail wherever she wished. As it stood now, with the Consortium dictating sailing routes, there was little to no commerce between the Horn of Africa and the Arab world. A highly lucrative slave market was being ignored. She planned on changing that. But Adiam— If he caught wind of what she was planning, he would certainly try to stop her.

Although Adiam was old and sick and on the verge of senility—as every member of the Consortium was aware—he still retained a firm hold on power. Talia, once the old Arab's lover and confidant, was now an unwilling adversary. And though she respected Adiam for what he had accomplished—the worldwide heights to which he had elevated the Consortium—she reluctantly understood that for her dreams to become reality, he had to be eliminated.

But that would present a new dilemma. Talia, as the only female member of the Consortium, was held in low esteem. Adiam had been instrumental in placing her in a seat of power, and without his continued support, she knew the other members of the controlling board would seek her removal. And she knew her ouster would not necessarily come peacefully. Her presence on the board had rankled more than a few male egos, and she was acutely aware of the predicament she would find herself in if Adiam were no longer backing her. Still, there was no disputing that the man needed to go if she wished to be regarded as anything more than a token. She couldn't simply wait for age and sickness to bring an end to his reign. Of that she was certain. But how could she remove him without putting herself in jeopardy? Talia took a deep drag on her cigarette and contemplated her avenues of action as she stared into the turquoise waters of the gulf.

*

Salat Al-Fajr—the prayer before dawn—found Mosi in the midst of a prolonged bow to Allah. For thirty-one years—as far as he could recall—he had dutifully paid homage to the Blessed One by strictly following the doctrine of the Quran. And now he was being rewarded. *Allah, blessed be He, truly provides for those who devotedly follow His teachings. See how the Supreme One rewards me for my incontrovertible belief. I have become rich beyond my wildest dreams. And whom should I thank for these worldly blessings? The One Creator of course: Allah, the divine and all knowing.*

With a kiss to the soil, Mosi pushed up into a kneel. As he stared at the brightening horizon, he embraced the belief that the coming day held infinite promise. Allah would make certain the skies were clear and the wind calm. The rich woman's plane would land and take off without incident. With the Creator's blessing, the cave would be emptied of the remaining tusks and he would be handsomely paid. Within forty-eight hours, he would be home, reunited with his wife and two young boys. With the money from the tusks, he would move his family from an impoverished region in South Sudan to a more prosperous and stable region north of Khartoum. There, he would purchase land along the White Nile and build a home. His remaining years would be devoted to teaching his sons how to become faithful warriors of Allah. Life would be good. He and his family would live out their days in peace. And he would attain all these earthly blessings because of Allah, the One Creator, He who provides for those who follow his teachings without question.

Mosi rose from his knees and stood as the first hint of the rising sun brightened the dark line along the eastern horizon. With the first glimmer of sunlight came the stirring of a morning breeze. The whiff of death it carried brought a smile to Mosi's face. Allah had given him the wisdom to foresee that Akmir would send men to the cave in the middle of the night to take the tusks. But Mosi and the two men the rich woman had provided were prepared. Under the heat of the African sun, the carcasses would soon begin to rot. Today the flies would be as thick as a dust storm. Vultures would darken the sky. The cackling rant of hyenas would serve as a backdrop to all other sounds.

All the more reason to work quickly. He would radio the rich woman and tell her to give him more men to assist in the loading. He would also tell her to send two planes, because Akmir would be sending other men— fully armed fighters who would not be taken by surprise. These men would offer great resistance. They would not be vulnerable to ambush, as the others had been. Haste would be paramount today. The sooner the tusks were transferred from the cave and loaded onto the plane, the better it would be for all concerned. The woman would need to understand this. If she didn't, he would make her. For Allah had whispered to him during Salat Al-Fajr.

"Be on guard," the Divine One had told him. "For the minions of Jahannam are near. They are watching, Mosi. Waiting for the opportunity to swallow the souls of the unbelievers."

*

Akmir smoothed the front of his thawb before placing a black and white keffiyeh on his head. As was his daily custom, he then placed a stiletto in the left sleeve of his robe and stuffed his prized pearl-handled revolver into the fabric gathered at his waist. As he did every day, he hoped neither weapon would be needed. But life had taught him to be prepared. And he intended to follow life's teachings.

As Akmir adjusted the weapons hidden within his garment, he gave a fleeting thought to participating in Salat Al-Fajr. Perhaps he should thank Allah for the events that were about to unfold. How else could he explain General Adhib's sudden agreement to meet with the other warlords, who controlled 80 percent of the city? He had been after the man for months to hear his proposal for the unification of Mogadishu, yet every appeal had been rebuffed. The sale of the white woman was supposed to have secured the man's commitment. But it hadn't. And he had been uncertain as to his next step. Now, literally overnight, the staunchest holdout against a meeting between the governing warlords had experienced a change of heart. What reason could there be, other than divine intervention?

Akmir straightened his keffiyeh and sighed. No, this was not Allah's hand. Adhib was a pig, an unscrupulous heathen who paid homage to none but his own reflection. To think the man would be swayed by a word from the Divine One was folly. Something else was behind the general's change of heart.

No, not *something*. Someone. *Someone* had persuaded General Adhib to change his mind. But who? And, more importantly, what had they promised? Akmir placed a hand on the butt of the pearl-handled revolver as he contemplated the many possibilities. Nothing he could think of put him at ease.

*

Juba glanced over her shoulder as she dragged the rifle behind her. Struggling to keep the two ammunition belts balanced across her shoulders, she wondered what she would find in the earthen groove the rifle was leaving in its wake if she stopped to examine it. Would she find nothing in the shallow trench? Or would she find the kind of nothing that melds into everything? But there wasn't time to decipher meaning in the turned soil. Dawn was near. The plane would likely return at first light.

Next to Juba, mirroring the girl's every step, the hyena she'd named *Eimlaq*—Giant—eyed her with what she perceived as amusement.

"*You* could drag the rifle, you know," she said to the animal, "instead of looking at me with that stupid expression on your face."

Eimlaq offered no hint of a reply. But the animal did glance at the bulky weapon as if she'd understood what Juba had said.

Without warning, Juba stopped and took a deep breath. Eimlaq stopped as well.

"This is heavy," she sighed.

Again, Eimlaq offered no response.

Juba studied the hyena as the animal surveyed the section of mountain they were ascending. Blue-head was close, camped out in front of the cave with two men. All were killers.

She'd been awoken by gunfire in the middle of the night. At first she thought she was merely dreaming, reliving the gunfight that had killed the ranger, but then she'd grabbed the horn and raced toward the mountain.

The darkness had prevented her from taking in the full scope of what had happened, but the three corpses she'd stumbled over at the first truck she approached gave her some idea of what had taken place. Blue-head must have known the men were coming. Perhaps he'd heard the truck's engines from his vantage point up the mountain. Perhaps he'd used the thunder gun from the plane, the one that had ripped both the ranger and a score of hyenas to shreds.

After discovering a second group of dead bodies by another truck, Juba decided there was no point in searching near the other half dozen vehicles in the area. She assumed the men who'd driven them were dead. And if they weren't, they soon would be. Many kilometers from a city or village, there was nothing she could do for any man who might still be clinging to life. Dawn would bring scavengers. The air was ripe with the scent of blood. The area would soon be overrun with flesh eaters. No dead or living creature within the immediate area would be safe.

Blue-head was a merciless killer. He must die. Blue-head must die.

Juba flinched and nearly bit her tongue when she felt something wet brush the back of her hand. The action swept away her thoughts and brought her back to the present. Eimlaq growled.

"What?" Juba sharply whispered.

The hyena looked further up the mountain.

Juba nodded.

"Yes," she murmured. "We must get higher before daylight."

With a pat to the animal's head, she resumed her climb.

*

"Early day?"

Startled by a man's voice, Talia grabbed the doorjamb and came to an abrupt stop.

"Or do you find sleep as troublesome as I do?"

Limned in the light of a small candle, the man sitting at the patio table nearest the harbor looked like a ghost. When the ghost put a cigarette to his lips, Talia let out a sigh of relief. Gathering the edges of a white shawl close about her shoulders, she stepped out of the building.

"There's a chill to the air. You should be in bed."

"Ha! Bed!" Adiam blew a stream of smoke from his mouth and chuckled. "A device of torture swathed in layers of cotton sheets."

Talia sat down in the chair across from him.

"There was a time when you enjoyed bed." She gave him a coy smile when he looked into her eyes. "Or have you forgotten?"

Adiam turned his attention to the burning tip of his cigarette, his face sad as he stared into the embers.

"What is it?" she asked. "What do you see?"

He took a drag off the cigarette, then held it at her eye level.

"Remember our first? You were—" Overcome with a short bout of coughing, he put his hand to his mouth.

Talia touched his arm. "I'll get some water."

He grabbed her wrist.

"No," he wheezed. "I have this." He tapped the tumbler sitting next the candle.

Talia shook her head. "When are you going to listen to the—?"

"Oh, please. Don't mention those people. They make me," he said, chuckling, "sick."

Talia opened her mouth but said nothing. With a disdainful glance toward the amber liquid in the glass, she muttered, "Whatever you say."

Adiam lifted the glass and took a small sip of the contents.

"Bourbon," he uttered with satisfaction. "Small batch. Arrived last week." He held the glass out toward her. "Care to try?"

She waved him off.

"No, no. Much too early." She glanced at her watch before nodding to the tumbler. "I would hope that's your last. Or are you forgetting the morning meeting you scheduled?"

"Meeting. Business." He shook his head and took a drag off the cigarette. Glancing over his shoulder, he asked, "What lies beyond the lights of the harbor, Talia?" Brow furrowed, little streams of smoke escaping from his nose, he looked pointedly into her eyes. "Do you ever wonder?"

Talia cast her eyes downward as she ran a finger under the gold band of her wristwatch.

"Wonder?" she repeated, irritated. "It's not in our best interest to wonder. You know that as well as I." She tapped the tabletop with her knuckles. "Open shipping lanes are vital to business. It's in our best interest to—"

Adiam raised a hand for her to stop. He looked dismayed as he shook his head.

"We've lost something, you and I." He tapped the excess ash from the cigarette and stroked his chin. "Do you remember?" His expression brightened and he said, "The alleys of Khartoum. Do you remember how alive they felt? How the energy to survive flowed through our veins?"

"Khartoum?" she scoffed. "Alive?" She shook her head. "Your recollections aren't mine. You forget who we were. Two different worlds." She raised her eyebrows and nodded to him. "You—a visitor. Me—one of the condemned."

"You took my breath away the moment I saw you."

She laughed, uncomfortable.

"I was a piece of filth in a tattered robe sucking men's penises for coins. The only thing flowing through my veins was the semen of drunken soldiers and old men."

Adiam shifted in his seat and looked away.

"Does that make you uncomfortable?" She reached over and grabbed his wrist. "As I said, we were of two different worlds. You were established, the right arm of *the* black-market dealer. I was a tramp, a starving orphan in a city of orphans." She squeezed his wrist before letting it go. "Don't let it upset you. I don't. I use the memories to keep me focused. To keep me in tune with the goals I've set for myself."

"Goals," he said with a shake of his head. "Yes, how important they seem…" His words trailed off as he looked toward the sky. "Is this what brings you out so early? Goals? What is so important that it cannot wait until dawn?"

Talia pulled the shawl close about her shoulders and ran a hand through her hair.

"I thought I would check the shipping manifests before going to the markets. Fresh fruit and some bakery items might soften the edge of our more ill-tempered colleagues."

Adiam lifted his glass.

"To a woman's touch," he toasted. He winked before taking a sip from the glass. "Either a welcomed flourish or a devious diversion." He paused to stare into the bourbon. "A woman's touch," he said with a wistful chuckle. "Two edges of a sword."

Talia refused to meet his gaze, checking the time on her watch and glancing toward the harbor.

"You need to rest before the meeting," she said. "Why don't I take you—?"

"You needn't go to the trouble of checking the manifest. The *Inshallah* departed on the tide last evening. And the *Jameel* left the US two days ago." He studied her face as he took a long draw off his cigarette. "Your cargo is well on its way," he added with a smile.

"My cargo? You mean ours—the Consortium's."

Adiam flicked ash from the tip of his cigarette.

"Yes. Of course," he replied.

"And what's the *Jameel* carrying on its return voyage? More overpriced farm equipment?"

Adiam turned and looked toward the harbor without replying.

"Well, I suppose I should—"

"Beyond the harbor." Adiam raised his glass as he turned back to face her. "May his spirit find its way to Jannah."

Talia frowned and shook her head.

"You're not making any sense," she said. "I think you should—"

"It was the woman." Adiam took a drag off his cigarette and then flicked the butt into the street. "The downfall of so many." He sighed heavily. "A brother gone."

"What are you saying? Who's gone? What woman?"

Adiam raised the glass to his mouth. "To Bin'ka," he said. He closed his eyes as he took a sip.

"Bin'ka? He's—?"

"Did you know her?"

"Her?"

"The white woman. The one Akmir sold to Adhib. The one you purchased from the imam in Kenya."

Talia felt the blood rush from her face.

"I didn't—"

"But how could you have known?" he asked as he reached inside his coat pocket. Withdrawing a pack of Camels, he said, "Who would have guessed he'd fall in love with a slave?"

Adiam reached into his trouser pocket and withdrew a lighter. He kept his eyes focused on Talia as he put flame to tobacco.

"It's possible he wasn't aware, I suppose." Smoke gushed from his nostrils as he exhaled. "The touch of a woman," he said with a chuckle. "Ah, well. Perhaps they will meet in another life."

Talia focused on the tabletop as she tried to collect her thoughts. Adiam had instructed her to pay for the nun's freedom when they dealt with the imam for Bin'ka's release. She'd told him they had been outbid. How did he know it was *she* who'd outbid him? Her transaction had been handled by a third party.

"You must understand," she said after a lengthy pause. "It was simply—"

"Yes, everything has a price," he interjected. He tapped his index finger atop the table. "Yet, Susenyo never spoke of cost, the penalty for dealing in devil's merchandise."

"I never intended for Bin'ka to be hurt. I never imagined he had feelings for the woman. Otherwise I would have—"

"Done as you were instructed?"

She looked past him toward the harbor. The sky along the horizon was brightening. Sunrise was near.

"How did you hear?" she asked in subdued tone of voice.

Adiam held the lit cigarette up between them.

"From the alleys," he replied. "From those who want more than they have." He took a drag and blew smoke toward her. "Perhaps your memories are not as strong as you believe. The eyes and ears of those in need have multiplied tenfold since we first shared one of these," he said, nodding to the cigarette.

Talia glanced at the cigarette before casting her gaze downward.

"I was… The woman…" She fiddled with the edges of her shawl. "I will transfer the funds from her sale to the company's account and make—"

"No need," Adiam interjected. "No action is required on your part." He took a drag off the cigarette and coughed. "The members will decide the repercussions of your transgression. That is why I called for this morning's meeting. The undercurrent of change swirling around us must be addressed, don't you agree?"

"Change," Talia absently muttered.

She briefly met Adiam's gaze before shifting her attention toward the harbor. As a cloud of cigarette smoke billowed across her view, the sun glinted at the horizon.

"Will I have the opportunity to speak?"

"Of course," he replied. He lifted the glass off the table and swirled the bourbon. "Who knows," he said. "Perhaps the members will see things differently than I. Perhaps the merchandise you continue to deal in will be accepted." He shrugged. "Perhaps I will find that I am out of step."

"Nonsense," she was quick to say. "Your leadership has been invaluable." She lightly placed a hand atop his. "Especially in the months following the assassination attempt by Akmir. I'm sure—"

"Akmir," he repeated with a disdainful sigh. "A buzzard with dreams of becoming king."

"From what I hear—"

He slid his hand out from under hers.

"When one carcass has been picked clean, the search begins for another." Adiam gave her a probing look and raised his eyebrows. "And everything is fair game."

Talia studied his face as he took another drag from the cigarette. Was he warning her? How much did he know about her dealings with the old Arab? And would his suspicions be brought up at the meeting? She checked the time on her watch as she thought about the pending gathering; she did not anticipate a favorable outcome on any vote that involved punishment for her.

"I best get to the bakery before the croissants are all taken," she said abruptly. Rising out of her chair, she added, "I called yesterday for the pistachio sweetmeat strudel you're so fond of." She eyed the tumbler and said, "I hope you'll have some sort of appetite."

She didn't know what to make of his furrowed brow as he turned to face the rising sun.

"The day is upon us," she heard him mutter. "The light has risen."

*

Juba snapped a magazine clip into the assault rifle and sat back on her haunches. Eimlaq, mirroring her movement, sat down beside her. Ears held high and turned toward Juba, the big hyena bent toward the girl and sniffed the weapon. Juba flinched when the animal snorted.

"It must be," she whispered. With a pat to the gun, she added, "I can't do it on my own."

Eimlaq's lip curled up, partially exposing the animal's bone-crushing teeth. Juba tapped the horn fastened to her waist and shook her head.

"It ends," she murmured. "It has to."

She leaned toward the animal and stroked it behind the ear. When Eimlaq jerked her head and looked to the sky, Juba didn't understand. A moment later she heard the sound of a propeller plane. She looked skyward.

"Washed out" was the best way she could describe the color of the morning sky. It was a tin roof on a misty day, metal-drab and worn, its luster lost to the pounding of dust-driven rain. Juba shivered and rubbed her arms. The weapon she held across her thighs suddenly felt heavy. Running a finger across the rifle barrel, she tried to remember everything the ranger had taught her about firing guns, but she couldn't get past the image of his face. Where was he now? To her, the possibilities seemed as vast and dreary as the sky. *Where do you go when you die?* she wondered. She smoothed the front of her kanga as the question drifted through her thoughts—where do you go when you die? Why the answer seemed important, she didn't know. But she wondered nonetheless, and she pondered the notions of heaven, hell, and reincarnation until a black spot appeared in front of the clouds.

Juba assumed the dark, winged object gliding across the dreary vista was a plane. But when another winged shaped appeared next to it, and then two more, she realized the objects were vultures—a score or more. Within a moment, they'd formed the circle of the dead. Thirty seconds later, the washed-out panorama was colored with a twisting swath of ever-expanding black.

Juba reacted to Eimlaq's sudden growl by placing a hand on the hyena's side and uttering a sharp, "Shush." When the animal abruptly stood and loosed a cackling, angry call, Juba became cross.

"Stop it" she hissed.

Eimlaq was a blur of gnashing teeth and fur as she charged forward. Startled by the hyena's action, Juba shimmied back and readied the rifle to fire. A glimpse of blue rising over the rock ledge where she and Eimlaq had taken cover preceded a sudden eruption of gunfire. The sickening squeal that followed twisted her stomach. Swept up in a moment of sheer terror, Juba pointed the rifle toward the patch of blue and squeezed the trigger.

The AK-47 came alive in her hands. The weapon's recoil sent her sprawling backward. She clutched her side. Pain shot through her chest when she touched her ribs. A gasp for breath felt like a dagger thrust into her lung. Blinking tears from her eyes, she gazed up at the sky. The swirling mass of vultures made her think the world was coming to its end. Resigned to the thought that her life was slipping away, she rested her head upon the ground and sighed. A yelp of pain brought her upright.

Struggling to sit comfortably, Juba tilted from side to side until she found an angle where the pain in her ribs didn't take her breath away. As she reveled in a moment of relief, she heard a man's voice intermixed with an animal's whimper. With a groan, she managed to get on her hands and knees. Slowly, she crawled forward, sliding the rifle with her as she moved.

The ledge where Juba and Eimlaq had been waiting was little more than a small outcropping of shale and hard-packed dirt some twenty paces above the cave of tusks. Juba had intended to use the rocks along the perimeter as support for the AK-47. But now she used them as cover. Slowly leaning her head over the ledge, she quickly surveyed the scene below.

Juba ducked as gunfire strafed the line of rocks. Shards of stone and dust flew into the air. As she covered her head with her arms, she visualized what she had seen: Eimlaq on her side; Blue-head a few meters to the right, lying face down on the ground; two armed men standing several meters farther down the incline.

She had thought Blue-head's death would be joyous—a cause for celebration. She'd envisioned standing in front of the cave of tusks and screaming with pride. Instead, the moment was inconsequential, an afterthought, barely registering as a matter that held the slightest bit of importance. Robbed of her moment of victory, she silently cursed the two men who'd fired upon her. Her ire now turned toward them. She slid the rifle in front of her and wriggled her body behind the stock.

Wincing from the pain in her ribs, Juba took a deep breath and slid the rifle barrel into a crevice between two large stones. As she tilted the stock of the rifle upward, she spread her legs wide and dug her toes into the soil. She could hear the ranger—Kamua—talking softly in her head.

"Take a deep breath and brace yourself for the jolt when you fire. When you're faced with more than one assailant, swing the gun from left to right as you shoot, and then swing it back. Keep your finger pressed against the trigger until the clip is empty. Remember, show no mercy. Or you'll be dead."

Juba took a deep breath and held it. Jaw clenched tight, she pulled the trigger. Calmly, remembering Kamua's instructions, she swung the rifle in increments from left to right and then back right to left. She was in the midst of a second rotation when the gun suddenly stopped firing. As she slowly exhaled, she closed her eyes. Though her shoulder ached from the force of the weapon's recoil, she remained still. She needed to listen and wait. The next sound she would hear would tell what she needed to do: reload or run, mutter her final words or stand in victory. Her options would be few. So, she listened and waited—and heard nothing. She lay in silence for a minute longer before deciding to move.

Again, recalling Kamua's instructions, Juba ejected the empty magazine before sliding the gun toward her. After several failed attempts to rise to her feet—the pain in her side took her breath away—she decided to kneel. She took a few shallow breaths before she leaned over and grabbed one of the two ammunition belts she'd carried to the ledge. Taking a fresh clip from the belt, she snapped it into place. Gritting her teeth, using the rifle as a crutch, she rose to her feet. Feeling strangely numb, she looked over the line of rocks and down the incline.

Before shuffling down to where one of the two men she'd fired upon lay moaning, Juba dropped to one knee where Eimlaq lay. She was grateful that the big hyena had passed and was now beyond suffering. Juba hoped she was loping through a plain of lush green grass with the wind in her face and the sun warming her fur. Having paid her respects to the animal, she stepped over to Blue-head. With the barrel of the rifle, she turned the man's head so she could see his face. Most of it—his face—was gone. In its place was a gaping, bloody hole. Without thinking as to why, she spat on his blue turban and kicked him in the side.

Juba cautiously approached the first of the two men she'd wounded. He was lying on his side, groaning, his hands on his blood-covered thighs. It appeared the bullets she'd fired had shredded his legs.

"*Sharmuta*," the man hissed when their eyes met.

Juba pointed the rifle at the man's head and squeezed the trigger.

Juba heard the sound of an engine cranking to life as the gunshot faded to silence. At the base of the mountain, she saw one of the trucks pull out of line and drive away. Sagging with exhaustion, she gazed, emotionless, at the dead bodies around her. Suddenly she felt very empty. She no longer wondered what toll killing took on a person. Physically and mentally numb, feelings of guilt and redemption conflicting within her, she sat down, placed her head in her hands, and wept.

*

Talia could sense the eyes of the eight men on the back of her neck as she placed boxes of pastries on the side table situated against the west wall of the room. Adiam, standing at the east window, facing the harbor, had barely acknowledged her when she'd returned from her errands. She glanced over her shoulder to see if he was looking her way, but he wasn't. As usual, he was smoking a cigarette as he stared out the window. Talia toyed with the idea that he was pondering who should take Bin'ka's vacant seat at the table. But he'd told her the meeting was to make the controlling members aware of her less-than-satisfactory behavior. How would the members react? And what punishment would they inflict? Given the Consortium's history in dealing with a member's disloyalty, a vote to put her to death was not out of the question. Nor was a vote for her banishment and the seizure of all her assets. Her only hope, she knew, lay in the manner in which Adiam presented her transgressions. If he was sympathetic, the other members might be swayed to feel the same way.

She had briefly entertained the idea that some of the members might be open to dealing in ivory and slaves. But she'd dismissed the thought after considering the age of each member and their allegiance to Adiam. There was only one member she considered somewhat young. He was the newest to have been offered a seat at the table, and he'd barely spoken at the handful of meetings he'd attended. No, she thought as she spaced the four boxes of pastries equally along the length of the table, she did not foresee the meeting going in her favor.

"I have espresso and fresh-squeezed juices being delivered," she announced as she turned toward the conference table. She did not make eye contact with anyone when she added, "I just have to run downstairs for plates. I'll be right back."

As she expected, she heard a few grumbles about time and getting on with the business at hand, but she ignored them. With a brief glance toward Adiam, she went down the stairs.

When she reached the first floor, she paused to address the three young women she'd hired for the occasion. "Take the espressos up when they're ready," she instructed. "And make sure each one is hot. I'll be back in a moment. When I return, we'll run the plates and the juices up."

She heard the obligatory, "Yes, ma'am," as she left the building.

Talia walked across the street at a slow but determined pace. After reaching the opposite sidewalk, she headed west. Taking a deep breath, she turned to face Adiam's three-story building. Understanding the opportunity for success had a short window, she extracted the detonating device she'd hidden in her underwear and without hesitation pressed the blinking button. She was planning her next move when the second floor of Adiam's building exploded in a ferocious blast. She waited for the dust to settle before screaming for help.

25

"TELL ME ABOUT your scars."

Teimbaka placed his fingertips on his face. From his forehead to his eyes, down his cheeks, and across his lips and chin, he lightly brushed numerous ridges of deadened skin. Some he recalled from the pain he'd suffered when the wounds were inflicted. Others he could not remember, little nicks and cuts that existed on the periphery of his memories. When he moved his hands to his chest and felt the jagged lines of flesh running from his left shoulder to his right hip, he winced. The memory of the starving lion that had raked its claws across his torso was as vivid as the reality on the day the attack had occurred.

From the pain associated with the scars brought the bittersweet recollection of recovery. As he thought of the days and nights in Claire's care, he turned his head, hoping the motion would prevent him from seeing her face. But there she was, leaning over him, dabbing water on his forehead as her lips silently mouthed a plea to the Father for mercy. How he longed to reach up, place a hand on the back of her neck, and gently bring her face toward his. To kiss her once more, to embrace her, to feel the beat of her heart against his chest—

Claire. The desire to be with her. The subtle sensation of her lips upon his.

The wondrous and obliterating torture of her memory produced such an ache in his heart he cried out as if he'd been skewered with a flaming spear. And then her image vanished—a ghost who'd slipped through his fingers. A memory whisked away by time. Try as he might, he could not conjure her back. The void he felt at her absence was incomprehensible. Suddenly, his blindness did not render his world nearly dark enough. His body shook as he choked back tears.

"You were whipped."

His back arched as if the bullwhip was at that very moment tearing into his flesh. Each lash had been delivered with laughter and a taunt. George Henry, a self-proclaimed prophet of God, had beaten him to a point near death and then left him bound to a tree. He'd found solace in the tears of a baby spirit-elephant. Redemption had come by way of the Mother. She was everywhere—the Mother—and he had let her down. Even now, as he struggled to make sense of where he was, whom he was talking to, and why he was still alive, he could hear the anguished cries of elephants as they lay dying on a blood-drenched plain.

"And your blindness?"

Teimbaka raised his hands to his eyes but hesitated to touch them. What purpose would it serve to feel the sightless orbs? Why did he need to be reminded that he had failed—again? Was Sarah alive or dead? He didn't know. If she hadn't drowned or succumbed to fire or a bullet in the head, she'd been captured. He did not want to think of what her captors might have done to her. Better if she'd died.

"Do you remember me?"

Immersed in a stupor of recollections and disjointed images, Teimbaka did not respond.

"We met when you were younger."

Teimbaka tilted his head to the side and turned his face toward the boy's voice.

"You were traveling with a woman. She was sick."

"Claire," Teimbaka rasped.

"Here," the boy said. "Drink."

Teimbaka felt a hand slide behind the back of his neck and gently lift his head. The show of kindness made him think of Lee as she lay dying in the cave of wraiths. But it was as though he was recalling the memory from her perspective rather than his, for his skin suddenly burned with fever, his lips felt dry and cracked. Water dribbled into his mouth as shadow demons danced on the inner walls of his head. He could sense an ominous presence hovering close by: dark angels waiting for his spirit to leave his disease-ridden body. The Serpent, Lee had told him, had laid claim to her soul some years before. She'd died asking the Father to forgive her sins. Remembering the horrible way in which she had perished, he wondered if forgiveness existed.

Water. Forgiveness. Teimbaka shook his head. Lee had refused a final drink. She'd left the world with a tortured scream. No mercy had been shown to her in the cave of wraiths. The water on his tongue suddenly tasted bitter.

"Yes, Claire. I believe that is what you called her."

Teimbaka felt the cup pull away from his mouth. The hand supporting his neck eased his head back to the ground.

"Where is she now?"

Teimbaka turned his face away. He found the question agonizing—the answer more so. He didn't want to utter the word, but inexplicitly felt compelled to.

"Dead," he murmured.

He waited to hear the boy's answer, but none was immediately forthcoming. In the absence of a reply, he listened to the distant cries of seabirds and the murmur of waves.

"Were you with her at the end?"

"No," he admitted.

"Her spirit holds strong," the boy remarked.

Too occupied with regret, Teimbaka ignored the boy's comment.

"Have you eaten?"

Teimbaka thought the question odd. He remembered John Too placing a hunk of bread and a handful of overripe grapes in his lap. That had been a day ago—or was it two?

"Will you share with me?"

"Share?"

Teimbaka flinched when something touched his hand.

"Cured fish and papaya," the boy said. "Here, I'll help you sit up."

Teimbaka crossed his legs as his back was propped against something solid. He opened his hands to accept the offered food.

"Will you say a blessing with me?"

"I am of the Mother," Teimbaka replied.

"Is She not part of the Father?"

Teimbaka took a bite of the fruit placed in his palm.

"Did you not say the words over the woman when Qudus pleaded with you?"

"The words," Teimbaka repeated.

"Say the words," John Too had implored. The words had kept the Serpent from taking Claire.

Teimbaka remembered shouting the words in hopes of breaking Satan's hold. At the sound of them, the dark angels waiting for her soul had scattered as though smitten by a mace swung by the Father's hand. A cloudless sky had shaken with thunder. The children who'd witnessed her awakening trembled in awe. And it was all because of the words. It struck him then that John Too had been the one who'd saved Claire, for it was he who'd told him where the words could be found.

"Qudus? I don't know anyone by that name."

"He's been with you the past weeks."

"John Too?"

"Will you help him?"

"I don't know where he is."

"He is in need of the Lion."

The Lion. Teimbaka grunted. He'd heard what some called him: The Lion of Djibouti. And for a time, he'd believed the nonsense. What a fool he'd been. He shook his head.

"The Lion is gone." He snorted dismissively. "Blind and worthless."

"You need only say the word."

Teimbaka heard the boy's reply but wasn't ready to acknowledge what he'd said. Blind, worthless, gone, fool: the words paraded themselves through his thoughts, leaving little room for others that might have clamored for his attention.

"He will be gone soon."

"What would you have me do?" Teimbaka tersely replied. "He left."

"Did he?"

Teimbaka pushed the back of his head against the surface behind him and took a deep breath.

"How was it I found you in the harbor?"

"I couldn't wait! The walls, the voice—I didn't know if he was coming back!"

"So you left him."

"I didn't! He—"

Teimbaka dumped the food onto his lap and placed his hands over his face.

"What would you have me do?" he cried. "What would you have me do?"

"What would the Mother say?"

The Mother: cheetah, owl, the beetles, the spirit-elephants, the hyenas linked to John's horn, the old woman in a hooded robe: The Mother was each of these and more. He understood that now. And understood how, with each form she assumed, she'd tried to protect him. In return, she asked the same of him. Protect her children, she'd told him; protect her children.

"Are you ready for the day to end?"

"The day," Teimbaka murmured.

"The day is not over until you are ready for it to end. Is this not a question Qudus has asked you many times?"

Teimbaka silently mouthed the name Qudus.

"The Serpent whispers amongst the branches so the trees cannot shake wisdom from their limbs," the boy softly said.

Wisdom—how little he had shown over the past year. If he had listened to John Too when they stood at his brother's grave, Claire might still be in Africa, might still be alive. But he'd listened to another voice, one that spoke in murmurs swept down from the peak of Ras Dashen. Had it been the Serpent's voice he'd heard? Had he left Claire at Satan's prodding? And she; had she left him under the same misguided notion that she was needed elsewhere? Had the Serpent duped them both, so in the end, they would be alone?

Teimbaka slid his open hands along the sand by his sides.

"Where is John Too?" he asked. "What would you have me do?"

*

Claire was staring at her hands when a grey-haired man dressed in a dark blue suit and royal blue tie sat down in the armchair opposite her. She glanced at the briefcase he placed on the coffee table between them.

"Hello, Claire."

Claire's brow furrowed. She tentatively replied, "Hello."

"May I offer my sincere condolences regarding your mother?"

Claire unclasped her hands and rubbed them along her thighs.

"It came as a shock to all of us. Just a horrible turn of events."

Claire glanced up at the ceiling for a moment. Her eyes narrowed. "Do I know you?" she politely asked.

"Forgive me," the man responded. "I thought, perhaps, you might remember." He chuckled awkwardly and fiddled with the knot of his tie. "We met in my office a few years ago, before you went to France. Roger Pembrook." He leaned forward and offered his hand. "Your family's lawyer."

After a moment, Claire leaned across the coffee table and briefly shook Mr. Pembrook's hand.

"I apologize, Mr.—?"

"Pembrook."

"Pembrook," Claire repeated. "I can't seem to recall…"

"As well you shouldn't," Mr. Pembrook interjected. "Not after all you've— What with your— Everything that's transpired." He stroked his chin. "I'm sure it's quite overwhelming."

Claire gazed at the coffee table before responding. "I'm not sure I understand what's happened." She looked up at Mr. Pembrook. "Can you— Would you— Will you tell me what you know?"

Mr. Pembrook pinched his ear lobe and cleared his throat. "Well, I would think the doctor or the police should be—"

"The doctor hasn't said much beyond that they're preparing to release me due to my mother's unfortunate death. And the police…" She wrung her hands. "They mostly ask questions. I haven't been able— Will you tell me? Please?"

Mr. Pembrook raised his eyebrows and sighed.

"Well, I…" he paused and stroked his chin.

"Please. I want to know what happened to my mother." She glanced around the room. "And me," she told him. "I want to know what happened to me. Why am I here?" She pulled on the fabric of the white blouse she was wearing. "Who gave me these clothes? And why am I in a doctor's care? Did I suffer a breakdown?"

Mr. Pembrook made a placating gesture with his hands.

"Please, Miss Waterman, you need to understand it's not my place to discuss the circumstances regarding your admission to this facility. Nor am I in a position to answer any inquiries pertaining to your present… um… condition. And as far as—"

"Then tell me what you can, Mr. Pembrook," Claire interrupted. "I want to know." She leaned forward and held his gaze. "I *need* to know."

Mr. Pembrook ran a hand over his thinning grey hair and pursed his lips, then abruptly reached into an inner pocket of his suit coat. "The Reverend Mother thought you might like this."

Claire placed a hand to her lips when Mr. Pembrook displayed a necklace adorned with a small silver cross.

"The Reverend Mother?" Claire muttered. "You spoke to her?"

Mr. Pembrook placed the necklace on the coffee table.

"I visited with her yesterday." He sat back in the chair and clasped his hands in his lap. "Lovely woman, as you are well aware. Lovely facility as well."

"Did she say anything about—" Claire reached out as if to gather the necklace in her hand. "I'm sure she's—"

She abruptly withdrew her arm. Turning her face away, she laid her hands on her lap.

"She's quite concerned for your welfare." Mr. Pembrook offered Claire a polite smile when she shifted her attention to him. "And looking forward to welcoming you home."

"Home," Claire muttered.

"As are the other nuns I met. They seem quite mesmerized by your—"

"How did my mother die, Mr. Pembrook?"

Claire leaned forward and scooped the necklace into her hand. She ran her index finger around the outer edges of the cross as Mr. Pembrook smoothed his tie and glanced down at the floor.

"I'm not sure I'm the one who should tell you."

"Then there's nothing left for us to speak of." Claire stood and extended a hand. "Thank you for coming, Mr. Pembrook."

Mr. Pembrook rose halfway out of his chair before clearing his throat and sitting back down.

"Please, Miss Waterman, please…" He motioned to the chair behind her. "Please have a seat, and I'll—" He took a deep breath. "I'll tell you what I know."

Claire smoothed her blue, knee-length skirt beneath her as she sat down.

"How did it happen?" she asked. "My mother."

"He—" Mr. Pembrook paused. "From what I've been told, your Mother was one victim of a triple homicide in the course of a drug-related robbery."

"Robbery?"

"Yes. From the information the police have released, it was an unfortunate byproduct of the suspect's living arrangement at the estate."

"The estate?" Claire repeated. "I don't understand. Who's living at the estate besides my mother?" She glanced down at the cross. "And the help, of course."

Mr. Pembrook rubbed his cheek and averted his eyes.

"What aren't you saying?"

Mr. Pembrook sighed. "Mr. Savage is the suspect's name. Though I believe that's his pen name."

"Mr. Savage?"

"Dirk, I believe he goes by. Dirk Savage." Mr. Pembrook regarded Claire through narrowed eyes. "The man who brought you home from Africa. The newspaperman. Or photo-whatever-he-calls-himself." Mr. Pembrook leaned forward. "Do you remember the individual?"

Claire silently mouthed the name *Dirk Savage* as she rubbed the cross between her thumb and forefinger. Mr. Pembrook appeared to be on the verge of saying something more when she responded.

"My brother."

Mr. Pembrook's eyes went wide. "You don't have a brother," he cautiously told her.

"He pretended," she said. "He pretended he was my brother. There was a nurse and a doctor." Mr. Pembrook reached out when Claire rose from her chair and looked toward the door. "Is this where he brought me? Did he bring me to this—?" She motioned to the room around her. "Place—clinic—whatever? Just where am I, Mr. Pembrook? Where did the—?" She clasped the cross to her chest. "What kind of place is this?"

"Now, now, Miss Waterman. Please don't upset yourself. The doctor said if you were to—"

Claire smoothed the wrinkles from her blouse and sat back down, saying, "Please excuse my outburst, Mr. Pembrook." Then, with a nod, "Continue with what you know about this Dirk Savage person and my mother."

Mr. Pembrook regarded Claire for a few moments. "Perhaps we should do this another day," he suggested. "The doctor was quite explicit about—"

"I assure you, I'm quite able to carry on with this discussion," Claire interjected. "I apologize for veering off track." She gestured with one hand for him to proceed.

Mr. Pembrook tapped his forefinger against his thigh and took a deep breath.

"Very well," he said. "But I'm not sure where to begin." He once again tugged at his ear. "No one has informed me just exactly what you've been told."

Claire dipped her head and dropped the necklace around her neck.

"Why don't we start with the day I arrived back in America? And then continue up until this moment."

Mr. Pembrook smiled briefly, then tapped his chin with a finger. He adjusted his cuffs and checked the time on his wristwatch. As he made a quick check to the knot of his tie, he cleared his throat.

"I received a call from Caroline—your mother—the day you arrived at the airport in Philadelphia. She sounded quite confused. Though she'd been informed of your impending arrival, she did not know you were arriving on a Red Cross transport, nor that you were in some kind of coma."

"Coma? I don't recall—" Claire shook her head. With a faint smile, she motioned for Mr. Pembrook to continue.

"As I said, Mrs. Waterman was a bit out of sorts over your condition. And while it was obvious you needed immediate medical attention, she didn't want you taken into the city, where she wouldn't be able to visit you as easily—" He smiled. "So, it was determined that you were to be brought here." Mr. Pembrook briefly motioned with his hand to the room around him. "Westchester Clinic. A private facility with a wing devoted to long-term care."

"Long-term care," Claire muttered. "How long have I been here?"

Mr. Pembrook scratched behind his right ear and raised his eyebrows.

"The good portion of a year." He paused. "Possibly a few months more." He glanced down at the floor. "It would be best if you heard this from Doctor Haraji. I'm not comfortable—"

"Mr. Pembrook." Claire clasped the silver cross dangling against her chest. "I appreciate your candor and your sensitivity. Please," she said with a slight nod, "please continue."

Mr. Pembrook sighed.

"Very well. As I was saying, you were admitted to Westchester Clinic, where you— I really think any discussion about your condition should come from Dr. Haraji. I'm in no position to—"

"Agreed," Claire quickly concurred. "That's not what I've asked you tell me. I'll get that information directly from the doctor."

Mr. Pembrook repositioned himself in the chair. With a glance at his briefcase, he continued.

"In the interim—while you were receiving top-notch medical attention—Mr. Savage—I believe his real name is Benson—somehow convinced your mother that it would be in your best interests if he were kept in proximity. And your mother—though I counseled otherwise—agreed to the man's—" Mr. Pembrook furrowed his brow "—suggestion and put him up in the guest room above the garage. With full privileges to the estate, I might add." He raised a finger to make a point. "Including meals, liquor, use of the estate vehicles. Your mother spared no expense."

Claire smiled and nodded when Mr. Pembrook stopped his narrative and looked at her expectantly.

"But it became clear after several weeks that things were not as they appeared."

"In what way?"

Mr. Pembrook leaned forward and cleared his throat. "Drugs," he said in a low voice. "The hard variety."

Claire shook her head. "I don't understand," she said.

"Heroin," he told her. "From what I understand, the man was an addict." Mr. Pembrook sat back the chair and crossed his legs. "An unsavory individual. I should have been more vocal."

"How could my mother allow—?"

"Oh, he's quite charming, from what I've been told." He uncrossed his legs and leaned forward. "And quite the smooth talker. Had your mother believing he was owed a substantial sum of money for 'saving' you, as he called it. Mr. Locket mentioned this to me on several occasions when I went out to the estate on family business."

"Saving me?" Claire questioned. She clasped the cross and stared off into space for a moment.

"Mr. Locket!" she softly exclaimed. "Dear Mr. Locket." She met Mr.

Pembrook's gaze with wide, bright eyes. "I can't wait to see him." She took a deep breath. "Such a wonderful man. Devoted." Claire smiled. "I can't remember a time he wasn't with us."

Mr. Pembrook pursed his lips and looked at his hands.

"Mr. Locket." Mr. Pembrook paused and stroked his chin. "Mr. Locket was taken the same night as your mother."

Claire gasped, a hand to her mouth. "Dear God in Heaven," she said as she made the sign of the cross. "How is this possible?"

"No one told you?" Mr. Pembrook gently inquired. He sighed. "I'm deeply sorry." He shook his head. "This is not what I expected. I should have never come. I should have waited until you were— Until the situation—" He shrugged. "Until you'd been made aware of everything that's transpired."

Claire leaned forward in her chair and swallowed hard. "Are you saying they were both killed? My mother and Mr. Locket? On the same night?"

Mr. Pembrook nodded slowly.

"The same—?" Claire shook her head. "The same person was responsible?"

"I'm afraid so."

"God have mercy on his soul," Claire murmured. She grasped the silver cross with both hands. "What would make a person commit such an act of…"

"It all goes back to the drugs." Mr. Pembrook nodded when she met his eyes. "Apparently he was running some sort of drug operation from the property. The police found a substantial cache of heroin and cocaine in the barn. Where Mr. Locket's—um—Mr. Locket was found."

"I can't believe it." Claire quickly crossed herself. "Bless those whose lives have been taken in an act of sin. And bless my mother for showing the charity of a true Christian heart."

Mr. Pembrook sat back in the chair and cleared his throat. "Indeed," he said. "A tragedy on many fronts, I'm afraid."

"And this Mr. Savage—where is he now?" Claire inquired. "In police custody, I hope."

"Oh, yes. He was apprehended at the scene of the crime. Apparently, your mother had been in touch with a DEA agent earlier in the day." Mr. Pembrook leaned forward in the chair. "An act of God, one might say, that he arrived at the estate moments after the—" Mr. Pembrook offered Claire a sympathetic nod. "After the acts had been committed."

"An act of God," Claire dazedly repeated. "Of course."

"Yes, no telling what—"

Mr. Pembrook drew back with a start when Claire abruptly leaned forward and grabbed the edge of the coffee table.

"And what was his explanation? What did Mr. Savage have to say for the sinful acts he committed?" She sat back with an audible exhale. "Did he exhibit remorse? Was he—?" She ran a hand across her forehead as her body drooped. "I'm at a loss." She sighed. "God forgive me, I'm at a loss."

"Anyone would feel the same, Miss Waterman—Claire, if I may. This must—" He scooted to the edge of the chair. "I can only imagine what you're—"

"You said triple," Claire blurted. She put her hand to her mouth. "Who— Who else?" she stammered. "Did he? Was it Mr. Savage?"

"Please, Claire, you needn't upset yourself with the man's barbaric behavior."

"Was it someone else who worked on the property? Someone in Mother's employ?"

"No, no, no," Mr. Pembrook was quick to say. "No one from the estate. No one you knew—unless, perhaps, you met here."

"Here?"

"A nurse," Mr. Pembrook replied. "She was employed here at the clinic."

Claire slowly shook her head.

"I don't— I don't recall any nurse. A woman? No. I seem to—"

"Tragic, quite tragic. It seems he was in some sort of delusional state. They—the authorities—have the terrible moment captured on videotape. Quite extraordinary." He shook his head. "Senseless, utterly senseless."

Both Claire and Mr. Pembrook were silent for a few moments. Then Mr. Pembrook cleared his throat.

"There are a few legalities we should discuss regarding the estate." Mr. Pembrook put a fist to his mouth and coughed when Claire didn't respond. "I know it seems unsavory to bring these matters up at this time, but it's in your best interest to take care of them now."

"Has he said anything?" Claire asked.

"He? Who do you mean?"

"Mr. Savage. Has he made a statement? Is he talking?"

"He's confessed to the egregious crimes, but from what I've been told—and that's very little—he hasn't said much about motive."

"Confessed? You said he was in a delusional state. Has he been examined?"

Mr. Pembrook made a dismissive gesture with his hands.

"You shouldn't take everything I've said to heart. In fact, I'm sure I've said some things that are purely conjecture." He put his hands on his knees and leaned forward. In a low tone of voice, he said, "Truth is, I don't know much more about the suspect than that he's incarcerated and awaiting a preliminary hearing. I'm afraid anything else I said was pure hearsay. I apologize for repeating it."

Claire rubbed a hand along her thigh as her eyes flitted from Mr. Pembrook to his briefcase to the silver cross.

"Confession," she muttered. "What would he have said? I would like to…" Her eyebrows pinched together as her voice trailed off.

"Most mentally disturbed have no idea why they commit acts against society," he said. "Or so I've been led to believe," he was quick to add. "But in this case—as the facts bear out—drugs and the man's addiction to them certainly played a part in—in—in his unraveling."

Claire opened her mouth as if to speak, but then put a knuckle against her bottom lip. She eyed Mr. Pembrook as she softly bit down on her finger.

"How was—? How was my mother killed?"

Mr. Pembrook sat back in the chair and sighed. "She was shot."

Claire raised her eyebrows. "Did she—? Did she suffer?" she asked in a quiet voice.

With a slight shake of his head, Mr. Pembrook said, "I doubt she even realized what happened."

Claire nodded. "And Mr. Locket?"

"Mr.—? Oh, the butler." He definitively shook his head. "No, no, he was shot the same way. I'm sure he—"

"The same way?"

Mr. Pembrook ran a hand over his head before clearing his throat. "Forgive my bluntness. They were shot in the head."

"Lord have mercy on their souls."

"I doubt they suffered."

Claire nodded.

"A senseless act," Mr. Pembrook commented with a sympathetic shake of his head. "Tragic your mother was lost in such a violent manner." He paused before adding, "I hear they'll be asking for the death penalty."

Claire crossed herself and shook her head. "Dear, God, no. That mustn't be. The Lord teaches us that a life should not be taken for a life." She looked earnestly at Mr. Pembrook. "No, no. Forgiveness is the way of the Lord. Forgiveness."

"Yes, of course," Mr. Pembrook replied. "Still, the state will seek the appropriate punishment as dictated by law." He offered Claire an awkward smile before adding, "No offense to the Lord, I'm sure."

Mr. Pembrook sat back in the chair. When Claire placed her hands together and began to murmur a prayer, he leaned forward and tapped the briefcase.

"It's really very important you sign a few documents," he said.

Claire reacted with a start.

"Forgive me." He gave a slight nod toward the briefcase. "Signing these will prevent your mother's estate—excuse me, *your* estate—from going to probate."

"Probate?"

"A long and oft times exasperating procedure where the court reviews your holdings and makes changes based upon their review."

"I'm not sure I understand."

Mr. Pembrook leaned forward. "They essentially rule on the validity of your mother's will. A needless and unnecessary procedural exercise in this case, as your mother's estate is in perfect order."

"Then why—?"

"Your mother had the foresight to draw up a living trust a few months back." Mr. Pembrook undid the clasp on the briefcase and extracted a small stack of stapled papers. "Your signature will free me—or, rather, the law firm representing your mother's estate—to oversee the distribution of funds and real estate holdings." He held the papers out toward Claire. "To you."

Claire hesitantly extended a hand to accept the papers.

"Distribution?"

"Yes, of what's rightfully yours. These will also prevent the state from tacking on needless legal fees and making dubious deductions from your holdings before releasing what has been bequeathed to the rightful heir."

Claire looked at the papers and then back at Mr. Pembrook.

"This is what my mother wished?"

"Yes," he assured her. "She was so very concerned with your wellbeing and wanted to make certain you were taken care of in the event something happened to her while you were in the clinic. She had no—" Mr. Pembrook chuckled "—fondness of paying money into the state." He nodded to the papers in her hand. "And this prevents the government from claiming any jurisdiction in the matter."

"I see."

Claire looked for a place to set the papers down.

"Here." Mr. Pembrook grabbed the briefcase and turned it over. "Use this as a tray," he suggested. Leaning across the coffee table, he gently placed the overturned briefcase on Claire's thighs. "I have a pen."

Claire placed the papers on the briefcase and then adjusted the posture of her legs so the papers didn't slide. When Mr. Pembrook offered a pen, she took it.

"I've taken the liberty of inscribing a small *x* where your signature is required. After you've signed—at a later date of course—we can discuss how you wish the estate to be—"

"You said the there was a videotape of the nurse." Claire put the pen to her cheek as she met Mr. Pembrook's eyes. "Was she— I mean— Did Mr. Savage take her life in the same manner as my mother's and Mr. Locket's?"

Mr. Pembrook blinked twice and sat back in the chair. "I dare say— I mean— Is that something you really want to know?"

He frowned when Claire placed the pen atop the papers.

"Mr. Pembrook," Claire began. "It's difficult for me to understand why a man who went to the trouble to bring me—" She paused to smooth the wrinkles on her blouse. "*Kidnap* me, actually—and bring me back to America would, after a year's time—so I understand—suddenly go berserk and kill three people."

"Drugs, of course." Mr. Pembrook leaned forward. "Claire, you must realize he was likely using drugs the day he, as you termed it, kidnapped you. And from that moment on, he was likely hard pressed to keep his addiction fed, as most addicts are. And I'm certain he experienced the highs and lows of navigating that course. That it took him a year before he snapped speaks of the charity of your mother and the staff." Mr. Pembrook placed his hands on his knees and took a deep breath. "The evidence is overwhelming. Your mother calling a DEA agent the night before she was—before the crime was committed—should stand as unequivocal proof of her belief that something had changed, something to make her fear for her safety."

Claire nudged the pen back and forth.

"The DEA agent—" Claire picked up the pen and tapped it against the papers. "Did he say why my mother called? You know, the reason she— Did she ask him to come out to the house?"

"I-I don't— I can't answer that."

"How would he have run drugs from the estate without Mr. Locket having known?"

"Who?" Mr. Pembrook scooted forward in the chair. "Mr. Savage? Is that who you mean?"

"And how did he take the life of the nurse and then get to the estate? Didn't the clinic call the police?"

"Claire, please, you're asking questions about things I know nothing about." He ran a hand back over his head as he said, "I'm sure all your questions will be answered in due time. In the interim—" he reached out and tapped the stack of papers "—you need to address *your* future." With a sigh, he scooted farther back into the chair. "That's the reason I'm here. To make certain you're taken care of as your mother wished."

"I'm sorry, Mr. Pembrook. It's just that I, just that I…" Claire covered her face with her hands and let out a sob. "It's just that I'm having trouble—"

"You needn't apologize, dear girl. Not after all you've been through, what your family has suffered. And here I am sounding like—" He shook his head and turned his hands up. "You have every right to be upset. Every right. But I hope you see I'm here to help." He leaned forward. "As your mother would have wanted me to be."

Claire laid the pen atop the papers and wiped her eyes with the back of her hand.

"It's just…" She shook her head. "I can't help thinking— Was there someone—I mean—Someone in Africa?" She put a hand to her mouth and sobbed. "I can't remember!" she cried.

"Claire." Mr. Pembrook leaned across the coffee table and touched her knee. "Let me call the doctor."

"No, no," she said. "I'm just— I'm being silly." She gave him a weak smile and wiped her eyes with the heels of her hands. "There's just so much to think of." She shook her head and sniffled. "So much to sort out." She clutched the silver cross. "I know it must sound odd, but I can't help thinking about what I left behind, what Mr. Savage took me away from. You must think me…" Her voice trailed off as she shifted her attention toward the floor.

"I see now what your mother would want me to do."

Claire looked back at Mr. Pembrook with a surprised expression on her face.

"She would want me to take care of both your past and future."

"My past? How is—"

"Allow me to hire an investigator, one who knows the city and area where you spent most of your time." Mr. Pembrook placed his hands together palm to palm and pointed his fingers toward Claire. "That way, while we take care of business here," he said, nodding to the papers, "we can start to piece together what you left behind in Africa." He opened his hands and turned his palms toward Claire. "How does that sound?"

Claire wrung her hands.

"I just— I don't know what to say." Her expression turned troubled. "I'm not sure what I left. I can't seem to recall…" She rubbed her forehead. "What is it I can't remember?"

"Claire, please. I'm here to help. As your mother wanted me to be." He bent forward and made eye contact. "Your mother went to great lengths to plan for me to be here." He glanced at the papers and nodded. "I know it would please her if you were to agree to her final wish."

"Her—?"

"The papers, Claire. Her living trust."

She stared at him in silence for a moment before her expression brightened.

"Of course," she said. As she picked up the pen, she asked, "Where should I—"

"There at the bottom, where I've placed a small *x*." Mr. Pembrook smiled and nodded as Claire signed her name.

"And three more times, if you would, on pages three, five, and seven. You'll see where by the mark."

Claire flipped over the top sheet of paper. She was in the act of flipping over the second when she stopped to address Mr. Pembrook.

"When—? The investigator— How soon, I mean, when do you think—?"

"Right after our business is finished here," he told her. "As soon as I get back to the office."

"But I don't see how—?"

"You leave it to me," he assured her. "I'll have someone on it before the sun sets."

Claire smiled weakly as she flipped over the second page of the document. Mr. Pembrook cleared his throat when she hesitated to put pen to paper.

"You mother placed her trust in me, Claire. I only ask you offer me the same opportunity: to earn your trust." He sat back. "Faith, Claire. Isn't that the pillar upon which all else is built?"

"Faith," Claire softly repeated.

"I hope to earn your faith, Claire. Please allow me the opportunity."

"Faith," Claire murmured.

With a nod of her head, Claire signed her name at the bottom of the page. Mr. Pembrook smiled as she signed her name twice more.

26

"I DON'T KNOW how to call the lion!"

Teimbaka heard the receding swish of a cloth garment. The boy was leaving.

"Where are you going?" he cried. "Why are you leaving?"

He strained to hear any reply, his hands bunching and twisting his robes in frustration. How could the boy lead him—a blind man—to an unfamiliar place and then leave him to fend for himself? The act was almost cruel. He simmered with anger. Where had the boy brought him? He'd asked to be taken to John Too.

"Hello?" he shouted.

He held his breath and waited for a reply. When he heard none, he sighed. What had the boy said before he left?

"Call the lion when you are in need."

Teimbaka took a deep breath and tried to set his angst aside.

Unconsciously, he placed his fingertips to his eyes. Slowly, as if an afterthought, his fingers slid from his eyes to his lips. There he let them linger as he hung his head and wept.

*

"Hurry. We have to go."

Tanya looked over the side of the freighter. The cable Chris wanted her to slide down was wafting in the wind. And the raft he wanted her to descend to looked like a dot bobbing on the waves. Though she knew one end of the cable was hooked to the small craft, she couldn't see exactly where it had been secured. Suspicious, she eyed Chris with disdain.

"You fucked up," she muttered.

Chris motioned for her to move toward him.

"Come on," he urged. "You need to go first. That way—" ·

"You crazy," she blurted. With a glance over the gunwale she said, "I ain't going down there on that." She pointed to the harness in his grasp.

"You want to get off this floating hotel, don't you?" he asked with a smile.

She grimaced.

"This is the only way." He looked down at the rubber raft outfitted with an outboard motor. "Unless a passport mysteriously materialized in your back pocket in the past few minutes."

Tanya shifted her attention from Chris to the little boy hugging his leg. Studying Marcus's expression, she couldn't tell if he was scared or bored. The boy had grown fond of Chris the past week. Looking at the two, she realized she'd be happy to be rid of them—and the sooner the better. But she wasn't keen on putting on a harness and sliding down a sixty-foot length of cable to what looked to be a toy raft being tossed about on a churning sea. She glanced at the sky. She judged that an hour or so of daylight remained before nightfall. The sense of uneasiness she was experiencing grew stronger.

"Why don't you go first?" she challenged.

He frowned and shook his head.

"You need to be there when I send the boy down." He shook the harness. "Besides, you don't know how this works."

She blew a pouty sigh.

"Come on, we're wasting time." He looked out toward the eastern horizon. "We need to be in position before the last of the fishing boats head to harbor."

She looked at Marcus. What was the boy thinking? He'd hardly said two words to her since they'd boarded the freighter. *Fucking stinkhole of a ship. Boy probably think he gonna die*, she mused. *Can't blame him*. The same idea had crossed her mind several times over the course of the past week.

"Look, you—"

Tanya recoiled and slapped Chris's hand when he grabbed her arm.

"Fine," he snarled. "I won't touch you." He shook the harness again. "But you better get in this before this tub starts moving again. Otherwise, we're going to be stuck—"

"Fine," she snapped.

Tanya grabbed the harness and slipped it on. Chris helped her secure the straps around her waist and shoulders. As she looked down at Marcus, Chris clamped a metal hook to the front cross-strap.

"I'll be there to catch you when you slide down," she said to Marcus. She bent and cupped his face in her hand. "Lady T be there like I always am, you hear?"

Marcus's blank expression didn't change.

"Come on," Chris interjected. "Time to go."

Tanya placed her hands on Marcus's shoulders.

"You watch how easy this is," she said. "Like one of those rides at the carnival, I bet." She patted his head. "You'll see."

With a heavy sigh, Tanya shifted her attention to Chris.

"I better not…" She glanced at Marcus.

"You won't—as long as you do as I tell you."

Tanya tried to focus on everything Chris told her as he prepped her to zip-line from the freighter to the waiting Zodiac. But his tone of voice was making it difficult for her to concentrate. He sounded like a drill sergeant. So much so, she was reminded of her father.

Her father. *My old man's dead.* She wasn't quite sure how she should feel. Part of her was relieved. The strict authoritarian was out of her life; she wouldn't have to listen to his shit anymore. But part of her understood her dad was gone—forever. She was parentless, alone. The realization left her feeling detached. Nothing seemed real. Nothing seemed to matter.

"Once you're over the side, hold the pulley lines tight. Keep your weight balanced."

Tanya gazed blankly into Chris's eyes as he lifted her above the handrail. She glanced at Marcus and shook her head. The boy looked like he was in a trance.

"Fall forward into the boat when your feet touch!" Chris shouted. "Once you're in, release the hook!"

She felt a tug on her chest, and then she was sliding. Her eyes went wide as she hurtled toward the sea.

*

Chris hugged Marcus to his thigh as Tanya zip-lined toward the water. A good part of him hoped the woman would fall out of the harness and drown. She'd been a pain in the ass since he'd paid their passage aboard the *Jameel*. Her belligerent attitude had nearly gotten him into a number of fights with the crew. Her constant complaints about quarters, the food, and the lack of freedom had gotten so bad he'd given serious thought to throwing her overboard. But every time he entertained the notion of getting rid of her, he thought of Marcus and how her disappearance might affect the boy. The kid had problems. More so than most his age. Parents killed by Rue Thompson and the drug cartel, Jim and Rochelle murdered in a botched robbery—by Tanya's boyfriend, of all people. No wonder the boy stared off into corners and mumbled like he was holding a conversation with someone. Probably lived in a make-believe world filled with make-believe people. And who could blame him if he did?

Chris gave the boy a reassuring hug.

"She's almost there," he said.

He glanced down at the boy and smiled. But Marcus was looking off to the side.

"We'll be on land before long." Chris patted the boy's head. "Where your daddy came from," he muttered. "Hmph.. Kinda weird, when you think about it."

When Marcus pushed away from his leg and went to stand at the gunwale, Chris shifted his attention to Tanya. She was in the Zodiac.

"You're next," he told Marcus.

But Marcus wasn't paying attention. He was staring at something off to the side.

*

Marcus gazed at his friend.

"You're coming, right?"

The baby spirit-elephant gazed back at him in silence. Marcus glanced toward the ocean.

"You know where we are?"

The baby spirit-elephant raised its trunk and placed the tip against the side of Marcus's head.

A vision of three boys scampering along the banks of a dry riverbed manifested in Marcus's thoughts. Though the boys were different ages, they resembled one another in dress and features. Two of the boys carried branches in their arms, while the third brandished a long stick. He—the youngest looking of the three—chased the two with the armloads of tinder. Marcus could see dust puffing from under the child's feet as he scurried from one boy to another with a wide smile on his face.

"Hi-yee!" he heard the sword-brandishing boy shout. "Pay homage to your king!" Marcus smiled when the boy swung his weapon in front of his chest and cried, "Kneel or face my wrath!"

Marcus unconsciously leaned toward the baby spirit-elephant as the two older boys stopped to face their giggling assailant.

The ferocious roar of a lion shook Marcus to the core, and he squeezed the guardrail in terror. He tried to shout to the boys to warn them, but when he opened his mouth to yell, he found he had no voice. He flinched as one boy dropped his armload of sticks and ran. He held his breath as the tallest of the three laid his branches upon the ground and took a step toward the hungry-looking lion. He blinked when a red mist burst from the boy's neck. And as he watched the lion clamp its jaws around the boy's shoulder, a wave of pain rippled through his body. Overcome with a sudden fit of shakes, Marcus wrapped his arms around his chest and gritted his teeth.

"Put this on."

Marcus stared blankly into Chris's eyes as the man buckled straps across his chest, around his waist, over his shoulders, and between his legs. He struggled to keep his hold on the spirit-elephant's trunk as Chris lifted him to the handrail and set him upon the uppermost bar.

"It's okay to be afraid."

Marcus flinched when Chris's face suddenly loomed in front of his.

"Tanya—Lady T—will catch you."

He didn't understand why Chris was smiling.

"Think of it as a ride."

Marcus tried to keep hold of the spirit-elephant's trunk when Chris pushed him from the rail, but it slipped from his grasp.

*

Tanya unhooked Marcus from the zip line, slipped the harness off, and set him down in the Zodiac. As she watched the pulley slide back up the cable, she thought about loosening the tether attached to the nose of the boat and leaving Chris stranded on the freighter. But as much as she had come to dislike the man, she understood she still needed him—as much for protection as for what he had promised.

"How am I gonna get back?" she'd shouted when he'd told her he'd booked passage for the three of them on a freighter to Africa. "Why the hell I wanna go there?"

"Don't worry," he said, worriedly scanning the pier. "I have plenty of connections. I promise, within a week, I'll have you and the boy on a plane back to the US."

She thought he was full of crap.

"LA, Miami, New Orleans—anywhere you want to go. I'll get you there."

Her instincts told her not to trust him, not to listen to his shit. But then he added, "Promise. Cross my heart."

And then he crossed his heart.

"What that do for me?" she scoffed. "Get me to LA or some such shit—fuck. Ain't got no money, no job, no crib. What that gonna do for me?"

"I'll take care of it," he told her. "Give you ten grand before you step on the plane."

"Shit," she sneered. "How you—?"

"Told you I was stationed in Africa for years. Got money here and there. Hid where no one would ever find it."

"You bullshittin'."

"And I have contacts just about everywhere in the States."

His condescending nod made her feel like he thought he was talking to a child.

"People who owe me. People who can set you up with a job and a place to stay."

"What? Like a whore in a crackhouse? That what you mean?"

She reflexively touched the spot on her arm where he'd grabbed it.

"We don't have time to stand here and argue. The cops could arrive any time and arrest us for murder. And if that happens, neither one of us is ever going see the light of day. So you gotta trust what I'm promising you and get on board the ship."

"And if I don't?"

She cowered when he made a sudden move with his arm. But he'd been reaching for his wallet. He placed his fist to his mouth before he opened his billfold and took out a wad of cash.

"All I got left," he said as he handed her the money. "Count it. Close to five grand." He placed the money in her hand. "Get you five more when we reach Africa. Another twenty-five before you get on the plane."

She squeezed the wad of bills. Money. She could start over. Miami—she'd always dreamt about moving to Florida, especially on those cold winter mornings when she was freezing her ass off. She'd given Chris a big *humph* as she'd stuffed the bills into the pocket of her jeans.

"What about the boy?"

"What about him?"

"He ain't got nobody." She shrugged. "And I ain't his kin."

Chris paused before responding.

"He's not the first," he muttered. Then he said something she found strange. "Small chance he might find someone where we're headed."

"What you mean?"

"Boy's father was African. Never know." He'd shrugged.

Tanya reacted with a start when she felt a tug on her hand. She looked down to find Marcus pointing upward past her shoulder. Following his finger, she observed Chris had traveled halfway down the zip line. She gave a quick pat to the pocket of her jeans, lifted Marcus into her arms, and carefully stepped toward the rear of the Zodiac. Within a minute after Chris touched down, he'd powered up the engine and cast off the lines.

*

Marcus stared at the shoreline in earnest. He was certain he saw his friend on the approaching dock, but as the boat drew near the old wooden structure, he lost sight of him. Maybe the long-nosed creature with the floppy ears was playing a game of hide-and-seek. If that was so, his friend wasn't playing fair. The place where they were headed—and all its best hiding places—was new to him. How was he supposed know where to look?

"Almost there, little man."

Marcus shifted his attention from the approaching dock to Lady T. It was the first time he'd seen her smile in, well—he thought back as far as he could—since before they'd got in the truck and driven to the big boat. That seemed like—well, it seemed like a long time ago.

"Recognize any of it?"

With what little daylight remained, Marcus couldn't make out too much of the approaching shoreline. The old dock where they were headed looked to be rickety and as long as five or six big trucks parked end to end. But the buildings behind it were just shapes. He gave Lady T a puzzled glance; what did she mean, did he recognize any of it? How could he? He'd heard Chris say they were in Africa, but he wasn't sure what that meant or where exactly Africa was. Chris had told him several times they were "crossing the Atlantic" over the course of the really long boat ride they had taken, but he didn't know what *Atlantic* meant either. So that wasn't helpful.

The sun was the same. At least it looked the same as it sank behind the buildings when Chris steered the rubber boat away from the freighter and followed a sailboat toward shore. But the place where he saw several big ships—off to his right as the speedboat rounded the end of the freighter—confused him. The pier, dotted with square cranes, looked a little like where they'd begun their journey. He wondered if they'd taken the long boat ride across the Atlantic just to end up where they'd started. But Chris and Lady T kept saying they were in Africa, so he was pretty sure they hadn't. Still, he wished he knew what the words *Africa* and *Atlantic* meant. If he did, maybe he'd have a clue as to where he was and where his long-nosed friend might be hiding.

"Chris say your daddy from here."

Marcus shifted his attention to Lady T. When she brushed a hand along his face, he sighed, because her touch gave him a peaceful feeling, like the world slowed down a little bit. He didn't really know how to explain it, but that's how she made him feel. So, as she caressed his face, he pressed his cheek into her palm and closed his eyes. He could hear water lapping against the side of the boat when the whine of the outboard motor suddenly stopped. With a tired sigh, he leaned against Lady T's leg and listened to his heartbeat. His eyes flew open when he realized that what he thought was a heartbeat was the beat of a drum.

*

Chris switched off the outboard motor and motioned for quiet. The sound of a drum troubled him. The captain of the *Jameel* had told him the old fishing pier would be deserted.

"Dhows and nets are all you'll find there," he'd assured him. "Once the fishermen tie up and unload their catch, there won't be a soul around."

But the presence of the drum meant otherwise. Street musicians drew a crowd. And crowds drew the authorities. Police, soldiers, customs officials—any type of government agent—raised the possibility of being stopped. He was running through a list of potential trouble when the boat's momentum brought it flush with a piling. He grumbled an exasperated "Fuck" when the Zodiac suddenly tilted to one side.

"What you doing?" he hissed as Marcus tried to get by him.

Chris grabbed the boy by the arm and jerked him to a stop. Placing one hand against the piling to steady the boat, he lifted Marcus up until he was at eye level.

"Nobody goes anywhere till I say," he hoarsely whispered. "You understand?"

"Don't hurt him," Tanya barked.

"Shut up!" he mouthed. He set Marcus down and made a fist. Shaking it at Tanya, he whispered, "You want everyone on the dock to know we're here?" He shook his head when Tanya averted her eyes. "Just stay put," he said to Marcus. "Can you do that?"

Marcus glanced at the dock and nodded. Chris shifted his attention to Tanya.

"Can *you?*"

Tanya reluctantly met his gaze.

"I suppose," she grumbled.

Chris sighed. "Good."

He bent and reached for the tether line coiled at the bow, then abruptly straightened.

"The drum," he whispered. "It stopped."

*

Tanya eyed Chris with disdain. *Well, la dee da*, she thought. *So somebody got tired of beatin' on a drum. Big shit. Who cares?*

"Can we go?" she asked him.

He shook his head. "Just trying to keep you alive. This place isn't what you're used to."

"Yeah, well, neither is that sweatbox of a room you kept me in the past week." She nodded toward the open sea. "Had enough of boats and shitty food. Marcus and me need to feel solid ground under our feet."

Chris glared at her for a few seconds before replying.

"Suit yourself. But…" he shook his head. "Never mind." And then he took Marcus into his arms and lifted him toward the dock. "Grab the ladder," he instructed the boy. "Wait for us when you reach the top."

*

Marcus scurried up the five-rung ladder with ease. When he reached the top rung, he jumped to the dock. Suppressing a giggle, he immediately raced toward the buildings at the end of the pier, where he'd caught a brief glimpse of his long-nosed friend.

*

Chris pushed Tanya aside as he clambered onto the dock.

"What the fuck," he muttered under his breath. "Marcus!" he hissed. He grabbed Tanya by the wrist and gave her arm a jerk. "Why didn't you stop him?" Muttering something unintelligible, he started after the boy, pulling Tanya behind him.

*

Tanya tried to break free from Chris's grasp, but when she saw a robed figure lunge out of the shadows and reach for Marcus, she stopped.

"Marcus!" she screamed.

She nearly lost her footing and fell into the harbor when she saw Marcus stumble.

"Help him!" she implored Chris. "Help him!"

*

Chris pushed Tanya to the side and sprinted ahead. Grabbing Marcus's assailant by the arm, he spun the person toward him, jabbing a forearm to the person's head and then a knee into his crotch. Chris flung the man harshly toward the railing. The man groaned as he landed between two stacks of crates and an oblong drum. Chris smirked.

"Fuckin' pervert," he snarled. He could barely make out the man's face as he glared at him. "Using your drum to lure—"

He coiled his arm for another blow, but someone grabbed his arm.

"Come on!" Tanya yelled, clutching at Chris's shoulder. "I can't find Marcus!"

*

Marcus scampered along the streetfront in pursuit of his long-nosed friend. Still a bit shaken from the man who'd appeared from the shadows, he repeatedly glanced over his shoulder to make sure the robed stranger hadn't followed him. He was pretty sure Chris could beat the guy up, but still. He could hear Lady T yelling, but from what he could make out, she was yelling at Chris. Maybe the man had gotten away from Chris and she was mad at him. But then again, she always seemed to be mad at Chris. Why were they always fighting? Grown-ups were always mad at each other. *Maybe that's what happens when you get older*, he thought. Maybe he didn't want to get older—ever.

A sudden burst of air and a fluttering noise right above his head prompted Marcus to duck. Startled, he caught a blurry glimpse of wings darting into a doorway several feet ahead—the same doorway where he'd last seen his long-nosed friend.

The abrupt boom of gunshot froze Marcus. He turned toward the dock. He listened intently. Nothing for a moment, then a chorus of loud, garbled voices. Marcus sprinted toward the doorway, where he was certain he would find safety and his long-nosed friend.

*

Chris stared into the barrel of the automatic rifle and raised his hands. He eyed the five armed men who'd burst out of a truck parked at the end of the dock.

"We don't have any—"

A rifle butt slammed sharply into his kidney. He nearly fell to his knees. But one of the men grabbed his arm and steadied him while another relieved him of the handgun stuffed in the waistband of his pants.

"*Ferenji*," he heard one of the men say in a dismissive tone.

"Hey!" Tanya shouted. "Get your hands off me, you son of a bitch!"

Chris heard a slap and looked over to see Tanya covering her face. One of the men stood in front of her with his hand poised to strike.

"Hey, asshole!" Chris snapped. "Leave the girl alone!"

When he saw the man glance his way, he spat at his feet. The man's eyes squinted to slits.

*

Tanya screamed when the man slammed the butt of the rifle into Chris's forehead. Horrified, she watched Chris crumple to the ground. She screamed again.

"Shut up!" one of the men ordered.

"You speak American?" she asked. Smiling, she pointed a finger at her chest. "I'm an American," she said. She glanced down at the seemingly unconscious Chris. "We're both American."

Projecting a friendly expression, she made eye contact with each of the five men. Noting their similar dress—dark khaki shirts and pants, maroon berets—she hoped they were some form of police.

"The captain of the ship we were on," she said, pointing at the ocean, "he said there's an American embassy here." She smiled and pointed toward the city. "Here. Djibouti," she went on, emphasizing the city with her extended finger.

One of the men chuckled. Another laughed. She sought out the man who'd told her to shut up—wiry, with a hooked nose—and took a tentative step toward him. Immediately, two of his companions grabbed her arms.

"I'm an American citizen," she protested to the man with the hooked nose. "I got rights. Take me to the embassy."

Frustrated when none of the men showed any sort of reaction, she stomped her foot.

"Where the police?" she demanded. She scrutinized the uniforms of the two men holding her by the arms. "You the police?" Shifting her attention to the wiry man, she inquired, "Are you part of the Djibouti police?"

"Djibouti," the man holding her right arm repeated.

"Yes! Yes!" she repeated. "Djibouti!"

All five men laughed.

"What's so funny?" she complained. "Why you laughin'?"

"*Amrikyia,*" the man with the hooked nose snickered. He shook his head. "You are ignorant, yes?" he said to Tanya.

"*Almudir!*" one of the men standing apart from the others shouted.

The men looked toward the end of the dock, where a set of approaching headlights was visible. Someone with authority was about to arrive.

"That your boss?" she asked.

The English-speaking man frowned and gave her a curt shake of his head.

"He gonna chew you all out for messin' with two Americans, I bet."

The man chuckled and turned his head.

Tanya grunted. "Well, whoever it is, you can bet your ass I'm gonna—"

One of the men clamped a hand over her mouth. When she slapped his arm, he grabbed a fistful of her hair and sharply yanked.

But the appearance of a white Mercedes four-door gave her hope. A Mercedes signified wealth. And wealth meant stature and—to a degree—sophistication. After being manhandled and laughed at, she was eager to speak with someone who had a little more tact and manners. So, when the rear door of the sleek automobile opened and a diminutive, elderly man exited, she wasted no time letting the man know who she was and where she was from.

"You the big man?" she called out. "Got two Americans here!" She gave a nod to the five men gathered near her. "And we ain't been treated right." She shook her head and added, "Uh-uh. No sir. Not treated right at all."

The elderly man gestured subtly with his left hand, and her arms were released. She smiled.

"That's right. That's better."

She noticed the boss man looking her over from head to toe. She'd been appraised like that before.

"Like what you see?" She gave the man a wink. "Then maybe we can do business. Like you take us to the embassy, and then you and me go on a date before I get on a plane and go back home."

"Home," the elderly man repeated with a smile.

Then he leaned toward the man who'd spoken in English and said, "*Majnoon.*" The men laughed. Tanya fumed.

"Why y'all so disrespectful?" She glanced down at Chris. "Man needs a doctor. And I need a room with a shower and a bed. And the boy…" Suddenly reminded Marcus had run off, she looked toward the buildings along the waterfront. "We need to find the boy," she said. She met the boss man's eyes. "Need to find the boy and get us where we need to be."

When the boss man didn't immediately respond, Tanya raised her voice.

"I said—"

"Enough!" the old man barked. "Bring her," he ordered. "And throw him in the trunk."

No sooner had he finished speaking than she was jostled over to the Mercedes while Chris was picked up by his arms and legs and shuffled over to the trunk of the car.

"What the hell you doin'?" Tanya yelled. "Didn't you—?"

The slap to the back of her head was swift and forceful. As she stumbled forward, she glimpsed the elderly man slipping into the back seat of the Mercedes. Pushed from behind toward the open back door of the car, she lunged backward in an attempt to break free. A punch to her stomach doubled her over and left her gasping.

"Bitch," the man with the hooked nose said. "No one hears you. No one cares." He spat at her feet. "Americans," he said. "Mogadishu will feast on your bones."

Still reeling from the punch to her stomach, Tanya struggled to stand erect.

"Mogadishu?" she sputtered.

With a nod from the man with the hooked nose, his companions pinned her arms behind her back and threw her against the Mercedes. Steel cuffs snapped over her wrists, a cloth was forced into her mouth, and Tanya was shoved into the back seat of the car. The old man acknowledged her presence with a nod. Once again, he scrutinized her from head to toe.

"You will do," he remarked in a pleasant tone of voice. "The general will be pleased."

Her stifled scream of rage sounded like a prolonged grunt.

"But your attitude." He shook his head. "The captain warned me you were—" he raised his bushy grey eyebrows "—troublesome. And some-what vulgar."

Tanya cowered back when the man reached over and placed a hand on her chest.

"Firm." He chuckled. "Adhib is partial to firm breasts." He nodded. "Yes, you'll do. You'll do."

Tanya's eyes went wide as the old man extracted a shiny-handled knife from the sleeve of his robe.

"I must remember to send the captain of the *Jameel* a little something extra." He tapped on the darkened partition between the front and back seats of the car before continuing. "For bypassing Djibouti and bringing you here."

She cringed when he squeezed her upper thigh.

"Young, firm, and American," he muttered with a chuckle. "Yes, the general will be pleased."

*

Marcus watched Lady T ride off in the white car. He was certain she would return, but he was happy she was gone for now. The past week hadn't been fun. Too much arguing between Lady T and Chris, too many days with no one to play with, too many crummy meals of runny stew served with flat pieces of bread that didn't taste like anything. Yuck. Maybe, after hide-and-seek, his long-nosed playmate would take him somewhere he could get some chicken and biscuits like gran-Jim used to make him. And maybe the bird that had followed his floppy-eared friend into the building belonged to someone who would show him around Africa—whatever Africa was. But first things first. A game of hide-and-seek was in progress. And his role in the game was obviously the seeker.

Marcus stepped away from the wobbly wooden door and moved farther into the narrow room with no windows. At the back wall, a dim blue light glowed from beneath a door. Intrigued, he took a few tentative steps toward it, stopping when the light went out.

At first, he was pretty sure the low rumbling he heard was coming from his stomach. Thinking about fried chicken and biscuits had made him hungry. But when he placed his hand flat atop his tummy, he didn't feel anything—no gurgling or growling. Redirecting his attention toward the back of the room, he was unnerved to discover that the vibrating sound seemed to be coming from behind the door. Curious, he moved two steps closer and listened. The soft, pulsing whirr grew stronger. He smiled. He thought he recognized the sound: a cat purring. Drawn by the sound, he darted across the room and grasped the doorknob.

The ferocious roar that met Marcus when he pulled open the door sent him tumbling backward. Terrified, he scurried across the floor until his shoulder slammed into a wall. Breathing heavily, eyes fixed on the open door, he waited anxiously, dreading to see what terrible dinosaur or dragon would emerge.

A tattered grey cat slinked through the door and came to a stop. Not certain whether he should be afraid of the animal or greet it with a wave, Marcus gave the cat with bright yellow eyes a smile and a nod. The cat made a dash toward the front door. Marcus bolted off the floor and sprinted to catch up. Pushing through the rickety door, he ran headlong into a person dressed in a loose-fitting, hooded grey robe.

"Would that I had been a tree," the startled woman said. "You'd be on your backside looking up at the stars."

Focused on pursuit, Marcus tried to go around the woman. But a strong hand gripped his upper arm.

"I would watch where you run," she advised.

Marcus looked up as she spoke, but he could see nothing of the woman's features inside the hood.

"There are slavers about," she told him. And then she shook his arm as if she was waking him from a deep sleep. "Nasty people, they," she went on. "Where is it you go in such a hurry? Have you lost a friend?"

Marcus tried to look around the woman, but her flowing robe blocked his line of sight. Frustrated, he looked up toward the woman's face.

"Hide-and-seek," he blurted.

"Hide-and-seek," she repeated, sounding amused. "And who is it you are trying to find?"

Marcus pictured his long-nosed friend. Not sure how to answer, he drooped one arm in front of his nose and let it sway back and forth before raising his hands to the sides of his head and flapping them next to his ears.

"A butterfly?" the woman guessed.

Marcus frowned and shook his head. He took a long step to the side and surveyed the area toward the water. He pointed out his long-nosed friend when he saw the animal standing near the head of the dock.

"Difireti?"

Marcus felt a zing of energy when the woman gently placed her hand atop his head.

"You see her?"

Marcus gazed up into the woman's hood with a puzzled expression.

"Her?" he asked. He glanced over toward his long-nosed friend. "She's a girl?"

The woman laughed.

"Difireti?" she asked with a chuckle. "Yes, she's a girl."

Marcus's face took on a thoughtful expression.

"Diff?" he muttered. He looked up into the hood. "Diff-diff-difter?"

"Difireti," she corrected.

Again, Marcus felt energy course through him when the woman lightly squeezed his shoulder.

"Differi-diff—" Marcus shook his head.

"Courage," the woman mildly offered. "Where you come from, she would be called Courage."

"Courage," Marcus repeated.

He glanced over toward where he'd last seen Courage and smiled. But when he didn't see her standing near the dock, he became distressed.

"She's gone!" he exclaimed. "I have to find her! We're playing a game!"

"There, there," the woman assured him. Pointing to an area of the dock where crates were stacked four and five high, she said, "I think I know where she is. I think I saw her…" The woman paused and placed her hands on her hips. "Well, I would need to be part of the game before I could tell you where she is, wouldn't I?"

Marcus took hold of the woman's hand as she began walking toward the dock.

"I haven't played hide-and-seek in quite some time," she went on. "Do you think it will be all right with Difireti if I play?"

Marcus looked up into the darkness of the hood and nodded.

"Then it's settled. We'll pretend—"

Marcus abruptly stopped and looked in each direction.

"Cat," he said. He pulled on the woman's hand. "Did you see a cat?"

"Cat," the woman thoughtfully repeated. "Why, yes." Resuming her walk toward the dock, she said, "I think I know where it might be. Should we make both the cat and Difireti It when we find them?"

Marcus nodded.

"Well, then. Let's hurry."

Marcus began to skip as the woman quickened her pace. And as he struggled to keep hold of her hand, he noticed the curious coloring of her skin: light shades of cream, sand, and soil ringed her fingers, hand, and wrist. Odd as he might have found the woman's skin to be, he barely gave it a second thought. For a game of hide-and-seek was at hand, and he intended to win.

27

"WHO'S THERE?"

Teimbaka tensed when he both heard and felt footfalls on the wooden dock. Anticipating another attack, he cowered farther between the crates where he'd taken refuge. His body involuntarily jerked as he waited for a kick to his side or a fist delivered to his chin. When neither materialized, he dipped his head and whimpered.

"Why must you torture me?" he whined.

A rumble of thunder accompanied a gust of wind. A drop of rain splattered against his brow. Steeling himself against an impending downpour, he wrapped his robe about his shoulders and curled into a ball.

"Do what you will," he muttered.

He closed his eyes and shook his head. Out upon the open water, he heard the snap of a rope and the bluster of a sail fluttering on the end of a broken line.

"I am worthless."

*

Claire stared at the man sitting across from her in conflicted silence. His appearance—blank stare within dark-ringed eyes, pale complexion, slumped posture, trembling hands—moved her to pity. Yet, knowing he had murdered her mother and Mr. Locket, she could not deny the anger she felt toward him or dismiss her troubling urge to seek revenge. Mr. Pembrook had told her the prosecutor in the case was seeking the death penalty. Though the prospect of the man dying by lethal injection was abhorrent to her, she could not dismiss her own recurring vision of the man burning in the flames of Hell for what he'd done. The vision was frightening. She'd prayed for it to be erased from her thoughts. But her prayers had gone unanswered.

"You shouldn't be here."

Claire looked blankly at the man. His voice, his words, barely registered.

"You should be on a plane." The man lifted his shackled wrists and shook the chain. "You should go."

"Go where?" she numbly asked.

The man looked at her strangely. Why did he seem so confused by her reply? The chain rattled as he rested his shackled wrists back on the table.

"I'm sorry I ever took you away."

She nearly reached out to him when she noticed his eyes were tearing up.

"I'm sorry for a lot of things," he added under his breath.

"Away?" She shook her head and looked down at the floor. "I was—" She glanced at him, suspicious. "Were we—? How do I know you?"

He offered no reply.

"They told me your name is Peter Benson." She fiddled with the cross hanging from the thin, silver chain around her neck. "I don't recall…"

The man chuckled sardonically.

"Peter Benson," he muttered. He stroked his whiskered jaw and momentarily closed his tired-looking blue eyes. "Had I never become Dirk Savage…" he wistfully murmured.

Claire shifted her focus to Dirk's unshaven face. Something about the cut of his chin, the deep blue color of his eyes, struck her as familiar. Suddenly his face was looming over hers, his eyes piercing as he spoke.

"I'm your brother," he'd told her.

"You," she whispered as though waking from a dream. "Why did you pretend… ?"

She couldn't finish her thought. She couldn't remember where exactly she had been when Dirk— She reached across the table and grabbed his hands.

"Where were we?" she blurted. She felt panic in her stomach. "When you—?"

A blast of crackling static startled her.

"No physical contact with the prisoner, Miss Waterman," a male voice commanded.

Claire whirled around and located the speaker hanging in the upper corner of the small room. Then she glanced over her shoulder toward a wire-backed window. Three men were on the other side of the window, peering in. Mr. Pembrook nodded to her when she made eye contact.

"You were warned."

Claire shifted her attention to the hanging speaker. She nodded and released her grip on Dirk.

"Ten minutes."

She slowly slid her hands back to her side of the table.

There was so much she wanted to know. Ten minutes! The time restriction seemed bizarre. Suddenly, asking—demanding—to meet with Peter Benson—the confessed killer of her mother and Mr. Locket—felt pointless.

"Why?" she asked, pained. She searched Dirk's eyes. "Tell me why."

She studied his expression as he glanced toward the window. He seemed detached, uninterested in what she'd asked. His head tilted from side to side as if he were listening to a conversation playing out within his thoughts. She was beginning to think he wasn't going to respond when he motioned with a finger for her to lean forward.

"They shouldn't know," he whispered. He glanced over both shoulders as if expecting to find someone standing behind him. "They shouldn't know why."

Utterly confused by his answer, Claire rubbed the cross between her fingers and shook her head.

"What are you saying?"

A stern expression swept across his features as he twice shook his head and motioned downward with a flattened hand.

"You confessed," she whispered. "Didn't you tell them?" She sighed when his brow furrowed. "Why— Why you—?" The fact that Dirk had murdered her mother suddenly became crystal clear. "Why you killed my mother!" she hissed. Almost as an afterthought, she added, "And Mr. Locket!"

His expression changed to one of bafflement. It dawned on her that he might not have full grasp of his faculties.

"That," he grunted. In a voice she could barely hear, he confessed, "That wasn't me."

As if he understood she was about to blurt out an astounded *"What?,* he rattled the chain binding his wrists and sharply shook his head. Claire sat back in her chair, mouth agape.

What could he possibly mean? she wondered. He'd confessed to the killings. His statement had been printed in the *Inquirer* several times. The police had replayed the audio of his confession for her—despite Mr. Pembrook's vehement objection—when they wanted to verify some of the minor aspects of the story. So, what was he saying? What was he telling her? That he didn't do it? Or was he saying he wasn't himself at the time?

"You—," she began quite loudly. She leaned across the table. "You confessed," she adamantly whispered.

He ran a hand over his head and blinked his eyes several times, looking surprised. Then, with an elongated sigh, he bent low toward the table and said, "I had to."

All at once his expression changed. Surprise transitioned to sadness. His air of resignation transformed to an expression of deep guilt. She recognized those emotions as if they were her own. She had experienced them before through a boy she once knew, a boy who had traveled for days to bring her medicine for a sick baby. The baby had died an hour before he'd returned. She'd watched his heart break at the news. He'd never forgiven himself.

"John," she murmured as she remembered. Sighing heavily, she made the sign of the cross.

"Who?"

"Never mind. I was thinking of someone…" She shook her head and looked toward the floor.

"It was time," she heard Dirk mutter. "She's been waiting."

Dirk was intently gazing at her when she looked up from the floor.

"She's been waiting," he repeated.

Unnerved by the intensity of his stare, Claire eased back into her chair and placed her hands on her lap.

"So I told them what they wanted to hear."

"She?" Claire whispered. "I don't—"

"Genevieve," he replied.

"Genevieve," she repeated. She shook her head. "I'm not sure—"

"I told you about her." He leaned forward. "The first time I visited you in the—" Dirk placed his fingers to his lips and glanced off to the side. "In the clinic," he said. "I told you about her."

She was on the verge of telling him she didn't recall, but his pained expression kept her from doing so.

"I see," she said instead. She grabbed the edge of the tabletop with both hands. "And what is it they don't—?" She nodded back across her shoulder, hoping he would understand she meant the men standing at the window. "What happened?" she whispered. "What don't you want them to know?"

She leaned closer as she waited for his reply. The vacant look in his eyes made her wonder if he'd understood what she'd asked.

"That night—" She hesitated. "The night you went to the house— my mother's—" She reached across the table to touch him, but slid her hands back with a glance to the speaker. "What did Genevieve see?" The silver cross lightly jingled when she leaned so far forward her chest nearly touched the tabletop. "What did *she* see the night my mother was killed?"

Dirk silently mouthed Genevieve's name, a glimmer of clarity in his eyes.

"We drove—" Dirk paused and rubbed his forehead. "There was a car in the driveway—black, official looking. Danny was surprised."

"Danny? You mean Mr. Locket?"

Dirk tilted his head to the side and furrowed his brow.

"Go on," Claire prodded. "Please."

"He said Cook had gone home. He couldn't imagine who it could be. I was—" She watched his eyes drift as he clenched and unclenched his hands. "I was—"

He paused to rub his left forearm. Claire put a knuckle to her lips when she noticed several unsightly needle marks on the underside of his arm.

"We went inside. There was a black man in the study with Caroline.

Caroline seemed upset. Danny's voice got loud. He asked the man to explain who he was."

Dirk sat back and rubbed his face. When he seemed to lose his concentration, Claire spoke up.

"The black man with my mother—with Caroline—who was he?"

Dirk immediately glanced toward the window. When he leaned in, Claire did the same.

"Said he was ATF. Danny didn't understand. Then Caroline pointed at me." He paused to take a deep breath. "I got angry. I'm sure I said…" His head drooped as his voice trailed off. "But she was lying," he muttered. Dirk looked up. "I've never dealt."

"Dealt? I don't understand."

"She kept looking at Danny—"

"Mr. Locket, you mean."

"Like she was afraid he was going to get angry. Kept edging nearer to him with her hand outstretched. Like she wanted to hold his arm or something."

"And what did Mr. Locket—Danny—say?"

"He gave me a dirty look. But when the ATF guy started going on about the estate being used as a path house for drug shipments, he snapped. Told the guy—Crenship, Crenshon, or whatever his name was—he knew everything that took place on the grounds and that he was horribly mistaken—or concocting an elaborate fabrication."

Claire and Dirk both jumped when the speaker suddenly crackled. "Five minutes," an impassive voice announced.

Claire shot the speaker a frown before continuing.

"Lying? What did he say to that?"

"He insinuated Danny was in on the operation. Said he had information from one of the other employees that he and I were partners. That he'd seen some unsavory people going in and out of the barn."

"The stables?" Claire repeated, confused.

"That was Danny's reaction. But then Caroline said she'd seen the same thing."

"Said the same—?" She shook her head.

"Said she'd seen a big fellow—very big, she said—coming and going.

Said she saw him hanging around the garage." Dirk chuckled derisively. "She pointed at me and said, 'Where he lives.' I laughed."

"Laughed?"

"I've never had a visitor—" His expression turned serious. His eyes glazed. "Not a person, anyway," he said. He chuckled uncomfortably. "Unless you mean Danny, or Mrs. Cavanaugh when she'd drop off something to eat." He shrugged. "In the beginning, anyway. Before she…"

Claire glanced over her shoulder. A fourth man had joined the three standing outside the wire-backed window. She noticed Mr. Pembrook pointing to his wrist as she turned her head back toward Dirk.

"My mother," Claire said in earnest. "You confessed to killing her. But now you're telling me it wasn't you."

Dirk sat up straight in his chair. Claire leaned forward.

"Who was it, then? Who killed my mother?"

"Sometimes she'd bring Irish stew and rolls baked fresh from the oven." He closed his eyes and smiled. "Sometimes a casserole of noodles with chicken in a—"

Claire slapped a hand atop the table. Dirk blinked several times.

"But when she found out I wanted money…" He shook his head. "But Caroline never intended to give me any. She was just stringing me along, keeping me where she could control me. I was stupid. Played right into her hands. I didn't see it until you were…"

Claire touched her cheek as Dirk's focus flitted from her nose to her chin to her lips and then to her forehead.

"They killed you," he uttered, confused. "I remember hearing someone— I saw you—" He stroked his jaw. "But you're here." His face took on a quizzical expression. "Why aren't you dead? That's what they wanted."

Claire placed a hand at the dull ache that had started just above her ear. She wasn't sure if Dirk was speaking about some fantasy he'd imagined or a garbled recollection misplaced from another person's memory. But regardless, she found what he said to be both hurtful and frightening.

"I'm…" She closed her eyes and took a deep breath. "My mother— You were—" Her eyes were filled with sympathy when she opened them to look at Dirk. "Genevieve. She saw who killed my mother. Ask her who it was."

Brow furrowed, Dirk looked down toward the floor.

"Who did she see?"

Dirk shook his head as though troubled by a nagging thought.

"He was just there," he muttered.

"Who?"

Dirk looked up and met her gaze.

"The big man—huge—just appeared, like he was— Knocked Danny to the floor with a vicious punch to the side of the head. Caroline screamed. I tried to—" He rubbed his neck. "He shoved a needle—"

When Dirk flinched, Claire noticed his eyes were blurry with tears. He looked like he was in pain.

"I must have walked—" He shook his head. "I don't remember. I found myself standing behind her. She was on the floor, kneeling." His right hand jerked as if a bee had stung his wrist. "He slapped a gun in my hand." He curled and uncurled his index finger. "I thought he was going to break my—" He leaned across the table with a desperate look on his face. "He forced me to squeeze it. The gun went off." His gaze drifted toward the floor. He shook his head. "Caroline." He slid a hand across the table like he was wiping something from the surface. "There was so much—"

"Time to wrap it up." The speaker crackled with a touch of feedback before the impassive male voice added, "Miss Waterman, if you'd slowly push your chair away from the table and stand."

Claire glanced at the speaker.

"And Mr. Locket?" she pressed. "Danny. What happened to him?"

Dirk looked over her shoulder toward the window at her back. A moment later, she heard a door open. She reached across the table and grabbed Dirk's wrist.

"What happened to Danny?" she urgently whispered.

"Time's up."

Claire gasped, startled, when a uniformed policeman grabbed her hand and forcibly pulled it from Dirk's wrist.

"Please," she implored, "a few more minutes?"

The uniformed officer placed her hand on the table in silence. His expression was neutral as he stepped around the table and stood behind

Dirk. Claire felt a moment of desperation as the officer gripped Dirk's upper arm and lifted him from the chair.

"Are you ready, Claire?"

Claire glanced over her shoulder to find Mr. Pembrook behind her. He smiled when she made eye contact with him. The sound of metal chair legs scuffing across a cement floor brought her attention back to Dirk.

"Wait!" she pleaded.

The officer calmly escorted Dirk toward the door. Claire looked frantically at Mr. Pembrook.

"Please! We must help him!" she cried. "Wait!" she yelled to the guard.

The officer halted for a moment and looked toward the two men standing at the window. Claire reached out and gripped Dirk's elbow.

"In the name of Jesus Christ, swear your innocence and I'll do everything—"

Claire flinched and fell silent when the officer curtly brushed her hand from Dirk's elbow and pulled him toward the open door. Mr. Pembrook touched Claire on the shoulder.

"Claire, you need to calm down," he gently advised.

"You sound like the other one," Dirk commented as he was led out of the room.

"What?" Claire asked. She glanced at Mr. Pembrook. "What does he mean?"

Mr. Pembrook shrugged and shook his head.

"The ramblings of a—"

Claire pushed by the elderly lawyer and hurried out the door. Dirk, she saw, was nearing the end of a short hallway with a barred security gate.

"What did you mean?" she called.

Dirk looked over his shoulder.

"What other one?" she shouted. "Who do I sound like?"

When Claire saw the gate begin to slide open she took a few steps toward Dirk.

"Claire!"

Claire came to a grudging halt when Mr. Pembrook grabbed her shoulder.

"Let him go," he advised as she turned to face him. "You've had your meeting."

"But he—"

"Why?"

Claire whirled back around at the sound of Dirk's voice.

"Why what?" Claire shouted back.

"Why do they send nuns to Africa?" Dirk replied.

He shook his head. Then the guard yanked him out of sight.

*

"Nuns," Dirk muttered. He looked at the guard. "They're so holy. Always citing Jesus, like he…"

Dirk fell silent as he glimpsed Genevieve waiting for him at the entrance of his cell.

"That's their job, ain't it?"

Dirk gave the guard a dismissive grunt.

"Myself, I never did know no nuns," the guard went on. "You go to religion school or somethin'? How many you know?"

Dirk extended his arms toward Genevieve's outstretched hands. The guard pulled him to a stop and turned him toward his empty cell. Dirk barely noticed the man unlocking his handcuffs because of the figure standing next to his bunk.

"Dirk," Doctor Haraji said in greeting, "how good of you to be so prompt."

Dirk glanced across his shoulder as the guard maneuvered him into the cell. Genevieve was no longer standing at the door. He felt a pang of anxiety.

"I'll let you know when I'm done," Doctor Haraji said.

Dirk shifted his attention back to the doctor. The guard nodded to the man before he turned and left.

"Be right outside if ya need me," the guard remarked.

Dirk wondered why the doctor would have need of the man. He also wondered where Genevieve had gone.

"How did your meeting go?" Haraji asked.

Dirk looked on in silence as the doctor bent toward the bunk and opened a black bag. He felt another pang of anxiety when the doctor extracted a needle and syringe.

"Time for your therapy booster." Doctor Haraji smiled as he nodded to the syringe. "Genevieve's been waiting."

Dirk tried to blink away the images forming in his mind. The torches, the sword; he covered his ears when he heard the mocking chants from the men in the alley.

"Dirk, I've told you it's okay," the doctor reassured him.

Dirk didn't resist when the doctor pulled his arms down.

"She forgives you for what you did."

Dirk shuddered and stifled a sob. He looked toward the ceiling when the doctor grabbed his left wrist and twisted his forearm upward.

"I've relayed her message to you a dozen times."

Dirk closed his eyes when he felt the needle puncture his skin.

"When will you go to her?" Haraji asked. "When will you find peace in her arms?"

"Genevieve," Dirk mumbled.

The sensation of her image zooming through his bloodstream was intoxicating. He could feel his body quiver as her apparition enveloped him.

"When will you go to her?" he heard a voice ask.

Too immersed in bliss, Dirk gave no answer.

*

Mr. Pembrook carefully placed a small paper cup into Claire's open hand and gently pressed her fingers around it. Satisfied the cup was secure in her grasp, he patted her wrist and sat down beside her.

"I'd prefer it be a cup of Earl Grey," he commented. "Tea is such a great relaxer."

He glanced at Claire's face; she looked spellbound.

"So many emotions," he remarked. "I wish you had taken my advice and dismissed the idea of trying to hold a coherent conversation with the man."

When Claire showed no outward sign she'd heard him, he cupped his fingers around her hand and guided the cup of water to her mouth.

"Go on, take a sip." He glanced at her and sighed. "Must have been terribly difficult for you." He eyed her with concern. "You certainly have more courage than I. Best let the judicial process play out now, I would think."

Claire took a mechanical sip of water, her expression vacant.

"Let's get you home," he said. "Nothing further to do here."

To his surprise, Claire slid further back on the wooden bench where they were seated and rested her shoulders against the uppermost plank. She took a second sip from the paper cup, a thoughtful expression on her face.

"There was no mention of an ATF agent or a—" Her eyes were focused, her intensity a bit intimidating when she turned to address him. "Was there any reference to a big man in the police report?"

Mr. Pembrook initially frowned but then raised his eyebrows.

"A big man?" he questioned. He shook his head. "None that I'm aware. Referencing what aspect of the report?"

Claire put a finger to her lips and then shook her head.

"I don't know. He seems so—" She ran the same finger along the ridge of her brow. "So troubled."

"I should say he is," Mr. Pembrook emphatically agreed. "And I would hope you'd consider whatever he told you in that light." With a gentle touch to her elbow, he added, "He's a confessed murderer, Claire. There's really nothing else to it."

"He said he confessed because he had to." She gave him a quizzical glance. "Said a woman—Genevieve—has been waiting for him." She shook her head. "Does that make sense? Waiting for him? Waiting where?" She took another sip of water. "Who is she, and what does she want him to do, exactly?"

Mr. Pembrook put a hand to his mouth and cleared his throat.

"Claire—three people are dead. Murdered. I doubt there is anything he could say that would make sense." He shifted his position on the bench so he could face her. "I set this meeting up—at your insistence—so you could find some closure to this— this *horrid* incident. Don't allow this man to plant doubt or sympathy toward him in your head. He's a confessed killer. I say let the judicial process run its course and let justice be served."

Claire clutched her silver cross with her free hand.

"Justice," she murmured. She looked down the hallway toward the room where the meeting with Dirk had taken place. "What justice is there if he's not guilty?"

"I hope that's a rhetorical question," Mr. Pembrook quickly replied. "You've read his confession."

Claire sighed and shook her head.

"I know, I know," she admitted. "It's just—why would he make it up? He seemed so believable, about there being a very large man who—"

"What about the nurse?" Mr. Pembrook interjected. "Did he invent someone else being present in the room when he stuck a needle in the poor woman's neck and shot an overdose of drugs into her system?"

"No, we didn't discuss—"

"Of course not, because there wasn't anyone. The only one in the examination room at the time of the incident was Mr. Benson." Mr. Pembrook slapped his knee. "Mr. Benson has even admitted he plunged a needle into the woman's neck. It was still lodged there when the doctor arrived. So please—" Mr. Pembrook shook his head and took a moment to compose himself. "Please, Claire—don't get caught up in the twisted babblings of a—" He gently grasped her hand and sighed. "Of a confessed murderer."

As he studied Claire's face for a reaction, Mr. Pembrook realized how vulnerable she was and how receptive she might be to falling back on her religious training. *Forgiveness*, he thought, *has no place here.*

"I'm— I'm troubled," Claire tentatively confessed.

Mr. Pembrook frowned. "By?"

"Oh, I suppose you're right about— Well—" She sighed. "Not about what transpired, I suppose, but the other thing—at the end, when he was walking out of the room."

"I don't follow. The other thing?"

"Nuns," she said. "He said something about me sounding like the other one." Carefully placing the cup of water on the bench beside her, she continued. "And then he asked about nuns. Plural. Did you notice? *Nuns* with an *s*."

Mr. Pembrook furrowed his brow. "I can't say that I did."

"Do you think—?" Claire glanced down at the cross. "You said you visited Reverend Mother." Mr. Pembrook nodded. "Did she mention another nun? One that was sent after me, possibly to locate me?"

Mr. Pembrook thought for a moment.

"Not to my recollection." He shook his head. "But that's not to say someone else didn't."

"Someone else?"

"If recollection serves me, your father said you were stationed in France when you were ordered to Africa. Is that correct?" When Claire nodded, he continued. "So, it would only follow that if someone was sent to look for you, the order would have originated from the con—" He cleared his throat and offered Claire a quick smile. "The facility where you were stationed. And not from the retreat in Maryland where you undertook your vows."

"My vows."

Claire placed a finger to the side of her cheek and sighed. Mr. Pembrook wondered what chord he'd struck. Did she recall her time in France? How much of her memory was intact after a year in the clinic?

"Dear God!" Claire exclaimed.

Concerned she might be experiencing some latent reaction to her therapy, Mr. Pembrook grasped her by the shoulders and gave her a shake.

"What is it?" he earnestly inquired. "What's wrong?"

She silently mouthed a name before she spoke it aloud.

"Angelique," she said. Mr. Pembrook felt a tremble run through her shoulders. "She was killed." She grasped Mr. Pembrook's forearm. "Her family— They don't know." Tears welled in her eyes as she asked, "How could they? Who would have told them?"

Mr. Pembrook took Claire's hands and held them.

"Angelique— What are you saying? Who is it you remember?"

"When we first arrived." Claire slipped her hands from Mr. Pembrook's grasp to rub the sides of her head. "We were in—" He saw confusion in her eyes when she looked at him. "When we arrived in Djibouti! We— Our driver—" She grasped his forearm again and squeezed. "He was killed. Shot on the road. Angelique was—"

He could sense her mind racing as she stared toward the floor. Her face seemed a jumble of emotions: surprise, anxiety, fright, anger, and finally sadness.

"She was younger than I. French," she said. "She was French." Mr. Pembrook felt the depth of her emotions when she looked into his eyes. "Her parents deserve to know. I need to tell them. I need them to understand her love for them and for—" She clutched the silver cross and sighed. "The Lord Jesus Christ." She wiped a tear from her eye and blessed herself. "They need to know. I need to—" She dipped her head and started to cry. "How do I find them?" she sniffled. "How would I know where to look?"

Mr. Pembrook lightly placed a hand atop Claire's knee.

"Perhaps I can be of assistance."

Claire wiped her nose with the back of her hand.

"I've utilized a number of agencies in Europe in the past. For clients," he explained when she looked up to meet his gaze. "When I needed to get in contact with a distant relative or locate a long-lost cousin who'd suddenly come into an inheritance."

"Agencies?" she questioned. "I'm not sure…" She shook her head.

"Investigative," he replied. "Missing persons, locating—" he paused and nodded toward her. "As in your case, finding someone's parents who live in a country where we don't have access to records."

He could see comprehension dawn in her eyes as she processed what he told her.

"So, you're saying—" she asked in a hopeful tone, "you could locate Angelique's parents?"

"Why, of course," he replied. "I have the name of the facility where you were stationed before you were assigned to your post in Africa, so we can start there. Surely, they'll have the name of the girl's—Angelique's—parents on hand. I can put a call in today once I get back to the office."

"Oh, would you? That would be—" she glanced down at the silver cross resting in her open palm "—such a blessing."

"And I'll make inquiries about the other matter."

"Other matter?" Claire uncertainly repeated.

"The nun. The one Mr. Benson referenced. The one who might have been sent to find you," he reminded her. "Do you think that's possible?"

"Another nun," Claire murmured.

She abruptly turned her head and looked down the hall as if someone had shouted her name. She stared for a few moments before shifting her attention back to Mr. Pembrook.

"'Why do they send nuns to Africa?' Isn't that what he said? Why *do* they send nuns to Africa, do you think?" She slowly closed her fingers around the cross. "I was sent there. I remember—" she rubbed a knuckle across her brow "—some of my stay."

Again, she glanced down the hall toward the room where she and Dirk had spoken. "He said I should go back. I should be on a plane." Mr. Pembrook leaned back onto the bench when she met his eyes.

"Do you know why he would say that?" She shook her head. "I feel as if there is a reason, but I can't seem to…" She lightly bit down on the tip of her knuckle. "Another nun… . Perhaps she could tell me why Mr. Benson…"

Mr. Pembrook shook his head as Claire lapsed into silence. *The poor girl is certainly out of sorts*, he thought. *Hopefully, she'll never remember—*

"Why can't I remember anything?" she asked, twisting the cross between her fingers. "Why was I placed in a clinic? Why did he say they wanted me—?"

"Claire!" Mr. Pembrook strongly interjected. "You're getting distracted."

"Distracted? How can—?"

"Might a trip to retrace your time in Europe and Africa be in order?"

"My time in…"

"Say, a few days in France before heading to Djibouti."

Claire's cheeks flushed as she massaged the sides of her head.

"I'm on good terms with one of the administrative attachés at the embassy. I'm certain he could help you—"

"Remember?"

Mr. Pembrook smiled and lightly grasped one of Claire's hands.

"I was thinking more along the line of reacquainting you with the area and the people." He raised his eyebrows. "And in the process, perhaps, you might run across someone who might have had some interaction with you when you were stationed there."

"Yes," Claire muttered with a nod. "Find someone who knows me."

She squeezed Mr. Pembrook's hand. "And then maybe…" She smiled and placed the tips of her fingers to her mouth.

"Let's not get ahead of ourselves," he cheerfully suggested. "First things first." He patted her on the knee. "Let's get you home."

He rose from the bench and motioned with an outstretched hand for her to do the same.

"Then I'll go back to my office and place that call."

"Call?" she repeated as she rose from the bench.

"About the nun," he clarified. "The nun who may have been sent to find you."

"The nun," Claire repeated. "Africa…" She glanced down the hall. "I wonder…"

She looked questioningly into Mr. Pembrook's eyes. "I wonder if she's still there."

<h1 style="text-align:center">28</h1>

THE SOUND OF a drumbeat coming from the direction of the harbor was a source of both hope and torment to John Too. Hope because it raised the possibility Teimbaka was nearby. Torment because even if the instrument were being played by Teimbaka and not some beggar pandering for coin, there was little his friend could do to help him out of his predicament. Teimbaka, blind and immersed in self-pity, was a shell of the man John Too had met in the desert. What had happened to the favored son of the Mother, the chosen of the spirit-elephants, the finder of the words that pulled Claire from the clutches of death and sent the Serpent slithering back to its smoldering pit of hate? How the Father and the Mother had turned their backs on the man.

As he rattled the chains clamped around his wrists and ankles, he couldn't help but wonder: was he, too, an object of their disappointment? No longer able to foresee events as he once had, he considered his slave chains a symbol of his failure. He equated the loss of freedom to the loss of their faith. Why did the Mother and the Father no longer trust him? What expectation had he failed to fulfill? And how was he to be of service to them bound in chains— a slave? He had to admit he didn't know. And that admission, in of itself, was disheartening.

Sister Lady—he thought of her in his state of hopelessness: where she was, if she was well fed, if she slept in a place free of the buzzing of flies and the weeping of the sick and starving. He missed her. Part of him felt empty without her. She was the spirit bond between the Mother and the Father, guardian of the infirm and destitute, nurturer of the words written by the Boy. Why had she been taken from the Mother's hand? What were he, Teimbaka, and John to do without her strength? They had fragmented upon her departure. He saw this clearly. Since that day, the Mother had gone quiet. The son of the Father had become distracted. As he mulled these observations, the chains around his wrists and ankles felt doubly heavy.

"When I say move, you will stand."

John Too's head swiveled with the crack of a whip. He watched the man wielding the instrument of obedience with a wary eye.

"And when you stand," the whip-wielder instructed, "you will do so in silence."

John Too dipped his head when the whip-wielder cast his gaze down the line of the enslaved and made eye contact with each, one by one.

"If any one of you causes trouble," the man said, snapping the whip close to John Too's feet, "all will feel the lash." John Too winced when the man snapped the whip for a third time. "Understood?"

John Too breathed a sigh of relief when the man walked farther up the line of human cargo toward the front of the warehouse where they'd been kept for the past day and a half. Cautiously, he surveyed the faces of those to either side of him: a score of women and children, with only one other man, who was chained next to him. The man, dressed in the clothes of a ferenji—a collared shirt with buttons down the front, pants made of denim, black boots—had recently been beaten. His face was swollen and discolored, his expression angry as he clenched and unclenched his fists. John Too sensed violence in him. This was no herder or farmer. And his clothes—his clothes were not those of a ferenji businessman. The man's dress and disposition made John Too wonder where the ferenji was destined. To life as a laborer in the oil fields in northern Sudan? Or perhaps he'd been purchased by a handler and would soon be competing in the fight pits in one of the Arab countries across the Red Sea.

The shout "Get up!" was accentuated with the snap of the whip.

Holding the slack of the chains close to his body so the links wouldn't clink, John Too slowly stood.

"Now move toward the door at the front of the building!" The whip snapped once more. "Move quickly!"

The line of enslaved moved as one, as if the chains that bound them served as both a conveyer of their actions and the vessel in which they moved. Slave.

Enslaved. The words held meanings John Too did not want to contemplate. Yet he could not help but imagine what the coming days held in store for him and for the women and children chained with him.

"Boy."

The word, pronounced with a ferenji accent, prodded John Too to glance behind him.

"Where are they taking us?" the man with the battered face whispered.

John Too ignored the question and faced front, searching for the man with the whip. He had no desire to feel its sting upon his flesh. He had seen the work of the lash on Teimbaka's back. How Teimbaka had survived George Henry's brutal beating, he could not fathom. Only by the grace and compassion of the Mother and the Father had he lived.

"Are you deaf?"

John Too closed his eyes. The clink of chain against chain sent a shiver up his spine.

"Answer me!" the ferenji harshly whispered, grabbing John Too's shoulder and spinning him around.

John Too glared at the ferenji. "Slave ship," he tersely told the man.

The loud crack of the whip near his ear buckled his knees.

"Did you not hear me, boy?"

A cuff to the side of his head made John Too cringe. Fear shot through him as the whip-wielder yanked him to his feet.

"I said silence!" The whip-wielder glared at John Too before shifting his attention to the ferenji.

"And you!" he barked. "Give me a reason to take the lash to you!"

John Too held his breath as the ferenji returned the whip-wielder's glare with one of his own. He was still clenching and unclenching his fists. John Too cowered as the whip-wielder lunged at the ferenji, slamming the butt of the whip into his chest.

"You'll wish you'd never left the US," the whip-wielder taunted. He shoved the ferenji back. "And that gash on your face?" He laughed. "The first of many." With a grunt and a smirk, he added, "The captain of the Jameel *did you no favors."*

John Too breathed a sigh of relief when the whip-wielder turned and walked toward the front of the warehouse. Cautiously, he glanced at the ferenji.

"American," he muttered. *"Like Sister Lady—"*

The whip lashed John Too's shoulder as its crack echoed down the line. He collapsed to his knees as the first of twenty lashes was administered to his fellow captives.

*

Blue: sky, water, a host of azure butterflies flitting from white-petaled flowers to an arch made of cream and red orchids. The settling calm of the color blue was a perfect backdrop to the yellow sun overhead.

Sarah leaned back on her elbows and stretched her bare legs. The lush grass felt soft against her thighs. Head tilted toward the sky, she closed her eyes. The warm rays of the sun sent a pleasant tingle through her flesh.

"Your god is a fable."

Sarah kept her eyes closed. She would not allow Bin'ka to disturb the perfection of the moment.

"As all gods are."

She could hear him shifting his great girth on the grass beside her. Was there a need for him to speak?

"Have you ever imagined what the people of the world would be like without religion?"

Past his voice, past the troublesome thoughts his question stirred, the sound of rushing water—a sapphire creek cascading through a rocky narrowing several meters from where she and Bin'ka had stopped to rest—captured her attention. She saw a mud-covered water buffalo, a blood-spattered hyena, and boy mounted on a donkey. All three animals dipped their mouths into the creek to drink the sky-colored water.

"What would have happened if you were never raped?"

The group at the creek raised their heads as if they'd been alerted to danger, and she assumed the boy, the donkey, the water buffalo, and the hyena were as dismayed as she by Bin'ka's rude question. But she soon realized their attention was focused not on Bin'ka but on her.

"Would you have killed?"

There was no escaping the memory: hardened penis in front of her face, a serrated hunting knife in her hand, a slash upward, a violent thrust of a blade into a man's throat. Though beset since the day of her capture with a pain that had rendered her emotionally paralyzed, she felt utter vindication and joy when she remembered her assailant's scream of agony. For a moment, she averted her eyes from the stares of the group by the creek. Killing, after all, was a sin. And then she wondered why.

"Would any of you not have done the same?" she asked.

The boy bowed his head. The water buffalo snorted. The donkey brayed. The hyena cackled.

"And you?" she asked, turning her attention toward Bin'ka. "Why do you mar such a day with this talk? Are you not in paradise when you look at the colors around you?"

Bin'ka rolled his shoulders and sighed.

"Paradise is dying," he lamented. With a nod toward the host at the creek, he added, "They drink at the feet of two people on the run, fugitives of slavery and war. Surely you see something must be done."

She studied his face as he plucked a blade of grass and scrutinized first one side and then the other. How easily he talks of change, *she thought.* How simple a remedy he must believe exists. *"The world is as simple or confused as the churning in your stomach," she wanted to tell him. "Which world do you walk?"*

"She asks if I am free," he went on. "But she doesn't wait for me to answer."

She watched his eyes as he released the blade of grass. There was a hint of sadness within them, as if he was witnessing the loss of something beloved. His expression, when he turned to address her, caused a small pang of hurt in her heart.

"So, I ask you: are you free?"

Sarah twitched at the hoot of the hyena, then grabbed hold of Bin'ka's arm when the water buffalo began to rake the ground with a hoof. The boy was standing calmly beside the donkey, scratching the beast behind one of its long ears. The way he was looking at Sarah gave her reason to believe he was waiting to hear her reply.

Blue—the sky, the water, a flock of sapphire-feathered birds flying from one emerald-topped tree to the next. The calming color of blue hummed along her senses. Relishing the moment, Sarah blocked the distraction of dialogue, closed her eyes, and concentrated on the hum. The low-level vibration was more a pulse. As if the color blue was alive. As if the color blue was life. Ever so slowly, she opened her eyes and looked toward the creek.

The cross of Sarah's faith dangled on the end of a chain. The chain in turn hung from the barrel of a rifle, which rested upright against a wall immersed in soft blue light. Sarah first viewed the cross as a solitary object suspended in the sky. But the weapon it hung from—an automatic rifle she had seen too much of during her stay in Africa—dashed her hope of being an active participant in a dream. Shifting her attention to her surroundings, she was at a loss as to where she was and how she had come to arrive in what appeared to be a subterranean cavern. Then, all at once, recent events came rushing back. She put a hand to her mouth and gasped. She remembered the sensation of falling. The floor beneath her, the one that had given way, had been made of wood. She looked up. The ceiling above her was intact stone. Caught in a moment of panic, she reached out for the cross. The instant her flesh touched the symbol of her faith, she heard Bin'ka's voice.

"Your cross." Reacting to the urgent tone in his voice, Sarah sat up. "I wrapped it around a latch." Distressed when she heard him cry out in pain, she raised her body to a kneeling position. "On a door. Close to the harbor." Sarah lifted the chain off the weapon and clutched it in her palm. "You must find it. They're waiting for you."

They're waiting for you. The words prompted her to stand and look anew at her surroundings. The walls of the cavern became the alleys she had run through. Men had been chasing her—a mob of torch wielding fanatics who'd taunted her by shouting her name. They'd killed Bin'ka. She was certain they would do the same to her. Or worse. Adhib. She remembered Adhib. The memory stirred feelings of filth and degradation. Boys had been murdered to coerce her into having sex with the man. The man—was he a man? Or was he a manifestation of Satan, a vile creature shielding his identity by taking on a human form and name?

"Say my name," Bin'ka had said. *Bin'ka,* Sarah thought.

"Bin'ka," she muttered aloud.

"You awaken."

Startled to hear a voice, Sarah instinctively grabbed the automatic rifle and dropped to a crouch. The feel of the weapon transported her back to the deck of the ship where she had first encountered Bin'ka. She touched her shoulder where the recoil of the weapon had bruised her flesh. Plumes of blood had risen into the sky the day she'd shot three men. Shouts of *Shange bahr!* had filled her ears. Bin'ka had smiled. She'd *killed* three men. Her mortal sins had increased by three. When the third man's bullet-ridden body had fallen into the sea, she'd wondered how God could ever forgive her. She still wondered.

"Come when you are ready."

Sarah concentrated on the voice—a woman's—reverberating between the stone walls. Blinking away her recollections, she followed the near wall of the cavern until she saw an opening to another chamber. Colored in the same blue light that had been the focus of her dream, the opening resembled a pool of water. Placing the cross around her neck, she shouldered the automatic rifle and walked cautiously forward.

Upon entering the room, she immediately came to a stop. Along the floor of the rough-hewn chamber—a crude rectangular space carved from stone—sat a group of what she first thought to be similarly dressed men, their backs resting against the rock walls, their faces obscured by strange masks. But as she scrutinized the nearest figure, she realized the shape had no bulk. The form was merely an empty uniform. The masks—sand-colored, with eyes of dark green glass, and a ribbed oval hose dangling below a presumed chin—conjured thoughts of alien invaders, characters out of a science fiction movie. Weapons of various designs stood next to each empty uniform, as though at a command, ghost soldiers would fill the outfits, grab their weapons, and march off to battle. Sarah found the setting both odd and frightening. Doubting she should be in such a strange place, she looked down at the silver cross around her neck and wondered if it was hers.

"I had to be sure."

Sarah whirled on her heels and leveled the rifle at the origin of the voice. A robed figure—hooded—stood to one side of another circular opening, an exact replica of the one Sarah had just walked through.

"Squeeze the trigger if you must."

Sarah glanced down at the gun.

"But there's only you and I," the figure said with what Sarah took to be a chuckle. "It's not loaded."

Sarah quickly glanced around the room. She counted a score of weapons perched along the walls.

"Oh, I suppose some of those may still be loaded."

Sarah jerked the rifle into a firing position when the woman abruptly moved her hands toward her head.

"I wasn't aware I'm to die, though." The woman pushed the hood of the robe off her head. "But I suppose you'd find the message regardless."

Sarah studied what she could discern of the woman's features. But since the woman stood with the glow of the blue light behind her, it was hard for Sarah to see much more of her than a head of bushy hair surrounding a thin face with eyes obscured by a pair of thick-framed, dark-lensed glasses.

"Who are you?" Sarah asked. "And where—?" She looked slowly around the room. "What is this place?"

"This place?" the woman questioned. "Why, it is nothing more than a staging area. A birthplace, if you will."

Sarah lowered the rifle to her side.

"Staging area?" She motioned toward the empty uniforms lining the walls. "These clothes—uniforms, masks. I don't—" She shook her head. "I don't understand." With a glance behind her toward the room where she'd awakened, she added, "How did I get here? And how did you get this?" She displayed the cross between her thumb and forefinger. "Bin'ka said he wrapped it around a latch. But I didn't see it when I—" Again, she glanced behind her toward the room where she'd awakened. "I went into a closet. Men—Adhib's men—were chasing me." She looked down at the cross. "They killed Bin'ka. They were going to—"

"Bin'ka," the woman said. "A loss to regret. A soldier to mold an army."

"Soldier? Bin'ka wasn't a soldier. He was—"

"No?" the woman questioned when Sarah's voice trailed off. "You met how?"

Sarah clutched her throat as she experienced a sudden shortness of breath. She felt the heaviness of water swirling around her torso and the sensation of waves lapping over her head. Instinctively, she dropped the rifle and began to thrash her arms. She searched for a glimpse of a sail.

"He saved me!" she blurted. "Pulled me onto a boat!" Sarah moved her hand from her throat to her chest. After taking a few deep breaths, she said, "Saved my life."

"And the others?"

Sarah relaxed as the feeling of asphyxiation subsided. After a deep sigh, she replied.

"Children," she said. "There were children. Freed from slavers. Freed—" Sarah paused to stare into the woman's spectacle-covered eyes. "*He'd* freed them." She glanced at the nearest uniform. "But he was alone." She shook her head. "And wore no uniform."

"Uniform," the woman scoffed. "The legion has no uniform. At least, not since—" Sarah followed the woman's gaze as she looked around the room. "These were a mistake," she went on. "They should have never adopted such a look." She slowly shook her head and added, "Too soon, too soon. They were impatient."

"Impatient? Who was impatient?"

"The first of the enlightened," the woman replied. "These," she explained with a sweeping motion of her outstretched hand. "The first to fight under the designation."

Sarah shook her head.

"Designation? I have no idea what you mean."

Sarah abruptly bent and picked up the rifle when the woman took a step toward her.

"The legion," the woman emphatically stated. "Didn't Bin'ka tell you?"

Utterly perplexed, Sarah shook her head.

"The Legion of God," the woman explained. "It's why you're here. To set the path forward."

Sarah's thoughts began to spin. *The path, the Legion of God, Bin'ka, the blue light, Adhib, his men, this place—* She placed a hand against the stone wall to steady herself. What in the world was the woman talking about?

"Who are you?" Sarah blurted. As if remembering the cross hanging from the chain around her neck, Sarah let the rifle fall to the floor and clutched the symbol in her hand. "Tell me how you got this," she demanded. "Tell me or I swear—"

She held the chained cross out in front of her and glared at the woman. A moment later she slumped her shoulders and sighed.

"I want to go home," she told the woman. "I can't—" She shook her head and slowly crumpled to her knees. "Help me," she pleaded. "Help me get home."

"Get home," the woman muttered. "And where would that be if not here?"

Sarah stared at the masks along the walls as if she expected them to offer guidance. But they remained expressionless and silent. She began to whimper.

"I must say you seem like an odd choice."

Sarah sniffled and wiped her nose with the back of her hand.

"But who am I to judge?" Extending a hand toward Sarah, she added, "I'm just the conduit. The message is for you. Come." With a crooked finger, she beckoned Sarah to join her. "Come and see. Read. Listen. Know your calling."

Sarah was hardly aware of being led into the brightly blue-lit room until the robed woman patted her on the forearm and released her hand. Machines—many as big as refrigerators, a few as small as a box of cereal— lined the entire length of one wall. Blinking screens, spinning tape reels, wires and cables of various widths running along the floor and strung across the ceiling—all were bathed in the color blue and hummed with electricity. The blue light, Sarah observed, came from a trio of monitors in bulky frames set intermittently on a long narrow table. Swivel chairs— high backed, with thick black cushions—sat in front of the three screens. Sarah could hear noises from the larger machines: bearings turning, pep- pered now and then with what sounded like plastic cards being slotted into metal compartments. Taken in bulk, the scene was overwhelming. Broken into segments, each individual machine was a peculiarity. Sarah had never before seen such a collection of equipment.

"I'll leave you to it, then."

Sarah dazedly shifted her attention to the robed woman.

"What?" she numbly asked.

"The far screen," the woman replied. She pointed when Sarah appeared not to have heard her.

"I haven't touched it since the words appeared. I use the other two for my work."

She touched Sarah on the arm and pointed once more toward the farthest of the three monitors.

"Where are you going?" Sarah inquired when the woman donned her hood and headed for the exit. "What am I supposed to do?"

Sarah could not see the woman's face as she turned to reply.

"Read. Listen. Understand your role," she said.

"But I—" Sarah glanced at the far monitor before blurting, "You never told me who you are. I-I— I don't know your name."

The woman turned toward the opening as if to continue walking, but then hesitated and turned back toward Sarah.

"I am the conduit," she said. "What other name I had is unimportant."

Before Sarah could think to reply, the woman walked quickly out of the chamber.

Left on her own, Sarah felt uncertain and thoroughly confused. What the woman had told her made no sense. The woman herself made no sense. *What am I doing here? And the machines—what are they? What purpose do they serve?* She scrutinized the nearest of the monitors; she noticed lines of words. Curious, she took a step closer. What she'd believed were lines of script were in actuality collections of letters, symbols, and numbers that held no meaning. Sarah blinked several times and then wiped her eyes as though clearing them of dust. When she refocused her vision and looked once more at the monitor, she saw nothing had changed; the screen still displayed continuous lines of letters, symbols, and numbers jumbled together in no logical order.

She glanced anew at her surroundings. *Nothing seems real,* she thought. The woman—the conduit, she called herself—the cavern, the machines. Sarah suddenly felt like Alice in Wonderland. Though, at the moment, her dream was more a nightmare than an adventure.

The far screen. Sarah looked over toward the third monitor. From where she stood, she could see a few lines of words. Curious and, like everything else she had confronted since awakening from her fall, senseless.

With a glance toward the exit the conduit had taken, she slowly walked
to the third monitor and stood before it. After reading the first word on
the screen, she sat down in the high-backed chair.

Sarah

Paradise is dying

Contrived worship has gone astray

Salvation will arrive

In bloodstained hands

The Mother cries out

For the Legion

Sarah read the words several times over, then stared blankly at the
screen. *The Mother cries out for the Legion. The Legion?* What could the
phrase possibly mean? *And who is the Mother? Mother Superior? Worship
gone astray—contrived, salvation—*she gazed down at her hands; *bloodstained—*hers? *Paradise dying—*hadn't Bin'ka said the same? Then she
remembered; it was in her dream that Bin'ka had uttered the phrase. The
boy, the donkey, the water buffalo, and the hyena—were these figures sym-
bolic? Of what? What did a boy, a donkey, a water buffalo, and a hyena
have in common? She examined her hands again as if they might hold
some clue. The word *bloodstained* returned, coloring every thought a sickening hue of red. Not wanting to revisit her past, she quickly shifted her
attention to the monitor. To her surprise, the words were no longer there.
The empty screen left her deflated.

Deflated. She shifted her thoughts to the unoccupied uniforms and
vacant masks. How odd they looked. How strange the men who'd worn
them must have been. As she continued to dwell upon the abandoned
outfits, she felt a stirring of recollection. Suddenly the uniforms seemed
familiar. But how could that be?

As she pondered, the blue light shining from the monitor flickered
several times and then dimmed to a subdued shade of azure.

An object appeared on the monitor. Initially small as a pinhead, the
cylindrical shape grew incrementally larger, as if emerging from a distance.
It was twisted and grooved, unfamiliar at first. But as it grew, Sarah saw
that one end of the object was pointed. When it finally filled the monitor's width, she realized she had seen the item before. It was the horn of

the hyena-man, the prized possession of John, the frightening character who had sutured the bullet wound in her shoulder.

"John," she murmured.

How long had it been she'd thought of him? She touched the shoulder he'd healed, a vison of John manifesting within her mind. He appeared to her as a boy dressed in decaying pelts, his body battered and bruised, an antelope horn held above his head as he ran down a hill surrounded by a pack of yelping hyenas. She'd heard explosions off in the distance as she'd watched him go. He'd run toward an area where smoke rose from a canopy of trees.

Sarah recoiled as a wall of flames burst onto the monitor screen.

Alarmed but spellbound, she placed her hand against the glass surface, then immediately pulled it away when she felt heat pulsing against her flesh. The horn, immersed within the heart of the blaze, turned fiery gold.

Sarah saw herself sitting on the crest of a hill as the sun broke the horizon. John's arm was wrapped around her shoulders, propping her up. He spoke of the Mother as he gave her water to sip. She—the Mother—was earth and water and all that lived within the two realms. Father—God— was the sky, the stars, the heavens and all that existed in one's soul. Together they held domain over all a person could see, hear, think, and feel. He spoke of the two as if he were a steward of their intentions, a protector of their children. Then the first of several explosions shattered the quiet of dawn. He ran to Teimbaka's aid without thinking what harm might befall him. The hyenas followed as if he were their spiritual leader. She remembered thinking, *Here is the basis of faith: an action performed without fear of consequence, a deed undertaken without thought of self.* She had equated faith to prayer for most of her life. John had shown her in one head-spinning act faith's true foundation. Subdued by regret, she placed her hand once more atop the flaming screen. To her surprise, the fire flickered and died.

A chill spread across her flesh. A new image materialized beneath her palm.

Dressed in a black robe, standing near a bright green hill, Teimbaka stared out from the screen as if he were expecting her to join him. Sarah removed her hand from the surface of the monitor to study the image more closely. The screen flickered anew. Blue faded to grey. Outlines appeared, crystal-white, bordered areas filled with floating particles colored ivory and gold. *Like stardust,* Sarah thought, masses of twinkling lights riding currents of solar wind against the backdrop of an endless sky. Then the lines bordering the stardust began to waver, twisting and bending into shape. Elephants—ethereal beasts as big as mountains, with stately tusks that pointed majestically toward the heavens—took shape behind Teimbaka. Enthralled, Sarah leaned toward the monitor. In that instant, the elephants began to weep.

Tears of blood flowed down the elephants' cheeks and pooled at Teimbaka's feet. In a matter of seconds, the pool swelled to a river with a current so strong it swept the black-robed figure off his feet. Instinctively, Sarah reached out and offered Teimbaka her hand. He in turn extended a hand toward her. But the monitor screen kept them from touching. A moment later, he was gone, the river of blood ferrying him to a destination Sarah could not guess.

Sarah lowered her hand to her lap and stared numbly at the screen. The river of blood continued to flow, expanding in width and depth. Within moments, the stardust elephants disappeared beneath a sea of blood. Soon after, the screen went dark. Sarah braced herself for what might appear next. But the monitor remained empty of images and light. Trembling and shaken, Sarah once more shifted her attention to the ghost platoon in the outer room.

Impatient, The first to fight under the designation. A legion—to combat what exactly? The many warlords in the country? Armies of governments rife with corruption? Slavers, self-righteous holy men preaching doctrines of hate? Or was it something more straightforward, simply those who prey on the innocent, perpetuating violence against those too weak to protect themselves? Sarah examined the masks, uniforms, and weapons in her thoughts. Though she knew little of weaponry and armies, she guessed the men who'd donned the outfits had been well equipped and prepared for whatever they might face. What had happened to those men? And what had Conduit meant by saying they'd been impatient?

Designation. She found the word perplexing. What was the designation under which the men who'd worn the uniforms had aligned themselves? Justice? Freedom? Righteousness? Equality? Then she remembered what

Conduit had said: *Legion of God.* The phrase drifted through her thoughts. *Legion of God.* Did she mean the Holy Father? Or was she referring to some false god: a warlord, a prophet, a self-proclaimed demigod? Or did she mean a god of another religion: Allah, Brahma, Yahweh?

Satan?

She closed her eyes and tried to wipe the notion from her mind. *The Lord is the Light and my Salvation*, she reminded herself. *Whom shall I fear?* But the river of blood she had witnessed on the monitor and the reference to bloodstained hands made her wonder all the more: just what legion of god was she here to supposedly lead? Near her wit's end, she covered her face with her hands and screamed.

"Paradise is dying."

Sarah jerked her hands away from her face and pushed the chair back from the screen.

"Who's there? Who said that?"

The monitor crackled with electricity. The screen suddenly radiated a brilliant blue light. Sarah gripped the arms of the chair and tensed her muscles.

"Will you not help it flourish?"

The voice emanating from the monitor was at once melodic, soothing, and powerful. It resonated in her bones. Its compassion swirled through her veins. Immediately she fell to her knees and made the sign of the cross. Bowing her head, she said, "Forgive me, Lord, for I have sinned. Say the word and I shall be healed."

Sarah clutched the silver cross in her right hand and lightly pounded a clenched hand three times against her heart. Faithfully, she waited for what she believed was the voice of God to say more. The intermediate silence brought both physical pain and a sense of spiritual fulfillment. Devoted to the words of God, she remained still, head bent with her hand over her heart, for several minutes. When she dared raise her face to peek at the monitor, the screen was dark. God, it seemed, had departed.

Trembling, she raised the cross to her lips. With a gentle kiss to the symbol of her faith, she said, "The Lord is my shepherd. I shall not want." Hopeful, she glanced at the screen; it remained dark. She covered her face with her hands and began to weep.

Sarah wept until her eyes were dry of tears. Disillusioned, her body sagging with exhaustion, she rose from her knees. She stared blankly at the dark screen for another minute, hoping the voice of the Lord would return. It didn't.

Little by little, Sarah became aware of subtle changes to the lighting in the room. Small, continuous fluctuations in the omnipresent blue glow drew her attention away from the monitor directly in front of her. The other monitors—the two with collections of letters, numbers, and symbols on the screens—were the cause of the change in light; the lines of notations looked to be in constant motion. More precisely, the lines of typescript seemed to be constantly changing, altering the blue glow as new white symbols appeared on the screen. Curious, she stepped away from the monitor God had used to communicate with her and moved closer to the other two. As before, she could make no sense of what the symbols meant or represented.

I use the other two for my work. The recollection of what Conduit had said entered her thoughts as she turned her head toward the chamber's exit. With a pensive glance to the dark monitor, she walked past the wall of whirring, clicking machines and stepped into the adjoining chamber.

Conduit was seated in front of long wooden table, typing furiously at a keyboard. Atop the table, to each side of the woman, were several calculators, stacks of books, and an array of papers, pencils, and pens. The table itself sat in the middle of a large, rectangular cavern containing a collection of scientific and engineering equipment neatly and compactly arranged so as to make best use of the space the chamber offered. Though it had been many years since Sarah had attended school, she understood she was standing in the entrance of a laboratory.

"What is this place?"

Surprised she had spoken out loud, Sarah placed a hand to her mouth. When it appeared Conduit hadn't heard her, she took a tentative step toward the woman.

"Why am I here?" she nearly yelled.

Conduit stopped typing and sighed. With a shake of her head, she turned to face Sarah.

"Didn't He explain?" she asked.

"He?" Sarah replied.

Conduit frowned.

"God. Didn't He tell you?"

Sarah glanced back at the room she'd exited.

"You mean the voice?" Reflexively she clutched the cross dangling from the necklace. "I'm not sure I—"

She averted her eyes from the woman. Again, Conduit frowned.

"Faith," the woman emphasized. "Everything He's put you through has brought you to this moment." She grasped the edge of the table with both hands and nearly rose from her seat as she said, "Paradise is *dying*. Isn't that what He said?"

Sarah moved another step closer to the woman.

"How did you know what I— What He—?"

"We're not the first," she said. "Did you think we were?"

"The first?"

"The chosen. The path," she clarified. "The conduit," she went on pointing a finger to her chest. "We're not the first." She glanced down at the keyboard on the table in front of her, then looked over to Sarah. "And we certainly won't be the last."

Sarah's attention wandered around the room, trying to match what the woman was saying to the array of equipment. But she couldn't grasp the connection.

"It will be a long process," she heard the woman say. "So much needs to be done."

So much needs to be done. The path. The conduit. Faith. What in the world did it all mean? Sarah looked blankly around the room. Out of chance, she noticed a faucet and basin along the wall across from where Conduit was working.

"You have running water?" she asked.

"Of course."

Conduit's reply prodded Sarah to examine her appearance. Her robe—tattered and filthy—was stained with blood. Her hands and forearms were equally soiled, with cuts and bruises scattered across her flesh. Placing her hands to her face, she closed her eyes. Gently, she traced the outline of her chin, cheeks, brow, and forehead. Where she felt lumps and abrasions, there was pain.

"I must look appalling," she said, embarrassed. With a nod toward the basin and faucet, she asked, "May I?"

"I don't care how you look," Conduit replied. "But suit yourself."

Sarah took a few steps toward the basin but stopped when she sensed Conduit studying her from behind her thick-framed, green-tinted glasses.

"I just want to clean up," she timidly remarked.

There was a long pause before Conduit replied.

"Will you be ready then?"

"Ready?"

"To begin."

Sarah clenched her hands when Conduit sharply exhaled.

"Your job," she told her. "To plot the path forward. To make use of my work."

Sarah shook her head. "Forgive me," she said. "I'm still in shock. And to be honest, I don't know why I'm here and what—"

Conduit screamed, "Paradise is dying! That's why you're here!" Sarah flinched and took a fearful step back when Conduit rose from her chair and pushed it aside.

"Don't you understand? Time is not our ally."

"Understand?" Sarah shouted. "I don't understand anything!" She opened her arms to encompass the contents of the room. "Why I'm here! How I got here! Who you are! What you're—"

The woman leaped to her and grabbed her wrists.

"Let go of me!" Sarah screamed. "You have no right to—"

"Right?" Conduit yelled. "You speak of rights?" The woman hissed a sardonic sigh. "Are you blind? Did you not look at the world around you on your way here? Did you not see what it has become?" Conduit squeezed Sarah's wrists before flinging them roughly to Sarah's sides. "That's *why* you're here: to *change* it. To put an end to the violence and disarray." She held Sarah's gaze for a moment before adding, "To restore order and balance. To bring peace." She reached out and gently took hold of Sarah's hands. "To save paradise," she softly explained. "To do as God has asked you and I to do."

Sarah stared blankly into the green-tinted lenses of Conduit's glasses. Though dim and fuzzy, the reflection on the surface of the glass unnerved her. She could hardly recognize her own swollen and discolored face. Confused and despondent, she shook her head.

"I am a sinner," she muttered. "I have killed." She lifted her hands, palms upward. "Tainted with blood," she said. "These are stained with the blood of my sins. Surely He can't want me to—"

"Help paradise live?"

Conduit smirked, then turned and walked back to her work table.

"But I'm tainted!" Sarah argued. "A sinner!"

Conduit abruptly turned back to face Sarah.

"All the more reason!" she hotly countered. "Innocence would wither in the path we pursue!"

"What path!" Sarah demanded. "What are you—?"

"Go wash up!" Conduit snapped.

Sarah shivered at the glare she sensed emanating from behind the green-tinted lenses.

"Make yourself pretty if you think it'll help," Conduit mocked. "Maybe you'll find your soul under the grime."

Sarah clutched the cross dangling at her chest as Conduit sat down and resumed typing. She heard a surge of activity from the machines in the next chamber. *Conduit. The way. A medium in which something is conveyed.*

How do I fit in? And what path has no place for innocence? Sarah crossed herself. As she walked toward the basin, she studied the equipment in the chamber with a new perspective.

"When you're finished, I'll show you the tools He has supplied us," Conduit remarked. "Then you'll need to decide."

Sarah slowed to a stop.

"Decide?"

Conduit glanced up from the keyboard.

"How and when to implement." She gave Sarah a brief smile before adding, "The job you've been groomed for."

29

MARCUS FOUND THE *ocean's various shades of blue pleasing. Where sunlight sparkled atop its surface, the water appeared to be the nearly transparent hue of an early morning sky. And where the edge of a cloud skewed the sun's rays or buffered them from reaching earth at full strength, the sea embodied sapphire as deep and pure as a star-whispered night. In between these realms of intense and pale lay mixtures of the two, a canvas of blue ever changing on the strength of a breeze or the swell of a wave. Yet, for all the pleasure Marcus derived from the intermingling effect of light, water, and wind, nothing held his attention more than a fleck of green atop a length of wood bobbing on the surf along the shoreline.*

Infatuation with the bright green bug had been instantaneous. As soon as Marcus had spotted the insect crawling along the edge of the dock, he'd quietly left the spot where he'd been sleeping next to the blind man and followed the bug down to where the ocean lapped against sand.

"Where are you going?" he asked the insect several times as he crawled alongside it.

And when the bug surprised him by spreading its shiny green shell and sprouting wings, he warned the little bug not to fly near the water.

"There's nothing for you there!" he'd urgently told it. "You'll drown or get swallowed by a fish!"

But the insect didn't listen. So he was left with no choice but to scramble down a wooden piling and race to the spot where he saw the beetle fly into the sea.

Hypnotized by the rise and fall of the staff as it rode the swell of the waves, Marcus slipped into a daydream where he imagined he was the bright green bug standing on the bow of a long wooden ship sailing treacherous waters. He sensed the waves and wind were dangerous, churned up by the spell of an evil shaman who wished Marcus harm. Why the shaman sought to drown him was unclear to Marcus, but the deeper he drifted into his imagination, reasons began to take shape. He carried a message—a message written by a holy man—entrusted to him to be given to the princess of a kingdom threatened by an army of winged serpents. The princess and all who lived within her realm would either perish or be condemned to a life of slavery if the note the holy man had written was not delivered to her by the time the sun was at its highest point in the sky. Marcus had been instructed by the holy man not to read the note, but he guessed its contents.

Faith you must keep
To squash the evil at your door
The boy whose hand carries this message
Is the key to defeat your enemy
Entrust him with the sacred sword
Have faith he will win the day

Marcus smiled as he visualized the words. And as he further fantasized over their meaning, he sensed the swell of the waves beneath his feet and felt the sea wind upon his face. Outfitted in a warrior's bright green suit of armor, he knelt before the princess with bowed head. Emboldened with honor, he opened his hands to accept the mythical sword.

"Do you swear, young warrior, to give all your energy in battle, to fight with courage, to answer the call of the gods, and defeat the forces of evil?"

Marcus sensed his destiny when she placed the sword in his open palms. As he clamped his fingers around the weapon, he could feel power emanating from its core. Beaming with pride, he looked up to address the princess. Confronted instead with a wave as tall as a mountain, he hastily rose to his feet.

To Marcus, the giant wave rolling in from the open sea appeared to be nearing the point where it would break over the shoreline. But as he stepped away from the water's edge and prepared to run toward the city, he realized the swell was still a long way from making landfall. Fearing for the life of the green-shelled bug, he quickly leaped to the shallows and pulled the wooden staff from the waves. Above him, shouts of warning rose up from a chorus of voices. Looking north toward the harbor where several large ships were anchored, Marcus saw a line of people on the old fishing pier. A handful of men—one wielding a whip—shouted in angry voices. Then the man with the whip snapped it at the woman at the front of the line. Marcus cringed when he saw the tip of the lash tear into the woman's shoulder. And when the woman fell forward, he saw those behind her come to an abrupt stop.

Marcus understood what he was witnessing when heard the sound of rattling metal. The people were bound to each other by chain, wrists and ankles shackled. Marcus remembered the pictures of slaves that Gran-Jim had shown him: old photographs in a book that depicted how black people were treated in America before the Civil War. Marcus hadn't understood what Gran-Jim meant by Civil War, but he remembered the word slave, *and he remembered the look on the faces of people in the pictures who were chained to one another. Gran-Jim had told him how terrible it was to be a slave, and he recalled how upset Gran-Jim had gotten when he talked about the pictures. Now, seeing what slavery looked like firsthand, Marcus experienced tightness in his stomach along with anger and nausea that spread through every muscle in his body. Clutching the staff tightly in his hands, he sprinted toward the line of slaves.*

A burst of gunfire brought Marcus to an abrupt halt. Crouching to the sand, he spied a man at the edge of the pier screaming something in a language he didn't understand. The man was pointing a gun at the onrushing wave and firing the weapon. Marcus turned his head to follow the path of the bullets. He saw little eruptions of foam appear on the underside of the wave. And then the monstrous wall of water broke upon the pier exactly where the man who'd fired the gun was standing.

The sound of the ocean crashing down on the pier reminded Marcus of a big jet rumbling down a runway just before lifting off into the sky. Stunned by the display of power, he watched, stupefied, as crates were thrust high into the air. To his dismay, he saw people floundering in the ocean as the wave retreated into the sea. Screams rang out above the din of rushing water. And though Marcus didn't understand the words people were yelling, he knew by the tone of their voices they were pleading for help. Suddenly cognizant the wave had not overrun the area where he stood, he ran toward the edge of the churning torrent with the staff held high above his head.

"Blind man! Lady! Difireti!" he called out. "Help me! Help!"

As his feet splashed into water and the swirling current wrapped around his ankles, Marcus came to an abrupt stop. Out of the corner of his eye he glimpsed a boy struggling near the shore. Instinctively, he waded into the churning surf until the water was waist deep. He grasped one end of the staff with both hands and then extended the shaft of wood out toward the child.

"Grab it!" Marcus yelled. "Grab the end!"

As Marcus stretched his arms to the limit of his reach, he saw the green bug crawl to the utmost tip of the staff. And then something wondrous occurred, for when the boy reached for the staff, its tip flashed green. Instantly, the waters of the ocean retreated. Awestruck, Marcus beheld the line of chained people, coughing and gagging on the ocean floor. The other men—the ones with the whip and gun—were not among them. Struck by what he'd witnessed, he gazed upon the ocean with a mixture of fright and wonder.

"Hurry!"

Marcus turned his head toward the dock at the sound of a woman's voice.

"Bring them!" the woman dressed in the grey robe yelled. "Bring them!"

Marcus raised his hand in acknowledgement as the blind man and Difireti joined the woman at the edge of the pier. Then someone yelled, "Teimbaka!"

Marcus glanced over his shoulder to find the boy he'd rescued standing next to him on the shore.

"John Too?" he heard a man shout in reply.

"I'm here!" the boy responded.

And then the man chained to the boy named John Too—a man Marcus recognized well—jerked the staff from Marcus's grasp.

"Find a hammer and a gun," Chris ordered. "Hurry. Hurry!"

*

Mr. Pembrook glanced at the dashboard clock as he maneuvered his Rolls Royce through a sharp curve. Though the steering wheel took a bit of moxie, as he called it, to turn the four-ton automobile, the car responded with the grace and ease one would expect of an impeccably crafted machine. And while a lesser man the same age and stature as Mr. Pembrook might have experienced some difficulty in steering the car, Mr.

Pembrook executed the turn with the ease of a man who regularly squeezed tennis balls to keep his hands and forearms strong.

As driving vintage cars had been a passion of Mr. Pembrook's for over a decade, he'd learned from experience that the pastime demanded a certain amount of physical strength. Pressed on the matter, he would often argue that driving was sport and thus required a participant with equal amounts of emotional passion and physical vigor—especially if that person wished to excel. To further his point of view, he would refer to his most prized possession—a 1964 Ferrari 250gt California parked in shiny display inside the six-car garage he'd had custom-built after Mr. Waterman passed away—and vehemently state while swirling his tumbler of single malt that "A man without heart and courage should neither possess nor attempt to drive a machine derived from the fabric of heaven!" He'd elaborate with, "To entertain the notion that a man of common quality should sit behind the wheel of such a godly machine would constitute a catastrophe within our social universe."

Arguing with Mr. Pembrook on the sport of driving vintage cars had proved an exercise in futility to those so disposed to try. Prideful to the point of annoyance, he was so taken with being part of an esteemed group of men whose stature in society allowed them the privilege to drive such artistic mechanical creations, he spent countless hours in his garage detailing the collection while at the same time keeping his body as buff and taut as time permitted.

"The appearance of both the car and the driver must be impeccable," he'd say. "If either is smudged or smeared, one might just as well banish himself to some lesser country, where ownership of a pig or a cow elevates a man to village leader. And if one can't keep every car in his showroom in tip-top condition, then he shouldn't have added to his collection."

Adding to the collection: Mr. Pembrook checked the dashboard as he reminisced past conversations regarding, "The treasures of man's mechanical genius," as he often referred to the production of sublime automobiles.

"Inconvenient time for a meeting," he mumbled under his breath.

Nine-forty pm. From his calculations, he'd be ten minutes early arriving at the clinic. *Meeting*, he silently scoffed. *More a stroking of egos*, he thought, *but if it serves as a means to acquiring...* He pictured the 1962

Austin Healy 3000 he planned on purchasing with his portion of the month's profit. Heartened by the thought of adding the British-made sport car to his collection, he pushed down on the Silver Cloud's gas pedal.

*

Claire sat quietly in a molded plastic airport chair trying to comprehend the activity around her. People—hundreds, she guessed: families, couples, friends, tour groups, servicemembers, and single travelers like herself— entered and exited restrooms; joined or left lines to purchase magazines, coffee, donuts, bags of nuts, neck pillows; waited to board impatiently or with blank faces or with eyes riveted to the pages of a book. Where was everyone going? And how was it they all decided to travel on the same day? What could cause such a mass exodus from Philadelphia?

Exodus. The word brought images to her mind. Were they memories? Had she and a group of boys sat by a fire near the face of a sheer rock wall while she was in Africa? Or was the imprint imagined, a false memory she'd concocted to help her cope with a time in her life she couldn't recall?

"My friend at the embassy, Mr. Frederick, will be at the airport when you disembark," Mr. Pembrook had told her. "No need to fret. I know how difficult this has been for you." He reassuringly tapped her knee and added, "But I see no other way, if you want to remember your time in Africa."

Africa. Claire tried to conjure an image of the continent, one that went beyond pictures in books or depictions from old Tarzan movies. But her recollection of the years she'd spent on the continent continued to elude her. Frustrated, she wondered for the thousandth time what had happened to her in the clinic and why she'd been placed in the facility in the first place.

"He'll get you settled at the hotel and then drive you to the various churches—Christian churches—in the city." Claire absently rubbed the hand Mr. Pembrook had lightly squeezed. "A logical place to begin, don't you think? Surely, someone will recall your arrival."

Her arrival. From what she'd been able to piece together from her conversations with Mother Superior at Sisters of the Holy Cross in Maryland, she'd been sent to Ethiopia on an exploratory mission of mercy. But records of her destination after the initial landing in Djibouti were incomplete or hadn't been chronicled. Which brought Claire back to the question she'd been asking herself since her release from the clinic: what had happened to her in Africa to warrant a year's stay in a mental facility?

Dr. Haraji—when she'd finally been able to meet with the man—had been less than candid. Citing psychiatric theory, he claimed her memory would return to her as soon as her fragile psyche was able to handle the emotional ramifications of recollection. When that would be, however, he couldn't or wouldn't venture to say. And though she had petitioned Mr. Pembrook for subsequent meetings with Mr. Benson, her mother's confessed killer, the lawyer had only been able to arrange one: an abbreviated, confusing encounter that, like the first, left her with more questions than answers.

*

"Danny wanted you to know!" Mr. Savage had blurted out when she stepped into the visitor room. She'd nearly tripped over her feet at his outburst, but the expression of excitement on his face had sparked her curiosity.

"He told me in the car the night we drove…"

When his voice trailed off, she imagined he might have reconsidered what he was about to say: "the night we drove to your mother's house and…"

"Tell me what?" she gently prodded.

He looked at her like he'd forgotten she was there and her question had reminded him. Or perhaps he'd noticed something about her he hadn't before—something important. He glanced at her necklace several times before answering.

"He told me he was your—"

Dirk abruptly reached across the table and tried to grasp Claire's silver cross. His sudden action produced a sharp pounding on the thick glass window at her back, and an authoritative voice blared over the speaker hanging in the corner of the room.

"No physical contact!" a male voice sternly warned.

Whatever Dirk had wanted to tell her seemed to lose its urgency after the loud intrusion. After the interruption, he would only murmur, "He loved you as a father loves a daughter," repeating the phrase several times when pressed.

The whole time, he stared at the cross dangling around her neck as if it were a lifeline and he a drowning man. She became so self-conscious of it that she covered it with her hand.

"Why the hell did you do that?" he shouted. "It's my only way of seeing her! The only chance she has to escape!" He pounded the table with his fist and yelled, "George Henry didn't care about the damn cross! And neither do you, obviously!"

She'd felt physically threatened by his sudden change of demeanor and the way his face contorted. Though the confrontation had taken place over a week ago, she could still feel his fury and despair. She began to tremble at the recollection. Embarrassed, she placed her hands between her knees and pressed her thighs together, glancing at the people sitting to either side of her.

"How could you take it from her?" he'd screamed.

And then his expression became melancholy, his demeanor subdued. It was as if he were acting out a scene in a play. He abruptly stood from the table and walked to the back of the room, arms held like he was carrying something heavy in his arms. The next moment, he set his burden down as though lowering a person into bed. She watched, mesmerized, as his fingertips traced the outline of an invisible face. Then, to her astonishment, he bent down and placed a kiss on what she supposed was the imagined forehead of someone he cared for.

"*Her?*" she inquired.

As soon as she asked, she regretted it; Dirk dropped to his knees and started to cry, his sobs prolonged and tormented. The door to the interview room opened behind her. Two uniformed guards rushed in and took Dirk out of the room. Mr. Pembrook met her as she exited.

"I don't know what to say," he remarked.

She fell against his chest, trembling, and rested her head on his shoulder.

"Perhaps we are seeing the true mental state of the man who—"

She silenced him with fingers against his lips and shook her head. To his credit, Mr. Pembrook said nothing more as he walked her out of the building to his car. They'd driven back to her mother's estate in silence.

She was grateful for his understanding, and she told him as much as she exited the car.

A week later, she called him to set up another meeting with Dirk. She had questions. Questions about things Dirk had said at their initial meeting. The court denied her request. Three more times she tried to arrange additional visits. In each instance, her request was denied.

Who really killed her mother and Mr. Locket? Why was Dirk's confession admissible if he was not of sound mind? And how had Dirk and Mr. Locket come to be in one another's company the night her mother was killed?

And why had Dirk kept repeating "Mr. Locket loved you as a father loved a daughter"? Near as important, why had Mr. Locket expressed those feelings to Dirk? Had the two become close in the year Dirk lived above the garage on her mother's estate? If so, what had Dirk told Mr. Locket about her time in Africa? In her first meeting with Dirk, he'd said that she should be on a plane. To Africa? To Djibouti? Ethiopia? She'd studied maps of each country as she tried to put the pieces of the last two years of her life into place. Ethiopia was vast—Djibouti less so—but each held numerous cities spread out over varied terrain. Why was her memory so shaded? What was she forgetting? Who couldn't she remember? And why had she been committed to a clinic?

Claire shook her head in frustration and rubbed her hands over her face. When she refocused on her surroundings, she noticed a young girl standing across from her, peering out one of the large windows that overlooked the airport runways. For a moment, she entertained the notion she was reliving a memory. Outfitted in a red beret, blue blazer, and a white and red plaid skirt, the girl was the spitting image of seven-year-old Claire in her school uniform. Claire closely scrutinized the girl as she raised an arm and pointed to a dozen Canadian geese flying across the sky. One memory fell away to be replaced by a vivid recollection of a moment in time that had never seemed important to her—until now. Hand at her mouth in surprise, she stood and remembered.

It had been a crisp spring day in early April; the chill of the air still turned a breath into a whimsical stream of fog. Mr. Locket—dear Mr. Locket—was serving Claire and her father tea in the study. She'd felt so grown up in the moment, sipping a blend of chamomile, honey, and mint as Father read a book in his favorite chair, facing the big picture window at the western end of the room. Claire felt so grown up in his presence that she decided to initiate a serious conversation. She wanted to impress upon her father how mature she'd become, how worldly the boarding school in France had made her. When a flock of Canadian geese circled low in the late afternoon sun, their destination the glass-like surface of the pond some thirty yards from where he and she were seated, Claire saw the sun-limned birds as what they were: a sign from God.

God. Claire pressed the silver cross to her chest.

Those who hope in the Lord will find new strength. They will soar on wings like eagles; they will run and not grow weary, they will walk and not be faint.

Closing her eyes, she could hear her voice ever so faintly as she recited the words to her father. A sense of calm washed over her as she remembered. God was with her—as He had always been. Even in the darkest of times, when she felt He had abandoned her, He'd been there for her, offering strength.

Faith. Oh Lord, where have I gone? I have strayed so from my calling.

Tapping the cross to her heart, she replayed the moment the geese had alighted on the pond. Only now did she realize what she had witnessed that day many years ago: angels setting down on the tears of a misguided world, a gift of a forgiving Father to those whose faith lay in the Trinity.

Faith. Claire got down on her knees and bowed her head.

"Dear Lord," she murmured in prayer. "Grant me the serenity to endure the things I cannot change and the courage to change the things I can. Give me wisdom to discern between the two. Bless me with patience and clarity. Help me see what is important and set aside worry. Through You, may the concerns of my past be forgiven. Amen."

Claire slowly crossed herself and raised her head. The little girl dressed in the blue blazer and red beret was no longer standing at the airport window. Troubled by the girl's absence, Claire rose from her knees and searched the concourse. The expressions on the faces of the people near her gave her reason to think something must be wrong with her appearance. She patted the sides of her head and then smoothed the wrinkles from her blouse.

"Get a room," a man snidely remarked.

To her embarrassment, she heard several people snicker. Blushing, she meekly turned and retook her seat. Head slightly bowed, she wrung her hands and tried to return to the memory of her father and the geese. But she could only visualize the image of Mr. Locket pouring tea.

"I hope Miss Claire finds the blend to her liking," he'd said as he placed the cup and saucer down on the table next to her chair.

Mr. Locket is dead, she suddenly thought. *Mr. Locket is dead.*

*

Mr. Pembrook took a seat, wondering if he'd gotten the time wrong. He checked his wristwatch: 9:55 pm. By his calculations, he was five minutes early. He cleared his throat.

"Sorry to be late," he said. And then, as if to prove he wasn't late, he tapped the face of the watch and smiled.

"Now that we're all here."

Mr. Pembrook eyed the woman seated at the head of the long conference table with a mixture of uncertainty and desire. Though beautiful in an exotic fashion, she had a ruthless reputation and a penchant for violence.

"Might I voice my objection to this meeting," Mr. Pembrook interposed with a deferential nod to Alexis. The eyes of the four other people seated at the table shifted in his direction. "Why couldn't whatever it is we are about to discuss have been addressed by phone? Surely each of us is aware of the consequences of being seen together."

Mr. Pembrook's gaze drifted to the giant of a man seated to Alexis's immediate right and suppressed an involuntary shudder.

"Wire taps," Alexis calmly replied. "I certainly understand your objection, Roger, but I felt it important we address a few items concerning our mutual interests now, before the situation can be rectified." With glances of acknowledgement to Mr. Pembrook, Agent Crenshaw, and Dr. Haraji, she said, "Hopefully, this is a one-time inconvenience." She gestured toward Goliath and added, "We're working to resolve the problem as soon as possible."

"Police?" Mr. Pembrook inquired. With a pointed nod to Agent

Crenshaw, he said, "I was led to believe that avenue of concern was put to rest some time ago."

"Didn't come from my end," Crenshaw bristled. "So don't be looking to cast blame my way."

"Overzealous assistant DA," Alexis explained. "One that doesn't seem to comprehend the ramifications of her actions."

"More violence?" Mr. Pembrook asked. Frowning, he added, "Won't that in itself draw attention?"

"Don't," Crenshaw said before Alexis could respond. "Don't tell me your plans. I don't want to know."

"Just read about them in the papers then," Mr. Pembrook commented. "After the fact, as the saying goes."

"Listen here, old man," Crenshaw shot back. "You're not innocent of what's gone down over the past couple years. So don't throw any of your holier-than-thou bullshit my way. Just because you wear an expensive suit and like to drive fancy—"

Goliath pounded the tabletop with his fist. A moment of nervous silence ensued before Alexis broke the tension with a laugh.

"Now that we're focused," she said with a smile at Goliath. Shifting her attention to Mr. Pembrook, she said, "Certain methods have immediate, lasting effects, Roger, and convey to those who might think of interfering with our business the gravity with which we run our operation. While we do our best to minimize theatrics, there are occasions where certain techniques return optimum results."

Mr. Pembrook looked to each of his business partners in an attempt to gauge their reaction before he spoke.

"Murder will always bring unwanted attention. The situation at the Waterman estate is a prime example." He raised his eyebrows and added, "I can only assume the wire taps have a direct correlation to that tragic affair."

"Tragic affair," Crenshaw scoffed. "Never would have happened if you hadn't brought the old bird into this. Coverin' your ass, like you always do. Makin' sure the gravy train don't bypass your door."

"That wasn't it at all," Mr. Pembrook protested. "You know it was just a stroke of bad luck she happened to walk down to the stables when a delivery was taking place." He shrugged and searched the table for a sympathetic face, glaring at Dr. Haraji when he made a noise of contempt. "The cook and gardener would have normally stopped her from straying that far from the house, but one was sick and the other was delivering food to our now-incarcerated killer."

"You wish to offer one of your esteemed medical observations?" Mr. Pembrook asked.

Dr. Haraji made a dismissive gesture with his hand. "Other options were available. I could have easily arranged for her food to have been—" he paused and smiled. "For her to have found herself in our debt."

"Addicting her wouldn't have solved the problem," Mr. Pembrook said.

"Are you done?" Alexis snapped. "Can we get on with it?" She glared, adding, "Or should I ask Goliath to put an end to your petty bickering in a manner that pleases him?"

With a raised eyebrow, a tilt of her head, and an appealing smile, she dared each man to reply. None did. Nor did any meet her gaze.

"Focus," she said.

Again, Alexis waited as Dr. Haraji, Agent Crenshaw, and Mr. Pembrook exchanged glances.

"For the past year and a half, the four of us—*five* of us," she said with a smile directed toward Goliath, "have nearly tripled the reach of our operation." A brief smile and a shrug, and she continued. "Now, however, we find ourselves with a bit of a problem on two fronts. First, because of the rise in crime resulting from our success, more resources are being directed toward uncovering and shutting down our—and our competitors'—operations. Obviously, because all of us—" she opened her arms as if she were welcoming a neighbor into her home "—enjoy the rewards of our labor, we can't let that happen."

"Can't we just buy off a few bureaucrats and a few more police officers?" Mr. Pembrook asked.

"I'm afraid the situation with the Waterman girl makes that avenue a bit complicated at the moment."

"How so?" Mr. Pembrook asked.

"If you'd kept the girl away from the courts and the jail like you were supposed to," said Crenshaw, "she wouldn't be askin' so many questions and prodding people to take a closer look."

"Look here," Mr. Pembrook countered. "She's on a plane heading to Africa right now." He paused to look at his watch. "Perhaps, by the time she returns, she'll be more focused on what she—"

"She won't."

Mr. Pembrook furrowed his brow and shifted his attention to Alexis.

"I don't follow," he said.

"She won't be coming back."

Mr. Pembrook shook his head and sighed.

"She booked a round-trip ticket. She intends to be back by the time the trial…" Mr. Pembrook's voice trailed off as it dawned on him what Alexis was implying.

"You gonna send *him* after her?" Crenshaw asked, nodding to Goliath.

"Nothing so blatant and obviously traceable," Alexis replied. Addressing Roger, she said, "I've asked a friend in Djibouti to see that she meets an unfortunate accident. Miss Waterman will no longer be a factor."

Mr. Pembrook's eyes shifted to the tabletop in front of him. He rubbed his chin, then checked his watch.

"So, our question to you, Roger—"

Mr. Pembrook felt a chill when Alexis said his name.

"What will happen to the estate once her unanticipated demise is verified?"

Mr. Pembrook stroked his chin as he glanced at the faces around him.

"The estate?" he repeated, confused. "I'm not sure I follow."

"As the property has served as a perfect distribution hub for the past eighteen months, we would hate for it to no longer be available."

Mr. Pembrook steepled his fingers, then placed them to his lips.

"Roger?" Alexis probed. "Roger," she repeated in a more forceful tone.

Mr. Pembrook blinked his eyes as if waking from a daydream.

"The estate, Roger. What will happen to the property when word comes of Miss Waterman's death?"

"The estate," he quietly muttered. "Yes. As Mr. Waterman decreed in his will, the estate house and adjoining acres will be bequeathed to Radnor Hunt. As his wife never bothered to pen a new will once her husband—"

"Radnor Hunt?" Crenshaw asked. "What's that?"

"It's an equestrian club," Mr. Pembrook replied. "A social club of wealthy patrons who gather at certain country properties during the fall season for the purpose of foxhunting."

"Foxhunting," Crenshaw sneered. "You mean to say—?"

He fell silent when Mr. Pembrook motioned with a finger toward the head of the table.

"How soon will the changeover take place?"

Mr. Pembrook put a clenched hand to his mouth and cleared his throat.

"Well, that depends," he replied. "First the court will have to rule on Claire's death. Which could take some time, seeing she will have died in another country. Her body will have to be flown back, and—"

"There won't be a body," Alexis interjected. She nodded to Roger and added, "Part of my instructions."

"Well, then." Mr. Pembrook cleared his throat again, then nodded and smiled. "Protocol would dictate the court review the will and then instruct me to execute the articles in due time."

"Due time—meaning?"

"The court allows the appointed attorney some leeway." He lifted a finger to stave off comment. "Anywhere from three months to several years. That being the extreme."

"Excellent." Alexis nodded her approval.

"Why the fixation on the estate?" Crenshaw asked. "Why not just move distribution to a warehouse somewhere in the same vicinity?"

"What are some of the first places ATF searches when they go looking for contraband?"

Crenshaw's response was a weak smile.

"The estate is perfectly situated to facilitate distribution to Philadelphia and Baltimore. We can unload raw product from the docks and then cut and package the merchandise on the estate grounds. Distribution of the estate's assets will be our cover for trucks entering and exiting the property over the course of the next several months. By that time, we will have established several other distribution centers, and the estate will no longer hold any value."

Mr. Pembrook heard Alexis talking, but his thoughts drifted to a meeting that had taken place many years earlier.

"If anything were to happen to me, Roger, see to it that Claire is well taken care of." Charlie had come to Mr. Pembrook's office to sign his will. The receptionist had referred to Claire as "the Waterman girl" when she'd announced that Mr. Waterman had arrived for his appointment. *The Waterman girl*—when exactly had his pristine legal practice devolved into a tainted quagmire? Roger eyed Alexis with anger. *She seduced me. Money, cars.* He'd willingly traded dignity for dishonor, honesty for lies. And now Claire was to be killed—*the Waterman girl.*

"Why does she have to die?" he blurted.

Alexis fell silent, a peculiar look on her face. Mr. Pembrook felt a queasy knot form in the pit of his stomach. Flinching under her probing stare, he sheepishly looked to the other men sitting at the table.

"Your pang of conscience is not welcome, Roger," Alexis said. "It reflects weakness. Claire has to disappear. Completely."

"Of course she does," Roger countered with a few definitive shakes of his head. "I was just—"

A glance exchanged between Alexis and Goliath rendered him speechless. When he regained a degree of composure, he stammered, "Of-of-of course she needs to be eliminated. I was just— I had— It was momentary, an idea we could control her through—" He nodded toward Dr. Haraji. "As the doctor said, there are other avenues."

"None that offers total finality, Roger. You see that don't you?"

"Yes," he quickly agreed. "Yes, of course." He smiled. "Yes, of course."

Roger glanced meekly at Alexis, and then his gaze drifted to Goliath. He breathed a sigh of relief when he saw the man's attention was fixed upon Dr. Haraji.

"So, the girl dies," Crenshaw remarked, shaking his head. "We're all in agreement. Now—" He checked the time on his wristwatch and frowned. "Can we get on with this? I got people gonna be askin' where I am soon."

"And they'll be thrilled to hear your announcement."

"My announcement? What are you talkin' about?"

Alexis waved him off.

"We'll discuss that in a moment. First, we need to rectify our second problem." She nodded to Dr. Haraji. "Can you give us an update, Doctor?"

"On?"

"On Mr. Benson—or Dirk Savage, as he prefers."

Dr. Haraji tapped his index fingers together. Eyes focused on the table, he said, "Treatment is nearly complete. He's approaching optimum stage. With the right stimulation, he will perform as conditioned." He glanced up from the table to make brief eye contact with Alexis. "The means of closure, however, need to be addressed. I can't afford a link to either myself or the clinic. My work here is too important."

"Your work," Crenshaw muttered. "That's rich."

Dr. Haraji closed his eyes and frowned.

"I don't expect you to understand the methodology of pharmaceutical cognitive research and conditioning, Agent Crenshaw," Haraji calmly replied. "Individuals in your line of work, I understand, believe every case begins or ends with the violence of a firearm. In the years ahead, however, the work I have undertaken at the clinic will offer society an alternative when confronted with what statistics show will be an ever-burgeoning criminal faction."

Crenshaw furrowed his brow.

"You talkin' about turning people into zombies?" He laughed nervously as he looked around the table. "You figurin' on changin' gang-bangers into lambs, pimps and dealers into puppies?"

All eyes shot to the head of the table when Alexis loudly cleared her throat.

"While we certainly support the work you are doing here, Doctor," she said, gesturing toward the people seated at the table, "our focus is geared toward the monetary rewards generated through your findings." She placed her palms on the table and leaned forward. "Meaning: which drug are you finding most compatible with your patients?" She kept her gaze locked on the doctor as she leaned back in her chair. "What drug, in your professional opinion, will most of the general population turn to for everyday use?"

"If you are speaking in terms of availability, physical acceptance, and affordability, the answer is quite clear."

Alexis leaned forward.

"An opioid derivative—OxyContin, say—or any formulation of the same product."

"A pain pill?" Crenshaw inquired. "You sayin' all the junkies gonna turn in their needles for a pill?" He chuckled and shook his head. "You dreamin'," he told the doctor. "Fuckers love their shit too much."

"That may well be at the moment," Alexis countered, motioning with her hand for Dr. Haraji to stay silent. "But we need to look ahead, Mallard, need to foresee the market five, ten years from now. As it is, we're running against the grain, so to speak, funneling cocaine and heroin, hallucinogens and marijuana into a compact area in the northeast. So why not look ahead? Why not expand?" She leaned forward in her chair. "Why not move toward legitimizing our operation?"

"Legitimizing?" Mr. Pembrook expressed his doubt with a shake of his head and a heavy sigh. "As much as I hate to admit it, we're criminals." He sputtered as he tried to find the right words. "Killings, drugs, kidnapping, coercion, robberies—I'm not sure how you think that can be legitimized."

There was an awkward pause before Alexis's response.

"Should we be worried about you, Roger? You sound like a man who's about to have a crisis of conscience."

"Not in the least," Mr. Pembrook forcefully replied.

"Then how else do you explain—?"

"I was simply making an observation." He looked from Alexis to Goliath before adding, "No offense intended, but our recent history—we *are* discussing the fallout from the Waterman affair right now—would seem to preclude us from becoming legitimate."

"Nonsense," Alexis was quick to say. "What government or large corporation doesn't have a finger—or a hand, for that matter—in unscrupulous behavior? From what I read in the papers and see on the news, there isn't a whole lot of difference between politics, corporate business, and what we're doing other than a name on a plaque over a building or a door. So, for you to infer—"

"Point made," Mr. Pembrook conceded. "I take it all back."

"Good," Crenshaw said. With a tap to his wrist he asked, "Now can we wrap this up?"

"Not before discussing your new vocation."

"What the hell are you talking about? I'm damn happy—and useful— where I am."

"True," Alexis agreed. "But you could be more useful in the state House."

"I ain't no politician," Crenshaw said. "So, you can—"

"Neither was Rue Thompson when he started out."

"That fat fuck?" He shook his head as he warily eyed Goliath. "Look what happened to him." He frowned. "Find somebody else to—"

"You're the perfect choice."

Crenshaw glanced from Alexis to Mr. Pembrook.

"Why not him?" Crenshaw asked, his gaze fixed on Mr. Pembrook. "He's got the politician look. And besides," he went on, shifting his attention back to Alexis, "he's a lawyer. He's already got the doublespeak down pat. Wouldn't need to—"

"He's not black."

Goliath chuckled.

"What's that got to do with it?" Crenshaw shot back.

"It's what the situation calls for," Alexis replied. "You'll be running for the seat vacated by our former competitor, Reverend Thompson. The district he represented is 95 percent black." She raised her eyebrows. "Need I say more?"

Crenshaw shook his head.

"I don't want to be no politician," he firmly objected.

"I'm not offering you a choice, Mallard."

Mr. Pembrook felt an immediate tension in the air. Crenshaw stiffened and grew visibly angry.

"Look here," Crenshaw cautioned.

"Don't," Alexis warned. "Don't make me…"

She paused and slowly looked around the table. As she held the gaze of each man, she rubbed the crescent-shaped ivory piece dangling from her right ear.

"When each of you accepted the invitation to this partnership, you did so with a clear understanding of who is in charge. Nothing has changed. You will follow directives—" she paused and turned her attention to Crenshaw "—or suffer the consequences."

Out of the corner of his eye, Mr. Pembrook saw Crenshaw slide a hand inside the front of his leather coat. Just as the ATF agent muttered,

"Fuck you," Goliath produced a big silver pistol from under the table and pointed the weapon at Crenshaw's head. Alexis abruptly held up her hand.

"Don't be stupid, Crenshaw," she said.

"No gunshots!" Dr. Haraji urged. "Not here. I can't afford—"

"Don't worry, Doctor. We haven't reached that point." She nodded toward Crenshaw. "Ego's no reason to lose control." With a smile, she laced her fingers and set her hands on the table. "As I was about to explain, we're entering a phase of great potential. The possibility of expanding beyond our immediate distribution area to the entire mid-Atlantic and northeast corridor is well within our grasp. But to reach such a level of market share, we need to ensure our distribution routes and staging centers are protected and stable. And the best way of maintaining a consistent production line is to run the operation within the boundaries of state and federal guidelines."

Alexis paused when Mr. Pembrook chuckled.

"Something you wish to say, Roger?"

Mr. Pembrook gave Goliath a wary glance before responding.

"I think that what you're saying sounds wonderful," Mr. Pembrook cautiously began. "But to legitimize a business—any business, much less the one we're involved in—is a painstaking legal process of adhering to state and county regulations as well as filing the proper forms with the office of the clerk in each state where you wish to conduct business."

"And?" Alexis pressed when Mr. Pembrook paused.

"Well, just what I said," he told her. "It would take the better part of a year to file for incorporation with numerous states. And it would require—"

"You will have everything you need," she interjected.

Mr. Pembrook stammered, confused, "I will? What do you mean?"

"I've appointed you head of the corporate legal department." Extending an open hand toward Crenshaw, she added, "As Mallard has graciously accepted *his* new position within the partnership, I'm certain you will do the same."

The pleasant smile on Alexis's face disappeared, replaced with a threatening look.

"In the coming days, I will speak to each of you individually about your new responsibilities—as soon as the little matter of the assistant

DA is taken care of and both the Waterman girl and Mr. Savage have been eliminated."

The Waterman girl—

Mr. Pembrook vaguely heard Alexis say something to Dr. Haraji about the need to open more clinics, but his thoughts drifted back in time.

The Waterman girl—

Claire had looked so angelic the day she visited his office with her father.

The Waterman girl—

He wondered how long she had to live.

The Waterman girl—

"If anything were to happen to me, Roger, see to it that Claire is well taken care of."

The Waterman girl—

Mr. Pembrook rubbed his chin and shifted his thoughts to the hunter green Austin Healy 3000 he intended to purchase.

30

WITH EVERY HAMMER strike, Teimbaka winced as if the claw end of the tool were gouging his skull. A man was shouting for shackles to be removed from the women and children. With every word, he felt areas of his flesh recoil, as if each scar marring his skin had suddenly been seared by a red-hot poker.

"Gunstard!" an inner voice screamed.

And with the man's name came the awful thought that the soul of the insidious German colonel had not died the day John had plunged the antelope horn into the man's throat. Claire had held that very belief: Satan could not be killed. She'd broached the unholy concept as she'd mourned the boys Peter Gunstard had murdered.

Confused and distraught by the implications of his thoughts, Teimbaka sought refuge in the folds of his robe. He covered his head and dipped it between his knees, waiting for the hammer to cease its pounding and the man's voice to go silent. And though he knew the clanging and shouting would end in the freedom of the slaves, he found the prospect unsettling.

*

"I'm getting too old for these early morning trips."

Talia made no effort to reply. While she normally enjoyed conversing with Akmir, she was distracted by the destruction visible through the car window: burned-out houses, piles of rubble where buildings once stood, mounds of refuse lining pocked roads. The level of devastation was difficult to comprehend.

"Are you certain we're safe driving here?" she asked.

"As long as the car flies that stupid flag." Akmir gave her a tired smile and pointed upward.

She took him to mean the flag of Islam he'd ordered the driver to attach to the car's antenna before they'd departed for the harbor. While familiar with the symbols of the Islamic crescent moon and star, Talia couldn't recall ever having seen them against a black background. The effect was chilling.

"Adhib's misplaced infatuation with creating an Islamic caliphate."

Talia glanced out the window and raised her eyebrows. What was left for the warlord's kingdom?

"I take it that unifying Mogadishu is not going well," she remarked.

Akmir shrugged and briefly picked the end of his hooked nose. "Given time—and the sudden disappearance of Adhib—the dream of a united Somalia may well yet be within my grasp," he said, laughing.

"Assassination?"

"Two failed attempts already," Akmir replied.

"A third?"

Akmir grunted. "The manner in which the first two failed has inhibited finding a willing taker for another attempt." He shook his head and turned a hand palm upward. "One was skinned alive before being set on fire. The other, slowly lowered into a vat of boiling oil."

Talia grimaced. "Gruesome."

"Effective."

"What is it he wants? Territory? Money? Power?"

Akmir motioned with a hand to what lay outside the window. "You would think by the destruction he wreaks and the ruthless manner in which he treats his people, he wants nothing but misery." Again, Akmir shook his head. "I supply him with slaves and women to appease him, to create opportunities for conversation." He shrugged. "But he wants nothing of talk. Except to babble on about a religious kingdom where the sword of righteousness rules." He softly chuckled and shook his head. "Zealots—there is no reasoning with them."

"Everything—everyone—has a price," she said.

Akmir eyed her for a moment before he smiled. "A philosophy we've embraced our entire lives. But what Susenyo professed seems to—" He stopped mid-sentence when he saw Talia's expression change. Lightly grabbing hold of her wrist, he asked, "What is it?"

"There," she replied. "Up the adjoining road." She gave him a worried glance. "We should turn around."

Akmir looked out the window.

"A sign of weakness," he muttered. "It would only provoke them."

Talia studied the group of armed men walking briskly down the center of the adjoining road. Some of the men carried torches. A few rode in an uncovered Jeep, waving black flags depicting the Islamic star and crescent moon. As the group edged nearer, she could hear yelling and sporadic gunshots.

"Pull over to the side of the street and back up," Akmir ordered the driver. "But don't make it appear as if we are hiding." He looked over at Talia. "I assume you're armed."

Talia patted the Glock she carried in a small shoulder holster beneath her robes. Akmir produced a big, shiny handgun from the sleeve of his *thawb* as the driver put the car in reverse.

"The flag should secure our safety," he said. Nodding to the muzzle of his weapon, he added, "But in case they're crazed on narcotics…"

Talia gave Akmir's weapon a favoring glance, then leaned forward and peered out the window. The group of flag-waving, gun-toting men was approaching the intersection just ahead of them. From her vantage point she counted nine men: four jogging in front of the Jeep, one on either side carrying lit torches, and three in the vehicle. One of the three in the Jeep was standing, waving a black flag and pointing to something on the road behind them. As the Jeep drew closer, Talia looked behind the vehicle and gasped. Tied to the vehicle's rear bumper was a body. From what she could discern, the poor soul was—or had been—a very large human being. She immediately wondered what crime the person had committed that such abhorrent punishment had been ordered.

"Look."

Talia glanced quickly at Akmir before shifting her attention toward the front of the passing Jeep.

"What is he doing?" she muttered in disbelief.

"The poor soul will be killed," Akmir said.

Talia put her hand on the butt of her gun as the Jeep came to an abrupt stop and the four armed men jogging in front of the vehicle converged on a robed figure who'd stumbled into the road. She unconsciously tightened her grip as the men assailed the robed figure, cursing and pushing him.

Although Talia was used to the sound of gunfire, when successive shots rang out—bang bang bang bang—she jerked with surprise. In a state of shock, she watched the torch on the far side of the Jeep tumble to the ground as the two men seated in the front of the vehicle slumped forward. The man standing in the back of the Jeep fell backward onto the road. In the same instant, a boy burst from a side street and ran toward the robed figure.

Reacting to the sound of gunfire, the four men in front of the Jeep turned with their weapons positioned to fire. In a blur, a dark-skinned man in Western clothes and armed with an automatic rifle jumped onto the hood of the Jeep and directed a prolonged strafing round at the four. The men jerked backward and crumpled to the ground. As the last of the four fell to the road, the dark-skinned man turned his weapon on the remaining torchbearer. A moment later, the man was lying face down in a pool of blood.

"What daring!" Akmir exclaimed with a clap of his hands.

Talia chuckled at his exuberance.

"Down!" the driver urgently shouted.

Talia chanced a glance out the car windshield before ducking her head. She saw the dark-skinned man aiming his weapon in their direction. She could feel her stomach tighten as she waited for him to fire. But nothing happened. Glancing over toward Akmir, she couldn't resist chuckling; the old Arab had his head between his knees, with both hands covering his skull. A second later, the driver announced, "Clear."

By the time Talia straightened and looked out the windshield, the dark-skinned Westerner was sitting behind the Jeep's steering wheel, yelling something over his shoulder. A few seconds later, she saw a little boy dressed in Western clothes climb up to the passenger seat just before the Jeep lurched forward.

"He's going to run them over!" Akmir exclaimed.

Akmir's shout drew Talia's attention. The boy who'd run out to help the robed figure was frantically pulling the person to the side of the road as the Jeep lurched forward. An instant later, the Jeep drove out of her field of vision. The boy, she saw, was safe. But the robed figure—a man, from what she could see of him—was prone on the ground and not moving. She wasn't sure if the Jeep had struck him or if he'd been hit by a bullet.

"Get us out of here," Akmir instructed the driver. "We'll have every lunatic—"

Talia put her hand on Akmir's arm as a dozen women and children ran across the intersection. Some, she noticed, had blood on their ankles and wrists.

"Slaves," she muttered.

"Ours," Akmir angrily stated.

"What?"

"I recognize—"

"How would they have gotten free?" Talia blurted. "Who would dare—?" Turning toward Akmir, she raised her voice in anger. "We have to round them up! The ship sails within the hour!"

"No!"

"But they're worth—"

"Do you wish to die?" he barked. Talia drew back when Akmir grabbed hold of her wrist. "Adhib will think we had something to do with this," he explained. "We can't recoup our losses if we're dead."

Talia nodded.

"Get us out of here," Akmir ordered the driver. "Hurry."

*

John Too anxiously pulled on Teimbaka's arm when he saw a black car suddenly appear and turn in their direction. Although he couldn't see who was driving, the vehicle flew the same black flag the men in the Jeep had been waving. Examining the carnage around him and recalling how angry the men waving the flags had acted before they were shot, he held little hope that the speeding car wasn't intent on running him and Teimbaka over.

"Teimbaka!" he cried. "Get up! Get up!"

John Too tugged on Teimbaka's robe. A quick glance toward the street showed the black car nearly upon them. The sound of tires crunching gravel twisted his stomach. Desperate, he pulled Teimbaka's hair in an attempt to rouse him. A glint of sun reflecting off the car's fender shot into John Too's eyes, temporarily blinding him. Unable to think of what else he could do, he flung his body atop of Teimbaka's and closed his eyes.

Squealing brakes. A gunshot. The sound of a car door swinging open.

"Get in!" he heard a woman shout.

There was a blur of movement, then someone clamped a hand around the back of his neck and lift him into the air. A moment later he was flung into the back seat of the car.

"Teimbaka!" he shouted.

A woman grabbed him by the shoulder. Frantic to reach Teimbaka, John Too slapped her wrist in an attempt to break her hold.

"Wait!" she yelled.

John Too flinched at a loud thud against the back window. He looked past the woman up toward the back of the car as two more thuds landed in the same area. A split second later, he heard glass cracking. Then he heard a door open and someone groan.

"Bulletproof," he heard a man say.

John Too looked over to see an older Arab with a hooked nose smiling at him.

"But not rocketproof," the Arab added, though John Too felt he was talking to the woman rather than him. "We shouldn't have stopped."

John Too punched the woman's hand from his shoulder when the car suddenly sped forward. Panic-stricken at the thought that Teimbaka had been left behind, he pulled and pushed the knobs and handles on the inside of the door.

"Let me out! Let me out!" he shouted. "Etiyopiya! I stay with Etiyopiya!"

A sharp blow to the side of his head knocked John Too off his feet and propelled him against the bench seat facing the rear of the car.

"He's in the front!" the woman barked. "Now sit down and shut up!"

From the expression of anger on the woman's face, John Too was certain she was about to hit him again. But a strafing round of gunfire tore into the metal roof just above the back window, prodding her and the Arab to flop to the floor and cover their heads.

*

Akmir swore under his breath, incensed that the bulletproof glass he'd spent a small fortune installing in the Mercedes was proving worthless.

"I will slit the thief's throat with my own hand," he hissed when glass fragments burst from the window into the rear of the car. "Selling me—"

He ducked his head and grumbled.

"Where should I drive, Master?" the driver yelled out.

"Back to our section of—"

"The airport!" Talia shouted.

Akmir looked up. He saw fear on Talia's face.

"Take me to the airport," she said in earnest. "This was a mistake. I should have never left Djibouti to come here."

Talia screamed when an explosion lifted the rear end of the car off the ground. She, Akmir, and John Too were thrown out of their seats.

"What in Allah's name is happening?" Akmir shouted.

"Soldiers!" the driver called out. "RPG!"

"Lose them!" Akmir ordered. "Get us off the road!"

"The airport!" Talia barked. "I must get to the airport!"

"There's no protection there!" Akmir forcefully countered. "No one controls—"

"I have men waiting," she reassured him. "And a plane equipped with a—"

A second violent explosion shattered the passenger window above John Too's head. Talia screamed again as the car shuddered from the impact. Akmir repeated his command to the driver to get off the road as automatic weapon fire erupted. Bullets tore into the buildings on either side of the car as the driver executed a sharp turn.

*

John Too looked up at the sky through the shattered window above his head and tried to make sense of where he was. That he was in Mogadishu, in the middle of a civil war, he did not dispute. But the question of where he was in this moment in time was not geographical.

The sky, he saw, was the palest blue. No different from yesterday, or the day before, or the day preceding. Somewhere in the back of his mind, he knew nothing would be different about it tomorrow, or the day after, or the one following, no matter if he was alive to see it.

Djibouti. He looked over at the lady. She'd said she should have never left. He glanced over his shoulder. She'd told him Etiyopiya lay in the front seat. *Djibouti.* Teimbaka had spent time there. From what John Too remembered, he'd traveled there in search of Claire. The story of Teimbaka—the Lion of Djibouti—had been born there, where he'd first done battle with the Serpent. The people who'd witnessed his actions had deemed him a holy warrior. They had praised his bravery. Spoken in awe of his strength. Some said that, through his heroic deeds, he had earned the trust of the Mother and the Father.

If that was true, what had gone wrong? Why had the Mother and the Father cast him aside? Why had they allowed him to be beaten to a shell of the man John Too had known? *Djibouti.* Perhaps if he could get Teimbaka back to the port city, some semblance of the man could be restored. As he stared up at the sky, he wondered if that was possible.

The woman. He turned his attention back to the woman, wondering who she was. She was beautiful, with almond eyes, smooth skin, and chiseled features that spoke of a mix of Arab and European lineage. That she was wealthy was apparent from her dress. He found her exotic. But her manner, her aura, radiated danger. And though John Too was still a boy, he nonetheless understood that the woman was a deadly threat.

"What are you staring at?" she snapped.

John Too quickly averted his gaze. Embarrassed the woman had caught him studying her, he turned his attention to the sky. It was the palest blue. Nothing about it had changed.

*

Chris parked the Jeep behind a tin-roofed maintenance shed on the edge of a runway and turned the engine off. Before addressing Marcus, he scoured the road for any sign of pursuers.

"Looks like we're clear," he said. He gave Marcus a brief smile. "Now all we have to do is…"

He tapped the steering wheel and sighed. As he shifted his attention from the boy to the area around the shed, he heard the stuttering cadence of automatic weapon fire in the distance.

"Shit," he muttered.

He touched Marcus on the shoulder.

"Come on."

Sitting stationary, his eyes focused on the floor between his feet, Marcus showed no sign that he'd heard.

"Marcus." Frustrated when the boy didn't respond, Chris shook his head. "Marcus," he said a little more forcefully. "Marcus! We got to go."

Drawn by the sound of another burst of gunfire, Chris grabbed the AK-47 he'd taken from one of the men he'd killed. As he slipped out of the driver's seat, he slung the weapon over his shoulder.

"Come on!" he ordered.

When Marcus didn't move, Chris leaned across the chassis of the Jeep and grabbed the boy by the back of the neck. In one swift, jerking motion, he pulled him from the seat and set him on the ground. As if he were addressing a misbehaving child, Chris bent down and looked Marcus straight in the eye.

"You either keep up or I'll leave you here to rot," he said.

Marcus stared back at him but said nothing.

"You understand what I'm saying?" He glanced toward an area where several planes of various sizes were parked. "Are you listening?"

Though he continued to stare into Chris's eyes, Marcus was silent and unresponsive.

"Fuck," Chris said. "You've lost it, haven't you?" He squeezed Marcus on the shoulder. "Done gone off the deep end." He shook his head. "Just my—"

The sound of rubber screeching on asphalt was quickly followed by the wobbling clatter of a hubcap falling off a tire and rolling across tarmac. Chris spotted a black Mercedes sedan swerving off the airport road just as a round of bullets ripped into the rear of the car and blew its bumper off. Chris slid a hand under Marcus's shoulder and lifted him off the ground.

"Let's go!"

*

Everything was a blur: objects, sounds, sensations—nothing made sense. Over and over, Marcus kept replaying what had happened to the men in the roofless car. A boom boom boom boom next to his ear. Blood—red, gooey, and warm—splattered all over his face. Everything went blurry after that. He remembered hearing more terrible explosions, but he had no concept of when they occurred. Then someone pushed him, pushed him so hard he had to run to keep from falling. Off balance, he'd looked over his shoulder. A woman; he remembered seeing a woman frantically waving her hands as if shooing flies from a batch of Gran-Jim's fresh-baked cinnamon rolls. Not looking where he was going, he nearly tripped over something. He didn't look to see what it was. He didn't want to look. Then he slammed into something hard and unforgiving. He remembered looking upward and seeing a man, his face frozen in an expression of horror. An instant later, the man dropped to the ground next to him. Then, somehow, Marcus had found himself sitting in the seat of the open-roof car. Splotches of blood had been everywhere.

Thinking he was in an unsettling dream, he closed his eyes and willed the dream to go away. Wind blew against his face. In the blankness of his thoughts an image appeared—Lady T.

"Lady T!" he cried.

As if waking from a terrible nightmare, he opened his eyes and unleashed a guttural wail. There was an earth-rattling boom and a sky-piercing flash, and he fell, his shoulder crunching against cement.

*

Chris flung Marcus to the ground when a twin-engine plane parked fifty meters from the Jeep erupted into a fireball. Out of the corner of his eye, he saw several armed men rush toward the inferno. In unison they opened fire. Chris first thought the men were shooting at the black Mercedes speeding toward a taxiing cargo plane. But the bullets flew past the car and strafed an area a few meters ahead of several vehicles that had followed the Mercedes into the airport. A large black flag inscribed with a crescent moon and star flew from the antenna of the lead car, which was painted in camouflage. Immediately behind the flag-bearing vehicle was an armored troop carrier fitted with a light-caliber machine gun. Shadowing the troop carrier—ten meters off the vehicle's passenger side—sped a Jeep transporting a team of soldiers equipped with a shoulder-mounted rocket launcher. Behind the Jeep and troop carrier drove three more vehicles. Each, Chris observed, carried two to three uniformed soldiers.

Reacting to a blur flashing across his vision, Chris dove to the ground and covered his head. What he assumed was a launched rocket detonated a millisecond later, sending a shockwave through the earth. The powerful whoosh of the ensuing fireball prompted him to take a tentative peek toward the runway. Where he recalled seeing a single-engine scout plane lay a blackened, fiery chassis with two smoldering wings.

The booming blast of a .50 caliber machine gun made Chris feel like someone was jackhammering the back of his neck. Momentarily confused by the deafening roar of the deadly weapon, he instinctively rolled several times to his right to get clear of the line of fire, finishing by sliding his AK-47 up past his shoulder. Guessing the heavy machine-gun fire originated from one of the pursuit vehicles, he swung the AK toward the lead vehicle and took aim.

Screams of pain and the sound of shredding metal accompanied the onslaught of high-caliber bullets tearing into the Jeep speeding alongside the armored troop carrier. Chris watched, awestruck, as .50 caliber shells turned flesh, bone, and metal into chunks of blood-tinged pulp. The armed group of men rushing out to meet the Mercedes cheered, but their celebration was short-lived. The armored troop carrier fired a sustained burst from its mounted machine gun, felling all but one of the armed men providing cover fire for the arriving sedan.

When the booming staccato of the .50 caliber erupted once more, Chris sprang to his feet and searched for the weapon. Muzzle flashes and smoke rising from the gun barrel made it easy for him to spot. A silver-bearded white man fired the big gun from a cargo plane sandwiched between two burning wrecks.

The Mercedes came to a sliding, tire-squealing stop meters from the cargo plane. The .50 caliber abruptly stopped firing as the back passenger door swung open. In the absence of the big gun's action, incoming fire hit the side of the cargo plane. Then the Mercedes's driver's-side door flew open. A man slipped out of the vehicle and opened fire with an automatic rifle. As the man strafed the line of oncoming vehicles with a barrage of bullets, a woman sprang from the back seat of the car and ran toward the plane. With the old man's help, she jumped up and into the cargo hold.

*

Talia gripped Yaroslav's forearm with both hands as he pulled her up into the plane.

"Who's manning the cockpit?" she yelled.

Yaroslav replied with a smile before shifting his attention to the massive gun mounted on a tripod in front of him. When he engaged the firing mechanism, Talia flinched and covered her ears. A glance toward the cockpit revealed no one in either pilot seat. She grabbed Yaroslav's upper arm and squeezed.

"Get up there!" she shouted. "Take off!"

She slapped his shoulder when he didn't react.

"I'll man the gun!" she yelled. With a nod toward the cockpit, she bellowed, "Get us out of here!"

Not waiting for a reply, she forcefully pushed Yaroslav aside and grasped the machine gun's double handles. As she watched Yaroslav jog toward the cockpit, Talia looked out over the barrel of the Browning. The pursuit vehicles—Adhib's men, no doubt—had maneuvered into a semicircle around the plane. Her cargo plane was boxed in. She was punched backward by a bullet grazing her shoulder.

"We're fucked!" she heard Yaroslav yell from the cockpit. "We're penned in!"

Talia grabbed her wounded shoulder and grimaced. A surge of anger shot through her when she brought her hand up to her face and saw her fingers covered in blood.

"Fuck," she said. "Fuck."

Furious, she stepped closer to the .50 caliber and grabbed the double handles.

"Get us out of here!" she screamed. She fired a concentrated burst at the flag-bearing Jeep and yelled, "Find a way!"

*

Yaroslav slid into the pilot seat.

"Find a way," he grumbled. He glanced out the window toward the burning wreck blocking the path forward. "Get us out of here," he mimicked.

Yaroslav looked toward the semi-circle of hostile vehicles. Taking a deep breath, he released the plane's parking brake and grabbed the throttle.

"You knew the woman would be the death of you," he muttered under his breath. "Knew it from the get-go." He shook his head as he nudged the throttle forward. "Your own damn fault. Now look at you. Stuck between two goddamn burning wrecks and a bunch of—"

A fresh burst of gunfire drew Yaroslav's attention to the tarmac. When he saw a Jeep speeding across the runway on the far side of the attacking vehicles, he leaned closer to the window and squinted.

"What in the Holy Mother?" he murmured as he watched a dark-skinned man fire on the soldiers attacking his plane.

"Seems we have friend!" he called back to Talia, laughing as three attacking soldiers fell to the ground. "A damn good shot!" he bellowed.

Talia must have noticed the mystery man as well, for no sooner had their unknown ally come under fire than the .50 caliber erupted in his defense. Firing right to left—from the lead vehicle flying the black Islamic flag to the last camouflaged-painted Jeep—the heavy weapon wreaked havoc. The mayhem brought a smile to his face. But it quickly faded when a new explosion produced a second wall of flames in front of the plane.

*

Chris instinctively ducked when a fireball spewed from a single-engine Cessna parked near the nose of the cargo plane. He fired one last strafing burst from the AK-47 before tossing the weapon aside and taking the steering wheel in both hands. With a quick glance at Marcus—who was lying on the floor—he stepped hard on the gas pedal and sped across the flames. As soon as he cleared the fire, he swung the Jeep around and braked. He grabbed a tarp he'd found in the maintenance shed and spread it over Marcus.

"Don't move," he told the boy.

Then he grabbed a second tarp and flung it over his shoulders. Tugging the heavy canvas over the top of his head, he took his foot off the brake and eased the Jeep forward.

"Let's hope this works," he muttered.

Chris dipped his head toward his knees, pulled the tarp up far enough so it covered his face, and gave the Jeep some gas. Holding an image of the burning plane in his head, he edged the steering wheel ever so slightly to the right. He could hear sparks explode over him as he nudged the front of the Jeep forward. Satisfied the grill of the vehicle was flush against the burning aircraft, he nudged the steering wheel left and eased the smolder-ing wreck toward the line of attacking vehicles. He could hear gunshots pinging off the hood, but he ignored them. He knew there was only one chance for Marcus and him to survive.

"Get ready to move!" he yelled to the boy.

Not knowing if Marcus had heard him, he gritted his teeth and pushed the gas pedal flush against the floor.

*

"What the hell is going on?" Yaroslav heard Talia yell.

"He going to push it!" he shouted with a laugh. "Damn negro is crazy."

Yaroslav watched plumes of sparks rise into the air as the Jeep method-ically pushed the burning wreck toward the semi-circle of vehicles.

"Almost clear!" he called back to Talia.

"Get us airborne!" she screamed.

*

Talia glimpsed a wall of moving fire out of the corner of her eye. Confused to see the burning wreck of a plane moving sideways, she leaned her head over the butt of the .50 caliber machine gun to get a better look. When she caught sight of a Jeep pushing the wreck off to the side she shook her head. Who was the driver? And where did he come from? Bullets rico-cheting off the cargo bay's open door prompted her to duck back into the hold. Glancing down at her wounded shoulder, she gritted her teeth and grabbed the heavy machine gun handles. With a muttered, "Fuck you," she fired off a twenty-round burst.

*

Teimbaka woke to the sound of gunfire and a man yelling, "Get us out of here!"

Using his fingertips, he examined the area directly below his body and then to either side. Rows of grooved, supple material linked by intricate stitching; he was lying on the seat of an automobile. How he had come to be in a vehicle surrounded by gunfire, he had no recollection. His last memory was of being pushed into a hard asphalt road. He'd heard the putter of a slow-moving car and men chanting in Arabic, "Death to the buffalo!" He'd sniffed the air, trying to locate the animal, but then someone grabbed him by the front of his robe and screamed for him to move. He'd been struck in the face—hard. Deftly, he felt behind him until his fingers discovered the inner panel of a door. When he located a handle, he pushed it down.

*

John Too heard a car door open.

"Etiyopiya!" he cried.

"Get down, boy!" the old Arab ordered.

John Too turned toward the man just as the old Arab grabbed his arm.

"You'll be safe with me," the man told him. "Hassan!" he yelled in the next moment. "Get us out of here!"

A chill ran through John Too's body when the old Arab looked into his eyes. Within the man's pupils, he saw the flicker of a Serpent's tongue.

Grabbing the old Arab by the wrist, John Too thrust his free arm out and upward and smashed the heel of his palm flush against the man's hooked nose. When the Arab cried out in pain, John Too yanked his arm free and scurried over the seat. Teimbaka was kneeling on the asphalt just outside the open door.

"Imp!" the driver yelled in Arabic.

As the man turned his weapon toward him and yelled, "Stay!" John Too slid out the open door and fell to the tarmac.

*

Marcus extended his arms outward from his sides and savored the rush of air buffeting his face. How and when he'd been changed into a bird, he didn't know, but he found the transformation utterly sublime.

"I'm flying," he joyfully muttered.

He flapped his arms and giggled. But when a thunderous round of explosions burst across his senses, the ecstasy of flight came to an abrupt and shocking end. Blinking to awareness, he dazedly surveyed his immediate surroundings.

Left and upward he saw a gun barrel sticking out of a big airplane. The gun was smoking and spewing fiery flashes. Ahead of him he observed a burning mound of metal with what looked to be wings on either side. Above him, holding him by the back of his shirt, was Chris, the man who'd sailed with him and Lady T across the ocean.

"Where's Lady T?" Marcus blurted.

When Chris glanced down with an angry expression on his face, Marcus averted his eyes. A shiny black car parked meters away caught his attention.

Sprawled on the asphalt next to the car was the boy he'd pulled from the ocean. "Boy!" he shouted. Pointing his finger in the boy's direction, he looked up toward Chris.

"Boy!" he shouted again.

"Get in!" Chris yelled.

And then he flung Marcus upward toward the big gun making all the noise. A woman, crouched in the open doorway, extended a hand.

*

John Too's head swiveled in the direction of the cargo plane when he heard a child yell, "Boy!" Immediately, he recognized the youth who'd pulled him from the ocean and the man who'd shoved Teimbaka in front of the soldiers.

"Help me!" John Too yelled to the boy.

But he was too late, for the man carrying the boy tossed him upward toward an open door in the big plane. The lady from the car grabbed the boy's wrist. And then the sound of squealing car tires—deafeningly close—compelled him to cover his ears with his hands and dip his head toward the ground.

*

Talia winced as soon as she grabbed the boy by the wrist. It felt as though someone had shoved a knife into her shoulder near her collarbone. She watched the boy fall back onto the tarmac with tear-blurred eyes. The man who'd handed the boy to her screamed "Fuck!" and then grabbed her forearm and barked, "Give me cover fire!"

Talia swallowed hard to suppress a surge of panic. Frantic, she grabbed the .50 caliber machine gun handles and fumbled to find the firing mechanism. She watched, detached, as Akmir's Mercedes sped away. The man who'd cleared the burning wreck from the tarmac and the boy who was with him were completely exposed. Overcome by a bizarre compulsion to help them, she spread her feet wide, bent slightly at the knees, and braced for the weapon's powerful recoil.

*

While all Chris's instincts had screamed for him to jump back into the plane and leave Marcus to whatever fate had in store for the kid, an image of Ed Taylor flashed through his thoughts. Whether it was a glimpse of Ed's compassionate expression that made him feel duty-bound to save the boy, or something he saw in Ed's eyes—something that reminded him of a father he barely knew—he sprinted to where Marcus was trying to help the two people still lying exposed on the tarmac.

*

Yaroslav eased the throttle forward as he maneuvered the plane into a slow turn. Grateful for the negro's efforts in clearing a path to the runway, he'd flashed a thumbs-up when the man used hand signals to ask if he and the boy could catch a ride. Though Yaroslav had no clue where the man had come from or why he'd decided to help free the plane for takeoff, it occurred to him that the negro might be some use to him in the near future. He figured there were still several tons of ivory hidden somewhere in the mountains near where he'd rendezvoused with the blue-turbaned

Arab; having another body around to help with loading would come in handy. Especially since the blue-headed bastard hadn't shown up at the last meet.

He leaned out the window and glanced toward the rear of the plane. Whoever the negro was and wherever he came from, he certainly seemed skilled with a weapon. And there was no doubting his daring and nerve. Following that line of thought, he eased off the throttle. Now in position to make a run down the tarmac, all he needed to hear was that everyone was on board. Once he got the order to go, he could have the plane airborne in thirty seconds.

*

"I told you to stay in the plane!"

Chris nearly slapped Marcus for his disobedience, but something about the other boy—the boy Marcus was helping off the tarmac—kept him from acting. The boy's eyes were so keen and aware that Chris sensed he could read the secrets of his soul. So instead of slapping Marcus, he helped him pull the youth to his feet.

"You carry Etiyopiya," the youth said.

Momentarily confused, Chris stood with his mouth agape.

"Etiyopiya," the boy explained, glancing down at the man prone by his feet. "The woman." The boy paused to point at the cargo plane. "She goes to Djibouti. Hurry."

*

Talia was mystified as to how the men and boys had not been struck by bullets. Though she was spewing cover fire from the Browning, incoming rounds from Adhib's men were heavy. The men and boys—positioned a dozen meters from the nearest of Adhib's vehicles—were almost point-blank targets. Yet, the four remained unharmed. It was impossible.

"What lies beyond the lights of the harbor?" Adiam said inside her head. So clear was his voice, so pervasive his presence, she felt as though she could turn from the machine gun to find him sitting at one of the little tables from his café, smoking a cigarette and sipping bourbon.

What lies beyond the lights of the harbor?

She'd assumed, when he'd first posed the question to her, he was referring to geography: terrain, ocean currents, and wind. Or perhaps trade routes, merchandise, or markets not yet tapped. Now, however, she wondered what Adiam had meant.

Teimbaka—the Lion of Djibouti. Whenever Adiam had talked of the man, he had spoken in tones of reverence, as though his old *azmari* partner was made of something more than flesh and blood. She had dismissed his talk as the ramblings of an aging, disease-ridden man viewing the past through a bourbon haze.

How charming Adiam had been when he talked of the Lion and the Mother. One could momentarily forget the ruthless manner in which he conducted business, the atrocities he'd committed in the name of profit. But now, as she watched the stranger lift the Lion and throw him over his shoulder, it occurred to her that Adiam's old friend might hold some value. The youth—the boy she'd stopped the car for—was certainly worth a good deal of money. He was the perfect age to be sold as an attendant to a wealthy businessman or marketed for sex.

"Hurry!" she implored the mystery man.

Firing a strafing round at Adhib's men, she glanced down at the ammunition box located at the base of the tripod. From what she could ascertain, it was nearly empty.

"Hurry!" she screamed.

*

John Too studied the black *ferenji* warily. Why was he helping Teimbaka after he had pushed him into the road? Shifting his attention to the plane, he was puzzled by the lady firing the powerful machine gun. Why had she come from Djibouti? And what business did she and the Arab share? Glancing between the woman and the *ferenji*, he felt very strongly that neither could be trusted. Yet what choice did he and Teimbaka have in reaching Djibouti if they didn't accept their help? Again, John Too studied the *ferenji* as they neared the plane; his sense that something was amiss grew stronger.

*

With a powerful heave, Chris thrust the blind man into the open space between the machine gun and the frame of the door. He shoved again to clear the entrance, then turned to locate Marcus.

"Let's go!" he shouted to the boy.

Lacing his fingers together, he cupped his hands and offered them to Marcus as a stirrup. Once satisfied the boy was safe on the plane, he repeated the maneuver for the unnerving youth. As Chris jogged alongside the open door in preparation to swing up into the plane, suddenly the Browning stopped firing and the plane sped up.

"Son of a bitch," Chris said.

*

Talia took her finger off the firing mechanism as soon as she saw the first of Adhib's vehicles speed away. Dumfounded, she watched as the remaining soldiers and vehicles followed suit.

"Get us out of here!" she shouted to Yaroslav. "Now!"

She heard the surge of the propellers, and the plane lurched forward. Dazed from the firefight and the pain shooting through her shoulder, she slumped to the floor, offering the briefest of nods to one boy and then the other. As she took a deep breath and let out a heavy sigh, the black Westerner vaulted into the cargo hold. Too tired to react, Talia watched the stranger come to a rolling stop, his body perfectly balanced on the balls of his feet. No sooner had she made eye contact with the man than he stood and approached her.

"Chris Mason," he said.

He smiled and extended his hand.

*

Yaroslav pulled back on the wheel and let out a sigh of relief when he felt the tires disengage from the runway. He took the plane to 500 feet before executing a slow turn to the left.

"So long, you desert hellhole," he muttered.

A commotion on the runway caught his eye. From what he could discern, the Mercedes sedan had been stopped by a slew of camouflage-painted vehicles. A person dressed in traditional Arab robes exited the back of the car and approached the nearest of the pursuing vehicles. When the robed individual suddenly thrust his arms out to his sides, Yaroslav had a good idea of what might occur. Sure enough, an instant later, he saw a rifle flash. The man dressed in the robes fell backward to the ground. With a slight shrug, Yaroslav nudged the throttle forward and began an ascent to fifteen hundred feet.

31

FLOATING—UP, DOWN, SIDE to side—Teimbaka couldn't tell. He felt as though he was suspended, hanging in air or drifting on water. The sensation reminded him of a certain morning near the Gulf of Aden when fog suddenly enveloped him, trapping him in the intersection of two streets. Surrounded by heavy mist, he'd become disoriented. Time—measured in anxious heartbeats—paused. Or, rather, it had become confused as to how to proceed. Like Teimbaka, it didn't know which direction to turn. He'd stood still, listening, waiting. After a few minutes of immobility, he felt weightless. He could smell salt water on the air, but he couldn't tell where it originated. The sound of waves—or what he thought were waves crashing along the shoreline— were entangled in the same web of ambiguity, their origin muddled by senses shrouded in doubt.

He'd been following John.

John—odd to think of the boy at this moment. Or perhaps it was appropriate. For as time had changed him, it had transformed John. He'd gone from boy to man—albeit one beset with demons—in the course of a year. Susenyo had crippled him with addiction, injected his veins with jealousy and hate. Yet Susenyo wasn't the only cause of John's dark transformation. John—the hyena-man—lived in angst, a product of spurned love. His infatuation and devotion to Claire had warped him. Teimbaka hoped—

He wasn't sure what to hope.

"Twenty minutes to Djibouti!" a man with an accent called out.

Claire—her name floated in Teimbaka's thoughts, turning and twisting, uncertain which direction to take.

*

Dirk's tears were tears of relief—joy realized after years of tortured memories. He felt his body go limp, as if his every cell had been given the capacity to sigh and then did so. That he was being offered the opportunity to join his beloved, Genevieve, was more than he could have ever hoped. How pathetic his life had become after her gruesome death. Years wasted in futility, in an existence tormented by false bravado and an ego that wouldn't accept responsibility. Only now, in this moment before reunification, did he understand that it was the weakness of his character that had led Genevieve to her gruesome end. Since that awful day, whether via his own imagination or through the powers of ethereal beings, her spirit had haunted him. In his mind he'd watched her raped, mutilated, and burned ad infinitum. Her decapitated head would stare into his eyes and plead for deliverance. Horror stricken, he'd been incapable of acting. What words or actions could he offer to rectify the end she'd suffered? Wishing nothing more than to be forgiven, he found himself choked with emotion when an inner voice told him he was about to be cleansed of all his sins.

The opportunity to undo all the meaningless years he'd spent on earth was upon him, a voice informed him. It lay in the length of rope resting in Genevieve's hand. How could he refuse? She was offering salvation. Forgiveness. She was asking him to join her. Willingly, he would oblige. How could he not, after what he had done?

He watched in joyous silence as Genevieve placed a noose around his neck and tightened the knot. Gently, he took her hands in his and kissed her fingers one by one. When he looked in her eyes, he saw paradise, a vast world of lush forests, azure skies, and rolling oceans tinted gold by a warming sun. Genevieve stood at the epicenter of this utopia, hand extended, beckoning. Sobbing in liberation, he took the step that would unite them. Bliss came with a rupture in his heart.

*

Dr. Haraji allowed himself the slightest of grins. Validation of his life's work dangled in front of him, hanging by a length of fabric torn from Mr. Benson's shirt. Years of research and experimentation had come to fruition in the form of an undeniable, practical result. To inform his colleagues of his findings was now paramount. He felt an urgent need to return to the clinic to begin work on his thesis. With a fleeting glance to Dirk's bulging eyes, he left the man's jail cell and walked a deserted hallway toward an unmanned security door.

*

Claire rested her head against the window and sighed, staring blankly down at the distant, passing terrain. Her thoughts lost in innumerable compartments of doubt, she did not consider what might be taking place in the country she once called home. Nor could she fathom the steps she would need to take to re-establish the memory of her years there. She had forgotten someone—or numerous people. She was certain of that. *Why* she had forgotten them was less clear. But snippets of images—places, faces, and events—stirred wild and frightful suspicions. Doubt, suspicion—she suddenly wondered why Mr. Pembrook had been so adamant she make the trip to Africa.

Claire rubbed her thumb along the face of the silver cross dangling against her chest as the ever-present ache in her head began to increase in intensity. *The cross*—it reminded her of... She wasn't certain *what* it reminded her of. Yet, she knew she was a nun—at least, that's what Mr. Pembrook and Mother Superior had told her. In that case, to wear the symbol of Jesus's resurrection was appropriate, wasn't it? And by wearing the cross, she felt— She wasn't quite certain *how* she felt. Complete? Secure? Inoculated? Steadfast? Confident? Empowered? Just how *was* she supposed to feel? *Jesus died on the cross and on the third day rose again.* Claire looked into the face of the cross. *What am I hoping to resurrect?*

Examining the vague image reflected in the silver of the pendant, she began to weigh what sort of nun she had been. Giving? Selfless? Merciful? Pious? What virtues had she held herself to? And what had she valued above all else: sacrifice, devotion, piety, mercy? Or had she been aloof and reserved, holding religion close to her heart instead of living life in mirror of the Lord's son?

Emerald eyes stared out at her from the surface of the cross as she mulled various aspects of her life. Slowly, in increments, she realized that her own eyes were amber. Unnerved, she quickly turned the face of the cross inward toward her chest and took a deep breath. *Am I going mad? Is that the reason I was in a clinic? Because I lost my mind?* Claire shifted her attention to the window. Beyond the tip of the airplane's wing, a canopy of clouds—cotton-ball mounds, smooth and level—gleamed pink-gold in the rays of an early morning African sun. Struck by the majesty of the vista, Claire bowed her head and gave silent thanks to the Lord.

Praise be to you, Almighty, you who give life to those who have no hope. Thank you for blessing this day. And thank you for the warmth of your grace and the depth of your love.

Embarrassed for having turned the face of the cross inward, Claire righted the symbol of her faith and gazed unconstrained into its arms.

Elephants—ethereal, translucent, their torsos imbued with a faint shimmering glow—materialized in succession on a moon-drenched pla-teau. Silhouetted against this ghostly landscape was a woman, kneeling, head slightly bowed. In one hand she held a rosary, the beads worn from prayer. Stars twinkled silver-white overhead as a shadow slowly took shape aside her. Claire bit down on her lower lip when, startled, the woman in the image abruptly rose from her knees and confronted the dark manifes-tation. Her hair cut short, her eyes somber and ringed with weariness, the woman angled her face upward and, to Claire's surprise, smiled. Claire realized that the barely recognizable woman was she. With her fingertips lightly pressed against her lips, Claire studied her own features in the reflected image with a mixture of sadness and curiosity.

What ordeal she had suffered that her image was so gaunt, exhausted, strained? How long had she gone without sleep? And food? Claire uncon-sciously touched her cheeks before sliding her fingers down her neck and resting her palm on her stomach. Guilt wormed its way into her thoughts as she acknowledged the meal she'd been served during the flight from Paris. Having read about the great famine across the horn of Africa and studying pictures of refugee camps—mile-wide ramshackle villages with no running water or sanitation—she wondered what had changed since she'd left. Had she been involved in one of the camps? And if she had, had she made a difference? And who—?

Claire glanced at the shadow figure in the surface of the cross before shifting her gaze back to the image of her face. From her image's expression, it was clear she was unafraid of whomever was standing beside her.

"What is it you pray for?"

Claire placed a hand to her heart as the voice of a man spoke within her thoughts. The voice—his voice—elicited elation and distress. And while she was certain she knew to whom the voice belonged, she could not assign him a face. The dull ache inside her head grew to a pounding hurt as she tried to conjure an aspect of the man's identity: his eyes, nose, mouth—or some memory of his touch.

"What you have asked."

Claire sharply inhaled at her image's reply. *What you have asked*—the words swirled inside her thoughts as she waited for her image to say more. *What you have asked.* Intuition told her she knew what her reflected self would say. Lifting the cross closer to her face, she racked her memory for the words she was certain she had spoken before.

"For the day to end," her image said.

For the day to end! Mimicking the actions of her reflected self, Claire raised a hand and placed her fingertips upon a face that was not physically present. Gently—as she watched her image do the same—she traced the outline of a brow and jawline with the edge of her thumb before hesitantly resting her forefinger alongside a mouth. In her imagination, she saw, as well as felt, numerous scars upon the skin she touched. *For the day to end.* She mulled the phrase in her thoughts. It struck her as being one she had heard many times before. Though she was distracted by the throbbing pain in her head, a vision of a crimson, violet-streaked sunset manifested within her mind. For a moment, the painful throb within her skull became the sound of a beating drum.

"Drum-man," she muttered, dazed.

Touching her lips as if something longed-for had brushed against them, she experienced the sensation of being kissed tenderly and with passion. Instantly, she felt shame. Yet, within the same breath, she felt a sense of fulfillment, as if something missing from her life—something vastly important—had been discovered.

"What is it you wish for?"

She remembered the asking, remembered the evening she put forth the question. She envisioned the outline of a man sitting on a flat-topped boulder. He was pounding on a drum. *The drum, drum-man*—the timbre of the instrument transported her to another image, one that placed her in a field of unmarked graves. She could hear hyenas cackling and hooting, their voices wild and haunting. Shivering at the recollection, Claire remembered how afraid she had felt the night she'd been beckoned to Angelique's burial ground by the sound of a drum. *Drum-man*—when she'd seen him, he'd told her not to be afraid. He'd said…

Claire looked deeper into the arms of the cross. The shadow standing beside her image began to take on substance. She peered closer. The shadow became a man dressed in a dark robe. In his hand he carried a spear. No, not a spear. A staff—a long shaft of wood that extended a foot or more above his head. His face—Claire pressed her palms against her temples as a sharp pain shot through her skull. His face—she could nearly make out his features as he began to turn toward her. His face—moonlight angling down from the sky illuminated a score of scars running along his jawbone. *Turn and look at me!* The pain in her head became unbearable. *Look at me!*

"Ma'am? Ma'am, are you all right?"

Look at me!

Claire bumped the back of her head against her seat when something touched her arm.

"Lady."

Disoriented, Claire looked numbly at a man peering into her eyes. Confused when he nodded upward and arched his eyebrows, she blinked several times.

"The stewardess," he said, nodding to a woman standing next to his seat.

Claire squeezed her eyes shut in effort to quell the pain in her head.

"Ma'am, are you all right? Can I get anything for you?"

Claire pressed her fingertips to her forehead and tried to place the woman's voice.

"Are you in pain?"

Pain. Trembling, she slowly lowered her hands to her lap and, out of habit, smoothed the wrinkles in her skirt. *Pain.* Though her head felt as though it might explode, she concentrated on keeping the man within the cross in her thoughts. *Pain.* She was certain she knew how the scars running along his jawbone had been made, yet felt tormented by her inability to recall any facet of the incident. *Pain.* Desperate to discover the man's identity, she grasped the base of the cross between her thumb and forefinger and held it up toward the uniformed woman standing in the aisle.

"Do you know who this is?" she blurted out.

The woman's brow furrowed. An awkward few seconds elapsed before the woman smiled. Claire straightened, anxious to hear what the woman would say.

"Jesus?" the woman volunteered in an uncertain tone of voice.

Perplexed by the woman's answer, Claire jerked the cross back to her chest. As though she were hiding something valuable from prying eyes, she cupped the cross within her palm and gave it a wary glance. *Jesus? Jesus?* No. No, it wasn't Jesus. But she gave the cross another quick glance to be certain. Forcing a polite smile, she addressed the uniformed woman.

"No," she told her. She shook her head before repeating more definitively, "No."

"Well, then," the woman cheerfully replied. "I suppose I'll—" She paused and glanced toward the front of the plane. "We should be landing in twenty minutes."

The woman fell silent but maintained eye contact. As Claire unconsciously rubbed the face of the cross with her thumb, the man sitting next to her cleared his throat.

"I'll check back," the stewardess said.

Distracted by thoughts of Jesus and drum-man, Claire nodded. A change of pitch in the plane's jet engines lured her attention to the window and what lay beyond. The wing—which had been, just moments before, gliding across a canvas of coral-colored clouds—appeared austere and dream-like, a length of silver-white metal suspended against a panorama of blue. *God has left me*, Claire immediately thought. Stung by the Lord's departure, she abruptly turned her attention toward the center of the plane. Perhaps the woman in the uniform was familiar with the Djibouti airport. Maybe the woman could tell her of an area designated for travelers to meet pre-arranged drivers. But to her dismay, the woman was no longer standing in the aisle. Nor could she locate any other uniformed person when she searched the cabin forward and aft.

"Are you familiar with the Djibouti airport?" she asked the man sitting next to her.

But the seat next to her was empty.

Flustered, Claire clutched the cross in her hand and took a deep breath. A sudden, heavy thud from a wide area beneath her feet sent a jolt of panic to her stomach.

"God have mercy," she muttered.

Seeking comfort, Claire raised the cross to eye level and peered into the center of its arms. Hoping the stewardess was correct, she anxiously anticipated the appearance of the figure she'd witnessed before. Perhaps the cloaked man within the arms of the cross *was* the Son of God, she told herself. Perhaps He was waiting for her to acknowledge His presence before He made Himself known. *Like Thomas*, she suddenly thought, *like Thomas after Christ's resurrection.*

Certain she'd unraveled the mystery of the man within the cross, Claire stared into the symbol's shiny silver surface and patiently waited for Jesus to reappear. Seconds passed. Nothing. No reflection, no figure, no vista of ghostly elephants bathed in moonlight. A minute elapsed—still nothing. Little by little, Claire began to doubt, her gaze slowly drifting from the cross to the window to the cabin of the plane to the empty seat beside her. Had anything she'd just experienced been real? Struck by misgivings, she placed the cross against her chest. She could feel her heart beating against her knuckles, the rhythmic pounding reminiscent of a drum.

"Drum-man," she muttered.

As she put her fingertips to her lips and closed her eyes, she couldn't help but wonder if she'd lost her mind.

*

Walking toward something, or walking away? Juba didn't know, nor had she been accorded the opportunity to ask. The old woman she'd been following—though Juba wondered how old the woman could be, given she'd maintained a half-kilometer gap between them for the better part of a week—seemed to have no specific destination in mind. Juba had followed her east one morning, north the next, west one afternoon, only to awaken after a night's rest and backtrack along the previous day's route. And while Juba was interested in catching up to the woman, she had admonished herself several times over the past few days for deciding to follow the woman at all.

It had all started one evening at sunset. The woman had appeared as a flaming apparition standing on a hilltop, dressed in a flowing grey robe, outlined in the eye of the setting sun. And though Juba couldn't clearly see the woman's distant face, she got the distinct impression the woman was staring at her in the expectation that Juba would join her. So Juba woke before sunrise the following morning and set off for the hilltop. But when she reached her destination, the old woman was not there. Which was peculiar, because Juba had seen the glare of the old woman's fire through the night. In fact, she had used the flickering beacon to guide her to the woman's camp in the pre-dawn twilight. Nonetheless, Juba found the fire extinguished, the embers cold to the touch. Slightly perturbed and somewhat confused, she sat next to the cold embers and folded her arms across her chest.

Dawn had been slow to arrive that morning. A somber shroud of grey mist had cloaked the earth in a dimness that had lasted unusually long. Annoyed by the sun's inability to break through the murky veil, she'd pulled the antelope horn from her waist-sash and plunged the tip into the soil. Each time she struck the earth, she raked the horn back toward her body. Soon, the ground was streaked with furrows. Absorbed in her annoyance, Juba didn't recognize the other shapes that lay etched in the ground until the sun broke through the fog.

A lion, a giraffe, an antelope, a wildebeest, and an elephant stood side by side along a river. The river ended at a waterfall near the base of a mountain. Trees covered an area from the base of the mountain to the edge of a barren landscape bordered by a line of twisting dunes. Along the far side of the dunes lay a wide swath of blackened earth.

Juba thought back to the time when she'd first encountered these figures, the evening she'd first met the old woman. The meeting had been somber—at least on Juba's part. Kamua, along with a dozen hyenas, had been killed earlier in the day. Juba had wanted to think of nothing, to drift into nothingness, but the woman's appearance had prevented her from doing so.

What did the old hag want of her? Why had she suddenly reappeared? Juba scrutinized the drawings for a clue. What meaning was hidden in the scene the woman had drawn? Juba didn't know.

Juba left the hilltop that morning giving little credence to the etchings. *The doodling of a silly old wanderer,* she thought. *Pictures scratched in the soil to pass the time.* Catching a glimpse of the woman on the plain some half kilometer west of the hill, she'd set off to catch her. By nightfall, however, she was no closer to the woman. Frustrated by her lack of progress, she'd fallen asleep early, determined to wake up long before dawn and reach the woman before the sun broke the horizon.

As on the previous night, Juba woke to see the woman's campfire flickering in the darkness some distance away. She immediately rose from her earthen bed and set off at a jog. But when she arrived at the spot from which the flames had beckoned her, the woman was nowhere to be found. The campfire was cold. Daylight revealed the same drawing in the soil: a lion, a giraffe, an antelope, and a wildebeest standing on the banks of a river, adjacent to a mountain, an area of trees, a swath of dunes, and a patch of blackened dirt. Juba sighed, suddenly feeling there was no sense in following the woman. She was being teased. She decided to set off for home.

Home. Juba's eyes teared up as she contemplated returning to her village—or what remained of it. Anger welled up from the pit of her stomach and spread to every part of her body as she remembered the slaughter of her family by the hands of some warlord she knew nothing about. She ground her fist into her eyes and admonished herself. *Tears are for children! I am no longer a child!* With a final angry glance at the animal drawings, Juba turned to go. But something tugged at her thoughts, compelling her to take another look at the etchings. Something was amiss, she realized: there was an empty spot where an elephant should have been.

Tembo—why aren't you there?

At the moment Juba questioned the elephant's absence, a pack of nearby hyenas hooted and cackled. Juba looked for them but instead spotted the old woman standing a half kilometer away, her robed figure encircled by the rising sun. Certain the woman was indeed trying to convey a message to her, Juba once more set off to reach her.

With several hyenas following, Juba trailed the woman for four more days and nights, each frustratingly similar save for the etchings in the soil. On successive mornings, the lion disappeared, then the giraffe, then the antelope, until finally, on the sixth morning of her quest to reach the old woman, the wildebeest was absent. More certain than ever that the drawings had been left by the old woman to convey a message, Juba set out on the sixth morning in a full sprint, determined to reach the woman before nightfall. But her effort failed. And by the time the sun set on the sixth day of her journey, she went to sleep no closer to the woman than she had been on the first.

On the seventh morning, Juba woke well after dawn to a foul stench in the air, her mind clouded by a disturbing dream that slipped from her consciousness as she stirred. Troubled, she was slow to acknowledge the presence of a lone hyena. The animal was pacing anxiously a few meters from where she'd slept. Juba's first thought was that something bad had happened to the old woman. Immediately, she looked west, the direction in which she'd last seen her. The flock of vultures she saw circling in the sky reinforced her misgivings.

With the single hyena running by her side, Juba raced toward the woman's campfire as wisps of the dream she could not recall floated in and out of her thoughts. Images of horror-stricken eyes and blood-smeared faces flashed through her head. Animal? Human? She could not tell.

Unpleasant as the visions was the rotten stench permeating the air. So pungent was the dreadful aroma, so bitter its taste upon her tongue, Juba covered her nose and mouth with a hand to try to keep the smell from invading her senses. But the stink grew more pervasive the closer she drew to the circling vultures. By the time she reached the knoll where the old woman had built her campfire, her throat and nose were so filled with the awful odor, she fell to her knees and retched. Gasping between violent bouts of heaving, Juba crawled to the crest of the little hill and looked out at the land below.

A cloak of shadows swirled from the base of the knoll to the banks of a watering hole some thirty strides from where Juba knelt. The ever-moving shadow cast by the vultures set gloom upon the land, tempering the figures that littered the terrain. Her eyes blurred, Juba imagined the hulking mounds dotting the landscape were crudely built huts. But as her spasms of vomiting slowly eased and her eyes cleared, the illusion dissolved.

"Tembo!" she wailed.

With a pain-filled shriek to the heavens, she pulled the antelope horn from her waist and ferociously plunged it into the ground.

*

The past, the future—John Too wondered which they were traveling toward. Neither offered any type of certainty, safety, comfort, emotional well-being, or sense that life would follow a path ending in unqualified happiness. Nor did either promise fulfillment of dreams, hoped-for reunifications, or assurance that friendships would survive or continue. Glancing at Teimbaka, he realized that neither past nor future offered hope of any kind. They were just destinations, after all, times one traveled toward or retreated to in hopes of finding something lost or not yet realized. What would Djibouti reveal to Teimbaka and him after the plane landed? Eyeing the small group of people sitting around him, he had his doubts.

The woman—he'd studied her reaction when the pilot informed her of the old Arab's death.

"Akmir," he'd said. "They shot him on the runway like a dog."

The woman had said nothing in response. Nor was there the slightest variation of her features. She'd remained expressionless.

"I'm sorry. I know he was a friend of yours," the pilot added after a pause.

John Too had waited for the woman to express some emotion. How could she not if the man the pilot spoke of—a friend, Akmir—had been murdered? He expected the woman to cry out in anger or hang her head and whimper. But she remained impassive. After a few moments of silence, the pilot raised his eyebrows, dipped his head, turned, and walked slowly toward the cockpit. The woman, John Too observed, didn't glance in his direction as he departed.

Yes, the woman was very beautiful, but she was also cold and without empathy. Someone to be wary of when the plane landed. A glance at the powerful machine gun looming next to her reminded him that she embodied two other traits: violence and danger.

The boy. John Too studied the child as he stared at a spot on the ceiling. His expression changed from vacant to highly animated over the span of several minutes, as if lost in a daydream one moment and watching someone or something entertaining in the next. Who was the boy? And what was his relationship to the dark-skinned *ferenji*? From the man's accent, John Too understood him to be American. But the boy—John Too shivered as he recalled the feeling he experienced when the child had reached out to him with the staff. The flash of green light brought with it a sense of unity, as if he and the boy were in some way linked or in accord. But how could that be if the boy was from America? John Too eyed him with curiosity; the boy was a mystery. As was the *ferenji*.

The man was, like the boy, an enigma. One moment he was taking a hammer to the shackles binding the slaves and leading them from the harbor to safety. The next, he was pushing Teimbaka in front of a Jeep, using him as a decoy to ambush and murder a group of soldiers. The slayings had been executed with precision and without mercy. He'd driven off from the scene, showing no concern for the women and children he'd freed. Surely he'd understood there'd be ramifications for his actions. Even a *ferenji* must know warlords exact revenge for the killing of their troops. Was the man willing to let the people he freed be imprisoned, tortured, or executed for what he'd done? John Too scrutinized the man's face: battle-worn, hardened, and chillingly detached. What part would the *ferenji* play when the plane set down? He'd saved Teimbaka and John Too from certain death or enslavement. John Too realized that counted for nothing.

And what would Djibouti bring Teimbaka? Peace? John Too thought not. The city, after all, was just a collection of roads and buildings. And from what Teimbaka had told him of his time there, what memories he held close to his heart were shaded with pain. Though he'd carried Sister Lady out of Djibouti's alleys and led John and her to freedom, the Serpent had followed. And the designs of the Serpent had not changed since. The beast of Jahannam was ever present, ever waiting for the chance to claim Teimbaka's soul. As aware as John Too was of the peril threatening Teimbaka, so too was he conscious of the toll the constant tug between good and evil had taken on the two of them.

Weary of the struggle to survive, disillusioned by the abandonment of the Mother and the Father, John Too had begun to imagine an existence without the weight of obligation upon his shoulders. Caring for a delusional and hopeless blind man was a responsibility he no longer wished to bear. But each time he looked at Teimbaka and entertained thoughts of leaving him behind, he could hear the Serpent whisper, "Betrayal, betrayal, betrayal." The beast of Jahannam was a master of deceit.

As the plane made a rough landing, an image of Claire, her face illuminated in firelight, appeared in his mind. Then came glimpses of the twelve—orphan boys like he—sitting near her, their eyes upon her face as she spoke the words of the Father. The image conjured the memory of her voice when the weakest and most downhearted of the group would seek her out, hoping she could provide the strength to get through the darkest hours of night.

"Faith," she would tell them.

And she would grasp the silver cross she wore about her neck and hold it up to the fire. With the cross glowing golden, she would speak from memory, recounting the words of the Father. Like a cooling breeze, her voice soothed and caressed, easing fear brought about by war, famine, and drought.

Faith—John Too hung his head as the *ferenji* stood and took a standing position behind the machine gun.

Faith—the image of Claire, cross in hand, consoling the twelve, was vibrant in his thoughts as he glanced at Teimbaka.

Faith—the powerful drone of the plane's propellers reminded him of nights along the Eritrean battlefront, huddled next to Sister Lady, the rumble of artillery filling their ears as the mountaintops flickered with the shadows of war.

Faith—remembering stirred feelings of regret, a lost time he wished had never ended.

Faith—the scars scattered across Teimbaka's face reminded him of the struggles the Lion of Djibouti had endured. Feeling less than what he hoped he'd become, John Too took a deep breath and murmured, "Faith."

*

"*Shange bahr.*"

Sarah smiled at the way in which Bin'ka spoke the phrase: teasing, but good-natured. For all the size of the man—shoulders as big as watermelons, chest as wide as a water buffalo—he more often than not displayed the heart of a child and the demeanor of a saint.

"Some lion of the sea you turned out to be."

When he chuckled, she did as well. His humor was contagious, his smile genuine and honest. He had one arm draped over the dhow's tiller, and the first light of morning was lending a silvery gleam to his deep-brown skin. Bin'ka was a contradiction: a frightening killer in the body of a gentle giant. And though she'd witnessed some of his more violent acts, there was nothing about him she didn't find appealing.

Sarah bunched her hand into a fist and pressed it into her groin. Troubled by her sudden pang of yearning, she quickly glanced over her shoulder. To her relief, Conduit was paying no attention to what was occurring outside the realm of her workstation. With a sigh, Sarah turned her attention back to the monitor.

"I can't imagine why they called me that," her image said.

"They see you for what you are," Bin'ka calmly replied. "Not for what you pretend to be."

Sarah's thoughts returned to the exchange depicted on the monitor. How a scene from her life could be replayed on something akin to a TV screen was beyond her comprehension. Yet, for the last few hours she had watched clips from the past—her own past, as well as the pasts of people she did not know—and viewed them as if she were present in the moment, positioned a few feet away, able to hear even the faintest whisper. She'd asked Conduit how such clear, vivid, and deep depictions could possibly exist. Conduit's response was a smile, a nod upward, and a couple of sentences Sarah was still grappling with.

"His gift to the chosen," she said. "So you may understand the course we must take to save paradise."

To save paradise—she could not fathom her part in such an undertaking. But Conduit had instructed her to watch and learn. And she did as the frizzy-haired woman with the green-tinted glasses asked.

"What do you mean, pretending? I'm a nun."

Bin'ka frowned.

"You're a woman," he said with a slight shake of his head. "Wearing a symbol doesn't change that."

"A symbol?"

Bin'ka nodded toward her chest.

"Your necklace—the cross." He grunted. "Doesn't change who you are. Doesn't erase what you've done or what others have done to you."

"The cross." Sarah lifted the symbol from her chest and held it flat in her palm. "It's a part of my faith. A symbol of my commitment to God, and His to man, by sacrificing his son."

Bin'ka studied Sarah's face for a moment before turning his attention toward the open water. The sun, nearing the horizon, cast a patina of yellow over the water far out to sea. The silver tint to his skin had transformed to burnished gold.

"I wear it not to make a statement, but rather to acknowledge Christ's suffering and to show devotion to my faith."

"Faith," he muttered.

"Yes, faith," she countered. Her expression questioning, she asked, "Why deny me faith?"

The dhow's sail fluttered in a gust of wind. Bin'ka glanced upward and momentarily closed his eyes. Before he replied, he took a deep breath and slowly exhaled.

"Faith in the sun, faith in the ocean, faith in the wind—these I can't deny. Nor do I deny the virtues of each." He shook his head. "But faith in religion? Faith in some hierarchy of men who preach moralistic principles they do not follow? No," he said with a definitive shake of his head. "No,

I cannot assign faith to such falsehoods. Nor hold faith in the contrived rules and platitudes created by men."

"They speak the word of God," she disagreed. "And follow the rules of His teachings."

Bin'ka smirked. Again, he shifted his attention toward the open water.

"To what end?" he asked, though he did not seek eye contact with Sarah.

"Are you being sarcastic?"

She didn't flinch when he abruptly turned his face toward her and glared.

"Or do you want an answer?"

With a brusque nod, he curtly repeated, "To what end?"

Sarah closed her hand around the cross.

"His words, His teachings are a blueprint—a path—so that we may find our way to paradise."

"Paradise." He shook his head and grunted. "How would you—?"

The sound of creaking wood accompanied Bin'ka's subtle shift of the tiller. The sail briefly fluttered as the dhow eased toward land. Sarah looked to the shore, her gaze following a swath of golden sunlight twinkling atop the water.

"I was once a slave," Bin'ka softly remarked. "My master—Susenyo was his name." He grunted. "He collected—"

Sarah glimpsed a brief smile on his face when she glanced his way.

"Everything," he continued. "He collected everything."

"I don't—"

"Old scrolls." He chuckled. "I remember sifting through a few of the piles he'd collected. Some were from as far away as—"

His brow wrinkled and his eyes glazed over. She remembered wondering what he was seeing in his mind.

"One was a drawing: a mountain towering above a river with a water-fall. Animals stood along the river's banks. I was drawn to it because the animals were the same I'd grown up with: lion, antelope, giraffe, water buffalo, elephant."

He paused to check the sail, their course, the children sleeping beneath the mast. With a sigh, he looked to her and met her eyes.

"One word was written above the scene: *paradise*." He raised his eyebrows and exhaled sharply through his nose. "No people," he said. "The artist—holy man, whoever—didn't include people in the drawing." He briefly paused before asking, "Does *your* paradise include people? And if it does, where do they fit?" He leaned toward her. "In what part of paradise do we belong?"

Sarah sat back in her chair and stared at the screen. The scene had frozen. She took the opportunity to study Bin'ka's facial expression; was it concern, inquisitiveness, innocence, wonder? She wasn't quite certain. If she were able to see *her* face, she would eagerly examine her reaction to his question. But her face was turned toward Bin'ka and away from the screen.

"What is paradise to you?"

Sarah nearly tipped backward in the chair. Bin'ka was looking directly out from the screen, staring at her.

"You say your god created paradise—*is* paradise, in a sense."

She gripped the arms of the chair as Bin'ka's face filled the monitor.

"What place do we have there after what we've done?"

Sarah wanted to look away but found herself incapable of turning her head.

"We butcher innocence, enslave children." She unconsciously clutched the cross when his face took on a pained expression. "We've sold paradise for handful of gold coins and a fancy crown." He shook his head and sighed. She could hear the sail flutter as his stare intensified. "Tell me how we belong," he challenged. "Tell me how we belong."

Sarah leaned forward and placed a hand atop the monitor as the screen went dark. *Don't go*, she found herself thinking. But he *was* gone, she knew. She'd watched him die. A vicious, brutal death he didn't deserve. And for what? Sadness came with the realization that Bin'ka had died to save *her*—Sarah. She found his sacrifice incomprehensible.

"Did you ever answer him?"

Startled, Sarah placed her hand to her chest and gasped. She blinked Conduit into focus.

"You scared me."

Conduit tilted her head to the side and shrugged. Uneasy in her presence, Sarah glanced between the frizzy-haired woman and the dark monitor.

"Did you ever give him an answer?" Conduit asked again.

Sarah looked at the screen and slowly shook her head. She *hadn't* given him an answer. She'd looked out to sea, toward the horizon, wondering what to say. Before she could formulate her thoughts, several of the children—the children he'd freed from slavers—awoke, asking for food. She'd left him, brooding and silent, at the tiller. A weak smile was all she could give him. He'd never broached the subject again.

"You need to answer him now."

Conduit's assertion came with a terrifying explosion that sent a shudder through the cavern walls. Sarah screamed and leaped out of her chair.

"What's happening?" she cried. She gripped Conduit by the shoulders. "What's happening?"

Conduit smiled and lightly placed her hands atop Sarah's wrists.

"The portal's been sealed," she replied. "The time of enlightenment begins."

"Time of enlightenment?" Sarah repeated.

Conduit brushed Sarah's hands from her shoulders and smiled. Sarah took a step to follow the woman, who turned and walked toward the table where she'd been working.

"What are you talking about? What are you saying?" Sarah extended a hand as if she intended to grab Conduit. "Are we trapped here?" she asked, panic in her tone. "Is there no other way out?"

Conduit stopped and turned to face Sarah.

"The way out is the path forward," she said.

Perplexed, Sarah stood in silence, shaking her head.

"When you are able to answer," Conduit explained, with a nod to the monitor Sarah had been watching, "the gates will open."

32

"THE DAY IS not over unless you wish it to be."

With help from John Too, Teimbaka felt his way down the flight of stairs and stepped onto solid ground.

"Do you wish it to be over?"

Turning east, he felt wind upon his face. Distant, almost imperceptible, ocean water scented the air.

"Take me to the harbor," he said. "There is someone there. Someone asking me…" He tilted his head to the side. "I must—"

The sound of squealing tires and slamming doors confused him. But he ignored the distraction and, using his fingertips, impressed upon John Too's face his desire to go.

*

Claire walked into the expansive one-story structure that functioned as the Djibouti airport terminal. Slowly, she looked around. Scrutinizing people, objects, and structures, analyzing smells and sounds, she hoped to find something familiar, something that would jar her memory. Perhaps if she came across such an entity, the pain in her head would cease. That was her hope.

But nothing about the Djibouti terminal seemed familiar to her. Nor did the people milling about—travelers, soldiers, airline personnel—strike her as former acquaintances. The absence of anything or anyone familiar left her depressed. It was a tiresome feeling that had been with her since

France, when her trip to find Angelique's parents had concluded in a dead end. She'd found nothing but a bouquet of wilted flowers lying at the doorstep of Angelique's parents' apartment. Would her trip to Djibouti have equally empty results?

"Claire Waterman?"

The vison of dead flowers dissipated when Claire heard her name. Slowly, she focused on the man who'd spoken.

"Do I know you?"

Claire studied the man's face—close-set eyes; large, pointed nose; skin wrinkled and darkened from the sun; protruding chin—hoping she would recognize him. But, like everything else around her, he was unfamiliar.

"Mustafa Harakan," the man said. Extending a hand in greeting, he added, "Mr. Pembrook said you would be arriving."

"Mr. Pembrook," Claire muttered, confused. "I'm not sure…" She looked to the surrounding area as if there might be someone else accompanying the man.

"I do some consulting work for the embassy." When Claire showed no reaction, he clarified, "The *American* embassy."

"Oh, of course." She smiled apologetically. "I was just…"

Djibouti—Claire closed her eyes and tried to remember what the city meant to her. Fragmented images of places and people whirled through her thoughts. Unconsciously, she rubbed the sides of her head.

"You must be tired."

Claire opened her eyes and lowered her hands to her sides.

"Come," Mustafa said. "Mr. Pembrook has everything arranged."

"Arranged?"

Claire stiffened when Mustafa lightly took hold of her wrist.

"But first we must collect your bags and go through Customs," he explained. "Then we will drive to the outskirts of the city, where the church of your faith has been rebuilt."

Claire glanced over her shoulder when she heard loud, sharp popping sounds from outside the building. Two uniformed soldiers ran toward the door leading to the runways.

"Or we could stop at the hotel first, if you'd prefer."

A small crowd of people congregated at the door the soldiers exited.

Though she did not understand the language they were speaking, from the excited tone of their voices and the animated expressions on their faces, she gathered something of interest was occurring.

"Thieves," she heard Mustafa remark. But she didn't correlate the word to what she was witnessing.

"Part of the world in which we live—yes?"

Claire felt a slight tug on her arm. Mustafa smiled politely, tilted his head toward the far side of the building, and began to gently pull her in that direction.

"Best you place that inside your clothing before we exit the building," he told her, with a nod toward her chest.

Claire grasped the silver cross and cupped it within her palm.

"Thieves are not the only unpleasantry we must contend with," he went on. "Zealots and fanatics have sprung up as late." Claire experienced a moment of uneasiness when Mustafa looked directly into her eyes. "I'm afraid Christianity is viewed unfavorably at the moment. Discretion might be best while you travel in the city."

"Zealots," she repeated. "I don't understand. You say the church we are going to was *rebuilt*?" She stopped and firmly but politely removed Mustafa's hand from her wrist. "Had something happened to it?"

Mustafa tilted his head to one side and shrugged.

"It was burned." He leaned toward her and quietly added, "Bombed by the followers of a radical cleric."

Claire felt a tightness in her stomach as Mustafa took a long, studious look at the people around them.

"They were lucky to have been allowed to rebuild where they did," Mustafa said, pulling on her arm as he began walking. "Disturbing talk of *jihad*," he went on. "As if there is not enough violence in the city already."

When he smiled at her, his face reminded her of a character from a childhood cartoon, his eyes two dark dots surrounded by a sea of wrinkles.

"Religious wars are the folly of mankind," he lightly remarked. "One need only look across the Red Sea for proof. Moderation and tolerance are what's needed in these times," he muttered. "Yes." He nodded. "Tolerance."

Claire looked on in silence as Mustafa collected her suitcase and carried it to Customs, where he proceeded to speak in Arabic to three armed, uniformed men standing near a large doorway—or perhaps guarding it. And though the three men, as well as Mustafa, both collectively and individually glanced in her direction from time to time, she was not questioned by them nor asked to show her passport. Surprised but grateful when Mustafa informed her they were free to travel, she gave a fleeting glance to what remained of the crowd standing by the entrance to the runway before following him outside.

"My car," he said as they approached a light-colored, four-door sedan parked near a sandbag bunker. "The church is no more than a fifteen-minute drive. The priest is expecting us." He opened the door to the back seat and nodded for her to get in. "Mr. Pembrook called ahead," he explained when she gave him an inquisitive look.

"The church—"

Claire frowned when Mustafa closed the door.

"The church," she repeated when he opened the driver's door. "What's the name of the church?"

"The church?" Mustafa asked as he settled into the driver's seat.

"The church you're taking me to," Claire replied. "The name. What's the name of the church."

"Oh, yes—the name," he said, as if he'd just remembered something forgotten. "The Church of the Holy Cross, I believe," he said. "Yes, that's it. The Church of the Holy Cross."

*

Talia seethed as she raised her hands over her head.

"What is this?" she snapped. She glared at the man walking toward her with an automatic rifle pointed at her head. "You taking over now, Mohammad?" she spat. "You think you have the—?"

The blow to her face was sudden and unexpected. The butt of the rifle clipped her square on the chin with a sickening thud. Somehow, she kept her balance. Blood trickled from the corner of her mouth as she fought to keep focus on the man's face.

"Shut up!" Mohammad ordered. He pressed the barrel against the underside of her nose. "You're done," he told her. "We—" he tilted his head back and to the side, gesturing to three, armed, uniformed men standing behind him, "we give the orders now."

Talia looked at the three men standing behind Mohammad. She knew all of them. They, like Mohammad, had been part of her personal guard for over a year. She'd thought they were loyal. With a grunt, she shifted her attention back to Mohammad.

"You don't have the brains to run the operation," she defiantly muttered. "All you're good for—"

The sharp blow of the rifle butt to her stomach caught her off guard. Talia doubled over, gasping for air.

"You talk when I tell you!" Mohammad barked. "Bitch," he muttered. "Whore."

Talia coughed and slowly straightened. She eyed Mohammad with contempt as the bearded, wiry man walked a few steps to her right.

"These are the riches you bring back from Somalia?" he mocked. He nodded toward the two men and two boys loosely grouped behind her. "This is all you gained from meeting with Akmir?"

"Akmir's dead," she told him. "I saw him—"

Talia cried out in pain when Mohammad slammed the butt of the rifle into the back of her leg. She slumped to the ground but managed to steady herself on one knee.

"Did I order you to speak?" Mohammad shouted.

"You're quite the man," said Chris.

Mohammad jerked the rifle up so it was level with his waist. He pointed the end of the barrel at Chris.

"Did you speak?"

"You're a piece of shit," Chris said.

Talia glanced over her shoulder in time to see Mohammad approach Chris with a menacing look on his face.

"You dare insult me?" Mohammad fumed. "You? Negro! Slave!" He pressed the barrel of the rifle into Chris's neck. "Nigger! Isn't that what you're called in your country?" he taunted. "Nigger-slave."

Talia glimpsed the flash of metal as Chris jerked his arms down from over his head and slammed a blade into Mohammad's neck. As Mohammad screamed and sought to pull the knife from his throat, Chris wrenched the automatic rifle from his grasp, swung it toward the three uniformed men, and fired off a short burst. Talia crouched and whirled. To her delight, the three men were prone on the ground, blood oozing from wounds in their chests. By the time she turned back to face Chris, Mohammad was falling face first to the tarmac, blood gushing from a wide gash across the front of his neck.

"Have a safe place in mind where someone's not going to try and kill you?" Chris calmly asked.

Talia glanced at the three men before looking down at Mohammad. With a smirk, she replied, "I'll drive."

*

The Church of the Holy Cross. Sisters of the Holy Cross. Claire rubbed the links of her necklace between her fingers as she stared blankly out the window. Nothing she had seen—people, buildings, trees—since getting into the car registered. Everything was a blur. Shapes had no substance. Figures had no features. A collage of color was rendered in grey. *Djibouti, Africa*—her surroundings made no sense. It was as if she were in a lucid dream—above, beside, and within every scene as the precise moment in time unfolded, but nonetheless separate.

Detached. Yes, she thought, *I am detached. Though I wear the symbol of my faith—my order—I am abstract of its creed.* A tear rolled down her cheek. Wiping it away, she thought, *I'm lost—I've lost my way.*

She felt the car slow and come to a complete stop. Outside her window—ten feet inside the entrance of what appeared to be an alley—an old woman squatted against a wall. The woman's hands covered her eyes. Claire could see her lips moving. *Chanting*, Claire thought. *Maybe begging.* The woman's clothes—her robe—appeared to be nothing more than a motley collection of rags thrown haphazardly over a hunched body. The impulse to leave the car and go to the woman came and went in a flash of indifference. The metal of the cross between her fingers suddenly felt cold.

Claire wiped a second tear from her cheek as she tried to remember how she'd felt upon arriving in a country that was in the throes of revolution, famine, and drought. *Wasn't I afraid? Did I have no concept of the danger I would face?* She stared at the old woman and watched her lips move. She imagined the woman was voicing what she herself was think-ing: *I was a fool. I was a fool. I am a fool.* Stricken by a pang of remorse, she clutched the cross to her chest and, for a moment, closed her eyes. *Or did I follow the intended path? Did I serve the Lord?*

Claire placed her fingertips against the pane of glass as the car began to move. She kept the old woman in sight as long as she was able. When the alley was no longer visible, she sat back in her seat and sighed.

"Almost there," she heard Mustafa say.

She stared at the back of the front seat and nodded.

"I just remembered."

Claire glanced up into the car's rearview mirror and made eye contact with Mustafa.

"I promised the priest I would bring fresh-pressed olive oil," he said.

Claire furrowed her brow and looked out the window.

"Freshly pressed—today. My apologies. It will only take a minute."

Claire swallowed and blinked her eyes in an attempt to focus on her surroundings. The structures passing by her window appeared dilapidated. She could see no people walking along the dirt road.

"I suppose…" She tried to think of what to say. "I guess—yes," she said after a slight pause. "If you promised."

The car came to a smooth stop. She heard the driver's-side door open.

"I'll be right back," Mustafa said.

What was she hoping to find in Djibouti?

*

Marcus went up on his tip-toes and looked out a window. The color of the ocean brought a smile to his face. *So blue*, he thought. *Bluer than…* He thought for a moment, picturing all the things he'd ever seen that were the color blue. After a few uncertain moments, he decided: *anything. The water is bluer than anything.* He giggled.

Conscious he'd made noise, he glanced over his shoulder. Not want-ing to get in trouble, he ducked down and slid across the floor until he reached a corner of the large room. The lady who'd been beaten up had driven them here. He wondered what she'd done wrong at the airport to be punished like that. He'd thought about it during the car ride. *Talking,*

I guess. Bad punishment, to be hit in the face and stomach with a gun just because you talked.

Chris had tried to make him talk during the ride from the airport. He'd asked if Marcus liked Africa—whatever that was. He'd asked if Marcus was hungry—he was. But Marcus didn't answer. He didn't want to get hit. He'd almost broken his silence once, however, when Difireti appeared.

He'd been staring at the blind man whose face was covered with scars. The little creature materialized in a spot right next to the man. Marcus giggled when the sparkly, translucent animal placed its long nose across the man's shoulder. But he quickly stopped giggling when the man placed a hand atop the creature's forehead and proceeded to pet the animal. The blind man could see Difireti! He'd thought no one but he and the old woman could see the little animal. But, obviously, the blind man could— or could sense its presence. This made Marcus wonder. And he'd almost asked the man all the questions he was thinking. Until he remembered the punishment for talking.

Who was the blind man with all the scars on his face? And who was the older boy—John Too—with him? And how did the blind man know Difireti? Thinking about these questions, Marcus suddenly wondered where the old woman had gone after the wave had washed the slaves into the sea. Had she been swept into the water as well? Had she drowned? The thought that she might be dead made him feel very sad. But the emotion confused him, because he didn't know the woman.

Why do I feel sad for someone I don't know? He didn't know why. But still, the question lingered. What *was* it about her that left such an impression upon him? Again, he didn't know—or wasn't sure. Ever since Gran-Jim and Gran-Rochelle had disappeared from his life, everything had gotten confusing. Thinking of his grandparents, he suddenly longed to be home, sitting in the apartment over the restaurant, eating one of Gran-Jim's homemade biscuits layered with strawberry jam. The memory of Gran-Jim—his cooking and the apartment over the restaurant—con- jured a hurtful pang of sadness. From his spot in the corner of the large room, he looked with melancholy at his new surroundings and the people that were now part of his life.

Marcus took a deep breath, held it, then slowly exhaled. When the blind man abruptly turned his head and looked in his direction, Marcus dipped his head and averted his eyes. *Can the blind man see me?* he wondered. *What does he want with me?* Just as the questions drifted through his thoughts, the blind man rose. And to Marcus's surprise, appearing to use Difireti as a guide, he began walking across the room toward the door.

"Where do you think you're going?" Chris challenged.

Marcus leaned forward as the blind man stopped and turned his head toward Chris.

"To the harbor," the blind man replied. "Someone is asking me…"

Marcus clenched his fists when Chris took a step toward the man.

"Sit down," Chris ordered. "You're not going anywhere."

Marcus stood as Difireti walked behind the blind man and nudged him toward the door.

"Are you deaf?"

Out of the corner of his eye, Marcus saw John Too stand. As the older boy moved between the blind man and Chris, Marcus darted to Difireti's side.

"And where do you think *you're* going?" Chris sharply inquired.

John Too extended a hand in front of his chest, motioning for Chris to stop. With a tilt of his head in Teimbaka's direction, he said, "There is someone on the docks. Someone whose voice he has not heard since Sister Lady was taken."

Marcus gripped the edge of Difireti's ear as he studied Chris's face.

"Really," Chris remarked. "Someone he hasn't seen or heard from."

John Too nodded.

"Then how do you know he's there?" Chris took a step toward John Too. "Did he call on the phone? Send a letter?"

Marcus felt his stomach tighten when John Too shook his head.

"Then, what?" Chris pressed. "Was there some invisible message delivered when we got off the plane?" He grunted. "You must—"

"She is the wind," John Too said. "And the rumble of the waves. The roar of the lion." John Too paused to look at Teimbaka. "She chose him," he told Chris. "And now she asks he return."

Chris shook his head. Marcus wasn't sure if Chris was getting mad or confused.

"She." Chris's face took on a mean expression. "What kind of shit you talkin', boy? Who the hell is *she*?"

Unfaltering, John Too replied, "The Mother."

"Whose mother?" Chris spat. "What kind of crap you—?"

Marcus turned toward the window when what sounded like a sudden boom of thunder rattled the building. From where he stood, he could see the sky; it was cloudless blue. Startled and confused, he abruptly stepped away from Difireti when Chris darted by him.

"What now?" he heard Chris angrily mutter.

Marcus felt a tug on his arm. Difireti was exiting through the doorway. He felt a twinge of panic when he realized John Too and the blind man had already left. He glanced in the woman's direction. She nodded toward the door. He didn't hesitate.

*

Claire lifted the cross from her chest and laid it flat against the palm of her hand. Her thoughts unsettled, she stared at the symbol of her faith, seeking guidance. *Do you know where he is?* She felt a jolt through her body as the question echoed in her head. Scrutinizing the surface of the cross, she once more wondered if she weren't losing her mind. *Do you know where he is?* She looked wildly to either side of her, then bumped her head on the roof of the car when something knocked against the window.

"Dear God!" she gasped.

"Do you know where he is?"

Claire cowered toward the middle of the seat while trying to make sense of the figure standing outside the car window. Hooded, body cloaked in rags… Then she saw locks of whitish-grey hair flowing from the edges of the hood. *The old woman from the alley.*

"What?" Claire asked, startled.

"Do you know where he is?" the old woman replied.

Claire leaned toward the car door and rolled the window down a few inches.

"Who?" she asked.

The old woman turned as if she were about to start walking away.

Claire was about to repeat her question when she saw the woman motion with a hand for her to follow.

"Hurry," she said, taking a few steps away from the car.

"Who are you talking about?" Claire asked, opening the car door and swinging her legs out.

"Quickly!" the old woman urged.

Claire caught a glimpse of the woman's eyes as she glanced over her shoulder: sparkling green.

"He needs your help!"

Claire slid out of the car.

"Who?" she stressed. "Who needs my help?"

Claire took a few hurried steps to follow as the old woman began to run toward the corner of a bombed-out building. Then, to Claire's surprise, the old woman came to an abrupt stop and looked back at the car. Claire followed her gaze. She suddenly wondered where Mustafa had gone.

"Mustafa!" she called.

"Quickly!" the old woman yelled, motioning with both hands for Claire to join her. "Come now!" she urged.

With a brief search of the buildings on either side of the street, Claire hurried to join the woman. She'd run several steps when a violent explosion blew her off her feet and hurled her through the air. Dazed, pain shooting through her hip and shoulder, she blinked several times. A wall of blurry orange wavered across her vision. Then she felt someone lift her off the ground. Unsteady, she placed her hand on the person's arm to catch her balance. As her head began to clear, she saw Mustafa's car on fire.

*

"Got any heavy ordnance stashed?" Chris asked her.

Talia tore off a long strip of medical tape and wrapped it over the piece of gauze she'd placed on her wound. She glanced up when Chris approached.

"Not here."

But as soon as she made eye contact with him, she wished she *had* stored explosives or grenade launchers in one of the safe rooms she had scattered about the city.

"Trouble?" she inquired.

"Truck exploded on the street below us. Couple of armed groups making their way toward this building." She studied his face as he glanced toward the window. "Looks like trouble. Wasn't sure if we—" He paused and grunted. "If *you're* the ultimate target."

"Vehicle detonations are commonplace." She smiled briefly. "Lately, anyway. And unless—" She fell silent when he walked hurriedly toward the doorway. "Going somewhere?" she asked in a sarcastic tone of voice.

He tilted his head slightly to one side before he answered. "Going to get the kid and bring him back."

"No need. He won't get far."

Chris stopped and abruptly turned.

"How the hell do you know how far he'll get?"

Talia smirked.

"I have eyes on every corner of the city."

She flinched at a burst of automatic gunfire from an area close to the building. Chris showed no outward reaction to the din.

"How far do you think he'll get?" She raised her eyebrows. "Seeing he's with a blind man."

Chris took a few hurried steps toward the window. She wondered what had drawn his interest.

"Get down!" he suddenly yelled, dropping to the floor.

Talia was about to ask why when the window and a portion of the surrounding wall blew inward. The force of the explosion knocked her off the chair.

"Son of a bitch," she said as she landed roughly on the floor.

When Chris grabbed her arm and yelled, "Is there a back way out?" she instinctively thrust the heel of her hand upward and kicked out with her foot. As one blow landed against his chin and the other struck the back of his calf, Chris retreated.

"Shit. Sorry," she said.

He rubbed the side of his face and grunted.

"Way out." he repeated.

"Bathroom."

He slid toward her as a second explosion detonated in the hall outside the doorway. Talia rose to a crouch. Chris grabbed her by the shoulders and spun her toward him.

"Bathroom's no good." He glanced over his shoulder. "RPG's not going to give a shit about a flimsy door."

She straightened and began running toward a slender door in a corner of the room. As automatic gunfire strafed the floorboards near the main entrance to the room, she glanced back at Chris.

"Hurry!" she shouted. "Trust me!"

*

The bursts of gunfire reminded him of Mogadishu. In particular, they reminded him of the final moments before he'd swung Sarah out into the water. Maybe it was the smell of the ocean air infused with the pungent aroma of sulphur and gunpowder. Or maybe it was the abrupt staccato of automatic weapons, the high-pitched whine of projectiles, the sudden booms. Or maybe, just maybe, images of Mogadishu had been conjured by a woman's voice and the aura of her fragrance. Women smelled different from men. He understood that now. More so than before, when he was younger, when he still had…

He dismissively wiped a hand across his eyes. *Before—* He wondered why he would entertain such an abstract notion.

But maybe it *wasn't* Mogadishu he was reminded of. Maybe the sounds, the smell, the proximity to a woman struck a different chord—one that, for him, contained enormous joy and sorrow: the bombardment of the orphan camp and the ensuing attack on the compound. Those incidents had been a nightmare of carnage, death, and suffering. Then had come Claire's abduction. He'd been devastated, empty and destitute. But during the quest to find her, his bond with the Mother had been strengthened a hundred-fold. With Her help, he'd been able to find Claire and free her.

But freeing Claire's person from Susenyo was not the same as freeing her spirit. Winning back her soul from the Serpent had proved grueling. Their faith—both in themselves and in each other—had been pushed to the breaking point. But they had persevered. From that point, they had fled to the mountains and taken refuge in the Palm of the Mother.

Palm of the Mother—a place of re-discovered joy, of hope reclaimed. A place of harmony. Where their love had been kindled, ignited by a moon-lit kiss as a herd of spirit-elephants looked on. Their hearts, their spirits, had bonded. The feeling was more than either could have ever dreamed. Bliss drifted within the mists that lay as a blanket over the plateaus. Palm of the Mother; how he yearned to return.

But the Palm had been ripped apart. Splintered in the arms of Bin'ka and a white-skinned man he knew nothing about. Where they had taken Claire and why they had taken her was a mystery. He'd spent the last year trying to uncover her whereabouts, but he was no closer to finding her now than on the day she'd disappeared. From what he'd been able to piece together, she'd been taken farther away then he could imagine.

Now he'd lost his sight—and, from his perspective, his life. His faith in the Father's words, in the words Claire so believed in, had dwindled to naught. And his faith in the Mother…

Teimbaka bowed his head, disappointment heavy on his shoulders. Inwardly, he wanted to perish, turn to dust, and let the wind scatter his ashes across the desert. What was left to him? *Darkness,* he silently replied. *Darkness and a life void of faith.*

"Difireti! Difireti!"

Teimbaka came to an abrupt stop at the child's cry.

"Come back, Difireti! Come back!"

"Who speaks?" Teimbaka asked.

Clasping John Too's shoulder, he asked again with more urgency, "Who speaks?"

John Too gripped Teimbaka's wrist. "The boy from the pier. The one who pulled me from the water."

"Who does he call?"

"No one," John Too replied. "He chases something I cannot see."

"Follow him," Teimbaka replied.

"But he's running away from the harbor."

Teimbaka turned his head and blindly gazed back toward the sounds of conflict.

"I can hear his footsteps." Tilting his head to the side, he said, "He runs as though—"

Teimbaka slid his hand from John Too's shoulder and rested it against his forearm. He glanced in the direction of the harbor before saying, "I once followed footsteps from the water. Could it be?" Once more, he turned his attention toward the sounds of violence. "Lead me to the boy," he said. "He follows someone I once knew."

*

Chris eased his body into the chute and peered into the darkness below his feet. Talia—who had already lowered herself into the cylindrical opening and disappeared—was nowhere to be seen. How far down the metal tube extended, he didn't know; Talia hadn't told him. Nor had she told him where the chute led. She'd simply opened the bathroom door, slipped her finger beneath a section of the tile floor, and lifted a perfectly concealed trap door.

"Close the door and lock the deadbolts," she instructed as he leaped into the bathroom.

And then, with a slight smile, she wiggled into the opening and disappeared.

Chris had stared at the spot she'd occupied for a few seconds before sounds from the adjoining room had stirred him to action. He could hear intruders, their voices drawing closer to the bathroom as he debated whether to follow Talia down the chute. Then a burst of automatic gunfire had prompted him to drop to the floor. To his surprise, no bullets penetrated the door. *Bulletproof,* he thought. Then he heard a man angrily shout, "Bring the RPG!" He hadn't needed any further persuasion. And though he hated confined, dark spaces, he followed Talia's lead. He gauged he was a dozen meters into his free-fall when there was a violent explosion above him.

Chris was in a deep sweat when he suddenly and without warning landed feet first on something pliant. Relying on his military training, he deftly rolled onto his side and tumbled several times to his right before coming to a stop. He lay motionless for a few moments to gauge his injuries and catch his breath. Slowly, he became aware that he couldn't see. His breathing quickened and his stomach bunched. Then he heard something stir close by.

"Hey!" he shouted, hoping to frighten whatever was making noise.

A moment of uneasy silence ensued before Talia said, "Relax."

A string of blue-tinted lights flicked on, dimly illuminating a section of an underground tunnel. Chris blinked his eyes several times and took a deep breath. Talia, he saw, was standing across from him, one hand resting atop a metal box.

"Can you move?" she asked.

With a grunt, Chris pushed off the ground and stood. He nodded. "I'm good."

"Then let's go. We have about ten seconds to clear this part of the corridor."

Chris looked to his left and then to the right. Left, he saw the blue-lit corridor, ending in darkness. To his right, he saw nothing but darkness.

"Follow the lights. Quick," she urged. "Move."

Chris counted off seconds in his head as he sprinted down the tunnel. Nine seconds had elapsed when he heard a muffled explosion.

"Sealed," Talia said as she slowed to a walk. "If they followed—"

Chris instinctively bunched his fists and took a defensive position when she abruptly moved away from him. She had a wide smile on her face when a second string of blue lights flicked on and illuminated a different section of the tunnel.

"Sweet," he said, with an admiring nod. "When did you do all this?"

She shook her head as she removed her hand from a metal box on the stone wall.

"Been here for centuries, as far as anyone knows," she said. She walked toward him. "I had lights installed on the sections we regularly use and," she said with a shrug, "added a few security measures here and there."

Chris studied the newly lit section of tunnel for a few moments before shifting his attention in the opposite direction.

"How far does it run?" he asked, nodding toward the section they'd vacated.

Talia shook her head. "No idea." She gave the section of tunnel he was gazing at a cursory glance and began walking into the newly lit segment. "We've never…"

"Never what?" he asked as he hurried to catch up to her.

She made brief eye contact with him before shifting her attention forward. "Felt the need to explore, I suppose."

Chris glanced back over his shoulder. "You mean you don't know where the other side of the tunnel leads or what it runs under?"

"No."

"Well, that's pretty dumb. I mean—"

"I've got other issues I need to deal with," she tersely said. "Your tunnel infatuation can wait."

"I was just—"

"Right now, I've got to find out who's trying to have me eliminated." She grunted. "Then slit the fucker's throat."

*

Claire gripped the old woman's sleeve as the two came to a halt. She wondered if the scene before her was part of some elaborate dream. Or perhaps she was hallucinating as a result of whatever illness had necessitated her hospitalization. Quickly making the sign of the cross, she muttered, "Dear God."

A dozen or so women and children knelt before a pockmarked wall. Hands pulled taut behind their backs, they faced a line of soldiers armed with rifles that, to Claire, appeared overly large. Glancing between the forlorn faces of the captives and the glazed expressions of the executioners, she realized that the weapons weren't too large. Rather, the soldiers were too small.

"They're children," she whispered.

"Look closer," the old woman replied.

Claire scrutinized the faces of the child-soldiers. Immediately, she was transported to a vision she'd once experienced—or was it a nightmare?—where she was one of the condemned. Was what she was witnessing now an extension of that same dream? She lightly touched her face with her fingertips in an attempt to gauge what reality she was in. The sensation of flesh upon flesh indicated that what she was experiencing was real.

"Do you see him?"

The child-soldiers raised their rifles and took aim. A taller figure dressed in a black robe, face covered by a swathe of the dark material, stood behind them, barking orders. How could she not have noticed the person before?

"Show no mercy! Send them to Jahannam! Let the Serpent devour their souls!"

The Serpent—coils of glossy black filled the hazy confines of a circular room. With eyes of flame and scales shimmering the color of a blood-tinged night, the leviathan rose to the height of the ceiling and gazed down upon the puny figure that stood before it. Tongue flicking in and out of its mouth, the Serpent seemed poised to strike.

"Leave her!" the man shouted. "We do not fear you!"

Her—Claire glimpsed an alabaster figure lying half-naked on a circular bed. The woman's appearance was unnerving, instantly stirring nausea in the pit of Claire's stomach. But the man's voice— It sounded familiar. Drawn to him, she studied his face. His flesh was covered with scars. As he swung a wooden staff above his head, she glimpsed sections of his bared chest. Jagged lines of pink skin ran diagonally from one side of his ribcage to the other. She felt she had seen the markings before.

There was some quality about the man that intrigued her. He was vulnerable yet at the same time courageous.

"Ready!"

"Do you not see him?"

Caught between the voices of the old woman and the figure dressed in black, Claire struggled to focus on the vision in her head as well as what was taking place in front of her.

"Aim!"

Then an image of Gunstard, armed with a handgun, suddenly flashed in her thoughts. Smiling directly at Claire, he placed the weapon against the back of a child's head.

"No!" she screamed as she recognized the child he was about to execute. "Not Thomas!" she pleaded. "Not Thomas!"

"He sees you."

Clarity came to Claire at the sound of the old woman's voice. Unaware that she had been gazing directly at one of the child-soldiers, she suddenly realized the identity of the boy.

"Thomas," she whispered in disbelief.

"Fire!"

*

"Why do you take me toward the sea?"

Teimbaka pulled on John Too's arm.

"I can hear the boy's footsteps; he travels *away* from the harbor."

Teimbaka heard John Too sigh.

"We're headed toward the edge of the city," he said. "I don't know what you mean by the sea."

Teimbaka closed his eyes and exhaled. The sound of waves lapping against a shoreline was unmistakable. The aroma of saltwater was pungent in the air. Touching his face, he could feel the moisture of sea mist on his skin.

"You are mistaken," he replied. "Listen, feel, smell."

John Too huffed. "Etiyopiya," he began. "We have been following the boy for several kilometers. You must—"

Teimbaka tilted his head to the side and listened for the reason John Too stopped talking.

"Perhaps you should wait here," John Too suggested. "I'll bring the boy to you."

A sudden gust of wind blew sand upon Teimbaka's face and brought the sound of a woman's scream to his ears. With her cry, the din of ocean waves inside his head swelled to a crescendo. The sea mist—what he'd sensed as dampness clinging to his flesh—became so dense he wiped away water seeping into his eyes. As he blinked away the moisture, he heard the roar of gunshots. Again, he heard a woman scream. Then a voice he'd yearned to hear for over a year cried, "Thomas!"

*

As the child-soldiers fired their guns, Claire screamed and sagged to her knees. Horrified to witness the execution of women and children, she placed her hands over her eyes and started to cry. But after the echo of the shots fell quiet, her sorrow and disbelief turned to rage. Angrily wiping tears from her eyes, she glared at the boy she'd once cherished, and she screamed his name.

"Thomas!"

The light shines in the darkness, and the darkness does not understand. The memory of the words came and went in a moment of anguish. Blood and tissue had stained the rocks the day she'd uttered the words to Thomas; Gunstard had murdered six boys without mercy. How could he—Thomas, one of the twelve who'd survived that evil day—be a servant of the Serpent, become the embodiment of evil, when he'd been innocence's charity?

Rifle barrel smoking at his side, Thomas gazed at her, expressionless. If he recognized her, Claire could not see it in his eyes.

"Thomas," she sighed, utterly disheartened.

"Infidel!"

Claire immediately shifted her attention to the man dressed in black robes. She did not understand his pointing finger nor why his eyes seemed filled with hate.

"Set her against the wall!" the man ordered. "We must purge the street of sin!"

Instantly, several of the child-soldiers shifted their rifles and stepped out of line. With determined expressions, they leveled their weapons to firing position and marched toward Claire. Thomas, Claire observed, was not among them. He remained stationary, his demeanor somber.

"Thomas," she said in a raised voice. "Thomas, you know me. You once read books while sitting on my—"

"Silence!" the man in black commanded.

Then the man took a step toward Thomas and clasped the boy's shoulder.

"Thomas!" Claire cried.

The boy flinched.

"Thomas," she said once more.

"Silence her!"

Claire pulled her necklace out from beneath her shirt and extended the cross toward Thomas. An instant later, a blow to her stomach felled her. Fighting through pain and gasping for breath, she looked up into the face of a child-soldier as the boy thrust the butt of a rifle toward her head.

*

Yaroslav nervously fingered the trigger of an AK-47 as he watched for movement in an open doorway across the street. The armed militia stationed at multiple points along the street to either side of him was cause for concern. Warily, he observed the men who had been part of Talia's private guard—up until a few days ago.

These darkies have no honor, he reminded himself. *They'd sell their own mothers for a handful of coins. The woman never stood a chance.*

The woman—Talia. It wasn't hard to convince the men on her payroll to betray her. Each and every man Yaroslav approached had voiced his displeasure at taking orders from a woman. Especially one who showed no respect to Allah and who was raised a prostitute, who had whored her way into a position of power within the Consortium. Their prejudice toward Talia—toward women in general—was apparent to Yaroslav as soon as he put out feelers concerning her overthrow.

He'd first entertained the notion of circumventing Talia after Blue-head had missed their last pre-arranged rendezvous. With Blue-head out of the picture, he wondered, why should the woman be the only one to benefit from the tusks? So he'd done a little snooping around the area where Talia had sent him and discovered Blue-head's corpse a few kilometers from the makeshift airstrip. A little more searching led him to the discovery of tusk fragments scattered through a big pile of rubble near the peak of a ridge. It had taken him some time, but he'd dug through the rubble and—with the help of few locals—moved some of the bigger boulders. The reward for his persistence was a massive collection of ivory tusks.

The decision to keep the cave of tusks a secret was an easy one. After dispensing with the local men who'd helped him dig out the cave entrance, he'd formulated the plan to eliminate the only other person with knowledge of the cave—Talia.

He urged himself to stay vigilant. The men he'd hired away from Talia couldn't be trusted. Greed was a powerful motivator. His days in the Soviet Union and, more recently, his time working in the Horn of Africa had reinforced that belief tenfold.

With his attention fixed on the doorway across the street—where, he'd been assured, Talia and the dark-skinned American would emerge from under the city—he spoke into one of three walkie-talkies he'd distributed.

"Anything from your vantage, Number One?"

He released the button and waited. The handheld crackled for a moment before a voice answered, "Nothing yet."

He depressed the Talk button again.

"What about you, Number Two?"

Again, the device crackled before a different voice replied, "Nothing."

"Keep your eyes peeled," he responded. "They'll be coming out soon."

*

Marcus placed his ear against the wall and listened. Then he patted the wall a few times before examining his palm. Glancing between his palm and the wall, he shook his head. How had Difireti walked through solid stone? He giggled. It was a trick, he decided. And what a good trick it was. Maybe Difireti could teach him how to do it. Having the power to vanish into solid objects would make playing hide-and-seek so much more fun.

"Thomas!"

A woman's shout drew his attention. Marcus cautiously inched his way along the side of the building until he reached the corner. He flinched when a man gruffly yelled, "Silence her!" but nevertheless peeked around the corner.

Dead people. He stared blankly at the ground. *Dead people.* Why were they always around? They were everywhere. So much so, he wasn't particularly alarmed at the bullet-riddled bodies strewn on the ground near Difireti. He was more perturbed by their unwanted presence. Dead people were everywhere. With a shrug of his shoulders, he murmured, "Difireti."

The sight of the little animal shimmering next to the woman kneeling among the dead people brought a smile to his lips. *How does Difireti do that? How can she make her body sparkle?*

With playful slap to the wall, he skipped around the corner of the building and shouted, "You're it!"

*

Yaroslav jerked the walkie-talkie to his ear when static crackled over the receiver.

"I've got movement," a garbled voice said.

Yaroslav pressed the Talk button.

"Is this position one or two?"

A long moment of static preceded "Two." He looked to his right. Two raised his hand and waved. Yaroslav quickly motioned for the man to lower his arm. Then he shifted his attention to the doorway across the street. As Number Two had reported, a figure moved just inside the doorframe. He figured it was the American. Though Yaroslav certainly admired the man's ingenuity and courage—and had planned on using his talents for his own benefit—it was clear he had to die alongside Talia. It couldn't be helped. No telling what she'd revealed to him about the cave and the ivory. And no telling what kind of deal they'd made to share it. He didn't really have a choice. The American had to die. *A necessary waste*, he told himself.

Yaroslav slowly positioned the walkie-talkie so the mouthpiece was touching his lips. When he saw the figure inside the doorway take a step across the threshold, he yelled, "Fire!"

Two explosions came in quick succession. The first blew the car containing Number One a foot off the ground. The second pulverized the window, frame, and wall where Number Two had been stationed. Yaroslav ducked back from the window. When the deafening roar of automatic gunfire erupted out on the street, he headed for the stairwell that led to the ground floor.

At the top of landing, Yaroslav swung the barrel of his AK-47 toward the room below him and descended the first few steps with caution. He caught the high-pitched whine of a projectile moments before the stairs under his feet exploded.

*

Teimbaka studied the sliver of flame flickering within his mind. He was certain he'd seen it before. But his memory of the flame was from a time so long ago, he wondered what relevance it held in the present. Having once embodied the mystery and power of the Father's words, the spark of light now appeared elusive, almost timid.

John Too tugged on his sleeve.

"Hurry," the boy said.

But Teimbaka knew from past experience there was no need to hurry.

The ethereal beacon could not be captured or contained. Proximity to the eternal fire could be accomplished only through faith and perseverance.

"Do you see her?" John Too excitedly asked.

Teimbaka stumbled as John Too pulled on him with greater urgency. Odd for the boy to refer to the light as *her*. But John Too—for a time, anyway—had lived in the grace of the Mother and the Father. Perhaps the flame appeared differently for people such as he. Perhaps, for him, the light manifested itself as a woman.

Woman—Teimbaka slowed to an uncertain stop and firmly pulled his sleeve from John Too's grasp. *Weeping*—he could hear weeping and sense tears sliding down cheeks weighted with sorrow. Had he once not experienced the same sadness? Did he not know to whom the tears belonged?

In his mind, the small flame glided across a smooth surface before pooling at the edge of a chasm, just as it had the night he'd searched for the words in the cave of wraiths.

"Hurry!" John Too cried.

And as he had done in the cave of wraiths, Teimbaka leaped toward the flame in a desperate attempt to grasp it. But before he could close his fingers around the fiery glow, the shimmering spark abruptly extinguished.

*

Claire's eyes went wide as a boy skipped toward her.

"You're it!" the child gleefully shouted.

"Go back!" she cried.

As she struggled to rise from her knees, she heard the man dressed in black shout the order she'd been fearing since being placed among the dead.

"Ready your weapons!"

Claire stood unsteadily as the boy ran to her side and tagged her on the thigh. Giggling, he looked up into her eyes and spluttered, "You're it."

"Aim!"

"Go!" she urged him. "Run! Save yourself!"

She thought the boy confused or daft when he simply smiled.

"But she's here," he said.

And he tapped her on the thigh as if trying to show her something.

"She went inside you."

"Send her and her false god to Jahannam!"

"Sister Lady!"

*

Teimbaka leaped toward Sister Lady. John Too reached out for him, but he was not quick enough. He could only look on helplessly as the man standing behind the child-soldiers lowered his arm and shouted, "Fire!"

The ferocious roar of a lion coincided with the firing of the guns. The sky, the earth, and the walls around John Too shook from the power of the beast's mighty cry.

*

Teimbaka bent low when he heard a flutter of wings near the back of his head. *They've returned*, he thought. *The dark angels have come.* As he acknowledged their presence, the ethereal flame reappeared.

The light—the spark suddenly reignited within the dark void of his blindness. Spellbound, he watched it rise out of a chasm. The glow pulled him forward, a beacon guiding him across a vast black abyss.

At the appearance of the flame, the dark angels wailed, their cries assailing Teimbaka like sand pelting his face. Beleaguered by the shrieking cries, he stumbled to one knee and shouted to the sky, "Mercy!" The flame burned tantalizingly close, flickering just beyond his reach. Desperate to reach it, he conjured what strength he could muster and lunged. As his flesh touched fire, a jolt of energy surged through his body.

*

Marcus saw the blind man stumble an instant before the child soldiers fired their guns. Emitting a terrifying roar, the blind man gathered himself and leaped to the woman's side. Bullets bombarded the wall as he pulled her down to the ground. What happened next, Marcus wasn't quite sure. But after a blinding ray of sunlight washed over the alley, Difireti stood shimmering by the woman's side.

"Do you see her, Etiyopiya?" John Too called out.

Marcus watched the boy he'd pulled from the water run toward the blind man. The blind man turned and looked directly at the youth, as though his sight had been restored.

"I see her, John Too," he said.

Softly placing his fingertips upon the woman's cheeks, he lovingly whispered, "I see her. I see her."

EPILOGUE

LINES: STRAIGHT, CURVY, circular, dotted, short, long—and those that join—angled, domed, sloping, pointed, and ridged. Funny how they are alone when they are first drawn, Juba thought: singular, waiting, lonely. But when they are joined, they become more.

Nothing becomes everything. Everything becomes nothing.

Juba watched, detached, as the horn drew another line in the dirt, her hand seemingly taking no part in the line's creation.

Stick figures: a man, a woman, a child, animals—several, of different species—a village, a mountain, a waterfall, trees on the edge of a grassy plain. *Drawn as though they are here,* she thought. When she knew, in a hurting, hollow-stomach kind of way, that they were gone.

"All gone," she sadly mumbled.

In a moment of indifference, she watched as the horn drew a line though them all.

"Dead. All dead," she softly proclaimed.

Eden—Juba raised the horn parallel to her chest. The girl—Enat, Juba had called her—was dead when she had taken the horn from the twine sash around her waist. So too was the man, Bouda, when she had found the horn in the black dirt near the burned-out air machine. Had the horn been cursed by an evil shaman? Would possessing it bring about *her* death?

She was inclined to drop the horn next to her gun and ammunition belts. But instead her attention returned to the figures drawn in the soil. Her mother and father, her village, the animals, the land—they had not possessed the horn or known of its existence. Yet, they were dead. Gone. All gone.

She breathed a troubled sigh.

The horn—it had powers. But they were not evil powers.

Curious, she tilted the horn up, down, and sideways, studying its grooves. Unable to unlock its secret, she decided the horn could only do so much. It wasn't invincible. It could not prevent death.

Death—the word, to her, was unfathomable. She understood the meaning, but she could not definitively gauge its scope. Scrutinizing the figures in the soil, she concluded that death did not make anyone more or less of what they were or what they might have been. It just made them nothing.

Nothing becomes everything. She thought about the old woman. What would *she* say about her mother and father being dead? Would she say their spirits had been lifted from the dirt and scattered by the wind? Or would she say their decaying bodies had seeped into the earth and spread over the land by the soles of people's sandals to be absorbed by the living?

Everything becomes nothing. She shook her head. Thinking about death confused her. Nothing was made better by it. Nothing was made worse. Except to those who remained. Those who felt the bad, empty feeling in their chest. But what did that matter to the animals, the mountains, the waterfalls, the trees, the grassland? Nothing. It didn't matter at all.

She sighed.

The horn drew a second line through the figures in the soil. Fittingly, a shadow appeared, encroaching slowly, steadily until it engulfed the world of the dead.

"That's quite a drawing you've made."

Juba frowned. Whose voice was talking inside her head?

"And the horn you're holding, is it—?"

Juba looked up. A woman. *Ferenji.* Dressed like a ranger.

"You don't want it," Juba told her. She tapped the etchings of her mother and father. "It can't stop people from being dead."

Juba didn't like it when the woman crouched next her. But she didn't tell her.

"Do you know them?" the woman asked, pointing to the figures of the man and the woman.

Juba focused on the lines drawn through the picture. She shrugged.

"Your mother and father?"

Juba continued to tap the stick figures but said nothing.

"And those huts," the woman inquired. "Your village?"

Dismayed when the horn abruptly scratch-erased the drawings of the huts, Juba lashed out at the woman.

"They're gone!" she angrily blurted. "All dead! Gone!" Juba huffed and gave the woman an angry look.

To her surprise, the woman nodded.

"I see. Dead. All dead."

Juba curtly nodded.

"Mother, father."

Juba tapped the corresponding stick figures.

"Village, mountain, river, the land."

As the woman said each name, Juba tapped the corresponding etching.

"Antelope, lion, dog."

Juba grimaced.

"Not a dog. Um, hyena?"

Juba nodded and tapped the figure.

"Rhino"

Tap.

"Elephant."

"Tembo," Juba sadly repeated.

Both her hand and the horn quivered over the earth-drawn depiction of an elephant.

"Tembo," the woman repeated. "Like the ones poisoned by the watering hole."

"They weren't supposed to die!" Juba exclaimed. "Blue-head is gone!" She gouged the dirt with the horn. "No more were supposed to die!"

"It's all right, it's all right. No one's going to— I mean…"

Juba huffed and tried to shrug the woman's hand off her shoulder. When the woman removed her hand, Juba scooted toward her rifle.

"Blue-head? Is that what you said?"

Juba blankly gazed at her gun.

"Is that yours?"

Juba grunted her displeasure.

"It's awfully big."

Juba shrugged.

"Do you know how to use it?"

Juba nodded.

"Blue-head. Is that the name of a man? A poacher?"

Juba made eye contact with the woman.

"Did you use it?" She nodded toward Juba's rifle. "On him?"

Juba pursed her lips and shifted her attention to the weapon. The woman stood.

"The tusks," Juba muttered. She glanced up at the woman. "The ranger."

The woman crouched and pointed to the stick drawing of the elephant.

"You tried to help, is that it? There was a ranger trying—"

"Kamua," Juba said.

Juba quickly etched a stick figure of a man and scratched a line through it.

"Dead?"

Juba glanced at the horn and nodded.

The woman sighed. "A damn war," she muttered.

"Tembo," Juba said.

The woman took a deep breath and rose.

"My name's Darleen," she said. "I'm headed to the south ranger station at the Gambella reserve. I'm working with the rangers there."

Juba stared at the lines in the dirt. *Nothing to everything, everything to nothing.*

"I've been scouting for poachers."

Juba glanced at Darleen, who was pointing behind her.

"I have a Rover."

Juba looked over her shoulder. She frowned when she saw a vehicle.

"I know. You didn't hear me when I approached. I didn't know what to think."

Juba watched, detached, as the horn began to scratch-erase the drawing of Kamua.

"Can I give you a lift?"

Juba looked at the woman, confused.

"A ride." She pointed toward the vehicle. "Do you want to come with me? To the ranger station."

Juba sniffled and wiped her nose with the back of her hand. Using the horn as leverage, she slowly stood.

"Oh, dear god," Darleen gasped, clasping Juba's shoulder. "Hurry. Get to the Rover."

Juba looked at her, perplexed.

"Hyenas."

Juba followed Darleen's gaze and smiled.

"I can't believe I didn't see them."

"They protect." Juba nodded to the horn. "They follow." She raised the horn to shoulder level. "It has powers."

"Powers?" Darleen shook her head. "That would be…"

"How far?" Juba stuffed the horn into her sash before bending to gather the gun and ammunition belts. Looping an ammunition belt around her neck, she said, "I'll help the rangers kill the bad men."

"Kill? No, that's not what rangers do. Only when they're forced to—"

"All dead!" Juba defiantly stated. She pointed to the ground where the drawings had been. "All gone." She definitively shook her head. "Bad men must die." She slapped the rifle and grunted.

Darleen raised her eyebrows and sharply exhaled. Casting a glance to the pack of hyenas a score of meters from where she and Juba stood, she said, "Let's get to the ranger station. They can explain their duties better than I."

Juba looped the second ammunition belt over her neck and grasped the AK-47 by the barrel.

"You help tembo?" she asked as the two began walking toward the Rover.

"Help the elephants? Why, yes, I'm on grant from university in London. I'm writing my thesis on—"

"Then you must learn."

"Well, that's what I'm doing."

Juba looked over her shoulder. Where she'd dragged the butt of the rifle across the soil, a wide, irregular line had been created.

"You must join," she said, recalling what she'd decided about lines.

"I don't understand. Join?"

Juba tapped the rifle barrel.

"To kill," she said.

"I don't think that will be necessary."

Juba stopped. When Darleen did the same, Juba shuffled in front of her so she could look directly into her eyes.

"I will teach you." She patted the gun. "If you wish to help tembo, you must learn to kill."

*

"If you wished for no other woman to experience the sins that have been committed against you, how would you accomplish this?"

Sarah gazed at Bin'ka—or what she understood to be an image of Bin'ka—with a pleading expression. How many different ways would he ask the impossible? And why? Why was he so persistent in seeking answers she could not give? How would you rid the earth of hunger? How would you stop men from killing their neighbor? How would you stop war? How would you save paradise? She shook her head; did he really expect an answer?

Paradise—that had been the hardest notion to contemplate. For God created paradise in His image. Scripture was clear on how it became tarnished and by whom: through the Serpent's subterfuge, Adam and Eve had eaten the forbidden fruit. It was the creation of sin. Saving paradise would mean the erasure of sin. But how could that be possible without God's guidance? More importantly, how could the task be approached without first seeking His forgiveness?

"Your ordeal. The decision you reached. You saw a way to end it."

She studied Bin'ka's image on the screen; he was depicted in the glow of a fire, waves crashing in the distance, as on a night en route to Kenya, Bin'ka and she camped along the Somalia coast. Though she was certain they had never engaged in this particular conversation, the emotions his questions stirred and the deep feeling of yearning she experienced as she gazed into his eyes were as real as any she had experienced during that journey.

"Tell me," he said. "Tell me how you ended it."

Sarah blinked several times as she struggled with his request. Unconsciously, she gripped the cross dangling from her necklace and lightly pounded the symbol of her faith against her chest. She searched for words—words that would explain what she had done, words that would ease and perhaps expiate her guilt—but she could not find them.

"I killed him," she simply explained. "I grabbed the knife while I absorbed his—" she briefly paused. "Evil. Then cut away his sin."

She placed her free hand over her fist. Trembling, breathing heavily, she closed her eyes.

"And when you removed his sin, what did he do?"

Startled to open her eyes to see Bin'ka holding a knife, she gasped. But as Bin'ka slashed the blade outward over fire, she visualized what she had done.

"He tried to stop me." Her eyes went wide as she relived the moment. "He wanted to kill me."

Jaw clenched, she wiped beads of sweat from her forehead and took a deep breath.

"I thrust the knife into his throat. Blood sprayed. I—" She examined her hands as if expecting to see them stained. "I was covered in blood. I stood in the shower and watched the water turn red." She gazed into Bin'ka's eyes. "I couldn't cleanse myself quickly enough."

Bin'ka said nothing. With a heave of his massive chest, he bent toward the fire and stirred the embers with the tip of the blade.

"And so it was done."

By the way he framed the comment, she wasn't certain if he was making a statement or asking a question.

"You ended evil."

Evil. Sarah mulled the word. *Evil.* Her neighbor, kidnapper, abuser was but one, she knew, a small part of the realm and reach of the foul entity.

"For a moment," she told him in a quiet tone of voice. "For me."

Images suddenly flashed through her thoughts: her clothes ripped from her body by the men who'd attacked them on the beach, hands pawing at her breasts, hot breath against her neck as she was pinned to the ground. Her eyes teared at the recollections.

"But only for a time," she glumly admitted. "Evil—" She looked past Bin'ka into the darkness beyond. "It's—"

Her consciousness searched the blackness at the periphery of the firelight. She could sense malevolence lurking, could sense its intent, its unwavering patience.

"Everywhere," she muttered. "Evil—" Once more she sought Bin'ka's gaze. "It's everywhere."

Bin'ka snorted.

"But you ended it." He twisted the blade back and forth as he extended the knife toward her. "For a time, you said."

"For a time," she repeated.

"And if there was a way…"

She bent toward his image as his voice trailed off, then reached out as if to take hold of his hand when she saw him place the knife into the center of the flames.

"If you could end it," he said. "How would it be done?"

Again, the impossible, Sarah thought. *Why does he ask?* She shifted her attention to the fire. When a trail of sparks suddenly exploded from the depths of the flames, she followed them upward into the night sky. There, each one burst into hundreds of sparkling particles.

Dirk—she'd been seated next to him as flares rose into the night sky. "A plague," he'd said a moment before the sky lit up. "It was if a plague had been loosed across the land." He'd meant evil. Evil had swept across the land, devouring all in its path.

"What must be done?"

She shook her head at his question. *Why does he keep pressing me?*

More images flashed through her mind: George Henry, Adhib, her neighbor, the men on the beach. Each was a small part of evil, each representative of an infinite number—*a plague*.

"Eradicate," she muttered. "It must be eradicated."

"With a blade?"

Her eyes were drawn to the knife in Bin'ka's hand. The blade blazed white-gold in the heat of the flames. As she looked on, it lengthened.

"A sword," she murmured.

"And would your god wield this sword?"

Eyes fixed on the weapon, Sarah contemplated the countless who, like she, had been raped, sodomized, tortured, and enslaved. Though faceless and of different ages and ethnicities, the women she envisioned shared a common thread, one which she herself had embodied before she'd been defiled—*innocence.*

"Many," she said. "Many hands would need to wield the sword."

Entranced by the image of the flaming blade, Sarah drifted into a vision of a field engulfed in fire. The sky above the field rained projectiles. The projectiles exploded as they hit the ground. She saw herself—dazed and disoriented—stumbling through waves of flames. A beast was at her side, guiding her, keeping her steady. The beast appeared as a fusion of hyena and man. Beneath their feet was a river of shiny green bugs. The river wound its way through the flames as it rushed toward a hill. Upon the crest of the hill stood a man in dark robes. The current of green beetles pooled near his side. Soon, the shiny green insects numbered so many, they engulfed the hill. Then a flash of lightning burst from the sky and struck the earth. The mound of green beetles ignited. Their bodies burned a luminous white-gold. The intensity of the light was so strong, Sarah shaded her eyes. Abruptly, the brilliant glow extinguished. In its aftermath, the dim light of embers remained. From within these embers, Sarah witnessed a child arise. Unconsciously, she lightly beat her fist upon her heart.

Slowly, Sarah awoke from the vision, shaken by what she'd envisioned, unsure as to what the images represented. She had told Bin'ka the Lord would need many hands to wield the sword that would eradicate evil, but she had witnessed only one child rise from the fiery embers.

Fire—Sarah closed her eyes. She revisited the moments before the mound of green beetles had been struck by lightning. The insects had functioned as a river, a current, a living conduit flowing toward a hill where a man waited.

The man in black—Teimbaka—he had sacrificed himself for her. Had protected her from countless assailants, thrown her into the water, where she was saved by—

Bin'ka—Sarah looked to his image with a sense of urgency. He appeared to her as a vague silhouette encased within fire.

"Who will eradicate evil?" he asked.

As her fingers touched the outline of his cheeks on the screen, his image dissipated into the flames.

"Bin'ka!" she cried.

The monitor flickered before going dark. Sarah continued to stare at it, hopeful Bin'ka would return. But nothing happened. After several minutes, she stood and left the chamber.

Sarah dazedly walked to Conduit's workstation. The frizzy-haired woman did not look up as she entered or show any indication that she was aware of Sarah's presence. And though Sarah had many questions for the woman—most pressing, when would she be allowed to leave the underground labyrinth—she passed her in silence, deep in thought, Bin'ka's unanswerable questions tugging at her conscience. From Conduit's chamber, she moved to the next, the one that held the weapons and uniforms of the failed legion. What had Conduit said about them? *Too soon*, Sarah recalled. *Too soon? In what respect? In what respect were they too soon?*

She studied the uniforms. The gas masks piqued her interest. Why had they been outfitted with gas masks? Sarah thought back to what little Conduit had told her about the group. *Too soon*—the assertion led her to the next train of thought. *We are not the first. We are here to save paradise.* The questions Bin'ka had pressed her on suddenly held some clarity. *How would I end evil? What method would I use to eradicate the sins of its spawn? Who would wield the sword of God?*

She scrutinized the uniforms of the first legion more closely. It suddenly dawned on her: perhaps the men who wore the uniforms were not the first legion. Conduit had referred to others who had come before. Would there be others after she and Conduit? And if Conduit had told her the truth about the part she was to play—to decide how paradise would be saved—then surely her visions held the answers to the questions Bin'ka posed.

The gas masks—had they been issued to the first legion because eradication was to be by an airborne poison? She thought of the consequences: death on an indiscriminate scale. Young and old killed without discernment, the innocent condemned equally with the guilty. Air, earth, and water tainted, defiled. *No*, she concluded, *poison cannot be the way. Then how?*

Bin'ka—he had held the knife to the fire; the short blade had transformed into a sword. *Who would wield the sword?* he'd asked. "Many," she'd responded. *And who will decide?* She shuddered as the answer became clear: *I am to decide.* She fell to her knees at the revelation. The responsibility was overwhelming. *How can this be so? How can God expect this of me? Who am I to judge?*

"Because you have been exposed to evil, experienced its sin."

Bin'ka stood at the far end of the chamber. In his hand, he gripped a sword of white-gold flame.

"Because you defeated it, killed it, sent it back to the hell from which it was born."

Sarah pounded the cross to her heart as Bin'ka's image multiplied. One became two, then three, then many, until what was once the figure of a man became an army that stretched far beyond the realm of her sight and comprehension.

"We wield the sword for you," they collectively said. And with a bow of their heads, they added, "We await your command."

The legion—the legion of God. She dipped her head, overcome with humility.

"How will you save paradise?"

Conduit's voice, her question, gently seeped into Sarah's awareness. In turn, Sarah looked to Bin'ka. But the image of him, of the legion, was no longer visible. His absence left her feeling empty. Conduit's question went unanswered.

"The time will soon be upon us," Conduit went on.

"The time?" Sarah half-heartedly inquired.

"For us to stand up to the evil that threatens all God has provided."

Sarah rose from her knees and slowly turned to face the woman. The cross gripped tightly in her hand, she said, "The burden is too great. And though I may understand what must be done, I cannot see how it can be accomplished."

Conduit smiled.

"Technology," she said.

Sarah did not understand the word.

"A tool the Lord provides," Conduit explained. Extending an open hand toward Sarah, she said, "Come. Let me show you."

As Sarah took her hand, Conduit bowed.

"You are the way," she quietly proclaimed. "I am the conduit."

*

"What will you do with Yaroslav?"

Talia twisted a lemon peel and dropped it into the cup of espresso resting on the table.

"Use him until he is no longer of any value," she casually replied. With a shrug, she added, "Then do what he intended to do to *us*."

"There must be a dozen other pilots you could hire," Chris countered. "After what he pulled, I'd just as soon slit his throat and move on."

Talia smiled and took a sip of the espresso. "What has he done that upsets you?"

Chris shook his head as though he hadn't heard her correctly.

"Tried to kill us?" he said. He shifted in his chair and glanced toward the harbor. "Doesn't that piss you off?"

"Piss me off—you mean, make me angry?" She chuckled and shook her head. "Business," she told him. "You get used to it."

Chris grunted. Ignoring her seeming indifference to their safety, he surveyed the perimeters of the outdoor café where they'd taken a table. Potential threats were everywhere: armed soldiers interspersed among passersby, merchants hawking their wares—no doubt prepared to protect their goods with weapons hidden beneath their stalls—and, of course, individuals within the crowd who could easily be paid assassins. *You get used to it.* He eyed her with disdain.

"Guess we view it a little different in the States."

Talia smiled. "Really?" Her eyebrows arched. "And your last employer—where is he now?"

Chris thought of Rue Thompson and frowned. From the fat preacher, his thoughts drifted to Yutanda and then to Tanya, Jim, and Rochelle. The sequence ended with Marcus. All but the boy were dead. And while he couldn't be certain of Tanya's demise, he was fairly sure she'd met her end in the company of the old Arab—or would, soon enough. Her big mouth, he knew, would cement her fate.

"I see your point."

He saw Talia's eyes narrow.

"As soon as we pinpoint the location of the cave where the ivory is stored, Yaroslav's use will end." She smiled and took another sip from her cup. "His fate will lie with you at that point."

Chris thought of the various ways he might deal with Yaroslav. Giving him a bullet to the back of his skull or slashing a knife across his throat, dumping him from a plane without a parachute, chaining his legs and hands to weights and throwing him into the ocean, or gutting him and then dropping him in the middle of nowhere. Letting the animals see to his end.

"Maybe I'll cut his Achilles tendons and leave him in the section of tunnel you won't venture into," he half joked. "Let whatever demons you think are there suck the blood from his veins." He chuckled.

Talia looked toward the water with a pensive expression. He wasn't quite sure what to make of her silence.

"Sore spot?" he probed.

She glanced at him with a furrowed brow.

"Want to fill me in?"

When she remained silent, Chris followed her gaze toward the water.

"Look, I didn't mean to—" He cleared his throat.

"Africa is changing," she said. She glanced into her cup and added, "Maybe quicker than it should."

"Change is inevitable."

"Is it?"

She wrung her hands as if massaging away pain, then sighed and shook her head.

"There are some aspects of Her that..."

He leaned toward her as her voice trailed off.

"Yes?"

She frowned and turned her attention back toward the sea. "Adiam," she began. "An old business—" She paused. "A friend." She briefly looked toward the sky. "He would sometimes refer to her as the Mother."

"Her?"

"Africa. Old magic. Things unexplained. Stories. Things you can't reason." She laughed nervously. "Stories you hear from people who've spent time in the wild." She looked toward the old dock jutting out into the harbor. "Some about this very city." She nodded toward the water. "Some about what has taken place on that old dock."

She paused and furrowed her brow.

As he waited for her to continue, he quickly surveyed the faces of the people milling about the café.

"But stories of the old magic are becoming less," she went on. "Waning as Africa moves forward, modernizes."

Finding the conversation of little interest, Chris scanned the people seated at the tables around them. Businessmen, mostly. Chatting up deals, he supposed. And what appeared to be a table of journalists. They were speaking French. In the far corner was a group of what he imagined were politicians or diplomats. From the tone of their voices, he guessed they were discussing some sort of urgent issue. He had just taken notice of a boy standing near the table of politicians when he caught a change of tone—an inflection of wariness—in Talia's voice.

"There's something there," she said. "Something old. Something not to be dismissed." Her expression was oddly intense when she added, "Not to be disturbed."

He pretended to cough to cover his smile.

"Sounds crazy, I know." She shrugged. "But Africa—there are parts of her you can't explain."

Chris's attention was drawn to the boy as he tried to understand what Talia was telling him.

"Something old," he muttered. He glanced in her direction. "Not to be disturbed; is that what you said?"

The boy—Chris scrutinized his face. He seemed familiar. But how could that be? He hadn't been to Africa in years.

"I know what you must be thinking," Talia said. "But I've known people who've gone into that section of tunnel."

The boy—what was he doing? He wasn't begging. Nor did he seem to be looking for anyone in particular.

"And they were never seen again."

Chris noticed the boy looking out toward the old dock. There were beads of sweat on his forehead.

"Don't you believe what I'm telling you?"

"What?" Chris replied. He offered Talia a sheepish smile. "Sorry. I was—" He glanced between her and the boy. "Something about—" He furrowed his brow and rubbed his chin. "That boy," he said.

Talia shifted in her chair. She followed Chris's gaze.

"A beggar, no doubt," she remarked.

"No," Chris muttered. "I haven't seen him—"

Chris fell silent as the boy looked directly toward him. His eyes were familiar. He was certain he'd seen them before. *But where?*

"If he's bothering you, I'll have him sent away."

Chris shook his head.

"The proprietor is a friend of mine," Talia went on.

The boy patted his chest. Chris continued to focus on the child's eyes. He was certain he had looked into them before.

"He's just a beggar," Talia said. "Here, I'll show you."

The boy's face was covered in sweat.

"Boy!" Talia called out.

Chris glanced across the table. Talia held a franc note in her raised hand.

"Come," she beckoned.

Chris stared into the boy's eyes as the child took a step in his direction. The boy, in turn, gazed directly at Chris. In the spark of a flashback, he remembered the son of the assassin, Mirko. The one family member he'd let live. The one who'd seemed to stare right into his eyes as he focused the telescopic lens on the boy's forehead.

Chris woke from the memory with a jolt; the boy was standing next to Talia.

"What do you say?"

Talia held the franc note just above the boy's head as she asked. The boy looked nervously toward the dock before he replied. Chris leaned toward him as he mumbled his answer.

"Speak up," Talia told the boy in a stern voice. "You must—"

Chris abruptly stood, overturning the table, and lunged for the boy. "He's wired!" Chris shouted.

"*Allahu Akbar!*" the boy screamed.

Death for Chris, Talia, and those seated at the nearby tables was violent and agonizing.

*

Goliath smiled as he watched Mr. Pembrook drive up the ramp toward the garage exit on the next level. The little sports car the man drove sounded like a super-charged lawnmower more than a fine-tuned racing machine. But no matter. He glanced down at the pair of wire cutters in his hand and grunted. As long as the steering cable broke somewhere on the freeway in the next half hour, the car could be whatever the old lawyer wanted it to be.

"Make certain it looks like an accident," Alexis had instructed. "There must be a dozen things that can go wrong on an old car like that. Find one."

Goliath frowned at the recollection. He didn't know much about cars, had never owned one. He didn't understand why he couldn't make the old man's death look like a robbery gone bad. He'd had to spend a few hours at a garage, picking a mechanic's brain. Time allocated to a problem he would have rather spent on *other* things.

"No police inquiries," she'd added when she'd noticed the look of disdain on his face. "Everything must appear above board. Logistics Ltd. is a corporate entity now, on the books in seven states and with access to every big city on the Northeast corridor. We can't afford a whiff of impropriety."

He remembered glancing at the wall of monitors behind her desk as she talked. He noticed a new boy in cell four. Twelve or thirteen years old. Goliath had nodded to that particular monitor when he'd shifted his attention back to Alexis.

"He's yours, of course," she told him. "When I get word you've accomplished your task."

Goliath shrugged. It was a stupid way to kill someone, he thought. A car accident was fifty-fifty at best. How could he be certain the old man would die even if the car ran off the road and hit a tree or slid down an embankment into the Schuylkill River?

He glanced at the pair of wire cutters again and shook his head. Fifty-fifty. But what did he know? He was just the executioner. Not the brains. That was her job—Alexis's. So far, so good in that department, he had to admit. She had a good handle on things. The lady was smart. Ruthless and perverted. But smart.

Crenshaw, as she'd predicted—and orchestrated behind the scenes—had won the special election for Rue Thompson's state congressional seat. As she had foreseen, the elimination of the punk Jaime Ain't had created an unspoken bond among the gangs and drug cartels running their respective businesses out of Newark/Port Elizabeth harbor. The drug trade was booming. And Dr. Haraji's recommendation to emphasize the opioid side of the business was proving a windfall. Moving merchandise between state lines had become pretty much risk free, thanks to the trucking corporation Alexis had set up. Logistics Ltd. had contracts with the likes of the New Jersey National Guard, the Pennsylvania Department of Transportation, and the Newark Department of Education. Alexis's latest coup was scoring a contract with FEMA to haul relief supplies to areas along the eastern seaboard damaged by powerful storms. Because of these connections, Logistics Ltd. trucks traveled along the highways without constraint and drove through weigh stations and police checkpoints without being stopped for inspection. The lady, Goliath had to admit, knew her shit.

So, as Mr. Pembrook's vintage sports car drove out of view, Goliath shoved the wire cutters into his pocket and headed for the stairwell. Alexis had insisted that a new Latino dude accompany Goliath, and the man was waiting on the fourth level to drive him back to HQ. Alexis had told Goliath she wanted his opinion of the man's temperament and capabilities. Which Goliath knew was a bunch of shit. But he'd played along. He always played along. That lwas his philosophy; play along with whoever was giving orders until the order-giver changed. Then pledge your loyalty to the new boss.

But watch out for yourself at all costs. No matter what.

The doorknob to the stairwell was cold as he turned it—as cold as his feelings about sabotaging Pembrook's car, as cold as his viewpoint on what the Latino dude had been ordered to do to him. *Try to do*, he corrected. Which, judging from the guy's look and build, wasn't going to be a problem. After all, Goliath had a seven-inch switchblade in his back pocket and a stiletto pin-blade in the buckle of his belt. On top of that, he'd watched Alexis slowly and systematically get rid of her partners. It was only a matter of time until she would try to get rid of him. But it didn't bother him much, knowing he would one day become the focus of her ill intentions. *Enjoy the moment* was his philosophy. *Enjoy who you are. Accept the good and bad.*

So, as he walked down the stairs toward level four, Goliath took the switchblade out of his pocket. As a precaution. Just in case. To be prepared. The teenage boy in cell four had given him extra motivation to stay alive. He'd already experienced several erections thinking about what he was going to do to the youth.

Suddenly, it dawned on him to go down to level five and work his way back to level four via the car ramp instead of the stairs. He was sure the Latino would be watching the door to the stairwell. He wouldn't be expecting Goliath to use the car ramp. And although he wasn't sure what he was going to tell Alexis about the Latino—about what had happened to him in the parking garage—he wasn't too concerned. Right now, the image of the teenage boy, naked in his grasp, consumed his thoughts.

*

"You must ask God's forgiveness."

Claire searched for a change in Thomas's expression.

"You need only ask, Thomas, and He will absolve you of your sins."

As she spoke, she peered into the boy's eyes, looking for a glimmer of understanding or guilt—a flicker of some emotion that might give her hope that Thomas felt remorse. She'd watched him take part in the murder of innocent women and children. Surely he understood the gravity of what he'd done.

"Perhaps while we travel," she continued, "you will use the time to reflect upon your actions."

Thomas stared blankly ahead, as he had done since Teimbaka had taken the gun from his hands and led him out of the alley. His eyes seemingly focused on nothing. Claire felt certain the shock of what he'd done was preventing him from communicating or displaying his feelings. Teimbaka did not share her opinion.

"The boy is under the Serpent's spell," he'd told her. "Did you not sense evil in that place?"

She glanced across the narrow courtyard where they'd taken refuge. Teimbaka was peering through the slightly open doorway, looking for the nonexistent people hunting them, she supposed. He seemed overly concerned about their safety. Perhaps even a bit obsessed. He'd argued against her leaving the courtyard to make a phone call to Mr. Pembrook. Told her it wouldn't be safe.

"Nonsense," she'd replied. Mr. Pembrook would send help from the American embassy. But Teimbaka had been firm in his objections. She was at a loss as to why he felt so strongly they stay hidden.

Glancing between John Too and Teimbaka, she couldn't shake the notion that each seemed different. John Too, from what little interaction she'd had with him, was certainly not the same as she remembered. He seemed guarded and reserved—wary of her and of her account of what had happened after Dirk flew her back to America. Why would he doubt her? He'd never done so before. He'd always been trusting and filled with hope. What had happened to change him? She shivered, thinking of what might have been the cause.

Before—she gazed at Teimbaka, not certain what to feel. Joy, gratitude, relief—love? Certainly, she felt some of each. At least she thought she did. But she'd envisioned more. A passionate embrace, a reaffirmation of their devotion, a declaration of love. But nothing like that had transpired. He'd simply looked into her eyes, rested his forehead against hers, and then kissed her on the tip of the nose before instructing John Too to take her out of the alley. For her part, she'd stared at him like he was a figure from a dream. She'd dazedly allowed John Too to lead her out of the alley without muttering a word.

Later, after Teimbaka had led them to an abandoned house on the outermost fringe of the city, they'd exchanged stories of the past year. She remembered nothing of that day Dirk and Bin'ka had whisked her from the firefight, she'd told him, and she had little recollection of the days preceding or following. To her, Teimbaka had seemed distracted as she spoke, nodding occasionally while his eyes drifted between Thomas and the little boy she did not know. He'd said nothing when she'd finished speaking. And it was only when she'd asked what he had gone through that he'd offered his story.

"We set out the very next morning. The nun—the one who'd been sent to find you—she knew the man who'd taken you. We were desperate to find both of you."

She had questioned him about the nun—Sarah was her name—but he offered little more than a physical description and the opinion that the woman was confused and seemed to be hiding some aspect of her past that influenced her every decision.

"We traveled through the heart of the Oromo conflict. Witnessed unspeakable carnage, endured hunger and thirst, were forced to take up arms to defend ourselves. Because of the color of her skin, we were hunted. It took months to reach Djibouti. We were exhausted when we arrived, but hopeful. Then, after searching the city for several days, we were told you'd been taken to Mogadishu. So we went south."

Claire tried to remember. She recalled Dirk's face peering down at her. Nothing more of what she could remember made sense.

"But you weren't there." She felt guilty as he spoke. "You never were. They'd flown you out as soon as you arrived. Sarah and I were—"

She sensed the severity of his disappointment. He ran his fingertips across his brow as the moon rose into the night sky. The angle at which the ghostly light fell upon his face illuminated the myriad scars etched upon his features. Each one was a testament to what he had endured. His was a face battered by war and encounters with Satan.

Somewhere beneath the wounds is the man I fell in love with.

She wondered if she could find that man again, if he existed beneath the scars.

Moonlight—how much softer it seemed the night he approached me as I prayed. How gentle he was when he lifted my chin, kissed me on the lips. I felt so torn, so hesitant. Falling in love seemed out place, forbidden. But the

*moonlight quieted my fears, soothed my trepidation. I saw it as a gift from the
Holy Father, a blessing to our union.*

She'd taken his hand in hers as she remembered the moment. It was
then—as he sat in silence and she in quiet recollection—that she realized
she was willing to try to find him, to rekindle what Dirk had taken from
them. But the changes she sensed in him, the year apart—she wondered:
did he feel the same?

"They came for us," he abruptly continued. "Hunted us through the
streets, cornered us at the harbor. There was a firefight. I tossed Sarah into
the water. I don't know if she survived. There was a massive explosion. It
lifted me off my feet and hurled me through the air. I don't know what
happened after that."

He paused then to glance toward John Too. She wasn't sure if she heard
anger or sadness in Teimbaka's voice when he said, "I don't know how he
found me. He pulled me from the water."

She felt slighted when he slid his hand from hers and shook his head.

"I was blind." There was a long pause before he said, "I should be dead.
I wonder if it wouldn't better if I—"

She'd hurriedly placed her fingertips against his lips to prevent him
from finishing. The sadness she'd sensed when she looked into his eyes
was overwhelming.

"God has seen us through," she'd softly reassured. "It is for us to go
on, to make the most of the time He gives."

He'd said nothing in response. And for a brief moment, as she'd gazed
longingly up at a star-filled sky, she'd wondered what God had planned
for them.

*

Teimbaka noticed Claire looking over toward him. She appeared to be
doting on Thomas, as she'd been doing since they'd reunited. And, no
doubt, thinking of how to persuade him to allow her to leave and find a
telephone. Did she not understand they were in danger? Did she think
her car had exploded accidently? Didn't she realize someone wanted her
dead? He shook his head. And Thomas—could she not see the boy had
been brainwashed? Turned into a killer by some warlord or imam to do

their bidding? The boy would no doubt try to kill them on their journey to Ethiopia. Of that he was sure. Thomas needed to be left behind. Or…

Ethiopia—back to his roots, back to the beginning, back to where he hoped the Mother's presence was still strong. The highlands and the plateaus—he felt a sense of relief as he thought of them. His relief quickly changed to concern when he thought of the obstacles they would need to overcome to reach their destination.

War—the borders between Ethiopia, Djibouti, and Eritrea were enveloped in conflict. They would need to navigate three warring armies, each with little regard for refugees. Food and water would be scarce and difficult to obtain. Thieves and robbers would be scattered along well-traveled routes. Slavers would be waiting to pluck up those who could not defend themselves. Tribal arguments, territorial disputes, tribal hunting and water rights would need to be respected. Airborne diseases—the result of rotting corpses—would make breathing the air risky. And then there would be the various warlords—those who claimed kingdoms within kingdoms—to steer clear of. If that was possible. He didn't believe it was.

Claire—his brow wrinkled as he thought of her. *She's changed*—that much he could see. In the little time they'd shared since being reunited, it was clear to him she was not the same person as the one he'd left the day he'd journeyed to his brother's grave. What had happened to her? Her story was vague and littered with holes she could not fill. *She didn't remember*—how can one not remember the good portion of a year? She said she'd been hospitalized, placed in a clinic. Why? What wounds had she suffered? Why did she have no scars? And why couldn't she explain the reason the white-skinned man had taken her back to America?

Dirk Savage—that was the man's name, she'd told him. But how was he connected to her? The other nun—Sarah—had told him she'd been sent to find Claire because a large sum of money was to be given to her. Dirk had offered to act as her guide. Yet Claire arrived back in Africa with nothing—no belongings, no money. *What am I to make of it? Of her?*

She spoke of the white-skinned man as though she owed him empathy, loyalty. But when he'd asked why the man hadn't accompanied her back to Africa, she'd told him he was in jail. He'd murdered her mother, she'd explained. *Murdered her mother*—he could offer no words of comfort. He didn't understand her sympathy for the man.

What am I to make of her? She talks of the Father as she did when we first met. Yet there is something different in her voice—a nuance of pain, a shade of doubt. Her faith is fragile.

From Claire, Teimbaka's thoughts drifted to the terrain beyond the courtyard. Peering through the open door, he noted the landscape was bleak, dry and unforgiving. No different than when they'd made their first crossing to the highlands over a year past. Yet he sensed everything about the land had changed. What would the journey bring? He wasn't sure.

Though the land appeared the same, they were not. *He* was not. Still— he glanced over his shoulder toward Claire and Thomas—she was the woman he'd fallen in love with. Did he not owe her the right to change? Should he not accept her doubts, her fears, her pain and embrace them as his own? Would she be as open to understanding his? Would they be able to find the moonlight again? Share a moment of bliss? Sense the Mother and Father had cast their blessing upon their union?

Unconsciously, he slid his fingertips across his brow, then lightly touched his cheeks. When he felt the blotches of scar tissue on his face— dozens of old wounds—he involuntarily winced. How unsightly he must look. *How ugly I must appear. What does she see in me? What can I offer her?* The life of a nomad, he concluded. One of a herder. Shepherding a flock of the misplaced, guarding against predators of both flesh and spirit.

How can Claire be happy with me?

The cling-clang of a small bell some distance away drew his attention. Curious, he once more surveyed the terrain beyond the courtyard. The wind had picked up, blowing east to west off the ocean toward the mountains. Sunrise to sunset. At dusk, the four of them would begin moving in the same direction. He wondered if it was a sign.

*

John Too studied the square of sky showing above the courtyard walls. Sunset was near. They would soon be departing. Traveling at night would hide them from those whose job it was to keep watch on what moved in and out of the city. But John Too knew darkness would also hinder their ability to stay on course. Becoming lost could prove fatal.

Lost—a sense of helplessness to see what lies ahead or behind. John Too's gift of seeing into the future had vanished, missing since he was brought back from death. He was fully aware he'd taken a bullet to the chest in the firefight with George Henry; he knew he'd died. Death had been a dark place. He remembered feeling disoriented and afraid, with no understanding of what to do. And then a spot of light had appeared, a bright green fleck hovering low in the darkness. Immediately, he'd been drawn to it and set out to reach it. But the speck of green drifted upward as he drew closer, taking a zig-zag course, staying just out of reach. He watched the light travel upward, ever upward toward a ceiling of swirling, silver-rimmed clouds. What he perceived as sky had rotated in a churning, circular motion, like a freak desert storm about to unleash a torrent of rain. Then the canopy began to spin out of control, siphoning what existed below up into its core. As the fleck of green vanished into the vortex, John Too was launched upwards, catapulted by an energy he could not fathom. Suddenly sunlight had broken over him as the sky exploded in a burst of white fire and a luminous flash of green.

But rebirth proved cold and dour. Once he'd shaken off the chill of death, he'd realized Sister Lady was gone. And with her, all hope of belonging. If that were not enough, he'd witnessed John—Bouda—repudiate Teimbaka and the path the Mother had set them on. The events had confused and disillusioned him. And over the course of a handful of days—as he set out to find the Boy—his faith in the people he believed and trusted had eroded.

Why had he been brought back from the dead? He'd wondered that countless times. What purpose was he to serve? And why had his ability to foresee events been taken away?

After several days of travel, John Too had come upon the boy, who was sitting on the edge of the Danakil.

"I've been searching for you," he'd said, distressed.

As he anxiously waited for a reply, John Too noticed the boy had grown into a young man. His hair was long and unkempt, his face gaunt and in need of shaving. The robes he wore were tattered and soiled. His feet were bare. He looked like he hadn't eaten for days.

"What are you doing here?" he pressed when the boy did not respond.

"Watching the salt traders," the boy softly replied.

John Too looked out upon the harsh landscape with a furrowed brow.

"I don't understand," he answered. "What do they—?"

"They enter the wasteland without fear."

John Too envisioned the landscape of the Danakil. Salt depressions; lava fields; endless kilometers of dry, cracked earth; volcanoes; geysers; boiling, chemical-fouled lakes. The terrain was unforgiving. In his opinion, it was hell on earth.

"It is a thankless job," John Too remarked.

"Is it?" the boy questioned.

John Too searched the wasteland to the horizon, his gaze intent.

"They toil long hours," he offered. "Endure unbearable conditions. Their reward is a trifling to what merchants of other spices reap."

John Too heard the boy sigh, noticed his shoulders slump.

"They care for their animals," the boy said. "Tend to one another's needs, hew worth from what others deem waste." There was a long pause before he added, "They walk a humble path."

John Too thought of all the caravans he'd witnessed: salt traders leading their camels, the beasts laden with supplies. Men and animal alike moving at a slow, deliberate pace. They passed through villages without drawing attention, reached their destination without fanfare. Often, they would embark on a few months' journey without anyone taking notice.

"They are few," John Too said. "And keep to themselves."

The boy nodded but said nothing in response. John Too felt the conversation had ended. But then the boy uttered a few more words, speaking so softly that John Too bent to one knee so he could hear.

"Angels watch them pass."

John Too immediately looked upward. The sun had fully risen. The sky was a glaring mixture of blinding light on a canvas of blue. There were no angels to be seen. He did not understand.

The remainder of the day passed in silence. Neither he nor the boy ventured to speak. Nightfall came with the emergence of a thousand stars.

The contrast between the land's bleakness and the majesty of the sky prodded John Too to comment, "The beauty of heaven, the desolation of hell."

"You speak as though the two are different."

John Too looked over at the boy, hoping to make eye contact. But the boy did not turn his head in his direction. Reflecting on what the boy had said, John Too looked out upon the vista that lay before them.

"One is bleak, the other inspires," he said.

"Look closer," the boy replied. "You will see they are the same."

John Too gazed admiringly at a sky filled with brilliant stars and luminous threads of what he'd always viewed as heaven's dust. Grudgingly, his eyes drifted lower, his vision focusing on the starkness of the terrain: an empty flatland dotted with dark silhouettes of broken mountain tops and cratered peaks. What had the boy meant?

"Soon, you will embark on a journey cloaked in darkness. You will walk beneath stars and feel earth beneath your feet. The sky will not shield you, the soil will not swallow you. No beacon will guide you, no promise will keep you on hallowed path."

The boy paused then, and after brushing back his hair, he pushed off the ground to stand.

"How will your path be decided?" he asked. "When heaven and hell share the same realm."

John Too studied the horizon. Though the darkness blurred definition, he could still perceive a faint line separating earth and sky. Yet where the two bodies met, there was a slender area of uniformity.

"The path will change as I travel upon it," John Too replied.

"Will it?'" the boy pressed. "Look closer."

John Too sighed. *Riddles*, he thought. *Riddles.* But although he questioned the boy's response, he did as he was instructed. Blinking to clear his sight as well as his thoughts, he once more searched the panorama that lay before him. And as he beheld the radiance of the night sky and the starkness of the landscape, he glimpsed a twinkling beside him, a subtle transformation of substance to light. Before he understood what he was witnessing, the boy shed the form of a man. Embodied within a sparkling mist of ivory and gold, what was once the boy drifted outward toward the horizon. Eager to follow, John Too stepped forward. It was then that a breeze stirred, a gentle current that blew from east to west. As John Too looked on, the sparkling mist was carried away. Within a matter of seconds, the ethereal cloud was absorbed by the night.

John Too recalled the incident with the boy as he watched Teimbaka turn from the doorway and look toward Claire.

"It's time," Teimbaka announced, signaling Claire with a motion of his hand.

Claire rose to her feet. She assisted Thomas in doing the same.

Teimbaka then addressed John Too.

"John Too."

John Too met his gaze.

"See to the boy."

*

Marcus ran out the open door as soon as the scarred man stepped away from it. He'd been waiting impatiently for him to do so, waiting to join Difireti, who'd been beckoning him to join her on the outer side of the courtyard wall. *An adventure*, Marcus thought. *She wants to have an adventure.* He didn't know where the ethereal animal wanted to take him, but he was happy to go. After having been told to sit quiet for a number of days—told to behave, told to hush, told to be good—he was eager to be on the move, eager to play.

"Why are you running?" he heard John Too shout.

Marcus glanced over his shoulder. John Too had followed him out of the courtyard. His arm was raised, his hand held aloft, signaling for Marcus to wait. Reluctantly, Marcus slowed to a stop. He anxiously glanced between Difireti and John Too.

"Why are you running?" John Too inquired as he approached. "Where are you going?"

Marcus looked in the direction of Difireti and smiled.

"I follow her," he replied. And as he spoke, he pointed west, where the young spirit-elephant waited. "She wants me to hurry."

Marcus observed John Too squint as he looked toward the western horizon. After a moment had passed, a wide smile formed on John Too's face.

"Teimbaka! Sister Lady!" John Too shouted.

Marcus clapped his hands. And as he skipped ahead, he heard John Too exclaim, "Come see! Come see! She's here!"

The End